Also by Barbara Wood

PERFECT HARMONY

THE PROPHETESS

VIRGINS OF PARADISE

GREEN CITY IN THE SUN

SOUL FLAME

DOMINA

CHILDSONG

YESTERDAY'S CHILD

THE MAGDALENE SCROLLS

HOUNDS AND JACKALS

NIGHT TRAINS (with Gareth Wootton)

THE WATCHGODS

CURSE THIS HOUSE

VITAL SIGNS

THE DREAMING

SACRED GROUND

the
BLESSING
STONE

Barbara Wood

St. Martin's Griffin ≈ New York

www.stmartins.com

Design by Patrice Sheridan

LIBRARY OF CONGRESS CATALOGING-IN-PUBLICATION DATA

Wood, Barbara, 1947–
    The blessing stone / Barbara Wood—1st ed.
    p. cm.
    ISBN 0-312-27534-X (hc)
    ISBN 0-312-32024-8 (pbk)
    1. Meteorites—Fiction. I. Title.
PS3573.O5877 B57 2002
813'.54—dc21   2002068364

First St. Martin's Griffin Edition: January 2004

10 9 8 7 6 5 4 3 2 1

This book is dedicated with love

to my husband George.

Acknowledgments

Special thanks go to some very special people: Jennifer Enderlin, my editor; Harvey Klinger, my agent; and two dear friends, Sharon Stewart and Carlos Balarezo.

What would I do without you?

the BLESSING STONE

Prologue

3,000,000 Years Ago

The Blessing Stone was born uncountable light-years from Earth, on the other side of the stars.

It came into being in a cataclysmic explosion of stellar proportions that sent cosmic fragments plunging across the gulf of space. Like a shining ship the searing hot chunk of star mass sailed across the sidereal sea, roaring and hissing through the dark night as it hurtled toward its inevitable destruction on a young, savage planet.

Mastodons and mammoths paused in their grazing to blink up at the flashing streak in the sky, the meteor's iron content creating a blazing wake as it burned up in the atmosphere. Witnessing the catastrophic event was a family of frightened hominids, small creatures resembling apes except that their brow ridges were not so prominent and they walked upright on two feet. They froze suddenly in their foraging at the edge of a primeval forest, and a moment later were knocked off their newly upright stance by the shock wave from the meteorite's impact.

The collision heated rock so that it melted and scattered fragments like rain. In Vulcan's furnace the meteor's stardust liquefied and fused with crystalline elements in the earth, homely quartz fracturing to embrace cosmic microdiamonds as if by the wave of an alchemist's wand. The crater formed by the impact gradually cooled and filled with rainwater and for two million years streams running off nearby volcanoes fed the crater lake, silting it up, covering the heavenly fragments with layer after layer of sand. Then a geological upheaval shifted the lake's drainage basin eastward, creating a stream that began to carve out a gorge that would one day, far into the future, be called Olduvai on a continent called Africa. The lake eventually emptied and subsequent winds carried off the layers of silt to expose the meteor fragments once again. They were hard, ugly pellets glistening only here and there. But one was unique, forged perhaps by chance or luck or destiny. Born of force and violence it was now smooth and ovoid in shape from its millennia of being buffed and polished by water and sand and wind, and it flashed with a deep blue brilliance like the sky that had delivered it. Birds flew overhead, dropping seeds that sprouted into lush vegetation, providing the stone with a protective blind so that only the occasional flash of sunlight reflecting off its crystal surface indicated its presence.

Another thousand years passed, and another, while the stone that would one day be revered as magical and horrific, cursed and blessed, waited. . . .

Book One

AFRICA
100,000 Years Ago

The huntress crouched low in the grass, ears flattened back, her body tense and ready to spring.

A short distance away a small group of humans scavenged for roots and seeds, unaware of the amber eyes that watched them. Although massively built with powerful muscles, the huntress was nonetheless a slow animal. Unlike her competitors, the lions and leopards who were swift and chased their prey, the saber-toothed cat needed to lie in wait and catch her quarry by surprise.

And so she remained motionless in the tawny grass, watching, waiting as the unsuspecting prey moved nearer.

The sun rose high and the African plain grew hot. The humans pressed forward in their endless search for food, stuffing nuts and grubs into their mouths, filling the air with the sounds of munching and crunching and the occasional grunt or spoken word. The cat watched. Patience was the key.

Finally a child, barely wobbling on upright legs, wandered away from its mother. The catch was swift and brutal. A sharp cry from the child and the huntress was trotting quickly away with the tender body in her lethal jaws. The humans immediately gave chase, shouting and brandishing frail spears.

And then the cat was gone, vanished through tangled underbrush to her hidden lair, the child frantically squirming and screeching beneath razor teeth. The humans, afraid to follow into the dense growth, flew into a frenzy, jumping up and down, thumping the ground with crude clubs, their shrieks rising to the sky where already vultures began to gather in the hope of leftovers. The mother of the child, a young female whom the others called Wasp, raced back and forth in front of the opening through which the cat had disappeared.

Then came a shout from one of the males. He gestured for them to leave and they all as a body loped away from the thorny patch. Wasp refused to move even though two females tried to pull her away. She threw herself to the ground and yowled as if she were in physical pain. Finally, frightened by the thought of the cat returning, the others abandoned her and made a swift escape to a nearby stand of trees where they hurriedly clambered up into the safety of branches.

There they remained until the sun began to dip to the horizon and shadows grew long. They no longer heard the cries of the stricken mother. The afternoon silence had been broken only once by a single, sharp scream, and then all was still again. With stomachs growling and thirst impelling them to move on, they climbed back down, glanced briefly at the bloody spot where they had last seen Wasp, then they turned toward the west and resumed their search for food.

The small band of humans walked tall and straight as they crossed the African savanna, their long limbs and slender torsos moving with a fluid, animal grace. They wore no clothing, no ornamentation; in their hands they clutched crude spears and hand axes. They numbered seventy-six and ranged in age from sucking infant to elderly. Nine of the females were pregnant. As they pressed relentlessly forward in their eternal search for food, this family of first humans did not know that a hundred thousand years hence, in a world they could not imagine, their descendants would call them *Homo sapiens*—"Man the Wise."

Danger.

Tall One lay motionless in the nest-bed she had shared with Old Mother, her senses suddenly heightened to the sounds and smells of dawn. Smoke from the smoldering campfire. The sharp aroma of charred wood. The air bitingly cold. Birds in the overhead tree branches, waking up to the day, whistling and cawing in a cacophony of birdcall. But no lion's growl or hyena bark, no serpent's hiss that were the usual warnings of danger.

Nonetheless Tall One did not move. Though she shivered with cold and wished to warm herself against Old Mother, who would be at the fire stones poking the embers to life, she remained in bed. The danger was still there. She sensed it strongly.

Slowly she lifted her head and blinked through the smoky dawn. The Family was stirring. She heard the raspy, early morning wheezing of Fishbone, so named when he had nearly choked to death on a fish bone and Nostril saved him by thwacking him hard between the shoulder blades, sending the bone flying across the campfire. Fishbone hadn't breathed right since. There was Old Mother as usual, feeding grass to the feeble fire while Nostril squatted next to her examining a nasty insect bite festering on his scrotum. Fire-Maker was sitting up and nursing her baby. Hungry and Lump still snored in their nest-beds while Scorpion urinated against a tree. And in the half-light, the silhouette of Lion as he grunted in sexual release with Honey-Finder.

Nothing out of the ordinary.

Tall One sat up and rubbed her eyes. The Family's sleep had been disturbed during the night by frantic shrieks from one of Mouse's children, a boy sleeping too close to the fire who had rolled over onto the hot embers and gotten badly burned. It was a lesson every child learned. Tall One herself bore a burn scar the length of her right thigh from when she had slept too close to the fire as a child. The boy, though whimpering now as his mother applied wet mud to the raw flesh, seemed all right. Tall One looked at the other members of the Family who were starting to shuffle down to the water hole to drink, their movements sleepy and sluggish. She saw no signs of fear or alarm in them.

Yet something *was* wrong. Although she could neither see it nor hear it nor smell it, the young female knew with every instinct in her body that a threat lurked nearby. But Tall One had not the mental intellect to grasp what it was nor the language to convey her fears to the others. In her mind she heard: *warning*. But if she were to speak the word, the others would quickly look around for the poisonous snakes or wild dogs or saber-toothed cats. They would see none and wonder why Tall One had alerted them.

It isn't a warning for today, her mind whispered as she finally left the security of her nest-bed. *It is a warning for tomorrow.*

But the young female in this family of early humans had no way of expressing her thought. They possessed no concept of "future." Danger that was coming was alien to creatures who knew only of danger that was now. The humans on the savanna lived as the animals around them lived, grazing and scavenging, seeking water, running from the predators, relieving sexual urges, and sleeping when the sun was high and their stomachs were full.

As the morning sun rose, the Family dispersed from the protection of the cattails and reeds and headed out onto the open plain, feeling safe now that dawn had broken completely over their world to dispel night and its perils. Tall One, her heart filled with nameless dread, joined the others as they abandoned the night camp and began their daily search for food.

She paused now and again to scan her surroundings, hoping to glimpse the new menace she sensed so strongly. But all she saw was a sea of lion-colored grass dotted with leafy trees and rocky hillocks stretching away to distant hills. No predators trailed the group of thirst-driven humans, no threat hovered on the wing in the hazy sky. Tall One saw antelope herds grazing, giraffes nibbling, zebras switching their tails back and forth. Nothing strange or new.

Only the mountain ahead on the horizon. It had been asleep just days ago but now was spewing smoke and ash into the sky. That was new.

But the humans ignored it—Nostril, as he caught a grasshopper and popped it into his mouth; Honey-Finder, as she yanked up a clump of flowers to see if the roots were edible; Hungry, as he scanned the smoky sky for vultures, which would mean a carcass and the chance for meat. Ignorant of the threat the volcano posed, the humans went about their relentless foraging, walking barefoot over red earth and prickly grass, roaming a world made up of lakes and marshes, forests and grasslands, and inhabited by crocodiles, rhinos, baboons, elephants, giraffes, hares, beetles, antelope, vultures, and snakes.

Tall One's family seldom encountered others of their own kind, although they occasionally sensed that humans lived beyond the boundaries of their own small territory. It would have been difficult to venture past the edges of their land for these were difficult barriers to cross: a steep escarpment along one edge, a deep and wide river along another, and an impassible marshland defining the third. Within these borders had Tall One's family, following instinct and memory, roved and survived for generations.

The Family traveled in a tight group, keeping the old ones and females with children in the protective center while the males kept to the periphery with clubs and hand axes, ever watchful for predators. Predators always targeted the weak, and this band of humans was weak indeed; they had been without water since the day before. They trudged beneath the rising sun, their lips and mouths parched as they dreamed of a river running clear where they would find tubers and turtle eggs and clumps of edible vegetation, or perhaps a rare, tasty flamingo captured among papyrus stalks. Their names changed as circumstances changed, for names were nothing more than devices for communication, a way to enable family members to call out to one another or to speak of one another. Honey-Finder received her name the day she had found a beehive and the Family had tasted sugar for the first time in over a year. Lump got his name after climbing a tree to elude a leopard, only to fall to the ground and receive a blow to his head that formed a permanent knot. One Eye lost his right eye when he and Lion had tried to scare off a pack of vultures that were feeding on a dead rhinoceros, and one of the vultures had fought back. Frog was clever at catching frogs by distracting his catch with one hand and grabbing it with the other. Tall One was so named because she was the tallest female in the Family.

The humans lived by impulses and instincts and animal intuitions. Few of them entertained thoughts. And since they had no thoughts they had no questions, and therefore they had no need to come up with answers. They wondered about nothing, questioned nothing. The world was made up of only what they could see, hear, smell, touch, and taste. Nothing was hidden or unknown. A saber-toothed cat was a saber-toothed cat—a predator when alive, a food source when dead. For this reason the humans were not superstitious and had not yet formed concepts of magic, spirits, or unseen powers. They didn't try to explain the wind because it didn't occur to them to do so. When Fire-Maker sat to start a fire, she didn't wonder where the sparks came from, or why it had occurred to an ancestor a thousand years prior to try to make fire. Fire-Maker had learned simply by watching her mother, who had learned in turn by watching *her* mother. Food was anything they could find, and because they possessed limited speech and social skills, hunting was so primitive as to be confined to the smallest game—lizards, birds, fish, rabbits. Tall One's family lived in ignorance of who or what they were and the fact that they had just completed a long evolutionary road that meant they and their kind would remain physically unchanged for the next hundred thousand years.

They were also unaware that, with Tall One and the new danger she sensed, a second evolution was about to begin.

As she searched for edible plants and insects, a vision haunted her: the watering hole they had woken to that dawn. To the Family's dismay, during the night the water had become so covered with volcanic soot and ash as to be undrinkable. Thirst had driven them on when they would normally have stayed to eat, and it drove them now, continually westward, doggedly following Lion who knew where the next fresh water lay, their heads rising above the tall grasses so that they could see the herds of wildebeest moving in the same quest for water. The sky was a strange color, the air smelled acrid and sharp. And directly ahead on the horizon, the mountain coughed smoke as it had never done before.

Tall One, her mind wrestling with an unaccustomed puzzle, was also plagued by a memory—the terror that had visited them two nights before.

Night was never quiet on the African plain, with lions roaring over fresh kills and hyenas emitting shrill cries to alert partners of the promise of food. The humans who sheltered at the edge of the forest slept fitfully, despite the fires they kept going against the darkness, to give light and warmth and to keep the beasts away. But two nights ago had been different. Habituated to lives constantly fraught with peril, the humans' fear had been heightened and sharpened, making them blink in the dark and listen to the pounding of their hearts. Something strange and terrible was happening to the world around them, and because they had no words for these new calamities, no cohesive thoughts in their primitive minds that might bring reason and therefore comfort, the frightened humans could only huddle together in the grip of sheer, mindless terror.

They had no way of knowing that earthquakes had shaken this region many times before, or that the mountain on the horizon had been shooting lava into the sky for millennia, going dormant occasionally, as it had for the past few hundred years. But now it was alive, its cone casting a terrifying red glow against the night sky, the earth trembling and roaring as if with life.

But only Tall One remembered these terrors as the others in her group swept their eyes over the ground and vegetation, watchful for termite hills, plants laden with seedpods, and trailing vines that might promise bitter berries.

When One Eye kicked a rotting log to expose squirming grubs, the humans fell upon the feast, grabbing the larvae and stuffing their mouths. Food was never shared out. The strongest ate, the weakest starved. Lion, the dominant male in the group, pushed his way through to seize large handfuls of the white morsels.

When he was younger, Lion had come upon the fresh carcass of an old lioness and had been able to skin it before the vultures descended. He had draped the bloody pelt over his shoulders and back, allowing it to mold to his body as it stank and became maggot-ridden and eventually dried, and because he hadn't removed it in years, the stiff skin was now part of him, his long hair had grown into it, and it creaked when he moved.

Lion had not been chosen as the Family leader, there had been no vote or consensus. He had simply decided one day that he would lead and the others had followed. Lion's occasional mate, Honey-Finder, was dominant among the females because she was large and strong and possessed a greedy, assertive personality. At feedings she would push weaker females out of the way to get food for her own young, stealing from others and gobbling down more than her share. Lion and Honey-Finder used both hands now to scoop the pale fat grubs out of the rotting wood and stuff them into their mouths, and when they had satisfied themselves, and Honey-Finder had seen to it that her five offspring had eaten, they moved away so that the weaker members of the family could scoop what was left of the sluggish larvae into their mouths.

Tall One chewed a mouthful of grubs and then spit the pap into her palm. When she held her hand out to Old Mother, who was toothless, the elder gratefully lapped up the masticated pulp.

The grubs devoured, the humans rested beneath the noon sun. The stronger males sat watch for predators while the rest busied themselves with the daily activities of nursing babies, grooming, napping, and engaging in sexual release. Sexual joinings were usually brief and quickly forgotten, even among couples who shared a temporary affection. Long term pair bonding did not exist, and the satisfying of the sexual urge was taken randomly at chance opportunities. Scorpion sniffed around the females, unaware that he was searching for the midcycle scent that would indicate a female was in her fertile phase. Sometimes it was the female who did the seeking, as Baby did now, instinctively hungry for a hurried joining with a male. Since Scorpion was already busy with Mouse, Baby chose Hungry and, although he was not initially interested, brought him to arousal and happily straddled him.

As the Family went thusly about their needs, and in the distance the mountain continued to spew fire and gas up to the sky, Tall One kept a sharp lookout, hoping to glimpse the ears or the shadow of the new danger that stalked them. But there was nothing there.

They trudged through the afternoon, thirst burning their mouths, the children crying for water and mothers trying to soothe them as the males made quick forays away from the group, shielding their eyes to scan the plain for signs of a stream or pond. They tracked eland and wildebeest, hoping the herds would lead them to water. They noted the direction of birds in flight, particularly wading birds: herons, storks, and egrets. They searched also for elephants because these were beasts that spent most of their time at water holes, rolling in the mud to cool their sun-dried skin or submerging themselves almost completely, leaving only the end of their trunks above the water's surface to allow breathing. But the humans saw no eland or storks or elephants that could lead them to water.

When they came upon the bones of a zebra they were briefly overjoyed. But when they saw that the long bones were already cracked open, the marrow sucked clean, their disappointment was acute. The humans did not have to examine the tracks around the carcass to know that hyenas had robbed them of a feast.

They pressed on. Near a grassy hillock Lion brought the group to an abrupt halt, silencing them with a gesture. They listened, and on the breeze heard nearby a "*yeow-yeow . . . yeow*"—the distinctive chirping noises cheetahs made when communicating with their young. Cautiously, the humans turned away, keeping themselves downwind so the cats did not catch their scent.

While the females and children scavenged for what vegetable and insect food they could find, the males with their wooden-tipped spears were on the alert for possible game. Although organized hunting skills were beyond them, they knew that a giraffe was at its most vulnerable when it was drinking at a water hole—it had to spread its legs wide so it could reach the water, and in that position was an easy target for humans acting swiftly with sharpened sticks.

Nostril suddenly cried out with glee as he dropped to one knee and pointed to a scattering of jackal spoor on the ground. Jackals were known to bury their dead prey and return to eat it later. But frantic digging in the immediate area produced no buried kill.

They pressed on—hot, hungry, thirsty, until finally Lion let out a whoop that the others understood to mean he had found water, and they began to run, Tall One keeping an arm around Old Mother to help her along.

Lion had not always been the Family's leader. Before him, a male named River had been the dominant member, taking the best food portions for himself, monopolizing females, deciding where the Family would sleep for the night. River had been named after a perilous encounter with a flashflood. The Family had managed to reach high ground in time, but River had gotten caught. It was only the chance passing of an uprooted tree that had saved him, depositing him on a sandbar days later, bruised and exhausted but still alive. The Family had named him for the new river that flowed through their territory and for a while he had enjoyed supremacy in the group, until Lion had challenged him over a female.

The fight had been to the death, with the two beating each other with clubs while the Family looked on, screaming and shouting. When a bloodied River had finally run away, Lion had shaken his fists in the air and then had promptly mounted an excited Honey-Finder with great vigor. River was never seen or heard from again.

After that, the Family had followed Lion compliantly and without question. Their crude society wasn't egalitarian for the simple reason that the family members were not capable of thinking for themselves. Like the herds grazing the savanna around them, or their ape cousins living in the distant rain forests, the group needed a leader for survival. One always rose above the rest, either through physical strength or mental superiority. It wasn't always a male. Before the leader named River there had been a strong female named Hyena, so called because she laughed like one, who had led the Family on their eternal and unchanging cycle of scavenging-gathering. Hyena remembered the borders of the territory, knew where the good water was, where berries could be found, and which seasons produced nuts and seeds. And when one night she had been caught separated from the others and, by great irony, had been torn limb from limb by a pack of hyenas, the Family had wandered aimlessly until a flashflood singled out River as their new leader.

Now Lion led them to the fresh water supply he remembered from four seasons ago—an artesian well protected beneath a rocky overhang. They fell upon the pool and greedily drank their fill. But when, thirst slaked, they looked around for food, they found none. No sandy bank in which to dig for turtle eggs or freshwater shellfish, no flowers with tender roots or vegetation harboring tasty seeds. Lion surveyed the scene with displeasure—surely there had been grasses here before—and finally indicated with a grunt that they had to move on.

Tall One paused to look down at the pool from which they had all just drunk. She considered the clear surface and then looked up at the smoky sky. She looked down at the water again and this time took the rocky overhang into account. She frowned. The water they had woken to at dawn had been undrinkable. *This* water was clear and sweet. Her mind struggled to make the leap. The sooty sky, the rocky overhang, the clear water.

And then the thought was formed: *This water was protected.*

She watched the Family as they trudged away—Lion leading with his hairy, hide-bound back, Honey-Finder at his side with a baby in her arms, a small child riding her shoulders, and an older child clutching her free hand—shambling, loping, their thirst forgotten now that their bellies ached with hunger. Tall One wanted to call them back. She wanted to warn them about something, but she didn't know what. It had to do with the new, nameless danger she had been sensing lately. And now she knew that, somehow, the nameless danger was connected to water—the soot-covered water of dawn, this clear pool, and the pond that Lion was leading them to farther along the ancient path.

She felt a tug at her arm. Old Mother, her small withered face turned up to Tall One with an expression of worry. They mustn't fall behind.

*W*hen the Family came upon a baobab tree laden with fruit everyone who could wield a stick swung at the branches, bringing down the pulpy seedpods. The Family feasted on the spot, sitting or squatting, or even eating standing up so they could keep a watchful eye out for predators. Then they dozed beneath the wide-spreading tree, feeling the heat of the afternoon settle into their flesh and bones. Mothers nursed babies while siblings rolled playfully in the dirt. One Eye was in the mood for a female. He watched Baby as she picked through the pod shells hoping to find one overlooked, and when he tickled her and stroked her, she giggled and fell to her hands and knees, allowing him to enter her. Honey-Finder picked lice out of Lion's shaggy hair, Old Mother smeared spittle on the little boy's burn wound, and Tall One, leaning somberly against a tree, kept her eyes on the distant angry mountain.

After their nap they roused themselves and, once again impelled by hunger, pressed westward. Toward sunset the Family arrived at a wide stream where elephants waded and sprayed water with their trunks. The humans approached the bank of the stream cautiously, searching for something resembling floating logs. These would be crocodiles, with only their eyes and nostrils and small hump of back above the surface of the water. Although crocodiles mainly hunted at night, they were known to strike during the day if they sensed an easy kill. More than once the humans had seen one of their own snatched from a river bank and carried under in the blink of an eye. Although they were dismayed to find the surface of the sluggish stream covered with soot and ash, they saw nonetheless an abundance of bird life along the banks—plovers and ibis, geese and sandpipers—which promised nests filled with eggs. And because the sun was dipping to the horizon and shadows were growing long, they decided to stay here for the night.

While some of the females and the children began gathering tall grasses and pliant leaves for nest-beds, Old Mother and Tall One and other females dug into the pond's sandy margins for shellfish. Frog and his brothers searched for bullfrogs. During the dry season bullfrogs laid dormant in burrows beneath the ground, coming out as the first raindrops of the rainy season softened the earth. As it hadn't rained here in weeks, the boys expected the catch to be good. Fire-Maker sent her children out to gather the droppings of whichever herd had grazed here recently and then she got to work with her sparking stones, using dried twigs to start a slow smolder. When wildebeest and zebra dung were added, a fire was soon burning, and the males set up torches made of tree limbs and sap around the perimeter of the camp to keep predators at bay. An hour of foraging also produced wild chicory leaves, nut-grass tubers, and the carcass of a fat mongoose not yet gone maggoty. The humans ate greedily, devouring everything, saving not a seed or an egg against tomorrow's hunger.

Finally they sat huddled against the night within the protection of a fence made of thorn bush and acacia branches, the males congregating on one side of the fire while the females and children gathered on the other. Now was the time for grooming, a nightly ritual that was impelled by the primal need for companionship and touch, and which in subtle ways established whatever crude social order existed among them.

Using a sharp hand ax that Hungry had fashioned for her from quartz, Baby chopped off her children's hair. If left untended, the hair would grow down to their waists and become a hazard. Baby was proof of it, having run from her mother when she was little because she hated to have her hair groomed, so it had grown down to her waist and stood out with grease until one day it became entangled in a thorn bush, trapping her. When the Family had finally disengaged a hysterical Baby from the sharp trap, patches of her scalp had been torn away and bled profusely. That was when she got her name, because she couldn't stop crying for days. Now Baby had scarred bald patches on her head and the rest of her hair grew out in frightful tufts.

Other females picked through their children's hair, cracking lice between their teeth, and plastered the little ones and other females with mud carried from the pond. Their laughter rose to the sky like the sparks from the fires, along with the occasional sharp word or warning. Although the females were thus busily engaged, they all kept their eyes on Barren, so called for having no babies, who was following pregnant Weasel around. Everyone remembered when Baby had given birth to her fifth offspring and Barren had snatched it away, placenta and all, and run off with it. They had all chased after her until they caught her, the newborn dying in the fracas when the women had nearly beaten Barren to death. After that, Barren always trailed after the Family when they went scavenging and slept far from the fire, like a shadow at the edge of the camp. But Barren was becoming bold of late, and hovering around Weasel. And Weasel was frightened. She had lost her three previous children to a snakebite, a fall from a rocky precipice, and to a leopard that had boldly sneaked into the camp one night and carried the infant off.

On the other side of the main fire, the males were gathered. Once a young male became too old to stay with the females and babies, he went to sit with the older males, to watch and to imitate scarred and calloused hands as they chipped flint tools and sharpened long sticks into rudimentary spears. Here the young males, no longer under their mothers' dominance, learned the ways of males: how to fashion wood into weapons and rock into tools; how to identify animal spoor; how to smell the wind and scent a prey. They learned the few words and sounds and gestures the males used for communication. And, like the females, they groomed one another, plucking live things from tangled hair and plastering mud on one another's bodies. The mud, as a protection against the heat, insect bites, and poisonous plants, had to be reapplied every day and was an important part of the nightly ritual. Young males jockeyed for the honor of grooming Lion and the older males.

Snail, so named because he was slow, was bellowing his protest at having to sit guard. After an exchange of shouts and angry fists, Lion settled the dispute by cracking a spear over Snail's head. The defeated man shuffled off to his post, wiping blood from his eyes. Old Scorpion rubbed his left arm and leg, which were growing strangely numb, while Lump tried to scratch an itch he could not reach, resorting to the nearest tree where he rubbed himself up and down the rough trunk until his skin broke and bled. Occasionally they glanced across the fire at the industrious females, creatures the males subconsciously held in awe because only females created babies, the males being unaware of their own part in the process. Females were unpredictable. A female who wasn't interested in sexual copulation could be vicious when forced. Poor Lip, who used to be called Bird Nose, had gotten a new name after an encounter with Tall One. When he had tried to penetrate her against her will, she had fought back, biting off part of his lower lip. It had bled for days and then oozed pus, and when it finally healed it had left a puckered gap so that his lower teeth always showed. After that, Lip left Tall One alone, as did most of the other males. The few who did try to mount her decided after an exhausting fight that it wasn't worth it, there were plenty of compliant females around.

Frog was sulking by himself. For the past year he and a young female, named Anteater because of her passion for honey ants, had enjoyed a special togetherness, like Baby and One Eye, who were currently cuddling and fondling and enjoying sexual pleasure. But now because Anteater's belly was swollen with child and she wanted nothing to do with him, Frog's advances were met with slaps and hisses. He had seen this happen before. Once a female gave birth, she preferred the company of the other females who had children. Together they would laugh and chatter as they nursed their babies and kept an eye on the toddlers, while the scorned males were left to their solitary pursuits of tool- and weapon-making.

The mother-child bond was the only real bond the Family knew. If a male and female paired, it was rarely for long, the course of their relationship running hot with passion and then dying out. Frog's friend Scorpion squatted next to him and cuffed his shoulder in sympathy. He, too, had experienced closeness with a female until she produced a baby and then wanted nothing more to do with him. Of course, there were those, like Honey-Finder, who remained affectionate to one male, especially when he tolerated her babies, as Lion did. But Scorpion and Frog had no patience with the females' babies and preferred females who were thus unencumbered.

Frog felt the heat rise within him. He looked in envy at One Eye and Baby, fondling and grooming each other. One Eye enjoyed sexual release whenever he wanted, Baby being so constantly willing to allow him. They were currently the only pair-bond, sleeping together, sharing affection. One Eye even tolerated Baby's children, something few males did.

Eyeing the females, Frog decided to try to interest a few by showing them his erection and giving them a hopeful look. But they either ignored him or pushed him away. So he went back to the fire and raked through the coals. To his delight he found an overlooked onion, charred but edible. He took it to Fire-Maker who immediately grabbed the morsel and got down on her hands and knees, supporting herself on one arm while with her free hand she chomped away. It didn't take Frog long. He was soon finished and shambling to his nest-bed for sleep.

When Lion finished eating, his eye fell upon Old Mother who was sucking on a root. Lion and Old Mother had been birthed by the same female, they had suckled the same breasts and tumbled together as youngsters. When she had produced twelve offspring, Lion had been in awe of her. But now she was growing feeble and the dim notion formed in his mind that food was wasted on her. Before she could even react, he strode past her, snatched the root from her fingers and popped it between his teeth.

Seeing what had happened, Tall One went to the dismayed Old Mother, making crooning noises and stroking her hair. Old Mother was the oldest member of the Family, although no one knew exactly how old since the Family did not reckon by years or seasons. If anyone had counted, they would know she had reached the advanced age of fifty-five. Tall One, on the other hand, had lived for fifteen summers, and she knew vaguely that she was the daughter of a female Old Mother had birthed.

Watching Lion as he circled the camp before settling down into his nest-bed, Tall One felt a nameless unease fill her. It had to do with Old Mother and how defenseless she was. A dim recollection came to the young female's mind: her own mother, having broken a leg, was left behind when she could no longer walk, a lone figure sitting against the trunk of a thorn tree, watching the Family move on. The group could not be burdened with a weak member, for the predators were ever watchful in the tall grass. When the Family passed that way again, they had found no trace of Tall One's mother.

Finally everyone began to settle down for the night, mothers and children curling up together in their nest-beds, the males on the other side of the fire, finding comfortable spots, lying back to back for warmth, tossing and turning to the sounds of growls and barks nearby in the darkness. Unable to sleep, Tall One left the nest-bed she shared with Old Mother and made her way cautiously to the water. A short distance away she saw that a small herd of elephants—all females with their young—had gone to sleep for the night, slumbering in the manner peculiar to elephants: by leaning against a tree or one another. When she reached the water's edge she looked at the surface of the pond covered in thick volcanic ash. Then she looked up at the stars slowly being devoured by smoke and she tried again to understand the turmoil in her mind.

It had to do with the new danger.

She looked back at the camp where seventy-odd humans were settling down for the night. Already, snores rose up to the sky, and nocturnal grunts and sighs. She recognized the moans and gasps of a pair engaged in sexual release. A baby wailed and was quickly hushed. The unmistakable sound of Nostril belching. And the noisy yawns of the males guarding the perimeter with spears and torches to protect the Family through the night. They all seemed unconcerned; for them, life was going on as it always had. But Tall One was troubled. Only she sensed that the world was not right.

But in what way? Lion was leading the Family to all the ancestral places where they had roamed for generations. They found the food they had always found; they even found water where it was supposed to be, albeit covered in ash. There was security and survival in sameness. Change frightened the Family. The concept of change never even entered their minds.

But now it was beginning to—at least in the mind of one young member.

Tall One's dark brown eyes scanned the night, watching for any suspicious movement. Ever alert, her guard never down, Tall One lived as the Family lived, by wit and instinct and a strong sense of survival. But tonight was different, as the past few nights had been, ever since the sense of a new danger had been born within her. A danger she could neither see nor name. One that left no spoor or prints, that did not growl or hiss, that possessed neither fang nor claw, yet which made the small hairs on the back of her neck stand up.

She searched the stars and saw how they were being gobbled by smoke. She saw the ash raining down from the sky. She surveyed the soot-covered water and inhaled the stench of sulfur and magma from the distant volcano. She saw the way the grasses bent in the night wind, how the trees leaned, and which way dried leaves flew. And suddenly, with a leap of her heart, she understood.

Tall One held her breath and froze as the nameless menace took shape in her mind and she grasped all in a staggering instant what no other family member had grasped: that tomorrow's water hole—

despite what generations of experience had shown them—was going to be covered with ash.

A shriek tore the night

Weasel, in the grip of birth pains. The females quickly helped her away from the camp and into the secrecy of the trees. The males didn't follow but instead jumped nervously to the periphery of the camp, clutching their crude spears and collecting stones that might be thrown at predators. As soon as the big cats and hyenas heard the cry of a vulnerable human being, and smelled the blood of birth, they would come. The human females instinctively formed a circle around Weasel, facing outward, yelling and stamping their feet to cover up Weasel's cries of pain and defenselessness.

She had no help. Clutching the trunk of an acacia, Weasel squatted and pushed, laboring hard while in the grip of cold terror. Above the screams of her female companions, had she heard the triumphant roar of a lion? Were a pack of cats about to fly through the trees, fangs and claws and yellow eyes, to tear her to pieces?

Finally the baby came and Weasel immediately brought it up to her breast, shaking and stroking it until it cried. Old Mother knelt beside her and massaged Weasel's abdomen, as she had done to herself and her daughters over the years, coaxing the placenta to be delivered swiftly. And when that, too, was born and the females hastily buried the blood and the afterbirth, the Family gathered around the new mother to look in curiosity at the squirming creature at her breast.

Suddenly, Barren pushed through and snatched the suckling infant from Weasel's arms. The females ran after her, hurling rocks. Barren dropped the baby but the females kept after her until she was caught. They tore branches from trees and beat her with them, mercilessly, not stopping until the bloody form at their feet was unrecognizable. When they were certain Barren no longer breathed, they returned to the camp with the baby that was, miraculously, still alive.

Lion decreed that the Family must move on, quickly. Barren's corpse and the birthing blood would attract the dangerous scavengers, particularly the vultures who could be determined and fearless. So they broke camp even though it was still night and, armed with torches, made their way across the open plain. As they trekked beneath the full moon, they heard behind them the animals rush in and growl savagely as they tore Barren's body to pieces.

*A*nother dawn, and light ash continued to sift down from the sky.

The humans began to stir, waking to noisy birdsong and the chatter of monkeys in the trees. Watching for predators now that the periphery fires had burned out, they made their way to the water hole where zebras and gazelles tried in vain to drink. The water could not be seen for the thick coating of soot that lay upon its surface. But the humans, able to scoop away the volcanic fallout with their hands, found water below, albeit gritty and foul tasting. While the others began to dig for eggs and shellfish, and search the shallows for frogs and turtles and lily roots, Tall One turned her eyes to the west, where the smoking mountain stood against a sky still dark with night.

The stars could not be seen for the great clouds of smoke that billowed out in all directions. Turning, she squinted at the eastern horizon, which was turning pale and where the sun would soon appear. There the sky was clear and fresh, the last stars still visible. She looked back at the mountain and experienced again the revelation of the night before when, for the first time in the history of her people, she had taken separate parts of an equation and fitted them together in an answer: *the mountain was spewing smoke . . . the wind was blowing eastward . . . therefore contaminating water holes in its path.*

She tried to tell the others, tried to find words and gestures that would convey the essence of this new peril. But Lion, acting only on instinct and ancestral memory, knowing nothing of the concept of cause and effect but understanding only that the world had always been one way and would always be so, could not make such a mental leap. What had the mountain and the wind to do with water? Taking up his crude spear he gave the command that the Family move on.

Tall One stood her ground. "Bad!" she said desperately, pointing westward. "Bad!" Then she gestured frantically eastward, where the sky was clear and where she knew the water would be clean. "Good! We go!"

Lion looked at the others. But their faces were blank because they had no idea what Tall One was trying to say. Why change what they had always done?

And so they abandoned camp once again and started their daily foraging while watching the sky for vultures, which could mean a carcass and the possibility of long bones filled with tasty marrow. Lion and the stronger males shook trees to bring down nuts and fruit, and seedpods that would be roasted later in the fire. The females crouched over termite hills, inserting twigs to draw out the fat insects and eat them. The children busied themselves with a nest of honey ants, carefully biting off the swollen nectar-filled abdomens while avoiding the ants' sharp mandibles. With the food coming in such meager portions, foraging never ceased. Only rarely did they come upon a newly dead beast not yet discovered by hyenas and vultures, and the humans would strip off the hide and gorge themselves on meat.

Tall One walked with dread: *The water will be worse ahead.*

Toward midday she climbed a small hillock and, shading her eyes, scanned the lion-yellow savanna. When she immediately started calling and flapping her arms the others knew she had found a clutch of ostrich eggs. The humans approached cautiously, espying the large bird guarding the nest. The black and white feathers told them it was a male, which was unusual, as it was normally the brown females that sat on the nest during the day, while the males sat on it at night. This one looked huge and dangerous. They kept a lookout for the female, who certainly must be nearby and who would be just as lethal defending her nest.

Lion gave a shout and Hungry, Lump, Scorpion, Nostril, and all the other males went running at the ostrich with sticks and clubs, yelling and hooting and making as much noise as possible. The giant bird flew up off the nest with a great flapping of its wings and confronted the intruders, chest feathers standing out, its neck extended forward as it attacked with its beak, kicking with its powerful legs. Then the mate appeared, an enormous brown menace racing across the plain at top speed, her wings outspread, her neck extended forward, her call high and screeching.

While Lion and the males kept the birds engaged, Tall One and the other females gathered as many eggs as they could and sprinted away. Reaching a clump of trees, they immediately began to crack open the enormous eggs and gobble the contents. When Lion and his companions came breathlessly back, having left two distraught ostriches to fret over a destroyed nest, they grabbed their share, hammering at the thick-shelled eggs to make holes, then scooping out yolk and white with their fingers. A few shouted with delight when they found ostrich chicks in their eggs, and popped the wriggling and squirming creatures into their mouths. Tall One took an egg to Old Mother, cracked open the top and placed it in the elder's hands. When she was certain Old Mother had eaten enough, Tall One finally sat back to eat the last egg she had saved. But no sooner had she cracked it open than Lion loomed over her. He snatched the egg from her and upended it into his mouth, swallowing the enormous yolk in one noisy gulp. Then he tossed the empty eggshell aside and seized her, turned her over onto her knees and holding her wrists with one hand and pressing her neck down with the other, thrust himself inside her while she howled in protest.

When he was done, he shambled off for a nap, looking for the nicest piece of shade. He came to the best spot only to find Scorpion defiantly sitting with his back to the tree. A raised fist and a roar from Lion, a brief clash of wills, and Scorpion sulked resentfully away.

At midday they slept, when the savanna was peaceful. A pride of lions lounged in the sun not far off, but the remains of a kill nearby—which was being finished off by vultures and which the humans had no interest in, themselves being full—told Tall One's people that the cats had recently fed and therefore posed no threat. While the Family dozed, Tall One rummaged through the shattered eggshells, hoping to find remnants of yolk and white. But worse than her hunger was her thirst. Once again she observed the smoke clouds in the sky and sensed that the farther they went in that direction, the worse the water was going to be.

The smoking mountain had gone to sleep, its plume of cinder and ash dwindling so that the air had cleared a little. After days of sub- sisting on roots and wild onions and the rare nest of eggs, the humans were now craving meat. They followed a mixed herd of antelope and zebra, knowing that the big cats would be doing the same. When the herd paused to graze, Nostril climbed a grassy hillock to stand lookout while the others crouched hidden in the grass.

Through the stillness of the morning, as the day warmed and the earth began to bake, the humans watched and waited. Finally, pa- tience was rewarded. They saw a lioness moving stealthily through the grass. The humans knew how she would hunt: since most animals could run faster than a lion she would stay upwind, undetected, and creep closer to the grazing beasts until she was in range to outrun her prey.

Tall One, Old Mother, Baby, Hungry, and the rest crouched motionless, their eyes on Nostril as he marked the progress of the cat. Suddenly she shot forward, sending startled birds to flight. The herd bolted. But the lioness was swift, running only a short course before catching up with a lame zebra. She flew into the air and sliced a massive paw across its flank, sending the animal onto its side. As the zebra struggled to get up, the lioness was upon it, clamping her jaws over its muzzle and holding it there until, gradually, the beast suffocated to death. As the lioness dragged her kill toward the shade of a baobab tree, the humans followed—upwind and silently. They squatted down again when they saw the pride of males and cubs rush forward for the feast. The air was filled briefly with savage growls and hisses as the lions fought each other before settling down to devour the carcass. Overhead, the vultures were already circling.

With stomachs growling and mouths salivating with anticipation of meat, Tall One's family waited patiently, hidden, watching. Even the children knew that silence was crucial, that it meant the difference between eating and being eaten. The afternoon grew long, shadows lengthened, the only sounds on the breeze the greedy feeding of the big cats. Nostril's back and legs ached. Hungry desperately wanted to scratch his armpits. Flies settled on bare skin and bit ferociously. But the humans didn't move. They knew that their opportunity would come.

The sun dipped to the horizon. Several children started to fret and cry, but by now the cats were too full to care as they shambled away from the shredded carcass for a long nap. The humans watched as the black-maned males loped away, yawning, following by fat little cubs with bloodied muzzles. Once the lions had thrown themselves beneath the baobab tree, the vultures moved in. Nostril and Hungry looked to Lion for the signal, and when he gave it, they all rushed forward, screaming and throwing stones at the vultures. But the giant birds, driven by a hunger of their own, would not give up the prize. Spreading their massive wings, they fought beak and talon to protect what was theirs.

The humans were forced to retreat, hungry and tired, a few bloodied from the encounter with the vultures.

They squatted again in the grass, this time listening for the hyenas and wild dogs that would inevitably come scavenging. After a brief twilight, night fell and the vultures continued to feast. Tall One ran a hand over her parched lips. Her stomach cramped with hunger pangs. Honey-Finder's babies wailed in protest. And still the humans waited.

Finally, as an effulgent moon lifted above the horizon, casting the landscape in a milky glow, the vultures flew off, gorged from their meal. Brandishing spears and howling at the tops of their lungs, the humans managed to keep the hyenas away from what was left of the zebra—little more than hide and bone. They worked swiftly, using sharp hand axes to hack the zebra's legs from its body. With their trophies over their heads, the humans ran off, allowing the hyenas to rush in to finish off tendon, ligament, and hair.

Within a protective stand of trees, Fire-Maker began at once creating fires to keep predators away. Lion and other strong men got to work stripping the skin from the zebra legs, and when they were clean, cracked the bones open swiftly and expertly to expose the precious creamy pink marrow within. Their mouths watering, the humans moaned and sighed at such a sight, and instantly their long hours of vigil in the grass, their painful joints and aching limbs, were forgotten. There was no feeding frenzy of the marrow. Lion apportioned the fatty delicacy out, and this time everyone received a share, even Old Mother.

$\mathcal{T}$all One tried again to protest the direction they were taking and this time Lion gave her the back of his hand, sending her rolling over the ground. Gathering up the children and babies and their few possessions, the Family started again to move westward. Old Mother came to Tall One's aid, making soothing sounds as she patted her granddaughter's angry cheek.

As they started to trek, breathing in the smoky volcanic air, Old Mother suddenly moaned and clutched her chest. Her steps faltered as she fought for breath. Tall One had her by the arm, holding her up. They went a few more steps when Old Mother finally let out a cry and collapsed. The others glanced at her but kept walking, their concern only for food. They watched for termite hills and berry patches, for nut-bearing trees and that rarest of all treats, a beehive. But they gave no thought to Old Mother who had given birth to half their mothers. Only Tall One cared as she tried to help the elder to walk, ultimately hoisting Old Mother onto her shoulders and carrying her. As the equatorial sun rose, the burden grew. Finally, after a strenuous trek Tall One, for all her stature and strength, could no longer carry Old Mother.

They slumped to the ground and the Family, forced to stop, milled around in indecision. Lion knelt over the unconscious female and sniffed her face. He tapped Old Mother's cheeks and pried open her mouth. Then he saw the closed eyes and blue lips. "Hmp," he grunted. "Dead," he pronounced, meaning that she was as good as dead. He stood up. "We go."

Some of the females started wailing. Others whimpered in fear. Honey-Finder stamped her feet and waved her arms and made mournful sounds. Big Nose gathered his unconscious mother into his arms and wept over her. Lump sat at Old Mother's side and tugged at her hands. The small children, terrified by the actions of the adults, started to cry. But Lion, taking up his spears and club, turned his back on the group and began to march resolutely westward. One by one they followed until the whole band was gone, the stragglers looking back as Tall One stayed by Old Mother.

Tall One loved Old Mother with a ferocity that she could not define. When her own mother had been left behind because of an injured leg, Tall One had cried for days. It was Old Mother who had taken her into a comforting embrace, and Old Mother who had fed her and slept with her after that. *Mother of my mother,* Tall One thought, vaguely comprehending her special connection to this female in a family that possessed no concept of kinships.

Soon they were alone on the vast savanna, except for vultures circling overhead. Tall One dragged Old Mother to the safety of trees and propped her against a sturdy trunk. Day was dying. Nightfall would bring out the golden-eyed carnivores that would close in on the helpless humans.

Tall One found two stones and, squatting over a pile of dry leaves, began knocking them together. It took endless patience and will, and her back and shoulders began to ache with the effort. But she had seen Fire-Maker do it successfully many times so she knew it could be done. Over and over, while the sky darkened and stars struggled to peep through the volcanic smoke, Tall One knocked the two stones together and was finally rewarded with a small flame. She gently blew it into life, feeding it more dry leaves until it flamed higher. Then she placed rocks around the fire, and twigs on top, and took comfort from the glow against the night.

Old Mother, still unconscious, continued to breathe with difficulty, her eyes closed, his face contorted with pain. Tall One sat next to her and watched. She had seen death before. It came to animals on the savanna. It sometimes came to members of the Family. Their bodies would be left behind and the Family would talk about them for perhaps a season or two before they were forgotten. The fact that she herself might someday die never entered Tall One's head. The concept of mortality and self-awareness were less a glimmer in her mind than the distant stars.

After a while Tall One realized that Old Mother would need water. When she saw a patch of flowers, almost as tall as herself, with speck-led bell-shaped blooms and fuzzy leaves, she reasoned that there must be water nearby. Dropping to her hands and knees, she dug into the soil, hoping to find moisture. She heard a pack of hyenas barking nearby, their bodies making rustling sounds in the bush. The hairs prickled on Tall One's neck. She had seen hyenas take down a human being, savagely devouring him alive while he screamed. Tall One knew that it was only the fire keeping the beasts at bay and that she must get back to it soon and keep the flames going.

Her digging grew frantic. Surely there must be water nearby to support such large flowers and fleshy stems. She tore her fingers on the hard earth until they bled.

She sat back out of frustration, fatigue creeping through her limbs, and a strong desire to sleep. But she must find water, and she must tend the fire. She must protect Old Mother from the predators lurking in the darkness.

And then she saw it, a flash of reflected moonlight. Water! Clear and blue, pooled at the base of one of the flowers. But when she reached out for it she found that the water was hard and not a small puddle at all. Scooping it up in her hand, she puzzled over the chunk of blue water that was matted with the dried leaves of the foxglove plant. How could water be solid? And yet it had to be water for it was transparent and smooth and looked as if it might at any moment be liquid.

She carried the stone, created three million years earlier out of a meteorite, back to Old Mother and, cradling the elderly female in her arms, gently slipped the smooth stone between her parched lips. Old Mother immediately began to suck, saliva appearing at the corners of her mouth, so Tall One knew that the water had turned to liquid again.

After a moment, however, to her surprise, the crystal slipped out from Old Mother's lips and when Tall One caught it she saw that the water was still solid. But now she could see it more clearly for the old female's tongue had cleaned the stone of its vegetative debris.

The crystal fit snugly in Tall One's palm, the way an egg would lie in a nest, and it was smooth like an egg, but with a watery surface that shot back the moon's light the way a lake or a stream did. When she turned it over and then held it up between two fingers, she saw deeper blues at its heart, and then deeper still something white and sharp and glinting.

A sigh from Old Mother brought Tall One's attention back from the crystal. She saw in amazement that Old Mother's lips had turned from blue to pink and that she was breathing more easily. A moment later Old Mother opened her eyes and she smiled. Then she sat up and touched her withered old breast in wonder. The chest pain was gone.

Together they stared at the transparent stone. Unaware of the curative powers of the digitalis in the plant, they believed it was the water in the stone that had saved her.

When they caught up with the Family at dawn, the others looked up from their foraging with mild curiosity, Tall One and Old Mother having already begun to recede from their memories. By gestures and limited words, Old Mother explained how the water-stone had brought her back from death and when Tall One passed the stone around to the thirsty members, they took turns sucking on it until they salivated. For a while, thirst was slaked and, for a while, everyone looked on Tall One with wonder and a little fear.

*S*he came upon the stranger by accident. She had been scavenging in the tall foliage that fringed the western lake for salamander eggs when she heard him at the water's edge. She had never seen him before—a tall youth with broad shoulders and muscular thighs—and as she spied on him she wondered where he had come from.

The Family had arrived at the lake the day before to find the water covered with ash and all the fish dead and rotting. Foraging for turtle and reptile eggs had proven fruitless, and the vegetation along the shore was so choked with volcanic ash that roots had come up black and inedible. Bird life had left so there were no nests filled with the good eating of crane and pelican eggs. There was only a small flock of ducks struggling for survival among the withered cattails and reeds. All able-bodied family members had dispersed in a wide area in search of food while the elderly and children remained at a camp on a rocky ledge that was relatively safe from predators. Tall One had spotted a small group of zebras kneeling at the water's edge, trying to drink through the ash, when she had espied the young stranger. He was doing a puzzling thing.

While holding a long strip of animal sinew, looped and fitted with a stone, with his other hand he tossed a pebble onto the water, causing the mallards to suddenly take flight. Then the stranger swung the sinew over his head and let loose the stone. Before Tall One's astonished eyes, the stone shot through the air and hit one of the ducks, causing it to plummet. The youth splashed out into the shallow water and retrieved the dead bird.

Tall One gasped.

The stranger stopped. He turned in her direction and peered intently at the wall of grasses until Tall One, inexplicably emboldened, stepped out.

She felt bold because she was wearing the powerful water-stone on a grass string around her neck. It lay between her breasts like a giant drop of water, its cloudy center, formed three million years ago when cosmic diamond-dust had melded with earth quartz, shimmering like a heart.

She and the stranger regarded each other warily.

His appearance was slightly different from that of the Family: his nose a different shape, his jaw stronger, his eyes an intriguing moss color. But his hair, like that of Tall One's family, was long and tangled and matted with red mud, but he had decorated it with bits of shell and stone, which Tall One thought very fetching. Most intriguing about him was the collection of ostrich eggs that hung about his waist on a belt of woven reeds. The eggs had holes in them and the holes were plugged with mud.

Although their languages were dissimilar, the young male was able to explain that his name was Thorn and that he had come from another family across the plain, in a valley Tall One had never seen. Through gestures and sounds, he told Tall One how he had come to be named Thorn.

As he hopped around howling in mock pain, mimicking his accident as he massaged his buttocks where many thorns had imbedded themselves, Tall One quickly grasped that he had gotten his name when he had fallen into a thorn bush. She laughed hysterically, and when he was finished, pleased by her laughter, he held out the dead bird to her.

She grew somber. A memory suddenly darkened her mind: long ago, before Lion was the leader, before the leader named River even, when Tall One had been very small, two strangers coming into the camp. They had come from over the ridge, where the Family had never gone. All were wary at first, and then the new males had been accepted into the group. But then something had happened—a fight. Tall One remembered the blood, and the Family's leader lying dismembered in the grass. One of the two strangers had taken his place and the Family followed him after that.

Was this stranger going to kill Lion and become the new leader?

While she watched him in silent curiosity, Thorn caught a few more ducks with his sling and rocks, and together they took them back to Tall One's camp.

The Family shouted with delight over the fowl, for they hadn't tasted flesh in days, and then they turned their curiosity to the newcomer. Children peered shyly from behind their mothers' legs while older girls eyed him boldly. Honey-Finder reached down and tickled Thorn's genitals, but he jumped back, laughing, his eyes on Tall One. When Lion gestured to the ostrich eggs around the stranger's waist, Thorn untied one and offered it to him. Lion puzzled over the plugged hole, figured it out, then dipped his finger in the hole and was stunned to find water inside instead of yolk. Thorn demonstrated by up-ending the egg and letting water dribble into his mouth. Then he gave the egg to Lion to drink. The Family was astounded. What sort of bird laid eggs with water inside? But Tall One understood: Thorn had put the water in the empty eggshells. From there she drew an even more startling conclusion, one that she had no words for and was only a struggling idea in her mind: *Thorn carried water with him against future thirst.*

They threw the ducks onto the fire, singeing off the feathers and partially cooking the flesh, and the Family enjoyed a feast that night, ending it by merrily throwing bones at one another. Old Mother happily sucked on duck marrow and gulped down the fresh water from the ostrich eggs. All the females in the group eyed the new young male, whose antics and strength aroused them. And even the males, for a while, were happy to welcome the intruder into their midst.

*J*he Family stayed by the lake, feasting on Thorn's ducks for as long as they lasted. Thorn didn't sit by the fire as the other males did, chipping stone tools and fashioning spears. There was a restlessness in him, and a need for attention. To Tall One he seemed like a big child, eager to make others laugh with his capers. Before their mildly curious eyes he gamboled and romped, jumped and mimed, for no apparent reason. But after a few nights of this, with Tall One being the first to understand what he was about, the Family began to grasp that there was meaning to the newcomer's shenanigans.

He was telling stories.

Audiences in a future age would call him a ham, but Tall One's family was held in thrall by his theatrics. Entertainment was unknown to them, and the recounting of past events even more alien. But as they began to understand his gestures and sounds and facial expressions, they began to see the stories emerge. They were simple tales, tiny dramas in which Thorn acted out a hunt with the people victoriously carrying a giraffe haunch back to the camp, or a near-drowning in which a child was saved, or a fierce struggle with a crocodile, resulting in death. Thorn soon had Tall One's family laughing and slapping their thighs, or crying and wiping tears from their cheeks, or gasping in fear or grunting in wonder. Food might be scarce on this lake abandoned by other animals, and the water might be foul and brackish, killing even the resident fish, but Thorn made the humans forget their thirst and hunger as he told over and over again the comical story of how he got his name. They never tired of seeing him fall into the "thorn bush" and suffer the thorns being plucked out of his buttocks.

And then one night he astounded them further by suddenly transforming himself into someone else.

He got up from his place by the fire and began to shuffle around the circle in a strange manner—his left arm curled up to his chest, his left leg dragging behind. At the first they gave him puzzled looks, and then they gasped. He looked just like Scorpion! Suddenly terrified, they looked around to see if Scorpion was still there—had he somehow taken possession of Thorn's body? But there he was, looking at the newcomer in shock. Scorpion's left side had been growing increasingly numb, rendering his left arm and leg almost useless.

And then, before their startled eyes, Thorn jumped into another stance, swaying his hips and pantomiming stuffing his face with food. Honey-Finder!

Nostril shouted out in anger and fear, but some of the children were laughing. And then when Thorn tugged at his long matted hair until it stood out, and walked with small mincing steps—and everyone instantly recognized Baby—others began to laugh.

Soon he had everyone howling with hysterics and it became a game. He would shamble along, examine a stick, and everyone would shout, "Snail!" He would scratch his back up and down on a tree and everyone would call out, "Lump!" And when he lifted a small boy onto his back, hooking the child's arms under his chin and the boy's legs around his waist in imitation of the putrid hide Lion wore, everyone clutched their stomachs and shrieked with laughter.

Thorn was happy to make them laugh. This family was not unlike his own: they foraged for the same food, followed ancient paths, lived by the same structure. Females and children grouped together, the males in their own separate group, and yet all strived for the survival of the Family. The females engaged in the same grooming and child-rearing sessions while the males whittled spears and cut hand axes from stones. Anger was swift to rise and quickly died. There were the familiar jealousies and envy, friendships and enemies. Old Mother reminded him of Willow in his family, with her bandy legs and withered breasts and toothless gumming of her food. Nostril and Lump reminded him of his siblings, and how he had romped with them when they were young.

And then there was Tall One.

She was different from the others, not just taller but also wiser. He saw how somberly she would observe the smoking mountain on the horizon, how her brow would furrow at the sight of the black clouds billowing across the sky. He himself had observed the same phenomenon and found it troubling. But more than Tall One's intelligence was Thorn drawn to her strong body, her long limbs and firm stride.

He liked the way she laughed, and how she treated the weaker females
with fairness and always made sure everyone had something to eat.
She made him remember the females in his own family, a memory
that was rapidly growing dim.

Thorn didn't know why he had left his family. One morning an
inexplicable restlessness had come over him. He had gathered his
hand ax and his club and had left. Other males before him had done
the same: his mother's brother, Short Arm, and Thorn's older brother,
One Ear. Not all males left Thorn's family. Most stayed. But the wan-
derlust gripped a few in each generation, and when they went away
they never came back.

Thorn had walked away from his sleeping family with vague images
in his mind: of the female who had given him life, of his female
siblings. Now, as he looked at this tall alluring female, he was not
aware that the shortage of willing females in his family had been at
the root of his departure, that he had left out of instinct, just as other
young males from other human groups had from time to time over
the generations joined his own family. Thorn hadn't said good-bye.
In time, his family will have forgotten him just as, in time, Thorn
would forget them.

*T*he lake finally became so polluted that the last of the ducks disappeared, forcing the Family to move on.

Conditions worsened. They started coming upon dead animals and
although at first it meant feasts of meat for the Family, as they continued their westward trek and found more and more dead eland and
wildebeest, elephant and rhino—hundreds and thousands of stinking
carcasses, the air thick with the stench of rotting flesh and clouds of
black flies—the flesh by now was too putrid for the humans to eat.

Tall One realized that the herd animals were dying because the
vegetation was covered with ash and cinders. Only the scavengers
were eating well, the jackals, hyenas, and vultures, all growing fat.
She and Thorn were in agreement that there was a connection between the volcano and the animals dying. But Lion insisted that the
Family keep moving westward to find water and food.

With each passing day, the water sources became increasingly foul.
Food grew scarce as small animals had vanished and plants were buried in soot. The sky grew darker and the ground rumbled with in-

creasing frequency. Each sunset Tall One would watch the smoking mountain with dismay and understand clearer than ever that Lion was leading them into danger.

Mothers' milk dried up and infants perished. After carrying her dead baby for days, Weasel finally sat down beside a towering termite hill that days ago would have provided a feast for the Family but that was now inexplicably devoid of termites, and she bent her head over her baby and stayed there while the Family moved on.

One night Tall One tossed in restless sleep, her dreams visited by the smile and comic antics of Thorn. She stirred in a heat she had never felt before, and a longing that was like hunger yet it was not food she desired. She awoke to the lone howl of a distant dog, and then she saw a silhouette moving through the sleeping camp. She recognized Thorn and wondered what he was doing. Perhaps just to relieve himself. Perhaps he would come to her nest-bed. But Thorn crept straight through the camp, past the periphery and out onto the open plain. Tall One followed, but only as far as the protective torches and acacia-branch fence, where Snail and Scorpion sat sentry. She waited for Thorn to return. By dawn he had not come back and the Family had to move on.

After four days and Thorn had not rejoined the group, Tall One wept silently in her nest-bed, fearful that her enchanting stranger was dead, and wondering why he had left when the Family had so welcomed him. The passion she had started to feel for him was replaced with pain and grief, emotions the young female had never experienced before.

And then suddenly he was there, standing on a hillock with the westering sun at his back, waving his arms and jumping up and down. The Family recognized his sounds and gestures as being good signs, and ran to him. He beckoned for them to follow, and they tramped en masse behind the young man as he led them along a curving streambed, now dry and waterless, and over another hill, along a narrow rocky canyon, until they climbed a slight incline and he pointed proudly to what he had found.

A grove of tamarind trees. And every part of the tamarind tree was edible.

The humans swarmed the tall, densely branched trees like locusts, grabbing for the pulpy seedpods, tearing at the leaves, stripping bark and stuffing their mouths. The fleshy fruit slaked thirst and the bark staved off hunger. Fire-Maker started a fire and everyone threw tamarind seeds into the hot stones for later consumption.

Now Tall One wept with joy, and with admiration. Everyone had thought Thorn ran away out of hunger and thirst. But now they knew he had gone in search of food for the Family—and had found it.

The balance of power shifted in an instant. Thorn was now given the plumpest tamarind fruit. Lion was given the leavings.

When the tamarind trees had been stripped clean and could yield not another leaf, seed, or piece of bark, the Family moved on. But this time they carried liquid with them. Before they could consume all the moisture found in the tamarind fruit, Thorn had shown them how to squeeze the juice into empty ostrich eggs to carry with them.

They still came upon rotting carcasses, but the marrow was good and sustaining. For a while, the volcano rested and the stars were briefly seen again. And when Thorn led the Family to an artesian well that gave them freshwater, he decreed that here they would spend the night.

Lion was not consulted.

The heat that had begun to burn in Tall One, the night everyone thought Thorn had abandoned them, continued to grow within her until thoughts of Thorn filled her mind night and day. She hungered for his body, for his touch. When the Family groomed by the campfire, it was Thorn she wanted to feel plastering mud on her skin. Tall One would glance shyly across the camp and see him there with the other young males, demonstrating to them how he made his sling, laughing with them. And when he looked her way, she felt the heat surge, like sparks shooting from the embers.

Overcome with restlessness, she left the group and went to the rocky outcrop where a few sooty herons waded in the artesian water. She was vaguely aware of being glad to see the stars and the moon, even though the sky was still hazy, and she was glad the ground hadn't rumbled in days. And she might have pondered these mysteries were she not in the grip of a strange spell.

When she heard footfalls through the dry grass she was not alarmed. An instinct told her who it was, and why he had followed her. She turned and saw Thorn's smile in the moonlight.

She had seen others act this way so many times without under-

standing why they did it, the touching and fondling, tasting and sniffing. But now it made her warm all over. Thorn pressed his mouth to
her cheeks and neck, and rubbed his nose against hers; Tall One's
hands found places on his body that made him moan. He grinned
and she giggled. They began to tickle one another until Tall One,
shrieking with laughter, suddenly pulled away and ran from him.
Thorn gave chase, howling and waving his arms. Tall One made sure
she didn't outrun him, although she could have with her long legs.
When he caught her, both screaming with laughter, Tall One dropped
to her knees and allowed him to thrust into her. Before he was finished, she pulled away and, giggling, rolled onto her back and pulled
him down. As he thrust into her again, she clasped him tightly and
rolled over and over with him inside her, her cries of pleasure rising
up to the sky.

They spent their days completely involved in each other. He sniffed
her all over. She tasted the salt in his armpits. Thorn jumped up and
down and pranced. He stood as tall as he could and expanded his
chest to show her how big he was. She coyly looked away, pretending
not to care. Although he had his pick of females, his affection was
only for Tall One. They groomed each other and slept in the same
nest-bed, arms and legs intertwined. Tall One had never known such
deep affection, not even for Old Mother. When she lay in Thorn's
arms she felt no fear, and when he caressed her and thrust himself
into her, she clung to him with an aching passion. There was something else, too: she was no longer alone in her fear of the new danger
because Thorn, too, looked up at the sky and saw how the wind blew
the smoke and knew that peril lay just beyond the next dawn.

*O*ld Mother finally died, closing her eyes as her head was pillowed
on Tall One's pregnant belly. The Family howled and beat the ground
with sticks, then finally they left Old Mother's body in the grass and
moved on.

One morning when the sky was filled with smoke and the ground
rumbled, Honey-Finder's oldest daughter, having recently entered puberty and discovering exciting new instincts blossoming within her,
watched Thorn while he created a new sling out of sinew stripped
from the carcass of an eland. She eyed his broad shoulders and strong
arms, then she approached him, giggling, and bent over, wiggling her

bare bottom. Thorn was instantly aroused. But she wasn't the partner he desired. Jumping up, he looked around for Tall One and, seeing her shelling seeds from baobab pods, ran up to her. He tickled her, played with her hair, jumped around and made comical noises. She laughed and pulled him down among the bushes where they coupled beneath the hot sun.

Lion watched in cold detachment. Ever since the stranger had arrived, the females had stopped offering themselves to him. Children followed the newcomer around, males looked upon Thorn with admiration. With his killing stones Thorn managed to bring down the occasional bird that braved the smoke-filled sky. At night he amused them with his comical miming. Everyone loved Thorn.

The idea was Honey-Finder's, since she too was unhappy with the way Thorn had upset the balance of power in the Family. Now that Lion had been deposed, so had she, with Tall One, now pregnant, taking her place as the dominant female.

They approached Thorn with smiles and gestures of friendship— Lump, Hungry, Nostril, and Honey-Finder, Lion's loyal faction. He was sitting beneath the shade of an acacia, working stiff sinews into new slings. Thorn had harvested the long tendons from the decomposed carcass of a giraffe, and now he chewed them and pounded them with rocks until they were pliant enough to make an accurate weapon.

He looked up into Honey-Finder's grin. She was offering him a handful of small withered apples. Thorn was delighted. This strong female had not warmed to him since he joined the Family. He was pleased to know now that she had finally accepted him. As he rose to his feet and reached for the apples, Lion and the other males suddenly appeared carrying clubs and sticks and big rocks.

Thorn gave them a puzzled look. Then he grinned and offered them a share of the apples. When Lion slapped the fruit away, Thorn's face went blank, and in the next instant they were upon him, five large males swinging their weapons against his slender body.

Holding up his arms to protect himself, Thorn stumbled backward and fell against the tree. As the blows came raining down upon him, he tried frantically to understand what was happening. He fell to his knees and scrambled for the slings lying in the grass. He held them up, but Lion's club slammed against his forearms. Thorn tried to do something funny, to make them laugh, but blood was streaming from his nose and scalp. As he fell to his knees, he held out his hands in a question: why? Lion swung his club hard to the side of Thorn's head, creating a loud *crack*. As he curled up and tried to protect himself, Thorn cried out beneath the rain of blows and kicks. Just before he lost consciousness, his mind came alive with images: of the female who had birthed him, of the camp in the valley where he had grown up, of laughing with his siblings, of knowing the freedom of the savanna beneath the hot sun. And then pain swept over him like a black tide. His last thought before death was of Tall One.

Having heard the cries, Tall One and the others came crashing through the brush, and when she saw Thorn's savaged body, she shrieked up to the sky. She fell upon Thorn and bellowed her outrage. She pulled at his shoulders, trying to wake him up; she licked his wounds and tasted his blood. She took his battered face in her hands and let her tears fall upon the bruised flesh. But he remained still and unbreathing. The family watched in silence as Tall One continued to wail and beat the ground with her fists. And then she, too, fell deadly silent, and when at last she rose to her feet, everyone fell back.

She was a vision of power—tall and pregnant with the blue waterstone flashing between her full breasts. She met the eyes of Thorn's killers one by one, and all of them except Lion and Honey-Finder looked away in shame.

Silence fell over the scene, broken only by the buzzing of insects and the distant sound of earth rumbling. The whole Family looked on, even the children held their tongues as Tall One challenged her adversaries with an unwavering glare.

And then, all eyes following her, she bent slowly and retrieved from the grass one of Thorn's slings and a stone. Lion drew himself up in preparation, fingers tightening around the grip of his club. But Tall One moved so swiftly and unexpectedly that she caught him off guard. In the wink of an eye, she had Thorn's sling fitted with the sharp stone and with one arching sweep of her arm, brought it squarely against Honey-Finder's skull.

Startled, the older female staggered back. Before anyone could react, before Lion could raise his club even, Tall One swung the sling again, this time catching Honey-Finder between the eyes. With a cry she fell, and in the next instant Tall One was standing over her, swinging the sling downward with great force, again and again, until Honey-Finder's face was bashed beyond recognition.

When it was over Tall One turned to Lion and spat contemptuously at his feet.

He did not move. With hot wind whipping volcanic ash and cinders about her, Tall One kept her eyes on Lion, fixed them on him, skewering him to the spot, even though he was bigger and stronger and carried spears and a club, and his back was armored with the rotten pelt of a lioness.

As they challenged each other with locked gazes, mutual hatred filling the air like sparks from the volcano, and the Family looked on, breathlessly awaiting the next move, the earth suddenly shook, more violently than it had ever done, knocking people off their feet.

Instinctively the Family ran for nearby trees, but Tall One did not move. Behind the forest rose the fiery mountain. Ash rained down, hot coals and incandescent debris. The top branches exploded with fire.

And suddenly it all came clear to her, the nameless danger that had begun to stalk her months ago, her growing sense of dread, of knowing something was wrong. Now she made another leap: *This place was not good.* And although her species had lived and evolved here for millions of years, it was time to leave.

She looked down at the water-stone hanging between her breasts. She lifted it up and held it in the flat of her hand like an egg, and as she turned her back on the fiery mountain, she saw that the narrow end of the blue stone pointed directly ahead, toward the east, and at its diamond-crystal heart she saw a river and the promise of water.

Raising an arm, she pointed toward the west where the sky was filled with black volcanic smoke and she cried, "Bad! We die!" Then she lifted her other arm and pointed to the clear sky in the east. "There! We go!" Her voice was strong and rang out over the rumbling noise. The Family exchanged nervous glances and she could see by their posture that many wanted to go with her. But they were still afraid of Lion.

"We go," she said more firmly, pointing.

Lion turned toward the smoking volcano in a gesture of defiance and fearlessness, and as he began to walk, others followed after him— Hungry, Lump, and Scorpion.

Tall One spat contemptuously on the ground again, then she took

a last look at Thorn, his poor battered body already disappearing beneath a fine coating of ash. She looked at the others—Baby, Nostril,
Fire-Maker, Fishbone—and when she saw that they were staying with
her, she turned her back on the lethal cloud filling the western sky
and took her first decisive step eastward, back the way they had come.

They didn't pause to look back at Lion and his small group heading
resolutely westward, but stayed close to Tall One whose long stride
nearly outpaced them. Along the way they stopped to collect ostrich
eggs and fill them with fresh water, and when they found food, Tall
One instructed her companions not to eat everything but to carry
seeds and nuts with them, against future need.

As they trekked eastward, the ground continued to rumble, and
finally the mountain exploded. Tall One and her group turned to see
an enormous black cloud rapidly spreading across the sky, blotting out
the sun and engulfing the west in a doomsday inferno. It was to be
the final eruption of a volcano that would, on a far future day, be
called Kilimanjaro. And it smothered in an instant Lion and his stubborn little band of followers.

Interim

𝓕illed with sadness over the death of the young male who had so
charmed her, and with the resolution never to forget him, Tall One
turned her back on the garden that had once been her world and,
armed with the water-stone, and believing that her power to lead her
people came from this rather than from within herself, continued to
take her Family eastward where, as she had predicted, they found
freshwater. She paused long enough to give birth to her first child,
not knowing that he was the progeny of the young male named
Thorn. Then they moved on until finally they reached a seashore
bountiful with shellfish and, when they dug into the ground, freshwater wells. They found here also a new kind of tree that provided
food, water, and shade: the coconut palm that grew in abundance.
Here the Family stayed for another thousand years until they grew
too populous for the local food supply and had to splinter again. Some
headed southward along the coast to settle southern Africa, but the
majority moved northward following the shorelines of lands that
would someday be called Kenya, Ethiopia, Egypt. They stopped for

generations, populating a place, and then moved on, always in search of new food sources and untouched territory. And with them went the blue stone, handed down from generation to generation.

As the millennia passed, the descendants of Tall One spread their seed along rivers and valleys, over mountains and forests, braving new territory that was far away from their origins, learning to build shelters or to live in caves, creating words and ways to communicate, developing new tools and weapons and hunting techniques. As language skills improved, so did social organization, which enabled the creation of planned hunting parties. Humans evolved from scavengers to predators. Thinking was born and therefore questions, and with questions came the need for answers. And thus were spirits, taboos, right and wrong, ghosts, and magic born. Thus did the blue stone, sparkling fragment of an ancient meteor, having traveled with the humans, revered and cherished, become no longer powerful in itself but powerful because of the spirit that inhabited it.

When Tall One's descendants reached the Nile, they split up, some to stay, others to push on, and the blue stone was carried northward to where glaciers coated the world in blinding white ice. Tall One's people encountered others who were already there—another race of humans who had sprung from separate ancestors and who were therefore slightly different, heavier, stockier, and hairier. Clashes over territory were inevitable and the magic water-stone fell into the hands of the foreign clan, who worshipped wolves. A medicine woman of this Wolf Clan looked deep into the crystal's heart and recognized its magic, and so she had it set into the belly of a stone figurine.

Thus did the water-stone become a symbol of pregnancy and female power.

Book Two

THE NEAR EAST
35,000 Years Ago

They had never seen fog before.

The frightened women, so far from their home and hopelessly lost, thought the white mist was a malevolent spirit creeping into the woodland on ghostly feet, cutting the fugitive humans off from the rest of the world, keeping them imprisoned in a silent, featureless realm. By afternoon the mist would dissipate enough to give the women a brief glimpse of their surroundings and then, when the stars came out, would sneak back and isolate the women once more.

But the mist wasn't the only menace in this strange new landscape where Laliari's tribe had wandered for weeks. Ghosts were everywhere—hidden, nameless, terrifying. Therefore the wanderers stayed close together as they moved through this hostile world, shivering in the swirling mist because they wore only grass skirts—adequate clothing for the warm river valley that had been their home but insufficient in this strange new land into which they had been forced to flee.

"Are we dead?" Keeka whispered as she held her sleeping baby against her breast. "Did we perish with the men in the angry sea and now we are ghosts? Is *this* what it is like to be dead?" She was referring to their blindness in the thick fog, the eerie way their voices carried, the dull sounds their bare feet made on the ground. It was as if they were moving through a realm not of the living. Keeka thought they must at least *look* like ghosts—certainly her companions did as they moved cautiously through the thick white mist, bare-breasted women with hair down to their waists, their bodies heavily ornamented with shell, bone, and ivory, bundles of animal hides strapped across their shoulders, their hands clutching stone-tipped spears. *But they hadn't the faces of ghosts*, Keeka thought. Their eyes, stretched wide with fear and confusion, were definitely human. "*Are* we dead?" she repeated in a whisper.

But Keeka received no response from her cousin Laliari who was too filled with grief to speak. Because worse than the menacing fog and the cold and the unseen ghosts was the loss of their men.

Doron's dark head disappearing beneath the violent water.

She tried to picture her beloved Doron as he had been before the tragedy—young, beardless, of slender build—a brave hunter who preferred to sit peacefully and carve ivory by the nightly campfire. Doron liked to laugh and tell stories, and he had a rare tolerance for children. Unlike the other men of the clan who had no patience with youngsters, Doron didn't mind them crawling into his lap and in fact enjoyed it and could be seen laughing (although he did turn red with embarrassment when caught). But mostly Laliari remembered Doron's embrace at night, how he would fall asleep afterward with his arms around her as he breathed softly into her neck.

Laliari choked back a sob. She must not think of him. It was bad luck to think of the dead.

The invasion had caught them by surprise. Laliari and her people had been going about their daily life in the river valley they had inhabited for countless generations when strangers from the west had suddenly appeared across the grassy plains, hundreds and thousands of them, saying that their land inland was drying up and becoming a desert. They had explained their plight while greedily eyeing the grassy expanses on either side of Laliari's river, the grazing herds, the plentiful fish and bird life. A bounty of food. But they had wanted it all for themselves. The ensuing territorial dispute had been long and bitter, with the stronger and more numerous newcomers driving Laliari's clan northward, forcing them to flee with their possessions on their backs—the massive elephant bones that formed the framework of their moveable tents, and the hides that stretched over the bones to make the tent walls. When the clan reached the delta where the river branched, they had encountered more people, much like themselves, but unwilling to share their food sources. And so another bloody battle over land and food had taken place, resulting in Laliari's people being pushed out again, this time eastward.

What had started as a large exodus of several hundred people had by then been reduced to a band of eighty-nine, with the women, children, and elderly going ahead while the men stayed at the rear to protect them from the pursuing delta-dwellers. They had come to a vast expanse of boggy marsh and reeds and had started across. Just as the women made it to the other side, they turned in time to see a monstrous wall of water come rushing from out of nowhere, a swift deluge racing across the vast marshland as it swallowed up the unsuspecting men who were halfway across.

The women, on their high ground, had stared in shock as they watched the hunters vanish in an instant beneath the turbulent water, arms and legs tumbling like fragile sticks, the men's cries silenced as water filled their lungs. And then the flood had grown calm and the women, not knowing that this marshy expanse was subjected to the vagaries of neap tides and spring tides—making it a swampland part of the time, an inundation at others—believed themselves to be standing at the edge of a newly formed sea.

Dazed and in shock, they had turned northward, following the eastern edge of the new sea until they had come to an even larger body of water—wider than their own river at its widest point, wider than the new sea covering the marshland of reeds and the bodies of their men. In fact, this vast sea went on to the horizon and the women could see neither land nor trees on the other side. It was also their first time seeing breakers and they screamed in fright at the water rolling toward them in huge waves, crashing on the beach, retreating, only to roll forward again, like an animal trying to attack them. Although they had found bountiful food here in the tide pools—limpets, periwinkles, and mussels—the women had turned and fled, moving inland away from the sea that would one day be called Mediterranean, and crossed a hostile wilderness until they came to a mist-filled river valley that bore little resemblance to their own.

Here, cut off from their ancestral land, from their men and everything they knew, their search for a new home had begun—a ragtag wandering band of nineteen women, two elders, and twenty-two babies and children.

As they trekked through yet another fog-shrouded dawn, having spent another moonless night in fear, the women kept hopeful watch for signs of their clan spirit, the gazelle. They had not sighted one since leaving their river valley. What if there were no gazelles in this strange land? Would the clan die without its spirit? Laliari, trudging along with her kinswomen through the unfamiliar valley, was haunted by an even more frightening thought: that there were worse things than losing their clan spirit. Worse things even than losing their men. Because in this strange mist-enshrouded world they could not see the moon. They had not, in fact, seen it in weeks.

Laliari was not alone in her fears. While the other women mourned the loss of their men, even greater was their grief over the loss of the moon. It had not shown its face in many days and they were beginning to fear that it might be gone forever. Without the moon there could be no babies, and no babies meant the ultimate death of the clan. Already the early signs were among them: in the weeks since they had been roaming on their own, not one of the women had become pregnant.

As Laliari shifted the heavy burden on her shoulders, she looked ahead at the two elders who led the small band through the fog and tried to take comfort from the thought that Alawa and Bellek, with their supernatural powers and knowledge of magic, would find the moon.

But Laliari could not know that Alawa was impelled by a deep terror of her own and that she harbored a terrible secret.

Old Alawa was Keeper of the Gazelle Antlers and therefore keeper of the clan's history. Her name meant "the one who was searched for" because when she was a small child she had gotten lost and the clan had searched for days for her. She had the honor of wearing the gazelle antlers on her head, strapped under her chin with strips of animal sinew. Alawa's earlobes had been so stretched over the years with ornamental plugs that they rested on her bony shoulders. Between her withered breasts hung necklaces of shell, bone, and ivory. Amulets covered the rest of her body, not for ornamentation but for ritualistic magic. Alawa's people knew that for survival every bodily orifice must be guarded against the invasion of evil spirits. In childhood, the nasal septum was pierced with an ostrich quill and kept open through adult-hood with an ivory needle. This prevented evil spirits from entering the body through the nostrils. Ears were pierced, top and bottom, as well as lips. Magic amulets were strung from belts so that they hung protectively over buttocks and pubis, for spirits were known to enter human beings through the rectum and vagina as well.

The other elder was Bellek, clan shaman and Keeper of the Mush-rooms. Like Alawa, his hair was long and white and strung with beads that clicked gently as he walked. His only clothing was a loincloth made of soft gazelle skin, and his body was as heavily decorated with magic amulets as Alawa's. Bellek carried dried mushrooms in a leather pouch, but he also searched for fresh ones in the wooded areas on the banks of this foreign river. Although mushrooms were plentiful and the band ate well of them as they traveled through this strange land of mists and ghosts, Bellek was looking for one mushroom in partic-ular, the one with a long thin stem and distinctive cap that he always thought resembled a woman's nipple. These were the mushrooms that, when ingested, transported a person into a metaphysical plane where supernatural beings dwelled.

Laliari was thankful that the clan still had Bellek and Alawa, for elders were the clan's most prized members and together, Laliari was certain, the old pair would find the moon.

As if sensing the girl's eyes on her, Alawa stopped suddenly and turned to peer through the mist at the younger woman. The others also stopped and looked at Alawa in alarm. The silence that engulfed them was terrifying, for it was the silence of ghosts holding their tongues, of evil spirits waiting to pounce. Several of the women gath-ered their little ones close to them and held babies tight. The moment seemed to hang suspended in time, Laliari held her breath, everyone waited. And then Alawa, having come to a secret decision, turned and resumed her weary trek.

Alawa's secret decision was this: that it was not yet time to tell the others of her new knowledge, which made her heart heavy with sad-ness. She had read the magic stones and studied her dreams, she had looked into the campfire smoke and tracked the flight of sparks, and altogether they had revealed a terrible truth that left no doubt in Alawa's mind.

For the survival of the clan, the children must die.

◆ ◆ ◆

$\mathscr{B}$y afternoon the fog cleared, as they had known it would, allowing the refugees a view of unfamiliar woodland and sandy river bank before the sun dipped to the horizon and robbed them of light.

They stopped to rest. While Keeka and other young mothers settled down to breast-feed and adolescent girls went to draw water, Laliari opened the last of their date reserves and distributed them among the group. The dates had been gathered days before, at a small palm grove on the river. With everyone throwing stones and rocks at the clusters of chewy fruit high overhead, they had reaped a rich harvest, feasting on the spot and then filling their baskets to carry on their backs.

While the others ate, Alawa separated herself from the group to find a partially sunny spot for the reading of her magic stones. At the same time, Bellek, stooped and nearsighted, scrutinized every twig and branch, every shrub and blade of grass to determine whether this was a lucky place to stay. So far, he had seen little good magic here.

Sixty-five thousand years in the past it had not occurred to a man named Lion that his people could alter their circumstances. But it *had* occurred to a girl named Tall One and it was her actions that had led to the survival of her race. This was her legacy to her descendants, to know that they need not be at the mercy of their environment. However, down through the millennia, as humans had multiplied and expanded the boundaries of their world, Tall One's descendents had grown extreme in their new knowledge of change and control, for now they tried constantly to manage every microscopic aspect of their environment through the appeasing and honoring of ghosts. They had to be always on the alert in order to keep their world in balance. The slightest misstep could upset the spirits and bring bad luck upon the people. If they crossed a stream they would first say, "Spirit in this stream, we wish to pass in peace." When they killed an animal, they asked its forgiveness. They were forever "reading" their surroundings. Whereas their ancestors of sixty-five millennia earlier had paid no heed to a smoking volcano, Laliari and her family read omens in the slightest spark from an ember. Which was why Alawa, as she interpreted the toss of her magic stones, wondered what they had done wrong at the Reed Sea to cause it to swallow up the hunters. Of course they hadn't known it was going to be a sea, so how could they have spoken the appropriate words? They hadn't even known its name so how could they have invoked its spirit? But surely there *had* been signs to read—there were always signs. What had they missed that would have prevented the catastrophe?

And, she thought darkly as she gathered up her stones, signs that could have prevented the catastrophe yet to come. For once again the collection of pebbles and small rocks that had been handed down through countless generations, all the way back to the very first Keeper of the Gazelle Horns, told the same message: the children were going to have to die.

She peered through the trees at the tragic collection of women and children. They were weary from lack of sleep. Nightmares plagued them, horrific dreams that Alawa believed were the result of the dead not having had a silent-sitting. If the silent-sitting had been performed, the unhappy ghosts would not now be haunting the dreams of the living.

Her own daughter, running, an invader close on her heels, grabbing her flying hair, pulling her off her feet, slamming her down onto her back, his club coming down again and again.

At first it had only been a few invaders and Doron and the hunters had been able to drive them off. But then more strangers had come, having heard of the lush green savanna teeming with wildlife, and then more invaders, swarming like ants over the western hills until Alawa's people were overwhelmed. Pushed north, they had encountered other settlements—kinsmen whom they saw at the annual gathering of the clans: Crocodile Clan, which Bellek had come from many seasons ago, and Egret Clan, which had been Doron's. There, with the help of kinsmen, Alawa's people had tried to stop and fight. But the invaders, stronger and in greater numbers, had kept up their assault, unwilling to share the abundant valley.

Little Hinto, child of Alawa's daughter, seized by an arm and flung into the air to come down on an invader's spear. Istaqa, Keeper of the Moon-hut, turning to throw a spear at a pursuer, to be struck by a rock in her face with such force that it split her skull open. The blood running into the earth. The screams of the stricken. The moans of the dying. Blind fear and panic. Old Alawa running for her life, her feet pounding in cadence with her thumping heart. Young Doron and the hunters staying behind to protect the women and the elders.

Perhaps they should perform the silent-sitting now, Alawa thought as she rose to her feet, her ancient joints creaking. Perhaps that would appease the unhappy ghosts who were haunting their dreams. But there was a problem: to perform the ritual meant speaking the names of the dead, and to do so would be to break the most powerful taboo in the clan.

She looked at the children and felt an immense sadness sweep over her. So many of them were orphans, their mothers having been killed during the battles with the invaders. And then there was little Gowron, son of her daughter's daughter, playing with a frog he had found. Alawa herself had pierced his little nose with the egret bone that prevented evil spirits from entering his body through his nostrils. It pained Alawa's heart to know he must die.

She turned her attention to Bellek, bent and wheezing as he explored the surrounding tamarisk thickets for signs and omens. He had to find the moon and so it was crucial that he concentrate and pay attention to every little detail. One mistake could spell disaster for them.

Even back on their ancestral land the people had lived in constant fear of the world around them. Death came often, swiftly, and brutally so that even there, among familiar rocks and trees and river, there was enough to be afraid of. The people had been constantly on the alert not to offend any spirits, constantly speaking the spells, carrying the right amulets, making the appropriate gestures that they had all learned since earliest childhood. But one of the problems they faced in this strange place was not knowing the names of things. They saw unfamiliar flowers and trees, birds with new plumage, fish they had never encountered before. What to call them? How to make sure no harm came to the survivors of the Gazelle Clan?

As Alawa watched the withered old shaman go about his readings, crouching to inspect a pebble, sniffing a flower, running dirt through his fingers, she wondered how he was going to react to her news. It occurred to her that Bellek might not like having to kill the children, even if it meant the survival of the clan.

It also occurred to her that Bellek was past usefulness.

Alawa had always been contemptuous of men anyway since they didn't create life, and she had often wondered why the moon even made male children. Perhaps back in their river valley the men had been good for bringing home rhinoceros and hippopotamus meat, work too heavy for women, thus feeding the clan for weeks. But this new place was filled with food for the picking. Hunters were no longer necessary. Was this why her dreams and the magic stones were telling her to sacrifice the children? As a way of cleansing the clan?

Alawa returned her attention to the children as they ate and played and tugged at mothers' breasts. She especially watched the boys, who ranged in age from nursing infant to the threshold of puberty. Boys older than this had left their mothers and joined the band of hunters, and so they had perished in the Reed Sea. As Alawa kept her eyes on the boys she thought again of the dead hunters and the lost moon and the nightmares that were plaguing the women, and the frightening thought that had formed in her mind days ago spoke louder now: that the drowned men were unhappy and jealous of the living. This was why they haunted the women's dreams. How could it be otherwise as there had been no silent-sitting performed for them? Everyone knew that the dead were jealous of the living, which was why ghosts were so greatly feared. And would the dead hunters not be especially jealous of the little boys who they could see growing up to take their places?

Reluctant though she was to carry out the deed, Alawa was firm in her resolve. As long as the hunters continued to be jealous of the boys and therefore haunt the women, the moon would not come out. And without the moon the clan would die. Therefore the little boys must be sacrificed to send the ghosts away. Then the moon would return and put babies into the women again. And thus the clan would survive.

At the next resting stop, the women sat with their backs to trees to nurse babies and cuddle their children. Some, having reached the end of their stamina, began to cry.

They had all lost loved ones in the Reed Sea—sons, brothers, nephews, uncles, sleeping partners. Bellek had watched his younger brothers perish; Keeka, the sons of her mother's sisters; Alawa, five sons and twelve sons of her daughters; Laliari, her brothers and her beloved Doron. A loss beyond comprehension, beyond counting. When the new tide had swallowed up the band of hunters, the women had run up and down the shore, screaming and shouting, hoping for a glimpse of survivors. Two had thrown themselves into the raging water to disappear forever. The women had camped on the new shore for a week until Bellek, after eating magic mushrooms and walking in the nether realm, had decreed the place bad luck and that they must leave. That was when they had gone north to encounter a vast, terrifying sea, and then had turned inland, to go in search of the moon.

But they still had not found it and the women were becoming disconsolate.

Seeing the tears streaking down Keeka's cheeks, Laliari reached into the pouch that hung from her belt and, bringing out a handful of nuts, offered them to her cousin.

Keeka had been plump, before the invaders came. She loved to eat. She had lived in a hut with her mother, her mother's mother, and her own six children, and every evening after the communal meal she would hurry back to the hut to store food away that she had hidden beneath her grass skirt. Keeka also loved coupling with men and didn't need to be coaxed. Nonetheless, the hunters who came and went from her hut with frequency brought her extra gifts of food and so dried fish and rabbit haunches hung from the roof of her shelter, onions and dates and ears of corn. But no one minded. Everyone in the clan ate well.

As Keeka snatched at the nuts and gobbled them down, Laliari looked back through the trees and saw a tragic figure lurking in the mist. *She Who Has No Name*. Laliari was amazed the poor creature had survived this far, being cut off from the clan as she was and having to trail behind the others through the thick fog. Laliari felt sorry for her. People were afraid of childless women because they were thought to be possessed by an evil spirit. How else to explain why the moon had not favored them with babies? Before the invaders came, She Who Has No Name had lived at the edge of the settlement, treated as invisible, eating tossed-away scraps. She had been forbidden to touch food that other people were to eat, or their drinking water, or someone's hut. And no man would embrace her, no matter how desperate his need for sexual release.

No Name had not been born with bad luck. She had in fact started out as any other girl. Laliari remembered when the clan had celebrated No Name's first moonflow, how special she had been treated, according to tradition, everyone speaking her name in joy, pampering her and lavishing her with gifts and food. An even bigger celebration was held when a woman became pregnant for the first time and her status in the clan was greatly elevated. But when No Name's moon-flow kept appearing regularly, and the seasons came and went and she produced no baby, the people had begun to look at her askance until finally she became a pariah, stripped of her name and standing in the clan.

Although Laliari had gotten used to the poor creature that had followed them from the Reed Sea, No Name's shadowy presence now sent fear shooting through her. Without the moon, would they all eventually end up like her?

Laliari curled anxious fingers around the magical amulet she wore about her neck, an ivory talisman that had been carved during the increase of the moon. She also wore a necklace made of over a hundred hornet bodies that she had painstakingly collected, dried, and cleaned smooth. They resembled small nuts and made a soft clacking sound as she walked. It was not for decoration but for the power of the hornet spirits to protect her and her clan, hornets being such fierce defenders of their own homes. And in a tiny pouch that hung from the woven waistband of her grass skirt were the precious seeds and dried petals of the lotus flower, her personal spirit-protector.

But Laliari found little comfort now in amulets and necklaces. She and her sisters and cousins had lost their land, their men, and the moon. If only she could speak the name of her beloved Doron, what a comfort it would be.

But names were powerful magic, not to be uttered frivolously, for a name embodied the very essence of a person and was directly con-nected to his or her spirit. Because names involved magic and luck and determined how a person's life was to run, they were not bestowed lightly but only after great thought and a reading of signs and omens. Sometimes a name changed at adolescence, or after a major event in a person's life. Or depending on a specific occupation they adopted, like Bellek, which meant "reader of signs." Laliari, meaning "born among the lotuses," had been so named because her mother had been drawing water from the river when her birth pains began. For the rest of her life Laliari was protected by the lotus flower. Keeka, "child of the sunset," since that was when she had been born. Freer, "hawk spreads his wings," had been the most powerful of their hunters. A name once used was never used again. Finally, it was bad luck to speak a person's name after death as this summoned his unhappy ghost. And so Laliari had to let Doron's name go unspoken, and therefore Doron himself, ultimately forgotten.

She drew the gazelle hide tighter about herself. When they had found they could stand the cold no longer, the women had untied the bundles they carried on their backs, animal skins meant for creating shelters. At home, when the river was low they lived by the shore, but when the river started its annual rise and flooding of its banks, the people tore down their shelters and relocated to higher ground, building new shelters out of skins and elephant tusks. When they had been forced to flee from the invaders, the women had tied the precious skins into bundles and carried them on their backs. Now they used them as capes against the chill of this foreign land.

As she shivered, Laliari thought of Doron again and how he had warmed her at night in her mother's hut. Tears sprang to her eyes. Laliari loved Doron because he had been so kind and patient with her after the death of her baby. Although most men grieved over the death of any child, since it was a loss to the clan, they quickly got over it and could not understand a mother's prolonged grief. After all, the men reasoned, the moon always gave a woman more children. But Doron had understood. Despite the fact that he himself could never know what it was like to have a son or a daughter, and that his only kinship to a baby could be through his sister's children, he understood that Laliari's baby was of her blood and that she would grieve the way he himself had grieved over the death of his sister's son.

Now Doron was dead. Swallowed up by a newborn sea.

*A*lawa cried out in alarm. The trees were weeping!

It was just the fog, so thick in the valley that moisture had collected on branches and leaves and dripped like rain. But Alawa knew what it really meant: the spirits of the trees were unhappy.

She made a protective gesture and drew hastily back. Her fears were growing daily. Despite Bellek's insistence that the farther north they went the better chance they had of finding the moon, Alawa was not so sure. Everything about their exile had been strange and baffling, starting with the inland sea that contained no fish, no life of any kind. When the women had trekked eastward from the sea that had no opposite shore and had found a body of water in which no fish swam, no algae grew, surrounded by a salt-covered shore that had produced no mussels or reeds—a completely lifeless sea—they had been alarmed. Even Alawa had sworn that she had never seen so strange a sight. But then they had followed the salty shoreline and had come to a river that flowed backward!

Too fearful to take even another step, the group had camped on the shore of the backward-flowing river while Bellek had eaten the magic mushrooms and roamed the land of visions. When he awoke he had decreed that this new river was safe, despite its backward flow, and that they must keep following it, for the moon lay northward beyond the mist.

And so they had gone, trekking first through a dry stretch where the ground was rocky and covered with sparse vegetation, and then to a place along the backwards flowing river where willow, oleander and tamarisk grew. But as they had made their way farther north, the river narrowed and grew winding with hills rising sharply up from the banks. So unlike their own wide and flat river back home! And this river flowed like a snake, switching back on itself so that sometimes Alawa's band was walking westward along its bank, then northward, and then eastward! As if the river couldn't make up its mind.

They had encountered stranger sights still. North of the dead sea they had come upon an open flat plain where rich grasses grew. But where were the animals? Bellek examined the ground and found traces of droppings. So herds had indeed once passed through here. Where were they now? Had the strange nightly fog carried the animals away as it had done the moon?

And now they had come upon trees that wept. With each moonless night, with each day that still produced no pregnant members in their band, Alawa's anxiety grew. The boys must be sacrificed soon or the moon might be lost forever.

At sunset they came upon a sight that stunned them. The women and children fell silent and stared, unable at first to take in the whole horrifying spectacle. At the base of a cliff rose a mountain of skeletons—hundreds of antelopes piled on top of one another, their skulls crushed, their bones broken. Alawa looked up and saw the sheer wall of a cliff rising above the carcasses. These animals had plummeted to their deaths from that plateau. *Why? What had frightened them so?*

The women hurried on, anxious to put the unhappy ghosts of the animals behind them.

Finally they came to the shore of a freshwater lake that future generations would erroneously call the Sea of Galilee. Densely bordered with trees and shrubs, tamarisk and rhododendron, its waters teemed with fish, and abundant bird life crowded the shore. Here the mist had cleared and late afternoon sunlight still warmed the earth. Sniffing the wind and studying the clouds, Bellek held up his staff that was decorated with magic amulets and gazelle tails, and decreed that here the magic was good, here they would make camp and stay the night.

While he and old Alawa went about their nightly ritual of making the encampment safe from malevolent spirits, inscribing protective symbols on the trees and arranging stones in ritualistic order, the women unfurled the hides to create windbreaks. As the elephant tusks had been lost when the hunters drowned, it would be impossible to build proper huts, so they used tree trunks, saplings, and sturdy branches wedged into the ground. The people of the Gazelle Clan practiced communal living—shelters were apportioned not to individual families but according to groups and ritualistic purpose. There were the larger huts where the hunters slept together separate from the women; the individual huts of the revered elderly; the shelters for the young women who had not yet had babies; the women's moon-hut; the shaman's hut; the hut for initiating young hunters; and a few small matriarchal units consisting of grandmother, mothers, sisters, and babies. And the shelters were always round so that there were no corners where spirits could lurk.

Their priorities on this night, as they hurried to make camp before sundown, were Alawa's hut and the moon-hut.

During menstruation women were vulnerable and needed protection from evil spirits and unhappy ghosts that were always waiting for a chance to possess a living human. This was the time of powerful magic, when it was decided if new life would begin in a woman's body. She would look at the moon and its phase would signal her time of separation from the others. She would take her magic amulets and special food, and retreat to wait and watch for the signs: if the moonflow came, there was no child in her. But if it did not show, then she was pregnant. So the moon-hut was erected first, with Alawa chanting protective spells around the entry, festooning strings of cowry shells, powerful symbol of female genitalia, and tracing magic symbols in the earth using red ocher to symbolize precious moon-blood.

The second shelter was for Alawa. Few women lived past menopause and so those who did were treated with the greatest respect for they were believed to possess great moon-wisdom.

As the group searched for food they came upon a tree that was new to them: knee-high and leafy, laden with pods containing white, fleshy seeds. After an experimental taste to make sure the fruit wasn't poisonous, the women began at once to harvest the chickpeas. In the meanwhile Bellek went to the water's edge and, poor though his eyesight was, nonetheless spotted life in the lake's shallows, causing him to smack his lips in anticipation of a meal of cooked fish. The children were sent in search of berries and eggs, with stern admonitions to observe the proper taboos even though they were in a strange land, and to make sure they did not offend any spirits.

Finally Alawa appointed someone to watch for the moon, with instructions to waken everyone at first sighting. With luck, this would be the night the moon rose before the fog came back.

While the women and children gathered around the comforting fire to eat and groom one another, to mend baskets and sharpen spears, to nurse babies and to try to forget their fears, Alawa slipped away to go to the water's edge. If the moon did not show itself tonight, she had decided, then she must act. Tomorrow, the little boys would have to die.

As Keeka fed her six children, she watched the old woman shuffle away from the camp, her once proud body now painfully bent beneath the weight of the gazelle antlers. Keeka had suspected for some time that a secret burdened Alawa. She knew what it was. Alawa was preparing to choose her successor.

And because the Keeper of the Gazelle Antlers was the clan's most important person, the Keeper always had the best hut, the best food. Keeka wanted to be Alawa's successor, but it wasn't something she could simply request. The choice was determined by omens, by reading the signs and interpreting dreams. Once the choice was made, the successor would live at Alawa's side constantly to learn the clan's history, to hear the stories and memorize them, as Alawa had done when she herself was a young woman many seasons ago. And now added to the clan's long history would be a new story—the invasion of the people from the west, the clan's flight up the river valley, the drowning of the men in the new sea, the loss of the moon, and this trek to find a new home.

As Keeka watched Alawa disappear through the lakeside brush, her attention was captured by a high-pitched laugh. Her cousin Laliari had taken one of the orphans into her lap and was tickling him. Keeka's thoughts grew cold. She had a suspicion that Alawa might choose Laliari.

Keeka's hatred of her cousin had begun two years earlier when the handsome Doron had joined the Gazelle Clan. Keeka had done everything she could to entice him into her hut, but he was interested only in Laliari. And that was rare. Physical joining between men and women was always random and serial, with few rules and no commitments. But Doron and Laliari had developed a unique affection that had rendered them disinterested in others, a relationship that foreshadowed marriage and lifelong pair-bonding, concepts that would not exist for another twenty-five millennia.

The more Keeka had wanted the handsome young hunter, and the more he ignored her, the more her desire had grown until having him had become an obsession. When he drowned in the Reed Sea Keeka had felt a secret glee for now not even Laliari could have him. Added to her feelings of triumph over her cousin was the fact that Laliari was childless, her baby having died before it had lived one season. And since there was no moon in this new land to give her another, Keeka, with her brood of six, looked upon her cousin with a sense of smug superiority.

Now she was loathe to think of Laliari being chosen as Alawa's successor.

Eating was done, grooming finished, so it was the hour for stories. The women waited for Alawa to appear in the firelight and begin her evening recitation. Laliari's people craved stories because stories connected them to the past and made them feel part of an otherwise baffling and frightening cosmos. Stories connected them to nature; myths and legends brought comfort in familiarity and explained mysteries. The women and children always fell silent when Alawa began in her frail, creaking voice: "Long, long ago . . . before there was Gazelle Clan, before there were people, before there was the river . . . our mothers came from the south. They were birthed by the First

Mother who told them to go north to find a home. They brought the river with them. With each moonrise they made water to flow, until they came to our valley and knew their wandering was over . . ."

As Alawa's absence from the campfire stretched on, the women tried to curb their fears. They knew she was searching for the moon. But now that night had fallen, the fog was creeping back into the valley and the women suspected Alawa would once again not catch sight of the moon.

Laliari looked up and tried to peer through the foggy ceiling. The moon was more than the giver of babies and regulator of women's bodies, it provided valuable light during the night when it was needed. Unlike the sun, which shone uselessly during the day when it was already light, and unlike the sun, whose face was too bright to be looked upon, a person could gaze at the moon for hours on end and not be blinded. The moon, depending upon its phases, caused flowers to open at night, cats to hunt, tides to swell. The moon was predictable, comforting, like a mother. Every month, after the terrifying days of the Dark Moon, the clan would gather at the sacred spot on the river and watch for the first rise of the Baby Moon—a fingernail sliver on the horizon. They would heave sighs of relief, and then cheer and dance as it rose in the sky, for it meant life was going to continue.

As Laliari cradled one of the motherless little ones in her arms, her thoughts drifted to the baby she had given birth to a year ago. The moon had given it to her shortly after Doron joined the clan. The infant didn't live long, however, and Laliari had had to take it away to the craggy hills in the east and leave it there. Many times after that, she would look toward the rising sun and imagine her baby there. She wondered if his ghost was unhappy. She had felt a curious tug to go back to that spot, but it was bad luck to be near the place of dead things. If someone died in a hut, the hut was burned down and the clan moved farther along the river to set up a new encampment.

Looking back on the time of her baby's sickness and death, Laliari could only blame herself, for surely she had unwittingly offended a spirit so that it punished her by killing her child. And yet Laliari was always so careful to follow the rules and obey the laws of magic and luck. Was that why their territory had been invaded by strangers followed by the death of their hunters in the killing sea of reeds? Had the entire clan somehow overlooked something? Then how were they to hope to survive in this new place when they didn't know any of the rules?

She knew it was bad luck to think of the dead, yet it brought such comfort to fill her mind with memories of Doron. How they had met, for instance. The annual Gathering of the Clans took place every year during the inundation when the river overflowed its banks. Thousands came from up and down the valley, erecting round shelters and hoisting clan symbols. It was during the Gathering that disputes were settled, kinship lines drawn, alliances formed and reinforced, news and gossip shared, debts paid, revenge meted out, and most important of all, family members exchanged. Those families with few women received women from families with a surplus. And those short on men, vice versa. It was a lengthy and complex process carried out by all parties, with elders intervening in instances of conflict. Doron and another young man had been exchanged for two young women from Laliari's clan. Laliari had been sixteen and she and Doron had spent a week covertly scrutinizing each other. It had been a time of shyness and excitement, of awakening instincts. Laliari had never noticed before what wonderfully strong shoulders men had—Doron in particular—and nineteen-year-old Doron had found himself flustered at the sight of Laliari's narrow waist and flaring hips. By the time the annual gathering had broken up and Doron had gone with Laliari and her clan to their ancestral land, they were spending every night in each other's arms.

Suddenly overcome with grief, Laliari rested her forehead on her knees and began silently to cry.

Down at the water's edge, another soul was racked with grief. Alawa, looking out over the expanse of water, had come to a painful decision: this was how the boys must die—by drowning, as the hunters had died.

She turned at the sound of footsteps and saw Bellek's familiar silhouette emerge through the tall reeds. He stood beside her for a long moment, his bony chest rising and falling in labored breathing. He had known for some time that Alawa was coming to an important decision. *She is getting ready to choose her successor,* he thought.

He would have liked to have a say in the choice, but only the Keeper of the Gazelle Antlers knew who the next Keeper should be. It had nothing to do with opinions and votes but with what the spirit

world wanted, what the gazelle spirit wanted. And only Alawa knew
what was in her dreams and what her magic stones were telling her.

"Is it to be Keeka?" he asked softly, hoping it was not. Keeka possessed a streak of gluttony that he feared might be detrimental to the
clan. If the choice were his, he would pick Laliari because the keeper
of the clan's stories had to be free of selfishness.

Alawa shook her head slowly because of the weight of the gazelle
antlers. When she was younger the horns had been almost weightless.
But with age, they had grown heavy so that her neck bent beneath
them. "Tomorrow the boys must die," she said in a croaking voice.

He looked at her as if he had not heard correctly. "What did you
say?"

"The little boys must die. The ghosts of the hunters are jealous of
them and that is why they haunt us and why the moon stays away.
If the boys do not die, then the clan will die. Forever."

He drew in a sharp breath and traced a protective gesture in the
air.

"We will do it in the lake," Alawa said resolutely. "The hunters
drowned and so the boys must drown." She turned sharp eyes to him.
"Bellek, you too must die."

"Me?" He blanched. "But the clan needs me!"

"The clan will still have *me*. And if the moon wishes us to have
men, it will give us new ones."

"But what threat am I? The boys, yes, because they will grow up
to be hunters. But I am an old man."

Her voice rose. "And you have made the hunters jealous by *staying*
alive. Selfish man! Would you threaten the extinction of our people
by not sacrificing yourself?"

He began to tremble. "Can there be a mistake?"

"You dare!" she cried. "You question my dreams! You question what
the spirits have told me. You bring bad luck upon all of us with your
doubt!" She waved her hands in front of her eyes as if to chase away
an evil spirit. "Deny what you just said or we shall all suffer the
consequences!"

"I am sorry," he said in a thin voice. "I did not mean to doubt.
The spirits have spoken. The—" He could hardly bring himself to say
it. "The boys will die."

◆ ◆ ◆

*W*hile Alawa slept beneath soft animal skins, Laliari sat with her back to the hide wall. She had been surprised when the old woman had asked her to keep her company in the hut, and Laliari had not missed the looks of admiration and envy among the others. Keeka especially, as everyone knew what this must mean: that Alawa was considering choosing Laliari as her successor.

But the old woman had gone right to sleep, and now it was warm and close in the hut. Laliari drew her knees to her chest and, folding her arms on her knees, rested her head on her forearms. She had not meant to fall asleep. But when she woke, the light from the misty dawn was creeping beneath the tent. And she knew without looking that Alawa was dead.

The young woman flew out of the shelter, her hair standing out in terror. She had never been in close proximity to a person at the moment of death before. Where had Alawa's spirit gone? Laliari remembered back at home on the river, a man and woman had been sleeping together and the man had awakened to find the woman dead. Bellek had done readings and proclaimed that the man was now possessed with the spirit of the dead woman. So the clan had driven him out of the settlement and wouldn't allow him to come back. They never saw him again.

In a panic, Laliari pinched her nostrils, belatedly trying to keep the old woman's ghost from entering her. Her wails woke the others. At once they tore down Alawa's hut and made preparations for the silent-sitting. Bellek examined Laliari with great scrutiny, looking into her ears, eyes, mouth, and vagina until he was satisfied. "No spirit there," he said firmly, putting her at ease. Maybe Alawa had been too old for her spirit to leave her body quickly, as it did with younger people. That old ghost might even now still be struggling to escape its casing of flesh. Bellek informed the distressed women that they must do a good silent-sitting, to ensure that when they moved on, old Alawa would not follow and haunt them.

It was a ritual as old as time, handed down through the generations from the first people to mourn the dead. Bellek traced a circle in the dirt around Alawa's corpse and chanted magic words. While he did this, the women ate and drank their fill, for they would be fasting during the next cycle of the sun. Even the children must sit silently with their mothers, leaving the circle only to relieve themselves when their bladders were full. The silence was to be absolute and no one was to eat or drink, for if they did it would upset the spirit of the deceased and make it jealous. Everyone knew that ghosts were un-happy—after all, no one wanted to die. And so being unhappy, ghosts would want to make the living unhappy, too, and therefore haunt them. The purpose of silent-sitting was to convince the ghost that this place was boring, no food or drink or laughter here, hoping it would move on to seek better places.

Bellek had covered the corpse with a gazelle-skin blanket, telling the others that it was to keep Alawa's spirit from trying to possess one of them. But he had done it for another reason. No one but he had noticed the marks upon the old woman's throat, and the look of fear that had frozen on her face at death—proof that Alawa had misinterpreted her dreams and had made a mistake about the hunters wanting the little boys to be sacrificed. Because how else could she have died of fright and strangulation if it hadn't been the ghosts of the hunters creeping into her tent and killing her?

Luckily, Alawa had not confided her plans to anyone else, and so Bellek kept the secret to himself. For as long as he was alive, the little boys—and himself—would be safe.

After the grieving women had sat in a silent circle for one day and one night, their stomachs growling from hunger, their mouths dry with thirst, their joints aching from not moving, the children restless and irritable, they divided up Alawa's possessions according to indi-vidual need, with the gazelle antlers going to Bellek, and, leaving her body where it lay, broke camp and resumed their trek north.

The nights grew colder, the fog rolled in again and again, and the women of the Gazelle Clan, unfamiliar with autumn and its mists and not knowing that it would eventually give way to winter rain, believed they would be trapped in fog forever. They shivered in their flimsy shelters, got little sleep and found little warmth until finally one night they were awakened by a fierce storm that was unlike anything they had ever experienced—a tempest that roared from the west, shrieked down the nearby mountains and blasted the frail encampment with an icy breath and rain that fell like spears. The women fought the wind to keep their shelters, but the malevolent gale, howling like a beast in pain, snatched away the protective gazelle hides and carried them out over the turbulent lake. Trees and shrubs were uprooted, sodden branches flew by while the terrified women clutched one another and tried to protect the children.

When it was over and daybreak exposed a devastated landscape, the women beheld a sight that struck them dumb: the mountains, once green, were now white.

"What is it?" Keeka said, holding her little ones close as other women cried and wailed in fear. Laliari stared at the distant peaks and felt a cold lump form in her throat. What *did* the white mountains mean? Were the mountains now ghosts? Did it mean the world was coming to an end?

Old Bellek, shivering with damp, his lips and fingers raw from the cold, looked mournfully out over the lake where the gazelle hides floated on the water. He wasn't afraid of the white mountains—long ago, in his boyhood, he had heard tales of something called snow. The world wasn't coming to an end, but the weather *was* changing. He decided that, for survival, the group must find sturdier shelter.

He turned toward the west and contemplated the cliffs that rose like sheer walls from the undulating plane. The cliffs were gouged with caves. Bellek suspected that they might be warm and dry inside, but the old man was wary of caves. His people had never lived in them and certainly had never explored inside them. Caves were where bats and jackals lived. Worse, caves were where the spirits of the unhappy dead dwelled. Still, he thought as he rubbed his freezing arms, without the elephant tusks, and now the gazelle hides, how were the women to make adequate shelters?

When he announced his decision to investigate the caves, a chorus of protests rose up. But Laliari, seeing the wisdom of the decision, offered to accompany him. However, she had been in the moon-hut during the storm, and her monthly flow had not yet ceased, so they had to wait.

By the third day it was safe for her to travel, and so they collected food and water and spent a day in spiritual preparation. They departed heavily armed with powerful amulets and with mystical symbols painted on their bodies as protection against ghosts and supernatural beings. With the women and children sobbing an unhappy farewell, the brave pair struck westward from the lake.

They reached the cliffs at noon, where they paused to eat dates and plover eggs, and to chant incantations to appease hostile spirits. Laliari started up first, finding the easiest route among the boulders, then stopping to help Bellek. They found a crude trail leading to the caves and their rocky ledges, a trail littered with animal bones and flint tools, indicating that people had once lived here.

Laliari chanted aloud as she went, more as a warning to possible humans than to appease spirits. If there were indeed people living here, she didn't want to startle them or catch them unawares. Best to let her presence be known, she decided, a noisy approach meant they had nothing to hide and came in friendship.

But they found no people.

The limestone caves were deep and dark, and inhabited only by formidable stalagmites. In each, Laliari and Bellek found stone tools littering the floor—hand axes, scrapers, and cleavers—as well as an-imal remains—horse, rhinoceros, and deer—which indicated that people had once lived here, and had eaten well, too. But where they had gone, the humans who had left charred hearths, broken tools and, in some instances, perplexing symbols painted on the limestone walls, the two explorers could only guess.

After a day and a night of investigating the caves, Laliari and Bel-lek grew discouraged. Although these were clearly excellent shelters—after all, other people had found them habitable—it was precisely *because* other people had lived in them that Bellek could not bring his clan here. The cave they selected would have to be untouched by humans or spirits or they might be inviting the worst luck upon their heads.

By the second sunset a light drizzle began to fall, making the rocks slippery. As they crept along the precipice to the next cave, Bellek lost his footing and fell. Laliari caught him, but not before the sharp edge of rock gouged into his shin. Laliari helped the old man up the rest of the way where they quickly delivered themselves out of the rain and into a warm dry cave.

Here they saw not only evidence of human habitation but the remains of a recent campfire. When they smelled the lingering traces of cooked food in the air, their ravenous hunger overrode their fear of strangers. Hastily looking around for inhabitants—the cave ap-peared to be deserted—they then searched for food. When Laliari saw what was obviously freshly turned dirt in the cave floor, she recalled how sometimes her people stored or "seasoned" meat in the earth. She fell to her knees and began digging. When her fingers encountered something both soft and firm that felt like an animal, she smiled up at Bellek. With luck they were going to eat. But when she scooped away the rest of the dirt and saw what was buried there, she screamed and jumped away.

Bellek limped forward and peered into the pit.

A small boy lay on his side with his knees drawn to his chest. Arranged around him were flint tools and goat horns, and scattered over the corpse were hyacinth and hollyhock petals and boughs of pine. Bellek quickly made a protective sign and staggered back. They were in the presence of a recently deceased child!

Laliari turned huge, frightened eyes to the old man, and before she could ask him what they must do to save themselves, a black shape suddenly came flying into the cave, enormous and hairy. It flung itself upon Laliari, sending her to the floor.

With fists and teeth she fought the beast, rolling over and over with it in a violent struggle. When she managed to scramble to her feet, the beast caught her by the ankle and dragged her back. Taking her by the waist, it lifted her into the air and with inhuman strength and a brutal roar flung her across the cave where she fell against the wall, hitting her head. Ignoring Bellek, who stood frozen in shock, the beast—which turned out to be a man wearing furs—ran back to the burial pit and began hastily covering up the dead child.

Moments later Laliari came to, and when her head cleared and her eyes focused, she found herself sitting with her back to the cave wall, Bellek crouched at her side, a hand over his bleeding leg. Then she looked toward the center of the cave where an astonishing scene was taking place.

The brute that had attacked her was crouched over the pit with the dead child in it and making eerie sounds, his arms flailing like those of a man possessed by a spirit. Laliari was instantly filled with terror. She wanted to run from the cave and get as far away from the corpse as she could, but Bellek's leg was bleeding badly and the old man had gone pale. She moved closer to him, put an arm around his shoulders, and tried in her confused mind to figure out what they must do to protect themselves.

In the meantime, as he continued to ignore the two intruders, the man in furs finished his chanting and sprinkled the last of a handful

of petals over the grave. Then he went back to his smoldering fire
and got it going again, the smoke curling up to disappear through an
unseen vent in the ceiling. He glanced once at the strangers, to see
the girl's large eyes watching him.

He had been out hunting and so now he peeled the skin off a pair
of rabbits and threw the carcasses onto the flames. When one was
charred, he picked the cinders off it and proceeded to wolf it down.
The man's name was Zant and he was the last of his people in this
valley.

As he ate, Zant looked sulkily at the two cowering against the wall.
The old man was moaning in pain while blood ribboned from a wound
and the girl kept her arms around him, fear in her eyes. He should
have killed them for breaking such a powerful taboo as desecrating a
grave. Maybe he still would, he thought as he continued to eat.

Hours passed. The stranger remained squatting by the warm fire,
his face cast in its glow. Laliari had thought at first he was an animal
because she had never seen a human wearing furs. He was ugly, too,
she thought, his prominent brow ridge and huge nose making him
look more like a beast than a man. Most unsettling was the color of
his eyes, which she could see even from this distance: they were blue,
like the sky. Laliari had never seen blue eyes before and she wondered
if they were the eyes of a ghost. Was that why he wasn't afraid of
being in the presence of a corpse?

When Bellek's moans grew louder, the stranger got up and came
toward them. Laliari jumped up and placed herself between Bellek
and the stranger. He pushed her aside and squatted down. Laliari
watched warily as he inspected the injury. At the slightest threatening
gesture, she would defend Bellek with her life. But all the stranger
did was to take something from a pouch on his belt and apply it to
the wound. When Bellek flinched at the man's touch, Laliari readied
herself to spring. But then Bellek's discomfort seemed to ease after a
moment, and the stranger went back to his fire. Laliari was instantly
at Bellek's side, closely scrutinizing the jagged tear on his shin, sniffing
the wound to determine what the stranger had applied to it. She gave
Bellek a questioning look, and he seemed unconcerned. A moment
later, the stranger returned with a skin of water and a roasted rabbit,
holding out both to Laliari.

Ravenous though she was, she hesitated. Food distribution in the
clan was governed by complex rules, and the eating of meat depended

upon many conditions: which hunter had caught the animal and under what circumstances, who the hunter's mother and mother's
mother were, which elders had the right to eat first, the phase the
moon was currently in. How could Laliari be certain this stranger had
spoken the correct spells when he had killed the rabbit? She certainly
hadn't heard him chant the proper invocations as he had skinned the
thing and thrown it on the fire.

The thought of consuming taboo flesh filled her with an uneasy
and vague sense of sacrilege, but the meat was charred and pink and
dripping with fat and juices, its aroma sublime. And poor Bellek was
licking his lips. Hunger won out. Laliari accepted the offering.

Her instinct was to gobble it right down, but clan law dictated that
Bellek eat first. So she bit off chunks, chewed, then spit the pap into
her palm for him to lap up. The process was slow and laborious, and
the whole time the stranger remained squatted on his haunches,
watching them.

Laliari's grass skirt seemed to baffle him as he tilted his head this
way and that, poking the long dry fibers with a curious finger. He
plucked at the woven grass belt, pulling it away from her waist, as if
puzzling over the mystery of how grass grew out of her skin. Then he
stared long and hard at the ivory needle piercing her nose, and when
he reached up to touch it, Laliari slapped his hand away.

When the old man had eaten his fill and closed his eyes in weariness, Laliari devoured the rest of the rabbit, sucking the bones clean
and licking the grease off her fingers, the whole time keeping her eyes
on the ugly stranger.

Finally he grew bored and went back to his fire. It was warm in
the cave and eventually they all fell asleep. Laliari wakened during
the night to see the stranger lying prone on the grave, sobbing. She
was puzzled. She understood grief, but didn't he know the bad luck
he was calling upon himself by staying so close to a corpse? Laliari
herself wished she could flee from this cave. But the rain was coming
down hard outside now, and Bellek's leg wound had rendered him
unable to walk. Visions of the dead child in the pit filled her head
again, and thoughts of his ghost lurking in the shadows made further
sleep impossible.

Eventually the stranger sat up and, after sitting for a long moment
on the mound of dirt, as if working out a decision in his mind, gestured for Laliari to join him at the fire.

She held back until curiosity overcame her. She looked at Bellek, who was sleeping fitfully, then went across to the fire, giving the child's grave a wide berth.

When she crossed her legs and sat, she glanced at the stranger's possessions clustered near his bed of furs: flint-tipped spears and hand axes, small leather bags bulging with mysterious contents, hollowed-out stone bowls filled with nuts and seeds. She held her hands over the fire to warm them. Keeping her head bowed, she studied the stranger from beneath her lashes. Necklaces of animal sinew and strung with bone and ivory lay upon his hairy chest. His hair, long and tangled, was knotted with beads and shells. Small purple tattoos dotted his arms and legs. In other words, he looked like any man from her own clan, except for his thick facial features.

She wondered why he was here all alone, where his people had gone.

Finally she looked directly at him and said, "Who are you?"

He shook his head. He didn't understand.

Using repetitive gestures, pointing to herself and then to him, she finally got her question across. He thumped his chest and from his mouth came something that sounded like "Ts'ank't." But when she tried to repeat it, the closest she could come was "Zant." And "Laliari" was so beyond him, no matter how hard he watched her lips and tongue as she pronounced it, it came out "Lali" and so Lali she was.

They attempted further communication with Zant naming other things—the cave, the fire, the rain, even Bellek—using words from his own language. But Laliari had difficulty repeating them. And when she said words in her own tongue, Zant tried to pronounce them but gave up after a while. Finally they fell silent, recognizing the limits of their communication abilities, both gazing into the flames to ponder this miracle of meeting a human from another world. But a question dominated Laliari's mind, and finally she could contain it no more. Pointing to the tender mound in the center of the cave floor, she gave Zant a questioning look.

She was startled to see tears fill his eyes. Few men in her clan openly cried, and when the tears fell down his cheeks, she grew alarmed. There was power in tears, just as there was power in blood and urine and saliva. But he merely wiped them away and uttered an incomprehensible word. When she gave him a puzzled look, he repeated the word, and as he repeated it over and over, pointing to the mound, she realized that he was saying the child's name.

Laliari jumped to her feet in horror and, quickly looking around the cave for the boy's ghost, made frantic magic gestures to protect herself.

Zant didn't understand. He liked saying the boy's name. It brought comfort. Why did it frighten her? Rising from the fire, he shuffled back to the grave where he knelt and lovingly patted the newly packed earth. But Laliari could only shake her head in fear.

Zant pondered this. He came back to the fire and, squatting again, reached inside the pelt that covered his torso and brought out a small gray stone. He held it out to Laliari.

When she didn't take it, he grunted a word and, to her great shock, smiled. It transformed his face. Suddenly the brutishness vanished and he seemed as ordinary as one of her own kinsmen. He kept offering the stone and she finally took it. Cupping it in her palm she frowned over it, uncomprehending.

The gray stone, which had clearly been shaped by tools, filled her hand. Pointed at the top and bottom, the middle part was comprised of smooth, rounded bulges. Laliari had no idea what it was until Zant touched her bare breast with a fingertip and then touched one of the rounded protuberances on the stone. She stared harder, and after a moment the shape became recognizable. It was a pregnant woman.

Laliari gasped. She had never seen the representation of a human before. What magic was this that she could hold a small woman in her hand?

And then the firelight glanced off the figurine in sharp flashes and Laliari saw that fixed into the statuette's abdomen was the most beautiful blue stone she had ever seen. It looked like frozen water, or a piece of the summer sky. It was like the blue of Zant's eyes, and when it caught the firelight, shot back such dazzling reflections that Laliari was mesmerized.

She brought the stone closer and gazed hard into its translucent heart. The fire crackled, Bellek snored in his corner. Laliari kept staring into the crystalline blue depths until she saw—She cried out.

Within the blue stone she could see a baby in a womb!

Zant tried to explain that long ago his forebears had taken the blue stone from southern invaders and a medicine woman of his people had had it set into the belly of this stone figurine. What Laliari could not know was that when Zant's ancestors had followed animal herds south into warmer climates, they had carried the blue stone back into the territories of its original owners, Tall One's descendants, of which, ironically, Laliari was one.

Now he was trying to explain a connection between the pregnant figurine and the dead child in the pit. But Laliari, for all her desire to understand, remained in the dark.

Suddenly a loud moan filled the cave, and Bellek cried out for Laliari. When she went to him, she saw that he was curled on his side and shivering badly. She tried rubbing his cold limbs and breathing her warm breath upon him, but his shaking only grew more violent, and his lips were turning blue. Gently pulling her away, Zant gathered the frail old man into his arms and carried him back to the fire. Laying Bellek in the circle of warmth, Zant took one of his own bedding furs and tucked it over the trembling body. After a while Bellek was quiet again, sleeping peacefully. Zant laid a huge clumsy hand on the fragile forehead and murmured words that Laliari, mystified, did not understand.

*B*ellek's condition worsened. His wound festered and he burned with fever. But Zant took diligent care of him. Despite the pouring rain, he ventured each day from the cave and returned with food that the old man could eat—soft roots, eggs, and nuts ground into an edible mush—and medicines—aloe for the wound, willow bark steeped in hot water for the fever. As Laliari watched how tenderly Zant ministered to the old shaman, cradling Bellek's frail head in his meaty arm as he helped him to drink and chanting softly in his foreign tongue, her initial wariness and revulsion of the stranger began to wane.

Still, he remained a man of mysteries.

Why was he alone? Where were his people? Had his clan died out because there was no moon? Was the child in the pit the last of his kind and now Zant was alone?

What had happened to the herds of animals in the valley, where had they gone?

Finally there was the little pregnant woman with the blue-stone baby in her abdomen. What did it mean?

As these questions crowded her mind, Laliari was also worrying about her own people in their camp by the lake. Without the powers of Alawa and Bellek they were defenseless and vulnerable. And surely they were terrified by now—never before had her people seen such days of endless downpour. As she looked toward the opening of the cave and the steady rain beyond, she thought of the lost moon, the animals gone from the valley, Zant the last of his kind, and she wondered, *Is the world coming to an end?*

While Zant continued to take care of Bellek and nurse him back to health, it was a time of exploration and discovery for the man and woman from two different races. Zant instructed Laliari in the knowledge of local healing herbs found in the valley, and Laliari collected roots and vegetables, demonstrating how her people cooked them. But these Zant scorned. His people ate meat only. He dismissed the greens with a contemptuous wave of the hand. "For horses," he said. "Not for men." He explained that he was a member of the Wolf Clan and wolves were meat-eaters. Laliari had never seen a wolf.

There were peculiar rock bowls scattered about the cave, each containing residues of burned animal fat. Zant demonstrated their purpose by setting fire to one and handing the bowl to Laliari. She looked on in astonishment. It was a steadily burning light. Since her people were not cave-dwellers and lived in shelters with openings to the sky—and therefore to the stars and moon—they had never invented lamps. And while her people had learned to carry embers to start a fire in the future, fire itself was never carried!

Zant carried things in bags fashioned from animal bladders, stomachs, and hides. Laliari, coming from a river valley rich in tall grasses and reeds, carried a basket, which mystified Zant, having never seen grass woven together before.

Because Zant and his people were meat-eaters, they had never been good at catching fish. Why should they with so much game around? But now game was scarce in the valley, and hunting was poor in the rain, so Laliari demonstrated how to fish with a net made of vegetable fibers and animal sinew. Choosing a day when the rain abated briefly and the sun broke through the clouds, they went down to a stream teeming with fish. Unfurling the net she carried in her basket, Laliari weighted it with stones and threw it into the stream. Zant, excited to see so many squirming fish caught in the net, splashed into the water to haul it up. But he slipped and fell in, causing Laliari to howl with laughter as he climbed back onto the bank and comically shook himself. His fur tunic was drenched, so he stripped it off and laid it on boulders to dry. When she saw his naked torso, Laliari's laughter died.

His skin was as white as summer clouds, but covered in fine black hairs that glistened with droplets of water. His chest was deep, his shoulders and arms powerfully muscled. A loincloth of soft leather covered his manhood, but his buttocks were exposed, firm and white, and pimpling with bumps as the sun went behind a cloud and the day turned cold. When Zant raised his arms to wring out his long hair, Laliari saw muscles and sinews ripple and move beneath his wet skin in a way that made the breath catch in her throat.

When the sun came out an instant later, Zant turned to it and lifted his face to receive the warm rays. He stood completely still, his nakedness dappled in sunlight and shadow, glittering with water, his long black hair streaming down his back. Laliari observed him in profile, the powerful chest pushed forward, the heavy brown and large nose thrusting skyward, and she wondered in bewitched amazement if this was what a wolf looked like.

And then clouds covered the sun, the day grew cold again and the moment ended, but Laliari's enchantment did not. As she watched Zant bend to retrieve his sodden tunic, she marveled at his power and dark mystery, and she felt a strange new heat begin to burn deep within her. When he turned suddenly and his blue eyes captured hers, she felt her heart jump in a way it had never done before, like a gazelle within her breast—joyous, happy, leaping with life.

But then she was immediately sad, for she remembered his loneliness.

Every day Laliari would watch Zant leave the cave, spear and ax in hand, and disappear into the rain. He would return a long time later, always with a kill, but cold and shivering, saying nothing, stripping the hide off the animal and throwing the meat on the fire. She would watch him crouch down and stare into the flames, a look of forlorn sadness on his face, and she would wonder about him. *Why did he stay? Why didn't he leave?* Once in a while he would look up, as if he sensed her watching him, their eyes would meet, and Laliari would feel something—she didn't know what—take place in the warm, smoky confines of the cave. After a while Zant would bring the cooked meat to her and Bellek. He would make sure they both ate before he himself ate any of it even though it was his kill. And while she ate, she felt his eyes on her, eyes filled with loneliness, questioning, yearning.

*T*hey spent their days in search of food, their evenings in awkward communication, their nights in restless sleep. Neither possessed the words to describe what was happening, neither could explain the alien emotions that had them in a grip. Laliari and Zant took care of Bellek, nursing him back to health, but both sensed something else happening in the cave, something taking shape, like a ghost, but not unfriendly, perhaps like the ghost of fire, because each felt a heat rising within them. Laliari wondered how Zant's people took pleasure, and Zant wondered how the men and women of her people came together. Unknown taboos stood between them, and the fear of breaking them.

*W*hen Laliari suddenly left the cave one day, taking her possessions and some food with her, murmuring words of reassurance to the old man, Zant understood. The women in his own clan practiced segregation during their moonflow.

When she returned to the cave five days later, Zant showed her a sight so astonishing that it opened her mind and explained so many things.

The rain had abated and the sun shone through the broken clouds. Making sure that Bellek was warm and comfortable, Zant took Laliari by the hand and led her from the cave and up a narrow trail that went to the tops of the cliffs. There, standing at the top of the world beneath a sky that went on forever, Laliari felt the wind invade her spirit and lift it to great heights. Below, she saw the rolling plains and hills, now starting to shade with the green of spring, and in the distance the immense freshwater lake where her people were camped. Laliari had never stood so high, had never had such a view of the world.

But this was not the sight that was to explain so many things. Zant wordlessly led her across the flat mesa toward its far, sharp edge. It terrified her to come to such an abrupt and precipitous drop, but Zant held her arm and smiled encouragingly. She moved to the edge and, terrified that the wind was going to carry her away, looked down.

There, she saw something that stopped the breath in her chest.

Below them, rising from the bottom of a deep ravine, was a mountain of horse carcasses. Whole animals, with only their bellies slit open, the skins and bones and tails left intact. The stench was dizzying for the carcasses were rotting. Through Zant's gesturing and miming, the horrific picture started to form in Laliari's mind: Zant and his people had driven this herd to its destruction. It was how they hunted. She remembered the mountain of antelope carcasses she and her kinswomen had come upon weeks ago, how they had wondered why the animals had galloped off the steep cliff to their doom. Now she understood that they had been driven by humans bent on slaughter.

But, she realized in dawning horror, they had used only a small part of the animals. As Zant spoke with his awkward words and clumsy gestures, Laliari envisioned the carnage: Zant's people cutting open the bellies of the beasts, many of them still alive, and crawling inside to pull out the tender organs, feasting on beating hearts and steaming livers, painting themselves with blood, empowering themselves with the spirit of the horse.

Laliari was at first horrified at the waste. Her own people would have made use of every organ and sinew, even the horse's manes. But then she saw that the most horrendous taboo had been broken: the majority of these animals were females. When her clan hunted, they only went after males, since males, unable to bear young, weren't needed for the survival of a herd. To kill females meant killing their future offspring and ultimately killing off the herd entirely. As she looked in dismay at the wasteful slaughter—some of the horses had been pregnant—she realized that her people had encountered no horses during their trek from the Reed Sea. Were these the last of them?

She turned to the man who both excited and mystified her, and now horrified and repulsed her, as he had done the night they first met. A man who could lay such a gentle touch on the festering wound of a frail old man, yet who could drive hundreds of horses to a useless death and think nothing of the waste of it. As he continued to talk, gesturing northward with his gnarled hand, thumping his chest, exhibiting pride and bravado, but his eyes betraying the stark loneliness that had dogged him these weeks, revelation like a dawn broke in her mind: that Zant wasn't the last of his kind after all. His people, having overkilled in this valley, were now forced to move northward in search of more herds. They were the Wolf Clan, he explained, and so they were following the wolf packs tracking the herds. His people were camped just a few days' journey northward, past the lake and into the mountains, where they waited for him.

*F*inally Bellek was healed and Zant declared that it was time for him to move on. He gathered his possessions and they began a sad good-bye. Now was the time of permissible touching, for they were parting.

"Lali," he said in such a forlorn way that it moved her heart, and his rough fingertips on her cheeks sent waves of heat through her body. She covered the hand with her own and pressed it to her face, turning her head so that her lips met the calloused palm in a long, painful kiss.

Beneath his heavy brows, tears shimmered in blue eyes. He spoke her name again, but no sound came out. Emotions without name, feelings without definition flooded her. Nothing had touched her this way before—not Doron's first embrace, nor witnessing his death. This dark and perplexing stranger from another world had found places deep within her that she never knew existed, and wakened a new spirit, one that hungered and burned and believed it would die without Zant.

He drew her into the circle of his arms and she brushed his cheeks with her mouth. His breath was hot on her neck; she felt his manhood hard against her. He lowered her to the cave floor, and she drew him down upon her. He called her Lali and feverishly stroked her limbs. She murmured "Zant" and opened herself to him. He was bigger than Doron in all ways, and the feel of him took her breath away.

Bellek, waiting outside on the rocky ledge, and understanding these things, hunkered down and began to pick nits out of his hair.

*Z*ant stayed with Laliari for seven nights and seven days, during which time they explored and discovered one another, spending the daylight hours in fishing and hunting and the nighttime hours in passionate embraces. When he finally departed they knew they would never see each other again. Laliari's place was with her own people where, although she did not yet know it, she would one day wear the gazelle antlers. And Zant must hurry north to join his clan, not knowing that because of their form of hunting, whole herds of mammoths, horses, reindeer, and ibex would be driven over the edges of cliffs, many of them to the extinction of their species. Zant and his people would migrate north in ignorance of the fact that their own race was on the verge of total extinction, for reasons that would still remain a mystery 35,000 years into the future, when he and his kind would be called Neanderthals.

After Zant had gone, Laliari sadly collected her things and prepared to go back to the lake with Bellek when she found tucked into one of her baskets the little figurine with the blue baby-stone in its belly. A final gift from Zant.

As they traipsed across the plain, Laliari assisting Bellek for now he limped, they both silently wondered if the camp would still be there since they had been gone for so long. But then they saw the smoke from the campfires and heard on the wind the laughter of children. And when they drew closer they saw—

Ghosts!

Bellek stopped short and made a strangled sound in his throat. But Laliari's eyesight was better and so she could see that the men in the camp were not ghosts but their very own hunters, once believed lost in the sea but now very much alive. They picked up their pace and soon Laliari was running, desperately searching for one familiar face in the group. And then she saw him.

Doron, who had survived drowning in the angry sea.

They had been swept miles downstream, they explained dramatically to their excited audience, and deposited on the shore—the *opposite* shore from where the women were. And so they had had to wait for the tide to change and for the Reed Sea to withdraw before they could cross. They had had no idea where the women had gone. It had taken them days before they picked up the band's trail, after that they had simply followed Bellek's magic symbols, which he had carved into trees during the women's progress up the river valley.

And now here they were, the clan reunited once again. Laliari looked at Doron with tears of joy but in her thoughts, Zant . . .

That night, as Bellek regaled everyone with the tale of their sojourn among the caves—even though he had spent most of it asleep—and as Laliari passed the fertility figurine around the circle for everyone to marvel over, there suddenly came a shout from the edge of the camp. One of the hunters who had been appointed to moon-watch came running into the light, waving his arms, a wild look on his face. Everyone jumped up and ran through the trees and into a clearing where they saw—

Everyone gasped.

The moon was rising big and round and bright in the starlit sky.

The Gazelle Clan held a big celebration that night in which Bellek dispensed the magic mushrooms. Soon, everyone around the campfire was delighting to hallucinations, intensified colors, and a glorious sense of well-being. Their hearts swelled with affection for one another, their pulses quickened with desire. Couples paired off, Doron guiding Laliari to the privacy of reeds and cattails. Bellek found himself cuddled in the arms of two rapturous young women. And Freer, Doron's fellow hunter, sought comfort between the hot and welcoming legs of No Name, forgetting her outcast status.

The next morning, everyone agreed that it could be no coincidence that the moon had returned with Laliari and Bellek. And Laliari, herself trying to explain the stupefying phenomenon, said the moon must have come with the blue stone the stranger in the cave had given her.

The others were dubious of Laliari's conclusion and quietly decided she was wrong, until a month later when most of the women in the clan discovered they were pregnant, including No Name. The figurine was examined more closely this time and now there could be no mistake: there were the breasts and abdomen of a pregnant woman, and at the center of the blue crystal a baby could clearly be seen.

The stone had brought the moon, and therefore life, back to the clan.

And so another celebration took place with everyone singing Laliari's praise. As she modestly accepted the honor, thinking sadly of Zant but happily of Doron, she failed to see on the other side of the circle a pair of eyes watching her—Keeka, who was not at all overjoyed to have her cousin back from the caves.

*R*evenge was on Keeka's mind.

She had been secretly glad when Laliari's exploration of the caves had stretched into weeks. Although she had been frightened, like everyone else, that Bellek might be dead and that they were now without someone to read the omens and guide them, she had secretly hoped her cousin would never come back. And then when Doron and the other survivors had shown up, Keeka had seen her chance to make Doron hers. It had almost worked, too. He had started sitting beside her during the evening meal and showing interest in sleeping with her—and then Bellek and Laliari had stepped out of the mist!

In the seven years since, Laliari had risen in status among the clan because they believed her fertility stone had brought the moon out of hiding. So powerful was the blue stone that even barren She Who Has No Name had given birth and now she had her old name back and was respected as a mother. The clan had elected Laliari the new Keeper of the Gazelle Antlers. Now she had three children, Doron slept in her hut instead of with the hunters, and everyone loved her. Keeka, in her jealousy, could stand it no more.

But the method of revenge had to be carefully thought out. Laliari must not know that it was Keeka who had killed her, otherwise Laliari's ghost would haunt Keeka for the rest of her life. But how to kill someone without their knowing it? All the methods she could think of—using a spear or a club, pushing Laliari off a cliff—lacked the necessary anonymity. And she couldn't fool her cousin the way she had fooled old Alawa. When Keeka had crept into the old woman's hut to strangle her—which she had been forced to do after she had overheard Alawa tell Bellek that they must kill the little boys, Keeka's boys!—she had covered her face with mud and disguised her hair with leaves, convincing the old woman that she was a ghost. But Laliari was of sharper mind and eyes, she would know who her assassin was.

The women were out on the rolling plains gathering spring plants. In their new home the clan had adapted to a new seasonal rhythm. Instead of being governed by the annual flood of a river, as they had been in their ancestral valley to the west of the Reed Sea, they were now regulated by the cycle of autumn fog, winter snow, flowering spring, and summer heat. They had had to learn new migratory patterns of game and birds, and when to go in search of edible wild fruits and grains. Grass skirts were no longer sufficient against the winter cold, and so they had learned to fashion tunics and leggings out of animal skins. In the winters they retreated to the warm, dry caves in the cliffs, but emerged in the spring to build grass shelters by the freshwater lake.

And so it was that Keeka, along with the other women, was foraging for food when she came upon a plant she had never seen before.

Its origin lay far to the north, in the mountains of a country that would one day be called Turkey, and over the centuries the seed of this plant had been carried on wind and wing to land and take root along the shore of Lake Galilee. Keeka, with her woven baskets and digging sticks, paused to contemplate the unfamiliar tall red stalks and broad green leaves. The clan had found many new foods in this valley, so this one was no surprise. However, as she bent to uproot one, she saw something that made her freeze.

Dead rodents lay on the ground among the new plants.

Keeka gasped and backed away. There were evil spirits in this place! As she traced a protective gesture in the air and hastily murmured a spell, something about the dead rodents made her stop and give closer scrutiny to them.

She realized after a moment that the animals must have been nibbling on the leaves of this new plant just before they had died. In fact, one was still alive, writhing in convulsions. An instant later it stiffened and lay dead. Keeka kept her distance, fearful of the poisonous spirit that inhabited the plant, but she didn't run away because an unexpected vision was forming in her mind: Laliari lying on the ground like the rodents, killed by the plant's evil spirit.

Suddenly she saw her instrument of revenge.

Filled with giddy excitement, Keeka rushed to the water's edge and coated her hands with fresh mud. She then chanted protective incantations as she gingerly coaxed the rhubarb from the soil. Hastily dropping the plant into her basket, she rushed back to the water to wash and scrub her hands clean. As she did so she smiled at her cleverness, for it would not in fact be she herself doing the killing, but the malicious spirit in the plant. As she hurried back to her basket and its lethal contents, she thought of how life was going to be after Laliari was gone, and her smile widened in delicious anticipation of luring the handsome Doron into her hut.

The clan's initial attempts at making clothing out of furs had been abysmal failures—for the pelts of such goats as they could find grew hard and stiff and unmalleable—and so Laliari's people had shivered all through their first winter in the caves. But Laliari had seen how soft and supple Zant's furs had been, so she and her kinswomen had experimented all the next summer in stretching and scraping the hides until they dried to a comfortable softness. Then she devised bone needles for piercing the skins in order to draw fibers through for seams. That was why she now stood on a windy hillock wearing a long tunic of warm and pliant goatskins, her feet clad in fur boots, her eight-month-old baby snug in a sheepskin pouch on her back. Laliari's two little boys, Vivek and Josu, were warm in capes and leggings made of soft gazelle skin as they chased grasshoppers.

Laliari was a distinctive figure as she stood tall and proud on the hillock, scanning the new green growth for the first fruits of spring, for on her head she wore the clan's gazelle antlers, tied firmly beneath her chin with animal sinew. She was thinking of a garlic patch that grew down by the stream, but unfortunately it was too early to pick them. Garlic had to wait for midsummer, which was too bad for the clan had developed a taste for it. She peered at the ancient, massive fig tree that grew on the hill, and studied the green fruit. Not yet ripe. It would be another cycle of the moon before the clan would taste of the figs' sweetness. Finally, she spotted a mulberry bush remembered from the year before, and she was delighted to find the first early berries ready to be picked.

As she collected the mulberries into her basket, the breeze shifted and bathed her in a delicate perfume—the scent of deep blue hyacinths, blooming in the thousands over the hills and meadows. Blossoming, too, almost overnight, were fields of blinding white narcissi. After spending dark months in smoky caves, the people of the Gazelle Clan were reveling in spring's rebirth.

Laliari herself was filled with inexpressible joy. The little baby girl asleep on her back, and close by, in the tall sweet grass, her two precious sons.

Her eldest boy, Vivek, was six years old with thick brows overshadowing his eyes, and already at such a young age was showing signs of the heavy jaw he would someday have. His resemblance to Zant came as no surprise to Laliari since it was Zant's fertility figurine, with the blue baby-stone in her belly, that had given Laliari the child. Laliari's second boy, Josu, was a bright little four-year-old with curly golden brown hair and chubby arms and legs. Tomorrow was the day of his nose piercing. There would be a big celebration and he would be given his own little ax and a shell necklace made of good-luck talismans.

It was hard to remember now the terror she had once felt in this land, or that her people had ever felt like strangers here. The clan had come to love this place by the freshwater lake. She lifted her face

to the breeze and thought of Zant. She hoped he had found his people, that he was happy now, and hunting with them. Laliari had never
gone back to the cave where she first met him, for a child lay buried
there and Bellek had declared the cave taboo.

Hearing a high-pitched whistle, Laliari turned to see her cousin
Keeka come walking up. Despite the chill in the air, Keeka was bare-
breasted and proudly displaying a beautiful periwinkle necklace one
of the hunters had made for her. Keeka had put on weight in the
years since their flight across the Reed Sea; once the clan had settled
here by the lake, Keeka had reverted to her old habits of hoarding
food.

However, to Laliari's surprise, Keeka had come to share this time.
She held out a basket containing broad green leaves and declared
that it was a wonderfully delicious new plant she had discovered.
Laliari gratefully accepted the basket and offered Keeka a basket of
mulberries in return. As Keeka went off smiling, already pushing
handfuls of mulberries into her mouth, Laliari took a small nibble of
the new plant and found the rhubarb leaf unremarkable.

"Mama."

She looked down to see Josu's little hands reaching, so she handed
a leaf to him and then gave one to the older boy. Vivek tasted the
leaf and, making a face, spit it out. But Josu happily munched on his
piece of rhubarb.

Having filled two large baskets with mulberries, Laliari called her
boys to her and they headed back to the camp on the shore. Other
women were arriving now with their gatherings: dandelion greens and
wild cucumbers, coriander seeds and doves' eggs, as well as a good
haul of bulrushes for making baskets and for their edible piths. Men
returned to camp with netted fish, baskets of limpets, and two young
goats freshly skinned. All would be apportioned out according to rules,
and everyone would eat well.

While ritualistic incantations were chanted, the meat was butchered and roasted and handed around, first to the hunters' mothers,
then to elders, and so on with the hunters themselves receiving the
last. Laliari breast-fed her baby and saw to it that her boys received
enough food. While Vivek happily scooped yolk from an egg, little
Josu continued to grasp the rhubarb leaf in his hand, nibbling at it
all the time. Someone had come upon a field of early wheat and had
shared it out. Each person bundled the stems together and held the

ears over the fire until the chaff was mostly burned off. Then they rubbed the ears between their palms to get the wheat grains out and pop them into their mouths.

After the meal, the camp turned noisy as usual, with the women attending to grooming and basket-weaving, the men to sharpen flint knives and talk of the day's hunt. It was some moments before Laliari noticed that Josu was complaining of pain in his mouth. She took a look and saw curious lesions on the insides of his cheeks and lips. She was instantly alarmed. Had an evil spirit entered him? Josu did not yet have the protective piercings in his nose and lips.

"And here," he added, pressing his hands on his abdomen.

"You have pain there?"

He nodded.

Laliari's heart jumped. The ghost had entered his mouth and was now in his stomach!

As she tried to think of what to do Josu started to shake. She drew him into her arms. "Are you cold, my precious one?"

Big round eyes stared back at her as the tremors suddenly grew worse.

Now other women came around, inspecting the boy, putting their hands on him and murmuring concern.

Laliari held him close and rocked him. When he suddenly started wheezing and gasping for breath, Laliari cried out for Bellek. By the time the old man arrived with his amulets and spells, the rest of the clan was gathering around to watch. Bellek examined the boy and set about immediately to working his medicine. As the flames from the various fires danced beneath the stars, casting the humans in alternating glow and shadow, he placed powerful talismans on Josu's body, chanting mystical spells as he did so. Then he dipped his fingers into jars of pigment and painted healing symbols on the boy's forehead, chest, and feet.

Josu's breathing grew worse.

At the edge of the group, as she tossed nuts with supreme indifference into her mouth, Keeka watched in detachment. Due to her own basic greed it had not occurred to her that Laliari would offer the rhubarb leaves to her children first. So now the evil spirit had entered the boy instead of Laliari. Keeka was intelligent enough to know she wouldn't have another chance and that Doron was not to be hers. Still, she derived some satisfaction from the look of terror on her cousin's face, and the tears streaming down her cheeks.

By now Josu was unconscious and the whole clan looked on, speechless.

And then suddenly he began to convulse.

"Save him!" Laliari cried as she held him.

As old Bellek quivered in indecision, the convulsions stopped. "Josu?" Laliari said in sudden hope.

The boy's chest expanded in a deep breath, then he released it in a long, ragged shudder. And then he was still.

*T*he silent-sitting was the most profoundly sorrowful sitting the clan had ever performed, and even when they started to tear down the camp—for now they must move on and leave Josu's little body to the elements—still no one spoke, their movements heavy and plodding, their faces etched with grief.

But it was urgent that they leave, now that the ritual had been performed, and while the others shouldered their burdens to begin the trek farther along the shore, Laliari did not move. She remained beside her son's corpse, her face whiter than the remnants of snow on the distant mountains. The clan members milled about nervously, terrified of the bad luck she was bringing upon them.

When she suddenly gathered the cold little body into her arms and wailed up to the sky, the others shifted in fear. We must leave her, half of them said. But she has the gazelle horns, argued the others. Doron squatted close to her, indecision shadowing his handsome face. He reached out but dared not touch her.

After several moments of bitter weeping over her son, Laliari finally fell silent and a strange mood settled over her. She became deadly calm, her eyes blank and staring. What they were fixed upon were the caves in the nearby cliffs. Suddenly she thought of the one in which she had met Zant, and the child buried there. Reaching into a small bag that hung from her belt she brought out the stone figurine with the blue baby-crystal in its abdomen. As she gazed at it she recalled the night Zant had first shown it to her, the night he had buried a child. She hadn't understood at the time what he was trying to tell her, but now it came to her: the crystal did not represent a womb with a baby in it—it was a grave with a child in it.

My son will not be left to wild animals. He will not be left to the wind and the ghosts. And he will not be forgotten.

While the others watched in bewilderment, Laliari first made sure her infant was safe and sleeping in its pouch on her back, then she gathered up Josu's body, instructed Vivek to hold onto her skirt, and she began to walk away from the camp.

The others hung back, wondering what she was doing. But when Bellek began to limp after her, the rest began to follow. But they remained at a distance, trailing behind the old shaman out of curiosity. Was he going to order her to leave the boy and come away? And where was Laliari going?

They had their answer when she reached the foot of the cliffs and began the awkward climb up the rocky trail they had used for the past seven years. She had to pause several times to allow Vivek to catch up, or to shift her awkward burden. It was necessary at times to lay Josu down and lift Vivek up and over boulders, then to pick up her tragic burden and resume her resolute progress.

She never once looked back.

The cave Laliari chose was one that had not been lived in for it was small and shallow, and the ceiling too low. But it was protected from the elements and the floor was soft and sandy. Gently laying Josu down, she took the digging stick that always hung from her belt and began to dig.

Everyone crowded at the entrance, peering in, whispering, none brave enough to go inside. After a few minutes Laliari's baby began to cry. She paused in her digging to unstrap the pouch from her back and bring her infant daughter to her breast. When the child had nursed and was asleep again, Laliari laid the baby in a safe spot and resumed digging.

When she had created a pit, she picked up Josu's body and tenderly laid it inside, arranging him in a comfortable position, as if he were asleep. Then she rose to her feet and went out of the cave, the others falling back to let her pass. They all stood on the rocky precipice to watch as she moved among boulders and shrubs collecting wildflowers and fragrant boughs. When her arms were full, she brought the foliage back and gently spread it out on Josu's body. The she covered him up with sandy soil, filling the pit and patting the earth down so that it was firm.

She then went to the cave entrance where her six-year-old son stood with Doron. Taking Vivek's hand, she led him to the grave where she said to him, "You are not to be afraid. Your brother is asleep now. He is safe from ghosts and from harm. And he can do no harm to you. His name is Josu and you will always remember him."

Everyone gasped. Laliari had spoken the name of the dead!

She didn't care what the others thought, or that Bellek had gone deathly pale, Laliari was aware only of the tremendous relief that washed over her to know that her baby was going to be kept here, safe in this cave, to dwell close by his family forever.

When she finally emerged into the moonlight, her baby strapped to her back, little Vivek at her side, Laliari held up the figurine with the blue stone for all to see. Everyone fell silent and listened, for she was, after all, Keeper of the Gazelle Antlers. "The Mother gives life, and to the Mother life returns. It is not for us to forget this gift she gives us. From this day forward, the names of the dead are no longer taboo."

Laliari knew that it was going to be no easy thing for her people to overcome a generations-old taboo. But she stood firm in her new resolve. No longer were her people going to grieve uncomforted as she and the women had once grieved for the drowned hunters without the solace of speaking the men's names. The dead should not be forgotten. She understood that now. Wisdom learned from a stranger named Zant.

Interim

*E*veryone was afraid of Laliari after that—at least for a while. But when they saw that no bad luck had come to the clan through her uttering the name of a dead child, that in fact the new season brought forth an abundance of food in the valley, they began to wonder if she possessed new power. When Bellek died the following spring, Laliari spoke his name during the silent-sitting, told of his deeds and his long life. Then he was laid to rest in the cave next to Josu. When once again no bad luck came to the clan for Laliari having broken the name taboo, others began to lose their fears and started to utter the names of those lost long ago—sons and brothers who had died at the hands of the invaders.

When ghosts did not haunt them and the valley continued to provide plentiful food, the people began to forget the old name taboo
until it became a regular part of the silent-sitting to speak of the
deceased—so that it was no longer silent-sitting but a remember-
sitting. Because it was the homely figurine with the astonishing blue
stone that had instructed Laliari in these new laws, it became the
custom at every remember-sitting to pass the stone around for each
member to hold as she spoke words of praise and remembrance over
the deceased.

When, years later, Laliari was laid to rest in the cave next to her
son, each member of the clan took turns saying what she remembered
best about the elderly Keeper of the Gazelle Antlers, but mostly it
was about the time, many seasons in the past, before most of the clan
members had been born, when Laliari had brought the moon and
fertility back to her people, and had taught them how to remember
the dead.

$\mathcal{N}$ow that the race of humans that had nearly hunted them to extinction had left, the wildlife gradually returned to the Jordan River
Valley and the people of the Gazelle Clan followed the herds, moving
with the seasons, summering by cool springs in the south, wintering
in the warm caves in the north. And always, wherever they went, the
little fertility figurine went with them.

The miracle of the blue stone lay in its beauty. If it had been more
homely like jasper, or dull and blunt like carnelian, it might have
eventually gotten lost or misplaced and forgotten. But its dazzling
sparkle enthralled people, and each successive generation was bewitched anew so that the shimmering nugget of cosmic meteorite was
handed down and kept safe, to be revered, worshipped, marveled over.

The blue stone eventually became so special that people stopped
carrying it around as if it were any ordinary amulet. Because the stone
was set into the abdomen of a stone woman, a miniature shelter was
constructed for her, a tiny little hut made of wood and mud and placed
in the care of a special caretaker. Like the Keeper of the Gazelle
Antlers and the Keeper of the Mushrooms, there was now a Keeper
of the Stone.

Ten thousand years after Laliari and Zant had lain in each other's
arms, a particularly cold winter hit the valley and the Galilee was

blanketed with snow. The people of the Gazelle Clan sat huddled in their caves and the Keeper of the Stone had a dream. In the dream the blue crystal spoke to him and it told him it was tired of living in a small body. So the clan elders conferred and decided that the stone should be transferred to a new body, better and larger, as was befitting its power. Artisans were appointed to carve out a new figurine, more detailed and lifelike, this time with facial features and even a woman's long hair etched into its head. The blue crystal was then lovingly placed in her abdomen, for the crystal was the statue's spirit. The statue's little house was also enlarged and constructed of more durable material, and because it was heavier, it now required two men to carry it on a platform between two poles. Wherever the Gazelle Clan roamed, thus was the statue, in her special house, carried and men vied for the honor to be its bearers.

As the size of the statue, and her house, grew, so did its spirit in the minds of the people. Twenty thousand years after Laliari buried her son in a Galilee cave, the people of the Gazelle Clan knew that a goddess dwelled in their midst. She lived in the crystal womb of a stone woman who lived in her own stone house.

*T*he clan grew in size and number until it became too large for local food sources to support it. And so smaller groups splintered off to claim other territories for hunting and gathering. But all remained members of the same tribe, revering the same ancestors and the same Goddess, and all coming together at an annual summer Gathering of the Clans at the place of a perennial spring, just north of the dead sea and west of the Jordan River.

There were two main clans now, the western and the northern, which were divided into families. Talitha's family was of the Gazelle Clan in the north, Serophia was Raven Clan in the west. It had become the custom, when the families and clans gathered annually at the oasis just north of the dead sea, for the Goddess in her house to be passed to another family for safekeeping for the coming year. Future generations would declare that it was no coincidence that the summer Talitha discovered the magic grape juice was also the summer the Goddess was in Talitha's safekeeping.

And that was when all the trouble began.

But really, the storytellers would say, the trouble had actually begun years earlier, when Talitha and Serophia were young and the clans were camped north of the dead sea, enduring the searing summer heat. It was not unusual for the occasional stranger to appear, hunters who preferred to live and roam alone, affiliated with no family or clan. Such men would come out of the hills with a fresh kill and search the camp for a hearth where they would share their catch with whoever skinned and cooked it for them. Talitha, a plump mother of five, was known for keeping a good hearth; her fire never went out, her cooking stones were always hot, and she knew secrets about spices. She also had a voluptuous body and enjoyed taking pleasure with men. So it was that the stranger who arrived that summer, a strong hunter named Bazel with a fine ewe on his shoulders, found his way to Talitha's tent where he stayed for a week, enjoying her bed and her cooking. When he made signs of moving on, for roving was in his nature, Talitha decided she wanted to keep him, and so enticed him with tasty roasted grains and juice pressed from grapes, skills she had perfected and would share with no one else.

He stayed another week in Talitha's tent, and then one morning went into the hills to hunt gazelle. When he returned, it was not to Talitha but to a grass shelter on the other side of the spring, where another clan was camped. This second shelter was kept by a woman named Serophia, younger and more slender than Talitha, and with fewer children. Here Bazel spent another two weeks of delight before turning restless eyes once again to the horizon. While the men of the two clans were only too glad to see the newcomer move on, for they coveted Talitha and Serophia for themselves, the two women were of a different opinion. Each wanted to keep the hunter for herself on a permanent basis.

The ensuing competition became the main entertainment of that summer and was spoken of for many years afterward. Talitha and Serophia launched a campaign that hunters declared rivaled the best tactics of any hunt or battle, with Bazel happily in the middle, dividing his time between tent and hut, sharing himself as democratically as he could. He had never been so well fed, nor enjoyed so much sex. It was a summer he would never forget.

But then the day came when the seers announced that it was time for the Gathering to disassemble and for clans to start off for their winter homes. Talitha and Serophia grew desperate, for Bazel had not yet made a commitment.

No one could really say afterward what happened. Accusations flew on all sides: some said Talitha had cast the evil eye upon Serophia, some said Serophia had brought bad magic upon Talitha. Both women came down with a bloody flux that caused painful urination, rendered them unable to have sex, and did not clear up until well into the winter. Neither the seers nor the medicine women could divine what the problem was, nor find a cure. Yet it was clear that each had been invaded by an evil spirit. One night, during the dark of the moon, deciding that he had better leave before everyone accused him of bringing this evil spirit among them, Bazel picked up his spear and slipped out of the camp, never to be seen again.

As the clans made their treks westward and northward to ancestral lands, both women were sick and miserable, each blaming the other for this misfortune, and each forming a grudge so deep and black that it was to have repercussions for centuries to come.

"And now we come to the Summer of the Grapes," was how the storytellers would introduce it. "The summer that all the trouble began."

By now the hunter Bazel was forgotten. Only the mutual hatred between the two women remained. Over the years each had risen in status among her clan. Both had produced a prodigious number of children and were now revered grandmothers full of postmenopausal moon-power. Talitha had grown thick-boned and heavy-set because she had the blood of Zant in her veins. Serophia was still slender although by no means frail. Both were made of tough fiber and indomitable personalities. As the seasons had passed and the clans had continued to gather annually, the war had quietly continued to rage. "Hmp! Serophia's chickpeas taste like pig shit!" Talitha would grumble to the women of other clans. "Every egg Talitha touches turns rotten," Serophia told anyone who would listen. Their rivalry became legend and a source of amusement for the clan gossips. Spies would run back and forth to report. When Serophia declared, "When a man lies between Talitha's legs, she falls asleep," Talitha countered with, "When a man lies between Serophia's legs, *he* falls asleep!" Even the men—those who were not currently involved with a female and who therefore were gathered outside the hunters' communal tent, men who rarely involved themselves in women's issues—became involved. Points were awarded to one side or another, wagers were made. At every summer gathering, the latest news on the Talitha–Serophia fight became nightly entertainment at all the campfires.

Because of the coincidence of a fever and a weakness, the stalemate ended during the soon-to-be legendary Summer of the Grapes.

Talitha's clan, on its trek from the northern caves, had been held up by an early summer fever that had spread through the children, so that Serophia's clan was the first to arrive at the southern spring. Seeing that they were alone, and knowing that Talitha had a passion for grapes, Serophia ordered her kinsfolk to gather all the wild grapes, stripping the vines clean. When the other, smaller clans arrived, Serophia happily traded the grapes for goods the others had to offer—flax from the south, salt from the east. But when Talitha's large band arrived, there were no more grapes for trade, and none left on the vine. When Talitha heard what had been taking place, her fury erupted.

She marched over to Serophia's tent and when she saw the fresh grape juice stains on Serophia's doeskin skirt, she exploded. "You let he-goats mount you!"

"Scorpions run when they see you coming!" Serophia spat back.

"Vultures wouldn't touch your carcass!"

"When snakes bite you, *they* die!"

Their families had to pull them apart, and while Serophia enjoyed the smug feeling of victory, Talitha secretly plotted retaliation.

The next summer, Talitha saw to it that her clan arrived at the spring first. There she had her people strip the vines of every last grape, some of which they ate, some of which they traded with the smaller clans. What was left over, Talitha had her people store in watertight baskets, and then hide the baskets in a nearby limestone cave. When the clans returned the following summer, Serophia could harvest all the grapes she wanted, for Talitha would already have a secret supply.

But when the clans gathered one year later at the perennial spring to erect their tents and huts, to light their many cooking fires and to commence the summerlong rituals of making deals, forming alliances, judging lawbreakers, Talitha's people experienced a shock. The baskets filled with grapes, so well hidden that they had indeed sat untouched in the cool dark cave for a year, had undergone a strange transformation.

The grapes had continued to ripen until they burst, skins mingling with flesh and juice so that the baskets now contained a sluggish mess. But the aroma was not unpleasant, and when one of the seers dipped a finger into the juice and tasted it, he found the flavor exotic and intriguing.

So Talitha dipped her hand in, scooped out the purple slush and sucked it up from her palm. Everyone waited while she smacked her lips and ran her tongue around her mouth, a look of indecision on her face.

"What do you think, Talitha?" asked Janka, the current Keeper of the Goddess, a stodgy solemn man given to airs of self-importance.

Talitha licked the rest of the mixture off her hand, then scooped up some more. She couldn't decide if she liked the taste of it or not. But there was something else, something she could not put a finger to . . .

She drank some more, thought about it some more, and found herself suddenly of cheery disposition. Declaring the grape sludge drinkable, Talitha ordered the men to haul the heavy, swollen baskets back to their camp that was but part of a massive encampment of hundreds of tents and shelters on the plain surrounding the bubbling spring. By the time Talitha's band arrived back with the baskets, numerous cook fires were sending smoke up to the stars, laughter and shouts were on the air, families were busy about the industry of life, and the people of the Gazelle Clan settled down to ponder the new mystery in their midst.

Sitting on a wide stool, elbows braced on monumental thighs, Talitha dipped a wooden cup into one of the baskets from the cave and drank again. While everyone watched and waited, she again smacked her lips and ran her tongue around her mouth. A strange taste, she thought, but palatable. There was none of the usual sweetness one found in grape juice, but rather a peculiar kind of dryness. Signaling to the others, they all dipped their wooden cups into the slush and all tasted, some hesitantly, some boldly. Lips smacked loudly, opinions flew around the circle, indecision drove the cups back into the juice again and again.

All agreed on one thing: they had no idea what they were drinking.

After a while, however, strange symptoms began to manifest themselves: slurred speech, staggered gait, hiccups, and outbursts of laughter for no apparent reason. Talitha became mildly alarmed. Had her people become possessed by evil spirits? There were her two brothers, holding on to each other as they stumbled about. And her sisters, one giggling, the other weeping. She herself felt strangely warm. When the normally reserved Janka broke wind, everyone roared with laughter. Enjoying this response, he did it again on purpose, and when everyone laughed helplessly at this funniest thing in their lives, he made rude sounds with his mouth until the whole group was rolling around clutching their stomachs. Talitha also laughed, but a fear nagged at the back of her mind. This was not how they ordinarily acted. What was possessing them? Unfortunately she couldn't think clearly and as she drank more of the grape juice, forgot what it was she couldn't think clearly about. And then when Janka, stodgy and solemn Keeper of the Goddess, suddenly grabbed her and started kissing her, instead of being outraged—Talitha certainly hadn't signaled to him that she was interested in copulating with him—to her great surprise she giggled and happily lifted her skirt for him.

He finished quickly and soon rolled off to snore at her side. Talitha helped herself to more grape juice and realized in shock that her knees no longer gave her pain.

For months now her knees had been bothering her, the joints swelling to the point where she had to be carried everywhere. Even the short jaunt to the limestone cave had afflicted her with such pain that it had taken two strapping men to carry her back. But now, strangely, her knees not only felt perfectly fine, they felt like the knees of a young woman!

This both startled and cheered her—surely they were drinking a magical drink. A drink filled with the spirits of happiness and health. A blessing from the Goddess!

But as she drank more, instead of continuing to feel young and cheerful, she started to feel maudlin and after yet another fortifying drink, managed to get to her feet and stumble through other camps, tripping over people, nearly knocking a tent over until finally she staggered into Serophia's compound where everyone fell into a shocked silence.

Talitha started weeping and beating her breast. "We are cousins, Serophia! We are kinswomen! We should love one another, not hate! I am at fault. I am so greedy and selfish." She fell to her knees. "Can you forgive me, my dear cousin?"

Serophia was in such a state of shock that she could only stare with her mouth hanging open. Two of Talitha's nephews, who had been out looking for her, came into the circle and, seeing their aunt in such a state, immediately took hold of her by the elbows, lifted her up and helped her out of the compound, Serophia and her kinsmen staring after.

By the time they reached Talitha's tent she was incoherent—as were most of the other family members. When her nephews laid her down on her bedding skins, she immediately fell asleep, her loud snores filling the night.

*T*he next morning it was a different story.

They all slowly started waking up to discover they felt absolutely terrible. Devils pounded their heads and churned their stomachs, evil spirits cramped their bowels and made them run with diarrhea. Their hands shook, their vision was blurred. Several declared they were on the verge of death. Mortification and embarrassment swept over them as they suddenly remembered antics from the night before. Worse, they were afflicted with memory loss.

When Talitha stumbled out of her tent, clutching her head, she squinted in the morning light to see Ari on his hands and knees, retching violently, Janka drinking from a water gourd as if all the rivers in the world could not quench his thirst, and absolutely everyone holding their heads and moaning. And several of the women were dismayed to find physical evidence of having engaged in sexual intercourse that they could not remember.

Talitha was both perplexed and frightened. How could they have all been so merry the night before, yet feel on the verge of death this morning? Clearly they had been possessed by spirits that had made them feel happy and joyous but then left them feeling sick and miserable afterward—evil trickster spirits!

Talitha herself had no memory of her visit to Serophia's camp until she saw the shamefaced look on her two nephews, the only two who hadn't drunk the grape juice the night before. As she was wondering why they wouldn't meet her eye, and why they looked like naughty children about to suffer a whipping, it came back to her. *She had been on her knees begging Serophia's forgiveness.*

"By the breasts of the Goddess!" she shrieked. Had they all been possessed by evil spirits?

Nonetheless, Talitha did not want to give up the new drink altogether. After all, there *had* been the good cheer. She instructed the seers and Keeper of the Goddess to read the signs and omens, to meditate upon what had happened and to pray to the Goddess for guidance. And after a day of retreat and prayer, fasting and ingesting magic mushrooms, the clan's prophets declared that the magic drink had been transformed by the Goddess and given to her chosen children as a special gift. After all, the seers and Keeper of the Goddess also remembered the good feelings of the night before. And so they approached the situation with care, regarding the transformed juice as a sacred drink, not to be taken lightly but with great solemnity.

Word spread throughout the vast encampment until everyone was talking about the magic grape juice. Talitha invited the heads of other clans to drink the juice and give their opinion. Serophia was pointedly not invited. They passed the bowl around and tasted the wine. They felt their veins run warm and their ears buzz pleasantly. The clan heads and seers conferred and discussed, drank more wine, and finally agreed that the enchanted juice was not a bad thing. After all, it made one cheerful, it drove away pain, and rewarded the imbiber with a peaceful sleep. In fact, it was clearly a holy drink, imbued with the spirit of life by the Goddess.

The Gazelle Clan wintered in the northern caves and the next spring arrived at the Gathering place before the other clans. They harvested the grapes and transported them straight away to the secret caves overlooking the dead sea. They waited a week and went back to taste the juice. But all they found were grapes. They waited another week, and still there was no magic juice. Finally Talitha declared that it must take a year for the transformation to take place, and so they stayed away from the cave, which they kept secret from the other clans, and when they returned the following summer, went straight to their secret cave where they tasted the juice with great apprehension. It had been transformed! This time Talitha shared the special drink with the other clans and accepted items in trade.

The fourth time the family visited the perennial spring, Talitha said that there was no point to going back to the caves for the winter when they could build sturdy shelters right here. Better to stay and guard the grapes, she reasoned, than to leave and risk other people taking them.

But their ancient tradition was: *what was, is; what is, will always be.*

They made the annual north-south-north circuit simply because they always had. But now, just as Tall One had determined that, for survival, her people must leave, Talitha decided that her people must stay. It frightened them not to return to the caves for the winter but at the same time they discovered that they liked staying by the perennial spring. They also secretly feared that if they left they might not ever again taste of the magic drink. So Talitha sent a contingent up north to exhume their ancestors' bones from the caves and bring them back for reburial. Her reasoning was: if the ancestors were buried here, then this was ancestral land.

So they built sturdy shelters and appointed themselves guardians of the cheerful vine and come next summer when the fruit ripened, Talitha led the family in the harvest, juice-making, and storage of the magic drink. Not knowing about the yeast that occurred naturally on the skins of the grapes, or its chemical action upon the sugar in the grape, turning it into alcohol, or that the process was called fermentation, they believed that it was the Goddess instilling the otherwise innocuous grape with properties that made men cheerful and women pregnant.

Talitha's family monopolized the vines but happily traded the wine for goods the other clans had to offer. But while she excluded Serophia's clan from this lively commerce, awarding herself a victory in her feud with her cousin, Talitha did not know that another secret discovery was taking place.

A second valuable crop grew naturally near the perennial spring, and every summer the clans helped themselves to as much of the barley as they needed, roasting the ears over their fires and eating the grains. Serophia decided that, in retaliation for Talitha's victory, she would monopolize the barley crop, trading with others but withholding the grain from Talitha's clan. She also decided that, like the Talitha bunch, her family would stay at the spring to ensure their ownership of the barley. But no sacred cave was involved; the harvested barley seeds were stored in baskets in one of Serophia's tents, and measured out to be eaten or traded.

And so more years passed, with the Talitha clan trading wine for goods on one side of the spring, the Serophia clan bartering with barley grain on the other, until the Summer of the Rain when a second miracle occurred.

Rain was rare enough in the Jordan River Valley, even more so during the summer, and so when a storm struck that sent a deluge upon the encampment that lasted for days, the miserable settlers discovered leaks in their tents they had never before had to contend with. Not only were bedding and clothing soaked, but rain filled the baskets of stored barley grain, ruining it.

Serophia, in her pride, would not have the baskets emptied. She kept the ruined grain supply a secret lest word got around to Talitha and gave her a reason to gloat. And then one day in the fall, a nephew remarked that the tent where the ruined barley was stored had a peculiar smell. Upon inspection, the family found the baskets swollen and distended and found inside, instead of the soaked barley seeds, a thick fluid that gave off a pungent aroma. Like Talitha, Serophia's clan knew nothing about airborne yeast and its effect upon barley soaking in water and the resulting fermentation. All they knew was that the transformed drink made people feel exhilarated and blissful.

In time, Serophia's descendants learned how to make beer on purpose and thus a new commerce was born.

Because the clans no longer roamed, the people discovered that they had extra time on their hands, and so they turned their time and energies to leisurely industry such as making jewelry, tools, musical instruments, and improving their methods of hide-tanning. Food became more sophisticated. Instead of eating wild wheat grains right off the ear, women found that grinding the grain between stones and cooking it with water made a nourishing gruel. One autumn day a woman named Fara was suddenly called away from her labors, and in her haste tipped the mixture of water and grain onto hot stones. When she returned she found a tastier treat than gruel, and one that stored well. And so a third family decided to make the perennial spring their permanent home, and they settled down to the lucrative industry of bread-making.

More families came, and once people started cultivating their own vegetables, which were watered by the bubbling spring, thus providing a ready food source, the people no longer found need to go roaming in search of fresh food. They began to erect permanent dwellings, and permanence meant that material wealth was no longer limited to what an individual could carry. Private mud-brick homes began to fill with personal goods and accumulations, baubles and trinkets, creating for the first time two new statuses of people: the rich and the poor.

And the Goddess, with her miraculous blue stone that turned grape

juice into wine and barley into beer, became the focus of a new trend
of prayers. No longer were there just prayers for the dead, fertility,
and health, now there were prayers for rain to make the crops grow,
prayers for an abundant harvest, prayers for more customers.

The poor prayed to become rich, and the rich prayed to become
richer.

Book Three

THE JORDAN RIVER VALLEY
10,000 Years Ago

---

*F*or all Avram knew, the night could have been filled with portents and apparitions, comets and an eclipsing moon—a night ominous and frightful, heralding Doomsday and Armageddon. Or, it could have been a peaceful summer's night. You would not know it by Avram—he was in a world of his own.

Such a dream he had had! Marit in his arms, luscious and supple, warm and giving, bending to him, lifting hips and lips to him. A dream so fueled with passion that even now, as he made his way through the vineyard in the cold light of dawn, Avram's skin still burned with fever. As he scaled the wooden ladder of the lookout tower, hand over hand, loaves of barley bread swinging on a cord from one shoulder, a skin filled with diluted beer from the other—for Avram would spend the day in the tower, watching for marauders—he felt his arousal start anew. By the time he reached the top he had a full erection again. Avram had never been so in love, or so miserable, in his entire life.

He was all of sixteen years old.

The object of his love was a girl of fourteen with budding breasts and eyes like those of a gazelle. She was long limbed, graceful as the wind, sweet tempered, and kind. The object of his misery was the fact that Marit was of the House of Serophia while Avram was of the House of Talitha. Their families had been feuding for two centuries and the mutual hatred between them was legendary. If anyone knew of Avram's secret love for the forbidden Marit, he would be publicly humiliated and cursed, beaten, locked up, and starved, maybe even castrated. At least in Avram's young mind that was how he imagined his punishment would be.

But he could not stop thinking about the words his *abba*, Yubal, had spoken three years ago when Avram had started noticing changes in his own body. "Life is hard, lad. It's a daily toil filled with pain and suffering. So the Goddess in her wisdom gave us the gift of pleasure to offset all that misery. She made it so that men and women can give pleasure to one another, to make them forget their unhappiness. Therefore when the urge comes upon you, lad, take your pleasure where you can, for it is what the Mother of us all wishes."

Apparently Yubal was right, for it seemed to Avram that the citizens of the Place of the Perennial Spring were singularly concerned with pleasing the Goddess in that respect. The traditional pastime of the settlement was an endless circle of falling in love, setting up house, and breaking up. Sporting citizens, who always loved gossip, would sit over vats of beer and make wagers on how long a new pairing would last, or who was going to be seen creeping out of whose hut. Sometimes the breakup of a relationship was mutual, but more often it was one partner getting bored and moving on. That was when fights broke out, especially if one partner had moved in with another. Everyone still talked about the day Lea the midwife had caught Uriah the arrow-maker with one of the Onion Sisters. Lea had pulled the woman's scalp right off her head and then had thrown scalding water on Uriah. The arrow-maker had fled the settlement never to return. But there were also those rare ones who stayed together for a lifetime—his own mother and his *abba* had been such an example—and that was how he saw it for himself and the delectable Marit: lovers for eternity.

As Avram stood beneath the shaded platform at the top of the tower—the grass canopy being vital for it was now summer and the days were growing hot—he tried to draw in deep breaths of chill morning air, hoping it would cool his ardor so that he could focus on the business of searching the hills and ravines for signs of raiders. He was determined to do a good job of it. The year before, when the raiders had come from the east, there had been no warning. His mother had been brutally slaughtered and his two sisters abducted. And so the tower had been built, and it was Avram's job to sit up here as a guard against future attacks.

The raiders didn't come every year, there was no predicting their attacks. A savage race, their land was on the other side of the eastern mountains and they lived by hunting and stealing. No one knew who they were or how they lived because no one had ever had the courage to follow them after a raid. But rumors flew. It was said the raiders ate rocks and drank sand, that they had no womenfolk of their own but perpetuated their race by kidnapping the women of other tribes. Their souls could leave their bodies while they slept. They were shape-shifters and often prowled among the people at the perennial spring disguised as crows and rats. They ate their dead.

And so vigilance was essential. But it wasn't easy constantly scanning the horizon for raiders, or searching the rows of vines for thieves, especially as Avram could not take his mind off Marit and the delicious dream he had had the night before. Surely no man had ever been so afflicted with desire as he. Not even his *abba*, Yubal, who had wept openly when Avram's mother had been killed, declaring her to be the only woman he ever had loved.

The boy squared his shoulders and began his vigil.

The sky was pinking up over the eastern mountains and the settlement called the Place of the Perennial Spring—and which lay half a day's journey to the west of the river the people called Jordan, which meant "the descender," for it flowed from north to south—was stirring awake in the early mist, cook fires smoking to life, aromas of baked bread and roasted meat filling the air, voices rising in anger, joy, surprise, and impatience. From where Avram stood he could see not only his *abba*'s vineyard and the barley fields of Serophia—and olive groves and pomegranate orchards and stands of date palms—he also had an excellent view of the central settlement, a vast encampment of some two thousand souls living in mud-brick houses, grass shelters, goat-hide tents, or just sleeping on the ground cocooned in furs with worldly possessions tucked beneath their heads.

While many people lived here permanently, some came yesterday and would be gone today, with others arriving today to be gone to-morrow. People came to the Place of the Perennial Spring to barter obsidian for salt, cowrie shells for linseed oil, green malachite for flax fiber, beer for wine, and meat for bread. At the center of this great beehive of humanity, with long irrigation channels radiating out like the legs of a spider, bubbled the perennial spring of sweet water, where even now, in the breaking light of day, girls and women dipped their baskets and gourds.

Avram sighed restlessly. All those females and not one of them was as beautiful or alluring as his beloved Marit.

Like most boys his age, Avram was not inexperienced when it came to sex. Although the sport consisted mostly of going into the hills with his friends to capture a wild ewe and take turns on her, he had engaged in some limited experimentation with girls. But with Marit, Avram had had no experience at all. They had not even, in all their years of living on adjoining properties, exchanged a single word. He was certain his grandmother would kill him if he even tried.

Avram wished he lived in the Old Days, which he imagined had been much better than today. He loved hearing the stories of the ancestors—not Talitha and Serophia, but the *very old* ancestors— when his people were nomads and had all lived together in one big tribe and men and women took their pleasure with whom they chose. But now they were no longer nomads traveling in great clans but instead small families that lived in one house on the same spot of ground and that somehow made people think that those who lived on one spot of ground were better than those who lived on another. "Yubal's wine tastes like donkey piss," Marit's *abba*, Molok, was always declaring. "Molok's beer was squeezed from the testicles of pigs," Avram's *abba*, Yubal, would counter. Not that the two men would voice these opinions to each other's faces. Members of the Houses of Talitha and Serophia had not exchanged words in generations.

So one could count on it that never, *ever* would a boy from one house and a girl from the other find their way into each other's arms.

Avram didn't think it was fair. The rivalry belonged to the ances-tors, not to him. The ancestors had had their day and their say. Now it was Avram's time. He fantasized about running away with Marit (once he figured out a way to talk to her first), taking her far from his vineyard and her barley field, far from the tents and huts and mud-brick houses, exploring the world together. For Avram had been born a dreamer and a quester, his soul restless, his mind forever questioning and wondering why. In another age he would have been an astronomer or an explorer, an inventor or a scholar. But telescopes and ships, metallurgy and the alphabet, even the wheel and domesticated animals were things as yet undreamed of.

Untying a loaf of flat barley bread, he broke off a piece and as he chewed, turned his eyes to the cluster of humble mud-brick dwellings that crouched at the edge of the Serophia barley field—the threshing hut, the shed where vats of barley grains fermented into beer, and the private house where Marit's family lived—and he released a sigh filled with longing, his ardor all the more acute because he had no idea how Marit felt about *him*.

He thought at times that he had caught her watching him. Just a few weeks ago, at the festival of the Spring Equinox, she had suddenly looked away and a flush had appeared on her cheeks. Was it a good-luck sign? Did that mean she shared his sentiment? If only he knew!

As the sun continued to break over the distant mountains, Avram scanned the settlement for Marit—he would consider a glimpse of her at this early hour a good-luck sign, which meant the rest of his day would go well. But all he saw were fat Cochava chasing after her children with a stick; two brick-makers locked in a loud argument over a vat of beer (apparently they had not stopped drinking all night); Enoch the tooth-puller and Lea the midwife engaged in hurried copulation against a tree. Across the way, he saw Dagan the fisherman scrambling miserably out of Mahalia's hut, his possessions flying after him as if flung by an angry hand inside. Last month Dagan had been living with Ziva, and the month before that, Anath. Avram wondered what it was about Dagan that made women get tired of him so quickly and throw him out. Poor Dagan—without a woman and her hearth, how was a man to live?

Then Avram saw a sight that made him laugh out loud. Here came crazy Namir with another of his goat experiments! Two years ago Namir had hit upon the notion that instead of chasing after goats in the hills, killing what was needed and then returning to the settlement, it would be a lot less work if he brought live goats home, kept them in a pen, and slaughtered them for food or traded them as needed. So he and his nephews had gone into the hills and trapped as many goats as they could. But since they wanted the herd to perpetuate itself, they took only she-goats, leaving behind the males. But after a year, the she-goats stopped producing young and the last of the little herd was eaten or traded away. While his neighbors laughed, Namir vowed to make his plan work. "After all," he told his friends over vats of beer, "goat herds perpetuate in the hills, why not in my pen?" So he went out again and trapped she-goats, bringing them back to his pen with its fences made of sticks, branches, and brush. This time, none of the goats produced young and in no time the captive herd was eaten or sold. So here he was again, determined to maintain a herd of goats, leading his embarrassed nephews through the awakening settlement as they carried squirming and bleating she-goats tied to long poles. Avram could just see through the gathering smoke, four men sitting under an arbor sharing a vat of beer, shouting insults at Namir and making bets on how long *this* captive herd would last.

It seemed to Avram that everyone in the settlement had a scheme, and not all as ludicrous as Namir's. He remembered when everyone had laughed at another man, Yasap, who had arrived ten years ago and planted fields of flowers. The people had laughed because what use were flowers? They stopped laughing when the bees found the fields and Yasap kept hives and collected honey. For the first time in memory, people had sugar all year round, and so great in demand was the sweet treat that Yasap was now the third richest man in the settlement.

More and more people, coming to the Place of the Perennial Spring for the first time, looked around and saw opportunities for an easier life, built shelters and went roaming no more. People with special skills traded their services for food, clothing, and jewelry: barbers and tattooists, soothsayers and star-readers, bone-carvers and stone-polishers, fishermen and tanners, midwives and healers, trappers and hunters. All came, most stayed.

If I were free and on my own, Avram thought, *I would not try to think of ways to stay here. I would pack bread and beer, take up my spear and see what was on the other side of the mountains.*

Hearing high pitched shouts, he looked down and saw his little brothers running up and down the rows of vines, chasing the birds away. Aged thirteen, eleven, and ten, the boys loved the vineyard and had made it their world. Come the harvest next week they would pull their weight alongside adult men in filling baskets with ripe fruit, and later when all the grapes were gathered, the boys' little feet would work hard in the winepress mashing the grapes into juice.

Avram was about to wave to Caleb, the eldest of his younger brothers, when he saw something that made him freeze. An elderly woman, bare-breasted in a long doeskin skirt, her braided hair showing white roots beneath the henna dye, shuffled along the path almost overburdened by the many stone and shell necklaces that weighted her withered body. But she was wealthy, and it was a woman's duty to thus flaunt her family's wealth.

Avram's eyes nearly popped out. Why was his grandmother making her way along the path toward the Shrine of the Goddess? It both startled and alarmed him. What was she doing abroad at this early hour? It could only be an urgent errand. Had she found out about his secret desire for Marit? Was she going to ask the Goddess to cast a spell on him? Like most boys, Avram was terrified of his grandmother. Old women possessed power beyond thinking.

He automatically reached for the phylactery that hung on a leather thong around his neck. By tradition, when a child reached the age of seven and it appeared he was going to survive into adulthood—so many children dying prior to that age—he was given a permanent name and a small pouch in which to carry precious talismans: one's umbilical cord, dried and shriveled, one's first tooth, a lock of mother's hair. Maybe a small animal fetish, a few dried leaves of a protective plant, all designed to keep one healthy and from harm. As Avram clutched the phylactery that held magic pebbles, pieces of bone and twig, he wondered if it was powerful enough to protect him from his own grandmother.

He watched as she made her way between huts and shelters, stepping around piles of offal and entrails, hurrying through the stink that surrounded the tannery where bloody hides were being stretched in the sun, and finally up the path that led to the small mud-brick structure that housed the Shrine of the Goddess. Avram saw Reina, the priestess, emerge from her small house to greet her visitor.

Even from here, Avram could see Reina's magnificent breasts. In the summer, all the women of the settlement went bare-breasted so the men could feast their eyes upon the treasures of their women. This was what had triggered his new lust for Marit: when had she turned from a child into a woman? Reina's breasts were high and firm, not the least bit sagging as were those of most women her age, because Reina had never had children. When she had been anointed priestess, she had dedicated her virginity to the Goddess. But that didn't make her any less of a woman. Reina rouged her nipples with red ocher and perfumed her hair with fragrant oils. Her hips were wide and the belt of her doeskin skirt was slung low below her navel, just above the blessed triangle that was no man's land.

Avram sighed again in youthful lust and confusion, wondering why the Goddess had created this confounding hunger between men and women. Reina, whom no man could touch thus making men want to touch her all the more. Marit, the owner of his heart and whom he could never have. Where was the pleasure in that?

When he saw his grandmother emerge a few minutes later from the Shrine of the Goddess, where the sacred statue with the blue-crystal heart was kept and cared for, he was surprised at the old woman's haste back to their house, as if she were filled with urgency. A moment later Avram heard two voices in the house, rising in pitch. Grandmother and his *abba* were having an argument!

A moment later his *abba* burst from the house, as if in fury, and set out on the dirt path leading to the barley fields and the house where Marit lived.

It upset Avram to see Yubal look so distressed. A memory: *Yubal carrying him on his shoulders, big hands holding tight to the boy's ankles, Yubal's long strides bearing them both through meadows and across streams. Avram had felt like a giant and had rode those broad shoulders with such pride that he never wanted to climb down.* Avram didn't know any other boys who enjoyed such a relationship with their *abba*.

Not all men deserved the honorific *"abba,"* which meant "lord," or "master," usually over a prospering business, sometimes over the house and children of a woman he had become devoted to. As few men stayed with one woman for long, especially once she started having children, Yubal was a rare exception, for he had been open in his affection for Avram's mother, and had lived in her house for twenty years.

Avram watched Yubal—handsome in fine buckskins, his long hair and beard richly oiled as befitting his high status—go a few steps, then stop suddenly, rub his jaw, and turn away to take the path toward the settlement, as if suddenly changing his mind. A few moments later Avram saw Yubal take a seat beneath the shady arbor of Joktan the beer merchant, where three other men were already sharing a vat of beer. Yubal was greeted with cheers of welcome for he was one of the most liked and admired men in the settlement. Then he signaled to Joktan who brought out a reed that was roughly two arm's-lengths long. Yubal dipped the reed into the tall vat, pushing it past the scum from the brewing process that always clogged the surface, and began sucking up the liquid underneath. Joktan's beer was far inferior to Molok's, but Yubal swore he would drink snake piss before he would let the beer of Serophia's bloodline pass his lips.

Seeing Yubal, Avram redoubled his efforts as lookout. It was for his *abba* that he wanted to do a good job. He wanted Yubal to be proud of him. However, for all his efforts to focus on being a good guard, there were reminders everywhere of his new obsession with Marit and sex.

Glowing brightly in the morning sun on the door of the stone-polisher's house was a freshly painted picture of female genitalia. The old man was hoping it would help his daughters get pregnant. Many families painted such symbols beside their front doors—usually breasts and vulvas—hoping to invite the Goddess's fecundity into their homes. Such hopeful women went to Reina the priestess for magic charms, fertility potions and herbs with supernatural powers.

Men had no part in the pursuit of fertility for Avram's people were not yet aware that men had any role in procreation. Conception was a mystery worked solely by women through the power of the Goddess.

A shout brought his attention back to the settlement and its activities. One of the criminals tied to a punishment post near the bubbling spring was yelling at the children who were throwing shit and rotten stuff at him. Although it was usually cheats and liars, trespassers and malicious gossipmongers who were tied to the posts, the man tied there now, naked and helpless, had gotten drunk on barley beer, climbed to a rooftop and urinated on unsuspecting passersby. His punishment might have gone easier if one of his victims hadn't been Avram's grandmother. Two other men were also tied to posts, punishment for raping a daughter of the House of Edra. Because these men were the target of wrathful women, who threw stones and dung at them, a group of bystanders were wagering on whether the rapists would survive until sundown.

Justice in the community was swift and brutal. Thieves suffered a hand chopped off. Murderers were executed. From Avram's vantage point in the tower he could see, on the other side of the wheat fields, the corpse of a murderer hanging from a tree, his execution so recent that ravens were still pecking out the eyes.

Avram froze.

Then he shaded his eyes and tried to sharpen his eyesight. Was that a column of dust? Coming from the northeast?

He felt a lump rise to his throat. Raiders!

But then his eyes widened and he gasped. It wasn't raiders at all but Hadadezer's caravan! "Blessed Mother!" he cried, and because he couldn't take the steps fast enough he fell the rest of the way down the ladder.

Avram ran shouting and waving his arms—the obsidian traders had come! There would be feasting tonight like no other. And in so merry a throng, with so many people drinking and taking pleasure, who would notice if two young people chanced to exchange a forbidden glance?

The caravan was always a sight to behold: a virtual river of humanity that had flowed over mountains, meadows, and streams, a thousand souls marching like drones, each man a beast of burden stooped beneath the weight of trade goods and supplies. Some bore wooden yokes across their shoulders with bundles suspended from each end; others hauled baskets on their backs attached to leather straps across their foreheads; heavier goods were hauled on sledges by teams of men yoked together. It was a long, slow, back-breaking endeavor to cover so many miles, tramping over thistle and rock, baking under the sun, freezing under rain, through mountain passes and scorching deserts. But there was no other way for it to be done. People in the south wanted what people in the north had to trade, and vice versa. Although a few brave men in the northern mountains were experimenting with cattle to tame them and train them to be draft and pack animals, the results so far had been unsuccessful. So upon the backs of men came malachite and azurite, ocher and cinnabar; goods made from alabaster, marble, and stone; pelts, furs, antlers, and horns; and the fine wooden tableware the north country was famous for— sauceboats and tiny eggcups, and platters with carved handles. All of this was being taken south where it would be traded for papyrus and oils, spices and wheat, turquoise and shells, to be hauled back north on the same bent backs.

There were women in the caravan, equally burdened with bedrolls, tents, live fowl, and cook pots—women who were following their men or who had joined the convoy along the way, some with children in tow, of which a few had been born during the caravan's impressive southward progress. Some of these women would leave the caravan when it reached the Place of the Perennial Spring, and local women, for their various secret reasons, would run away from the Place of the Perennial Spring and disappear southward with the caravan.

Ahead of this enormous human convoy rode its captain, an obsidian trader named Hadadezer, Hadadezer's personal mode of transportation was another wonder to behold. Hadadezer did not walk—anywhere. And certainly not the two thousand miles comprising his caravan circuit. A carrying platform devised of two sturdy poles with a webbing of branches and reeds was hefted on the shoulders of eight strong men. Here Hadadezer rode in splendor, sitting cross-legged on woven mats with soft doeskin pillows stuffed with goose down supporting his arms and back. Since everyone knew that a fat man was a wealthy man, judging by Hadadezer's generous girth, he must be the wealthiest man in the world.

Hadadezer's long black hair was impressively oiled and braided and reached his waist, as did his great black beard, likewise oiled and braided and threaded with a wealth of beads and shells. He wore a knee-length leather tunic that was covered entirely in cowrie shells, collar to hem, a garment so splendid that it made people gape in awe. Six thousand years hence, Hadadezer's descendants would adorn themselves with gold and silver, diamonds and emeralds, but in this time, when precious metals and gems lay as yet undiscovered in the earth's secret places, cowries were the ornament of choice. They were also the coin of commerce.

Hadadezer was known far and wide as being a shrewd man. In his younger years he had started a trade in frankincense, a resin collected from a tree called *lebonah*—which means "white"—that grew in the north. When lighted, the incense gave off a beautiful perfume and so it had become instantly popular and in high demand in both river valleys. However, although Hadadezer charged highly for the product, he in turn had to pay the resin collectors a high cost, too, which left him little profit. But one season, as he was passing through the heavily forested country in the north, he had discovered that the fragrant wood of junipers and pines, when powdered, adulterated the frankincense in such a way that no one could tell they were receiving a diluted product. In this way he stretched his supply of the resin, charged the same price and made a much larger profit.

Hadadezer never missed a thing. One reason for his success as a trader was that he employed a complex form of bookkeeping that only he understood. Since paper and writing still lay four thousand years in the future, the obsidian merchant relied upon a system of tokens made out of hard-baked clay, imprinted with symbols only he could identify, and strung on various cords and twine dangling from his belt.

The people of the settlement rushed out to greet the caravan in eager anticipation of the coming night when old acquaintances would be renewed, lovers reunited, enemies found and dealt with, contracts made, promises fulfilled, and all manner of goods and services traded. As the sun climbed and delivered a scorching day, tents were pitched, cook fires lit, wineskins and beer vats broken out. And just as the citizens of the settlement would seek entertainments and pleasures in the caravan encampment, likewise would the work-worn members of the caravan, having been laboring for so long, go into the town in search of bread, beer, gambling, and sex. Hadadezer would camp at the Place of the Perennial Spring for five days, after which his men would pull up stakes, shoulder their burdens, and continue southward to the Nile River Valley where they would camp again before turning around and making the northward journey home. Hadadezer made the two-thousand-mile circuit from his mountain home in the north to the Nile delta in the south and back to his home all in a year, coinciding his visits to the Place of the Perennial Spring with each summer and winter solstice.

Every man and woman who could walk, crawl, or be carried would be at the evening feast, for it was going to be a night of pleasure and diversion. The hardworking citizens of the Place of the Perennial Spring spent both halves of a year looking forward to the arrival of Hadadezer's caravan. Tonight they were going to enjoy themselves.

With one unhappy exception.

After being allowed to observe the Procession of the Goddess as she was taken around the caravan encampment to bless the visitors and all commerce that was going to take place there, Avram had been sent back to the vineyard where he and his younger brothers were to patrol for thieves.

Carrying his flaming torch as he went up and down the rows of vines, Avram thought longingly of the men in the caravan and the wonderful stories they always told of savage hunts and seas that drowned men, of women with fire between their legs and giants as tall as trees. They had traveled up the Nile and encountered people with skin as black as night. In the far north, they had seen an animal that was neither horse nor antelope but something in between, with two humps on its back. Avram longed to be a trader. He didn't want to smash grapes with his feet for the rest of his life.

He also knew that Marit would be somewhere in that great collection of happy humanity, perhaps buying henna or admiring a shell necklace. Perhaps she would stroll away from the company of her mother and sisters to watch a trained monkey perform antics, or to purchase one of the spicy meat delicacies mountain women were so famous for. And while she was there, out of the watchful eye of her family, beneath the moon and the stars, amid the sounds of laughter and brawling and revelry, and surrounded by the heady aromas of smoke and perfume and food being cooked, perhaps she would not mind if a certain boy stood close to her, perhaps even accidentally brushed her arm.

Passion was stronger than obedience. Avram could stand it no longer. Handing his torch to his brother Caleb with a muttered excuse, he stole like a shadow out of the vineyard.

The encampment covered the plain beyond the corn and barley fields and stretched nearly to the Jordan River, the smoke from its hundred cook fires rising to the stars. There was so much going on, so much to see and do that, as Avram delivered himself into the press of merrymakers, his mind was nearly distracted from its obsession with Marit. He stopped now and then to watch such entertainments as acrobats and magicians, dancers and jugglers, snake charmers and tricksters—all eager to separate the gullible onlooker from his precious cowrie shells.

Everywhere Avram went, food was offered. Massive spits held roasted pig and goat, reed mats were heaped with mountains of flat barley bread and bowls of honey, and one could not even count the number of vats of beer with long straws for drinking. He continued his search for Marit.

He came upon a crowd watching a dancer who wore little except bead necklaces and a belt made of shells. She was beautiful and voluptuous, all curves and sweat and flesh, shimmying and sashaying most seductively to a drum beat and the accompaniment of clapping hands. Avram did not know who she was but he wanted to burrow into her, set himself on fire in her deepest part. He felt aggression rise in him, and a heat that burned hotter than a thousand suns. His throat ran dry. His tongue filled his mouth. His eyes went like arrows to her thighs. He thought of Marit. Aching hunger filled him.

He turned away from the dancer and saw, a short distance away, Marit's *abba* passionately haggling with an ivory vendor. Molok was a short, compact bandy-legged man with a generous belly hanging over his belt, a sign of his prosperity and love of his own beer. A man of quick temper who would cut the testicles off any male descendant of Talitha who even looked in the direction of a Serophia woman.

Avram felt his heart rise to his throat. What madness was this? Why did he persist in this obsession when clearly it could have no good ending?

He was just about to decide that his search for Marit would only bring bad luck and that he should go back to patrolling the vineyard with his brothers as he was supposed to, when he espied a group of ladies clustered around a henna-seller. It wasn't how the women looked that caught his attention, rather how they sounded: their laughter and one in particular, high and lilting, like the song of a certain small bird that lived in the willow trees on the banks of the river.

In an instant the encampment vanished. The earth beneath Avram's feet dropped away. The sky above dissolved into nothingness. Until all that was left was sweet Marit and her delightful laugh.

"Out a the way, boy!" boomed a butcher who was trying to haul a sheep's carcass past him.

But Avram was made of wood—dumb and immobile. His lovesickness washed over him like warm rain. His lungs labored to breathe. He wondered if it was possible to die of being in love.

And then Marit turned and looked at him. And a miracle occurred.

The night suddenly returned with all its stars and moon, shining more brightly than they had in millennia, and the earth slammed up against his feet, good and solid and filled with promise; the encampment materialized again with all the laughing people and the music and dancers whirling and such a festive feeling in the smoky air. Avram's heart slid back down to his chest while another part of him rose, and heat sprouted all over his skin. Because Marit was looking at him—right at him, her dark eyes locked with his, holding him, drinking him in, taking him into herself as she had done so many times in his dreams.

He gulped. There could be no mistaking that look.

*T*he Valley of the Ravens was a riverbed that ran with raging water during winter storms but was dust-dry during the summer. Avram's moonlit shadow followed him like an accomplice, sharply outlined on the rocky walls of the narrow canyon. He listened to the silence, to the lonely wails of jackals, to the wind whistling through the rocky ravine. There was a chill in the night air but his skin burned with fever. He watched the moon, full and bright, trace her eternal course across the sky.

He held little hope that Marit would come. The subterfuge was a simple one: he had enlisted the aid of a friend to give Marit a secret message when she visited the well. He was to tell her Avram had found a rare flower in the Valley of the Ravens that he would like to show her. Marit would know it was a lie, but it was the necessary excuse she would need, *if* she wanted to come.

Avram hunkered down and waited. When the breeze shifted he heard the music and laughter of the caravan's farewell feast, and his nose picked up the occasional ribbon of cooking aromas. His stomach growled but he wasn't hungry. His impatience and nervousness grew.

Time passed. The moon continued across the sky. Avram jumped to his feet and paced. Marit wasn't going to come. He had been a fool to think she would.

And then there she was, as if she had slid down a moonbeam and landed silently on her feet.

They stared at each other across the brief rocky space. It was the first time the two had been alone together in their lives—always there were her sisters or Avram's brothers, or other people in the settlement. But now it was just them, alone beneath the stars.

Avram realized that he was shaking, from both fear and excitement. In all his fantasies he had not reckoned with the fear. It suddenly, and belatedly, occurred to him that the ancestors would be here with them in this canyon, Talitha and Serophia, ghostly combatants watching to see what taboos their progeny were going to break. He felt a cold sweat break out across his back and trace icy paths down his spine. Avram was certain that if he turned suddenly he would see Talitha standing behind him, angry, wrathful, ready to separate his head from his body.

He saw Marit rub her arms and glance furtively to the right and left, as if she too expected to see her vengeful ancestress loom over her to deliver a lethal blow.

But the moment stretched and all they heard was the wind whistling through the rocks, and all they saw were shadows, moonlight, and each other. Avram cleared his voice. It sounded to him like thunder.

Marit looked down at her hands. "The flower," she said softly. "Did you—?"

He swallowed. "I—"

She waited.

He thought flames were going to erupt all over him. "I—" he began again. All his fantasies about them speaking their first words together had not prepared him for reality. Suddenly he felt the eyes of his grandmother and his *abba* on him, and his ancestors all the way back to Talitha, and he was stabbed with fear. Cold sweat doused the heat on his skin and he shook badly. What was he doing? Breaking his family's most serious taboo!

And then he saw that she, too, trembled and realized what a risk she had taken coming here, how dangerous it must be for her as well. Molok would lay red stripes on her bare back if he knew!

They could turn away now and still save themselves. He should run up into the hills and let Marit flee back to her house. No one would be the wiser.

But neither moved. They were prisoners of the moonlight and of their mutual desire, the fourteen-year-old girl and sixteen-year-old boy on the brink of becoming woman and man.

Later, neither could say for sure who took the first step. But one step was all that was needed, for the rest of the steps followed in quick order and in an instant that winked out all the centuries and eons of time that had come before them they were in each other's arms. Avram pressed his lips to hers, Marit curved her arms around his neck. In their desperate, hurried, and very awkward first kiss, each imagined the canyon walls breaking apart and tumbling down to bury the two in an avalanche. They imagined they heard the howls of outraged ancestors and thought they felt the cold breath of death rush over them.

But in the end it was only Avram and Marit, embraced and on fire, oblivious to any ghosts that might be watching, mindless of taboos and repercussions, of bloodlines and revenge. And when they drew breath long enough to utter a word, both chose the word "love."

The next morning Avram watched for signs that he had brought bad luck on the family. He awoke expecting to find the house in ruins, or the roof on fire, or his skin an eruption of pustules. But the morning was calm and his grandmother was drinking her breakfast beer as usual. She did not complain of bad dreams, did not show any signs that anything was amiss. Yubal, however, seemed in a more pensive mood than usual, but Avram attributed it to the coming grape harvest.

Avram consumed his beer and bread in nervous silence, and before he left the house, paid extra obeisance to the ancestors, leaving a larger portion of his breakfast for them than usual, praying they wouldn't haunt the house because of his transgression with Marit.

Although he lived in constant fear of retribution, of the ground suddenly swallowing him up, or lightning striking him from the summer sky, the days went by with no evidence of bad luck coming into the house, and so Avram grew confident and arranged to secretly meet Marit again in the Valley of the Ravens. She, too, reported nothing out of the ordinary in their house—no hauntings, no bad luck—so it must be all right with the ancestors that they do this. "It is the Goddess's wish that we take pleasure," Avram reasoned as he drew her into his arms. "So who are the ancestors to disobey the Goddess?"

How they managed to keep their clandestine activities a secret was a miracle that convinced them the Goddess must be on their side, for in the weeks and months that followed, days filled with stolen kisses, nights of forbidden embraces, no one in their families suspected and the two were never found out. Avram was able to get away on the pretext of going fishing and no one found Marit's behavior odd for she was at the age when girls grew dreamy and took walks in the moonlight. Her mother even encouraged it because such walks often resulted in pregnancy.

While Avram and Marit expressed their secret love through the seasons, oblivious to the rest of the world, lost in each other's eyes, a change took place in the sixteen-year-old. When he was with Marit he felt complete, as if they were one soul sharing two bodies. And when they were apart he felt hollow and without purpose. Worst were the five days each month she spent in the moon-hut in special communion with the Goddess—at those times Marit was not only separated from him physically but spiritually as well, for the sequestered days were spent in prayer and ritual and in direct communion with Al-Iari.

Avram and Marit shared not only their love and their bodies, but their dreams as well. He told her that he longed to be a trader like Hadadezer. He didn't want to smash grapes with his feet for the rest of his life. The problem was, his dream was in conflict with his heart, for if he adopted the trader's life then he would never be at home and he would not see Marit for long stretches at a time. How was he to reconcile the two?

Marit's vision was different: "I love being part of a long chain of life, to know that I came out of my mother, who came out of *her* mother, all the way back through Serophia to the Goddess Al-Iari herself. It gives me great comfort and also a sense of wonder to know that *my* daughters, when I have them, will grow up to continue the chain."

Avram was suddenly struck by the unfairness of life. A woman's bloodline continued while a man's did not, except through his sisters.

By the time half a year had passed, and it was nearly time for the winter solstice and the return of Hadadezer's caravan, Avram and Marit were proud of how well they had kept their secret. They had even managed to pretend in front of others that they didn't like each other. In their youthful naiveté they believed they could keep this up forever.

*T*here was no greater proof of the life-creating power of the Goddess than in the making of wine. For wasn't the cave the Earth Mother's womb? And wasn't the grape juice from Yubal's vineyard like a woman's monthly moonflow? Everyone knew that when a woman's moonflow was held within her womb, a child began to grow. And so did the miracle of wine come about: the grape juice was carried into the cave-womb and held there in mystery and darkness until, six months later, men went in to find it had been miraculously transformed into a drink with "life."

Therefore the tasting of the vintage was the most important and solemn religious rite at the Place of the Perennial Spring. The Goddess herself, carried upon the shoulders of four sturdy men, her blue-crystal heart glinting in the first rays of sunlight, led the procession to the sacred cave in the south. The statue had been carved a hundred years ago from a single block of sandstone. It stood three feet tall and was marvelous in its detail, from Al-Iari's large, all-wise eyes to the delicate sandals on her feet. The crystal stone, ancient and magical and powerful beyond all knowing, was seated between the Goddess's bare breasts.

The morning air was crisp and chill, the winter solstice being just days away as the parade marched solemnly across the plain and down to the river, continuing south to the dead sea where the sacred wine caves were. The cliffs were reached at noon, whereupon Reina the priestess brought everyone to a halt. Seeing that the Goddess was placed upon her throne of rock, Reina conducted a prayer. A sheep was sacrificed and placed upon the altar. Then Avram's grandmother, his *abba*, Yubal, Avram, and his three younger brothers proceeded alone up the narrow path to the mouth of the cave.

Not a sound was heard among the hushed gathering, for the first tasting of the summer vintage would tell the people how the rest of the year would go.

Avram's grandmother paused at the entrance and, lifting her arms, prayed aloud to the Goddess and to any spirits or ghosts that might be nearby. She spoke words that had been passed down from Talitha's day, when the first wine was created in this cave, then she dusted the threshold with frankincense and bay leaves, a sacred mixture meant to sanctify the area. She went in first, to strike flints and light the oil lamps that had been placed there in the summer. She stepped with a light foot lest her intrusion disturb the sacredness of the cave.

When she satisfied herself that the wineskins were untouched, that no sacrilege had been committed here during the months of fermentation—for it was death to anyone who entered the sacred wine cave—she beckoned to Yubal. He was the *abba* of the house, he was also the *abba* of the vineyard, he must take the first taste.

To Avram's surprise, Yubal touched his arm and indicated that he should join them. Avram had never set foot over the threshold of the sacred cave. He was filled with awe as he followed Yubal into the darkness and could *feel* the presence of Goddess-power all around him. He thought of Marit outside among the onlookers, and how filled with pride she must be to see him enter the sacred cave.

Yubal paused before the wineskins, stored on limestone shelves carved out of the cave walls, and looked at the boy beside him, tall and handsome, the first signs of a beard on his cheeks. Yubal could not explain why he felt the way he did about the boy. It had happened while Avram's mother was pregnant. They would lie together on their sleeping mat and Yubal would stare in wonder at the great mound of her belly, watching it move when the baby was active. Yubal would lay his hand on that marvelous mound and feel the child move beneath his fingers, and something miraculous would come over him—it almost felt as if the child were moving within himself.

"Before we proceed, Avram," Yubal said in a quiet, resonant voice that went no farther than the entrance of the cave. "I have something to tell you." He grinned. "Wonderful news."

He looked into the boy's expectant eyes and grew somber. He had never had trouble talking to Avram in the past. They had been close and never awkward with each other. Even that one time, when Avram turned thirteen and Yubal had had to explain the rules and taboos of being with women, about the special tent the women retired to once a month, the moonflow that created new life and that was the sole purview of women. It had been difficult to explain it all to the boy. Just the power of woman's mystery nearly stopped the words in Yubal's mouth.

For all his wealth, Yubal was a simple man. He understood his vineyard and his wine, but women baffled him. There was that secret about them . . . that hidden place within them where a man took his pleasure but also where life began, where the Goddess dwelled. The fear of menstrual blood was strong in Yubal, as it was in most men. To even come into contact with it, so the myths said, meant instant death to a man, for the moon-blood carried the power of the Goddess, the power of life and death. When a woman's blood stopped coming, it meant a new child was being formed. But when the flow appeared, it meant a life had died.

"Our house is to receive a new member," Yubal said now amid the flickering lamps in the cave.

Avram looked at him in surprise. In his infatuation with Marit

Avram had been so blind to everything that he hadn't been aware his *abba* was involved in plans to unite their family with another. But of course, it was a move that must happen eventually.

The traditions and laws of family alliances began with the first families of the settlement, generations ago, when raiders came and plundered crops and houses. The ancestors had decided that, for the survival of the settlement, families must protect one another. Over the generations, it had been discovered that the most successful way of guaranteeing mutual protection in times of invasion or disaster was the periodic swapping of sons and daughters. In the case of Avram's family, they had too few males to work the vineyard and protect the harvest from marauders. Yubal often hired men to help, but they tended to eat the grapes, and when invaders came, they ran. By the same token, there were now no females in the House of Talitha, just the very elderly grandmother. With just Yubal and Avram and the three younger boys, the house would die out. So a female would be added to their family, preferably one with many brothers and uncles, for such men would willingly protect the vineyard and not steal from the family they had been allied to.

"Who is it to be?" Avram asked, several candidates crowding his mind—the daughters of Sol the corn-grower, the nieces of Guri the lamp-maker, the youngest Onion Sister.

Yubal cleared his throat and shifted his weight. "A daughter of the House of Serophia is to join our family."

Avram stared at him. "Serophia," he said dumbly.

Yubal held up a hand. "It is a shock to you, I know. But the Goddess was consulted and she spoke through Reina. We also consulted the star-reader and the seers. All agreed that a family so ancient and noble as ours can only ally itself with a house of equal standing. Who else but Serophia?"

Yubal had not been happy with the idea himself, and had argued with the grandmother about it. Edra was a good House, he had argued, and the bloodline of Abihail. But she, and the Goddess, had prevailed. No other house would do. And so, through a representative (since it was unthinkable the rival *abbas* should actually speak), Yubal had approached Molok on the issue of creating an alliance between the two families. But Yubal had had an advantage. He had heard from the trader Hadadezer that Molok was getting worried about his beer trade. It was becoming easier and easier for other men to make beer—

all they had to do was buy barley bread, crumble it into water to form a mash and leave it alone until it fermented, without having the bother of a barley field that needed cultivating, harvesting, and protection from locusts and thieves. The rumor was, Molok's business was starting to fail and he was looking for ways to diversify and keep the family prosperous. But Molok was rich in another area: his house had many strong sons, and so Yubal decided that the protection of another man's sons in exchange for a winepress and a portion of the grape harvest was a good bargain. The alliance, after centuries of rivalry, was agreed upon.

"Even though the sons of Serophia might still hate us," Yubal said, "they will nonetheless protect their sister in case of raider attack, protecting us and our vineyard as well."

"Which daughter, *Abba?*" Avram said in a whisper.

"The youngest. The girl Marit."

Avram felt as if he had been struck by lightning and stuffed with honey at the same time. His shock and his joy collided to strike him dumb.

Yubal hurried on, misreading the shocked look on Avram's face. "I don't blame you for being angry. But it is for the ancestors and for the bloodline. But now, I have even better news!"

Avram tried to find his voice, to say, "What could be better than having my beloved Marit beneath my own roof?" but Yubal was speaking quickly. "I have entered into an agreement with Parthalan, of the House of Edra, and we are to unite with them by sending you to live with them. Think of it, Avram! Living with the shell-workers! A very enviable position since their work is clean, no sweat, no calluses, their hands are always soft and clean. And they have several beautiful daughters with whom you can take your pleasure."

Yubal was pleased with his own cleverness—just look at the expression on the boy's face! He was clearly about to faint at the suddenness of this good fortune. Since Avram was a dreamer, always wondering what was on the other side of the hills and wasn't interested in the vineyard or making wine, Yubal had found the perfect solution in Parthalan for he and his daughters traveled yearly to the Great Sea where they collected cowries, conches, clams, scallop, and abalone shells that they brought back to be carved into jewelry, fetishes, amulets, and magic ornaments. Parthalan was rich and had been looking for a new healthy male to add to his family. So Yubal struck a deal with Parthalan: Avram was to join the House of Edra and in return, Parthalan was to pay annually in abalone shells to the House of Talitha.

Yubal's face glowed with joy in the flickering lamplight. "Finally you will see what is on the other side of the hills! What better life could you ask for!"

"Oh *Abba*," Avram cried, his voice resounding off the cave walls. "This is terrible news."

Yubal's face fell. "What do you mean? You should be rejoicing. You have never been happy working the vineyard or the winepress. Now you are being given a chance to see what is on the other side of the horizon. I am handing you your dream and you are angry?"

"My dream is Marit!" Avram blurted.

Yubal stared at him. "What are you talking about?"

"Marit. I love Marit."

"You have a passion for the girl? I had no idea. You certainly kept it a secret."

Avram hung his head. "*Abba*, I cannot leave her."

"But you have to."

"I cannot be parted from Marit."

"You're young yet, lad. Once you set your hands upon the luscious thighs of Parthalan's daughters—"

"I don't want the shell-worker's daughters. I want Marit!"

Yubal's face darkened. He loved the boy but Avram was overstepping bounds in this sacred cave. "You cannot have her, Avram, and it breaks my heart now to know what I have done. But all the arrangements have been made with Parthalan, the agreements are set. We spoke vows before the Goddess. We cannot go back on our word." Yubal laid a heavy hand on Avram's shoulder. "But think on this then, that Marit will be in our house, safe and protected, and she will be here when you come back from the Great Sea."

Avram was utterly miserable. "The abalone hunters are gone for a year at a time."

"But then they come back to carve and sell their shells. You will be with Marit then."

"I shall die at the Great Sea."

Yubal sighed. The day had not gone as he expected. Still, there was nothing to be done about it and Avram was young, he would get over it. Time to move on and remember why they were in the cave. But first, there was something else Yubal wanted to do.

He wore a wolf's fang on a leather thong around his neck. He had been hunting in the hills one day and was attacked by a wolf. Yubal had nearly died—his body still bore the scars. The men who brought Yubal home, covered in blood, had also brought the dead wolf with Yubal's knife buried in its chest. Yubal later removed one of the beast's fangs as a trophy and made it into a pendant: a big yellow canine tooth with the faint rusty stains of his own blood still on it. It was very powerful protection against harm because it possessed the spirit of the wolf.

He now lifted the thong over his head and draped it over Avram's. "To protect you while you are away at the Great Sea."

The youth was speechless. He looked down at the powerful talisman and felt his throat constrict. He had difficulty finding voice. "I vow to honor the family and your contract with Parthalan, *Abba*." And in his mind he saw Marit, waving farewell on a hilltop, her figure growing smaller until she was no longer in sight.

*I*t would take a blind man, Hadadezer thought cynically, *not to see that Yubal has made a terrible mistake.*

As the obsidian-trader gnawed on a mutton joint, occasionally wiping his greasy hands on his generous beard, he looked around and thought this feast was more like a funeral than a celebration. The Serophia girl's brothers looking dower. Molok drinking too much. Marit's mother too loud, braying false laughter, wearing so much bone and shell jewelry she looked as if she might collapse beneath the weight of it all. The Talitha grandmother putting on a nauseatingly sweet face, fawning over the guests. And too much food, even for these rich families. What did they expect? That a few gestures, a prescribed ritual, vows before their goddess and suddenly all the hatred that had been ingrained in them since birth would vanish? Great Maker, there was much bad luck hanging over this feast. For the first time in all his years of eating and drinking at the Place of the Perennial Spring, Hadadezer was anxious to get back to his own tent and away from this bad luck.

Unfortunately, he was an honored guest—his caravan was due to depart tomorrow for the north—and so he could not leave. He must sit through this painful feast and then be expected to follow the procession from the girl's house to her new home. It was but a short distance from the Serophia homestead to that of Talitha, but in Hadadezer's mind it was going to take forever. He sighed. At least he wasn't expected to delay his departure and join the procession taking the sullen Talitha boy, Avram, to his new home with the shell-workers.

At least the girl seemed happy, sitting on her little throne festooned with winter flowers, her hair wearing a crown of bay leaves, her chest barely rising and falling beneath the weight of so many cowrie shell necklaces, gifts from family and friends. But her new kinsmen, Yubal and Avram, looked about as miserable as two souls could be. And they were drinking too much, even by Hadadezer's standards.

The evening dragged on with false merrymaking until finally Reina the priestess gave the signal that the final stage of the unification of the two houses take place. Hadadezer belched his relief and signaled to his bearers who immediately jumped up and hoisted his carrying platform onto their shoulders. They followed the girl and her family a discreet distance, then the trader gave another signal and his bearers veered away from the procession, carrying their master back to the caravan encampment where two lovely young females were waiting to share his bed.

Yubal could hardly walk. He was so sorry about the contract he had made with the abalone hunters—he had truly thought Avram would be filled with joy at the news—that he had poured far more wine down his throat than he was accustomed to. A deeper pain also afflicted Yubal that no amount of fermented drink could assuage: the reality that he had had to go to Molok and ask for this alliance. Although at first he had felt smug about knowing of Molok's desperation to save his failing beer business, and had even come away from the negotiations thinking he had done the man a favor, the reality of what he had done now stuck in Yubal's throat like a thorn. No amount of Goddess blessings or good wishes from friends, no assurances from the seers and star-readers that he had done the right thing, could get the sour feeling out of Yubal's stomach. He still hated the Serophia Clan, Molok most of all, and now regretted that he had not found another way to protect his vineyard.

Avram was also miserable because he was leaving in a week and would be gone for a year. And so he, too, had drunk more wine than he was used to.

When the procession reached the Talitha house, Reina invoked the blessings of the Goddess and the gathered company cheered and wished both families well. Molok and his sister kissed Marit good-bye, her sullen brothers glowered at Yubal and sent him a silent message that they were going to be closely watching out for the welfare of their sister. And then the gathering broke up with Yubal and Avram stumbling drunkenly to their pallets while the grandmother took Marit to the women's side of the house.

The moon was fat and yellow and gibbous, more like a spring moon than a winter one, and it pierced the straw roof in a thousand tiny rays. The radiant light also found its way through the small window in the mud-brick wall and fell across Marit as she lay wide-eyed in her new bed. She was waiting for Avram. They had agreed that once everyone was asleep, he would come to her bed.

But where was he?

She listened to the silence in the house, broken only by the snores of the old woman and the younger brothers, then, deciding she could wait no longer, she slipped out of bed, naked, and tiptoed across to the other side.

At that same moment, Yubal tossed and turned in a moon-affected dream in which his beloved bed partner, Avram's mother, appeared to him, saying she was not dead after all and that she had come back to him. But as he took her into his arms and they started to make love, he awoke suddenly and blinked in a drunken fog, unable to distinguish between dream and reality. Where had she gone?

Hearing a sound, he rolled his head to the side and saw her— Avram's mother, young and slender and naked, tiptoeing across the communal room. She was coming to the men's side of the house, to him.

Yubal managed to get to his feet and stagger over to her, roughly pulling her into his arms.

Marit's cry wakened Avram. He blinked in darkness and frowned at the two human figures captured briefly in broken moonlight. He had trouble keeping his vision from going double. He rubbed his eyes and looked again. Two people in a clinch, naked.

He got up and fell to his knees. No, he must be dreaming. It was a hallucination.

He looked at them again. The image swam before him, as if the house had somehow sunk beneath the perennial spring and was underwater. He saw pale arms writhing like snakes, and two heads performing a strange dance. Legs stumbling, bodies squirming. Lovers in an aquatic embrace.

And then he experienced one of those moments of absolute clarity in the midst of a drunken stupor: Marit! In Yubal's arms!

He tried again to get to his feet, but the floor beneath him swayed and swooped like the watchtower in a storm. His stomach rose to his throat and he realized he was going to throw up.

He rushed outside in time, vomiting in his grandmother's small cabbage garden. He gulped night air and when he started back for the house, nausea rose again.

Yubal's hands on Marit's body.

He tried to go back but a sickness worse than that caused by the wine overwhelmed him. *Yubal and Marit!* His thoughts flew and collided, finding no cohesion, just a jumble of blurry concepts and feelings.

So he turned and ran. Sweating and feeling sick, with the world spinning around him, he plunged into the vineyard where his intoxicated brain exploded with a shower of irrational thoughts. It came into Avram's jumbled mind that Yubal had planned this all along so he could have Marit.

"No," he whispered as he fell to the ground. "It cannot be."

He tried to make sense of what his eyes had seen, but his brain was soaked in too much wine, thoughts did not come in a logical order. Suddenly, anger and jealousy exploded within him.

Raising his fist skyward he shouted, "You betrayed me!" He choked on his sobs as he swayed on unsteady legs. "You did this on purpose! Bringing my beloved into the house and sending me away to the Great Sea. You have wanted her for yourself all along! Curse you, Yubal! May you die a thousand terrible deaths!"

Sobbing, filled with nausea, the world twirling around him, Avram ran again, crashing through vines, his eyes blinded by tears, sickness of soul and body overwhelming him as he plunged headlong into a darkness that finally swallowed him entirely.

◆ ◆ ◆

*B*right light. Moans.

Avram lay perfectly still, wondering why he felt so sick. His head pounded and his stomach churned. His mouth felt as dry as dust and tasted sour.

Another moan. He realized it had come from his own throat.

Bit by bit he lifted his lids and accustomed himself to the light. Sunlight, pouring through an opening in a tent.

Why was he in a tent?

When he tried to sit up, nausea rolled over him in such a powerful wave that he fell back onto the bedding. A bed of furs. Not his own bed.

Whose tent was this? And why was he in it? How did he get here? He tried to remember, but his mind was as murky as a mud pond. Memory came to him in vague recollections: the feast celebrating the alliance of the two families, the procession to his house, his grandmother leading Marit to the women's side of the house, he and Yubal dropping to their sleeping mats.

After that, nothing.

When he heard a humming sound, he turned toward it and saw a dusky-skinned woman packing cookware into a basket. He tried to speak, and when she saw that he was awake, gave him a water skin to drink from, explaining as she did so that she and her sisters had found him outside their tent, lying in his own vomit. They had brought him in and cleaned him up, and then left him to sleep it off.

He sat up and cradled his head, which was filled with angry demons. The sixteen-year-old could not recall having ever felt this rotten in his life. *I was sick? Vomiting? But why here in the caravan encampment, why am I not at home?*

He managed to get to his knees, and then to his feet, but he swayed unsteadily and his head pounded mercilessly. In confusion, he watched the dusky-skinned woman busily carrying things out of the tent. In fact, all that remained was the bed he had slept on. Then he remembered: Hadadezer's caravan was leaving this morning.

I must get home before they notice I am gone.

But at the tent opening, the blinding sunlight stopped him. Slapping a hand over his eyes, he fought down rising nausea and tried to pull himself together. His bladder was full and he urgently needed to relieve himself.

There was privacy behind the tent, and as he urinated, saw the vast encampment breaking up. Then he turned toward the settlement where he realized a great chorus of wailing and crying was being lifted to the sky, a sound made only when someone important had died.

Going around to the front of the tent where the dusky-skinned woman was pulling up stakes, Avram asked her what had happened in the settlement. She explained that a wine-maker had been making love to a girl and had died in her arms.

Avram blinked at her. Wine-maker? Making love to a girl?

It all came flooding back: Avram waking to see Yubal kissing Marit. The flight into the garden, the raised fist and curse shouted to the sky. And then—

Now he remembered, a twisted horrid scenario that he had watched from his hiding place among the vines: a scream, followed by Marit running from the house. His grandmother coming out, crying and beating her breast. Avram's brothers stumbling about as if they had been struck by lightning. Other people arriving, going into the house. The neighbors shouting, "Yubal is dead! The *abba* of the House of Talitha has gone to his ancestors."

Avram now remembered his drunken shock at the time, hidden in the vines, rooted in stupefaction. Yubal was dead?

And then the memory: *Avram, shaking a fist to the sky. "May you die a thousand horrible deaths!"*

He had run blindly from the vineyard, sick and confused, finding himself at the shrine of the Goddess.

The memory came back dim and murky. Al-Iari's house, small and low-ceilinged, its dark interior illuminated by oil lamps casting light upon shelves stocked with magical amulets, healing herbs, potions, powders, and fertility charms. And upon her altar—

The statue.

And dazzling in the lamplight, the blue stone. The Goddess's heart. Her *forgiving* heart. Avram in drunken desperation had impulsively thrown his arms around Al-Iari's stone legs, losing his balance and taking the craven image with him. A loud crack.

Avram now staggered against the tent as if he had been struck. *The Goddess lying shattered on the floor.*

It could not have been real! It was all a monstrous, twisted night-mare.

When he heard someone asking him a question, he blinked at the dusky-skinned woman. "Did you know the wine-maker?" she repeated.

But all he could think of was the shattered statue of Al-Iari. No nightmare, it had been real. *He had killed the Goddess!*

And then another memory: the blue crystal, his hand blindly reaching for it, curling around it, fumbling for his phylactery, pressing the stone inside the soft leather pouch.

Breathless with shock, Avram brought his hand up now and laid it upon his chest where he could feel, beneath his tunic, the bulge of the phylactery. But now it was larger and had a new hardness.

The blue stone, the heart of the Goddess.

He tried to move, tried to cry out, summon tears, impel his lungs to voice his outrage and grief. But nothing within him moved, his body would not obey. Like a man under a spell he watched the women tear down their tent and pack it onto a sledge, and when they started walking with the rest of the members of the caravan, a mass exodus moving away from the Place of the Perennial Spring, Avram without thinking fell in with them.

They were a family of seven women: grandmother, mother, three daughters, and two female cousins. They told him they were feather-workers and that he was welcome to accompany them. And so he went with the feather-workers, a mute, nameless boy who might have made the women wary were he not so pleasant of countenance and clearly the son of a wealthy family.

*T*he days and weeks went by in a haze. Avram did hard labor for the women during the day and at night they stroked him and kissed him, saying he was a very pretty boy, and drew him into their lush bodies. After a while the numbness wore off and Avram recognized the utter wretch that he was. He had killed his *abba,* brought disgrace to his bloodline, broken a contract with Parthalan, abandoned Marit, and, by stealing the heart of the goddess, had as good as killed her as well. And so he let the feather-workers, who did not know the details of his tragedy, console him and offer him refuge.

They did not know that the boy traveling with them was but a shadow, a soulless shell that had no purpose. His body moved with instinct—sleeping, eating, urinating. When a cup was placed in his hands, he drank, and when the women visited his sleeping mat at night, his body reacted as a man's and he took his pleasure. But Avram himself felt no pleasure, no hunger or pain. He moved in a realm that was of neither the living nor the dead.

Northward the caravan went, a slow moving river of burdened humanity, stopping at small settlements and then continuing on, past the freshwater lake and the Cave of Al-Iari, into the lush woodland where the *lebonah* tree grew. Avram pulled the feather-worker's sledge and pitched their tent at night while his feminine companions fed him and delighted over his youth and innocence. And though he had lost all care for his own safety and well-being, something in him made him stay hidden from Hadadezer, who had been Yubal's friend.

Numb of mind, body, and spirit, Avram watched the feather-workers at their skilled labors. Their talent, known the length of the caravan route from the mountains in the far north to the delta of the Nile, lay in their instinct for layering feathers on leather the way they are layered on a bird. They were also skilled in use of color so that their fans, capes, belts, and headdresses commanded the highest prices.

Knowing there was an evil spirit of sickness inside him, the matriarch fed Avram medicinal concoctions designed to drive evil spirits away. She crooned over him and laid healing hands on him. Her daughters and nieces gathered around him in a loving circle and sang to him. Especially when he woke from bad dreams in which he found himself running after Yubal, trying to call him back.

Maybe it wasn't an evil spirit inside him after all, the grandmother finally decreed when their ministrations did not help. Maybe the boy's own spirit had died. And once dead, a spirit could not be revived.

It was spring when the caravan finally emerged through a mountain pass and wound down to a vast, grassy plateau where other families were camped beside a shallow lake. The feather-workers invited Avram to continue on with them to their village of stone houses just a day's journey away, where he could live a life of leisure with them for two years before they joined Hadadezer's caravan again. But he felt a compulsion to move on, the setting sun beckoning for reasons he did not understand. He learned that this was a winter camp and that once the rains ceased the families camped here would pull up stakes and follow the herds that went in search of spring grasses. So he went around the tents and offered himself as a hard worker in exchange for being allowed to travel with them.

Thus did Avram continue his flight from the Place of the Perennial Spring. The feather-workers gave him a tearful farewell and a handsome feathered cape lined with goose down, and with the new family he traveled across the Anatolian plateau, a gentle plain of short grasses and stunted willow trees, wild tulips, and peonies. They followed large herds of horses, wild asses, and antelopes. Avram saw the two-humped camels, fat marmots basking in the sun, rose-colored starlings that flocked in the thousands, and cranes that built nests on the ground. But these wonders might as well have been ash and stone for all they moved him. Avram did not tell the nomadic family his name or his story, but he worked hard for them and kept his peace. When the women crept into his bed his response was as objective and automatic as it had been with the feather-workers. He gave them pleasure with his body, but gave nothing of his heart.

When they reached the western edge of the plateau, he bade the family farewell and continued on down to the coast, where he reached a narrow body of water that he mistakenly took for a river, not knowing that it was in fact a strait connecting two major seas and separating two continents. Avram also did not know about shrinking glaciers on the European continent and the resulting rise in sea level that would, over the millennia, turn this small strait into a major shipping lane that would one day be called the Bosporus.

Here he saw boats for the first time, and found a man who would take him across to the other side. Avram had just turned eighteen and thought his life was over.

*H*e journeyed alone.

If he encountered signs of humans, he went the long way around to avoid them. And in his new self-sufficiency during his relentless trek westward Avram the dreamer gradually became Avram the hunter, trapper, fisherman. He fashioned snares to catch rabbits and spears to catch salmon. He dug for shellfish along beaches and slept beside a lonely fire at night. The feather cape protected him from wind and rain, and during the hot summer he propped it on poles for shade. His skinny adolescent body began to build muscle, and his beard came in. He continued west when he could, but when he encountered coastlines and found himself at the edge of seas with no opposite shores, he moved northward, not knowing he was tracing routes that eight millennia hence would be followed by men named Alexander the Great and St. Paul.

In an estuary on the east coast of what would one day be called Italy, he came upon a village where people ate a tremendous number of cockles; they even had a special flint tool expressly for opening them. They lived in grass shelters that blew down with each storm. Because Avram had by then journeyed to exhaustion and needed to rest, he stayed with them for a season and then moved on. But he had not told the cockle-eaters his name nor his story, nor had he learned their language, for he considered life now a fleeting impermanence and the knowing of names and stories was no longer important. Whenever he yearned for his home at the Place of the Perennial Spring, or felt warm feelings in that direction, he hardened his youthful heart and reminded himself of the crime he had committed and the dishonor he had brought upon his family, that he was a cursed man and fated to be cast out from his own people forever.

The horizon continued to beckon, just as it had in his childhood, except that now he followed it not to see what was on the other side but because there was nowhere else to go. And in his mindless need to put miles beneath his feet, nowhere did he find another settlement like his own at the perennial spring. He had once thought that people everywhere lived in mud-brick houses and kept their own orchards, but he saw now, as he trekked northward, crossing nameless rivers and meadows, climbing hills and peaks, that the citizens of the Place of the Perennial Spring were unique in the world.

He also knew something else: because of the wolf's fang Yubal had given him in the sacred wine cave, he could come to no harm. In the days and weeks traveling to the source of the Jordan River and beyond, and then westward across the Anatolian plain, and finally the treacherous crossing in a shallow boat, no harm had come to him. The cockle-eaters had welcomed him, others treated him warily. Animals let him pass in peace. And so he came to realize that it was the power of the wolf spirit that was protecting him.

But the protection brought him no joy or succor for there was a cruel irony in Yubal giving him the wolf's fang. Had Yubal kept it for himself, Avram's curse might not have killed him.

He continued northward, following mighty rivers and surviving in mountains higher than any he had ever seen. He found dense forests of birch and pine and oak where the principal game was red deer and wild cattle. Here he came upon a race of bison hunters. He traded his feather cape, which was no longer splendid but still a novelty, for furs and boots and a proper spear. He joined hunting groups, stayed a while, and then moved on. He never revealed his name, never told his story. But he hunted well, always shared, respected the laws and taboos of others, and never lay with a woman without her consent.

In all this time he kept the blue stone close to his chest, hidden, a symbol of his crimes and his shame. Since his flight from the Place of the Perennial Spring he had not brought it out of the phylactery. But not a day went by in which he was not aware of its presence there: cold, impersonal, judging. And at night when he was visited by dreams—of Marit searching for him in the Valley of Ravens, Yubal calling him down from the watchtower—he told his companions nothing of his torment.

The day arrived when the restlessness came over him again. Looking northward, he asked the bison hunters what lay in that direction, and they said, "Ghosts."

So Avram said farewell to the bison hunters and headed north to the land of ghosts.

Bundled in furs with spears and arrows strapped across his back, and trekking on snowshoes the bison hunters had given him, Avram finally came to the edge of a vast, white wilderness. It was more snow than he had ever seen, endless snow with no mountains opposite, not even a horizon, and the winds blew more fiercely than he had ever imagined, howling gusts that sounded like the shrieks of a thousand demons that cut through his flesh to freeze his very core. He thought, *I have come to the end of the world. This is my destiny.*

As he started across, the wind shifted and blew his fur hood back, blasting his face with an icy breath. Quickly pulling the hood back up and holding it securely beneath his frozen chin, he proceeded forward, unaware that he was in fact crossing a sea, that he was no longer on land. What lay at the end of this journey he had no idea except a vague notion that he was going to the land of the dead. As it occurred to him that he might have already died and this was a mere formality, the ice beneath his shoes suddenly gave way, plunging him into the icy water.

Avram frantically fought for a handhold on the ice, but it kept breaking beneath his fur gloves. As he thrashed about in the water, something bumped against his legs, and he glimpsed a big brown monster swimming around him. Terror filled him. He no longer wanted to be dead but very much alive. But his efforts were futile as he felt his legs go numb in the water, a numbness that began creeping up his body. When his last handhold on the ice broke away and the frigid water closed over his head, his last thought was of Marit and warm sunshine.

*A*vram was flying. But not like a bird, he realized, for he was half-sitting, half-reclining, his arms tucked snugly across his chest beneath a pile of furs. *Is this how the dead travel to the land of the ancestors?*

As he blinked through a ring of fur around his face, he saw the white-on-white landscape rushing past. He frowned. Not flying, yet he wasn't running either, for his legs were stretched before him and likewise swaddled in warm furs. He looked directly ahead and when his eyes were able to focus, he saw that he was being carried away by a pack of wolves. *I am to be their dinner.* Maybe it was revenge for Yubal killing that wolf all those years ago. So, the fang was no longer protection.

Eat me then, his muddled mind cried out. *It is what I deserve.* And he lapsed again into unconsciousness.

When he awoke next, the flying sensation had slowed and he saw small, round, white hills drawing near. He looked at the wolves again and this time realized they were no ordinary wolves, and they appeared to be tethered together with leather straps. When he heard a yell, he realized someone was standing immediately behind him, towering over him, calling commands to the wolves. Avram tried to see a face but it was hooded with fur.

Deciding that he wasn't sure he liked being dead, he fainted again and the next time he awoke it was to find himself in a small dark place that smelled of burning oil and human sweat. He blinked and tried to focus. The ceiling was made of ice. Was he in an ice cave? But no, he could see the seams where the blocks of ice came together. A house—made of ice. And he was lying in a bed of some kind, and beneath the furs he was naked. Someone had taken his clothes! He tried to feel for his phylactery but there was something wrong with his arms. He could not move them.

A voice nearby, and then a shadow on the wall. He blinked again and saw a face come into focus. Old, wrinkled, and grinning tooth-lessly. She spoke. At least, he thought it was a she. And then, to his shock, she suddenly threw off his blankets, exposing him to the air. "Indecent woman!" he cried, only to realize that the cry had been inside his head. He couldn't move his jaw, nor even open his mouth. As Avram lay limp and helpless, the old woman pried open his mouth and peered inside, then she inspected his navel and prodded his tes-ticles. Finally her rough hands started to work on his frozen flesh, first clasping and pressing his fingers, then gently massaging life back into them. She lifted his hands to her mouth and blew on them. He felt neither the warm breath nor the touch of her hands. And when she moved down his body, he continued to feel nothing.

She stopped and gave him a worried look. After uttering a few incomprehensible words, she crawled out of the shelter through an opening he had not noticed before. "You didn't cover me up!" he wanted to cry, but his lips and tongue would not obey.

She did not leave him for long and when she returned, another person was with her, a tall, broad-shouldered figure. Avram watched in puzzlement as the second person divested itself of layers of clothing to reveal full breasts, narrow waist, and flaring hips. She laid herself alongside Avram and took him into her arms. The old woman covered them up and left the ice hut.

Avram drifted in and out of consciousness many times before he came fully awake. The first thing he noticed were golden lashes lying on the crests of pale cheeks, a fine long nose and wide pink mouth. He would learn much later that her name was Frida and that it was she who had saved his life when she pulled him from the ice.

*H*is recovery took weeks and was mostly left to Frida and the old woman, who massaged him and fed him fish and soup and healing herbs. Men came to look in on him, squatting inside the small ice house and asking questions that he did not understand. Each night he fell asleep in Frida's warm arms and woke the next morning to find her flaxen hair spread across his chest. The morning he awoke with an erection, the old woman declared him cured and Frida did not sleep with him after that.

Later he would learn why they had saved his life and why they had shared with him what small food stores they had. Before he had fallen into the ice, before he had started his trek across the frozen sea, a wind had blown his hood back from his head, and Frida had seen it. Unaware that there were people nearby, Avram had pulled his hood back up and started across the frozen waste, but not without Frida having seen the black hair and swarthy skin. Among their gods, she would later explain when Avram had learned their language, were dark-haired ones who were the guardians of the woods and caves and who possessed wondrous powers.

Finally one morning the old woman set his clothes before him, dried and soft again, and which he eagerly donned. He was overjoyed to see his phylactery, still on its leather thong, and it appeared to have been untouched. But he opened it anyway, to make sure he had lost nothing valuable in his mishap with the ice, and although the old woman watched in curiosity as the objects spilled out—the string that was his withered umbilical cord, a baby tooth, Yubal's wolf fang—it wasn't until she saw the blue crystal that she cried out.

To Avram's astonishment, she hurriedly crawled out of the ice house and he could hear her shouting outside. A moment later, the biggest man Avram had ever seen squeezed his way inside. For an instant Avram thought the stranger was going to steal the crystal. Instead, the man squatted on the ice floor and stared in wonderment at the stone. He looked at Avram and asked a question, to which Avram could only say, "I do not understand your language." The man nodded and started to leave. Then he stopped and beckoned for Avram to follow.

With the phylactery securely around his neck and hidden beneath his fur tunic again, Avram took his first steps outside to discover that the "morning" had only been in his imagination, for he found himself in a land of constant darkness.

The people clustered around him, shyly curious about the newcomer. They wore hooded jackets, pants and boots of waterproof sealskin, and they all looked so alike that he wondered how the men and women found each other for their pleasure. But most of all they resembled ghosts, for their skin was like white smoke and their hair the color of pale wheat. And they were tall! Even the women towered over Avram. They seemed to find novelty in his short stature, black hair, and olive complexion.

The leader of the clan introduced himself as Bodolf.

In his journey across the continent, Avram had encountered bears. They were what Bodolf reminded him of—a huge, pale bear with a thunderous laugh. Bodolf did not oil his beard as the men in Avram's clan did, but he did braid his long blond hair. However, the braids were not ornamented with shell and beads, but rather with human finger bones. "Plucked from the corpses of our enemies," Bodolf later boasted.

Avram was then introduced to a man named Eskil, whom he thought was Bodolf's brother, the resemblance was so strong. But then he realized that Eskil was considerably younger—uncle and nephew perhaps? And then it was cleared up when Bodolf said, "Eskil and I are not blood-related. He is the son of my hearth-mate, the woman I have spent all my winters with." For Bodolf was one of those who did not seek variety but found contentment with the same woman every year.

That night—although the sun had never risen—the clan held a feast in honor of their visitor who possessed a piece of the sky. Avram dined on seal for the first time in his life, and whale oil and the meat of a bear whose fur was as white as snow. They sought to impress him with their favorite delicacy—a roasted goose that had been fed only rotten fish, which supposedly imparted to the meat an exotic flavor but which Avram found revolting. Still, he was thankful to be alive and in the company of so hospitable a race. Especially as the women, with hair like corn silk and skin as smooth as fruit, found him an intriguing novelty.

He continued to share the old woman's ice house and earned his keep by entertaining the clan with what they called lies: descriptions of palm trees and sandy deserts, giraffes and hippopotamuses, and summers so hot that water dropped onto a rock sizzled and evaporated.

At the first signs of spring, Bodolf's clan, who called themselves the People of the Reindeer, left their ice houses and traveled by sled to a mountainous region where pine and birch trees were shedding their snowy burdens. Here the people got to work chopping trees for logs. The work went night and day until a mighty timber house was built, large enough for all to live and sleep in. Avram helped, wielding axes and applying pitch, and eating with them at mealtimes but sleeping alone at night. He didn't want to learn their language, he didn't want to know their names.

When he had moments to himself, he would look at the new green growth and, thinking of springtime at the Place of the Perennial Spring, turn his eyes southward. Since he could no longer press northward nor westward—he had come to the edge of the world—perhaps it was time to turn back.

But . . . to where? Back to the Perennial Spring where he would only know dishonor? There would be only one reason for him to go back: he pictured Marit living in his house with his grandmother and his brothers.

"Stay with us," Bodolf said, laying his arm across the young man's shoulders. "We will tell you our stories and you will tell us yours. And we shall drink together and gladden the hearts of our ancestors."

They introduced him to mead, a drink made of fermented honey that they consumed in copious amounts in the summer months. When Avram tasted the drink and saw how attractively Frida's hair caught the firelight, he decided there was no urgency to leave.

He watched them hunt, listened to them talk, and gradually, despite himself, learned their language. "How did your people come to live in such a place?" he asked, thinking of his own sun-blessed homeland that seemed a more sensible place to live.

"Our ancestors originally lived in the south. When the reindeer heard go-north voices, they went and my ancestors followed them." Bodolf pointed to the mountains rising like knives from the earth and the great rivers of ice in between. "The voices came from those glaciers. They were retreating north and left behind the lichen and moss that our reindeer love so well. So, you might say those glaciers brought us here."

"Why are they retreating?"

Bodolf shrugged. "Perhaps the sky is calling them back."

"Will they come again?" Avram asked, trying to picture a world blanketed entirely in ice.

"It depends on the gods. Maybe. Someday."

Avram looked at the compound where the strange wolves were kept. To his astonishment, men were feeding them and the beasts were not attacking.

"How is this possible?" Avram said.

"Do you not have dogs where you come from?"

"What are dogs?"

"Cousins of wolves."

"You tamed them?"

"They tamed *us*," Bodolf said with a smile. "They approached our ancestors long ago and said, 'If you feed us we will work for you and be your companions in the dark nights.' "

Avram learned that Bodolf's people worshipped the reindeer, as a provider of food and hides, but also as the creator of life as well.

The magnificent beasts were kept in a large compound where they were free to roam, handsome animals with long dark fur and white mantles, and antlers so splendid they resembled trees. To see such animals kept tamely by men was a marvel to Avram, but even more astonishing was how the reindeer allowed themselves to be milked. He thought of Namir and his experiments with keeping goats, and suddenly Avram had new respect for the man, because he had not thought the taming of animals possible.

Bodolf told him about the days of the ancestors when they used to chase reindeer herds across the ice and how one man had gotten cut off from his hunting party. As he lay in the snow, frozen and starving and near death, a reindeer materialized and crouched down next to him, keeping him warm with her massive body, and then she allowed him to drink her milk. And while Reindeer was nursing him back to life, she said to the man, "Do not chase us and hunt us down. Bring some of us to live with you and we shall feed you and keep you warm. But let my herds roam free." So they captured females and brought them back. There was milk for a time, and then Reindeer came to the ancestor in a dream and spoke again: "You cannot separate my females from the males, for as with men and women, my reindeer must have pleasure." So the ancestors brought a male to live with the females, and the people had milk forever after that.

Avram frowned. "But how do animals take pleasure?" he asked, trying to imagine it.

Bodolf laughed and made a gesture with his hands. "The same as we humans do! Animals are no different!"

Having only ever seen animals when he had hunted them in the hills, chasing after them with spear and bows and arrows, Avram had never seen this behavior. It made sense, he supposed. The Goddess created the act of intimate pleasure for people, why not for animals as well?

"Come the spring," Bodolf said with satisfaction, "calves will be born."

Avram's eyebrows shot up. "How can you know this? The moon chooses when young will be born. Men have no way of predicting this."

Bodolf gave him an impatient look. "Do you not have animals in your land?"

"We have many."

"And they bear young?"

"When we hunt in the spring, we see babies among the herds."

"And so it can be predicted! Because in this way," Bodolf said, again making a crude copulating gesture with his hands, "the Reindeer spirit begets females with offspring. She does the same with humans. When a woman dreams of a reindeer, or inhales the smoke from reindeer meat on a fire, or if she wears a reindeer amulet around her neck, she will get pregnant. Reindeer is the life-giver of all things. Is it not the same among your people?"

"In my land, it is the moon that gets a woman with child," Avram said, still unconvinced about animals and sexual pleasure.

But more intriguing to Avram than the puzzle of the reindeer was the people themselves. He observed more permanent pair-bonding among the People of the Reindeer than among his own kind. There were no alliances between families but rather between two people: the woman provided the hearth and shelter while the man provided food and protection. Perhaps it was because of the long and harsh winters that made life harder here and so survival depended upon cooperation. Avram thought, *A man can't very well go roaming at night for a woman, not like during the hot sultry nights at the Place of the Perennial Spring, where copulating is random and beneath the stars.*

When summer waned and winter approached, Bodolf suggested to Avram he choose a winter-mate. When Avram said he was used to sleeping with men, Bodolf and others boomed with laughter and said, "Choose a woman. What better way to keep warm?"

He thought of Frida, and learned that she had not yet chosen a winter-mate. However, to gain entrance to a woman's shelter a man must first prove himself a good food provider. And so Bodolf and Eskil took Avram on his first hunt.

The hunters skimmed across the frozen wastes on skis and dog-drawn sleds as they raced after polar bear and elk. Avram threw his hood back and lifted his face to the sky. Such speed! Such freedom! He called to the others and they waved back, and for a while he forgot his wretchedness and accursed state, that he was a murderer, a breaker of oaths, a man who had abandoned his beloved and sullied his family honor. For these few hours he was clean and free, and for a brief time he allowed himself sentimental thoughts of his three brothers, thinking how they would have enjoyed this adventure on the ice.

But when he saw Bodolf and Eskil together, and their special bond, it reminded him of his relationship with Yubal, and it made his heart ache anew with grief. He could tell these people something: that it was possible to kill a man with an uttered oath.

The days grew shorter and the People of the Reindeer left the timberland and headed out onto the frozen waste to build their ice houses. Bodolf tested the snow with his knife at several places before he found the right weight and texture for building blocks. "The snow is very poor here—too soft on top and too hard at the bottom—but it is the best we can find." He and Eskil cut the first block. Avram helped them turn the big chunk over, then Bodolf carved a usable block from the middle of it. The blocks were laid layer by layer in a spiral and when the dome was completed, Bodolf excavated a sleeping platform by digging out the floor and shoveling the excess snow out the small entrance hole at the base of the dome.

After they had built their shelter, Bodolf and Eskil took Avram seal hunting, which was done through the frozen ocean ice. Bodolf explained that since seals needed to breathe, they scratched holes through the ice as it began to freeze and then periodically returned to them for air. Avram watched as the hunters used their half-wolves to locate these holes by smell, then they slipped a slender whalebone through the thin ice and waited. When the whalebone quivered it meant the seal was surfacing and so the hunter swiftly threw his harpoon. It required a man to stand very still for several hours, a task Avram was good at due to his long hours in Yubal's wooden watchtower.

Although they laughed at Avram's failed attempts to harpoon a seal, they finally joined together and helped him to catch one, so that he would not have to spend the winter months sleeping with snoring old men. It was the custom to bring a seal carcass directly to a woman for she must offer it a drink of water as a sign of hospitality, thus propitiating the seal's spirit. So Avram brought his seal to Frida. She offered it a drink and invited Avram to stay at her hearth.

*T*hey gathered in the ice house of Bodolf and his woman of many years, Thornhild, along with Eskil and a girl with a shy smile, and Avram and Frida who sat holding hands. They listened to wolves howling in the night and Bodolf's explanation to Avram. "No one knows why wolves howl. Perhaps they see ghosts, or they are possessed by the spirits of the men they kill. Perhaps they like the sound of their own voices," Bodolf said with a smile. They were drinking the last of the summer mead and enjoying the warmth of furs and a smoky brazier in the cozy ice house. "Wolf packs take great pleasure in howling together. I have seen them howl when they greet each other after a hunt."

"Like people," Avram said with a grin.

He was growing comfortable with the People of the Reindeer, even though he felt superior to them and knew that they thought themselves superior to him. Their rivalry was good natured. When he tried to describe his house, Bodolf said, "You live in the same house all year?"

"Yes, and for many years."

His companions were shocked. They pinched their noses and made faces.

"We sweep them out," Avram said defensively. "We keep the houses clean."

"Why do you stay in one house?"

"To watch the vineyard."

"You have to watch the vineyard?"

"That is what I said."

"If you do not watch it, the grapes will not grow?"

"Oh, the grapes will grow."

"Then why do you watch the vineyard?"

"To prevent others from taking the grapes."

"Why would you prevent other people from taking the grapes?"

"Because they are ours."

Bodolf exchanged glances with the others. "So when strangers come, the fruit is not for them?"

"That is so."

"Why not? The fruit is on the vine."

"But my *abba* grew the vines and so the grapes are his."

Eskil frowned. "If your *abba* were to die, would the vines die?"

"Well, no."

"Then how are they *his?*"

He explained the story of Talitha and Serophia, which he told with great solemnity. To his indignation, they roared with laughter. But then as he continued to drink the fermented honey and tell the story, he also began to find it humorous and after a while was clutching his stomach and howling at the antics of those impossible women long ago.

In the end, despite their differences, Avram and the People of the Reindeer agreed on one thing, that fermented drinks were wonderful.

Finally they wanted to hear his own tale, and when he told them, he finished with: "I do not know why I ran or why I kept going. I could have stayed with the feather-workers and lived a comfortable life. But I was impelled westward and now I seem to have come to the end of the world."

"Perhaps you are on a vision quest," Bodolf said, and the others solemnly agreed.

Thus did Avram pass his second winter among the People of the Reindeer, hunting seals and bringing them back to Frida, sleeping in her arms at night, laughing with her in the day—although night and day were all the same. She showed him lights in the northern sky, dancing phantoms of fabulous colors. He told her about the desert and sea of salt with no life in it. They made love in their cocoon of fur and ice, and in Frida's arms Avram forgot for a while the shame that had driven him here, and the crime he had committed. He buried his face in her corn-silk hair and declared her to be the love of his life, but she only laughed and teased him for she had heard him call for Marit in his sleep, and she knew that a dark-haired dream-woman was her competitor.

Avram learned to live by a new rhythm of light and dark. The days were brightest from spring to late summer, and darkest between autumn and spring. For three months the sun never dropped below the horizon, and for three months it never rose. The cycle of changing seasons was the appearance and disappearance of solid ice on the sea. He learned about Bodolf's gods and the superstition of his people, and Avram respected their beliefs. He learned to like the taste of seal meat, and in the summer followed Frida up to snowy peaks from where they could see the entire world. The People of the Reindeer tattooed themselves by using a fine bone needle to draw soot-covered thread under the skin, and one spring Avram bravely suffered the needle-art on his forehead. The Place of the Perennial Spring became a dream, Marit and the others seemed like people he had made up. That land of warmth and sunshine, so far from this land of cold and snow, could not possibly exist.

When one of the sled dogs gave birth to a litter of pups, Avram found one little dog more endearing than the rest, and began visiting the pen where they were kept. The feeling must have been mutual for the pup began to whine every time Avram left, and finally jumped out of the pen and followed him back to the timber house. Avram named her Dog and she became his constant companion after that.

It was during his fifth summer with the People of the Reindeer that the dreams began. Scenarios involving Yubal and Marit, Reina the priestess, his brothers, even Hadadezer; warm, seductive dreams colored in the greens and golds of the Jordan's springtime. Avram's sleeping mind swam like a baby toward the warmth, his fingers reaching for red poppies and pink peonies, for sweet dates and juicy pomegranates. Dreams so real that when he awoke he was astonished to find himself back in the frigid north, and he wondered how his soul was able to travel such great distances in so short a time.

The dreams increased in frequency and intensity until they made him weep and mope like a sick dog. Bodolf and Frida grew alarmed. So they sent for the stone-caster.

The reader of stones was small and old, her body like a withered brown nut inside its shell of seal and reindeer furs. But her eyes were as sharp as the North Star, and twinkled with an intensity that made Avram believe she would have the answers.

Everyone sat in a circle and watched as the oracle blew into a leather bag and then tossed stones onto a square of soft sealskin. She pointed with a crooked finger to each. Her voice crackled: "This stone holds your hopes and fears. This stone is what cannot be altered and must be expected. This stone tells your present situation." She looked at Avram. "You wish to stay. You wish to go. This is your dilemma."

"Can the stones tell me which to do?"

She breathed softly, slowly. "There is an animal spirit at your side. One I do not recognize. A small beast with tall horns that curl like smoke. Its hide is the color of mead, black stripes outline its white belly." She raised her eyes. "It is your clan spirit."

"The gazelle," he said in wonder. How could she describe it so well when she had never seen one before? "What does it want me to do?"

She shook her head. "Not what *it* wants you to do." She stared at him for a moment, her starlight eyes two pinpoints in her aged face. "There is another stone," she said at last. "Not of these. There." She pointed to the pouch lying on his chest. "Blue like the sky, transparent like the sea. This stone possesses the answer."

Avram lifted the phylactery from beneath his fur jacket and opened it with care. Bringing the crystal out, he cradled it in the palm of his hand, this powerful stone that had been given to his people by Al-Iari herself before the beginning of time. When he looked into its heart he saw the cosmic diamond dust and realized that it was the bubbling spring that was the heart of his home. He thought, *The crystal is the heart of the Goddess, it belongs in the shrine at the Place of the Perennial Spring.*

It was also where his own heart belonged, back among his own people. He knew that now. During his sojourn among the People of the Reindeer, Avram had been unaware of the change slowly taking place within him. His grief had faded, and with its ebbing a new emotion had flowed into its place: a longing to go home.

When he said good-bye to the People of the Reindeer, he gave the wolf's fang to Bodolf, because the wolf was their enemy. Bodolf in turn gave him a chunk of amber carved in the shape of a polar bear. He kissed Frida, who was nine months pregnant, and wished her well. Then he hefted his bundle on his back, clasped his spear and bow and, with Dog loping at his side, struck off southward toward the ice bridge that would take him to the other side of the sea, back on the track that had brought him here five years prior.

*B*y the time Avram reached the mountain village that was Hada-dezer's home, it was a year since he had left Bodolf and his people and over nine years since leaving the Place of the Perennial Spring. He and Dog had spent an adventure together, journeying back across the mountains and rivers that Avram remembered from before. They were good companions for each other, sleeping together for warmth, Dog sounding the alarm if danger was nearby, Avram sharing his nightly catch with the faithful canine. They had also saved each other's lives—once, when a bear attacked Dog and would have killed her had it not been for Avram's skillfully thrown spear, and another time when a wildcat jumped on Avram and would have clawed him to death had it not been for Dog's strong jaws. For Avram, it had also been a time of discovery. His only relationship with animals had been to use them as food or clothing. But this new contract between the dog and himself brought a quiet joy he had never known before.

When they arrived at the stone fortress in the mountains, the pair caused a commotion as men on watch wanted to kill the "wolf." But Avram was able, by invoking the name of Hadadezer, to force them to spare the dog. And when he was led through a maze of high stone walls and tunnels, people gawked and murmured about the wild animal in their midst.

The fortress town was a peculiar assemblage of houses so clustered together that they shared common walls, forming a strange honeycomb of dwellings that had no windows or doors, the entrances being openings in the rooftops. Avram was led into a courtyard so overshadowed by walls and surrounding mountain peaks that no sunlight touched the paving stones. Here Hadadezer was living out his final days, on a splendid platform littered with pillows and furs, attended by servants who saw to his every need. His face was as round as the full moon and gleaming with sweat, his body huge and ponderous with swollen feet that looked as if they had not touched the ground in years. His eyes nearly bugged out of their folds of flesh when he saw his visitor. "Great Maker, it is my old friend Yubal!"

Avram stopped short and wondered if the trader were seeing ghosts. And then he realized Hadadezer was looking at *him*. "You are mistaken, for I am Avram, son of Chanah of the House of Talitha. You would not remember me—"

"Of course I remember you!" the old man boomed. "Great Maker, what a blessed day it is to see the son of my good and dear friend, may his spirit know peace!"

"Son?" Avram said.

Hadadezer waved arms as large as legs of lamb. "I speak figuratively, since obviously a man cannot have sons. But your resemblance to Yubal, may he rest with the Goddess, is proof of the dear man's strong spirit and influence upon you!" He snapped an order and a most amazing object was brought out into the courtyard: a slab of obsidian almost as tall and wide as a man, knife-thin and as flat as the dead sea, and encased in a shell frame. When angled just right, Yubal's ghost materialized inside the volcanic glass. Avram jumped back and traced a protective sign in the air.

Hadadezer laughed. "Do not be afraid, lad! It is only yourself, a mirrored reflection!"

Mystified, Avram turned his head this way and that, lifted one fur-clad foot and then the other, and realized that the image was indeed himself.

It made him suddenly nervous. The only place one could see one's reflection was in water, and it was considered very bad luck to stare into water for it might steal one's spirit. Now he stared in fascination at the bearded man observing him from the black glass. It was Yubal, to the last hair.

"Come come, sit," said Hadadezer. "We will eat and drink and talk about the old days, which were better than these days. Since the beginning of time, the old days have always been the best."

While his host's servants brought out an enormous vat of beer with two long straws, Avram reported on his long, extraordinary journey, leaving out only the reason why he left.

"And what is *that?*" Hadadezer said, noticing the dog for the first time. She had curled up by Avram's feet and rested her head on her paws.

"She is my faithful companion."

"You travel with a wolf? And I thought I had seen everything! What is the world like?" Hadadezer asked after sucking up a good quantity of beer and running his hand over his mouth.

"It is as different as people are different. There are men who live as bears, men who live on ice, men who crawl into caves on their bellies and paint the images of animals they have slain."

"And towns? Did you see towns?"

"Only here and the Place of the Perennial Spring." He was suddenly filled with melancholy, to speak of his birthplace, and to be again in the company of someone from his past. Memories rushed back and thickened his throat.

Perhaps Hadadezer saw the mist come into Avram's eyes, for he said quietly, "We all wondered where you went to. Most people thought you were dead. Did you run away because Yubal was dead? Yes, I thought so. You were young and frightened. It is understandable.

After Yubal died and you disappeared, it was obvious to everyone that it had been a big mistake to try to unite the two families. Clearly the curses of Talitha and Serophia were upon everyone."

Platters of food were set before them: fowl cooked with stuffing, vegetables in oil, flat bread, tiny bowls of salt, and a revolting concoction called yogurt.

"Yes, I suppose it came as a shock to you, poor lad," Hadadezer continued as he helped himself to a roasted pigeon stuffed with mushrooms and garlic, "to hear of Yubal's death. It did not surprise me, though. Not a bit."

Avram's hand, holding a pickled walnut, stopped at his mouth. "What do you mean?"

"Yubal had a complaint of the head for a long time. I gather he did not tell you? Perhaps not to worry you. Whenever he got angry or exerted himself his head would pound most painfully. He asked me if I had a medicine and I said I did not. However, I warned him to go easy on his temper and his body as I had seen this affliction fell much younger men. They say he died while exerting himself with a young girl." Hadadezer nodded sagely. "That would do it."

Avram stared in frank astonishment at the mountain of a man whose beard was flecked with yesterday's dinner. Yubal already had a condition that was waiting to kill him? Then it wasn't Avram's curse that did it?

He was thunderstruck. After carrying the burden of guilt all these years, and having it suddenly lifted—

Yubal had already had death within him.

I did not kill my beloved abba.

Avram could barely keep from crying out with joy. Suddenly ecstatic, he wanted to sacrifice immediately to the Goddess and to whatever local gods there were. He felt like jumping up and throwing his arms around the mountainous Hadadezer. He wanted to dance and tell everyone what a beautiful place the world was. Instead he took a long draw on the beer and smacked his lips with pleasure.

Hadadezer shifted his great weight on the platform that served not only as his carrying chair but as his bed as well, and said, "A lot happened after that, my boy. Two years after Yubal's death, the raiders came. This time they were more thorough. Many people died. And then locusts the next year."

Avram was suddenly solemn, and ravenous for news of home. "Is my grandmother still alive? How are my brothers?"

"As it turned out, the night Yubal died was my last visit to your home. When I returned here to the mountains I realized my journeying days were over. I turned the caravan trade over to my sister's sons so that I could enjoy what years are left to me. My nephews report only the broader news—raiders, locusts, withered crops. But the names of who are alive, who are dead—" He spread out his hammy hands. He went on to explain how his caravan trade had fallen on hard times, due in part to the misfortunes of the Place of the Perennial Spring. "They no longer trade in wine," he said, "and that is one thing I sorely miss."

The drinking straw fell from Avram's hand. "What happened to the wine?"

Hadadezer shrugged. "They make only enough for themselves."

Avram envisioned his brothers toiling in the vineyards, men now, no longer boys, struggling to cultivate the vines, bring the grapes to harvest, fill the winepress, and then transport the skins to the sacred cave. All without the wise and unflagging supervision of Yubal.

"You say you are going back?" Hadadezer asked as he discreetly slipped an empty goatskin under his tunic and urinated into it. Avram wondered how the man emptied his bowels, and tried not to think of it.

"Yes, I am going home. It has been nearly ten years."

Hadadezer nodded, handing the goatskin to a servant and wiping his hands on his beard. "I wonder, my young friend, if we can work a business deal together, you and I." And when the shrewd trader laid out the plan that was in his mind, Avram had to concede that it served both their purposes. When the caravan next struck southward for its annual circuit, Avram would walk at its head.

He spent the summer in Hadadezer's peculiar mountain town, enjoying the trader's hospitality and accepting the coy invitations of Hadadezer's nieces into their beds. While he was there he saw many new wonders, for these hardy people were an industrious and inventive race: experiments in pottery made of clay and baked in an oven; nuggets of copper being melted and molded into tools; men starting to train cattle to pull plows. When Avram exclaimed over a woman suckling a lamb at her breast, Hadadezer said: "We have observed that a young kid or lamb forms a quick attachment to its mother. When separated from the herd at birth and suckled by a human wet nurse, it bonds with its human mother and lives tamely with the human family. We learned this by accident. A woman who had lost her baby took a wild kid out of grief and suckled it, and it followed her around the village ever after. Now we have tame goats. No need to hunt," added Hadadezer, a man devoted to finding ways to conserve his energy.

Avram was taken to a string of stone structures where female cattle were housed, cows that had not been born in the wild but here in the mountain stables where they were kept for their milk, just as Bodolf's reindeer had been.

"You have noticed that we worship the bull, Avram," Hadadezer said, who had been brought to the milking stables on his carrying platform. "The bull is the creator of life. Our women bathe in bull's blood in order to get pregnant."

Avram had noticed the steer horns that were present in many homes, and symbols of the bull everywhere. He stared in astonishment at the placid beasts who allowed men to handle them. What magic did these people possess that they could tame animals?

"In the time of our ancestors," Hadadezer said as he offered Avram a cup of yogurt, "before we built this mountain town, when we still lived in tents and roamed the plain, we worshipped the earth and the sky for we knew nothing of how the bull gives the cow its calf. And then our ancestors were told by the gods to stop roaming and to build this place, and to bring animals in from the plains and keep them here so that the spirit of the Great Bull could make our people fruitful. This is what makes my people so strong, Avram, the spirit of the Great Bull, whereas *your* people are born of the moon, which makes them weak. I mean no insult but speak only the truth. You will see for yourself how life at the Perennial Spring has lost vigor and vitality. I would send a bull with you if I could, but they are impossible to manage."

Avram noted that Hadadezer spoke of bulls the way Bodolf had spoken of the reindeer, so that he wondered if each race was propagated by a different god. It would explain why people over the world varied in their appearance and characteristics—the People of the Reindeer with their pale hair and skin from drinking reindeer milk;

Hadadezer's people with their reddish complexions from the blood of the bull. *And my people are small and dark, for we are born of the moon and her realm is the night.*

As he dwelled among the stone walls and ruddy-skinned people, learning their ways and sleeping with their women, accustoming his stomach to yogurt, cheese, and milk, a strange disease began to creep into Avram's soul. It was not an illness of the flesh, not heralded by physical signs or symptoms, but rather a disorder of the spirit. It entered Avram's body by way of dreams that were sinister and turbulent, and memories that came unbidden, dark and disquieting, all centered upon one theme: the night Yubal died. In slumber was Avram forced to relive that night over and over, seeing himself wake up, discovering the two naked figures embraced in the darkness, realizing that Yubal had engineered everything so that he could have Marit for himself. The pain of that discovery came back with fresh force every morning that Avram wakened from dreams that left him drenched in sweat. In all his years of journeying across strange and foreign lands he had given little thought to Yubal's duplicity, the very thing that had caused Avram to curse Yubal in the first place. But now that he knew it was not his curse that had killed Yubal, now that he was free to remember the other aspects of that fateful night, Avram was plagued with the inescapable and brutal truth that the man he had loved and revered had arranged for Avram to go away with the abalonehunters so he could have Marit to himself.

*F*inally the heat of summer passed and Hadadezer consulted the local seer who declared it was a propitious time for the caravan to depart.

On the night before departure, Hadadezer confided in Avram that he would rather not have turned the caravan business over to his sister's sons because they were a shiftless lot who despised hard work and had no business sense. He frankly admitted he thought they were cheating him. Unfortunately, tradition dictated that inheritance must stay within the family. "But that does not mean that I cannot place agents along the route, men whose loyalty I can count on."

Avram would be Hadadezer's representative at the Place of the Perennial Spring. The four other agents were the sons of the woman with whom Hadadezer had lived for many years. The eldest bore such a strong resemblance to Hadadezer that Avram was reminded of Yubal and himself, and Bodolf and Eskil. Hadadezer trusted these young men for they loved and honored him and would keep honest accounts of trade in the settlements where they would live: in the country of the *lebonah* trees, on the coast of the Great Sea, at the mouth of the Nile delta, and at the village that was flourishing and rapidly growing on the southern banks of the Nile. Hadadezer offered his guest gifts and Avram chose carefully, thinking of Parthalan, Reina, and Marit. These gifts would be the beginning of his atonement to them. In return, he gave Hadadezer Bodolf's amber polar bear, which Hadadezer delighted over like a child.

On the morning of departure Avram saw another curiosity: donkeys trained to carry great loads. Although the People of the Reindeer had half-tamed their reindeer for milk and dogs for pulling sleds, they had certainly not attempted to burden the animals. This was astonishing. "There are limits," Hadadezer warned. "Treat the donkeys well, feed them well and they will carry your burdens for you. Do not try to ride them yourself, for you will meet with a most unpleasant return to the ground." Avram laughed and thought the old trader must be drunk, for who ever heard of a man *riding* a beast? Hadadezer had the donkeys and men loaded with goods to trade—seeds for cultivation, obsidian for tools and weapons—as well as provisions such as salt fish, beer, and bread. "As an investment," he said to Avram, puffing from the exertion of having to give so many orders even though he had not left his carrying chair. "Refortify the settlement at the spring, Avram. Make it a prosperous place again, thereby making my caravan profitable again."

Avram kissed Hadadezer's plump nieces good-bye and as he led the caravan through the main gate of the walled town and toward the southern mountain pass, he hardened his heart and braced his spirit. He was prepared to beg his brothers' forgiveness for running away and dishonoring the family; he would throw himself before Parthalan and restore the family's honor; he would beseech Marit for exoneration and rededicate his heart to her. But he would never beg forgiveness from Yubal's ghost, for it was Yubal who must ask forgiveness of Avram.

The caravan traveled the same route southward that had carried a bereft youth northward ten years prior, but now Avram saw the countryside with open eyes. On that journey in the past, when he was in the company of the feather-workers and he was a boy without a soul, he had looked at the landscape through soulless eyes and had seen nothing. But now he saw forests of cedar that were fragrant and magnificent, the Cave of Al-Iari and the home of his ancestors, and a river so sweetly familiar that he fell to the earth and wept with remorse-filled joy.

The sky was gray and a light winter rain fell when the caravan arrived at the Place of the Perennial Spring. The welcoming crowd on the hill was smaller than in times past, and Avram wondered if it was because there were no watchtowers, no one to alert the citizens that the caravan was arriving. But as he drew nearer, walking ahead of his pack donkey, he saw that the settlement itself was much smaller than when he had seen it last, and realized in shock that there were no mud-brick structures, not even the house he had grown up in. He recognized the man who came running to greet them as Namir, the goat-trapper, older and grayer, and shuffling with a limp. Behind him trailed people unfamiliar to Avram, so that he wondered if perhaps the entire population had changed in ten years.

Then Namir stopped suddenly, blinked owlishly, and cried, "It is a ghost!" and ran back to the settlement before Avram could assure him he was not Yubal returning from the dead.

Others, the older citizens, likewise stopped and gawked at Avram, their faces white with fear, while the younger ones ogled Dog and the laden donkeys, having never seen such things before.

Avram gave the signal for the caravan to make camp. Weary men unloaded their burdens, grumbling loudly as was their right, cook fires were lit—although more smoke than flame rose from the damp twigs and dung—and tents went up in the light drizzle. Avram thought it was a sad, ragtag affair, not at all like the grand days of Hadadezer. But his spirits were high as he anxiously searched the growing crowd for familiar faces. His brothers, would he even recognize them? His grandmother would not still be alive. But Marit, still a girl in his mind, surely she was here?

Finally a man of short stature but with the strut of a rooster came forward, walking with an impressive wooden staff. It took Avram a moment to recognize Molok, Marit's *abba*. "Welcome, welcome!" he shouted with enthusiasm, but Avram saw the look of curiosity on the old man's face as he stared at Avram with the frown of a man trying to identify something. Now they all came to greet the caravan as word spread through the settlement and more people arrived.

Three men came running, digging hoes still in their fists. Avram barely recognized them. In all his years of journeying, his brothers had remained boys in his mind, he had never imagined them growing up. But they were men now, robust and handsome. To Avram's shock, Caleb fell to his knees and wrapped his arms around Avram's legs. "Oh blessed day that brings our brother home! We thought you were dead!"

"Rise up, brother," Avram said, lifting Caleb by the elbows. "It is I who should be at *your* feet."

They embraced and shed tears on each other's shoulders, and then the younger brothers welcomed Avram, openly crying with joy.

"Do I know you, man?" Molok said, squinting at Avram with eyes clouded with cataracts. "You look familiar."

"*Abba* Molok," he said respectfully, "I am Avram, son of Chanah, of the House of Talitha."

"Eh? Avram? They said you were dead. But you are too meaty to be a ghost!" Molok raised his arms in a self-important way and declared the rest of the day to be one of celebration, an unnecessary announcement since already vats of beer were being rolled out, freshly slaughtered goats and sheep arrived on men's backs, flat barley bread materialized along with jars of honey, platters of salt fish and fruit aplenty. The sound of flutes and rattles filled the air before all of the tents had been erected, along with shouts of reunion and recognition and welcoming laughter as people from the caravan mingled with people from the settlement.

It was, after all, like the old days.

By sunset the entire settlement, it seemed, had turned out, sharing food and cook fires, gossip and news. But the two faces Avram watched for had not yet appeared. He was afraid to ask his brothers what became of Marit and Reina the priestess.

Although the settlement was his home, Avram set up a small camp within the caravan, uncertain as yet of his status among his people. Although no longer guilty of Yubal's murder, there was still the matter of dishonor. But nothing seemed amiss as his brothers happily brought ducks to roast on the fire, baskets of bread, and skins of wine. They were full of news, but were also eager to hear Avram's news, remarking on his forehead tattoo and wanting to know where he had been all these years.

When Avram saw how his old friends and neighbors merrily launched themselves into the impromptu celebration, their misfortunes momentarily forgotten, their worries about tomorrow flown like a bird, something occurred to him that had not occurred to him in all the years of his absence: that the people in this settlement did not know it was he who had stolen the blue-crystal heart of the Goddess. Further, they did not know he had run away out of cowardice, or that he had purposely dishonored the contract Yubal had arranged with the abalone hunters. The reputation of disgrace and shame among his people had been in Avram's imagination only, because as Hadadezer had said, they had no idea what happened to him. *They thought I had been killed, or kidnapped, or wandered off out of grief and somehow died. How can I ask them for forgiveness when they do not know what there is to forgive?*

And then he saw something else in their hope-filled eyes: that they did not want to know the truth. He realized in a shuddering moment that so great had been their burdens and misfortunes during his absence, that it would be the worst cruelty to introduce dishonor, shame, and guilt into their lives now. So he made up a lively tale involving grief, getting lost, losing his memory, being captured, and fighting his way back—an epic story filled with gods and monsters, lusty women and feats of heroism, all of which everyone found suspect but loved for its entertainment, and as they passed around the wineskins no one blamed Avram for what happened ten years ago. The past was gone. Getting happily drunk was all that was on their minds now.

And then his brothers told him their own sad tale.

There were other bad-luck times while he was away, they told him, not just the raiders, but some bad-luck summers and then locusts one year devouring all the crops so that a lot of families pulled up stakes and resumed the nomadic life. The settlement, once so large and thriving, was reduced to a few hangers-on. "What is the use in planting and cultivating a crop only to have it stolen?"

He asked about the summer grape harvest as it was nearly the time of the winter solstice and they would be going to the sacred cave soon for the tasting of the new vintage. But Caleb sadly shook his head, saying that there had been a pitiful grape crop that summer, just enough to make raisins to trade to passing travelers. "The nomads come, camp here, and help themselves to our grapes. How do we three stop them? We cannot be vigilant night and day."

"But what of the sons of Serophia?"

"After Yubal died, Marit went back to her family," Caleb explained bitterly, "and so we no longer had the protection of her brothers. When the raiders came, the sons of Serophia did a good job saving their barley crop while our vineyard was stripped clean. It took us two years to have a good crop again, and then locusts came and ruined us once more. Since then we have barely been able to produce enough wine for ourselves, with a little extra to trade."

This was alarming news, for the wine trade was the mainstay of the settlement, wine was what had made the people prosperous and was in fact what had caused people to end their nomadic ways and settle down in the first place. "That will change now," Avram assured his brother. "We will make the vineyard flourish again, and the next time the raiders come we will be prepared." He was already formulating a plan in his mind: he would offer local men a skin of wine in exchange for night patrol of the vineyard.

"Where is Reina the priestess?" he finally asked in a cautious voice, afraid of what they were going to tell him.

Reina was tending her shrine, they said. The Goddess no longer came out among the people, her processions ceased ten years ago. But she was still there, as was her faithful handmaiden.

Excusing himself from the company of his brothers, inviting them to eat and drink their fill and to stay by his fire, Avram rose on unsteady legs and made his way out of the noisy encampment. He went first to what was left of the Talitha vineyard and was dismayed to find it shrunken and impoverished in the dying light of a gray day. His brothers had erected what defenses they could around a small parcel of vines, but the rest of what had once been vast and flourishing fields lay weedy and untended. There was no evidence of the wooden watchtower that had once stood here, and where their fine mud-brick house had once been was now a large tent made of goatskins.

With a growing sense of dread, Avram continued into the settlement, which was quiet as most of the citizens were making merry in the caravan camp. Here he received an even greater shock. Conditions were worse than he had first thought. Guri the lamp-maker's dwelling, the tent of the six linen-maker brothers, the abode of the Onion Sisters, the house of Enoch the tooth-puller and Lea the midwife, Namir's mud-brick home and that of Yasap the honey-collector—all gone. The settlement had the temporary, ramshackle look of the days of the ancestors with no sign of permanence.

When he found Parthalan the abalone hunter, Avram nearly broke down. The old man was alone and almost blind, barely subsisting in a grass shelter and managing to carve the few shells that came his way. He cried when he saw Avram and laid no blame on the young man for his own misfortune. "Life is a curse," Parthalan said. "Death is a blessing." Avram thought of the gifts he had brought back for Parthalan: beautiful shells for carving that would be ruined beneath the blind man's shaky hands.

As he left the old shell-worker, Avram tasted bile in his throat. Nothing happened by chance, he knew, everything had a cause. As he looked around at the impoverished settlement and the stamp of bad luck upon everything he saw, he knew the cause. This was all Yubal's fault. If it hadn't been for Yubal's duplicity, working bad-luck alliances to obtain Marit for himself, he might not have died and today the vineyard would be flourishing, the settlement prosperous.

His heart heavy with bitterness, Avram took the last path he knew he must follow: to the residence of Serophia. To Marit.

Here, too, the mud-brick house was gone, its crumbled foundation visible at the edges of the tent that had been erected in its place. She was by the entrance, feeding grass into the oven, flat barley bread browning on the hot stones. She did not look up, but Avram sensed she knew he was there.

Marit had grown beautifully plump in his absence. No longer slender, she was womanly, with flesh and curves to fill a man's arms. But not *his* arms, he thought resolutely, for though his heart still ached with love for her and his body hungered for her touch, the memory of that last night, seeing her in Yubal's arms, was more painful than a thousand knife wounds. He knew that he would never be able to look at her again without remembering Yubal's deception, nor be able to lay a hand upon her skin without seeing the pair of them, naked and clasped in a feverish embrace.

"Why have you come?" she said in a voice as flat as dust.

Avram did not know what to say. He had thought she would be pleased to see him. Or at least glad to know that he was alive.

She turned and beheld him with eyes like stones. Her face, still round and beautiful, was etched with lines, and the corners of her mouth were turned down from too many years of hardship and disappointment. "I knew you were alive, Avram. Everyone else said you must be dead, but I knew in my heart what happened to you. You saw us that night, Yubal and me. You woke up and saw us and then you ran out. I waited for you to come back and when you didn't, and days and weeks passed, I realized that you had run away, and why."

"I had every right," he said in righteous indignation.

"You had no right! You were jealous of Yubal and me without even knowing what it was you saw. You jumped to a conclusion and judged both of us. You thought that Yubal and I were taking pleasure together."

"It is what I saw."

"Avram, did you stare at the moon too long? If you had but watched a moment longer you would have seen me pull myself from Yubal's embrace, you would have heard him call me by your mother's name. You would have seen him apologize in embarrassment, you would have seen him start back for his bed, and then you would have seen him clutch his head and fall to the floor. Had you no better faith in either of us? Your *abba* and your beloved?"

He blinked. "I thought—"

"That's your trouble! Too much thinking!" She dashed a tear from her cheek.

He stared at her, too dumbstruck to speak.

"No man would lie with me after that. I became an untouchable woman because they believed I was cursed and that I made men drop dead with my touch. In all these years I have not known the comfort of a single embrace."

"Why did you not set everyone right?" he cried.

"How does one fight a rumor, Avram? People will believe what they wish to believe, whether it is the truth or not." She added bitterly, "Certainly *you* did."

"All these years," he whispered hoarsely, "how you must have hated me."

"I did at first. And then I grew to feel only contempt. While everyone else said you must be dead and prayed for you, I kept my counsel. Who would listen to me anyway? A woman with a curse upon her!" Placing her hands on her hips, she tipped her chin and said in a challenging tone, "You are the only man I have lain with. Can you say the same, Avram? In these ten years, how many women have you lain with?"

He stared at her, a helpless fool, as his mind counted off the women: the feather-workers, the nomads, the cockle-eaters, the bison hunters, Frida, Hadadezer's nieces.

She turned away from him and threw more grass into the oven. "Ten years wasted. You and I are in the midway of our lives, Avram. Your grandmother lived to be sixty-two, but she was blessed. No one lives that long. All we can hope for now is a few more years of good health before we become a burden to our families. And a burden I shall be, for the Goddess has chosen to withhold children from me. I am barren, Avram, and there is nothing less deserving of food and shelter than a barren woman. Now go away. Feel sorry for yourself elsewhere. You will find no pity here."

He stumbled out into the night, dazed and confused. Great Goddess! cried his mind. What have I done?

His feet led him to the only place left for him to go. The shrine of the Goddess was smaller and humbler than the mud-brick one he remembered and was made only of timber and grass with an adjoining hut where the priestess lived. He had heard from his brothers that Reina had been reduced to low circumstances, even though she was still the priestess of Al-Iari. She had been raped by the marauders, they said, and the experience left her bitter. On top of that, because the blue stone had vanished, many people turned away from the Goddess—especially after the raiders, and the locusts, and then the bad-luck summer when all crops failed. People blamed the priestess for misinterpreting the signs and so Reina no longer received the generous gifts from the past but was getting by on bare subsistence.

He found her stirring a pot of gruel over her fire, adding herbs by the pinch. Her hair was gray now, but carefully combed and braided. She no longer wore a dress of fine linen; stained doeskin covered her thin frame. She looked tired, defeated. Avram was suddenly at a loss. He had come to her for comfort and guidance, to have his world set right again. But the priestess looked more in need of succor than himself. He didn't know what to say, so he shuffled his feet to announce his presence.

She looked up. Her eyes widened. "Yubal!"

"Be calmed, Lady Priestess," he said quickly, "I am not Yubal, I am not a ghost. I am Avram."

"Avram?" She picked up a lamp and brought it closer to him. In the light he saw the dark circles under her eyes, the age that the past ten years had placed upon her, and the hollows in her cheeks. It alarmed him. Even the priestess was not immune to the bad luck of this place.

Her eyes filled with tears as she inspected every inch of his face, taking in his long braided hair, his man's beard, even the gray at his temples, though he was not yet thirty. Her eyes seemed to feast on him as they took in his broad shoulders and thick chest, then they returned to his face, lingered for a moment on the curious tattoo, and she smiled. The smile softened her features and made her look younger. "Yes, it is Avram. I see that now. But how like Yubal you are! I heard that the caravan had arrived, but no one told me that you had arrived with it. Come, we must drink and reminisce, and thank the Goddess for your safe return."

She didn't ask him why he went away or where he had been or why he had come back. It was as if all curiosity was gone from her. Or perhaps, he thought, ten years of hardship had taught her to accept and no longer to question. She had no wine to offer, and the beer was diluted and flat, but he accepted it with gratitude and sat with her beside a smoky brazier, for the winter night was growing cold.

Reina drank, and it shocked him that she did not first pour out a libation for the Goddess. "It is good to see you again, Avram," she said warmly. "Seeing you is like having Yubal back. I was in love with him, you know."

This caught him off guard. "I did not know."

"It was my secret. But although I never took pleasure with him, the desire was there in my heart, and so I think the Goddess punished me for breaking my vow of chastity. When the raiders attacked and brutally used me, it killed within me all desire for Yubal or for any man, and taught me that pleasure between men and women is not pleasure but pain."

He looked into his wooden cup, at the meager ration of beer with debris floating on its surface, and felt his heart tumble within his chest. "I am so sorry," he whispered, feeling as bereft as the wastelands of Bodolf's people. "How did such bad luck come to our people?"

She shook her head. "I do not know, or even when it began. Perhaps it started with something small, maybe someone stepped on someone else's shadow, or a servant girl broke a pot, or an ancestor was insulted."

"I ran away," he said.

She nodded, her eyes fixed on the small flame of the oil lamp.

"I saw something that I mistook for something else and like a coward—"

Reina held up a hand hardened with calluses. "What is in the past is gone. And tomorrow may never come. So we must live for this moment, Avram."

"I came seeking forgiveness."

"I have none to give."

"I meant from the Goddess."

She gave him a startled look. "Did you not know? The Goddess has abandoned us." She spoke simply and without rancor, as if all rage had been drained from her. This alarmed him more than if she had vented her fury at him as Marit had done.

And suddenly he realized the magnitude of his transgression. The bad luck of this place had not been brought on by a broken pot or an aggrieved ancestor. It was *his* fault. Avram, son of Chanah, of the bloodline of Talitha. *He* had caused this calamity. "Great Goddess," he murmured, as the terrible picture unfolded before him: his misjudgment of Yubal and Marit, his stealing of the crystal, and his cowardly flight to the north.

Drawing the phylactery out from under his tunic, he pulled it open and spilled the blue stone into his hand. He held it out to Reina, the crystal catching lamplight and shooting it back like stars.

She gasped. "You brought the Goddess home!"

"No," he said. "She brought *me* home. You must show the stone to the people so that they know the Goddess has returned to them."

She wept for a moment, her face buried in her hands, her thin shoulders shaking. Then she composed herself and took the stone from him, gently, as if it were eggshell fragile. "I shall not tell them yet. For there are those who will remember that the stone disappeared the same night you disappeared, and will calculate that it came back the same day you returned. I shall plan a special moment and reveal the miracle to them in a way that casts no suspicion upon you. I will build her a bigger shrine, a new one, better than the old. I will throw a huge feast and let the people know that the Goddess has returned to them."

Avram said, "I thought I had returned with new wisdom, for I have seen the world and the people in it. But I discover that I have no wisdom at all and that I am as wretched as I was when the feather-workers took me north. All this bad luck happened because of me.

What must I do to atone and bring good luck to our people once again?"

She laid a hand on his arm. "Have you paid your respects to Yubal since your return? You must do so, Avram. Honor him at once, and pray to him. Yubal was wise. He will show you the way. And," she added with a tremulous voice, "bless you for bringing the spirit of the Goddess back, for now she will bring prosperity to her children."

As he started to leave, he paused and said, "Marit is without children. Can you help her?"

"She came to me and we tried, year after year. I gave her amulets and potions, prayers, and spells. I gave her placenta to eat and smoke to inhale. But month after month her moonflow appears." Reina held the blue crystal to her breast and her smile shone as it had done in the old days. "But perhaps now there is hope, for Marit is yet in childbearing years."

Avram returned to his brothers' tent and found the ancestral niche where the small statues of the ancestors lived. The one for Yubal was in the shape of a wolf and Avram remembered the wolf's fang Yubal had given him. He said now to his revered *abba*, "In all those days and nights of my westward flight, as I traversed foreign and hostile places, I thought it was the spirit of the wolf that was protecting me. But now I know it was you, *Abba*, walking with me, guiding me, keeping me safe." He picked up the tiny stone wolf and kissed it.

"I vow, *Abba*, upon your spirit and the spirits of our ancestors that I shall reverse the bad luck I have brought upon our people."

He had a dream in which Yubal spoke to him. Yubal was holding the blue stone of the Goddess and saying, "You must build defenses for the settlement. A wall and a tower."

"I shall get to work cutting trees," Avram responded in his dream.

"Not trees. The defenses must not be made of wood for wood can burn."

"Mud-brick, then. I shall get to work at once."

But Yubal shook his head. "Mud-brick dissolves in the rain." He handed the blue stone to Avram. "This is how you must build. The walls must be as durable as the heart of the Goddess."

When Avram woke, he knew what he had to do.

Breakfasting on bread and beer, he dressed in his fur leggings and boots, but left himself naked from the waist up. Then, before the sun had broken over the eastern cliffs, he took Hadadezer's donkeys and went up into the nearby hills. As the sky clouded and a cold wind blew, Avram labored all through the day. He dug into the earth with his bare hands and hauled out rocks and stones of such a weight that they made him puff with exertion. Hour after hour he laboriously unearthed stones and loaded them into the panniers on the donkeys, and when he returned to the settlement he went straight to the bubbling spring and emptied the panniers onto the ground. Then, without a word to the puzzled bystanders, he turned around and went back into the hills.

Back and forth he went, toiling beneath the gray sky, going wordlessly about his labor as he brought rocks and stones to the place near the spring while the citizens gathered and watched. He toiled until well past sunset, saying not a word to anyone, leading the donkeys out of the settlement, and returning with rocks and stones. His only companion was Dog, who trotted faithfully at his side.

That night Avram fell into bed exhausted, slept only a little, then roused himself before dawn to feed the animals, stroking them and whispering into their ears, and then he led them back into the hills.

More people gathered to watch this perplexing activity. Someone dragged a vat of beer to the spot and sold straws. Men began to wager on what Avram's insane project was. A pile of stones beside the bubbling well. Had he gone mad?

When they finally started calling out to him, asking what he was about, Avram did not respond. His face was set in a look of grim determination. And when he paused, it was only to dip his hands into the spring's runoff, for his palms were raw and bleeding. When Caleb and his other brothers arrived, Avram would not speak to them. Only when the wall and tower were finished would he be forgiven his sins.

He worked to the point of exhaustion, never resting, barely eating, until he finally collapsed by the spring, beside his mountain of stones.

Bystanders were afraid to touch him for they thought he was possessed. When Marit came running and saw him lying unconscious in the dirt, she spat at them and said, "Have you no pride? Have you no honor? You do not move to help your friend?"

Caleb appeared and helped her to carry Avram back to her tent where he was laid on her bed, in the women's half of the shelter. Her brothers, who had come in from the barley field for their noon meal,

looked at their old rival with contempt, but a ferocious look from
their sister silenced them. "Take your bread and get back to work,"
she said, and they obeyed, for Marit had been the head of their family
ever since their mother died and Molok had gone simple in the head.

Marit bathed Avram's hands and applied a healing salve, then
wrapped them in strips of linen. She wiped his face and washed his
chest and limbs, and as she did so her tears fell onto his bare skin.
She swore at him and told him that he had looked at the moon too
long, but his body was wasted and his skin was gray, and she knew
that demons had driven him to dig up rocks in the hills. Dog curled
up at his feet and Marit couldn't get the animal to move.

When Avram woke, Marit was stroking his forehead and saying,
"Avram, I cannot begin to understand what has happened to all of
us, or why the Goddess chooses the fates for us that she does. I am
only a simple woman. But I *am* certain of one thing: my love for you."
She stretched out alongside him and Avram weakly took her into his
arms. Already he felt the good luck returning.

The next morning he wakened to the sounds of cheering. "What
is going on?"

Marit was combing out her hair and braiding it. She smiled at him
and looked almost young again. "Reina says the heart of the Goddess
has returned." And she went into his arms, to express her joy.

When he was strong enough, Avram returned to his task of collecting stones for the wall and tower, and Marit joined him, carrying
two baskets. By noon, Caleb and the two other brothers had joined
them. And still the citizens watched.

The third day Namir arrived with a basket, and four of his nephews.
By nightfall the mound of rocks was most impressive.

The next morning, Avram awoke to find men and boys already at
work going steadily in and out of the settlement, dropping stones and
returning to the hills. The sight of the blue crystal in the breast of
the Goddess had heartened the citizens at the perennial spring and
given them new hope.

*A*vram ordered a trench to be dug, which would be the foundation
for the wall. The women took part in this, tucking the hems of their
skirts into their belts and bending over with digging sticks and baskets. As the trench carved a huge perimeter around the well, men

quickly decided that they wished their homes to be within the wall, and so the industry of brick-making was commenced until the entire settlement was alive with the business of rebuilding itself, the power of the Goddess in them once again. They toiled through the winter and spring, with boys in temporary wooden watchtowers keeping a lookout for marauders. And the first layer of stones went up.

In the meantime, Avram had hired men to patrol the vineyards in return for wine. His brothers brought the vines back to life and now they were flourishing and producing fruit. Other citizens joined in helping to keep the vineyard healthy, they weeded and pruned, fertilized and watered, for everyone craved wine, and they set upon any grape-thief with sticks and clubs.

And then two miracles occurred for which Avram was not prepared.

The first occurred after Dog disappeared one afternoon. It worried Avram for days until one morning she materialized at his door, her coat covered with the nettles found in the nearby hills, and fell down exhausted at his feet. After a passage of time, Avram noticed her belly start to swell, and when she gave birth to a litter of pups, he knew that a new population had taken up residence at the Place of the Perennial Spring.

Then the second miracle happened. "I am pregnant," Marit said with such wonder in her tone that one would have thought she had looked upon the very face of the Goddess.

It was indeed a miracle, a sign that the Goddess had brought her blessings back to her people. But as Avram made tender love to Marit that night, he was aware of something at the back of his mind, like a transparent butterfly, annoying and teasing, but he could not catch it.

That summer, as more layers were added to the perimeter wall, and mud-brick houses were being erected within the circle, and a sturdy stone tower began to rise beneath stonemasons' hands, Avram's vineyard produced a bountiful crop, and everyone took time off from building to trample the grapes in the winepress.

Reina and the Goddess led the procession to the sacred cave, and as they approached, a wind came up, soft and lulling, sweet-scented and fresh. Avram paused to look out over the plain that stretched to the dead sea, and he had the odd sensation that someone with perfumed breath was breathing on him. His hair and beard stirred in the summer breeze, and then sunlight shot off the dead sea in spears of golden light. The day took on a surreal air. Suddenly he heard the heavy droning of insects, colors stood out brighter than before, as if the nature all about him were trying to tell him something.

He brought the procession to a halt at the base of the cliffs and squinted up to the shadowed opening of the cave. It struck him again as it had struck generations before him how like a womb it was. And into the womb of the Earth Mother the grape juice would be carried and placed on carved-out shelves, there to stay safely in the dark while the Goddess worked her magical transformation and imbued the juice with life, turning it into wine.

As Avram stared at the cave, the transparent butterfly returned to the edges of his mind, to flit about with maddening elusiveness: it was a thought waiting to be formed, an idea on the verge of being known. But hard as he tried to grasp it, it would not come to him.

After the wineskins had been placed in the cave, everyone returned to the settlement to continue working on the walls and mud-brick houses. But Avram's mind was distracted. He helped with the mixing of straw into mud for the bricks, inspected the progress of the stone wall, and labored with other men to set the inner stairway of the new tower, but always part of his mind continued to chase the will-o'-the-wisp that had taken up residence in his mind.

Then one evening as he sat beneath a bower and drank beer while Marit mashed chickpeas and onions for their supper, his eyes fell upon Dog nursing her pups. And something struck him that he had not noticed before: that four of her puppies were white like herself, but two were gray like the wild wolves in the nearby hills.

Avram wondered for the first time how she had gotten pregnant. Dog came from a land far from the moon's sovereignty. She came from the territory of the reindeer god. Did the reindeer god's fertility power extend this far? Moreover, how had the spirit of the *wolf* entered Dog's womb?

Avram's mood waxed philosophical as he looked at Marit, far along in her pregnancy, and asked himself, What is it that creates life? Bodolf and his people believed it was the spirit of the reindeer. Hadadezer believed in the spirit of the bull. And the people of the Perennial Spring knew that it was the moon that created life. But could there possibly be a broader, more pervasive power than reindeer, bulls, and local moons? He thought again of the wine cave and the grape juice lying in fecund darkness, being transformed from juice to wine, being given "life" by the Goddess. And once again the elusive thought, that teasing butterfly, refused to be captured.

Over the next weeks, Avram found himself taking long walks in meadows and deserted canyons, to be alone with himself and his elusory thoughts. At night he tossed and turned in strange dreams involving Bodolf and Eskil, Yubal and himself, Hadadezer and the sons of the woman with whom he had lived for many years. When Avram awoke, the meanings of the dreams escaped him until one autumn afternoon, as he was impelled to separate himself once again from the company of men, with only Dog trotting faithfully at his heels, Avram came to a pond. He squatted and looked in, and saw Yubal looking up. It was then that the meaning of the dreams came to him: the younger men resembled their elders.

Like Dog's pups resembling their mother, but resembling the wolves in the hills as well.

One afternoon he paid a visit to Namir, who was grumbling over a quiver of arrows, trying in vain to straighten them. After offering Namir a skin of wine and taking a seat in the shade, Avram asked the old man what he had observed among goat herds. "Have you seen them do this?" and he made a gesture with both hands.

Namir shrugged. "I have seen the goats do many things. They run and play and fight, as people do."

"But you have seen this?" and he made the gesture again.

Namir brought an arrow shaft close to his eyes and inspected it with displeasure. "Yes, I suppose."

"Why do they do it?"

"How should I know?"

"Is it male and female that do it?"

He finally looked up from his work. "Avram, have you stared at the moon too long?"

"When you trap your live goats, do you only trap the females?"

"Of course! The males are useless. Unless it is to eat them directly."

Avram told him about Bodolf's reindeer and Hadadezer's bulls. Namir scratched his head. "Are you saying that animals take pleasure as we do? Did one of those donkeys of yours kick you in the head, Avram?"

"When we hunt, the animals run from us. As soon as they pick up our scent, they scatter, they do not pause to take pleasure with one another. How do we know what they do when we are not around?"

Namir wrinkled his nose. "Eh?"

"Animals in a pen, fed and tamed, do not run from us. Namir, I have seen with my own eyes animals taking pleasure in the same manner as humans."

"Lunacy!" the old man said with a laugh, but Avram saw the curiosity creep into Namir's eyes.

The notion would not leave Avram's mind. He thought back to the reindeer compound—the male mounting the females. He had not known at the time that animals did that. He explored his memories of the early days of his flight, when he had journeyed across the Anatolian plain with the nomads. They had camped among wild herds and occasionally he had seen animals mount one another. Avram had thought perhaps it was a form of fighting, or play. Finally he thought of Hadadezer's bull giving pleasure to cows. And Dog, disappearing into the hills to return with half-wolf pups.

Was *that* the act that created new life? Not spirit-created but by male and female, man and woman. But how? For it did not occur every time. There was old Guri the lamp-maker who liked to take his pleasure with young girls, and they never got pregnant. And the oldest of the Onion Sisters who lay with many men and never got with child. And then he thought, *girls and older women do not have the moonflow.*

He was stunned. Was that it? Everyone knew that moonflow was what the Goddess used to create babies. But what if the moonflow was like grape juice? For this was the essential miracle of life: the grapes did not ferment on the vine, nor did grape juice ferment when contained in a wooden cup. Grapes were grapes and juice was juice. It required the power of the Goddess in her cave to change it to wine.

But it requires men to carry the grape juice into the cave.

Avram stood as if thunderstruck. Turning his face to the breeze, he peered into the distance and saw on the rolling plain that surrounded the bubbling spring the new fields being plowed for planting. And he saw what he had not seen before: how the furrows in the ground resembled a woman's private place. And then he pictured the seed being scattered by the hand of a man.

Did men and women together create life?

No, he corrected himself. *It is the Goddess who creates life—that power is hers alone. But she takes from both male and female to form that new life.*

He nearly fell beneath the weight of the revelation: *Wine is made the way babies are made, through the power of the Goddess. But just as grapes placed in the cave do not transform into a holy drink, but require the collaborative effort of man for them to become wine, then it follows that the moonflow on its own cannot become a child but requires the involvement of a man. And seeds scattered willy-nilly on unprepared ground are not as likely to sprout as those sown into plowed fields. Cave and field and woman: they are all Mother. They each bring forth life. But not on their own, each needs the contribution of a man.*

And then came the most staggering realization of all: Marit, who had lain with no man in eleven years, was now pregnant.

Avram went to the shrine of the Goddess to seek her counsel. He prayed and silently asked, *Am I entertaining blasphemous thoughts?* But then he saw Reina and recalled how, long ago, he had looked on her with youthful lust, and he had asked himself then why the Goddess had created this confounding hunger between men and women. Because it seemed to him now, as it had seemed to him as a tormented youth, that intimacy between men and women wasn't *all* pleasure, as Yubal would have had him believe. "The Goddess gave us this pleasure to help us forget our pain," his *abba* had said long ago. But now it did not make sense to Avram. So often the pursuit of intimate pleasure was accompanied by pain and often followed by tragedy. Why then had the Goddess created this inescapable magnetism between men and women?

And then she spoke to him: *It is to ensure that life is created, Avram.*

He began to tremble with excitement. His next question almost terrified him: *And so it is man and woman, male and female?* he asked of the statue with the meteorite heart.

As if in response, the blue crystal seemed to shimmer and shoot out points of light. Avram stared at the mystical stone and looked deeply into its heart, struggling to see an answer. And in the next instant his mind opened in a blinding epiphany: where he had once seen the milky essence at the crystal's core as the perennial spring, he now recognized it as a man's essence when he takes his pleasure with a woman. *The moonflow and man's fluid, combining in the cave of the woman, for the Goddess to work her miracle.*

Suddenly everything fell into place. As if he had observed the world through blurry eyes all of his life and suddenly his sight was sharpened. It all made sense, the entire wondrous miracle of it. Now he saw it everywhere he went: birds building nests together, male and female, to produce eggs and feed their young; fish swimming in the streams, the females to lay eggs, the males to swim over them and bless them with their procreative essence. He felt connected to all of humankind and all of nature in a way he never had before. No longer a bystander in creation but an integral part of it. He recalled what Marit had once said about being one link in a long chain. Now he was part of a chain as well, without whom subsequent links could not be connected to those preceding. Marit, pregnant—*with his child.*

It was as if the sky had opened up. For all his life Avram had wondered *why*, and he had wanted to delve the mysteries of nature. As he looked around himself, suddenly everything made sense, suddenly he *understood*.

He went straight away to his tent where he prostrated himself before the avatars of the ancestors, and he spoke to Yubal, pouring out his heart and bearing his soul, declaring his love and reverence for the man, shedding tears of relief and joy as he called him *abba*, this time adding a new meaning to the word, for though it had always meant "master" or "steward of a house," from now on it would also mean "father."

$\mathcal{A}$vram did not make public his new knowledge for he knew people would only laugh and declare that he had stared at the moon too long. But he did quietly advise Namir to take he-goats along with the females the next time he trapped a herd, and he remarked to Guri the lamp-maker that his plan to raise pigs was not an outlandish notion. He did tell Marit, however, the miraculous news, and she accepted it for it had come from the Goddess. Avram knew that, in time, as men raised donkeys and dogs, goats and pigs, they would make the same observations as he had, and reach the same conclusions.

At last the wall was finished.

Everyone gathered to celebrate the dedication of the new tower, which they were going to call Jericho, which means "blessed by the moon." Avram climbed the new stone stairway nearly twelve years to

the day after he had climbed the wooden ladder of his father's watchtower in the vineyard on a fateful dawn that seemed so long ago.
Then, he had been a beardless boy, filled with uncertainty and lacking
purpose, pulling himself up rung by rung, trying to make sense of a
confusing world. Now he was a man, confident and purposeful, planting his feet firmly one after the other on the stone steps.

Among the proud onlookers was Marit, holding their child on her
hip, a strapping boy of thirteen months. At her side was Dog, her
belly swollen again, and flanked by a new generation of puppies.
Avram had seen Dog's first pups grow to maturity, and then romp and
play and mount one another until the females were pregnant so that
a third generation of domesticated dog was about to join the settlement. Namir was smiling in the sunshine, the fat and prosperous and
very proud owner of a flourishing herd of goats, because he had taken
Avram's advice. Guri the lamp-maker was experimenting with pigs
again, and the Onion Sisters were adding a duck pen to their plot of
ground, discovering as Avram had discovered that there was a greater
harmony in nature than they had previously thought, a wondrous
interdependence that was like a beautiful, shimmering spider web,
with animals and spirits and humans all connected in a sacred contract.

Avram reached the top of the tower, and when he emerged into
the brilliant sunshine, a roar rose up from the crowd. The citizens of
Jericho looked upon their achievement with great pride and feelings
of security, for nowhere in the world were there walls such as these,
walls that they knew no invaders could pull down. As he welcomed
the deafening roar, feeling at peace and exonerated of his past sins,
Avram allowed his thoughts to float away over the miles until they
reached the People of the Reindeer—Frida, and the child she had
been carrying when he left. His child.

Avram had left his blood up there in the frozen north, the bloodline
of Talitha, the bloodline of Yubal, to be carried on by others, so many
miles away.

Interim

*A*vram never understood why it was to him that the knowledge of
fatherhood had been given. But the Goddess had her reasons and for
the rest of his life he thanked her morning and night, his prayers full

of praise for the Mother of all. In time, although not in Avram's day or in the days of his sons and grandsons, the Mother of All would be joined by a Father of All, until someday, in the not too distant future, the Mother would be supplanted entirely by the Father.

Jericho prospered. Avram and Marit had more sons, Namir's goat herd increased, more litters were born to Dog and to Dog's puppies, Guri ceased being a lamp-maker and became a prosperous pig farmer. More crops were planted, wheat and corn, cotton and flax, more animals were domesticated and raised for their milk, eggs, and wool. With increased bounty and good luck, the people made sacrifice to the Goddess. Her shrine was enlarged and her priestesses grew in number. As the centuries passed, the wall gradually bore no more resemblance to the one engineered by Avram for, as it turned out, down through the ages the walls of Jericho would fall many times to be rebuilt again and again.

The manufacture of textiles came to Jericho, and the alphabet and writing. Two thousand years after Avram and Marit joined their ancestors, a man named Azizu was at his potter's wheel and accidentally knocked it over. As he watched it spin away on its side, an idea came to him. It took many attempts and failures but Azizu succeeded in making two wheels roll on an axle, upon which he placed a cart. He could now transport ten times as much pottery as before, and he credited his inspiration to a visit to the shrine of the Goddess where he had kissed her blue-crystal heart for luck. Four thousand years after Hadadezer dazzled Avram with copper nuggets scooped out of a streambed, men were mining copper and tin and smelting them together to form bronze. A thousand years after that, men discovered iron and how to master it, and the world changed forever.

As populations increased, settlements became villages and villages became towns. Leaders rose from the masses and called themselves kings and queens to rule over others. Al-Iari's power grew, her shrine became a tabernacle and then a temple with priests and priestesses. Her people called themselves Canaanites, and travelers from Babylon and Sumer recognized her as their own beloved Ishtar and Inanna. Alongside Baal, she was worshiped for her fertility, and though her countenance changed over the years and her statue replaced many times, the ancient blue crystal remained her heart.

And so she had lived, protected and adored, for thousands of generations from the time of Laliari and Zant. And then invaders came from the valley of the Nile led by a ferocious conquering pharaoh named Amenhotep who brought back not only human captives but captured gods and goddesses as well. Among them was the patron Goddess of Jericho, who was housed temporarily and out of respect in the shrine of a lesser Egyptian goddess, where her crystalline heart caught the eye of an adulterous queen.

When the queen was laid to rest in a tomb splendid beyond imagining (due to the guilty conscience of the king who had poisoned her) the blue crystal went with her, and there queen and crystal slept in a dark, airless world, anonymous and forgotten for a thousand years until tomb-robbers, drunk on beer, smelling of urine and covered in fleabites, smashed their way into the tomb and brought the ancient blue stone back out into the light of day. The teardrop of sky-hued meteorite changed hands over a succession of years as it was bought, sold, stolen, fought over, and gambled away until it wound up in Alexandria, in the possession of an important Roman official who had the stone set in a beautiful gold necklace for his wife.

He intended the gift to be a punishment.

Book Four

ROME
64 C.E.

*L*ady Amelia's prayer was a desperate one.

Please let the child be healthy.

The shrine of the household gods held several Roman deities, therefore Lady Amelia had her pick of some of the most powerful in the pantheon. But since the circumstances called for the special intercession of a goddess who empathized with a mother's plea, Lady Amelia had chosen one whom people called Blessed Virgin (because she had conceived a child without assistance from a man), a goddess who had known suffering when her son was hung on a tree to die, to descend to the underworld and to rise resurrected. Therefore it was to this compassionate mother, the Queen of Heaven, to whom Lady Amelia now made her plea. "Please let the child be without blemish or flaw. Let my daughter's husband find favor with it and accept it into the family."

Her whispered words died in the morning silence. Died because there was no meaning behind them, no faith. Her prayer was a sham, lip service to a piece of marble. Lady Amelia was going through the motions of piety because it was expected of her; as a model Roman matron she always did the right thing, always kept up appearances. But in her heart she was completely without faith. How could a woman believe in goddesses when men had the right to dispose of women's babies?

Her prayer finished, she crossed herself, touching shoulders, forehead and breast because she had once been a follower of Hermes, the ancient savior-god known as the Word Made Flesh. The signing of the cross was from years of habit. Lady Amelia no longer believed in its power. She remembered a time when prayers were a comfort, when the gods were a comfort. But now the gods were gone and there was no comfort in the world.

Cries suddenly filled the house, echoing off walls and columns and statuary. Her daughter had been in labor for a day and a half and the midwives were beginning to despair.

Lady Amelia turned away from Blessed Virgin Juno, mother of the savior-god Mars, and delivered herself into the shaded colonnade that enclosed the villa's interior garden where a fountain splashed sweetly on this warm spring day. Lady Amelia did not bother to visit the shrine of the ancestors. She hadn't prayed to them in years. Without gods there could be no afterlife and without an afterlife the ancestors could not exist.

She slipped silently past the atrium where young men were playing dice and laughing, unconcerned about the screams that tore the morning peace. They were Amelia's three sons and two sons-in-law, as well as close friends of the youth whose child was struggling to come into the world. As she passed the open doorway she saw her daughter's husband, a young father-to-be reclining at his ease, drinking wine and rolling dice as if he hadn't a care in the world.

Perhaps he hasn't, she thought in uncharacteristic rancor. Childbirth was the concern of women alone.

A thought flew like a shadow across Amelia's mind, swift and dark like a raven: *We women carry children inside our bodies, we feed them with our breath and our blood, our beating hearts pump life into them, and for nearly ten months the child and the mother are one. And then come the birth pains, the tearing of the flesh and rush of blood, the agony of pushing the new life out into the world. However, for you, young father, there is no pain, no blood. A moment of pleasure and nine months later you drink wine and roll dice and decide the fate of the newborn.*

Amelia experienced a pang of resentment. Not just toward her son-in-law but toward all men who decided life and death as blithely as if it were the toss of dice. She had not always felt this way. There was a time when Amelia, wife of the powerful and noble Cornelius Gaius Vitellius, had believed in the gods and had thought life was good, that *men* were good. But all joy and faith had been extinguished the day death had been chosen over life.

A day not unlike today.

Her path was blocked suddenly by an elderly man. The Bird Reader, whom she had hired to interpret the signs. The old Greek plied a lucrative trade because Romans were a superstitious people, always watching for signs and omens, reading meaning into every cloud and thunderclap. For a Roman the day could not begin without first determining if it was an auspicious day for conducting business, for getting married, for making fish sauce. And of all the instruments of augury, from knucklebones to tea leaves, the flight of birds was the most important—even the word "auspicious" was derived from *auspicium*, which meant the divination of flights of birds.

"I have read the auspices, Lady," the Bird Reader began. "I see a man. His arms are opened wide, ready to embrace you."

"Me? Surely you mean my daughter. Or her newborn."

"The signs were very clear. A man is coming into *your* life, Lady, and he is holding his arms out in welcome."

The only man she could think of was her husband, Cornelius, due back from Egypt any day. But that wasn't possible. He hadn't opened his arms to her in years.

"What do the birds say of my daughter?"

The soothsayer shrugged—a quick gesture—and held out his hand for payment. "They say nothing of her, Lady, only of you."

Amelia gave the man a gold coin and hurried along the colonnade to the bedchamber where her daughter was laboring to bring new life into the world.

Lady Amelia had taken every precaution to ensure the success of this pregnancy, her youngest daughter's first. As soon as Cornelia had announced she was with child, Amelia had insisted she come and stay at home during the pregnancy, home in this case being the country villa where the patrician Vitellius family had produced wine and olives for generations. Amelia would have preferred their house in the city, but whenever her husband Cornelius was away, as he was now on a trip to Egypt, he insisted she and the household retire to the country. Only Amelia knew his secret reason for this unbending rule. Only Amelia knew that it was a form of punishment.

She went into the bedchamber that was crowded with midwives and their assistants, Cornelia's aunts and female cousins, her older sister and two sisters-in-law, and the astrologer who sat in the corner with his charts and instruments, ready to record the moment of the child's birth. Following a very old tradition among aristocratic families, Amelia's daughter had been named after her father, hence Cornelia (just as their eldest son was Cornelius), which sometimes led to confusion. Amelia would have liked to name her daughter after herself, but it wasn't done.

Amelia's heart went out to Cornelia who, at seventeen, was the same age she herself had been when she had given birth to *her* first child, a son who would now be twenty-six had he lived. Amelia's second pregnancy had ended in miscarriage, but her third pregnancy, when she was twenty-one, had resulted in her eldest son, Cornelius, twenty-two years old and studying the law in the hopes of following in his father's illustrious footsteps. Amelia had been pregnant seven times after that: one that had given her twins, now twenty years old, the one producing Cornelia, two producing babies that died in infancy, the one that had given them Gaius, their thirteen-year-old son, another ending in miscarriage, and the final pregnancy, six years ago when Amelia was thirty-seven, the pregnancy that had altered her life and her universe forever.

She went to her daughter's bedside and, looking down in sympathy and concern, placed her hand on Cornelia's feverish forehead in a sincere wish that she could take her pain upon herself.

The young woman pushed her mother's hand away. "Where is Papa?" she said fretfully. "I want Papa."

Amelia felt a stab of pain. Cornelia had not finally agreed to stay at the country villa because she wanted to be with her mother but because she had wanted to be there when her father returned from Egypt. "I sent word to Ostia," Amelia said. "As soon as his ship arrives, he will be told."

Cornelia turned away from her mother and lifted up her hands to her sister and sisters-in-law. The other young women crowded around until Amelia was pushed out of the circle. She did not protest. Lady Amelia had been pushed out of the family's circle years ago, when grief had driven her to commit an unforgivable act. Little girls that had once worshipped her and followed her around like sunbeams, had turned their backs on a woman they decided was no longer worthy of their love.

Yes! she wanted to cry, as she had wanted to cry for the past six years. *I committed adultery. I sought comfort in another man's arms. But it was not for need of sex or love—I was driven to him out of grief because my baby was born lame and my husband threw it away!*

But the cry went unspoken, as it always did—no one cared why Amelia had slept with another man, only that she *had*—and she clasped her hands tightly as she watched the midwife at her work. The woman had lubricated the birth canal with goose grease, and still the baby would not come, so now she drew a long white feather from her bag, climbed onto the bed to straddle the laboring mother, and proceeded to tease Cornelia's nose into a sneeze.

Lady Amelia closed her eyes as a painful memory flashed in her mind. Her own labor during the birth of her last child, the baby Cornelius had refused to acknowledge, ordering a servant to take it, only minutes old, to a rubbish heap to be left exposed. Amelia had never even seen the child. It had been taken straight from her womb to Cornelius, who had taken one look at the crooked foot and declared the child unfit. Amelia had spent the years since trying to understand what she had done to cause it, for surely she must blame herself. How else to explain the baby's malformed foot? With a grief-filled heart she had relived the months of the pregnancy over and over, trying to discover the one mistake, the one slip she had made that had caused the deformity. And then it had come to her: the day she had been sitting in the garden of their city house. She had been reading a book of poetry and had not felt the butterfly land on her foot. It was only when she glanced down that she had seen it, and because she had been so entranced by its proximity and its beauty, and its apparent lack of fear—for it had lingered there, glorious in the sunshine, fluttering its fragile wings—she had not shooed it away. How long the butterfly had rested on her foot she did not know, but clearly it had been enough to leave a mark on the baby that had been taking shape in her womb at that moment, for three months later the child was born with a twisted foot, marking it for disposal on a waste heap.

This was why Lady Amelia had been so protective of her daughter these past months, reading the auspices several times a day, watching for signs, being careful not to break any taboos or to bring bad luck into the house. When a black cat had appeared in the garden, she had had it destroyed at once. But a stray white cat had been brought in and pampered for good luck. Lady Amelia could not bear to have her daughter go through the agony she herself had gone through with that last, lost child.

Since the feather had not produced results, the midwife dug again into her bag and brought out a measure of pepper that she emptied into her hand. Bringing it up to Cornelia's nose, she said, "Inhale deeply." The girl did and produced such a forceful sneeze that the baby was pushed down and the assistant cried, "There is the head!"

Moments later, the infant slithered onto the waiting blanket. While the midwife tied and severed the umbilical cord, Lady Amelia stood apprehensively at the bedside.

"Is it a boy?" Cornelia asked breathlessly. "Is he perfect?"

But Amelia would say nothing. The baby having been born, the matter was now out of the hands of women. What happened next was up to her daughter's husband. If he rejected the child, then it was best Cornelia knew nothing about it, for it would be taken from the house and laid on a rubbish heap to be exposed to the elements.

As soon as the midwife bundled the newborn in a blanket, Lady Amelia took it from her and, cradling the child gently, hurried from the room. Behind her, Amelia heard Cornelia asking the midwife if it was a boy or a girl. But the woman, from experience, wisely kept silent. The less a mother knew of her baby the better, just in case.

Lady Amelia entered the atrium and immediately had the attention of the young men gathered there: her eldest son, Cornelius, who already had two small children of his own; her next son, twin to Amelia's twenty-year-old daughter; her youngest son, only thirteen; the young husband of her twenty-year-old daughter; male cousins and close friends; and finally Cornelia's husband, nineteen years old, drawing himself tall and proud, aware of the solemnity of the ancient tradition he was about to follow and the gravity of his next actions.

She laid the baby at his feet and stepped back. No one moved or breathed as he bent to part the blanket to see the child's sex. If it was a girl, and she had no flaws, he would acknowledge the child as his and then leave it for slaves to take to a wet nurse, as custom dictated. But if it was a boy, and unflawed, he was to lift it up and declare it his son in front of family and friends.

The moment stretched. Amelia was nearly sick with fear. *Six years ago, Cornelius parting the blanket, seeing that the baby was a girl, and then seeing the crooked foot that would make her lame for life. Turning his back. Gesturing angrily to the slave that whisked the infant away like so much spilled garbage. And Cornelia, only eleven years old, rushing into the bedchamber, saying, "Mama, Papa has ordered the baby thrown away! Was it a monster?"*

And now Cornelia herself was waiting for the same news . . .

The newborn was a boy, perfect and unblemished. The young father broke into a smile and lifted the baby off the floor. "I have a son!" he cried, and the others in the room cheered and offered congratulations.

Lady Amelia nearly collapsed with relief. But as she was about to hurry back to her daughter with the good news, there was a sudden commotion outside. Philo, the majordomo of the villa, materialized in the doorway with his wooden staff and dignified manner. "Lady, the master is home."

Her hand flew to her mouth. She was not ready!

Amelia did not go directly to greet Cornelius but instead watched from the shadows as slaves rushed forward to welcome their master with wine and food, to relieve him of his toga, to fuss about him in transparent excitement: when the master was away, life in the country was deadly dull. He accepted their adulation with the graciousness of a king. At forty-five, Cornelius was tall and handsome with just a brush of gray at the temples. Amelia could almost remember what it was like to be in love with him.

But that was before she had discovered his cold, unforgiving heart, when he had learned from friends of her brief indiscretion with a poet who had been passing through Rome, and she had confessed, and begged forgiveness, and told him it was because she had been so filled with grief over the loss of her last baby and the poet had crooned the words she needed to hear. But Cornelius had said he would never forgive her, and everything changed.

She silently followed him as he went straight to the birthing chamber where he congratulated his son-in-law and took the infant from the wet nurse to fuss over it. Then he sat on the bed and bent over

Cornelia. She had always been his favorite. When those two were together Amelia had always felt left out. What secrets was he whispering to her now?

A little boy came running in then, shouting, "Papa! Papa!" Lucius, a plump and pampered nine-year-old, was followed by an old hound he had named Fido, Rome's most popular name for a dog as it meant "faithful." Fido could be a good name for the child as well, for he worshipped his father and followed him everywhere. Amelia watched as Cornelius scooped the child up in a loving embrace. He wasn't really their son, only by law. Cornelius had adopted the boy when he was orphaned at age three. Lucius was the child of distant cousins and therefore family. Amelia tried to love Lucius but could not find it in her heart to do so. It was not the boy's fault. Amelia could never forget the fact that Cornelius had embraced another woman's child while discarding her own.

Amelia was thirty-seven when she had conceived her last child. Already she had been feeling the changes in her body, signs that her fertile years were coming to an end. And so it had been a special pregnancy because it would be her last, and she had loved the life in her womb more deeply than any of her other children. It was to be the companion of her older years when her other children were grown and gone, the special child that receives an older mother's attention and wisdom.

And then Cornelius had thrown it away.

Amelia had tried to remind herself that she should in fact be thankful: to have five living children out of ten pregnancies was a sign of favor from the gods. Roman children weren't even given names until they reached their first birthday, infant mortality was so common. Had that precious one survived the rubbish heap? Was there a little orphaned girl somewhere in Rome hobbling about on a lame foot? People who scavenged rubbish heaps to salvage broken pots, and lamps, and scraps of papyrus and cloth, sometimes took babies that still breathed. Such rescues were not out of compassion but for profit: a small child could be raised on minimal food and care, and then, if it lived to see its third or fourth birthday, could be sold at the slave market for nearly pure profit. If she was lucky, the girl would grow up to serve a gentle master. More likely she would be sold into a life of harsh servitude, and if at all comely, for sexual entertainment.

After watching the family reunion as if through the eyes of a stranger—for she knew she would never be included, no matter that she was wife and mother—Amelia left her place in the shadows and went to give instructions to the cook for the evening feast. The morning's tension dispelled, the house was alive with activity. That the young master had accepted the newborn into the family was reason enough for celebration, but now there was the added and exciting prospect of moving back to the city.

But as Amelia inspected the fresh game and discussed sauces with the cook, to her great surprise, Philo the majordomo appeared unexpectedly to announce that her husband wished to see her. Amelia didn't trust Philo. She knew that his sleepy eyelids belied a keen intellect. She suspected he spied on her and reported her activities to Cornelius.

Amelia did not go straight to her husband's private chambers but stopped at her own suite first to check her hair, her dress, her perfume. She was suddenly nervous. Why had he asked to see her? Amelia and her husband barely talked, even after a seven-month separation.

Cornelius Vitellius, one of Rome's most popular lawyers and a current favorite of the mob, had gone to Egypt to oversee family business there. Amelia and her husband were very wealthy. While Cornelius owned copper mines in Sicily, a fleet of cargo vessels, and grain fields in Egypt, Amelia owned several blocks of tenement apartments in the heart of Rome.

She found him seated at a small writing desk. Freshly home from such a long journey and already he was catching up on correspondence and news. She stood patiently. Then she cleared her throat. Finally she said, "How was Egypt, my Lord?"

"Egyptian," he said dismissively.

Amelia wished she could have gone with him. Ever since she was a child she had dreamed of visiting the ruins of Egypt, but of course such dreams were now beyond all hope of coming true. As she waited nervously for him to state his reason for summoning her, she thought frantically over the past seven months to see if there was anything he could remotely take to be an infraction of the rules he imposed upon her. But it was impossible to recall what it would be. Cornelius could take her slightest word or gesture as an act of rebellion. Whatever it was, what would he do to her this time? Leave her behind in the country when he returned to Rome? She did not think she could bear much more of this seclusion.

His punishment was always manifested in the most subtle ways. And part of his control over her was that he would not even allow her to bring up the issue for explanation. He had judged her and that was the end of it. She wanted to say, "Let me tell you why I did it." But the subject was closed, even though it was *her* subject, part of her life, and she should have control over whether it was discussed or not. Cornelius hadn't interrogated her as other husbands might do. He hadn't raised his voice or called her names. Amelia often thought that if only he would do these things then the "monster" could be brought out into the open and perhaps be put out of their lives. But Cornelius had sealed every avenue, making sure the nameless phantom couldn't escape, that it would continue to exist between them as Amelia's private torment.

The adultery was something that had simply happened. She had been disconsolate over the loss of her baby. The love affair had lasted only a week, but it had been enough. Instead of divorcing her and banishing her to exile as was his right, Cornelius had surprised her by staying married to her. At the time she had thought it was his way of forgiving her. The real reason was in fact quite the opposite.

He now controlled her life utterly, and periodically, as part of her continued punishment, sent her to stay in the country. Amelia loved the city, all her friends were there, and her beloved bookshops and theaters. Whenever she was forced to stay in the country she was reminded of Julia, the daughter of Augustus, who had been exiled to the island of Pandateria, a barren volcanic outcropping in the ocean that was so small she could walk the length and breadth of it in under an hour. Julia had been allowed no wine, no favorite foods, no pets or entertainments or companionship—no luxuries whatsoever. And there she had died after years of never seeing another soul except the old man who brought fish up from the beach. Such was the fate of adulterous wives, if they were not in fact executed for their crime.

But Cornelius had chosen a slower, more painful punishment. Instead of just cutting her down with one blow and banishing her to exile, he kept Amelia so that he might slowly whittle her down, chipping away at her self-confidence and pride. There was a goddess statue in the garden exposed to the elements, and every season it would be a little smaller, a little more diminished as the wind and rain slowly eroded it. Long ago it had been a beautiful, perfect statue with distinct chiseled facial features but now her nose and cheeks and chin were all worn away, her face formless so that it was no longer known which goddess she had been. That was how Amelia saw herself: she was a statue exposed to her husband's harsh elements. And like a statue, she was immobile and could not run away. Someday, she feared, she would be so featureless that her identity would no longer be known.

Cornelius finally rose from the writing desk and held a small ebony box out to her.

She stared at it. "What is it?"

"Take it."

He had brought her a gift? Her heart leaped with brief hope. Had his months in Egypt, and absence from home, given him pause to reflect and reconsider? She thought of the Bird Reader's prophecy of a man welcoming her with open arms, and she wondered in a rush of excitement if Cornelius had forgiven her at last.

She drew in a sharp breath when she opened the box and saw what was inside: the most exquisite necklace she had ever laid eyes on.

Giddy with joy and sudden hope, she carefully brought the gold chain out of the box and held it up to the light. Set in expertly crafted gold was a stunning blue stone, egg-shaped and smooth, shot with hues from skies and rainbows and lakes. As she fastened it behind her neck, Cornelius said, "The legend is that it was found in the tomb of an Egyptian queen who deceived her husband and was put to death for it," and Amelia's hopes and joy collapsed.

She saw the truth of her life, all in an instant: a woman whose children no longer needed her, whose husband was cold and cruel, and whose few friends gossiped about her behind her back. An intolerable situation. Yet she could never leave for the law gave Cornelius absolute right of life and death over her. Besides, she *had* done wrong. She deserved to be punished.

*A*melia woke with a start.

She listened to the night and heard, beyond her open window, the never-ending noise of the city. Wheeled traffic was not allowed in the streets of Rome during the day and so the night was always filled with the clip-clop of hooves and the creaks and groans of wagons. But it wasn't the city that had wakened her. "Who's there?" she whispered in the darkness.

When there was no response she continued to lie still, holding her breath. She was certain she felt a presence in the room. "Cornelius?" she said, knowing that would be impossible.

Her skin suddenly rose in bumps and she felt her scalp crawl. Filled with nameless dread, she sat up. Her bedchamber was flooded with radiant moonlight. She looked around the room but saw no one there. Yet she was certain someone was there.

Creeping from her bed, she stole across the room to look out the window. Rome slept. Rooftops, towers, hills, and valleys covered with buildings glowing in moon- and starlight. And the relentless traffic in the streets, strangely solemn and muted, as if ghosts drove the horses and mules.

She felt an icy breath on her back. Turning with a start, she surveyed the bedchamber once more. Her senses were heightened. The furniture seemed to stand in eerie relief in the supernatural light of the moon. Suddenly it didn't look like her bedroom at all. It made her think of tombs and death.

Crossing the cold floor, she reached her dressing table and looked at the ebony box Cornelius had brought from Egypt. And suddenly she knew: *There lay the nameless presence.* The hateful blue crystal that had lain a thousand years upon the bosom of a dead woman. It terrified her. When Cornelius had first given it to her, Amelia had gazed long and hard into the blue depths of the stone, and what she had seen there had so filled her with dread and terror that she had put the necklace away, swearing never to bring it to light again.

For she had seen the ghost of the murdered queen.

*A*s morning sunlight streamed through her window, Amelia sat at her dressing table as she always had, applying makeup, inspecting jewelry, getting her hair arranged: a necessary ritual. Amelia kept her sanity by keeping up appearances. By ordering the arrangement of her hair she had order over her emotions. By doing what was expected she didn't have to think or make decisions. As a woman of a certain station, there were rules she must follow, and Amelia followed those rules almost obsessively. She was like a mime in the theater, all gestures and no substance. She had loved Cornelius once, long ago, but now she could not recall what it had felt like, loving Cornelius, or loving at all. She had not been in love with her lover, a man she had known for exactly one week and whose face she could barely conjure now. Looking back, she could not recall the emotions that had driven her to his embrace, and certainly no trace remained of their fleeting, physical passion.

Adultery was a strange thing. It all depended on who committed it, and with whom. Among the lower classes, spousal cheating was almost a national pastime and a great source of jokes for the theater. But the nobility was held to a different standard and a straying wife was looked upon as cheating not only on her husband but upon her social class as well. As Lucilla, the beautiful widow of a famous senator, had once snippishly told her, it wasn't the adultery that was the sin, it was getting caught. Amelia had acted in the highest stupidity, and for that the lords and ladies of Rome could not forgive her.

"Beware the number four, my Lady," the astrologer croaked in an ancient voice as he took readings from a star chart.

Lady Amelia looked away from her mirror. She had been applying rice powder to the dark circles under her eyes because once she had gotten back to sleep, nightmares had plagued her with terrifying scenarios of tombs and sarcophagi and vengeful dead queens. "The number four?" she said.

"It is your bad-luck number today," said the old man who read Amelia's horoscope every morning. "It is to be avoided at all costs."

She stared at her reflection. How was she to avoid a number that was so prevalent? The universe was made up of fours: the four elements, the four winds, the four phases of the moon. And people: four limbs, four chambers of the heart, four passions.

Her slave girls were dressing her hair for the day and they were doing a beautiful job for they liked their mistress. Amelia was gentler than many ladies of her station and didn't stab her slave girls with hairpins if they didn't do things exactly right. The two young women labored with care as it was necessary for a lady to vary her hairstyle; having the same style day after day simply wasn't done. This morning Amelia's long curls, dyed with henna to cover the gray, were layered like a tiara on her head. As the wife of a Vitellius it was important that she always looked her best. Amelia wore dresses made of Chinese silk, necklaces made of pearls from the Indian Ocean, and jewelry made of Spanish silver and Dalmatian gold. A stranger might even envy her.

"Is there anything in your charts about a man greeting me with open arms?" she asked.

The elderly seer arched his bushy white eyebrows. "Open arms, Lady?"

"As if to embrace or welcome me."

He shook his head and gathered up his instruments. "Nothing, Lady," he said and left.

She bit her lip. The Bird Reader at their country villa was never wrong. His prophecies came true with uncanny frequency. Unfortunately the reader of auspices had not accompanied the household back to the city.

Amelia shivered—not from cold but from fear. The necklace. It frightened her, even sitting concealed in its box. The blue crystal, hard and cold, made her think of death. It was the color of cruelty and intransigence. There was no mercy in the stone, just as there was none in the giver. Pleasing to the eye but hard and cold with an unreadable core, like Cornelius himself.

She thought of his power, of the power of men in general. What power did women have? Amelia's virginity and therefore her sexuality had been guarded by her father and her brothers. When she married she had been handed over by her father to her husband. At no point in her life had she owned her own person. When her brothers came to visit, they greeted her, as all Roman male relatives greeted their kinswomen, by kissing her on both cheeks. This was not a gesture of affection but rather a covert way to detect wine on a woman's breath, for drinking alcohol was considered unseemly. *I have not even any say in what goes into my stomach!*

She shivered again, almost afraid to look into her mirror for fear of what she would see—the specter of the dead queen hovering behind her. That horrible necklace. It was as if Cornelius had brought a ghost into their home. If only she could pray. There was a time when prayer had been a comfort. But now there was only a spiritual desert inside her where faith had once flourished.

How she envied her friend Rachel, so devout, so active in her religious community, and so certain of her place in the world. Rachel knew of Amelia's loss of faith and had tried, in her gently persuasive way, to bring her friend into Judaism. But Rachel's religion only baffled and confused Amelia. If a hundred Roman gods could not inspire faith, then how could just one?

Her thoughts now upon Rachel, Amelia recalled again her surprise of the night before when she had received an invitation to come to Rachel's house today, a day Amelia would not normally have seen her friend for it was Rachel's holy day, called the Sabbath. Even more astonishing was that the invitation was to come to a *meal*. Because rabbinical law prohibited Jews from eating with gentiles, in all the years of their friendship, not once had they broken bread together. And so Amelia was excited and looking forward to the day. But she must be careful not to show her joy to Cornelius, or he might order her to stay home.

Amelia knew why Cornelius allowed her to continue her friendship with Rachel, when he had stripped her of every other privilege and freedom: it was to have one thing to hold over her, one precious thing he could take away and therefore keep her afraid of him. If Cornelius were to deny her all pleasures and make her truly a prisoner, he would have nothing left with which to threaten her, to control her. The outings to Rachel's house were his constant reminder of his power over her. And he kept her in suspense. Amelia never knew until the last minute if he was going to give her permission to leave the house. So, while she was happy to be seeing Rachel again, there was still that cloud: was this to be the last time?

*T*he day is most favorable for you to argue your case in court, Excellency." Cornelius's personal astrologer nodded with satisfaction over his calculations. "Most favorable indeed. I should say the case will be settled by noon."

As three slaves took pains to arrange their master's toga just right, draping it this way and that, measuring the folds precisely, Cornelius glanced toward the open doorway. He knew she lurked just beyond, Amelia, hovering like a sparrow.

She had not always been timid. There was a time when Amelia had been a strong woman with a personality befitting her high station in Roman society. The sad ruination had been her own doing. And divorce with banishment was proper punishment. But only Cornelius knew his secret reason for staying married to her. Romans didn't like bachelors, especially wealthy ones. Emperor Augustus had even gone so far as to almost make bachelorhood a crime. If Cornelius were to divorce Amelia, every mother of an unmarried daughter, every widow and divorcee, every marriageable female in the Empire would be after him. This way, Amelia was his shield. He was in fact pleased with the way he had worked his life out so well. Amelia was no longer a meddling wife and hindrance, no longer on his agenda of duties—he could in fact ignore her completely—yet she was a convenient barrier against marriage-minded women. Very tidy indeed.

And that necklace! A stroke of genius, if he did say so himself. The moment the Egyptian dealer had shown him the necklace stolen from a tomb, Cornelius had known it was perfect for Amelia—the garish bauble of an adulterous queen. And the timing could not have been better. His wife's indiscretion was six years old and people were starting to forget. The blue crystal with its scandalous legend was the perfect way to refresh people's memories. It was also an excellent way of subtly advertising his own growing power in Rome, for the crystal said, *If I can do this to my wife, imagine what I can do to* you.

There was a small crowd waiting for him in the atrium. Cornelius had been back in Rome only two days and already word had spread that the wealthy patron was back.

They always arrived at dawn, hungry young men looking for favors, referrals, introductions. They hurried from their mean lodgings in the tenement blocks to come and pay respects to their patron upon whom they depended for their subsistence living. In return for gifts and meals, these eager clients were expected to accompany him on his rounds in the city. It was Roman tradition: the larger the following, the more important the patron. And Cornelius Gaius Vitellius had one of the largest followings in Rome.

Cornelius was a lawyer, successful and influential, with many highly placed contacts. Whenever it was announced that he was going to be arguing in the law courts, crowds came to listen. His generosity was also well known. Cornelius sponsored free days at the baths, with his name prominently displayed on a banner over the entrance. At the arena, one of the awnings for blessed relief from the sun had Cornelius's name on it, informing the populace that this shade had been provided by him free of charge. He sent slaves into the streets blowing pipes and proclaiming his greatness, followed by more slaves dispensing loaves of bread. Cornelius aspired to being consul someday, least in power only to the emperor, and giving him the right to have a year named after himself so that he would be remembered for eternity. Loaves and awnings were a small price to pay.

He thought of Amelia, standing just outside his door, waiting.

A man had only one true possession: his good name. Strip away his lands and his fortune and his accomplishments and he still hadn't been touched as long as he still had his good name. It was the one thing a man had a right to defend at any cost. And there was no worse humiliation in Rome than to be a laughingstock. To be the butt of jokes was for other men, not for Cornelius Gaius Vitellius, whose patrician blood ran purer than that of the emperor himself (although Cornelius would be the last to remind Nero of this fact). Banishing his adulterous wife to exile would have been too easy, the coward's way out. Cornelius showed Rome what stern stuff he was made of by keeping her and making her a continual example to other wives.

Their marriage had been an arranged one, the unification of two powerful families through the betrothal of Cornelius and Amelia when they were eleven and eight years old respectively. Eight years later they were married and within five years they were parents. After the first son, named for his father, there came a succession of pregnancies resulting in miscarriages, stillbirths, and healthy infants—a normal mix. Over the years Cornelius established his reputation for oratory and for winning cases in the law courts, and Amelia was an exemplary wife. A man could not ask for more.

And then she had become the friend of Agrippina, mother of Nero and the most powerful woman in the Roman empire—a woman who had once attended the games wearing robes woven entirely of golden thread so that she had blinded the spectators! Agrippina was dead now, thank the gods, but Cornelius would never forget that humiliating moment six years ago at the circus, when he and Amelia, pregnant at the time, had entered the imperial box as guests and the crowd had jumped to its feet with a roar of approval. Cornelius had lifted his arms in acknowledgment of the adulation, and Agrippina had said out of the corner of her mouth, "They are cheering for your wife, you idiot, not you."

How was he to have known that Amelia had personally persuaded Rome's most favorite charioteer to come out of retirement for one last race? A wife's activities were of no concern to a husband, as long as his children were raised properly and his house run well and she kept her husband's name and reputation sterling. Whatever else wives engaged in—charities, parties, shopping—were not a husband's concern. So how was Cornelius to have known that Amelia had headed a delegation of patrician ladies to flatter and cajole and plead with the arrogant charioteer to come back for one more race? Since Amelia had been successful where others had failed, and because Rome adored the chariot driver to the point of nearly deifying the man, the mob had lifted Amelia herself to heroine status.

And her husband had not had a clue.

Cornelius had been the butt of jokes for months afterward. People recited rhymes and jingles, and scrawled ditties on public walls, making "Cornelius Vitellius" a euphemism for witless husband. And there was nothing he could do about it without making himself look even more foolish. The humiliation and resentment had eaten at him like a cancer until an idea for revenge had come to him. He might not be able to knock Amelia from her public pedestal, but he could certainly topple her from her own personal one. Even if the baby had been a perfect boy he would have declared it unfit and sent it to the waste heap. Fortunately it had been a girl, and no one had looked closely enough or had had the nerve to challenge the existence of a deformed foot. Out went the child, despite Amelia's hysterical pleadings, to be exposed on a rubbish pile to be consumed by birds and rats and the elements, and Cornelius's dominance was established once again.

And then the silly woman had gone and slept with another man—a poet of all people! And then had been stupid enough not to be discreet about it so that her indiscretion was found out. Once again, Cornelius had had to act. But not to banish her from Rome. Since she was such a darling of the mob, let the mob be constantly reminded of the whore that she was.

The slaves finally done with his toga, Cornelius stepped away from them and went to examine himself in a full-length mirror of polished copper. "I suppose you want to visit the Jewess?" he said to no one in particular. Cornelius never referred to Rachel by name. He disliked Jews and was opposed to the imperial policy of tolerance toward them and their secretive sect. He had also conveniently forgotten that it was the Jewess's husband, a physician named Solomon, who had saved the life of one of their children.

Amelia finally stepped into the open doorway. "If I may."

He fussed with his toga, turned this way and that in front of his reflection, snapped an order at the slaves, inspected his perfectly man-

icured fingernails, then said, "Is this something you really wish to do?"
She bit her lower lip. "Yes, Cornelius." She desperately wanted to
be allowed out of the house. After visiting Rachel, she hoped to stop
at the bookshops near the Forum and see if a new collection of poetry
was in. But it would have to be a quick stop, and she would have to
be sure to hide the book from Cornelius.

He finally looked at her. "You aren't wearing my gift."

Her heart jumped. The necklace! "I thought—it seems too expensive for—"

"The Jewess is your best friend. I would have thought you would
wish to show it to her."

She swallowed with a dry mouth. "Yes, Cornelius. I will wear it, as
you wish."

"In that case, you may visit her."

She tried not to show her intense relief.

"You will be home before sunset," he added. "We are having guests
tonight."

"Who—"

"No stopping at the bookshops near the Forum. You are to come
straight home from visiting the Jewess, and I shall know if you do
otherwise."

She bent her head and whispered, "Yes, Cornelius."

He dismissed her and she returned to her bedchamber where she
drew the gold necklace with the hated blue crystal out of its box and
placed it over her head. As she felt its heaviness settle against her
chest, she felt shadows gather around her. She had no choice but to
take the ghost of the Egyptian queen with her.

*A*s Amelia rode through the streets in her curtained litter, she welcomed the noise and smells of Rome. Accustomed to the fresh air of
the countryside, Amelia's nostrils were shocked, as always during her
first days back in the city, by the odors and miasmas that enveloped
this metropolis that stunk in all weather. She didn't have to draw
aside the curtain to know that they were on the Street of Fullers, for
fullers used urine in the treatment of wool and so they always set jars
outside their shops for passersby to urinate into. The stench was as
familiar as that of baking bread. In other streets feces, both animal
and human, baked in the sun to give off a fetor that mingled with

the odors of cooked as well as rotting fish. But the most pervasive and, to Amelia, welcome smell of all was that of humanity.

Rome's streets were congested with people looking for excitement and diversion; people buying, people selling, men wishing to be seen, or out to see who they could see, women causing scandal, or searching for gossip. Every street corner had its itinerant entertainers—jugglers, clowns, fortune-tellers, and snake charmers. The way might be blocked by a crowd watching a sword swallower or a trio of acrobats hoping to pick up a few coins. Magicians with pigeons competed against midgets with monkeys. There were singers and sidewalk artists, fire-eaters and mimes. Orators stood on boxes and expounded on everything from the virtue of spicefree food to the evils of sex. One-legged sailors entertained with parrots trained to spout obscene words; poets recited in Greek and Latin; hucksters sold potions and elixirs and cure-alls. Be it the marketplaces, the parks, or the Forum, streets narrow or wide, the Roman mobs milled about like schools of restless fish, forever in search of entertainment and distraction. They filled shops and taverns in their appetites for wine and meat; they gossiped and flirted and fought and met in amorous assignations in a thousand colorful venues. The dark alleyways offered baser amusements: savage dogfights, naked dancing girls, child prostitutes. Sex was bought cheaply and consummated swiftly and without sentiment. Destitute women offered themselves, their daughters, even their infants for a loaf of bread. And murders were committed, in fits of emotion or through cold calculation.

Lady Amelia, who sailed through it all in her curtained litter carried by four stout slaves who shouted to make way, loved it all with a passion. Rome made her feel alive again, and helped her to forget the ghost that traveled with her.

By the time the litter was brought to a halt before a high wall with a solid gate set in it, the sun had reached its zenith. Amelia pulled a rope and heard a bell chime somewhere within. As the gate swung open and she started to step across, Amelia reached out and brushed her fingertips over a small piece of clay inset in the stone wall. It was called a mezuzah and it contained a scrap of papyrus with sacred words written on it. She touched it automatically, in the same way she crossed herself now and then, not because she believed in the power of sacred words but out of respect for Rachel, who did.

For Amelia, the best part of being with Rachel was the ease. Rachel was not a competitive or gossipy woman, Amelia never felt she was being silently judged or criticized as she was among others in her social circle. With Rachel, one could either be talkative or silent in her company. Their favorite pastimes together were taking walks along the Tiber, browsing the book stalls, watching street entertainments, or spending endless hours in Rachel's garden over a friendly game of hounds-and-jackals, very often the only sound to be heard the rolling of the dice and the click-clack movement of the game pieces. But they had never eaten together, and so Amelia was looking forward to a new experience.

Her friend came down the path to greet her, an older woman, plump and round-faced, with a wealth of silver necklaces shimmering on her bosom.

"My dear Amelia," Rachel said as they embraced. "How I missed you!" Tears shimmered in her eyes. "And you have another grandchild!"

"A healthy boy."

"God be thanked. Cornelia is doing well?"

"She and her husband are still in the country and will return to Rome in a few days. But you, Rachel, you look well!" It had been seven months since they had seen each other, and while her friend always appeared in the peak of health, Amelia could not help notice that the older woman fairly glowed. Draped in expensive dark blue silk edged with silver embroidery, Rachel actually looked years younger. Hooking her arm through Amelia's, Rachel explained that she and her daughters had just returned from the synagogue and that Amelia was the first of the guests to arrive.

"Today is Shavuot, a holiday celebrating the day when Moses received the Ten Commandments and the Torah from God at Mt. Sinai. In Jerusalem, people are taking offerings of the first fruits from their harvests to the temple. This is why my home is decorated especially with flowers and plants, to remind us that this is a harvest holiday. It is a pilgrimage festival, and Solomon and I had always hoped one day to celebrate Shavuot in Jerusalem."

She paused on the path because something had glinted in the sunlight and caught her attention. A gold chain around Amelia's neck. "What is this? A necklace that you hide?"

When Amelia brought the blue-crystal pendant out into the light, Rachel started to touch it but Amelia drew back and said, "Don't."

"Why?"

"There is a curse on it."

Rachel's eyes rounded in shock.

"This necklace was taken from the mummy of an Egyptian queen."

Rachel placed her hand on her bosom. "Robbed from the dead? God protect us. Amelia, why do you wear such a thing?"

"Because Cornelius told me to."

Rachel said nothing. All the words she had to say about Cornelius had been uttered long ago.

"I feel her presence."

"Whose?"

"The dead queen. It's as if Cornelius brought her ghost home."

"There are no ghosts in this house," Rachel said as she linked her arm through Amelia's. "You will be safe here."

$\mathcal{A}$s they entered the coolness of the atrium, Rachel paused and took Amelia's hands between hers and said with a special warmth in her voice, "I cannot keep the good news from you a moment longer. Oh my dear dear friend, what a wondrous thing happened while you were away in the country! You know how bleak life has been for me after Solomon's passing."

Rachel's husband had been a physician trained in the Greek school—a Hippocratic physician, which were in high demand for their skill and honesty. This was how the two women had met, when one of Amelia's children had gotten hurt and Solomon had come. He and Rachel had just moved to Rome from Corinth. Solomon had explained that his father and brothers were physicians there, and he had not wanted to take patients from them so he had come to Rome where he discovered a great need for good doctors. Rachel and Solomon had enjoyed one of those rare relationships in which the spouses love one another. In Rome it was highly unfashionable for husbands and wives to be in love, and it was especially frowned upon to demonstrate affection in front of others. Amelia recalled how shocked she had been to see Solomon kiss his wife on the cheek. Rachel had not been the same since his death, as though his passing had left an emptiness in her that could not be filled.

But now she seemed ebullient with joy. She said to Amelia, "I used to think, if only I could be assured I would see my Solomon again.

And now I have that assurance." Rachel went on to tell of a Jewish hero she called the Redeemer, of a coming kingdom he heralded, of a promise of eternal life. "Christ is our means of having spiritual peace. He made both Jews and gentiles one in his death by breaking down that which divided them, the old law, resulting in the creation of a new one."

When she saw Amelia's puzzled look, she laughed and said, "It is confusing, but soon it will all come clear. There are answers here for you, too, my dear friend."

Others began to arrive. Amelia was surprised at the mix of guests for Rachel had once told Amelia that she was her only non-Jewish friend, and yet there were gentiles in this group. Nor were they confined to Rachel's upper-class status but seemed to have been drawn from all walks of life, including slaves who, to Amelia's astonishment, were greeted with the same warm welcome. It was a noisy affair. Because Judaism was such a mystery to most Romans, Amelia had imagined their religious rituals to be silent, solemn affairs, like those in the temples of Isis and Juno. But Rachel explained to her bewildered friend that these gatherings were patterned after the weekly meetings at the synagogue, which were for social as well as spiritual purposes.

There were three dining tables surrounded by nine couches, with three guests per couch. In this way did Rachel exhibit her skill as a good hostess, for it was considered bad form to have less than nine people at one table, or more than twenty-seven people at a party. All fires had been kindled the night before for it was forbidden to light a fire on the Sabbath.

When everyone was settled, Rachel said, "It is my joy to welcome the gentiles among us today."

An elderly man wearing a skullcap and a fringed shawl, protested loudly about the presence of non-Jews, and walked out.

Sending a young man to go after him, Rachel explained to Amelia: "Many of us are still divided on matters of practice. Each community has its own rules and tenets of belief. The elders are trying to unify the communities, but the world is a big place. Our brothers and sisters in Corinth hold to different practices than do we, and our brothers and sisters in Ephesus hold to different practices from those of us in Rome and Corinth!"

Amelia saw that the old man was being coaxed back by the young man who was saying, "Remember the words of the prophet Isaiah when he said, 'I will make you a light for the Gentiles that you may bring my salvation to the ends of the earth.' " The elder took his place on a couch, but he still didn't look convinced or happy about the presence of non-Jews.

Rachel led them in prayer. She sang out, *"Sh'ma Yisrael: Adonai Elohenu Adonai Ehad!"*

And the rest sang back, *"Barukh Shem Kevod Malkhuto le-olam vaed!"*

Rachel then smiled at the new guests and repeated the prayer in Latin for their benefit: "Hear O Israel: The Lord our God, the Lord is One! Blessed be His glorious Kingdom forever and ever!"

The meeting seemed to consist of reading letters and telling stories. Amelia recognized some of the stories since the resurrection of gods was nothing new. The god Mars had been martyred and descended into the underworld for three days and rose again. Other saviors had done the same in prior ages; even Romulus, the first king of Rome, had appeared in the flesh to his followers after his death and told them he was being taken up to the gods. Julius Caesar and Augustus were now gods. Men becoming gods was a commonplace occurrence. And as for an afterlife, Isis already promised this. The group spoke of the crucifixion of their redeemer. This meant nothing to Amelia for criminals were crucified everyday. Crosses lined the roads leading into Rome, and it was rare to see one unoccupied. And as for Jesus performing miracles and healing the sick, these too were nothing rare, for in Rome one observed miracles in the streets on a daily basis, magicians who turned water into wine, and faith healers making the lame walk. Still she listened politely and marveled at how rapt the listeners were.

Rachel's cousin from Corinth was there, who had brought letters to be read out loud. Rachel explained quietly to Amelia, "We do not have synagogues or temples or structured centers of worship. We gather in private homes. My cousin, like me, is a patroness of the new faith and holds feasts in her home in Corinth. Her sister-in-law, who lives in Ephesus, is also a wealthy patroness and holds feasts in her home. This is how we gather. But we are not uniform in our rules and beliefs. There is a group in Alexandria, for example, that is comprised entirely of gentiles, and so they have chosen to hold their gatherings on Sunday, the holy day of Mithras, instead of the Sabbath. And they do not follow *kasher* food rules but eat what they have always eaten—pork and shellfish, milk with meat. The companions who knew the Master send letters to the many communities in an attempt to bring us all together under one ideology. But it is difficult, the empire being so vast."

Amelia didn't see much of a gentile influence at this gathering. Most of the members were Jewish. There was a menorah on the table. Rachel's head was covered, as were the men's, and most of the men wore fringed shawls and phylacteries on their foreheads. They recited prayers in Hebrew first, and then in Latin. And the dishes, while varied and plentiful, contained no pork or shellfish, no milk or cheese. But there was steamed fish in a tasty sauce, boiled chicken, and a sweet, tender veal.

Rachel, presiding, explained to the newcomers that this was a feast honoring the arrival of the One Who Has Been Awaited—the Messiah who will bring God's kingdom to the Jews. "We have new friends with us here today." She introduced them. "Some of you protest the gentiles in our midst. But Paul has told us that before God we are neither Jew nor gentile, but all equal before Him."

Rachel broke off pieces of bread and passed them around. "Blessed are the meek," she sang out, and the others sang in response, "For they shall inherit the earth." On and on, in beautiful antiphonal chanting.

Amelia noticed that they addressed their prayers to one called Abba. "Abba is the name of your god?" she asked.

"Aramaic was the language of our Lord, and 'abba' is the Aramaic word for 'father.' Jesus addressed God as Abba, and now so do we."

Although their mood was one of joy, Amelia sensed an underlying tension. There was a strange anxiousness among the group and as she listened to their stories, she began to understand the source of this anxiety: their redeemer was crucified thirty years ago and few of his original followers were still alive. Everyone said this meant Jesus's return was soon. "Any day now," Rachel assured the group. This was new to Amelia, for she could not think of a single savior god who had promised to come back, or who had in fact come back after his resurrection. Rachel went on to report of tribes on the borders of the empire fomenting rebellion against Rome, and then she cited signs and portents that heralded the end of the world.

The closing words were spoken by an elderly man among them whom they addressed as Peter, which sounded strange to Amelia, for they were speaking Latin and therefore calling him Rock. She had never heard a man called Rock before. When asked why he had such a strange name, Rachel replied, "Because he is Simon the Rock, which refers to his steadfastness and loyalty. He was our Lord's first disciple."

Peter did not resemble his namesake. Small and old and frail, he had to be helped to the couch where he began to speak in a voice as soft as feathers. He first praised God and then spoke on the holiness of life. Much of it held little meaning for Lady Amelia, who listened politely to such exhortations as: "You are a chosen people, a royal priesthood, a holy nation. Once you were not a people but now you are the people of God," and "The end of all things is near, therefore live your lives as strangers here in fear."

Finally there was a collection of money, some of which would be shared among the poor of Rome, the rest to be sent to needy Christian communities in the empire. When everyone was preparing to leave, Rachel asked Amelia to stay, for she was anxious to hear her friend's thoughts. But Amelia had to confess that she did not understand this new belief, nor could she accept that the world was about to end. "Thank you, my dear friend, for including me today. But this is not for me. I have not the faith that you require among your members. Nor do I feel that your redeemer would interest himself in me." She stopped suddenly.

The frail old apostle named Peter was preparing to lead the group in a final prayer, and before Amelia's astonished eyes he rose to his feet, held out his arms and began to recite, "Blessed Father in Heaven . . ."

She stared in shock at the outstretched arms and remembered the prophecy of the Bird Reader. Was *this* the man foretold?

*T*he heat of summer was upon them and so Rachel was preparing the peristyle garden for the Sabbath meeting. The group had grown in numbers and she could no longer keep the feast to three sets of three couches. Now the guests sat on the ground or on benches and ate from bread trenchers that she passed around. Since they had no formal place of worship, no temple or synagogue, but met in private homes, they called their group an *ecclesia,* a Greek word that meant "summoned to assembly" and that future generations would call a church. Rachel's house was now a house-church, as was Chloe's home in Corinth, Nympha's in Laodicea, and so forth. And all the scattered house-churches together were starting to be called the Universal Church.

The Christian faith was growing so rapidly that Rachel was now almost daily performing baptisms in the fountain in her peristyle garden with its little statue of Bacchus on top spouting water upon the Christian converts. She carried out the ritual the way her cousin Chloe had taught her, who had learned it from the missionary Paul, who had learned it from Peter in Jerusalem. There was comfort in the ritual and in the unbroken chain, for Jesus himself had been thus baptized in the Jordan River, and now, nearly forty years later, his followers were doing the same. Rachel had yet, however, to baptize her best friend.

She looked over at Amelia, whose contribution to the communal meal was small loaves, baked with her own hands and stamped with the cross of Hermes.

Amelia had no idea how hard Rachel prayed for her. And it was no longer just to bring her friend into the joyous fold of Jesus the Christ, but a more urgent reason fueled Rachel's prayers: literally the saving of Amelia's immortal soul. Rachel's own conversion had occurred back in January, on a rainy day that she would never forget, when she had heard the glorious message from Palestine—that the long awaited savior of the Jews had come at last, and that when he came again, people were going to be reunited with the deceased, for as Paul promised, death was only sleep, a "night between two days," and that those baptized in the Lord's name would live again. Peter had laid his knobby old hands on Rachel's head and she had felt an instant lifting of her grief. She wished the same joy for Amelia.

When Solomon died, it was Amelia who had been Rachel's mainstay and empathizer, coming to the house in all weathers, with words or silence, depending upon Rachel's mood at the time, but always there, sharing the grief and the burden of being suddenly alone in the world. Many times in those dark days Rachel had wondered if she would have even gotten through it all without Amelia.

And then the tables had turned. "I feel as though I am losing my soul," Amelia had confessed one evening as dusk crept softly into the private garden. "Cornelius is draining me, Rachel, and I haven't the strength to fight him."

Rachel wished she could pull that necklace from Amelia's neck and grind the poisonous blue crystal beneath her heel. But Cornelius made sure his wife wore it every day; worse, Amelia believed she deserved it. "I did commit adultery," she said unhappily.

"Amelia, listen to me. One day the Lord came upon a group of people about to stone a woman caught in adultery. He stopped them and offered the first stone to anyone in the mob who had not themselves committed a sin. And Amelia, no one took the stone! Is Cornelius without sin?"

"It is different for him. It is different for men."

Rachel could not argue with that, for the inequality between men and women was the same in both Roman and Jewish traditions, which placed the father or husband above the women in the house. But Jesus had preached of equality between men and women, and wasn't Rachel herself proof? In the synagogue she must sit in a balcony, hidden behind a screen, and not take active part in the service, whereas at the Sabbath feasts in her home, celebrating the life and death and resurrection of the Lord, she was the deaconess, the one who presided over the service, the prayers, and the breaking of the communal bread. And when Jesus returned and the new kingdom of God commenced, it was going to be a new age for women as well as for men.

Rachel was not going to give up on her friend. When Jesus returned, only those who were baptized would be admitted to the new kingdom. And he was going to return soon, for Peter said the Lord had promised to come back in the lifetime of his disciples. Jesus had died over thirty years ago, those of his followers still alive were of extreme age, like Peter, who was so frail that it looked as if each breath might be his last. As Rachel tasted the stew that had been simmering since the beginning of Sabbath the night before, with morsels of lamb so tender they melted on the tongue, she vowed that no matter what it took, whatever strength she had and purpose of mind, she was going to save her friend's soul.

Amelia hummed as she arranged the small loaves of bread on platters. Such little tasks made her feel useful. In her own home, she was no longer needed. Cornelius was spending more and more time at the imperial palace as he had become a member of Nero's inner circle, and although Amelia had five children, one son-in-law, two daughters-in-law and four grandchildren, her house on the Aventine Hill was a strangely silent and deserted place. There was just the two boys left, Gaius, who was to receive his toga of manhood in two years and no longer a little boy and who spent most of his time with his schoolmates or his tutors and had no time for his mother; and little Lucius, who wasn't really her son, who had his nanny and tutors and the attention of Cornelius when he was home. Amelia would roam the rooms and colonnades and gardens of their hilltop villa as if searching for something. Rachel told her that it was faith she sought but Amelia was not so sure. If it were faith she was seeking, then would she not have found it by now in this hotbed of zeal and religious fervor? At some meetings, people fell to the ground in religious fits of ecstasy, speaking gibberish or prophesying the end of days. The group prayed and sang and baptized new converts, they witnessed the Lord as their savior and pledged their souls to God. But so far none of this had touched Amelia.

She turned her attention to preparing special food for poor Japheth who, having no tongue, had difficulty eating. His tongue had been cut out by a sadistic master and he had joined Rachel's house-church because the God of the Jews listened to silent prayer. A priest at the temple of Jupiter had demanded a fee for reciting Japheth's prayer out loud to the god, saying, "How do you expect the god to hear you if you can't talk?"

When Amelia handed a plate of bread to Cleander, a young slave with a clubfoot whom Rachel had recently freed, she could not help but think of her lost baby, wondering again if it had survived the rubbish heap or if she was already in the afterlife waiting to be reunited with her mother, as Jesus had promised. If only she could believe! Amelia had not joined Rachel's group out of faith but for the friendship. She felt needed again, and part of a family: Gaspar, the freed slave with only one arm; Japheth, the tongueless mute; Chloe, the evangelist from Corinth; Phoebe, an elderly deaconess who lived here in Rome. It didn't matter to Amelia that Jesus was many things to many people—wise man, rebel, teacher, healer, redeemer, son of God—for had not Jesus himself spoken in parables that each might interpret his message according to his own belief? Amelia saw Jesus as a teacher of a moral life. She saw no divinity in him, no miraculous powers, with perhaps one exception: his message had brought happiness back into her life. *That* was a miracle.

She wondered if Cornelius had noticed the change in her. And if he thought about her at all, what did he suppose she was up to? Did he picture her and Rachel sitting like two contented hens comparing grandchildren and complaining about current hairstyles? He could not possibly imagine the weekly assemblage Amelia found herself in, especially the social mixture. She shuddered at the thought of his reaction to his wife sharing bread with men and women of low birth, or to learn that she had given up a bracelet that had been his wedding gift to her twenty-seven years ago to help bail a Jew from Tarsus out of prison.

Cornelius. After all these years, she still did not understand him. Why, for example, after six years, was he stepping up his punishment of her, taking every opportunity to humiliate her, when surely it was time to let the matter fade from memory? But then she had started seeing the sideways looks in her direction and hearing the whispers behind her back. After being back in Rome for only a few days, the rumor finally reached her: Cornelius had taken the beautiful widow Lucilla to Egypt with him. Amelia felt sick. The blue-crystal necklace was a means to keep her past sin in the forefront of everyone's mind while he quietly got away with his own.

Upon their return from the country, she and Cornelius had plunged back into the social whirl of nightly dinners and holiday galas, Roman high society having little else to do. Cornelius always insisted Amelia wear the Egyptian necklace, and though she concealed it beneath her dress, he made her bring it out to show others while he told the legend of the adulterous queen. Nero's wife, Empress Poppaea, had lifted the heavy gold pendant in her hand, narrowed her eyes at the blue crystal, and said with delicious glee, "Scandalous!"

Nightmares plagued Amelia, and during the day, whether gardening, weaving, or inspecting the house, she felt the dark shadow of the Egyptian queen at her heels, a malevolent phantom to remind her of her sin. But when she came to these joyous Sabbath feasts at Rachel's house, where the guests were noisy and pious and followed the laws of their god, Amelia felt light of heart. She wished she could say to Rachel, "I am a believer." But how did it happen, this miracle of faith? What was it that worked through people who experienced sudden epiphanies, right here in Rachel's garden, causing them to fall to their knees and speak in an incomprehensible tongue? And why did the mysterious power work in some but not in others? Every week, congregants sang and clapped their hands and shouted "Hallelujah!" and worked themselves into a frenzy, they grew fevered with devotion and many fell into fits of religious ecstasy and hysteria, while others simply looked on in bafflement.

They were all so convinced that the world was coming to an end— not just Rachel's group, but visitors from house-churches all over the empire—that many had given away all their possessions. Even Rachel's house was changing: she had freed her slaves, much of her expensive furniture was gone, and her silk dresses had been replaced by ones made of homespun cloth. She was constantly collecting money to send to their poorer brothers and sisters in Jerusalem, and her exquisite collection of silver necklaces had been sacrificed to finance evangelical missions to Spain and Germany.

But Amelia had discovered that the lack of a unified belief among the Christians was growing. More gentiles were joining, people from all walks of life and bringing with them their own beliefs, so that when Rachel finished leading them in the "Hear O Israel" prayer, several crossed themselves, or made the sacred sign of Osiris. Occasionally special visitors came to speak to the assembly, some who had even known Jesus, but these were very old men who spoke in croaking voices, their Greek so colloquial that they needed translators even in a group that spoke Greek! To Amelia's puzzlement, even these men could not agree on what happened in Galilee over thirty years ago. There were the followers of a man named Paul, who had never met Jesus in person but who was popular because people took his preaching to mean that, once they had embraced the Christian gospel, they could live as they liked (Paul kept writing letters to set people straight on this issue, but they seemed to keep misunderstanding him). Another group, made up mostly of Greeks, interpreted the Christian message in accordance with Greek philosophy. The followers of Peter, the man most popular in the Christian movement, believed in strict observance of Jewish law and that gentiles must convert to Judaism before becoming Christians. And then there were the mystics, people who had come from mystery religions, who claimed that the new sect should not develop around ordinary men but through mystical union with Christ only. Each group believed itself to be more correct and superior to the others.

Individual beliefs varied as well: although all believed in Jesus's imminent return, some said he would arrive in a chariot made of gold, others said he would come humbly on a donkey; some argued he must come to Rome, others said he would appear first in Jerusalem. On the

Kingdom of God, they differed as to its nature, where it was and when it would be established. Some regarded Jesus as a prince of peace, others as a prophet of war.

Adding to the confusion were the many gospels that were being circulated in scrolls, letters, and books, each declaring to be the "true" message of Christ, though none had been written until long after his death. Compounding this confusion further was the fact that few men who had actually known Jesus in his lifetime were still alive. A new generation who had never heard Jesus preach were interpreting thirty-year-old events against contemporary issues and moods. The debate over conversion of the gentiles continued to rage: baptism or circumcision. Those advocating circumcision claimed it was too easy to join the faith, that converts were not giving up their old gods, merely adding Jesus to their pantheon. Gentile Christians were starting to praise Jesus's name on the twenty-fifth day of December when they celebrated the birthday of Mithras, and followers of Isis, Queen of Heaven, said that Jesus's mother Mary was the Goddess incarnate. Each person believed that it was *their* god whose kingdom Jesus proclaimed.

There was even an argument over the Lord's name. He was Joshua, Yeshua, Iesous, or Jesus, depending upon one's nation and tongue. Some called him Bar-Abbas, which meant "son of the father," while others argued that Bar-Abbas, whose first name was also Jesus, was a different man altogether. And those who called him Jesus bar-Joseph were met with opposition by those who claimed that if the Lord called himself the son of God then he had no earthly father, like other saviors before him.

But Amelia wasn't concerned with rules and ideology, or who was right and who was wrong, or what the Lord's real name was, for unlike the others she did not believe in Jesus or his god or the promises he had made. Amelia came to the weekly gatherings for the friendship and good company, to be among people who did not whisper or gossip about her, who did not judge her on past misdeeds, who joined hands and sang together and shared a bountiful feast in the name of a crucified martyr. Most of all she came because as Rachel had promised, the evil phantom that dwelled in the blue crystal she wore beneath her dress was left outside the door—for the spell of an afternoon Amelia knew peace and love, and freedom from fear.

Finally, everyone had arrived and this Sabbath's meeting was about to begin. Rachel was preparing to read from the Torah. She had chosen a passage from Deuteronomy: "What other nation is so great as to have their gods near them the way the Lord our God is near to us whenever we pray to him?" Rachel had finally made a break with the synagogue where it was forbidden for a woman to read from the Torah to the congregation. When the rabbi had told her she must stop this practice, she had reminded him that Miriam was a prophetess in her own right and that she had helped to lead the Israelites out of Egypt as her brother Moses's equal, not as one subordinate to him.

Before she could unroll the scroll, one of her freed slaves came hurrying into the garden to inform her that a latecomer had arrived. When everyone heard the identity of the guest, great excitement erupted.

Amelia turned to the elderly Phoebe and said, "Who is it?"

"Her name is Mary, and she knew the Lord," Phoebe said with reverence, and disbelief in her voice, that such a great personage would honor their humble assembly. "A woman of means, and of influence, who fed and housed Jesus and his followers that they might spread the message." Amelia knew that Jesus had had many women among his followers, women who gave their wealth to him and to his cause, just as Rachel, Phoebe, and Chloe did today. But she hadn't known that any were still alive. Phoebe continued: "Mary was his closest companion, his first apostle. When Jesus was arrested, Peter and the other men denied knowing him. When Jesus was crucified, it was only the women who wept at the foot of the cross. The women took his body down and placed it in the tomb. And after the tomb was sealed, it was the women who held vigil outside, because Peter and the men were away hiding in fear. When Jesus came out of the tomb, it was to this woman that he first appeared and told of his resurrection. It is my secret belief," the elderly woman said with a light in her eyes, "that when the Lord returns, he will come to this woman first, to Mary."

The visitor was unremarkable in appearance. A woman of extreme age, she was small and bent and draped in white homespun cloth. She walked with a cane and the aid of a young woman, and when she spoke it was in a voice as thin as a butterfly's wing. Her Greek was the colloquial dialect of Palestine, and so her young companion translated into Latin for the gathered company. She spoke plainly, but from the heart.

The July day was hot; flies droned in the garden, bees filled the air with their buzz. A breeze hardly stirred so that people had to fan themselves. In the corner, an old man began to nod off.

Mary first asked everyone to pray with her. They stood with their arms outstretched and heads back in imitation of the Crucified One, their eyes open and heavenward as they chanted loudly and in unison. Afterward, several crossed themselves. Then Mary began her story. "My Lord was the kindest of men. He loved little children and his heart wept at the sight of sickness and poverty and injustice. He healed and blessed and taught goodness."

The heat of the day settled in the garden, like a guest wishing to hear the story, bringing with it a kind of magic warmth, a soporific effect that transformed the old woman's words into hypnotic chant. Lulled by the heat and the cadence of Mary's words, Amelia felt herself slip into a kind of altered consciousness, as if she had drunk unwatered wine, and after a while she began no longer to hear words but to see images instead. She saw herself walking with Jesus in the green hills of Galilee; standing at the lakeside and watching him preach from a fishing boat; she sat among boulders and grass as he spoke from a hillock about mercy and kindness and turning the other cheek; she tasted his wine at a wedding and felt his smile brush her cheek as he passed by.

Mary spoke of money changers and priests, a little girl in a coma, a man named Lazarus. Amelia saw a feast of fish and bread, smelled the dust of the roads and byways of Palestine, and heard the clip-clop of hooves as Roman soldiers rode by.

Heavy air and heat and the buzzing of bees, and the garden slipped into another age, another place, taking Amelia with it. Mary's frail voice painting vivid pictures. And then suddenly—

He was here! In Rachel's garden! The renegade Jew and the peaceful preacher, the armed zealot and the son of God, his multiple images swirling up from the hot paving stones, shimmering like phantoms, finally coming together and coalescing into a *man*.

Amelia was transfixed. Mary's words, riding on the turgid air with the bees and dragonflies, had brought the man into their company and Amelia *saw* the flesh and blood and sinew of him. When Mary spoke of how Jesus wondered why God had placed this burden upon him, Amelia saw the doubt in his eyes and the sweat on his brow.

When she told how he prayed, Amelia saw the glory radiate from his face. All the Jesuses that had been preached about and debated over were here now among the blossoms and greenery of a Roman peristyle garden, in the form of a man, no longer a myth or mystery, but a human born of a mother and burdened with all the hopes and doubts and foibles that were humankind's lot.

"And then he was betrayed," Mary said, her voice breaking. "Roman soldiers stripped him and mocked him, pierced his brow with thorns and flayed his back with whips. And then my Lord was forced to carry the beams of his cross through Jerusalem as people jeered and threw dirt at him. Nails were driven into his wrists and feet, and then he was hoisted high for all to see. My precious Lord hung there like a pitiable animal, bleeding and helpless, humiliated and shamed. As flies began to feast upon his wounds, as the air began to leave his lungs and his face was twisted in the utmost agony, he spoke. He asked the Father to forgive the men who had done this to him."

Some in the garden began to weep, a soft whispering sound, more anguished in its suppression than all the loudly wailing mourners of the earth. Others were too shocked to even breathe. Amelia found herself profoundly moved. Not any of Peter's preachings nor Paul's exhortations, nor reading of scrolls and letters and gospels had achieved what the softly spoken words of the elderly Mary had done: brought Jesus to life.

Amelia pressed her hand to her chest for the breath was caught in her lungs. When she felt the necklace beneath the fabric, she wondered what it was. Then, remembering, drew the pendant out and looked at the blue crystal in the diffracted light of Rachel's garden. As she gazed into the crystal, she saw the poor creature who had been tortured by Roman soldiers, his body emaciated from months of self-denial and sacrifice, his face streaming with blood, his tender skin bruised and torn, his feet slipping and staggering on the rough stones of a Jerusalem street. So many crucified criminals Amelia had seen, yet she had never seen the *man*, she had never stopped to think about the mind and heart beneath the tortured flesh. How many of them, those poor creatures hanging on beams along the Via Appia, had been innocent of crimes? How many had had families, women they loved, children they had dreams for? How many had hung on their undeserved crosses while their families wept at their feet?

"Yes," Mary repeated, her voice strained with the memory of that tragedy thirty years ago, "after all he suffered, our Lord asked God to forgive those who had tortured him."

Amelia felt her throat tighten. She saw the blue crystal through tears; it seemed to turn liquid in her hands. *Jesus, after all that had been done to him, with his dying breath had asked his god to forgive the men who had so ill-treated him.* And suddenly she saw clearly the heart of the crystal. It was not the ghost of an Egyptian queen after all, nor Simon Peter in prayer, but Jesus, hanging on the cross, his arms open in welcome, ready to embrace her. As the Bird Reader had prophesied!

Amelia cried out. She had been carrying him with her all these weeks against her breast and had not known it—the man with welcoming arms.

*S*he was baptized.

Everyone attended, all her new friends, and they feasted afterward, and prayed and cried and laughed together. Rachel had the honor of performing the ceremony in her fountain pool, with tears of joy streaming down her cheeks as the water streamed over Amelia's head. It didn't matter to Amelia that her family knew nothing of her religious conversion. They wouldn't understand and so she would not try to explain. Perhaps in time, she told herself, she would start to speak of her personal experience, and perhaps she could bring one or all of her children into the new faith. That was her secret hope: to see Cornelia and the others kneel in joy in Rachel's baptismal fountain.

"What is this?" she heard Cornelius say as he came into the garden. As was his habit, he spoke without greeting or introduction.

Amelia was tending her flowers and wondering if summer roses had always smelled so exquisite. She felt as if she were seeing the world through new eyes, as the evangelist Paul was said to have done when the scales fell from his eyes. Everything around her took on new color, new vibrancy. Like these roses. She decided she would cut a bouquet for Phoebe, who was down with a summer cold, and pay her a visit. It was one of the duties of house-church members to perform the Bikur Cholim—the great mitzvah, or praiseworthy deed, of visiting the sick—but Amelia didn't think of it as a duty. She had come to regard Phoebe as a sister.

Amelia's faith wasn't firm yet, like Rachel's. Although she felt empowered, she was still baffled. It wasn't anything she could explain to anyone, there were no words sufficient. Total acceptance was not instantaneous. There was still much to think about. The concept of an all-seeing yet unseen god, for instance. He had no statues, no images. Amelia had never prayed to a spirit before. Her blue crystal helped, for she could see the image of the crucified Redeemer in it. Others in the house-church employed imagery as well, for people loved their familiar and comforting symbols and saw no reason to give them up: Gaspar prayed to his statue of Dionysus, who himself had been a crucified savior-god; Japheth continued to wear his old cross of Hermes; and a newcomer from Babylon, who had once worshipped Tammuz the Shepherd, had painted a small mural in Rachel's garden depicting Jesus as a shepherd with a lamb on his shoulders. The concept of there being only God and no Goddess was also difficult for Amelia to accept, for was not all of nature made up of male *and* female? Therefore, like Christians who still prayed to Isis, Amelia retained her belief in Juno, the Blessed Virgin. Other tenets of the new faith were also new to her and a struggle to accept, but one thing she had no doubt about, that she had been forgiven by Jesus for her sins and weaknesses and that a new life awaited her.

"Amelia," Cornelius repeated impatiently, "what *is* this?"

"Good morning, Cornelius." She did not turn around.

"I want to know what this is."

"It's an interesting thing about summer roses," she said, gazing at the fragile blossoms in her hands. "I was always taught to remove any spent blossoms to encourage the plant to rebloom. But not all roses rebloom. Did you know that? Some are spring-blooming only and for that type of rose, even if you cut the old flowers away, it doesn't help. But for those that rebloom, such as these yellow tea roses, removing what is left of dead flowers will definitely encourage the next wave of bloom."

"Amelia," he said in exasperation, "turn around when I am speaking to you."

She turned, and his eye caught the glint of blue sunlight on her bosom. She was wearing the necklace outside her clothing. "Don't you find that interesting, Cornelius?" she said. "That by removing dead flowers you prompt the growth of new ones?"

"Tell me what this is."

She glanced at the object in his hand. "It looks like a scroll, Cornelius."

"It's an accounting of the rents collected at the tenement block in the Tenth district. Or rather, the rents *not* collected. You have not pressed for these tenants to pay. Why?"

"Because they cannot. There are mothers with children and no one to provide. There are freed men with no employment. There are sick and elderly. They cannot afford the rent."

"That is not our concern. I want these rents collected at once."

"The building is mine, Cornelius. *I* shall decide on the rents."

Her words, her tone, silenced him for a moment. Then he said, "You never did have any business sense, Amelia. I shall send Philo with the city guard to collect those rents."

"The building is mine," she said again, gently but firmly. "My father left it to me. I am the legal owner. And I say who pays rent and who does not."

"Do you realize how much money we are losing?"

She looked him up and down, taking in the fine white toga with the purple edging draped in precise folds over his body. "You do not look any the less fed for it."

His eyes flickered. "Very well," he said, slapping his palm with the scroll, as if to punctuate his words. "I shall collect the rents myself."

It took Cornelius a month with big strong guards to squeeze the exorbitant rent out of the frightened tenants; it took Amelia an afternoon to give it all back.

"All our friends are talking about it, Amelia. You have made me a laughingstock." They were in the garden again. Cornelius wore a stormy expression.

"Cornelius," she said, using the tone she often did with ten-year-old Lucius, "I told you I would not collect rent from those people. Not until their circumstances improve."

He narrowed his eyes at the necklace, again worn outside her dress. "I don't know what's gotten into you, but I think you need to stay at home for a while. You will not be seeing the Jewess." He turned to walk out. Then he stopped. "Amelia? Did you hear me?"

"Yes, Cornelius, I heard you."

"Very well then. It is understood. You will not visit the Jewess."

As she looked at Cornelius she thought of Rachel's belief that the world was coming to an end. Most Christians shared the belief and therefore many debates during Sabbath meetings revolved around the nature of that final end. Was the world going to go up in a ball of fire? Were there to be earthquakes and floods? Would nations rise and fight until only the saved were left? Many saw angels with trumpets on the way, others saw plagues and death. Whichever of these took place, Amelia wondered how Cornelius would react. She pictured him strutting about, as he did in the law courts, and shouting, "Now just a minute, you can't do that!" It almost made her smile.

"Amelia? Did you hear me?"

"Yes, Cornelius, I heard you."

"Very well then. You will not go to the house of the Jewess any more." He started to turn away once again, then stopped. "Amelia?"

"Yes, Cornelius?"

His eyes flickered down to her bosom, where the Egyptian necklace was boldly displayed, the blue crystal casting sharp reflections in the sunlight. "Do you think that's appropriate?" he said, pointing to it.

She looked down. "It was a gift from you, Cornelius. Don't you want me to show it off?"

After the apostle named Mary had left, on that remarkable day of Amelia's epiphany, she had asked Rachel how she could obtain this forgiveness that Jesus had asked for his torturers and she was stunned to learn that one did not have to pay fees to a temple or sacrifice an animal. Nor did one have to go through an intermediary such as a priest or a priestess. Simply speak directly to God, Rachel had said, ask His forgiveness, mean it in your heart, and you will be forgiven.

She had come away from Rachel's in a maelstrom of emotions. Thankful that there had been no one home when she returned, she had gone straight to her private sanctuary, a small garden with a fountain and a statue of Isis, and had thought far into the evening and night about what had happened. For hours she had been filled with rage at men who torture innocent beings. And then her anger had grown more focused and closer to home: Cornelius, refusing to forgive her. But by the time she had slept and woken to a fresh sunrise, her passions had distilled to one singular element: a new power. No longer filled with fury, no longer in pain or confusion, no longer feeling weak and helpless, Amelia had wakened to a new dawn and a new self. She had slipped the hated necklace over her head and let it lie there exposed outside her dress. And she had thought: if I am to be branded, then let all the world see.

Cornelius narrowed his eyes. It wasn't like Amelia to play games. He would drop the matter of the necklace for now. "So it is understood then," he said. "You will not see the Jewess again." He waited. "Did you hear me?"

"I heard you."

"Then you will obey."

"No, Cornelius. I will continue to visit my friend Rachel."

"Amelia!"

"Yes, Cornelius?"

She noticed for the first time that he had started to comb his hair forward from the back. Baldness was not admired in Rome, it was in fact considered a sign of weakness. Men therefore went to great pains to compensate, the same men who ridiculed their wives for spending so much time with their hairdressers. This observation startled Amelia, all the more because it aroused in her not a feeling of contempt for her husband but pity. Busts of Julius Caesar showed him to be a man of very thin hair, yet he was a hero, a god, no one thought of his scalp when they admired the man. She wanted to say to Cornelius, who spent hours with his comb and oils: polish your scalp, make it gleam, and then go on to greatness.

"I forbid you to go there anymore."

She examined her roses.

"Amelia, did you hear me?"

"I am not deaf, Cornelius."

"Then you will not go to Rachel's house anymore."

Again she kept snipping blossoms and placing them in a basket.

He frowned. "Are you unwell?"

"Why do you say that, Cornelius?"

"You're feverish."

"I am not."

"Then why are you acting so strange?"

"Am I?"

"What is the matter with you!" he boomed, and instantly regretted it. Cornelius prided himself on never losing his composure. Skilled orators and crafty lawyers had tried as much and had never caused so much as a fracture in his composure. Now his wife, of all people, was discomfiting him. He would not have it. "You heard me," he said in a final tone. Then he turned on his heel and walked out.

The perplexing exchange stayed with him all that afternoon and into the evening, but he refused to be drawn into whatever game she was up to. He knew he had nothing to fear. Not in a thousand years would Amelia disobey him.

And yet, the very next morning, she did just that.

"Where is Lady Amelia?" he asked of Philo, the majordomo.

"The Lady is gone, Lord."

"Where to?"

"Where she always goes on Saturday, Lord. To the house of the Jewess."

Cornelius saw red. She had dared to disobey him. There would not be a second time.

That evening, when she returned, he was waiting. "Remove that necklace."

"But I've grown to like it."

"I know this is some sort of ploy to force me to forgive you—"

"Why Cornelius, I don't need you to forgive me. I have already been forgiven by someone greater than you."

"Who?" he said with a dry laugh. "The Jewess? Take it off, Amelia."

"If I am to be branded an adulteress, Cornelius, then let all the world know of my shame."

"I want you to remove it."

"You wish me to be reminded of my sin, do you not?"

"This is about that damn baby, isn't it?"

Her eyebrows arched. " 'Damn baby'? Do you mean our daughter, our last child? Yes, I suppose this moment has its roots in that other moment, six years ago. I tried to be obedient when you threw away my daughter, but I went into a depression. And you did not care, Cornelius. So I sought solace in another man's arms. Perhaps this was wrong, I do not know. But I do know that what you did to my child was wrong."

"The law says—"

She lifted her chin. "I do not care what the law says. Laws are written by men. A baby belongs to a woman and to no one else. You had no right to send my child away to be exposed and die."

"I had every right under the law," he said dismissively.

"No. That is man's law, a fabricated law. The birth of a child to a woman is *nature's* law, and no mere man can subsume that."

When she turned to leave, he said, "Stay, Amelia, I have not finished talking to you," but she kept walking, right out of the room.

◆ ◆ ◆

*A*melia's blatant wearing of the blue crystal became the talk of their social set and sparked not a few jokes about Cornelius—again. He finally demanded she give the necklace to him and she refused. To be safe, she placed it under her bedding each night so that should he try to take it, she would waken and catch him. But he never tried.

The next time they spoke Cornelius was going through the house and barking orders at the slaves to start packing for a move to the country. Amelia assumed he was punishing her again, but when he said, "There has been an outbreak of malaria. Until the Campus Martius has been drained, we are not safe," she heard a ring of truth in his words.

Malaria had plagued the city for centuries and while no one knew of a solution to eradicate the disease altogether, it had been noted that when the marshes in Campus Martius were drained, the disease abated. Rachel's physician husband Solomon had suggested that the disease was not in fact caused by bad air—the *mal aria* that gave it its name—but rather by the mosquitoes that bred in the marshes. However, as Solomon was a Jew, the city magistrates hadn't listened to him.

What ultimately convinced Amelia that this move had nothing to do with her recent defiance was that Cornelius was insisting the rest of the family move to the country as well—Cornelia with her baby and young husband, Amelia's twenty-year-old twins and their spouses and babies, twenty-two-year old Cornelius Minor with his wife and two children, thirteen-year-old Gaius, and Lucius, the adopted son, with Fido at his heels. Accompanied by nannies and tutors, personal servants and a huge retinue of slaves and guards, the Vitellius clan set out from the city of Rome on an early July morning, the majority of them looking forward to getting away from the heat and stench and noise of the city for a while.

Only Amelia had misgivings.

*A*lthough the Vitellius estate, like that of all wealthy Roman families, had slaves who did nothing but spin yarn, weave cloth, and make the family's clothes, Amelia believed, as most Roman matrons did, in the old-fashioned virtue of performing such labors herself.

And so she sat beneath the shade of a sycamore tree in their country garden, a bag of wool at her feet, carding the fibers in preparation for turning them into yarn. She was not alone. Her two daughters and two daughters-in-law, each rocking a cradle or holding a squirming infant, her young sons Gaius and Lucius, and assorted little boys and girls, the children of slaves, were gathered around her to listen to a story she was telling of a man named Jesus and the three magi who brought gifts to him when he was born.

It was another of the new faith's divisions that, while the Jewish Christians emphasized obedience to God and to God's law, the gentile Christians craved stories of their redeemer. And since little was known of the life of the Lord prior to his final years of ministry, and since few who actually knew him were still alive, the gaps were happily filled in by followers who provided stories they felt *suited* Jesus. Other savior-gods such as Dionysus, Mithras, and Krishna had been visited by magi and shepherds at their birth, so then must Jesus have been, for it only made sense. And what did it matter anyway if the stories were historically true or not? They served, in their universal familiarity, to make it easier for the newcomer to accept Jesus.

When Amelia finished the story, little Lucius scrambled to his feet and, putting his arms around her, said, "Does Jesus love me, too, Mother?"

"Children, go play," Cornelia snapped suddenly, complaining it was too hot to have children around. Her sister and brothers' wives, bored with the stories and the heat, gathered up their babies and drifted toward the house where splashing fountains offered relief. But Cornelia remained beneath the sycamore, ordering one slave to bring more cool wine and another to apply more vigor to the ostrich fan he was wafting. Rocking the cradle where her baby fussed in his damp cloths, she said, "I had a dream last night. Something is wrong in the city."

She had her mother's instant attention. Dreams were important. Their messages were not to be ignored.

"It was nothing specific," Cornelia said, squinting at the garden wall, as if she could see beyond it, over the miles and hills to where Rome baked in the July heat. "I just wish Papa would join us."

"He has many duties."

"Duties!" Cornelia said sulkily. "He's in Rome with his mistress.

You did know that, didn't you, Mother, that Papa has a mistress?"

Amelia had suspected as much. Cornelius had a healthy sexual appetite, and since he had not visited her bed in years, she assumed he was finding release elsewhere. She resumed carding the wool.

"How can you tolerate it?"

Amelia stared at her daughter. Cornelia was acting the injured party, as though her father were being unfaithful to *her*. "What your father does is his own business."

"You know who it is, don't you? It's Lucilla. He took her to Egypt with him. Did you know that?"

Amelia did not want to speak of it, for it was in bad taste to do so and besides, it was none of her daughter's business.

Cornelia looked at her mother and said with a frown, "You're putting on weight."

Amelia looked down at herself. It was true, she was plump. But what woman wasn't after ten pregnancies? "It happens as one gets older, Cornelia," she said, wondering at the unexpected criticism.

"Still, it isn't becoming." Cornelia gestured impatiently to the wet nurse to take the fretting infant away. "And this new religion. Worshipping a dead Jew. It's unseemly."

Amelia put her carding down. "Cornelia, why are you so angry with me?"

"I'm not angry with you."

"Well something has put you in a bad humor."

Cornelia, seventeen years old and hating the monotony of country life, brushed a bee from her arm. "Papa's mistress. You drove him to it."

"That is between your father and me."

"Then why do you wear that necklace? It isn't right that you should flaunt it."

Amelia curbed her impatience. "It was a gift from your father."

"Really, Mother, I am not a child. I know why he gave it to you. All of Rome knows why. It's unbecoming that you should wear it so."

Amelia ran her hand over the carded wool, feeling the rich lanolin on her fingertips. The subject of what happened six years ago had never come up between her and her youngest daughter. She had hoped it never would. "Cornelia, dear," she began.

"Don't try to defend yourself," Cornelia said as she felt for an errant curl on her damp neck and forcefully tucked it back up into her chignon. "You drove Papa away from you," she said petulantly. "He's only a man. With your infidelity, you drove him to another woman."

"Cornelia!"

"It's true. Papa would never commit adultery otherwise."

Amelia stared at her daughter in frank shock.

"And he is still seeing her," Cornelia continued peevishly. "And it's all your fault."

"What your father does in his private time—"

"It isn't just that. It's that boy, Lucius." The orphan whom Cornelius had adopted.

Amelia looked over to where Lucius was playing fetch with Fido. "What about him?"

"He calls you Mother."

"I am his mother, legally anyway," Amelia said, and a terrible foreboding began to steal over her. "And he *is* a blood relative," she continued, her throat tightening with a chilling presentiment. "His parents were Vitellii."

"Oh Mother, how can you be so blind?"

Suddenly, there it was, out in the open. What Amelia had unconsciously known for a while but which she had been fooling herself into ignoring: she had told herself that the boy's resemblance to Cornelius was due to his Vitellius blood. But now she saw it clearly, what Cornelia was about to reveal: that Lucius was Cornelius's son.

Pressing her hand to her necklace, drawing comfort from the feel of the blue crystal beneath her fingers, she recited a silent prayer: *God give me strength . . .*

"We will speak no more of it," she said in a tight voice, reaching for more wool.

"And it doesn't bother you that Lucius is Lucilla's son? That everyone in Rome knows that Papa adopted his mistress's bastard and that he is still seeing her?"

"That is enough!" Amelia said. And as she met her daughter's challenging glare, she noticed for the first time that the strong resemblance Cornelia bore to her father wasn't a natural one. Amelia recalled a time when Cornelia had had softer features, a more forgiving face. But as the years went by she had developed the habit of pinching her nostrils and firming her lips as though in constant disapproval, the way Cornelius did. The result was to shape her face to look like his. "Cornelia, what did I do to make you despise me so?"

The girl averted her eyes. "You cheated on Papa."

"After he threw away my baby." There. It was out in the open.

"He did the right thing! It was deformed! *You* must have done something wrong!"

Amelia was stunned to see her daughter on the verge of tears. And just as Cornelia blurted, "It's all your fault. The baby—everything!" a slave came running from the house, shouting, "Lady! Lady! The city is on fire!"

They watched the fire for six days, receiving reports from runners who brought daily updates. The villa was in an uproar, its daily schedule brought to a halt as the family and slaves climbed to the roof and saw the red sky in the distance. Rome, burning . . .

Was it the end of the world? Amelia wondered. *Was this what Rachel and her friends had been prophesying? Is Jesus about to enter Rome?*

Cornelius sent word that he was all right. He had ridden to Antium to give the news to the emperor. But it was her friends Amelia was worried about: Phoebe, who was old and infirm, Japheth who, being mute, could not call for help, and Gaspar, with one arm. How were these to escape the flames?

They would later learn that the fire began in the circus, where it adjoined the Palatine and Caeline Hills. Breaking out in shops selling flammable goods and fanned by the wind, the conflagration instantly grew as there were no walled mansions or temples to stop it. The fire swept first across the level spaces, then it climbed the hills, outstripping every effort to stop it. The ancient city's narrow winding streets and irregular blocks made its progress swift and easy. But the worst horror was the panic among its citizens as the avenues and alleys were clogged with people trying to flee. Eyewitnesses brought reports of utter chaos among the population as those intent upon their own survival trampled the helpless. When people ran blindly down smoke-filled streets, shrieking, they would find a wall of flames before them or outflanking them. When they escaped to a neighboring quarter, the fire followed—like a beast with a will. Finally, the terrified populace crowded onto the country roads and poured into the fields and farms.

There were bizarre reports of menacing gangs preventing firefighters from dousing the flames. Torches were openly thrown by men declaring that they acted under orders. And then there was the obscene and unhampered plundering. People lying in the streets, still alive, were stripped of clothing and jewelry. Men trying to save their homes were bludgeoned as vandals rushed in to loot.

When Nero returned to the still-burning city, making certain everyone knew that he had left the safety of Antium, thus risking his own life because he loved his people so, he threw open the Campus Martius, Agrippa's public buildings, even his own gardens for the relief of the homeless masses. He had food brought from neighboring towns, and the price of corn was reduced. Yet these measures earned him no praise. For a rumor began to spread that while the city was burning Nero had performed for his inner circle, singing of the destruction of Troy. And an even worse rumor: that Nero himself, desiring to build a new city, had ordered the fire started.

By the sixth day the raging flames met only bare ground and open sky, and the fire finally died out at the foot of the Esquiline Hill. Of Rome's fourteen districts only four remained intact. Three were leveled completely to the ground, the others were reduced to scorched ruins. To count the mansions, blocks, and temples destroyed was impossible. And the number of homeless people, orphaned children, widowed spouses was beyond count.

For a week Amelia's heart was in her throat as she thought of her friends, and waited anxiously for word. She would have gone herself had she not had her own family to think of, for streams of refugees were now clogging the roads and begging at the villas of the rich. She would have opened her doors to them were there not an unruly element among them, brigands who, taking advantage of the disaster, took to marauding the countryside, attacking refugees and homes until finally a cohort of soldiers was dispatched to restore order.

Until she received word from Rachel herself, Amelia could do nothing but wait and worry and pray.

Cornelius finally returned to report that while their own city property had been spared, much of their hill lay in blackened ruin, and their house had suffered smoke damage. He was having a new residence built at once, he said, and in the meantime the entire family was to stay in the country, where the air and water were pure and fresh, and they were safe from the diseases that were now sweeping through the destroyed city.

It was to be nearly a year before they returned, but in the meantime Amelia received a letter from Rachel saying that her own house had been spared and that most of the house-church members, praise God, had gotten through the disaster unscathed. They were resuming their weekly Sabbath meetings and would include Amelia in their prayers. Rachel also managed to send visitors and letters from Paul, and because Cornelius was in the city for most of the time, Amelia organized a small house-church of her own and invited family and slaves to take part. Cornelia would have nothing to do with her mother's activities and spent most of her time being fretfully pregnant with her second child, keeping to a summer pavilion adjacent to the villa, where she entertained her own friends.

In the meantime, Rome was rebuilt and many profited from it. Nero contracted with private entrepreneurs to have rubble removed and dumped in the Ostian marshes by corn ships returning down the Tiber. He decreed that a portion of every new building be made of fireproof stone from Alba. Householders were obliged to keep firefighting apparatus in their homes, such equipment being purchasable from local distributors. Rome was alive with the sound of money changing hands.

After a time, Amelia began to wonder at Cornelius's new cheerfulness. Every time he visited the villa, he announced that they were going to become incredibly rich on the rebuilding of Rome. His ships were the ones that had gotten the contract to bring in new building materials. He had had the foresight, he bragged, to monopolize the stone market at the quarries. After a while, recalling how he had insisted that the *entire* family move to the country, and the haste of that move, a terrible thought began to haunt her: had Cornelius known about the fire ahead of time?

And then finally the day came when he announced that they were to return to the city. None went with a happier heart than Amelia.

*I*t could get stolen," Cornelius said, frowning at the blue crystal that shone so boldly upon Amelia's breast. "A thief could yank it from your neck. You should have left the necklace at home, Amelia."

But she merely said what she always said. "It was your gift to me, and I shall wear it always."

"Then at least conceal it beneath your dress."

But she made no move to hide the blue crystal.

They were arriving in their curtained litter at the great circus on Vatican Hill. It was a big day for the emperor and all of Rome was going to be there. Amelia hadn't really wanted to come but she knew her absence would be noticed by the imperial family. Besides, her husband was one of the sponsors of today's events; she could hardly miss it. She had never been fond of gladiatorial combats or the contests of killing wild game. But she would get through the day: Cornelius had promised that tomorrow she could go to Rachel's.

They had been back in Rome for less than a week and Amelia had had little time to catch up on the latest news among her Christian friends. As Cornelius had promised, their new home on the Aventine Hill was even more spacious and luxurious than their old mansion had been, and Amelia had had her hands and hours full with purchasing furniture, arranging for the painting of murals, buying new slaves. And then Cornelius had announced that Nero was offering games in thanks to the gods for the rebirth of the city.

Enormous crowds poured through the chutes and into the ascending rows, pushing, shoving, and scrambling to fill the top half of the immense number of seats looking down into the huge arena. Excitable and noisy, unhampered by education or good manners, they were squashed together, men, women, and children, crying, shouting, laughing, and sweating in their passion for diversion and entertainment. Lower down, the first rows were filled with senators, priests, magistrates, and other officials of distinction. The next rows were crammed with citizens of wealth and standing. Here was where the Vitellius clan had a private box.

The whole family had come. Filing in behind Cornelius and Amelia were Cornelia and her husband, Cornelius Minor and his wife, the twins with their spouses, and young Gaius and Lucius trailing behind. The young women already had their heads together, gossiping over who was there and with whom; who was dressed in the wrong colors this year, wearing her hair in an old-fashioned style, who was looking older, fatter, less socially acceptable. Amelia tried hard to ignore the presence of the beautiful widow, Lucilla, who sat only two boxes over, the guest of a senator. Lucilla dazzled in the sun with her dyed blond hair, stunning gown, and stole of pink silk.

In the year since the day the Great Fire had broken out, Amelia and Cornelia had not discussed Cornelius's mistress again. Nonetheless, Amelia sensed it still between them, a pocket of chilly air that kept mother and daughter distant.

A flawless blue sky stood overhead; later, the awnings would be rolled out to protect the spectators from the sun. Cooking aromas drifted over the crowd as vendors prepared offerings that would be sold throughout the day: pork sausages and hot bread, roasted pigeons and steamed fish, warm fruit pies and honeycakes. And heard over the buzz of the arrivals was the roar of frightened and restless beasts in their cages. The mood was at fever pitch, for word had spread through the city that Nero was offering a special surprise today, one that he and his financial sponsors had managed to keep under wraps. Not a seat was left when the trumpets announced the arrival of the imperial family. Latecomers had to stand on the top tier of the stadium, and that too was packed. A riot broke out at the entrance gates to the arena, as an angry mob was told there was no more room. City guards using spears and clubs drove them off, with people being trampled in the process. A typical day at the circus.

The games opened with great pomp and fanfare and religious ceremonies, for the games had their roots in ritual propitiation of the gods centuries ago. Priests and priestesses slaughtered lambs and doves and offered them to Jupiter and Mars, Apollo and Venus. Incense floated on the air, holy water was sprinkled on the sand. Every single one of the spectators knew that there was a solemn side to the arena entertainments, that such blood sport was necessary for the health and continued prosperity of the empire.

Nero arrived, crossing the sand with great ceremony, sending the mob wild. Once situated in the imperial box, he ordered the games to begin. A fanfare of trumpets introduced a rough-and-tumble pantomime show, followed by conjurers and magicians, acrobats and clowns, dancing bears and daredevil horseback riders, troupes of dancing girls in lavish costumes, marching bands and parades of elephants, giraffes, and camels. A jolly show with ostriches, held in captivity for so long that when released they literally frolicked around the arena, was a great crowd pleaser for archers suddenly appeared and chased the frightened, comical birds with arrows until they were slaughtered to the very last. Then the bloody games began: gladiatorial combats, beast hunts, mock battles, all turning the sand crimson. In between shows, slaves came out with hooks and chains to drag corpses and carcasses away and to spread fresh sand, while the spectators ate and drank and relieved themselves.

The day wore on and grew hot. The overflowing latrines began to stink and the stench of blood, no matter how covered by sand, began to fill the air. Just as the mob was growing restless, trumpets blared and Nero announced that by will of the gods, he had found the perpetrators of the fire that had destroyed their beloved city and killed and injured so many of their loved ones. Gates opened and a ragtag group of people staggered out blinking in the sunlight. Amelia looked at them in surprise. She had expected to see surly brigands, army deserters, the sort one always saw at these criminal executions. But this group seemed comprised of—

Women! Old men! Children!

"Cornelius," Amelia said sharply, but quietly so that no one heard, "surely Nero does not believe these people are responsible for the Great Fire?"

"He has proof."

"But look at them," she said. "They are hardly—"

She frowned. Did she see familiar faces among them? She leaned forward and shaded her eyes. That old man . . . he bore a strong resemblance to Peter, the fisherman, who had been a guest at Rachel's church-house.

She gasped. It *was* Peter! Being whipped along by a soldier until he fell to his knees and the crowd roared with approval. And there was Priscilla! And Flavius, and old Saul. "Blessed Mother Juno!" Amelia whispered. "Cornelius, I know these people!"

When he said nothing she looked at him and was stunned to see the smug smile on his face. He did not meet her eye but kept his gaze forward on the entertainment he had taken part in organizing. The execution of the so-called perpetrators of the Great Fire.

And then Amelia saw something that made her stomach rise and her throat tighten. Her hands flew to her mouth. She gave a cry. Rachel, down on the bloodied sand, being prodded along by the tip of a spear. Her hair was loose and streaming over her shoulders. Even from up here, Amelia could see the cuts and bruises. Her friend had been tortured.

She sat frozen and speechless as she watched the group stumble to where crosses had been laid on the sand; as the guards knocked the old men and women and children to their knees; as they were forced to crawl onto the wooden crossbeams and lie on their backs while two hundred and fifty thousand spectators laughed and jeered, and cried, "Death to the Jews!"

Amelia found her voice. "Cornelius, you must stop this."

"Hush! The emperor."

Amelia looked up at Nero who at that moment happened to be looking her way. When he gave a friendly wave and she saw no malice in his smile, no spite in his eyes, she realized the emperor had no idea of her connection to the people about to die.

She looked again at Cornelius, his handsome profile presented to her like that on a coin. "Stop this," she said again, more firmly. "You cannot allow this. Those people are innocent. They are my friends."

He finally turned to her with a look that chilled her to the marrow. "Why should I do as you ask? Have *I* not made requests of you which you chose to ignore?" His gaze flickered significantly to the blue crystal on her chest.

Amelia was suddenly sick. "Are you doing this to punish me? You are killing innocent people because . . ." Nausea swept over her. "Because of your anger with *me*? By all that is holy, Cornelius, what sort of monster are you?"

"The kind, dear Amelia," he said with a smile, "that knows how to please a mob." He waved an arm over the spectators. Their roar of approval was deafening.

The deaths of Rachel and the others were made farcical. Those not sentenced to be crucified were dressed in wild animals' skins and torn to pieces by dogs or lions. The crucifixions were saved for last, for sunset, so that the effect of the burning bodies was all the more spectacular. Amelia sat in shock as she watched the crosses rise into the air on ropes pulled by other condemned Christians. She heard the singing and praying and wailing of the pitiful creatures hanging from the crosses as one by one they were set afire. The audience cheered its approval as the victims screamed and writhed beneath the flames. "Die!" they shouted. "Die, you burners of our city!" Amelia saw vengeance-lust in their faces, for many had lost their homes or loved ones in the Great Fire. After this they would go home appeased, a little less grievous, a little less miserable about their lot, and rumors that Nero himself had torched Rome would gradually fade away.

"I have to stop this!" Amelia started to bolt from her seat, but Cornelius took her arm in a tight grip.

"Are you mad?" he hissed. "Think of your family!"

She looked over her shoulder at Cornelia and her sister, their heads together as they pointed at someone in a magistrate's box. The two boys, Lucius and Gaius, having gotten bored, were up on the top tier, spitting on people below. Her grown sons and sons-in-law were lounging with arms hooked over the backs of their chairs, half-watching the spectacle with wine cups in their hands.

Amelia began to sob. As the smoke and stench of burning flesh reached her nostrils, she felt the fire from the crucifixes fly down her throat and sear her heart. She felt her soul catch flame and burn as her friends burned on the sand below. Sickness rose up in her, and pain raced along every nerve and fiber in her body. Rachel was already unrecognizable, and though her charred body still moved, Amelia prayed that it was only reflex and not because her friend was still alive.

No one questioned the slaughter. No one stopped to think that, to put an end to the rumors of his complicity in the Great Fire, Nero had decided to blame someone else. No one questioned his choice of a group of renegade Jews called Christians, who already had a bad reputation in the city. Of the areas that had escaped the fire, one was the region across the Tiber River where a large Jewish population lived. And everyone still remembered when, only fifteen years before, Emperor Claudius had banished some upstart Jews from Rome for causing near-riots in the synagogues with their disputes about Christ.

Her pain fading to shock and numbness, Amelia looked at Cornelius's face while her Christian friends burned. His features held a look of such pure, undiluted hatred that it shocked her. And then she realized it was not the first time she had seen such a look on her husband's face. It had surfaced once before, also at the arena, when they had been guests in the imperial box and the crowd had cheered for Amelia. Cornelius had raised his arms, mistakenly thinking the adulation was for him, and Nero's mother had set him straight, calling him an idiot, and for an instant Cornelius had turned this same dark poisonous look upon Amelia—

Suddenly she knew the truth.

◆ ◆ ◆

*A*melia wept as she had never wept before. Not even when Cornelius had discarded her baby had she shed such anguished tears. While the household slept and all was silent, she lay prone on her bed, her face buried in her pillow, her lungs heaving great sobs, pain racking her body. For as long as she lived she would never get the image of Rachel's death out of her mind. Nor did she want to. It would be her private memorial to her dear friend, the daily reminder of Rachel's martyrdom.

Other emotions flooded her besides the grief: fury, bitterness, hatred. They came out with her tears like poisons, soaking her pillow until, well past the midnight hour, her crying finally began to abate and she sat up on the bed feeling a strange new hostility in her heart. It was not directed toward Emperor Nero, nor the mob at the arena, but toward one man: a monster named Cornelius.

She crept to his bedchamber and stood over him as he slept, questions whispering in her mind: *Why did Nero punish the Christians? How had he even heard of us? There are as many religious sects in Rome as there are street corners. And we are but an offshoot of the Jews. News of our group would not have reached such lofty ears as Nero's . . . unless someone named us to him. Someone who wanted to see us destroyed. Was it you, Cornelius? Was this another of your ways of punishing me? What a monster you are. Jesus, hanging on the cross, was able to forgive his tormentors. But I cannot forgive you, Cornelius.*

It occurred to her then that she could kill him in that moment, as he slept at this midnight hour. She could stab him where he lay, and then raise the alarm, rip her gown and tell the house guards that an intruder had done it. She would get away with it and be free. But she knew she would never kill Cornelius. Freedom would not come from his death, because she was already free.

She lifted the blue crystal in the moonlight and saw the benevolent spirit housed in its bosom. The ghost of the Egyptian queen was gone. A savior was in its place.

*S*he had come with only one slave, a large African who was a Christian. He lighted her way with a lantern and was big enough to deter any would-be thieves and attackers in the night streets. When they reached the noisy tenement house, one of the few untouched by the Great Fire, the African led the way up narrow stone stairs filled with rank smells, scurrying rats, walls covered with angry graffiti. There were no doors in the doorways, just ragged hangings for a bit of privacy.

Amelia was unafraid. She was a changed woman. And she had come seeking answers.

Coming to the doorway that she had been directed to, she parted the cloth and peered in. The occupant, an old crone, looked up, startled. She was eating gruel from a wooden bowl, her only light coming from the moon.

Amelia drew her veil back from her face and head and brought her lantern close to her face so that the woman might clearly see her. "Do you know me, mother?" she said, using the respectful title for elderly women.

The woman stared in fear and shock.

"Do not be afraid. I have not come to harm you." Amelia drew out some coins and laid them on the table. "Tell me, do you recognize me?"

The midwife looked at the coins, then at her astonishing visitor. She lowered her bowl, wiped her fingers down her dress and said, "I remember you."

"You delivered me of a child, seven years ago. A girl child."

The old woman nodded.

"Was the child deformed?"

The woman bent her head. "No . . ."

And so much fell into place then. Her daughter's anger. Crying: "It's all your fault. The baby—everything." Cornelia had been eleven years old when the baby was born and laid at Cornelius's feet. She had come running back into the bedchamber, fear in her eyes, demanding to know why her papa had rejected the infant. Now Amelia understood. The child had been perfect and little Cornelia, blind worshipper of her father, had not understood how her father could have done such a thing.

Now Amelia knew the truth: it was not her mother whom Cornelia hated.

◆　◆　◆

*A*s Cornelius arrived at his house on the Aventine Hill, he felt good about life. He had just won a court case and the crowd had cheered. His home was peaceful again and Amelia was behaving herself. Ever since witnessing the punishment of the Christians in the arena she had become quiet and docile once more. She had even stopped wearing that damned necklace for all to see.

As he entered the atrium he wondered where the slaves were. It was the majordomo's habit to greet him, yet Philo was nowhere to be seen. He was about to call out when he heard voices chanting in unison. He drew nearer to the garden and heard the Latin words: "Father in heaven, blessed is your name. Your kingdom comes. We do your will on earth. We pray, give us daily bread, forgive our sins, and rescue us from evil."

Cornelius stepped through the open doorway and peered into the garden. A group of people—mostly strangers, but his own slaves among them, Philo included—were standing with their arms held out, their heads back and eyes closed as they chanted. Then he saw Amelia, facing the group, leading them.

When they all crossed themselves and said "Amen," Amelia opened her eyes and leveled a direct gaze at him.

Both knew they had reached a turning point.

*B*ecause Rachel's house and all her slaves and goods had been confiscated by Nero, this week's Sabbath meeting was to be held at Phoebe's house. But Phoebe was elderly and her arthritis was bothering her, and so she needed assistance. Amelia was in the marketplace purchasing food for the feast. Despite what had happened to Rachel and the others, more people than ever were joining the Christian faith, especially when Nero had abandoned his persecution of them, and so a good-size crowd was expected. As she selected moderately priced wine, Amelia's thoughts were upon those sacrificed in the arena.

Rumors had flown through the city. After the Great Fire, everyone said, Nero had tried to appease heaven. After consulting the sibylline books, prayers were addressed to Vulcan, Ceres, and Proserpina. Juno, too, was propitiated. But neither human resources, nor imperial munificence, nor appeasement of the gods could eliminate sinister suspicions that the fire had been started on purpose by the emperor himself. To suppress this rumor, Nero needed scapegoats. He chose the Christians.

No one knew why he chose that group in particular, although Amelia had her own dark suspicions. People said it was probably because Christians were mostly rich, and Romans were always jealous of the rich, and suspicious of them, too, asking, how did they get to be so wealthy? Rumors of black magic and child sacrifice circulated. Strangely, after the arena event, the Christian persecution ended. Nero's plan had backfired as the victims had ultimately been pitied by the people who felt innocents were being sacrificed to one man's brutality rather than to the national interest. And anyway, no one cared about such an insignificant sect, even Nero had forgotten them because of his own personal problems. And so Christians were safe again.

"You are the Lady Amelia, wife of Cornelius Gaius Vitellius?"

Amelia looked up to see a member of the Prefecture Police standing over her, his face shadowed by the visor of his helmet. He was accompanied by six large guards. "I am," she said.

"Will you come with us, please, Lady?"

The Roman Prefecture, which housed Rome's main prison, stood near the Forum as an imposing presence. Outside, an impressive white marble facade with beautiful fluted columns and statuary faced the open square, but inside it was a warren of dark, forbidding corridors and cells.

"Why have I been brought here?" Amelia demanded to know as she was led down into the bowels beneath the main building. Her escort did not respond but marched grim-faced at her side, the jingle and clank of their armor echoing off dank walls.

They came to a halt before a heavy wooden door. The guard dragged it open and then stepped to one side, indicating that Amelia should go in. "Am I a prisoner?" she asked in disbelief. By the light of the guard's torch, she saw a grim cell inside, small and foul smelling.

"Please, Lady," he said, gesturing again.

Amelia's impulse was to protest, to run even. But she knew it would be to no avail. Whatever mistake had been made, it would be soon cleared up. With head held high, she entered the cell as if entering a sunlit temple.

The door clanged shut behind her and she heard the turning of keys in a lock. As the guards tramped away, taking with them the torch, darkness descended over her and Amelia was immediately gripped with panic. She ran to the door and pressed herself against it. There was a small opening just above her head, covered with bars and beyond her reach. Even on tiptoe she could not see out. But a wan light filtered in from sconces in the corridor, and presently her eyes adjusted to the dark.

The cell was dark and smelled of mold and urine, with chains on the walls and rotten straw piled in the corners. She saw old blood-stains on the floor, she could hear the faint cries of other prisoners. Fighting the fear and panic that were threatening to grip her, she tried to think with a level head. Surely this was a mistake! But . . . the guards had known where to find her in the marketplace; they had identified her on sight and had known her name. That meant some-one had told them. But who? And more puzzling, why?

Suddenly she was filled with a terrifying presentiment: could they possibly keep her locked in here forever? She sank to the stone floor, her ear pressed to the thick door, and sat with her knees drawn up. The darkness closed in around her, and the myriad foul odors filled her head. She felt something run past her foot and she cried out. Surely her family would miss her and come inquiring! But she had heard of people being locked up in this prison forever, forgotten . . .

She clasped her hands and began to pray.

*C*ornelius Vitellius arrived at the prison wearing his purple-edged toga, a garment allowed to only a privileged few, and he wore it now on purpose, not so much to impress the prefecture guards but to re-mind Amelia of his position and power. "Is she here?" he demanded of the man on duty.

"Been here since the first watch, your Lordship," the watch com-mander said, giving Cornelius the kind of brief salute career army soldiers offered to civilians of importance. "That's ten hours."

"No food and water?"

"Not a drop or a bite, as you ordered. We did give her a bucket to piss in, though. How long you want us to keep her?"

"I'll let you know. For now, say nothing to her."

The watch commander had learned over the years that a silent mouth was a profitable one. The popular lawyer—the guard himself had consumed more than one of Cornelius Vitellius's free beers—wasn't the first man to have a pesky relative held under arrest as a way of curbing unwanted behavior. He winked and turned back to his game of dice.

Cornelius followed the jailer down the stench-filled corridor and paused outside the metal door to get into the right frame of mind, as he often did before a trial. Then he gave the signal to the jailer.

"By the gods, Amelia!" he said as he rushed in, the door clanging shut behind him.

"Cornelius!" She flew into his arms.

"I couldn't believe it when they told me you were being held here!"

"Why am I here? Am I under arrest? No one will tell me anything."

"Now sit down. Be calm. Apparently someone named you as a Christian."

She stared up at him. "But Cornelius, my being a Christian is no secret. And it is not a crime to be one."

"I'm afraid Nero is still waging his revenge against the Christians, but he is doing it secretly, due to public antipathy." When he saw that she believed him, for she had gone very white and looked frightened, he added, "Nero has allowed me to talk to you before the real interrogation begins."

"You mean . . . torture?" she said with a mouth so dry she could hardly speak.

"Renounce this new faith, Amelia. Give me the names of the members, and you will go free."

"And if I do not tell?"

"Then it is out of my hands." He spread them for emphasis.

She thought of the people who had become dear to her—Gaspar and Japheth, Chloe, Phoebe. . . . She began to tremble violently. Would she be able to withhold their names under torture?

"How far—" she began. "How far will Nero pursue this?"

He let his shoulders slump, the way she had seen them slump during a court trial. A gesture more expressive than words.

"Cornelius, help me! I want to live! I want to see our grandchildren grow up. I want to see Gaius receive his toga of manhood." In that moment, life had never looked so sweet. And never had she felt so desperate. "Please, Cornelius! I beg you on our children's names. Help me!"

He took her by the shoulders. "I want to, Amelia. By the gods, for all that has been between us, I would never wish *this* upon you. But Nero has his mind set. Tell them what they want to know and you will walk out of here with me this day."

She looked at him with eyes filled with terror. "I . . . can't."

"Then tell me, and I shall tell the guards. They will allow that. When and where do the Christians next meet? And who are they?"

Amelia had no way of knowing that Cornelius would do nothing with the names. He would not tell the guards, her friends would go unharmed. She believed they would come to harm and so she remained silent. He tried another tack: "Give up this new faith, Amelia, and we can go back to the way we were, years ago, when we were happy. I'll take you to Egypt. Would you like that?"

She searched her husband's face in the torchlight that flickered through the small grate in the door. He looked genuinely upset. Finally she said, "Nero can kill my body, Cornelius, as he did my friends. But they are not dead. So he has no power over death. In the end, what does he really have?"

He eyed her sharply. Was she referring to Nero, or was it a veiled reference to himself? No, he saw no guile in her eyes. "If you allow this to happen, you cannot love me or your family. You are not thinking of our children!"

"But I am!" she cried. "Oh Cornelius, it is for my children that I do this!"

"If you will not listen to me, Amelia, then there is nothing I can do." He turned to walk out.

"No!" she cried. "Don't leave me here!"

"It is a simple thing to obtain your freedom, Amelia. Any child could see it."

She regarded him in horror. "Are you truly going to leave me here in this horrible place?"

"As I said, it is out of my hands."

Cornelius made sure he looked as powerless and abject as possible when the door to her cell was closed and locked, but as he followed the jailer down the corridor he felt slightly annoyed at her refusal to cooperate. He had hoped for last minute begging and crying and then his victory. So he told the watch commander to keep her for the night, no food, no water. He thought for a moment. "Can you arrange for her to hear sounds of torture?"

"I can do better, your Lordship," said the soldier who often relieved the boredom of his job with sadistic diversions. "I can go into her cell with blood on my hands. Works every time."

*A*melia awoke to the sound of the key in the massive iron lock. She slowly sat up, feeling aches in all her joints for having slept on a stone floor. There were bites on her skin; some itched, some were painful. She had never known such thirst. "Cornelius?" she whispered.

But it was her daughter. Amelia was surprised at how terrible Cornelia looked.

"Mother," the nineteen-year-old said as she gathered Amelia into a tearful embrace. "What a terrible thing!"

"Have you—" Amelia began. She was shocked at her own physical weakness. "May I have some water?"

Cornelia banged on the door and shouted her demand. A minute later the jailer—not the same guard as the night before—was back with a jug of water, a lighted torch, and two stools for sitting. He had the look of a man not at all pleased with his job.

"I heard from Cornelius," Cornelia said, referring to her brother, not her father. "He was here at the prison visiting a client and heard about your arrest. Oh Mother, I could not believe it! Why are you here?"

Amelia first had to quench her thirst, gulping directly from the pitcher and relishing the feel of water running down her hands and arms and neck. She thought that a hundred baths would never get her clean. Finally she related the conversation she had had with Cornelius, wondering why *he* wasn't there.

"But," Cornelia said with a frown, "I have heard of no new persecution. Nero is too worried about his own neck these days to contemplate those of others."

And so Amelia knew. What she had really known, deep in her heart—what had visited her in dreams and whispered to her in cadence with the rustling of rats and the endless cries of other prisoners—that this was all Cornelius's doing. By forcing her to renounce her new faith, he would be triumphant over her again.

And in the next instant, Cornelia also knew. "It's Papa, isn't it?" she whispered. "Why? Why does he hate you?"

"It's all because of wounded vanity. I was the cause of a great blow to your father's pride. I did not do it on purpose. The crowd in the arena—"

"I remember that! Everyone talked of it for weeks. Papa thought the mob was honoring him, when it was you. Is that why—?"

"Why what, Cornelia?"

The young woman bent her head. "I saw the baby. She was perfect. There was no crooked foot. But Papa ordered her to be taken away. I was so horrified. I didn't know what to think of him."

"Your father was your hero and he turned out to be only a man."

"And he continues to punish you. Don't let him, Mother. Give him what he wants and you can be free."

Amelia shook her head. "If I give Cornelius what he wants, then I shall never be free."

"Yes you will. I'll help you! He can't persecute us both. Mother"— Cornelia's tone grew frantic—"it isn't as though it's Nero! It's only Papa who's doing this to you."

"Daughter, listen to me. It doesn't matter if it is Nero and a stadium full of people, or just one man. I cannot renounce my faith."

Cornelia dropped to her knees and, laying her head in her mother's lap, sobbed. As Amelia stroked her daughter's hair, she marveled that a mere two years ago, the day Cornelia gave birth to her first child, Amelia had been a woman without faith. But now she had faith in abundance and wished she could share it with her daughter, handing it to her like a goblet of sparkling hope.

"Go now, child," she murmured. "Take care of the family for me. See that they are well. And little Lucius, treat him as your brother, Cornelia, for he is indeed that."

They embraced and kissed and said good-bye, with Cornelia protesting that she would see to her mother's release. But Amelia knew it would not be so, that Cornelius held all the power here.

Her daughter had been gone only a few moments when Cornelius arrived, so that Amelia suspected he had been outside, waiting.

"Once and for all, wife, will you renounce this madness?" he asked, and when she shook her head, she saw the genuine bafflement on his face.

"Cornelius, I think when you took me to the circus it was to frighten me," Amelia said. "I think you were hoping that my witnessing Rachel's death would make me give up my new faith. But it had the opposite effect. Because of what I saw, because of what you forced me to witness"—her voice grew in strength—"because *you* murdered my friends, I am more firm in my resolve than ever. I shall never tell the names of my fellow Christians. And I shall never renounce my faith."

He towered over her in his impressive toga of office—a garment that made crowds part before him—and she saw rage seethe in his eyes. But he said not another word, and as he turned on his heel and left, the door shutting behind him, Amelia knew that her cause was lost. Whether or not Nero was involved, whether or not the charges against her were true, she knew that somehow Cornelius was going to exact his final revenge on her. He was going to see her punished in the arena. And she would not be alone: he would crucify Japheth and Chloe and all the others, saving her for last.

Down the dank corridor and up the slimy stairs that were to have struck such fear into his wife as to make her obedient to him again, Cornelius marched with fury in every step. But already a new idea was beginning to form in his mind, a way to turn this ruined situation into an advantageous one. He would tell Amelia that he had managed to obtain her release by using his political weight and the prestige of his name and reputation. She would then gossip about it to her friends until, within a very short time, Cornelius would come out looking the hero.

So it was with some impatience that he wanted to give the order to the watch commander to have her released, as the two men had previously arranged. But the commander wasn't there, but an underling who explained that his officer was away for the moment, and the key ring with him.

"Go find him then!" Cornelius barked, anxious now to get on with Amelia's release and the gilding of his reputation.

Back in the dark cell, Amelia sat sick and terrified. She had broken out in a sweat and was shaking all over. She thought of the years still left to her, her family, the babies that were going to grow up, her house in the city, even the villa in the country was suddenly precious to her. She wanted to attend the toga ceremonies of Gaius and Lucius, to watch their eldest son win his first case in the law courts, to cradle her daughters' new babies, to grow old and wise and cherish each blazing sunset. How she had taken it all for granted, her life, her family, when she should have praised every sunrise, embraced every day!

She prayed as she had never prayed before, this woman who had once been without faith but who was now so filled with faith that she prayed not only to her new redeemer but to Blessed Mother Juno as well. She prayed for a sign. *What should I do?*

She listened for the answer, but all she heard was the oppressive silence of the massive walls that imprisoned her, and the faint cries of prisoners begging for release, for food, for water. She listened to the beating of her own heart, to the whispered fears of her own conscience. She prayed and listened. And finally, exhausted from fear and hunger and thirst, Amelia lifted the necklace from beneath her dress and gazed into the heart of the blue crystal, the cluster of cosmic diamond dust that had taken the shape of a crucified savior. And just like that, the answer came to her.

It was this stone that had given her faith in the gods again, and it strengthened her faith now. She knew what she must do.

With trembling hands she worked at prying the crystal free from its gold casing and when it was free, she held it up to the faint torchlight and nearly cried out at its beauty. Because of the gold backing, she had not seen its beautiful transparency, the utter sharpness and clarity of the image of Jesus within. How strange now to think she had thought this stone cursed, that the image was that of a ghost. But of course, that was what Cornelius had wanted her to think.

And then she thought of the pain that was to come, the torture and agony, and finally an ignominious death in the arena. She knew she hadn't the strength to keep from revealing her friends' names and whereabouts under torture. Her heart thumped. Her spirit wanted to be strong but she knew the flesh could be weak. But perhaps here, now, she would have the strength, before the torture began.

Suddenly she was thinking back to a day eight years ago when Cornelius, deciding over life and death, had chosen death. Now Amelia faced that same choice. Thinking of the innocent baby left exposed to die, she chose life: eternal life.

Having made the decision, she felt a strange calm steal over her, and suddenly all mysteries became clear. *Perhaps,* she thought, *when Jesus spoke of the end of the world, he had not meant that the end would come to all people at once, but rather to each in his time, as one dies and a new life begins. For me, tonight, the world comes to an end.*

She held her breath and listened. She heard murmured voices at the far end of the corridor. She had to move quickly, before they came for her.

Swallowing the stone was not easy. As soon as she placed it on her tongue she broke into a sweat and became sick to her stomach. And she thought of all the life that was yet ahead of her, the beautiful house and her husband now wanting to be loving toward her, wanting to start fresh, to lavish her with gifts. But all she could think of was the man on the cross who had forgiven those who crucified him, and who had cleansed her through spiritual baptism.

She put the stone farther into her mouth and still could not swallow it. So she pushed it with her finger and when she started to gag she was afraid she would vomit it back up or she would black out and the guards would pull the stone out before it had done its work.

Gagging and bent over and in excruciating pain, she worked the crystal farther down her throat, mentally praying, "God forgive me for taking my own life but I am made of weak flesh. I cannot bear to lead my beloved friends into the arena with me, though our deaths be those of martyrs."

And then the fierce instinct for survival rose up, and she panicked. Her heart raced and her hands clawed at her throat. Though it was her will to die, her body fought. Her lungs struggled for breath, her mouth stretched wide for air. Stabbing pains shot through her chest, and her head felt as if it were about to burst. She fell to the floor and flailed about like a fish pulled from water. She felt fire in her lungs, and bells clanged in her ears. *Dear God, end my misery!*

And then finally a strange peace came and life ebbed from her body like the petals of a summer rose, dropping one by one. And thus did the blue crystal, this fragment of the cosmos—marvelous in its mystery and perfection, having long ago directed a girl named Tall One out of Africa, having led a woman named Laliari to lose her fear of the dead, and having shown a young man named Avram his place in the world—lodge firmly in the throat of a woman of tremendous faith. As blackness began to engulf her, as she prepared for death and her reunion with Rachel and cherished friends, and perhaps with the abandoned child who had been born perfect, Amelia did not miss the irony that the object with which her husband had intended to punish her turned out to be the instrument of her redemption.

Interim

The guards didn't know how she had died but her face was engorged with blood, her tongue purple and protruded. The prison physician said that Lady Amelia had the look of someone who had died of a heart attack. The fear of torture in the arena must have been too great for her, he said. Cornelius remembered what she had said about his taking her to the circus backfiring. It was true. He *had* wanted to put the fear in her, but not to the point of killing her.

Then he saw something the others did not—the stone missing from the necklace, and he knew in that moment what she had done.

But not wishing his wife to achieve martyrdom status, preferring people instead to believe she had died of cowardice, he did not point out the missing blue stone and her heroic method of death. He kept his silence and became the model grieving husband.

Cornelia, on the other hand, went wild with grief, blaming her father for the tragedy. She forbade him to cremate her mother but instead had Amelia laid to rest in a fine tomb that resembled a house, complete with false windows, doors, and a garden, and Cornelia went every week to visit, making a great demonstration of her grief. As private revenge against her father, Cornelia took up her mother's faith, although she did not believe in it, and practiced Christianity openly, turning her home into a church-house, flaunting it wherever she could until the day came when she realized she really was a Christian. In her new zeal she campaigned to keep her mother's memory alive and so insisted that Christians commemorate her mother's martyrdom on the day of her death every year, with Cornelia delivering an annual eulogy on how Amelia had defied the authorities and died for her faith.

When Cornelia's first child—the baby that had been born the day Cornelius returned from Egypt, bringing with him the blue-crystal necklace stolen from a queen's tomb—grew to manhood and he became a passionate Christian and a prominent deacon of the church, he ordered a silver reliquary to be fashioned to house his grandmother's remains, and on a day of great veneration, before a gathered company of hundreds of Christians, the shroud-wrapped bones were reverently moved from coffin to reliquary and placed in a shrine where all could come and worship.

In her later years, Cornelia followed her mother and became a Christian martyr under Emperor Domitian who had her tongue ripped out during a spectacle in the circus.

Cornelius, having suffered no great loss from his wife's death, was eventually appointed to the office of consul, thus getting a year named after himself and guaranteeing, he smugly believed, his memory in history. Unfortunately, the empire eventually passed into a new rule and the roster of consuls faded into oblivion. While his wife Amelia went on to become known for her martyrdom and even to have a church named after her, Cornelius Gaius Vitellius disappeared from history.

The bones of St. Amelia were moved from the family crypt during the golden era of Emperor Marcus Aurelius and placed in a newly built church where thousands came to venerate her. There she slept peacefully, her descendants commemorating her memory each year on the day of her martyrdom, until the final and most brutal of Christian persecutions broke out under Emperor Diocletian in the year 303 c.e.

The first edict of Diocletian was that Christian assemblies were forbidden, churches and sacred books were ordered to be destroyed, and all Christians were commanded to deny their religion and sacrifice only to the state gods. The penalty for failure to comply was death. During a secret meeting of bishops and deacons it was agreed that, although death meant instant martyrdom and therefore union with Jesus in heaven, it was also necessary to the faith that certain members survive and carry the word beyond the empire. Lots were drawn to select these missionaries. Relics and books and holy objects, among them the silver casket containing the remains of St. Amelia, were gathered up and spirited out of Rome in the middle of a stormy night, and launched in a ship upon a choppy sea.

There, upon waves as tall as buildings and in a night as black as ink, Lady Amelia, former wife of Cornelius Gaius Vitellius, was transported to the Roman province of Britain where Christian sympathizers lived in a settlement called Portus, once a Roman military garrison but now a thriving town known for its eels.

Book Five

ENGLAND
1022 C.E.

---

*M*other Winifred, prioress of St. Amelia's, looked out the window of the scriptorium and thought: *spring!*

Oh, the blessed colors of nature, God's paintbrush at work: pale pink cherry blossoms, red and black mulberries, scarlet hawthorn berries, and sun-yellow jonquils. Would that her own paint palette were as rich and varied. The illuminations she could create!

The colors gave her hope. Maybe *this* year the abbot would allow her to paint the altarpiece.

Her ebullience abated. She had had the dream again, although she couldn't really call it a dream for it had come to her while she was awake. A vision, then, while praying to St. Amelia. And in the vision she had seen what she had seen countless times before: the life of the blessed saint, from girlhood to conversion to Christianity, from her arrest by Roman soldiers to a martyr's death at the hands of Emperor Nero. Although Winifred had no idea what Roman soldiers looked like, or a Roman emperor for that fact, nor how people dressed and lived a thousand years ago—and of course no one knew what Amelia had looked like, certainly her bones had not been looked upon in centuries—Winifred nonetheless felt certain that the vision was accurate, for it had come from God.

The problem was, how to convince Father Abbot. Like a bone between two dogs, the altarpiece was an issue that had been worried about by the two of them for longer than Winifred could recall. She would ask permission to work on something more challenging than a manuscript, and the abbot (both the present one and his predecessors) would counter that her ambition was unseemly and in fact verged upon the sins of pride and ambition. Although Winifred would acquiesce every time, for she had taken vows of obedience, her rebellious mind would secretly think: men paint great paintings, women are only good for capital letters.

For that was precisely what Mother Winifred and the sisters of St. Amelia's did: they painted capital letters, known as illuminations, which were famous the length and breadth of England. The only problem was, illuminations were not what Winifred wanted to paint, it was what the *abbot* wanted her to paint.

She sighed and reminded herself that the life of a nun was not about wanting but obedience.

Folding her hands into the voluminous sleeves of her habit, she started to turn away from the window where the rainbows of spring had distracted her, when she saw Andrew, the elderly caretaker of the priory, hurrying through the garden waving his hands. When she saw the look of worry on his face, Mother Winifred leaned out. There was no glass in the convent windows since the nuns could not afford such an expense.

Tugging at his gray forelock, Andrew begged the prioress's pardon and said as how he'd been up a tree cutting off old limbs for wood when he'd seen Father Edman on the road, coming this way. "Reckon it'll be quarter of an hour afore he gets here."

Winifred reacted with mild alarm. Why was he coming *now*? The abbot came only once a month to St. Amelia's, to hear confessions and to pick up manuscripts. He used to say the Mass as well but was too busy and important now to be wasted on a handful of elderly nuns. Lesser priests were assigned to that onerous duty.

"I'm thinkin' it be bad news, Reverend Mother."

Winifred pursed her lips. She had never known the abbot to alter his schedule for *good* news. Still, there was no need to spread alarm.

"Perhaps he has come to tell us that our roof will be repaired this year."

"That would be blessed news indeed."

"In the meantime, do not tell the others. We need not trouble them unnecessarily." Thanking the man, and asking him to let her know when Father Edman had reached the gate, she left the window. Keeping news of the abbot's visit to herself, for she feared it would worry her sisters, she moved along the row of nuns who were already at work on this glorious spring morning in this eleventh century of our Lord.

The convent scriptorium was a large room containing a long central table and writing desks along the walls where the sisters of St. Amelia toiled at their exquisite labor. The window shutters were open to admit the morning sunshine. The sisters worked in silence, their black-veiled heads bowed over their work. Winifred had once visited the scriptorium at Portminster Abbey, where silence was imposed upon the Benedictine monks there, although copying sacred texts was not a silent occupation. A few monks were starting to experiment with the new silent reading, but most still read to themselves the way people had done for centuries: out loud.

While the monks at Portminster Abbey penned the actual text of a book, they left a space where the first letter on a page was to go because it was added last, here at St. Amelia's. But even though it was the illuminations and not the text that were famous all over England, it was the monks who received the credit. Mother Winifred accepted this as the order of things, for she was obedient to the church and God and men. Still, she sometimes thought it would be nice if the skill, talent, and devotion of her sisters could be acknowledged just once.

Which brought her thoughts back to Father Abbot. Her dream-vision had been so strong this last time that she felt an urgency to speak with him about it. Of course, she could never go to the abbot but rather must wait for *him* to come to *her*. In forty years of living at the priory, Winifred had rarely ventured beyond its walls, and even then it was to go only a short distance—on those occasions when members of her family died and were buried in the village churchyard. Once, she had attended the installation of Father Edman as the new abbot of Portminster.

Father Abbot . . . How strange that he should be making this un-
scheduled visit on this particular morning. Dare she hope that this
was the hand of God at work? Was it a sign that the abbot was finally
going to relent and grant her wish? Was he going to understand at
last that the altarpiece was not for Winifred's own pleasure or pride,
but a gift to the blessed saint in gratitude for what she had done for
Winifred?

When Winifred was a child living at home in her father's manor
house she had possessed an uncanny knack for finding lost things—a
pin, a brooch, once even a meat pasty that had been carried off by a
dog. Her granny told her she had the sight, inherited from her Celtic
ancestors, but had warned her not to tell anyone for they might think
she was a witch. So Winifred had kept her second sight a secret until
it came out one day by accident, when the whole manor house had
been turned upside down to search for a silver spoon that had gone
missing. Fourteen-year-old Winifred had "seen" it in the buttery behind a churn, and when it was recovered, everyone had demanded
an explanation as to how she had known it was there. She couldn't
explain and so had been deemed the malicious little culprit. She had
received a beating, and the father of the boy to whom she had been
betrothed called off the engagement, citing weakness of character on
the part of the girl. That was when she had gone to the chapel at St.
Amelia's and prayed for help.

While her mother and sisters had continued to offer prayers in the
chapel, Winifred had gone exploring, and when she had stumbled
into the scriptorium where the sisters were bent over their labors, and
she had seen their palettes and pigments, their parchments and pens,
she had known that this was where she was meant to be.

Winifred's father had been only too happy to grant the girl's request
to enter the convent, and here Winifred had lived ever since. Not a
day went by in which she did not offer a prayer of thanks to St.
Amelia who had rescued her from a deplorable future: an unmarri-
ageable daughter, producing no grandsons, contributing little in return
for her keep, eventually to become that most despised of worthless
creatures, the maiden aunt whom families were required to support
and to suffer in return for bad moods and bad embroidery.

The scriptorium at St. Amelia's smelled of oil and wax, soot and
charcoal, sulphur and vegetative matter. A haze hung in the air as
lamps burned day and night, not for illumination but for the har-

vesting of lampblack necessary for the making of inks. The nuns also made their own pigments: the finest deep blue was made from lapis lazuli, which came only from Afghanistan; to make red ink they used red lead, vermilion from cinnabar, or crushed kermes beetles; and a few colors the making of which were a secret known only within these walls.

At the head of the central table was Sister Edith who was most deft at applying gold leaf, the first stage of illumination. It took a special hand to apply the gesso base and then the gold leaf on top of that; a keen eye to know when the foundation was *just* moist, to breathe on it only *just so*, to press the silk cloth *thus*, to wield the dog's tooth burnishing tool *to a point*. A heavier hand or a dimmer eye than Sister Edith's and the gold leaf decoration would be second rate at best.

Another sister was painting a miniature of Adam and Eve in the Garden of Eden. They were both naked, both feminine with rounded hips and bellies, the nun having no idea what a naked man looked like. As for the genitals, fig leaves were a godsend, for the sisters had no notion of how men were constructed beneath their clothing. Mother Winifred herself, for all her years, was ignorant of human anatomy, even female, having never assisted at childbirth or otherwise seen a woman exposed. She was familiar with the metaphors: the man's key for the woman's keyhole, his sword for her scabbard, and so forth. But the business of copulating and procreating was beyond Mother Winifred's ken.

She never thought about sex, or wondered what she had missed. As far as she understood it (mostly from tales she had heard from the lady guests at the convent), sex had been created as a sport for men and a misery for women. She remembered when her older sister had gotten married and the female cousins had come to help her pack for her journey, how the girls had giggled over the *chemise cagoule*, a voluminous nightgown with a small hole in the front, to allow impregnation with minimal body contact.

"Why don't you rest for a spell, Sister?" Winifred said now to the elderly nun who was about to paint the serpent.

"I am sorry it is taking me so long, Mother Prioress, but my eyesight . . ."

"It happens to all of us. Lay your brush aside and close your eyes for a few minutes. Perhaps a few drops of water would help."

"But Father Abbot said—"

Winifred pursed her lips. She wished that Father Edman, during his last visit, had not been so loud in his complaints about the increasing slowness of progress. It wasn't necessary to distress her sisters with his criticism. And it wasn't as though the ailments could be helped. Agnes was getting on in years, it was only to be expected that her work would take longer.

"Never mind the abbot," Winifred said gently. "God does not wish us to work ourselves right out of His service. Rest your eyes and resume later." She mentally added one more item to her list of requests to be made of Father Abbot: a medicinal eyewash for Sister Agnes.

Bells chimed then, calling the convent members to terce, the third of seven canonical hours set aside during the day for religious song. Carefully laying down their brushes and pens, the nuns whispered a prayer over their unfinished work, crossed themselves, and silently filed out.

After passing through the centuries-old cloister, they gathered in the choir that was the heart of their chapel: to the east of it was the altar where the sisters celebrated Mass; to the west, behind a wooden screen, was the nave where local people, pilgrims, and guests of the convent came to participate in the mass. The chapel, a small, modest building made of stone, was the heart of the collection of humble structures that comprised St. Amelia's priory, built three hundred years ago. The sisters, living by the Rule of St. Benedict, which called for silence, celibacy, abstinence, and poverty, slept in cells in a dorter and ate in a large refectory. A slightly more splendid dorter was meant to house permanent residents who were not nuns but ladies of means who had gone into seclusion. There was also a guest house for pilgrims and travelers, although it stood empty these days. Next to the small church was the chapter house where the nuns gathered to read the Rule and confess their sins, and finally the scriptorium where they spent the majority of their hours. All of these stone structures were arranged around the cloister, a rectangle of arched colonnades where the sisters took their exercise. From out of these cold, gray, silent walls came the most astonishingly beautiful manuscripts in all of England.

Winifred observed the handful of sisters as they filed into the choir box to sing. Once they had been a large group, but now it was dwindling, the members frail and elderly with not a single young novice among them. Nonetheless, Winifred was a strict disciplinarian and inspected her nuns every morning to make sure their habits were spotless: black tunic, scapular, and veil; white coif, wimple, and crown band. In inclement weather or for rare trips outside the convent, they wore black cowled capes. Each had a rope belt around her waist from which hung a rosary and a bread knife. Their hands were never to be seen but tucked inside sleeves, arms clasped at the waist behind the scapular. Eyes were always cast downward in modesty and humility. Although speech was allowed, voices were to be kept low and words to a minimum.

As in all convents in England, membership was open only to noblewomen. Middle-class women had little hope of being allowed to join, and peasant women had no chance at all. Winifred would have liked to open the sisterhood to middle-class women of means and vocation, and perhaps even to the occasional worthy peasant girl. But those were the rules and she could not change them. St. Amelia's was also equipped to take resident schoolgirls—daughters of wealthy barons—there to learn embroidery, etiquette, and, those with liberal-minded fathers, to read and write Latin and work basic sums so that they could someday capably run a household. St. Amelia's also used to house widows with money and no place to go and women seeking sanctuary from abusive husbands or fathers who could afford to stay there—a feminine haven, free of men and male dominance.

They had once been a thriving community of nearly sixty souls. Now there were only eleven, including Mother Winifred herself. The rest were seven veiled sisters, two elderly noblewomen who had been there for too many years to move to the new convent, and Andrew the elderly caretaker, raised at the convent from infancy when he had been left at the gate in a basket.

It was because of the new convent ten miles away, built five years ago and housing a relic far more important than the bones of a saint, that St. Amelia's was dying. The other convent was attracting the novices, lady guests, schoolgirls in search of instruction, pilgrims, and travelers, all filling the rooms and money coffers of the Convent of the True Cross. Winifred tried not to think of the empty writing desks in her scriptorium, the inkwells long since gone dry, and the remaining sisters who toiled over the illuminations and who, like herself, were growing old. The priory of St. Amelia had lost pupils and novices to the Convent of the True Cross because there had been reports of miraculous healings over there: wives getting pregnant, barons coming into fortunes. The abbot had told Winifred that it had been a long time since St. Amelia had performed a miracle. But Winifred thought Amelia performed miracles every day—just look at the illuminations!

Nonetheless, the pilgrims had stopped coming. How could one compete with the True Cross? Pilgrims rarely visited *both* shrines— when one treks many miles for a blessing or a cure, one will choose a splinter from the tree of Christ's suffering over the bones of a woman—and so St. Amelia's was bypassed more and more each year.

And finally, who could compete with youth and wealth? Winifred was in her fifties with no family left. When her rich and politically connected brother had still been alive, her place was secure. But he was dead now, her sisters and brothers-in-law all dead, her family penniless and just about gone. The new convent, however, was supported by the new prioress's father, Oswald of Mercia, who was very rich and very generous. And of course, it had the full support of the abbey.

Portminster Abbey, set high on a hill overlooking the small town of Portminster and the River Fenn, had its origins in a Roman garrison established in 84 c.e. on the east coast of England that had grown into a port town aptly named Portus, famous for its protected harbor and trade in eels, an industry that continued into Winifred's day. In the fourth century, the remains of St. Amelia had been brought from Rome to Portminster by Christians seeking refuge from persecution by Emperor Diocletian. A group of hermit monks, living in a *monasterium* outside of Portus, embraced the fugitive saint and gave her refuge. Over the centuries Anglo-Saxon influence corrupted the word *"monasterium"* to *"mynster,"* and when a newly built church went up, it was given the name Portus Mynster. In the year 822, Danes pillaged and burned Portminster, but the remains of St. Amelia were once again rescued and hidden away in a small community of holy sisters who lived in a priory that hugged the end of a forgotten Roman road.

A century later, when Benedictine monks arrived and built an abbey at Portminster, there was debate over what to do with the bones of St. Amelia. Finally, it was decided they should be allowed to remain at the modest priory because by then a reputation had already been established about the miracles the blessed saint performed, drawing pilgrims and visitors from far and wide. Patron saint of chest ailments, Amelia was said to cure everything from pneumonia to heart failure— some even went so far as to declare that the blessed saint cured other afflictions of the heart, namely lovesickness. As a result, the priory had grown in fame and wealth. At the same time Portminster Abbey, which was eight miles away and governed the priory, had gained a stunning reputation of its own for producing exquisite illuminated manuscripts.

As the nuns sang the religious chant for terce Winifred's eyes strayed to the altar where the small reliquary containing St. Amelia's bones stood. She pictured her imagined altarpiece behind it: a triptych of three wooden panels with gilt edging, each four arms' lengths tall, three arms' lengths wide. In the first she would depict Amelia's conversion to Christianity; in the second her missions to the sick and poor; and lastly, Amelia clasping her bosom as she commanded her heart to stop in her breast before the Roman soldiers could force her to denounce her faith.

Winifred's eyes moved up to the dusty scaffolding that embraced the ceiling above the altar. The struts and braces had been erected five years earlier, when the abbot had promised roof repairs. However, with the opening of the new convent, and all of Oswald's money pouring in that direction, the abbot had seen this repair project as a waste and it was called off. But the workmen had left the wooden scaffolding, and to Winifred its presence was almost a mockery.

As the sisters lifted their voices in the "*Salve Regina*," Winifred glimpsed a shadow on the other side of the screen meant to separate civilians from the nuns. It was Andrew. "The abbot's at the end of the path," he said quietly, his eyes round with worry.

"Thank you, Andrew," she murmured. "Go and admit him through the gate."

Leaving the sisters at their song, Winifred hurried across the cloister to the kitchen where a gray-haired woman in a plain gown was stirring porridge over a fire. She was Dame Mildred, who had come to the convent twenty-five years earlier upon the death of her husband. As none of her children had survived to adulthood, and her own relations were dead and buried, she had adopted the community of nuns as her family. When her fortune ran out and she could no longer pay for her keep, she happily took up duties as cook, and had long since forgotten that she had once been a knight's lady. "We shall need ale for the abbot," Winifred said. "And something to eat."

"Dear me, why has he come? It is too soon!"

Although Dame Mildred had been given an order to fetch ale, she left her station and followed Winifred to the visitor's gate where they both anxiously watched the abbot's approach.

"Reverend Mother!" Mildred said in sudden joy. "Look! Father Abbot brings a brace of pheasants!" Her face fell. "No, 'tis but one pheasant. There are eleven of us, hardly enough to go around, and if the bishop should decide to sup with us . . ."

"Do not worry. We shall manage."

Mother Winifred watched the abbot's progress as he rode his fine horse down the garden path. She could tell by his posture that her fears had been justified. The abbot carried more than holy books in his rucksack. He also carried bad news.

God's blessings upon you, Mother Prioress," he called out as he dismounted his fine horse.

"And upon you, Father Abbot." Mother Winifred eyed the paltry pheasant, thinking that there would be no generous supper tonight, while at the same time the abbot discreetly sniffed the air but detected no enticing cooking aromas. He remembered a day when he could look forward to Winifred's famous *blankmanger*, which she personally made from chicken paste blended with boiled rice, almond milk, sugar, and anise. She used to cook delicious fish dumplings and fritters that made one's eyes water. And her plum tarts . . . He sighed at the memories. Sadly, those days were gone. Now, if he stayed to dine, he could expect stale bread, thin soup, wilted cabbage, and beans that would make him fart into next week.

Together they entered the chapter house with stomachs growling.

As they walked they spoke of the weather and other inconsequential things, "roundabout topics," as the prioress thought of them, for she knew the abbot well enough to know when he was putting off distasteful news, and while they talked Winifred's keen eye did not miss the fact that the abbot was wearing new robes. His cloak, though black, fairly dazzled in the sun, as did the shiny spot on his scalp where his hair had been shaved for a tonsure. She also noticed that his girth had expanded since she last saw him, a mere two weeks ago.

But foremost on her mind was the purpose of this unexpected visit, the subject he was avoiding. He needn't bother, she already knew what the bad news was: there would be no repairs to the roof again this year. She and her sisters were to suffer another winter of buckets and pans and soaked beds.

Perhaps she could turn this dismal visit to her advantage. Delivering such disappointing news, the abbot could hardly follow it up with a refusal of her request to paint the altarpiece. She would appeal to whatever grain of charity dwelled in his heart.

Winifred believed in the Bible to the letter, but with room for interpretation. While she believed that God had created men *first*, she didn't believe he had created them *smarter*. Nonetheless, she had taken vows of obedience and so obey the abbot she would—within reason. If he could not give her a new roof, then he must acquiesce on the subject of the altarpiece. She deserved that much consideration. At nearly sixty Winifred was one of the oldest women she knew. She was in fact older than most men she knew—older certainly than Father Abbot—and she thought that this alone entitled her to special privilege.

As they entered the chapter house, a drafty hall furnished with straight backed chairs and dominated by an enormous sooty fireplace, Winifred asked the abbot if he had brought willow bark tea. "It is not the first time I have made this request, Father Abbot."

As he lowered his bulk into the one comfortable chair, the abbot wondered if Winifred wore her wimple too tight or if her face was naturally pinched like that. Then he caught a glimpse of her hands and could tell by the blue-black stains that she had spent the morning gathering woad leaves. The shrubby broad-leafed herb, which contained the raw material of a blue dyestuff, was an excellent substitute for the imported Indian indigo that went into the nuns' pigments but which was rare and expensive.

"You must not think of your comfort, Mother Winifred," he chastised gently.

Her lips firmed into a hard line. "I was thinking of Sister Agatha's arthritis. The pain is so bad she can hardly hold a paintbrush. If my sisters cannot paint . . ." she said, leaving the threat to hang in the air.

"Very well. I shall send willow bark tea as soon as I return to the abbey."

"And meat. My sisters need to eat. They need their strength to work," she said significantly.

He scowled. He knew what she was up to. Winifred had a way of holding her illuminations hostage in exchange for creature comforts. But he was in no bargaining position. Demand for the illuminations was growing, although he took great care not to let Winifred know this.

It would be incorrect to say that Abbot Edman hated women. He simply saw no purpose to them and wondered why God, in His infinite wisdom, had chosen to create such an adversarial means for reproducing His children. For Edman was convinced that men and women would never, into eternity, learn to get along. If it were not for women, Adam would have stayed in Eden and all men would be living in Paradise right now. Unfortunately, England was no paradise and this convent fell under his purview as abbot of Portminster and so it was his duty to pay regular visits. But he never lingered, getting the business over with and departing as quickly as politeness allowed.

As he tried to relax in this thoroughly feminine atmosphere—why did women have such a frivolous passion for flowers?—he thought of the brothers in his order who had difficulty holding to their vow of celibacy. Edman was celibate, although as a priest it was not required of him. Most priests were married, which was beyond his comprehension, and more amazing was the incident back in 964 when Bishop Ethelwold gave the married priests at Winchester Cathedral the choice of keeping their wives or their jobs, and to a man they chose their wives. Celibacy had never been a problem for Edman because he had never had any desire to enter into a carnal state with a female, and it was completely beyond his comprehension why any man of reason would want to. Born into poverty with only the vaguest memories of his mother and orphaned early upon the death of his fisherman father, Edman had survived in the port town by wit and cunning, and allowing himself to be used as a work animal by farm women and fishwives. He had received more undeserved clouts to his head than he could count, which taught him that there was no compassion or tenderness in any woman alive. It was only the kindness of a local priest, who taught him to read and write, that had rescued Edman from a life of humiliation and grinding desperation. He entered the holy orders and with ambition, a quick mind, and the ability to make the right friends, had climbed the clerical ladder until he now headed an illustrious abbey and a prosperous order of Benedictine scribes.

Thus he chafed at these obligatory visits to St. Amelia's priory. Certainly it could be carried out by an underling, and he had in fact once sent one of his subordinates to the convent to pick up an illuminated manuscript. Mother Winifred had been so affronted that she had said the manuscript wasn't finished and as much as insinuated that it would not be until the abbot himself came to collect it. The creature had a strange way of being obedient and defiant at the same time. But on some issues Edman stood firm—her request to paint an altarpiece, for instance—and on this she acquiesced to his orders. Thank God, for the abbot could not spare the time she would spend on St. Amelia when her arts were needed to fill the growing demand for illuminations.

Still, despite his distaste for visiting the convent, he had to concede that places like this served a useful purpose. Many an unwanted female was sent away to a convent to live out her life respectably, in safety and without being troublesome to their menfolk. And of course there were the creatures who preferred the company of their own kind, women who bridled at having to obey men, women who thought themselves the equal or superior to men, women who had the strange notion that they could think for themselves. Convents therefore served the purposes of both men and women alike. The abbot just wished the creatures weren't so fanatical about cleanliness. The smell of honest sweat never hurt anyone, but Winifred and her coterie always reeked, like all highborn ladies, of sweet lavender and tansy, which they strew on their mattresses to keep fleas away.

"How was your visit to Canterbury, Father Abbot?" Mother Winifred asked, not at all interested and hoping his response would not be too long winded. She could tell by his bulging rucksack that he had brought more work for her sisters, which meant she must get to the business of preparing fresh pigments.

Edman thought so hard that he squinted. At Canterbury Cathedral he had witnessed a strange sight. Something called a play in which men dressed in costume and acted out a story. It had been held as part of the Easter services and was a new invention by the priests there. When a monk dressed as the Devil came onto the stage, the congregation had erupted in fear and fury and had nearly killed the poor man when they rushed at him. The argument went that such enactments would help people learn Bible stories more easily, but the abbot had reservations. If people could simply *watch* a story, then would they stop listening to sermons? Would educated men stop reading the Bible? Perhaps this "play" thing would not catch on. He certainly had no intention of putting on such enactments in his abbey.

He wondered if the plays were a sign of the changing times. Although, there was a day, just twenty-two years ago, when the Church had thought times were going to change so drastically as to literally herald the end of the world.

What a disappointment the millennium had turned out to be. All the buildup and hysteria, the feasts and orgies, people flocking to the abbot for confession, the suicides and doomsayers, everyone thinking Jesus was coming back and the world was about to end. And the endless debates! Do we count a thousand years from the birth of Christ, or from his death? Did the millennium mark the second coming of Christ, or the beginning of Satan's reign? Was the Muslims' destruction of the Holy Sepulcher in Jerusalem a sign? But that event had occurred in 1009. Could nine years later still be the millennium? Abbot Edman, at the time a young clergyman, had joined the Peace of God movement in an effort to curb the rampaging of feudal lords. Of course, Judgment Day fever had had its benefits. A wealthy baron in the county had given all his lands and wealth to Portminster Abbey and headed off to spend millennium eve in the Vatican dressed in sackcloth and ashes. And then, the morning of January first of the year 1000—nothing. Just another cold morning with the usual aches and pains and flatulence.

"My journey went well, God be thanked," he finally said, hoping these inanities weren't leading up to her request to paint the blasted altarpiece again—such a tiresome subject. No matter how many times he told her that it was out of the question. Didn't she know that to go against an abbot's will was to go against God's?

Of course she knew it, which was why she never disobeyed. The woman was a model of Christian compliance, although she did use the occasion of confession to sneak her little rebellions in. "I am guilty of the sin of hunger," she would murmur through the screen in the confessional, "and wish Father Abbot would provide more food for my sisters and myself." He would ignore the gibe and order three Our Fathers for the sin of gluttony.

But the abbot's annoyance was tempered with pity. Poor Winifred. As soon as word had spread about the new convent and its generous amenities, there had been an embarrassing exodus of nuns, lady guests, and pupils from St. Amelia's. But how could it be otherwise? Winifred was hardly known for her bountiful table. She was parsimonious with wood and coal, and didn't allow pets. The lady guests often complained to him of lacking conditions. And now they were comfortably housed in the new place where fires kept out the cold and the supper table groaned with meat and wine. Poor Winifred was left here in these drafty rooms with a meager, loyal following. Were it not for their continued production of fabulous illuminations, he would have closed down this old place long ago.

Dame Mildred had baked honeyed oatcakes, a much needed healthful treat for the sisters. But because the pantry was low on both oats and honey, she had made precisely eleven walnut-size cakes, one for each of the sisters and one for Andrew, the caretaker. Since she could not allow Mother Prioress the embarrassment of not offering something to the abbot, she brought the plate out, thinking that she would sacrifice her own oat cake that the abbot might know their hospitality. To her shock, and to Mother Winifred's, the Abbot scooped up three of the cakes at once and popped them into his mouth. They watched his jaw and cheeks work away at the precious oats and honey, and when he gave a great swallow, reached for three more. The cakes were gone in no time and Mother Winifred was filled with outrage.

As Father Edman washed down the rather tasteless cakes with a cup of weak ale, he did not miss the glance exchanged between the two women. He ignored it. The abbot made no apologies for his appetite, for he believed that God wanted his servants to be well fed. How could he expect to make converts to Christianity if he were a scarecrow himself? Would not the pagan say, "How good can your Christ be if he lets his children starve?" And Abbot Edman was serious in his evangelizing, for although England had all the outward markings of Christendom, the Abbot was only too aware that many folk still worshipped trees and stone circles. Ancient superstitions and heathen ways lay beneath a very thin surface of pretended piety and so the fight for men's souls was a never-ending battle. He saw himself as Christ's warrior, and everyone knew that soldiers must eat.

Wiping his fingers on his habit, he got down to the business at hand and reached into his carrying bag for the new pages that needed capital letters. He had also brought a book for Winifred to illuminate—it was yet another sign of the changing times that people other than the clergy were starting to show an interest in books. "The patron wishes to have his picture on the front page, dressed in armor and seated atop his horse with shield and jousting staff. He wishes his lady to be illustrated at the beginning of one of the psalms."

Winifred nodded. This was a common request. She usually chose Psalm 101 for a gentleman's lady. In Latin it began with the letter "D," which lent just the right shape and room for a human figure. Plus the opening phrase, translated into English, was, "I will sing of your love," which the ladies always liked.

Although a variety of books was currently being illuminated in England and Europe, from Gospels and liturgical books to works from the Old Testament and the collections of ancient authors copied from Carolingian copyists, Father Edman's regional specialty was psalters—psalm books—decorated with biblical scenes and of a quality found nowhere else in England, thanks to Winifred. The decoration was executed in a lively style, with human figures in animated postures and wearing fluttering draperies. Since Winifred had been schooled as a girl by an artist trained in the Winchester style of illumination, her artwork was manifested in rich blue and green coloring, sumptuous borders of leaf ornamentation and animals, but she had also added her own trademark style in the spiral patterns, interlacing, knotwork, and intertwined animals reminiscent of Celtic metalwork.

Competition among the book-producing centers was fierce, each rival abbey or cathedral wanting its books to be the most popular among kings and nobles. But illumination manufacture was slow, with most cathedrals and monasteries producing only two books a year. It was one of Edman's predecessors who had hit upon the idea of putting the nuns of St. Amelia's to work, for with their smaller hands, keener eyesight, and gift for detail, they could labor over capital letters while the monks churned out the main text. Pride had kept that former abbot from revealing that the artwork was done by women and so everyone thought it was the monks of Portminster Abbey who produced such miraculous artwork and at such phenomenal speeds. "They work at the speed of God," the abbot liked to say.

But now there was a problem: no new novices were coming to St. Amelia's and the original artist-nuns were dying off. It was the bishop who had come up with a solution. And a reasonable and brilliant solution it was, Edman thought, but he knew Winifred would not see it that way.

He had to move carefully next, for he had no idea how she was going to react to what he had to say. There was that rebellious streak in her to be minded. If he did not handle her with care, all could be lost. And the abbot was an ambitious man. To govern an abbey was a measure of success, to be sure, but he felt destined for greater things. A new cathedral was being built at Portminster, which meant a bishop would be installed there. Father Edman intended to be that bishop. But much of his success depended upon Winifred's continued production of illuminations.

While the abbot had been devouring cakes meant to feed eleven, Winifred sent for the completed manuscripts to be brought to the Chapter House. Edman now examined them. As always, the colors were breathtaking and alive. He could swear that if you touched the red you would feel a pulse, that if you sniffed the yellow you would smell buttercups. The abbot found it a strange irony that Winifred herself should be so dour and colorless while her creations were breathtakingly vibrant.

He did not praise the work—he never did, and Winifred never expected it. But she saw the admiration nonetheless in his eyes and felt a moment of pride. Therefore she thought this would be a good time to bring up her request once more to paint an altarpiece.

He patiently listened to her explanation—"I wish to give St. Amelia something in return for all she has given me"—but he already intended to turn her down. Edman couldn't afford to have Winifred take on a project that would take months—precious time stolen from teaching young nuns how to do illuminations.

He cleared his throat and tried to sound as if he had given her request serious thought. "I am sure St. Amelia feels you have done enough in her service all these years, Mother Prioress."

"Then why can I not stop thinking about the altarpiece? It is in my mind day and night."

"Perhaps you need to pray on it," he suggested.

"I have done, and the only response I seem to get is more thoughts about the altarpiece. I even dream of it now. I feel the hand of God directing me."

He pursed his lips. This was dangerous thinking, that a woman take her orders directly from God. What if *all* women got this notion? Then wives would not obey husbands, daughters would not obey fathers and society would be thrown into chaos.

"As it turns out, Mother Prioress, St. Amelia's will not have any use for an altarpiece."

Her nearly nonexistent eyebrows arched. "How so?"

"I am afraid," he cleared his throat again, nervously this time, "that St. Amelia's is to be closed down."

She stared at him. Silence descended over the chapter house. Through heavy doors came the sound of whispering footsteps. Finally she said, "What do you mean?"

He stiffened his spine. "I mean, Mother Winifred, that these old buildings are beyond redemption and a waste of good money to attempt repairs. I have conferred with the Bishop and he agrees that you and your sisters should be relocated to the Convent of the True Cross and this place closed up."

"But our work—the illuminations."

"That will carry on, of course. And you will teach your skills to a younger generation of nuns that they can continue the tradition."

She went numb. Of all the possible bad news she had anticipated, this had not even brushed her mind. "And what of St. Amelia?"

"She will be given her own chapel in the new cathedral at Portminster."

*T*he hour was late, the chapel stood empty and silent, except for a lone figure illuminated by the flickering of a single candle. Winifred, on her knees.

She had never known such despair. The day that had started out with so much color and promise was now as bleak as an English winter. To be moved from the only home she knew! To have to start, at this late stage in her life, to teach a lifetime of skills and knowledge to young girls. To have to tell her own dear, elderly sisters that they were to be relocated to unfamiliar lodgings where they were going to have to adjust, after years of familiar routine, to new ways and customs. How could such a thing have come to pass? Did not decades of servitude count for anything?

But the worst, oh the worst, was to be separated from her blessed saint.

For most of her life Winifred had prayed daily to St. Amelia. She never started or ended a day without a dialogue with Amelia. Winifred had never traveled far from the priory because she didn't like to go far from her saint. It was Amelia who gave her wisdom and strength. Amelia was more than a woman who had died a thousand years ago, she was the mother Winifred had barely known, the daughter she never had, the sisters she had buried in the church graveyard. And now, as she sat alone in the chapel amid flickering candlelight and silent stone walls, Winifred was being forced to say good-bye. She felt as if she sat at the brink of a great, terrifying abyss.

"Father Abbot," she had managed to say when she recovered from hearing the shocking news, "I have lived here for over four decades. I know no other home. Here was where blessed St. Amelia gifted me with my talent for painting. How can I leave? If I am separated from St. Amelia I shall lose my gift."

"Nonsense," the abbot had said. "Your gift comes from God. And you can still visit St. Amelia at the cathedral now and then."

Visit St. Amelia now and then. *I shall perish . . .*

Now her heart was torn in conflict. From infancy she had been taught to obey father, husband, priest, church. But there were times in her life when she had felt she possessed better sense and could make better decisions than others. Take the midnight of the millennium for example: Father Edman's predecessor had ordered her and her sisters to go to Portminster Abbey to pray, and to be safe. But Winifred had felt strongly that they were safer with St. Amelia and so she had disobeyed the abbot. As it happened, hysteria had broken out at the abbey on New Year's Eve, there was a riot and people had been seriously injured because the abbot had not handled it well. His own panic over the impending millennium had merely inflamed the already impressionable people. Yet, because of Winifred's willful disobedience, her sisters and lady guests had been spared.

But what was she to do in this case? The issues were less clearly defined. She lifted her eyes to the reliquary on the altar, glowing dully in the candlelight. The burden of governing and caring for sixty nuns, lady guests and pupils, plus overseeing daily the physical and spiritual needs of flocks of pilgrims had not been half as great as the responsibility she now faced for her diminished family of eleven.

Winifred experienced a moment of bitter recrimination: it wasn't really about closing down an antiquated place, she thought, because with a bit of money and a bit of fixing up, St. Amelia's could be self-sufficient again. It was about women outgrowing their usefulness, for what the abbot wanted was for Winifred to start teaching the younger sisters how to paint illuminations. "Let Agnes and Edith rest their weary hands and enjoy their final days in peace. Let younger hands take on the burden of work," he had said. And she had argued that her sisters loved their labors and that to take them away would be to rob these women of their reason for breathing. But the abbot had refused to listen.

It made Winifred feel ancient and decayed, a useless discard, like a broken sewing needle. Age counted for nothing; youth was all. And like a rotten pile of leaves must be swept aside to allow for new, green growth to bud up from the ground, so must she and her aged sisters be swept aside.

For the first time in decades, Winifred was on the verge of despair. This sweet, humble priory had survived three centuries of storms, floods, fires, and even Viking raids. Now it was being toppled by a splinter of wood!

Suddenly fearful that her thoughts were sacrilegious—for it was no ordinary sliver of wood the new convent housed!—Winifred clasped her hands together and cried, "O blessed Amelia, I have never asked you for anything." It was true. While people came to the saint for favors and cures and answers to wishes, Mother Winifred, the saint's caretaker for forty years, had only ever offered prayers of thanks. But now she had a request, and it wasn't a material one, she wasn't seeking relief from physical pain or asking for love advice or a husband—what Winifred begged for now was guidance. "Tell me what to do."

Forty years of self-control finally gave way. "Please help me!" she cried and did something she had never done before, she threw herself upon the altar and clasped the silver reliquary to her bosom.

Realizing in horror what she had done—the reliquary was only ever touched with a feather duster—she quickly righted herself from the altar, mumbling apologies and making the sign of the cross, and in so doing caught her foot on the hem of her habit. Suddenly sent off balance, she grabbed for a handhold, clutching at the altar cloth without meaning to and, in falling, brought everything down with her—flowers, candlesticks, reliquary, and all.

She hit the stone steps with a painful shock, did a half roll, banging her head so that she was knocked momentarily out of her senses. When her head cleared a minute later, Winifred found herself supine on the altar steps, her glazed eyes staring at the scaffolding overhead, a sharp pain in her skull. When she tried to move, she found her right arm pinned under a weight.

The reliquary. Which had broken open.

And the saint's bones lay exposed for the first time in nearly a thousand years.

Winifred shot to her feet and whispered, "Mother of God!" as she stared in horror at the defiled relics.

Her heart thumped wildly as she tried to think what she must do. Had desecration taken place? Was there a special ritual for the replacement of saint's bones? The abbot. She must let Father Abbot know at once.

And then something stopped her. Checking her impulse to run from the chapel, Mother Winifred slowly lowered herself to her knees and gazed in wonder at the delicate objects strewn on the steps. Like seashells, they were, or tiny rocks found in a stream—fragile and vulnerable, a fingerbone here, a slender armbone there. To her amazement, the skeleton, for the most part, was complete, although all ajumble now, and crumbling to dust. The skull was still connected to the neck, the neck to the collarbones. The ribs had collapsed long ago, and the pelvis was in a hundred pieces. But it was the neck that now drew Winifred's attention, for there was something about the bones there . . .

She bent closer and squinted in the dim light of the chapel. At the base of the skull where the first two vertebrae joined . . .

Her eyes widened. Scrambling to her feet, she seized the lit candle and brought it down to the bones. She held her breath as she watched how the flickering flame danced on the pale bones and caught the tiniest, strangest glint within them.

She frowned. Bones weren't supposed to sparkle.

She brought the candle closer and bent nearer, narrowing her eyes, focusing, delving into the crack between the two vertebrae. A draft whispered through the chapel, making the flame dance, causing the glimmer to happen again. It was like the spark one sees when striking a flint, she thought.

What was it?

An eerie feeling crept over her as she knelt alone in the silent chapel with the thousand-year-old bones. Winifred suddenly had the strongest notion that she was no longer alone. She looked around and saw that the chapel was empty. No one, no *thing*, lurked there. Yet the hair beneath the back of her wimple stirred as if to stand on end; her neck crawled as if someone breathed upon it.

Someone *was* there.

And then she knew. All in an instant, in the most astonishing mental clarity she had ever experienced in her life: it was St. Amelia, wakened from her long sleep by the disturbing of her bones.

"Please forgive me," Winifred whispered tremulously as she tried to think how to gather up the pieces and replace them to the reliquary. It would have to be done as religiously and reverently as possible— and without anyone knowing. This much she knew for certain: that the bones had been meant for her alone to see, and no one else. It was a sign. St. Amelia was trying to tell her something.

When the candle flame flickered again and once more caused a spark within the neck bones, Winifred reached out a trembling hand and, with outstretched forefinger, gingerly touched the dry, chalky spine. The vertebrae fell apart, so old and desiccated they were. And as they fell away, like the halves of a walnut, they exposed an object of such astonishing wonder that Winifred, with a cry, fell backward and landed on her buttocks.

For imbedded in Saint Amelia's neckbones was the most beautiful blue stone Winifred had ever seen.

*S*he kept it with her, secretively, hidden in a deep pocket of her habit. The blue crystal from St. Amelia's throat. She told no one about it, after restoring the bones to the reliquary and the reliquary to the altar, for she needed to ponder the mystery she had uncovered. Why was the crystal there? How it had gotten lodged in the saint's neck bones? And was it a sign from St. Amelia? But what else could it be? The bones had been sealed in their reliquary for centuries, for a thousand years for all Winifred knew, why should they have chosen that moment to reveal themselves? The answer was obvious: after the abbot left, she had been filled with such utter despair that she could have believed the sun would never rise again. And then Amelia had spoken through the blue crystal.

But what was the message? Did it have to do with the move to the new convent? If so, was Amelia telling her to go, or to stay? Nothing had ever weighed so heavily upon Winifred's mind and heart as this new turn of events. The women in her charge were depending on her to make the right decision.

And they were all so helpless! There was poor Dame Odelyn, elderly and lame, waiting by the well for someone to come along and draw water for her. Odelyn had come to St. Amelia's long ago when a Viking raid had wiped out her entire family. Heirloom jewelry, hidden in the well behind the manor house, had bought her a permanent residency at the convent. But ever since that day when she had had to climb down to retrieve the treasure hidden there by her father, barely able to make the descent for she had just crept out of her hiding place and seen the butchered corpses of parents and siblings, Odelyn had been terrified of wells. And then there was Sister Edith who was so forgetful that she had to be escorted out to the *necessarium* every night because she always lost her way. And Agatha whose arthritis was sometimes so bad she needed assistance in eating. The list was endless. How could Winifred tell these women that they were to be uprooted from the only life they knew, from all that was comforting and familiar, to be thrown into strange and unfamiliar surroundings?

In searching for the answer to her conundrum, she focused on the blue crystal. She became obsessed with its colors and tried to recreate them when she mixed pigments. Holding the semitransparent stone up to light she saw explosions of cyan, ribbons of sky blue and cornflower, lakes of sapphire, ponds of aquamarine. But the color kept changing. She looked at it in sunlight and candlelight, during a storm and at sunset, and she saw azure, turquoise, marine blue, ultramarine, lapis, navy, indigo, teal. Winifred was fascinated by the color and composition of the crystal. The stone was not entirely transparent for there was a clouding in the heart, a gathering of particles that sparkled when the sun caught them just right. Whitish silver, taking a different shape depending upon which angle one observed it. She suspended the crystal on a fine thread and let it twirl slowly in the sunlight. The soul-substance seemed to move and change. It was mesmerizing. As

Winifred stared, she almost believed she saw the phantom of a woman there, beckoning . . .

She would have liked to capture it on parchment but that would take a miracle, for where on earth was she going to find such blues, such light and transparency, such liquid hues?

"You did not touch your breakfast," Dame Mildred said with great concern after the sisters had left the rectory for the scriptorium. It was unlike frugal Mother Winifred not to clean her plate; she had not even drunk her morning tonic. Winifred believed in the age-old health practice of chasing winter out of one's blood by drinking a concoction of seven spring herbs. Ever since her days as a young novice she had annually revitalized her body by drinking a tea made from burdock root, violet leaves, stinging nettles, mustard leaves, dandelion leaves, daylily shoots, and wild onion. Foul tasting but so invigorating. "You've been out of sorts since the abbot's visit."

Dame Mildred had always reminded Winifred of the small lap dogs that ladies preferred, the kind that could be carried in a sleeve and that peered out with big, liquid eyes. Winifred suspected that nothing eluded Mildred's notice, especially as her domain was so central to the convent. Sisters came to her with their ailments and woes, asking for liniments, tonics, cures, and bracing nourishment. Dame Mildred was a tiny woman, but sharper for all her size than the cumbersome abbot. "Was his news so upsetting?" she pressed.

"We are not to have our new roof this year," Winifred finally said. It wasn't the entire truth, but it wasn't a lie either. She hadn't told her sisters the bad news yet, wanting to pray on it. She had bought a little time by telling the abbot that her nuns would not be able to work on the latest manuscripts if they knew about the impending transfer to the new convent, and so he had given her two month's grace period, after that time the move must take place. In the meantime, Winifred pondered the miracle and mystery of the blue crystal, and tried to discover its message.

Leaving Dame Mildred with a skeptical look on her face, Winifred went to the scriptorium where the sisters were already at work, silent and reverent, creating biblical scenes of such glorious color and vibrancy that they would be the talk of England. The pigments were the secret of creating remarkable illuminations. What good, after all, was the artist's skill when inferior paints were used? But now they were low on supplies, and what was there was of poor quality. Winifred

had tried to wrest some coins from the abbot for the purchase of new
supplies, and he had refused her request, knowing that she would work
miracles with what little they had, as she had always done in the past.

Winifred thought now of the new ring she had not failed to notice
on the abbot's hand. A gift from a patron of the abbey, no doubt.
The value of that one piece of jewelry could have kept her nuns in
the best quality pigments for a year, perhaps she could have even
purchased malachite from which to create breathtaking greens. But
she and her sisters must be satisfied with obtaining greens from buckthorn and mulberry, and if really pressed, from the berries of honeysuckle and nightshade leaves. Probably they were going to have to
resort to the juice of iris flowers, which was a delicate process and
took patience and skill. The dark blue flowers did not appear to be a
likely source of green for the purplish color that was first squeezed out
was not promising. But as soon as it was combined with alum a clear
and beautiful green appeared. The secret, Winifred knew, was to remove all the pollen.

Was it fair that the abbot, with his beautiful ring, should force her
sisters to go through so much extra work?

And clearly they were going to have to make their yellows from
apple-tree bark this year. If only she could afford saffron. Saffron was
the indispensable element for imitating gold. A pinch of dry saffron
in a dish, covered with egg white and allowed to infuse, produced a
beautifully transparent strong yellow. Winifred liked to use this glassy
saffron to strong effect for ornamental pen flourishings around colored
initials, for goldlike frameworks of illuminated panels in books, and
for golden glazes and touches in lines of writing in red and black.

But they had no saffron, and the abbot had a beautiful ruby ring!

She nearly cried out with frustration and despair. The abbot expected her to make silk from sows' ears, and now she was to teach
all that she knew to young nuns! Not just how to draw or paint or
make pigments, but how to purchase the ingredients and keep from
being swindled. Did the abbot not see that during this learning process
the students were going to turn out very poor illuminations? Could
he not anticipate that the reputation of his books was going to suffer
until the skill of the novices had reached the level of excellence of
the very sisters he was determined to put out to pasture? His lack of
foresight infuriated her. Typical of most men, she thought sourly, the

abbot thought only of today. Leave tomorrow for the women to worry about.

"Mother Winifred!" Dame Mildred's voice rang out. She came hurrying into the scriptorium, her sandals making slapping sounds on the paving stones. "The gypsy peddler is here! Mr. Ibn-Abu-Aziz-Jaffar!"

Winifred's joy was instantaneous. "Praise God!" she cried. Surely this was another sign from God: just when they are at their lowest in supplies, the Almighty brings the pigment-seller to their door!

"God's blessings, Mr. Jaffar!" she called out as she hurried down the path with her black veils billowing around her.

"And to you, dear lady!" he called back, sweeping his hat from his head and bending with an elegant bow.

A man of foreign origin with an olive complexion and close-cropped silver beard, the peddler always greeted the prioress in a way that made her think of courts and kings. He wore a long robe embroidered with stars and moons; his cap was padded and edged in fringe. He was tall and stately, and though she guessed he must be near sixty, he held his back straight and shoulders square. His old horse drew a most curious wagon, painted with celestial symbols, zodiacal signs, comets, rainbows, unicorns, and large, all-seeing eyes. The peddler was known far and wide as a purveyor of dreams and magic, stardust and hope. People liked the way his name, Ibn-Abu-Aziz-Jaffar, rolled from their lips; children followed his wagon, chanting his name, bringing wives out of their cottages. In reality he was Simon the Levite, and he was a Jew. He told everyone he was from "far off Araby" but had in fact been born in Seville, Spain. To his customers he was a gypsy Christian, but beneath his long robe he wore a tasseled shawl and at night when he was alone he solemnly recited "Hear O Israel." Simon did not hide his identity because of local prejudice (persecution of the Jews would not blossom fully in Europe for another three hundred years, when the Black Death had to be blamed on *someone*), but because he had found he enjoyed playing the exotic persona and the notoriety that went with it. He liked selling mystery and illusion; he delighted in seeing children's faces light up over his prestidigitation and magic, for Simon was himself youthful at heart. He had come to the isle of Britain by accident on a ship bound for Bruges that had been blown off course. When he discovered that he was different—at home he was simply one of many like himself, but here he was unique—he decided to stay, for there was profit in uniqueness. He lived a solitary life, making an annual circuit from London to Hadrian's Wall and back, and looked forward to the day when he could retire in his own small cottage and put old Seska, his faithful companion of fifteen years, out to pasture.

Mr. Ibn-Abu-Aziz-Jaffar had but one weakness that on more than one occasion had nearly been his undoing: he loved women. Be they young or old, fat or thin, slow or quick, he found joy and wondrous mystery in every female he met. He sometimes wondered if this was because he had been one of eight brothers. Females were God's gift to men, he avowed, despite what the Torah said about Lilith and Adam's unfortunate dalliance with her. He loved the softness and smell of them, their mercurial moods, how they could sometimes be weaker than a man, sometimes stronger. Their ferocious instinct of motherhood. Their flirtatious smiles. Their long hair—oh, their long hair. Although Simon was getting on in years, he was not so old that he did not still appreciate a firm thigh, a full bosom, and a warm heart. He never forced or compromised a woman; she came willingly or he would have none of it. But women everywhere were intrigued by foreignness and reasoned in their blessed hearts that a man who had come from so far must know more about the art of love than the local pickings. And the thing was: he did.

He traveled alone and was rarely accosted, for even brigands respected the healer and themselves sometimes needed the fool, or the fortune-teller. Although people could not read, symbols painted on the sides of his wagon advertised his skills as an alchemist, fortune-teller, dentist, magician. He sold and traded everything—buttons, pins, thimbles, and thread, potions and ointments, bottles and spoons—with one exception: he did not deal in relics and religious goods. For Simon the Levite belonged to that rarest of breeds: he was an honest peddler. Therefore he left the selling of saints' hair and teeth and bone to charlatans and priests and sometimes thought there was no difference between the two. He also harbored his own private opinion of the splinter of the True Cross that was housed in the new convent up the road, for he had encountered other such splinters in his travels across Spain and France, and had heard tell of others throughout Europe and in the Holy Land, and decided that the mental calculations of any idiot would reveal that all so-called splinters of the True Cross laid end to end would reach the moon.

He recalled the madness that had gripped England twenty-two years ago when something called the millennium was supposed to have occurred. It puzzled Simon for there was no thousand-year mark according to the calendar of the Jews, nor to the calendar of their racial brethren the Muslims, who reckoned their years from the time of Muhammad. Had that meant only a third of the world was to come to an end while the rest went on as before? It turned out to be a moot question for the significant midnight came and went without incident, and now priests were declaring it was the *next* millennium, a thousand years hence in the impossible-to-imagine year 2000, that Jesus and his angels were to descend.

As Simon traveled the English countryside, he was many things to many people, but whenever he stopped by the priory of St. Amelia near the river Fenn he was himself. He admired the prioress and knew that she saw through his sham and recognized and respected his wisdom and learning. And so off came the fringed hat, away went his wand and mystical gestures. But he kept the wizard's robe on because he thought it lent him dignity.

It had been a year since he last came this way and the reduction in the nuns' circumstances alarmed him: the tumbledown walls, the fields gone to seed, the absence of geese or hens, weeds growing over a path that had once been trampled smooth by the feet of pilgrims. He had known the new convent was growing in popularity, but he had not thought the nearby abbey would abandon these women so. Surely the fat abbot could see that these devout sisters needed food on their table and ale in their cups.

When Winifred saw the white-toothed smile in the olive face, she realized she was very happy to see Mr. Jaffar. Winifred was very unworldly, having been born twenty miles from the priory and never in her life having traveled farther than that. She knew a rudimentary Latin and had read the Bible, but that was the extent of her reading. Winifred and her sisters knew nothing of the rest of the world, only what they heard from pilgrims and travelers. And since both had stopped coming to St. Amelia's, the visits of Mr. Ibn-Abu-Aziz-Jaffar were so much more precious, for the itinerant tinker brought news and gossip.

He was a strange man, almost repellent in his foreignness, yet pos-

sessing a curiously compelling personality. Had she allowed herself
such worldly thoughts, she would have noted that he was very handsome. While Winifred suspected he was not a Christian, she knew he
had the highest respect for God. And he had a way sometimes of
saying things that lit small candles in her mind. Mr. Jaffar was unlike
the other peddlers who came this way. Those men were filthy and
thieving and unrefined, whereas Mr. Jaffar was clean and graceful,
with a foreign charm. More than anything, he was trustworthy.

In the past, other merchants of pigment materials had swindled
her. Inexpensive azurite was easy to pass off as costly lapis lazuli. To
tell them apart with certainty the stones had to be heated red hot:
azurite turned black, lapis remained unchanged. Azurite was purchased as a powder, and there were swindlers who put sand into the
ground pigment to increase the weight for sale and it was the ruin of
the color. Likewise, dishonest dealers would put all the best blue at
the top of the bag and the poorer quality at the bottom. Not so Mr.
Jaffar who now opened a box on the side of his wagon and displayed
such richness of paint materials that she eyed them as if they were
platters at a feast.

"The good Lord has brought you at a most propitious time, Mr.
Jaffar, for my sisters and I are in need of fresh supplies. We are desperate for yellows."

To her delight he produced gallstones.

Winifred reached into a deep pocket and brought out the water-
filled glass globe she used to magnify her work. Mr. Jaffar had once
tried to sell her a new invention from Amsterdam—polished glass
called a lens—but she had turned it down as being much too expensive. As Winifred examined the gallstones through the globe, Simon
thought: herein lay the woman's true gift, for Winifred was more than
just talented at drawing and painting, she possessed the most uncanny
sense of color. Beneath her nimble fingers and keen eyes the most
prosaic of elements became the most glorious hues in all of God's
creation. Take the pigment known as sap green, a substitute for ver-
digris, which was rare and expensive. Sap green was made from the
juice of the ripened buckthorn berries mixed with alum and allowed
to thicken by evaporation. The result was an olive color, transparent
and rich. Although other monasteries had mastered the color, Winifred's skill lay in creating durability. Normally, sap green did not last
long, which was evident in poor quality manuscripts made only decades ago. Mother Winifred, however, knew the secret of thickening

the juice just right, and then keeping it in bladders as a dense syrup rather than allowing it to dry. When used thus on a manuscript, the color was not only beautiful to the eye, but durable.

While she took her time looking over the powders and minerals, the raw materials that would create living animals on a page, Simon watched her closely and thought she looked different today. There were shadows on her face, disturbing currents in her eyes. He had always thought the prioress a placid creature, if a bit dour and humorless. He had never thought her capable of being disquieted.

She carefully chose her purchases, then she said, "I have not the money at the moment. I trust you will be in the neighborhood for a few days as is your custom?"

He stroked his impeccably clipped mustache and thought somberly. It was apparent to Simon that the Prioress could not possibly afford the items she had chosen. How was she to pay? Nonetheless, he would not embarrass her by raising the question—Simon knew only too well the importance of keeping one's pride. If only she would see her way to parting with one or two of her illuminated books. Men in London had inquired of him if he could lay hand to Portminster manuscripts. One illuminated book from Winifred and she could have all the pigments she needed. But he knew she would not part with one, for she believed the books belonged to the abbot. "Very well, dear lady, we shall conclude our transaction three days hence." He wondered now if he would be invited in for ale and possibly a cake, and mistakenly took her hesitation to mean she was thinking the same thing. Instead, to his surprise, she asked him if he, being an alchemist, could comment on a rather strange object that had come into her possession.

Expecting a tooth from a saint or a clover with four leaves, Simon was stunned when she handed him a blue crystal that was as deep and blue as the Mediterranean Sea. He sucked in his breath and whispered an oath in his native tongue, then he brought the crystal up to his keen eye and examined it closely.

Simon could barely speak, the stone was so beautiful. In an age when it was considered ruinous to cut a gemstone, for it was said to destroy the stone's magic, gems of such clear transparency rarely existed. Simon had seen only a few—he had once even seen a cut diamond and could scarcely believe that such a cloudy piece of crystal could harbor such brilliance within. Yet this stone appeared to be uncut, for it was smooth and vaguely egg-shaped, just slightly larger

than a robin's egg, but of a more spectacular blue. Could it be aquamarine? He had once seen an emerald from Cleopatra's mines. That,
too, had been cut and dazzled the eye with brilliance. But no, this
was not as green nor as pure at heart as that emerald had been.

Though he could not identify the stone, he sensed that it possessed
great value. "I know a man in London," he said, "a dealer in gems."

Winifred had heard of London. Most people possessed scant knowledge of the world beyond five miles in either direction from where
they lived; few were even aware of other countries, and their only
familiarity with foreigners was to know that the Vikings who had once
been the scourge of England were devils from beyond the sea. But
Winifred knew that London was a town to the south, a prosperous
trade center where the king lived.

Mr. Jaffar added, "London is the perfect place to sell such a gem."

"Sell!"

"Why yes," he said, handing it back to her. "Is that not what you
were asking of me?"

"To sell Amelia's stone?" she said, as if he had just asked her to
hack off her arm. And then common sense took over. "Is it so valuable then?"

"My dear Mother Prioress, I could fetch you a fortune for this stone.
Its uniqueness alone would bring a ransom in gold."

Her eyes widened and her practical brain suddenly buzzed with new
thoughts and plans. With a ransom in gold she could repair the roof,
reinforce walls, provide new beds, and then perhaps plant some crops
and purchase a few goats, hire some local lads to help out, make St.
Amelia's self-sufficient again, attract new novices and lady guests with
their donations and patronage of their families. All in an instant, in
the dazzling blue flash of a crystal, Winifred saw a bright new future
for St. Amelia's.

And then she frowned. "I must confer with the abbot."

"What does he say to do with the stone?"

"He does not know of it yet."

Mr. Ibn-Abu-Aziz-Jaffar stroked his beard. "Hmm," he said, and
Winifred read his meaning.

"I *should* tell the abbot," she said in an unconvincing tone.
"Shouldn't I?"

He asked how she had come by this gem and when she told him,
Simon the Levite said, "It would seem to me, my dear Mother Pri-

oress, that it was to you alone this stone was given. A gift from your saint."

When she bit her lip in uncertainty, Simon said gravely, "You are caught in a struggle."

She bowed her veiled head. "Yes, I am."

"It is a struggle between faith and obedience."

"I feel that God is trying to tell me something. But He has told the abbot the exact opposite. How am I to choose?"

"That, dear lady, is up to you. You must look inside your heart and listen to what it is saying."

"I refer to God, not my heart."

"Are they not the same thing?" He asked further about the crystal, specifically how she thought it came to be lodged in the saint's neckbones. Winifred then told him how Amelia had commanded her own heart to stop before the authorities could torture her into revealing the names of other Christians.

"Then," he said, "it would seem, if this stone is delivering a message as you believe, that the message is one of following your own counsel."

Her face brightened. "This was my thought!" And suddenly she was confessing to him about her dream to paint an altarpiece for St. Amelia.

"And what troubles you most," the wise foreigner said, "is that if you go to live in the new convent, you will lose this vision."

"Yes," she breathed. "Yes . . ."

"Then you must listen to your heart."

"But God speaks through the abbot."

When he said nothing, and she saw the skeptical look on his face, she said, "Mr. Jaffar, I suspect you are not Christian."

He smiled. "You suspect rightly."

"In your faith, do you not have priests?"

"Not as you do. We have rabbis, but they are more spiritual advisors than intermediaries to God. We believe that God hears us and speaks to us directly." He wanted to add that Winifred's crucified lord had been a rabbi, but decided this was neither the time nor the place for such a topic.

He said, "I will be camping by the stream for a few days while I visit the farms hereabouts, after which I shall continue on to Portminster. Before I leave, you can tell me your decision. I pray, my dear Mother Prioress, that it is the right one."

◆ ◆ ◆

$\mathcal{M}$other Winifred decided to go to the abbey alone. Although it was customary for the members of her order to travel in pairs or groups, this was one journey she knew she must take by herself. She still had not broken the bad news to the others, despite the abbot's orders that they must vacate St. Amelia's as soon as possible. Perhaps she would have complied without hesitation if it had not been for the incident with the reliquary and her discovery of the blue crystal. But the incident *had* occurred, and she *was* in possession of St. Amelia's remarkable talisman, and now she was under a compulsion to confer with the abbot over what to do next.

She had prayed all night, and though she had not slept, she felt strangely refreshed. Her foot was firm as it took to the path leading from the convent, her resolve and spirit strong, for with her she carried the blue crystal of St. Amelia.

When she arrived at the main lane, Winifred saw that she was not going to have to travel alone after all. She joined a group of pilgrims headed for the Convent of the True Cross—*they had walked right past St. Amelia's.* "Got to get to the convent by noon," their leader explained. "That's when the sisters put out their table. I'm told we'll have our fill of mutton and bread today." Then he saw Winifred's habit and, slow-witted soul that he was, her identity finally dawned on him. Turning bright red, he said lamely, "We didn't want to impose on you good ladies of St. Amelia's, being the ragamuffins that we are." And he moved to the head of the group where he could let his embarrassment subside.

They encountered more people on the road: farmers taking produce to the Portminster fair, knights traveling with guards, ladies in curtained litters. The road wound through forests of hawthorn, elm, and beech where glens suddenly opened to reveal patches of bluebells and streams collecting in dark, sun-dappled pools. Trails lead off the road to farmhouses and meadows with sheep grazing. And every now and then they encountered paving stones of ancient manufacture, reminding them that Roman legions had passed this way. And amid all these people, and the hues of spring, inhaling the woodland air and buoyed by morning birdsong, Winifred felt her confidence grow. She was doing the right thing, even though, had the abbot known, he would have called it disobedience.

The older ones in the group talked of Vikings, tall yellow-bearded devils who wore red cloaks over ring mail and were known to fight with bloodthirsty frenzy, like mad wolves. Memories of the Vikings gave these elders a kind of prestige, for it had been thirty years since the decisive Battle of Maldon when the Danes, with the help of Norway's most feared Viking King, Olaf, defeated the Anglo-Saxons and laid waste to England. And even though the overthrow of King Ethelred by Danish king Sweyn, putting the Dane Canute in power, was of more recent memory, the younger members of the traveling group had no experience with such fear. Although there were still rumored attacks here and there by Vikings who refused to accept the new peace with England, the constant terror of the past one hundred years was over at last, England had learned to sleep easy at night, and the verse, "From the fury of the Northmen, good Lord deliver us," had been stricken from the litany.

They came to a signpost with one arrow marked "Portminster," pointing ahead, another bent to the left, pointing down a narrow lane, marked "Mayfield," the third, a newer arrow, was aimed to the right and said "Convent of the True Cross." It had not been Winifred's intention to visit the new convent, yet she found her feet turning onto this new lane, along with the knot of pilgrims whose topic of conversation now shifted to speculation of what they could expect on the nuns' dinner table.

They glimpsed the walls through the trees, and the first thing Winifred heard was laughter. Feminine laughter, coming from the convent. And then she heard voices—chattering, calling out, like excited hens. She frowned. How was one to concentrate upon spiritual matters in all that noise? As they passed through the outer meadow, she stopped and stared: two young women in novices robes were tossing a ball to one another, laughing, their habits blowing immodestly in the breeze. A third was teasing a little dog with a bone, pretending to throw it and then laughing as it ran to fetch. Two more young nuns stood on ladders in apple trees, their skirts tucked up as they called out merrily to one another while they plucked fruit. Passing through the main gates and entering the inner yard, Winifred was stunned to find a world of commerce busily at work with pilgrims, townsfolk, lady guests, and holy sisters all mingling. Wooden booths had been erected for the sale of convent trinkets—embroidered badges for pilgrims to prove they had visited the shrine, vials of holy water, rosary beads, statues, good-luck charms, sweets, and breads—with nuns involved in the exchange of money!

As Mother Winifred passed through the crowd that resembled a village fair, her initial shock turned to worry. There was no piety in this place, no dignity or decorum. The abbot had assured her these sisters followed the Rule of St. Benedict, but Winifred saw no modesty, poverty, humility, or silence here.

As she went up the steps of the chapter house, a certain irony struck her: that wealth attracted wealth. Whereas it should be obvious to any casual observer that it was St. Amelia's in dire need of money, Abbey expenditures were clearly being squandered on this new place, founded by a wealthy baron who was himself sparing no expense. The orchards outside the walls! Winifred pressed her hand to her growling stomach as if to calm a petulant child. The thought had crossed her mind to steal a few apples and take them back to her hungry sisters.

The interior of the chapter house was like that of a wealthy man's home, with silver candlesticks, handsome furniture, tapestries on the walls. And when Mother Rosamund came in to greet her, Winifred received a second shock.

This was what people were told: when the Dane Canute became king of all England, Oswald of Mercia led other Englishmen in declaring their allegiance to him. For this he was rewarded with lands in the shire of Portminster. And when Canute, in his zeal to become "a most Christian king," announced his intention to build new monasteries, Oswald requested the privilege of building a convent in honor of his new liege. What persuaded the Danish conqueror was Oswald's recounting of a tale about the year he had traveled to Glastonbury where it was said Joseph of Arimathea had brought the Holy Grail of Christ, and there, camping one night along the road, Oswald had had a dream in which the location of a precious relic was revealed to him. Deep in a cave was an iron chest containing a piece of Christ's cross, buried there by Joseph himself. Oswald had brought it back to house it in his family chapel. It also happened that Oswald's oldest daughter, Rosamund, was devoutly religious and had prayed, all during the battles between the Danes and the English, for Danish victory for she had felt it was God's will—or so Oswald said. Because of the daughter's prayers, and the piece of the True Cross, Canute graciously consented to the founding of the new convent in his name.

So the story went. But this was the truth: Oswald of Mercia, a coward to the bone, was fighting on the side of English king Ethelred when he saw which way the war was going. So he switched sides, turning on his fellow Englishmen. As for his daughter Rosamund, she was not so much religious as she greatly disliked men and, preferring the company of women, refused to marry, no matter how much her father threatened or bribed her. She also wanted power. So he hit upon the perfect solution: let her run a convent. It could be no ordinary convent but must have prestige and significance. And what better way to imbue an institution with significance than planting a very important relic within its walls—and what could be greater than the cross upon which Christ Himself had died? There, of course, had been no visit to Glastonbury, no dream, no cave, no iron chest containing the True Cross. The reliquary on the altar in the new convent's chapel contained nothing but air.

Winifred now found herself face to face with the governess of the convent that was leading St. Amelia's to ruin. Mother Rosamund was appallingly young. She could not have been in the order for more than six years. It had taken Winifred nearly thirty years before she had succeeded to the post of prioress. A stray lock of beautiful red-gold hair had escaped the confines of Rosamund's wimple, and Winifred had the uncharitable thought that it was on purpose. She pictured the vain young woman standing before a mirror and burrowing beneath the starched white fabric with a sewing needle to snag just the perfect curl. But most shocking of all were the young woman's hands—they were all over the place, like frantic butterflies tied to her wrists by threads. They fluttered up and down, in and out, her sleeves falling back to expose her arms past the elbows! Clearly Rosamund had had no formal training in the Benedictine discipline. And if this were so, then how could she, as the prioress, train her sisters?

Winifred's heart was heavy. How was she to teach these frivolous girls the art of sacred illumination? She simply could not. She would tell the abbot that this new convent was an affront to the order and that he must personally step in and restore discipline. Winifred didn't care how rich Rosamund's father was; this convent was an offense to God.

"My dear Mother Winifred, how pleased you must be to face years of rest after all your service to God. To shed the mantle of prioress and be a sister again."

Winifred stared at her. What was the girl talking about? And then it came as clear to her as the crystal blue of Amelia's stone: of course there could not be *two* mother prioresses in one convent! Since the abbot had said nothing about this, it was obvious he was expecting Winifred to make the logical deduction herself. But it came as a shock nonetheless. That she should be stripped of her title and reduced to an ordinary sister again, and compelled to address a girl who was young enough to be her granddaughter as "Mother"—it was unthinkable.

"Not that you won't be having responsibilities!" the young woman added lightly. "My girls are looking forward to learning how to paint those lovely illuminations."

Winifred's head swam. Rosamund made it sound like a child's game. "There is more to it than just painting pictures," she said. "I will have to teach the making of pigments, their proper use—"

"Oh, but my father is going to provide us with paints! The very same paints that are used at Winchester! He will have them brought up each month special!"

Winifred felt her bones freeze. To use pigments that had been mixed by someone else? "But I always purchase my raw materials from Mr. Jaffar," she said in a tone that sounded almost pleading.

"We have nothing to do with him," Rosamund said with undisguised contempt. "He offended my father. That blackguard is not permitted to set foot on our property, and it extends all the way to the main road."

Winifred felt the floor tilt beneath her. The edges of the room grew dim. She was near faint with the shock of what had just transpired. To no longer be prioress, to no longer have control over the manufacture of pigments that was her very reason for being. And now: never to see Mr. Jaffar again!

As Rosamund escorted her guest on a tour of the new convent, cheerily pointing out all the wonderful amenities and luxuries, Winifred barely heard a word. She stumbled with the gait of a woman who had suddenly aged by two decades. Her head spun with grief and disappointment and shock.

But as she was taken from room to room, through a cloistered garden and down flagstone paths, her shock turned to awareness, until gradually her eyes were opened at last and she was asking herself: how could she have even thought that she and her sisters would never move here?

It was another world, a wonderful world. Each guest room had its own *necessarium*—a little closet built off the outer wall with a pipe carrying the waste to a trench below. Such luxury, not to have to trudge through all weather when nature called! There were special amenities found only in the homes of wealthy nobles: candles marked to tell time, lanterns of transparent ox horn, the freshly swept floors covered with sweet-smelling rushes. And luxuries: in the yard behind the kitchen, hired servants were boiling sheets, cloths and undergarments in a wooden trough containing a solution of wood ashes and caustic soda. Boys working in the vegetable gardens, women feeding flocks of fat hens and geese. An old man hired to fashion bars of sweet-smelling soap.

The kitchen was five times the size of that at St. Amelia's and its fully stocked pantry and buttery, for all of being five years old, still smelled of fresh wood and whitewash. Winifred's eyes bulged at the sight of the noon meal laid out: a whole ham, slabs of rare beef, crusty bread, barrels of ale and wine. When Rosamund put a generous plate in front of her, Winifred said she had eaten fully before leaving St. Amelia's, but so as not to offend, she would carry this meal back in a cloth and save it for later. In truth, it would be divided among the others, who had not tasted jam in a very long time.

She was then taken to the grand chapel where the pilgrims— knights and paupers, lords and clergy, the sick and the lame—all waited in line to pray before the magnificent shrine of the True Cross. This church had something her own little chapel did not have: a stained-glass window. And so much gold! So many candles, all white and straight. All for the reverence of a piece of wood, whereas the bones of a real woman, a woman who suffered martyrdom for her faith, were housed in a homely place where the candles were squat and smoked badly. Winifred did not feel bitter toward this contrast, only sadness, and suddenly wanted to gather St. Amelia into her arms and whisper, "This might be grander but you are loved more."

Finally: this place had an infirmary, which St. Amelia's did not. Eight beds and a nursing sister who specialized in ailments. Winifred's eyes bulged at the sight of the medicine cupboard: the potions and lotions, ointments and salves, pills and powders. Several vials of curative eyewash. Remedies for arthritis. Rose-hip tonic for kidney troubles.

Marveling at the generous stock of medicines, and thinking of the private *necessarium* that Sister Edith would have, right off her own room so she did not need a nightly escort, and the young man in the outer yard who was ever ready to draw water from the well, thus putting fear of wells out of Dame Odelyn's mind . . .

Winifred sighed. There was no denying it. This would be a haven for her elderly sisters. They would be well fed, taken care of. Never mind that they would no longer have duties. Peace and comfort mattered more.

She had been invited to stay the night, in the guest quarters where the mattresses were filled with eider down, but Winifred was eager to get back to her own home before dark. Thanking Mother Rosamund for the tour and hospitality, Winifred hurried from the chapter house as quickly as decorum allowed. After she passed through the main gates and followed the path back to the main lane, she paused beneath a leafy beech tree and, alone in the shadows, retrieved the blue crystal from her pocket.

As it lay in her hand, catching sunlight that filtered through the branches overhead, Winifred realized that the crystal had not been a sign after all. There was no message from Amelia, no significance to the stone's discovery. It had been an accident, nothing more. Winifred knew now that she and her sisters must come here and live out their lives in this place. She would strive to do her best teaching the art of illumination to the novices, but she knew that the excellence that had once gone into her labors would not be there, for already she felt the creative spark fading. The gift St. Amelia had bestowed upon her many years ago had run its course. From now on, Winifred would be an ordinary illuminator; she would teach ordinary girls to execute ordinary paintings. And she would set aside once and for all her foolish dream of creating a splendid altarpiece for St. Amelia.

◆ ◆ ◆

$\mathcal{M}$r. Ibn-Abu-Aziz-Jaffar returned after three days as promised. And Winifred had the money she owed him, for she had sold their one last item of worth, a handsome unicorn tapestry that had hung in the chapter house—what need was there for it now that St. Amelia's was to be closed?

He said he was sorry to hear that she was losing her home, and said he would pray for their happiness and success in the new place. And then he did a surprising thing: he gave her a gift, something he could have clearly sold at a good price, a chunk of costly Spanish cinnabar. He placed it now freely in the prioress's dye-stained, work-roughened hands.

Winifred looked at the offering speechlessly. The red stone, crushed, would make excellent vermilion paint, which they were badly in need of. "Thank you, Mr. Jaffar," she said in all humility.

He further shocked her by taking her hand and holding it between his. Winifred had not felt human touch in forty years, and certainly not a man's! And in that instant the strangest moment occurred: Winifred felt the warm skin beneath her fingers and for the first time in her life saw a member of the opposite sex not as a father or a brother, a merchant or a priest, but as a *man*. She looked into Simon's dark lively eyes and she felt something unfamiliar move within her breast.

And then she saw a vision, a function of the Celtic sight that had once led her to lost spoons and meat pies, but this time it was something lost in the past: all in a flash she saw herself meeting this same man on the day before she first visited St. Amelia's over forty years ago. But now he is an itinerant young man carrying juggling balls and a box of magic tricks. Their eyes meet as they pass in the lane, and then they are gone. But later, in the chapel at St. Amelia's, instead of going exploring, fourteen-year-old Winifred thinks instead of the handsome young man she met on the road. She does not wander through the convent and happen upon the scriptorium, but instead returns home with her mother and sisters, to travel the next day to the market fair in town, where she encounters the young man a second time. On this occasion they speak, and the magic between them is instantaneous. He speaks with a thick accent and his clothes are foreign. He says he comes from Spain and wishes to travel the country and bring dreams and joy to folk. He promises to come back someday and so Winifred waits for him. Five years pass before she sees him again, and there he is at the gate of their manor, with a brand new wagon and horse, and he is asking her to go with him. They will travel the world together, he tells her, and have many children and many adventures. So Winifred runs off with the stranger and never looks back.

She blinked and caught her breath and looked into Mr. Jaffar's dark eyes. And she realized she had just been given a glimpse of *what might have been*.

"Where do you go from here?" she asked suddenly.

The question surprised him. "To the abbey, Mother Prioress. I sell medicines to the monks there."

"Go inland," she said. "Travel first to Mayfield."

"But Mayfield is far out of my way, another two days' journey. And then to make my way back—"

"Please," she said urgently.

"Can you tell me why?"

"I have a presentiment. A *feeling*. You must turn inland from here, travel through Bryer Wood."

He considered her words. "I shall discuss it with Seska, Mother Prioress," he said, referring to his horse. "If she agrees, we shall make the detour." Then he climbed onto his wagon, took up the reins and waved good-bye for the very last time.

*W*here is Sister Agnes? It is time for us to leave."

Dame Mildred came into the chapter house with the last of her packed goods—ancient pots and pans, a broken rolling pin, useless items that had sentimental value, which she could not bear to leave behind, even though Winifred had informed her she would no longer be doing any cooking. "Agnes is in the graveyard," Mildred said, breathing heavily from the exertion. She had refused to leave even a spoon; her entire kitchen had been picked clean and packed into sacks. The man who was to transfer the sisters to the new convent was going to need more than one wagon. It was ironic: although the sisters had taken vows of poverty, the requirement to get into a convent was a payment in money and goods, to be held for common use.

And so although Winifred and her ladies were themselves poor, they nonetheless had the accumulated effects of generations of women going with them.

Winifred was not surprised to hear that Agnes was in the convent graveyard. She had visited it every Sunday for sixty years. Now she must say good-bye to it.

The prioress found the elderly nun kneeling at a tiny grave that was shaded by an elm tree that had recently been stricken with leaf blight. She was brushing away dead leaves with her arthritic fingers. And she was weeping.

Winifred knelt beside her, crossed herself and closed her eyes in prayer. The miniature coffin beneath them contained the corpse of a baby that had lived only a few hours. Sixty-one years ago, during a Norse raid on Portminster, Agnes and her cousins had been caught at the river by a gang of Vikings. While the other girls had managed to escape, Agnes had been seized and raped. When she turned up pregnant a few weeks later, she had been brought to the convent of St. Amelia's and ordered to stay there for, in her father's eyes, she had dishonored the family. The nuns had taken her in, but her child had not lived long. After he was buried here in the convent cemetery, Agnes stayed and never saw her family again. She took holy orders and learned to paint illuminations, and spent every Sunday for the rest of her life pouring love into a grave that was marked simply, "John—d. 962 Anno Domini."

She squinted up at the bare branches and wondered why God would inflict the tree with the blight just now, for its leaves were raining onto the little grave and within hours it could be completely covered. Once the sisters left, there would be no one to keep the grave clear of blighted leaves. "Soon my wee Johnny will be covered up and forgotten." There was already a pile near the grave that Andrew had intended to burn later. Except that Andrew wouldn't be here; he was moving to the new convent with them.

Winifred helped the elder nun to her feet. "Andrew says the new convent is very large," Agnes said.

"It is, Sister Agnes, but it is also nice and new. And"—she peered up at the blighted maple tree through her own tears—"all the trees are healthy and green."

"I shall never find my way around it."

Winifred had heard the same fear expressed by the other nuns. She herself dreaded having to learn her way through that maze of corridors and courtyards and buildings.

"And I shall never paint again," Agnes said, drying her eyes.

"It is time for you to rest. You have spent your life in the service of God."

"Retirement is for old horses," Agnes said petulantly. "Am I so useless? I can still see. I can still hold a pen. What shall I do with myself? And who will look after my wee Johnny here?"

"Come along," Winifred said gently. "It is time for us to go."

They gathered in the chapter house, which was dominated by an enormous fireplace that had been installed two hundred years earlier by a mother prioress who had been particularly sensitive to the cold; her wealthy brother had paid for the ostentatious hearth that was much too large for the room, but had failed to provide the constant wood and coal it required, and so the fireplace had fallen into disuse. Carved into the massive mantelpiece were the words of Christ by which Winifred and her sisters tried to live: "*Mandatum novum do vobis: ut diligatis invicem*"—"A new law I give you, that you shall love one another."

Dame Mildred was bemoaning leaving her giant stewpot behind. It hadn't been used in years because of the diminished population of the convent. "It's a good pot," she fretted. "It fed us through many a hard winter. We shouldn't leave it behind."

"It's too big, Sister," Mother Winifred said gently. "We cannot manage it ourselves. Perhaps later we can have some men come back and fetch it."

Dame Mildred looked uncertain, her woeful glance cast back toward the kitchen as if she were leaving a child behind.

They were interrupted by shouts outside and the sound of horse's hooves clattering in the yard. Andrew hurried in, white-faced and blathering something about an attack. As Winifred rushed to him, another man flew in, his face flushed from his hard ride. He wore the emblem of the abbey over chain mail, and he carried a halberd. "Begging pardon," he said breathlessly. "Vikings have attacked and I've been sent to bring you and the ladies to the abbey for protection."

"Vikings!" Winifred crossed herself and the others started wailing.

He told them in rapid order what had happened: the Norsemen had landed at Bryer's Point and marched the short distance to the Convent of the True Cross. Reports were sketchy, but it was believed the entire complex had been ransacked and put to the torch. Of the pilgrims and sisters he had scant knowledge, only that Mother Rosamund had managed to escape and make it to the abbey to give the alarm.

"She said her nuns had run to the chapel for safety and there the devils had found them, all huddled together, and they had been slain where they were, like geese in a pen. And now I've been sent to fetch you and your ladies. Come quickly, we've no time."

"But the abbey is some distance from here!" Winifred protested. "Mightn't we encounter the Vikings along the way?"

"Well you certainly would not be safe here, Mother Prioress," the man said impatiently. "Hurry! I will escort you. We'll take the man's wagon." The man who had been hired to transfer them to the new convent.

While her sisters cried and milled about in a panic, Winifred tried to think. The invaders had not attacked the harbor town nor the abbey but had chosen an unprotected convent. What was to prevent them from turning in this direction and hope for a second easy kill? If so, then the soldier and his helpless charges would run smack into the invaders.

Every instinct told her that they were safer staying put. To meet the Vikings on the road was certain suicide, but to stay at St. Amelia's gave Oswald's soldiers time to give chase and perhaps rout the invaders in time.

Winifred felt the blue stone in her pocket and recalled how St. Amelia had faced her fate with courage, how she had not succumbed to the tortures of men. St. Amelia had done more than defy the orders of a mere abbot, she had rebelled against the authority of the emperor of Rome.

"No," Winifred said suddenly. "We shall stay."

The guardsman's eyes bulged. "Are you mad? Now look, I've been given orders and I mean to carry them out. All of you, now, please, into the wagon."

It was as if he hadn't spoken. The elderly nuns and two ladies clustered around their prioress like chicks around a hen, saying, "What should we do?" Winifred recalled a report from many years ago, when she was a girl and the Vikings had attacked a village northward along the coast. There the villagers had gathered in the church and had huddled together. The Vikings had set fire to the building and all within had perished. Remembering also when she was very young and lived at home with her brothers and sisters, how they would all huddle together during a frightening storm. *We must not huddle together, for that is what they will expect of us.*

"Now listen to me, dear sisters. Remember how our blessed saint faced a trial worse than this, for it was her faith that was put to the test, as well as her flesh. But she found the courage to outwit her tormentors, and so shall we."

"But, Mother Winifred," said Dame Mildred in a tremulous voice. "How?"

"Each of you must find a hiding place for yourself, one that the invaders would not expect to find a lady in. Do not hide under a bed or in a clothes wardrobe as this is the first place the Danes will look."

"Can we not all hide together?"

"No," Winifred said firmly. "Above all, we must not hide together, not even in pairs."

The soldier from the abbey spoke up. "Mother Prioress, it is the abbot's direct or order—"

"I know what is best for my women. And you will stay, too."

"I!" He put his hand to his chest in shock. "I must return to the abbey."

"You will stay," she commanded. "You will find a hiding place and there you will remain, silent and still, until I give the all-clear signal."

"But I take my orders from—"

"Young sir, you are in *my* house, and I am the authority here. Do as I say, and do it swiftly."

After a moment of ineffectual milling about, the women finally fled the chapter house, each running to the place they loved best, thinking this would protect them, or to that which they feared most, believing that a villain would fear it too, and so Dame Mildred ran to seek shelter in her beloved kitchen, Sister Agnes to her beloved Johnny's grave, Dame Odelyn to her loathed well in the yard, and so on until the eleven members of St. Amelia's priory vanished before the astonished eyes of the guardsman from the abbey, who was thinking it could not be done and that they were all going to be slaughtered like sheep.

But he underestimated Mother Winifred's ingenuity. Her nuns, being smaller than Vikings, were able to squeeze into hiding places the invaders could not, like mice in wall cracks. And so Dame Mildred carefully swept away the cobwebs that had grown over the mouth of her enormous stewing pot, climbed in, and restrung the cobwebs over her head. Sister Gertrude, finding untapped strength and ingenuity, climbed up into the chimney of the enormous fireplace in the chapter house and clung like a frightened bat to the hinges of the flue. Sister Agatha ran to the dorter where she ripped open the seam of a mattress, pulled out some of the straw stuffing, threw it out the narrow window, then climbed inside the mattress and held the split seam closed with her fingertips. Dame Odelyn thought of lowering herself on the bucket down into the dreaded well, but then she realized that the bucket down inside the well might be a give-away, so she arduously climbed down, using the uneven stones of the well wall for handholds. Sister Agnes threw herself upon wee Johnny's grave and then raked blighted leaves over herself and trembled under the pile. Sister Edith, who always had a hard time finding the *necessarium*, rushed straight to it and squeezed into the foul-smelling space between the seat and the wall.

It was not until she made sure that each was securely hidden, including Andrew and the man from the abbey, that Winifred finally climbed up into the scaffolding over the altar and secured herself there.

No sooner were they hidden than the Vikings arrived, bursting into the forecourt with fierce yells and cries of blood-lust. They barged into the chapter house and chapel, the dorters and refectories, kitchen and scriptorium like stampeding bulls. As Winifred had predicted, they searched relentlessly for the hidden sisters: in the confessional, behind the altar and tapestries, inside cupboards and storage chests, under beds. Dame Odelyn in the well, kept her face downcast and saw in the water below the reflection of a red-hair-haloed face look briefly in from above, but not seeing her for her dark blue gown blended into the deep shadows. In the kitchen, no man bothered to look into the giant cookpot with the threads of spider web across its mouth. Gertrude, in the mattress, heard heavy footfalls and held her breath. She heard the door being flung open; felt a pair of eyes scan the room; then heard the footsteps tramp on to the next room. Each terrified woman hunched in her special hiding place, heard or saw the villains barge through, ransacking and plundering, and shouting curses when no women were found.

Winifred, hiding in the scaffolding, clutched the blue stone as she watched with held breath the Viking leader tramp through the chapel, slowly looking around. He was the biggest man she had ever seen with muscles like melons and hair like fire. He seized Amelia's silver reliquary and forced it open, dumping the bones out and scattering them with his feet. After a search under and behind the altar, in the confessional, in every nook or recess where a woman might hide, he tucked the box under his arm and stormed out.

Winifred did not relax her posture. Although every joint and muscle ached from her awkward position among the crossbeams, she kept as still as she could, praying that the invaders would make quick work of their destruction and leave. She felt sweat break out over her body. It trickled down her scalp and under her veil. Her hands grew damp. Suddenly, to her dismay, the blue crystal slid out of her wet fingers and hit the floor directly below.

She had to bite her tongue to keep from crying out, and she prayed with all her might that no more Danes came into the chapel. But to her horror the Viking leader came back, as though he had forgotten something or had sensed something amiss in there. She watched in terror as the tall blond giant in the horned helmet strode slowly down the central aisle and to the bottom of the altar. He gave a turn, and his foot kicked the crystal.

Winifred stifled a gasp.

The Dane looked down, retrieved the sparkling gem, then looked around, knowing it had not been there a moment ago. He turned his face upward and peered into the overhead shadows, the construction of planks and struts and supports. He stared for a long moment. Winifred saw a pair of keen blue eyes but she couldn't tell if he could see her.

Suddenly his roving gaze stopped and his eyes met hers. She held her breath as she clung to the rotten wood and tried not to disturb the dust on the beams.

The moment stretched on, with the savage below staring up at the terrified nun.

And then in his foreign tongue he shouted an order to his men and Winifred saw, through the clerestory window, the others gathering up their plunder. When two men came in with torches, he barked orders at them and gestured for them to leave. When they ran out, he looked up again, and this time there was a flicker in his eyes, a slight lift of his mouth. Another person might have read the look as a salute to courage and ingenuity; Winifred saw it only as the power of St. Amelia at work.

She waited a long time before climbing down. Her bones protested as she finally unfolded herself from the cramped position, and she nearly lost her foothold as she made her way to the floor. Then she hurried up the narrow stairs to the top of the belltower and looked out. In the distance she heard the thunder of horses' hooves—Oswald's men riding after the fleeing invaders. And then the thunder faded and the afternoon was quiet and still.

She called the sisters from their hiding places, helping them to climb out of tight spaces they had only hours before slipped into with ease, and they all gathered in the chapel to pray. When they told of how they had escaped detection, each in her own peculiar place, and as Winifred thought of the scaffolding erected five years ago, when roof repairs were to have begun, how she had cursed it all this time and in the end it had saved her, and thinking of Odelyn's dreaded well and the *necessarium* that had been the bane of Edith's life, and the leaves that were going to obscure poor Johnny's grave, she thought: the scaffold, the cook pot, the blighted elm, the well—items that had brought irritation and heartache, these were no accidents. They were miracles. There to save us had we but the courage to use them. Amelia's courage.

Winifred thought of the blue stone that the Dane had picked up and she hoped that the grace of St. Amelia went with it and that it would somehow, someday bring light to the heart of the barbarian.

*A*s the abbot rode down the lane on his fine horse, he thought how much more convenient the newer convent had been to the abbey. Unfortunately it had been utterly destroyed by the Vikings whereas St. Amelia's, by some miracle, had been spared. And having been spared it was now the only convent in Portminster. Ironically, if both had been destroyed, rebuilding would have been done on the other site and St. Amelia's let go to ruin.

When he took the turn-off he joined the stream of pilgrims heading for the priory. The splinter of the True Cross had been consumed in the fire at the other convent, so Amelia was once again the only relic in the area. The abbot knew a miracle had occurred here. Why hadn't the Vikings burned this place down as well? Everyone said it was St. Amelia who had stopped them. But, thinking of the indomitable Mother Winifred, he wondered . . .

Changes had taken place since the miracle of the Danes. Wonderful cooking smells now came from the kitchen where a tasty stew was simmering in Dame Mildred's enormous cookpot. Outside, a young man was at the well drawing water and handing the bucket to Dame Odelyn. Another youth was raking leaves off a little grave. There was industry everywhere, and new prosperity.

But the abbot wasn't coming here today to congratulate the nuns of St. Amelia's. He was here because he had heard disturbing news: Mother Winifred was not herself training the young novices in manuscript illumination but was leaving the task to the elderly nuns. And what was the prioress doing with her time? Painting that blasted altarpiece!

Well, he was going to put a stop to it once and for all. He would brook no more disobedience from that woman.

He expected Winifred to be at the gate to greet him as she always had in the past, but she wasn't there. It was Sister Rosamund, now a resident of St. Amelia's and demoted from mother prioress, although she did not seem to mind. She was the prioress's assistant, and happily had her hands full seeing to the comforts of travelers, pupils, and lady guests, as well as supervising the renovation of buildings, the housing of goats, sheep, and hens, and seeing to it that the dinner table always groaned with food.

Rosamund cheerfully escorted the abbot to the new solar where Mother Winifred was seated at an easel, painting. He was about to speak up when he looked at the panel and was rendered speechless. And then he saw something even more dumbfounding: Mother Winifred was smiling!

He took a seat and remained quiet while she worked. Winifred had created an exquisite St. Amelia, radiant and humble, serving the poor, spreading the word of Christ. In the fourth panel of the new altarpiece, St. Amelia was holding a blue crystal, cupped in her hand, to her throat. The abbot could make no sense of it, but it was beautiful and compelling and it took his breath away.

When a novice brought him ale and he sipped it absently, Father Edman not only decided that he would let Winifred finish the altarpiece after all, he was already thinking of future paintings he was going to commission her to paint, and the patrons who were going to pay handsomely for them.

Interim

*W*hen the abbot had seen the magnificence of Winifred's altarpiece, he had done a quick turnabout and claimed all credit for encouraging her, and then commissioned a triptych for his own church. He never made bishop, but died two years later when he choked on a fishbone during his third helping of Easter dinner.

Mother Winifred lived another thirty years, spending her days producing a prodigious number of breathtaking paintings, altarpieces, and miniatures—madonnas, crucifixions, and nativities—all identified as hers by the ubiquitous crystal, for artists did not sign works in those days.

Shortly after the Viking raid, Mr. Ibn-Abu-Aziz-Jaffar returned to St. Amelia's for one last visit, to thank Mother Winifred for warning him against going to the abbey that day, as his decision to turn inland and journey instead to Mayfield had diverted him from the direct path of the Vikings, thus saving his life. Mother Winifred, forgetting the sight she had inherited from Celtic ancestors, gave all credit to St. Amelia, and invited the itinerant merchant to rest at the priory for as long as he liked. He decided to retire there, in a small cottage on the grounds with his faithful horse Seska living out her days in a paddock. Simon the Levite occasionally helped out around the convent, was popular among visitors and pilgrims, and continued to be Mother Winifred's friend and adviser. They developed a ritual of meeting every afternoon for a quiet talk—Simon the Jew and Winifred the nun—until his death fourteen years later. Though he never converted to Christianity, she insisted her old friend be given last rites and be buried in hallowed ground.

As Mother Winifred continued to execute her paintings, her hand and eyesight finally fading with age, she sometimes paused in her work to think of the Viking who had picked up the blue stone, and wondered what he had done with St. Amelia's power.

What had happened was this: when the Vikings returned to their ship, they found it ablaze and surrounded by Oswald of Mercia's soldiers, who slaughtered the Danes to a man. Oswald himself took part in the pillaging of the bodies, and he found a curious blue stone, beautiful beyond belief. He had it mounted on a sword that later accompanied an ill-fated Crusader to Jerusalem where the stone was pried out of the hilt and carried to Baghdad as a gift to the caliph where it was fitted, for a while, into his favorite turban. In a moment of weakness, the caliph gave the crystal to a temple dancer who wore it in her navel as she danced for him and then fled during the night with her illicit lover. The crystal was carried in pockets and purses, knew masters and mistresses, was sold and bought and stolen again, until it was brought back across the English Channel by a soldier returning from the Crusades. Having been blinded in battle near Jerusalem and hoping to find a cure, he joined a group of pilgrims headed for Canterbury. They were set upon by brigands who sold their booty in the north. Here the crystal was set into the lid of a mother-of-pearl jewel box by a young man who hoped to win a young lady's affection with such an extravagant gift. But when the young lady rejected her suitor's marriage proposal, he took himself off to Europe where he vowed to kill himself once he had found a suitable spot. There he met a man from Assisi named Francis, who was founding a new brotherhood based on poverty, and on an impulse the dejected young man joined the order, giving away everything he owned, including the cursed jewel box.

The peasant who found the box in the Franciscans' pile of charitable offerings pried the blue stone loose from the lid and bought a loaf of bread with it, and when the baker's wife saw the captivating gem, she exchanged it for another novel invention, a glass mirror, believing that an object that showed her reflection was more precious than one that did not.

In 1349 the Black Death killed one third of the population of Europe, and in that time the blue crystal was blamed for seven deaths and six cures as it passed from deceased to survivor, from patient to doctor. Almost a hundred years later, when a young girl named Joan was burned at the stake in France for heresy, a man in the crowd that was watching was unaware that his pocket was being picked, the thief relieving him of two gold florins and a blue crystal.

In 1480 on a warm summer day, a crowd gathered in the hills near Florence to watch a twenty-eight-year-old artist-inventor demonstrate his newest creation, which he called a parachute. Witnesses merrily placed wagers on whether the young idiot would break his neck, but when Leonardo da Vinci landed without mishap on a grassy field, the blue crystal passed from the hands of a Medici prince to a traveling scholar who took the glittering gem back to Jerusalem as a gift for his beloved daughter, only to find she had died in childbirth during his absence. So bitter was he over her death that he hid the hated crystal away, for it reminded him of his only child, and there it lay, in a gold box, in a beautiful home on a hill overlooking the Dome of the Rock, awaiting its next owner, its next turn of fate.

Book Six

GERMANY
1520 C.E.

---

*I*f asked, Katharina Bauer would say she was marrying Hans Roth because she loved him. But in truth, it was her passionate wish to become part of a family.

To call a woman sister, or aunt, or a man brother, or uncle, to hail someone as cousin, niece, or nephew, this was the stuff of Katharina Bauer's dreams. Seventeen years old and the only child of a widow who lived in a humble room above a *hofbrauhaus*, Katharina wished upon every star, every good-luck piece that she would belong to a large, happy family. And Hans Roth, twenty-two years old with eyes the blue of cornflowers, just happened to possess such a family.

One of three sons and two daughters to Herr Roth, the stein-maker, and his hausfrau, Hans lived in a beehive of a house that was filled with relatives, in-laws, and assorted extended family members, all involved in the making and selling of beer steins. And now that Katharina had been allowed to help out during their busiest time (although she was not paid for it) and made to feel part of the Roth family, she secretly hoped that by this time next year she would be addressing Herr Roth as "Papa."

This was what true love was like, Katharina told herself as she blissfully helped Hans in the drying room. This feeling of quiet joy, peace, and contentment. She had seen it in older couples, people who had been married *forever*. How lucky for her and Hans that they should start out this way already. What a perfect road lay before them!

As for that other aspect of marriage—the bed and babies—Katharina preferred not to dwell on it, for kissing Hans was as far as she desired to go. During those few stolen moments when they were alone together, in the woods or down by the river out of sight of anyone, and Hans became more eager than usual, Katharina had to stay his hands and remind him that they were not yet wed. But when the proper time came, she would do her duty and suffer the brief physical union necessary for producing children.

As they lifted the newly carved beer steins from the drying shelves, they detected delicious aromas drifting through the open window: pork cutlets sizzling on a fire, cabbage simmering in a pot, potatoes roasting, bread emerging fresh from the oven—Frau Roth was preparing their usual heavy midday meal. Katharina knew she would not be invited; Frau Roth was not noted for her generosity. But Katharina would not have dined with them anyway, not while her mother was at home making do with cheese and an egg. Once in a while a satisfied customer would pay Isabella Bauer in sausages and potatoes, which she would stretch into a week of meals for herself and Katharina. But bread was plentiful, they always had bread, and because they were fortunate to live above the *hofbrauhaus*, and because the owner Herr Müller was smitten with Katharina's mother, they always had beer.

"These are going to Italy," Hans said as they placed the dried steins into the burn oven. Katharina did not miss the note of reverence and wonder in his voice as he said "Italy," for Hans had a yearning to see the world. To Katharina, however, the world was Badendorf, where the central market square was dominated by a fountain and surrounded on two sides by shops and houses with half-timbered facades; on the third side was the *hofbrauhaus*; and on the fourth side, the three-hundred-year-old *rathaus* with its front door on the second story, reached by a stairway that could be removed in case of danger; next to it the Romanesque church that dated back to the fifth century, with foundations, it was said, that went back to the ancient Romans. The *marktplatz* was the venue for annual festivals, weddings, celebrations, fruit and vegetable vendors, and the occasional religious play. As far as Katharina Bauer was concerned, Badendorf *was* the whole world.

She didn't know what lay around the river's bend, or at the end of the road, or on the other side of the mountain, nor did she care. She had not heard of a coronation that had just taken place, in a town called Aachen, of a king named Charles V, and that it was the biggest such event since the coronation of Charlemagne. Nor was she aware that another man, an Augustine monk named Martin Luther, had just been branded a heretic by the pope for spreading new and dangerous ideas, and that his protestations were going to spread like wildfire across Europe due to the timely invention of a third man named Johannes Gutenberg. Katharina Bauer knew only her town, the forest, the castle, and the citizens of Badendorf. It was enough.

As Hans took a stein from her, their fingers brushed and she saw a flush rise in his cheeks. No flush rose in hers for the love Katharina felt for the young man was not the "sparking" kind, as she thought of it. She wasn't even sure that kind of love really existed outside of songs and poems and romantic tales. What counted was fondness, affection, and a deep feeling of being comfortable with someone. Since she had known Hans all her life, this love had slowly grown as they had and when his parents had mentioned marriage, it had seemed only natural to Katharina that the pair should continue their lives together. And it would be a perfect marriage, she knew, with Katharina becoming the most in-demand seamstress in Badendorf and Hans carrying on the famous Roth beer stein manufacture.

Centuries ago natural hot springs had brought Romans to this area for their health. Although the springs had dried up, in their place was a clay that was perfect for making stoneware. And so Badendorf was noted for its beer steins. Each one started as a handful of raw clay that was formed and carved and painted by hand, and then fired and colored with glaze. In order to dry out the clay and give the stein its consistency, the steins were air dried in the drying room for many hours before they went into the burn oven. The overall process took several days and required a lot of patience. This was the secret of the Roth steins: the slower the water was driven out of the clay, the sturdier the final stein became. And so Roth steins were in demand all over Europe and beyond. Which meant that someday, Hans was going to be a very rich man. Then Katharina would be able to buy her mother a grand house and see to it that she didn't have to work anymore.

Their morning's labor done, Katharina followed Hans into the atelier where the most recently fired batch was being fitted with pewter tops.

Two hundred years ago, doctors had deduced that the plague was transmitted by flies and so, to prevent the disease from spreading, a law was passed requiring all beverages to be covered. The problem was, a removable lid distracted from the pleasure of drinking beer, for the stein would then require two hands. A one-handed solution was needed and thus the hinged lid was born, allowing people to drink with one hand and still comply with the law. Roth steins were known for their ornate, decorative lids that always complemented the design on the stein itself.

As Katharina helped a pair of Roth cousins with an unwieldy bale of packing straw, Hans came up behind her and, putting his hands on her waist, whispered something in her ear. Katharina giggled and slipped out of his grasp, pretending to have enjoyed the flirtation. But she secretly hoped that once they were married he wouldn't touch her so much. And anyway, it wouldn't be seemly, once they were a respectable married couple.

As she was about to comment on the hour and that her mother would be expecting her, they suddenly heard a shout outside. Someone was frantically calling Katharina's name.

She stepped out to see Manfred, the son of the *hofbraumeister*, running across the square, waving his arms and looking for all the world like a windmill.

"Katharina!" he yelled. "Come quickly! There has been an accident. Your mother—"

Katharina broke into a run. Manfred fell into step beside her. He was out of breath. "She was standing behind the beer wagon when the horse bolted! A barrel rolled off the wagon. It struck your mother. The Arab doctor is with her."

Katharina silently thanked God for that. The elderly doctor was the man she most trusted in all the world.

Dr. Mahmoud had fled Spain twenty-eight years earlier when the Moors were expelled by Queen Isabella. He had been in the north

buying medicines when the news reached him that his entire family
had been wiped out and that it was too dangerous for him to return
to Granada. After a year of wandering in Europe, he had found haven
in Badendorf, where Isabella Bauer, knowing what it was like to be a
stranger in a strange town, had shown him kindness and had helped
the citizens to accept him.

Now Dr. Mahmoud was the first person Katharina saw when she
reached the open door of their room over the *hofbrauhaus*—his aged
body, draped in the exotic robes of his culture, a turban on his white
hair. Friar Pastorius, a young religious brother with a weak constitution and a clubfoot, was in the corner, praying. When she saw her
mother lying on the bed unconscious, a bloody bandage on her forehead, Katharina ran to the bedside and fell to her knees.

Isabella Bauer, the finest seamstress in Badendorf and the surrounding countryside, was thirty-eight years old and although she had
known a life of deprivation and hardship, still retained her youthful
looks. But now, her eyes closed in a deathly coma, she looked even
younger, her face smoothed of the lines of worry and age, her complexion pale and unblemished. "Mama?" Katharina said, taking her
mother's cold, limp hand. "Mama?" she said a little louder. She looked
up at Dr. Mahmoud whose expression was grim.

Katharina felt her heart stop. Her mother was the only family she
had known. Katharina knew little about her father. She had been just
a baby when he had died of a virulent fever that swept through their
village in the north. There wasn't even a grave for her to visit. The
dead had had to be burned, to halt the spread of the fever. She and
her mother had escaped and come south to settle in Badendorf, and
when Katharina grew older, she would every so often turn her green
eyes northward, to the bend in the river and the world she had never
seen, and picture the village and the handsome smiling man who had
been her father.

While Katharina and her mother did not belong to the prospering
German merchant class, and their existence was a daily struggle and
they often had to do without (Isabella frequently had to go to her
patrons and almost beg for the payment they owed her), they did not
consider themselves poor. They lived in a small room above the *hofbrauhaus*, the only home Katharina had ever known, and made do
with mended dresses and patched shoes, and sometimes went hungry,
or without heat in the winter, but they considered themselves blessed

for they were not of the peasant class that was overworked and over-
used by the nobility. Isabella Bauer often told her daughter that while
they might not have money, they had their dignity.

And life, on the whole, had been good. There was a small walled
garden behind the *hofbrauhaus* where Friar Pastorius taught Latin to
boys and Dr. Mahmoud saw patients. It was also where the light was
best and so Katharina and her mother did their stitchery there while
the elderly Arab consulted with patients behind the privacy of a port-
able screen that he carried down from his room, and Friar Pastorius
hammered rudimentary Latin into the stubborn skulls of merchants'
sons. On any typical morning, as Katharina and Isabella stitched their
fine patterns, the air would be filled with birdsong and the chanting
of the friar's pupils, "*Anima bruta, anima divina, anima humana . . .*"
punctuated by an occasional cough from behind the doctor's screen.
Thus did Katharina's young and agile mind, as she wove roses and
leaves into linen, absorb lessons meant for boys, "*Leone fortior fides.*"
Now, as Katharina anxiously knelt at her mother's bedside, she heard
birdsong drift up from the garden and through the open window, and
she was suddenly struck by a feeling of premonition—that the idyllic
days in the garden had come to an end.

Finally, Isabella's eyelids fluttered open. Her gaze was momentarily
unfocused, then she saw Katharina, her golden hair forming a halo of
light in the sunshine that poured through the window. Isabella smiled.
How beautiful the girl had grown. The hair, once as pale as cornsilk,
now a deep gold. Flawless skin. Clear green eyes. Isabella lifted a hand
to the smooth cheek and said with great effort, "God has decided to
call me to Him, daughter. I had thought I would have more time . . ."

"Mama," Katharina sobbed, pressing the cold hand to her face.
"You'll be all right. Dr. Mahmoud will see to it."

Isabella smiled sadly and rolled her head on the pillow. "I know
that there are but minutes left to me. I had hoped for years, but God
in His wisdom . . ."

Katharina waited. Dr. Mahmoud kept keen, dark eyes on his patient, while Friar Pastorius did not cease his murmured chanting. A
curious crowd had gathered outside the door but Herr Müller was
keeping them out.

Presently Isabella drew in a deep breath and spoke again. "There
is something you must know, my child, something I have to tell
you . . ."

Tears fell from Katharina's eyes onto the bloodstained sheet.

"There," Isabella whispered, "in the chest." She pointed to the one piece of good furniture they owned: a wooden chest that held their fabrics and threads, needles, and scissors. "The box of ribbons. Bring it to me."

When Katharina returned to the bed with the ribbon box, Isabella said, "Now I must . . . tell you. Katharina. Be strong. Ask God for strength. It is time for you to know the truth."

The girl waited. Dr. Mahmoud leaned forward. A bee flew in through the open window, buzzed about as if searching for something, and then flew out.

"What is it, Mama?" Katharina prompted gently.

Tears sprouted in Isabella's eyes as she said, "I am not your true mother. You are not my true daughter."

Katharina stared at her. Then she frowned. She looked up at Dr. Mahmoud, and at Friar Pastorius, who had halted his chanting. Had she heard correctly?

"It is true, Katharina," Isabella said with great effort. "You are not a child of my body. You came from another woman."

"Mama, you are not well. Dr. Mahmoud said you had a nasty blow to your head."

"I am in my right mind, Katharina. Now listen to me for I haven't much time." Isabella drew in a labored breath, released it, drew another. "Nineteen years ago a plague wiped out my village in the north, taking my husband and two babies, leaving me alone. We few survivors scattered. I ended up at an inn where I worked as a maid and also did some needlework. A family came one night, the wife was pregnant. They commissioned me to embroider a christening robe for the baby. But the mother died in childbirth. The husband came to me—he was so grief-stricken. I had never seen a man weep so."

Another labored breath. "He told me that he was on a journey . . . that he and his sons were going far away and could not take an infant with them. He came in the middle of the night, Katharina, and wept like a child and asked me to keep his baby for him, promising that he would come back for her. That baby was you, Katharina."

The crowd outside the door murmured until Herr Müller raised his arms for silence. Dr. Mahmoud took Isabella's wrist and felt her pulse. His expression grew even grimmer. His look told Katharina that there wasn't much time.

Isabella continued: "So I took the baby for him, promising to take good care of her until he returned. Afterward, I left the inn. I didn't trust the owners and thought they might steal from me, for the stranger had given me gold coins for your care. I made my way here to Badendorf where I told everyone I was a widow, which was true, and that the baby was mine, which was not true. I thought your father could still find me, for I hadn't gone too far . . ."

Isabella's voice died and she ran her tongue over dry lips. Gently, Dr. Mahmoud slipped his hand under her head and held a cup of water to her mouth, but she was unable to drink.

After a long moment, she spoke again. "The man . . . your father, Katharina, gave me something. . . . Open the box now and lift out the ribbons. The bottom of the box . . . lift it up. There is something in there. It belongs to you."

Katharina was surprised to find a false bottom in the ribbon box, and when she lifted it, found an object wrapped in a handkerchief. Unwrapping it, she saw through eyes filled with tears a miniature religious painting the size of her hand.

"This is one of a pair—a diptych, like the one above the altar of our church. But so much smaller, as you can see. Do you see the blue stone in the picture, daughter? It is in the other painting as well. Together they tell a story."

"Mother—" Katharina's voice broke. "I don't understand."

"Your father . . . he had a pair of small paintings . . . a miniature diptych joined by a hinge. He broke it in half . . ." Isabella closed her eyes, picturing the solemn ritual that had taken place in the middle of the night seventeen years before. ". . . and gave me this half, this little painting, saying that in case he himself could not come back for you, if he was unable to travel and had to send an agent for you, the man would present the other half, and when they matched, I would know."

Katharina looked at her mother in confusion, then she frowned at the small painting in her hands. "Is this the Blessed Virgin?" In the panel, a woman dressed in medieval clothes was holding a blue crystal to her throat. A mysterious gesture. But there was no mistaking the value of the stone, for it was glorious in its color and transparency.

Isabella's voice came from far away, as if her spirit were already taking its leave. "He showed me the other painting. . . . In Latin, across the top, it said, '*Sancta Amelia, ora pro nobis.*' "

" 'St. Amelia, pray for us,' " Katharina murmured, unable to take her eyes off the miniature painting that had belonged to her father.

"He said . . . the blue crystal in the painting is St. Amelia's Stone and has magical healing properties because it was given to Amelia by Jesus himself."

Katharina was mesmerized by the painting. How to describe the color of the stone? Not sky blue, for that was too pale, nor ocean blue for that was too deep. And it wasn't just one hue but layer upon layer, as if it weren't a painting of a stone but the actual stone itself. Katharina had no way of knowing that the painting had been executed in England by a prioress named Mother Winifred five hundred years ago.

"Your father was dressed like a rich man," Isabella said in a whisper. "He might have been a noble. He left a bag of gold coins. I spent only a few, just to get us established here in Badendorf. After that, I never touched the money for it is your legacy. Each year, on your birthday . . . I promised myself that I would tell you the truth. But I couldn't bring myself to do it. You came into my life at a time when I was filled with grief and pain over the loss of my own babies. God forgive me, but part of me hoped the man would never come back for you. But now that I am dying, you have a right to know the truth."

"Hush, Mama. Save your strength. We can talk later."

Isabella shook her head, a gesture that took great effort. "You were never mine to keep, Katharina. I was to take care of you until he came back. But he hasn't returned and it might only be because he is injured, or ill, or is in prison somewhere. Perhaps even now he is praying to God to bring you to him." She reached up and touched Katharina's golden braids. "His hair is the color of yours. He had a magnificent yellow beard, like a sunburst. Look on the back of the painting."

Katharina turned it over and read the inscription: "Von Grünewald."

"That is your family name," Isabella said. "You see . . . you were never meant to be mine. Your destiny lies elsewhere. You must find your father, Katharina. He could be hurt. Perhaps he is ill. You must go to him."

"But I cannot leave you!" Katharina cried.

"Child, all this was not meant to be. Perhaps, if I had told you the truth long ago, things would be different. But in my selfishness I kept silent. Now I must make restitution. The stranger . . . he deserves to have his daughter."

Katharina began to sob. "But how will I find him?"

"He said he was going in search of the blue stone that is in that little painting. He told me he was going to Jerusalem, where he thought the stone was. Find it . . ." Isabella said, struggling for breath. "Find the blue stone, and you will find your father. When you match this miniature painting to its mate, you will have found him, God willing."

Her frail hand, that had stitched so many beautiful flowers and birds and butterflies, trembled against her daughter's cheek. "Promise me you will go, Katharina. For wherever this blue stone takes you, there you will find your destiny."

With those words, Isabella breathed her last breath. Katharina threw herself across her mother's body and wept while Dr. Mahmoud and Friar Pastorius saw that the crowd and Herr Müller were quietly dispersed. Isabella Bauer was buried in the local churchyard after a funeral, during which her many customers praised her skill and boasted owning many of the fine collars and handkerchiefs and linens decorated by her talented hand. They especially offered condolences to Katharina, men and women who had once made Isabella Bauer and her daughter wait for hours at the service entrance of their homes, and who often did not pay the seamstress for her weeks of work, but who now, once they had heard that the girl might be of noble blood and had come into a small fortune, treated her with great respect and deference.

Katharina moved woodenly through the days that followed, numb with shock over this sudden and unexpected turn in her life. And when she began to emerge a little from her grief, she started to wonder about the incredible story her mother had told her, wondered if it was true. So, with Dr. Mahmoud and Hans Roth accompanying her for protection, Katharina left Badendorf for the first time in her life, traveling north to a village that was only ten miles away but felt like another world to the seventeen-year-old girl.

There she found the inn where she had been born. Then she went to the nearby church and the elderly priest remembered a woman dying in childbirth, a noble lady, not of this district. She was buried in the graveyard. Katharina found the gravestone: the date of death was Katharina's birthday. And the last name was von Grünewald.

As Katharina knelt beside the grave she tried to feel something for the woman buried there but she could not. Her sorrow was for the seamstress who had been her real mother. Nonetheless, here lay the bones and dust of the woman who had given her life, and Katharina felt a strange new emotion flood her. As she laid her hands on the gravestone of Maria von Grünewald, dead at the age of twenty-six, Katharina vowed to search for her father—this poor woman's husband—and that no matter what obstacles might lie before her, she would be reunited with her true family.

*I*t was the talk of Badendorf. Katharina Bauer was going to Jerusalem!

Hans was less than happy. "*Why* must you go?"

As it was unthinkable she should travel alone, Katharina had first asked Hans to go with her but of course he could not; he was indispensable to the running of the stein factory. And then she had asked Friar Pastorius, but the poor young man was not of strong enough constitution to make such a journey, as dearly as he would have loved to see the holy city. Finally she had gone to Dr. Mahmoud for advice who had responded by saying that knowing one's father, and paying respect to him, was very important. He had gone on to say that by coincidence he had been thinking of going to Cairo, where he wished to die, and that he must not put it off too much longer as he was already an old man. And so it was decided that they would travel together.

"I made a promise, Hans," Katharina said resolutely as they returned from their last walk together in the woods that surrounded Badendorf. "I must find my family."

"But *I* am your family. When you marry me—"

She took hold of his hands and smiled sadly as she said, "Yes, I know, Hans. But my father intended to come back for me. It can only be because of great calamity that he did not. I have dreams—I see him in prison, alone and forgotten, or sick in a village far from here. I must find him. I owe it to him. And to my mother. My *two* mothers. When I have done this, I shall come back to you."

Frau Roth, who never believed anyone was good enough to marry her children and who had only grudgingly witnessed their vows at the altar, had always harbored the secret hope that Hans, her baby, would never marry. It was common knowledge that Herr Roth suffered from a heart ailment and that Frau Roth, being of robust constitution and iron will, would most likely outlive him by many years. She had no intention of being alone, and certainly none of being at the mercy of a daughter-in-law—let alone the daughter of a mere seamstress (Frau Roth did not for a moment believe the story of a rich nobleman). "Katharina must go, my son," she said in the warmest tone she could muster. "She was meant to be with her father."

"Then promise you will come back to me," Hans said with such passion that it embarrassed Katharina. "Do what you must, find your father, make peace with your past. And then come back and be my wife."

And so, on top of the two weighty promises Katharina had made to her mothers—one at a deathbed, the other at a graveside—she added another: to return to Badendorf and be Hans Roth's wife.

*T*he merchant train arrived and all of Badendorf turned out to see Katharina off. Frau Roth made a great display of the purse filled with silver talers and pfennigs she was giving to Katharina as a surprise gift. The bag was passed around as everyone looked in and remarked upon Frau Roth's generosity, and then, when no one was looking, she removed half the coins, secretly pocketed them, and handed the lightened purse to Katharina.

The massive merchant train had been formed by a league of merchants and investors who pooled their resources to protect their goods on the road: furs and amber from the north coast to be exchanged in the south for fruit, oil, and spices, which would then be taken back up north. The train was heavily guarded by hired soldiers, who rode alongside the huge wagons drawn by massive horses. Along the way, certain fierce brigands would receive "insurance" payments, and they in turn would keep other thieves away. Civilians joined such enormous trains, for it was the only safe way to travel.

Katharina and Dr. Mahmoud were to travel with Herr Roth's latest export shipment of beer steins, and as they said their tearful goodbyes, Hans gave Katharina a special stein: the centerpiece was a mountain scene with a small cameo of the town of Badendorf, meticulously crafted and painted by Herr Roth himself. Friar Pastorius, shy and red-faced with embarrassment, also gave Katharina a gift: a flat leather pouch, oiled and waxed so that it was waterproof, and strung on a leather thong to wear concealed under one's clothes. It was a perfect size for the miniature of St. Amelia.

And then they were off, a mile-long caravan that had originated in Antwerp and would continue on through Nuremberg, the financial trade center of Europe. It followed one of the major overland trade routes and expected to arrive at the Alps in the summer, when the passes were clear. The trail was known as the Amber Route and had been established long before even the Romans had invaded Europe, thousands of years ago when Stone Age people in the far north collected precious amber and transported it overland from the North Sea to the Mediterranean and Adriatic coasts. Roman legions had added roads and bridges and made the Alps passable. The Crusades and the sudden popularity of pilgrimages in the Middle Ages increased traffic on the route, and by the time Katharina and Dr. Mahmoud set out, they were part of a parade of merchants, wayfarers, pilgrims, beggars, vagrants, knights, and even royal postal wagons. It was a colorful procession with men playing pipes, women carrying bread and babies, children chasing dogs, a noisy group hauling creaking wagons, carts, and drays, some on horseback but most on foot, changing constantly at each crossroads where travelers left and others joined. Their way was impeded by many stops, as each new frontier and border crossing required an inspection of papers and proof that the traveler was free of the plague. Nightly stops were either in the open or at crude hostelries that charged exorbitant prices. At the Alpine passes they were helped by local people trained especially for the strenuous cartage.

Katharina thought it a wonderful adventure, for she enjoyed the safety of traveling under the protection of prosperous merchants who hired archers to guard them, and she enjoyed the comfort of traveling in an enclosed wagon that was also her bed at night. And in the evenings, quietly by the campfire, Dr. Mahmoud taught her his native tongue, for he believed knowledge of Arabic would be an asset to her in the Holy Land. As he told her stories of his youth, his memories were all literally sweet for he spoke of a golden fruit in Spain called an orange, and a rich fruit in Egypt called a date, neither of which Katharina had ever tasted. But the relative ease of their southward journey ended when she and Dr. Mahmoud had to part company with their fellow travelers in Milan, for the Roths' export agency was in Genoa, and they were advised not to sail from

Genoa for it would take weeks longer and they ran the risk of being attacked by Barbary pirates. So they joined a merchant train carrying French textiles to be exchanged in Venice for Venetian glass, and followed the fertile plain of the Po River until they turned north to Padua, and from there to the Adriatic coast. Although from Baden-dorf to the Alps they had been among friends, now they were with strangers, and so they kept to themselves. Dr. Mahmoud had learned long ago that there was survival in silence. He never let on that he was Muslim, for in this day and age he was the enemy, especially as they drew closer to the Mediterranean where the hated Turks ruled the seas.

Venice came as a shock. Although along the way they had passed through larger towns, and even the breathtaking metropolis of Nu-remberg, these had been but passing spectacles compared to Venice. Katharina had never seen a town so *flat*. There wasn't a mountain or hill in sight; people lived on canals and got about in small boats with curious curved prows; and the citizens were more sumptuously dressed than any she had seen in the northern towns. Upper-class women tottered about on tall platform shoes and did not cover their hair, as was the fashion in Germany, but proudly displayed their locks and tresses with gold nets and ribbons. Katharina had never seen such long hair on men, especially the young men who seemed to Katharina to be very feminine. But there was nothing feminine about the way they cast suggestive glances her way. Her own hair was also an at-traction. Even though her golden coloring was somewhat distinctive in Badendorf, it wasn't unusual. But the farther south she went, the more unique it became. Although she did see women with blond hair, it was dyed and obviously artificial, so that Katharina frequently drew the admiring glances of strange men. She stayed close to Dr. Mah-moud keeping a grip on their bundles, and they made their way to the harbor in the vast lagoon.

As they progressed through narrow streets and along canals, they chanced upon a wedding party in progress in one of the magnificent mansions. From a balcony, the bride and groom were merrily throwing food to the crowd below: Katharina saw whole roasted pheasants, golden loaves of bread, candied fruits, and sugared almonds rain down upon the happy recipients. At Dr. Mahmoud's quick thinking, they joined the crowd and grabbed a small wheel of cheese and a cluster of purple grapes, which they feasted on as they continued their trek toward the harbor. Such displays of wealth and largesse, they were later to learn, were typical of this powerful maritime city. Equally excessive, Katharina and Dr. Mahmoud learned, was the Venetians' sense of justice. For as they rounded a corner they came upon an angry mob that had moments earlier set upon a pair of men. The victims' chests were ripped open and their steaming hearts nailed to the doors of a small church. It was an act of revenge, Katharina was told by one of the bystanders. The two men had just the week before assassinated the head of one of Venice's most powerful families.

They hurried on to the harbor where they were met by more astonishing sights. Through a forest of forecastles and masts, sails and rigging, Katharina saw the water afloat with caravels, carracks, galleons, square-riggers, lateens, merchant ships, vessels of war, canoes, dinghies, launches, rafts, and even a pair of weather-beaten red-sailed Chinese junks. The quays were choked with mobs of pilgrims, both Christian and Muslim, embarking for and disembarking from their holy places. There were sailors of all navies, merchants, scholars, officers, lowly crewmen in rags, and longshoremen hauling bales, barrels, animals, and goods on board. The air was filled with the Babel of a hundred foreign tongues and the miasma of a thousand strange smells. Katharina even saw something called a bookstore. While she had seen printed books before—the church in Badendorf was proud that its Bible had been produced on a printing press—she had never seen as many books as this shop boasted: over four hundred in stock!

Katharina had never dreamed of travel and adventure and now they had been thrust upon her. Her spirit was a curious dichotomy of sadness and joy, for she both grieved for the loss of her mother and Badendorf and Hans, and at the same time she was thrilled at the thought of meeting her real blood family. She had not believed a person could look backward and forward at the same time, and yet she was doing just that.

They went to shipping offices, where Dr. Mahmoud's Arabic and rusty Spanish were of little use but Katharina's German and smattering of Latin stood them in good stead. Unfortunately, everywhere they inquired, they received a variety of responses, from captains refusing to take a Muslim, captains refusing to take a female, captains refusing passengers altogether. Superstition ran second to fear in a sailor's life: if a heathen didn't sink the ship, then a woman would.

The day was starting to wane, and so was their hope. Dr. Mahmoud suggested they find lodgings for the night and try anew in the morning.

That was when Katharina saw the stranger. He caught her attention because he was different from the others on the dock, although she could not pinpoint exactly why. There was the look of the nobleman about him in his white, padded doublet, blue, padded breeches and blue stockings. He wore a strange mantle, which was old-fashioned, since men didn't wear cloaks these days. It was all white with an eight-pointed blue cross embroidered on the back, as if he belonged to a religious order. Closely cropped brown hair and closely cropped beard above a white ruffed collar. Tall, fit. Elegant sword slung from a belt on his left hip. Clearly a man of wealth. But there was something about the way he looked out to sea; an air of mystery about him, or perhaps it was longing, that held Katharina's interest. He turned suddenly to speak to one of the porters, and Katharina caught a shadow of sadness in his eyes. *Tragedy haunts this man*, she thought, and was surprised at herself. Strangers to Badendorf had rarely caught her attention, let alone her imagination. Yet this man had done just that and she had no idea why.

As she turned to Dr. Mahmoud to ask where they were to go next, ruffians suddenly appeared from nowhere and knocked them aside to run off with their parcels. Katharina cried out and caught her elderly companion as he fell.

The stranger in the cloak, seeing what had happened, immediately took chase. "Right there, you maggoty bastards!" he shouted, catching up with them and dragging the two back by their collars. As soon as the thieves dropped their booty, they bolted, vanishing in the throng.

"Are you hurt?" the stranger said to Katharina, addressing her in Latin, the universal tongue of Christian travelers.

"We are all right, thank you, sir," Katharina said, breathless more from the stranger's proximity than from the assault by the ruffians.

"I am Don Adriano of Aragon, a knight of the Brotherhood of Mary. Is he a Turk?" He jerked his head toward Dr. Mahmoud.

Katharina filled her eyes with the stranger. Close up he was even more striking. Not so much handsome as possessing interesting features. And the shadows of longing and loneliness were even more evident. "Dr. Mahmoud is from Spain, sir, like yourself."

This seemed not to interest him. "Where are you bound?"

"For Haifa and then to Jerusalem."

He studied her again. A girl, with hair like spun gold and the naiveté of a newborn babe. What was she doing in the company of an old Arab, and heading to Jerusalem? It would be none of his concern except that she was a Christian bound for the Holy Land and he had taken a vow to aid pilgrims on their way to Jerusalem.

"I can take you to Haifa," he said, and quickly added, "But only you. Not the old man."

"But I cannot leave Dr. Mahmoud!"

Don Adriano was surprised to hear the passion in her voice and see it in her clear green eyes. There could be no blood relation between the girl and the old man, so what was their bond? He gave it further thought. Don Adriano's family had fought to push the Moors out of Spain. His father had died fighting the Muslims. And the brotherhood he belonged to, housed in a fortress on the island of Crete, was dedicated to wresting the Holy Land back from the barbaric Muslims and restoring it to Christendom.

But finally, deciding that his duty was to a Christian pilgrim, he nodded curtly. Let the old man tag along. He would not be Don Adriano's responsibility.

"Wait here," he said and he strode off, his white mantle with its blue cross billowing in the breeze. Katharina watched him engage a ship's captain in what looked like an angry debate for the captain kept shaking his head. But Don Adriano, being tall and of impressive bearing—and there was no mistaking his rank and status—finally won and the captain reluctantly nodded assent.

When the Spaniard returned he said, "I convinced the captain that taking a Muslim on board could be good insurance should we encounter Barbary pirates, for they will let one of their holy men go unscathed, as well as anyone in his company. The fact that your friend is also a doctor helped. But the captain says his crew won't have a female on board. Sailors are a superstitious breed. Any trouble and they'll blame you, señorita. He says there's only one way he'll take you. That you disguise yourself."

"Disguise myself! How?"

"You will travel as the old man's grandson."

Don Adriano took them to a small tavern and left them there, giving the proprietor a florin to keep an eye on them. When he returned a short time later, he took Katharina and Dr. Mahmoud out into the alley where, after making sure they were alone and unseen, he handed her a bottle of foul-smelling black paste. "It will turn your hair brown," he said, and then left her to do the work.

While Katharina massaged the dye into her scalp and long hair, Dr. Mahmoud dug into his traveling bag and brought out a spare galabeya, a long straight Egyptian robe that hung loosely and without shape on the body. From Katharina's shawl he was able to fashion a decent turban to cover her newly dyed hair, which she coiled on top of her head, tucking stray ends up. When she was dressed she emerged from behind the privacy of a stack of barrels. It was with a physician's eye that Mahmoud studied the finished product. He saw a problem with the feminine breasts, so he brought out a roll of bandages from his medicine kit, handed it to her and told her to bind her chest as flatly as she could. He discreetly turned his back while Katharina completed the disguise.

When they returned to the dock they saw Don Adriano striding toward them, and when his eyes fell upon Katharina, his mouth opened in mild surprise. She was so slim and tall and well disguised that one would mistake her for a boy.

He had purchased bottles of water, loaves of bread, wedges of cheese, some fruit, and strips of dried beef, for passengers were to provide for themselves. By the time they climbed the gangway, the elderly Muslim, his grandson, and the Christian knight, the sun was slipping to the horizon and the sailors were in the rigging.

She was a Portuguese ship that had recently brought elephant ivory from Africa and was now headed for India with a hold full of copper ingots bound for the coppersmiths of Bombay. There was a brief delay as the captain ordered some of the cargo removed and reloaded, for a cargo that shifted under sail could cause a shipwreck. Once he was satisfied that the copper was stowed low enough to stabilize his ship, he gave the order to set sail. He led his crew in prayer, and Katharina heard earnestness in their paternosters, for although ocean travel was the fastest way to travel, it was also the most dangerous. And then two boys played a flute and a drum while the seamen got busy with the ropes and winches, the rhythm of the tune helping them to work together. Finally they were sailing out of the lagoon and into the open sea. Katharina stood in the bow, her face into the wind as she thought, not of the people and village she had left behind, but of the family that awaited her in some unknown land.

◆ ◆ ◆

*T*hey slept as the sailors did, in hammocks strung between bales of cargo in the ship's hold. Space was so cramped that meals were taken on a small table wedged between two cannons. But most of the time, weather permitting, the three passengers spent their time on the deck in the fresh air.

Katharina wondered about their rescuer, for although Don Adriano stayed with her and Dr. Mahmoud at all times, and advertised by his imposing presence that he was their protector, he otherwise had nothing to do with them. She noticed that he touched neither meat nor wine, and wondered if it had to do with the vows of his brotherhood, and when she watched him pray—down on one knee, holding his sword in both hands before him, the hilt resembling a crucifix—she suspected he was a deeply religious man.

But a troubled one.

There were lines in his face that she thought at first had been created by wisdom and experience. But then she thought, *no, they were etched by pain.* And there was the look of longing as he stared out to sea for hours on end. What was he seeing? What was he searching for? Adriano watched the sunset, watched the sky darken and the stars come out one by one, his face uplifted as if expecting to see some message written up there. He carried silence around himself like the knight's cloak he wore. He was wrapped in it, that silence. Was it to keep things out, or to keep things in? Maybe both. Katharina had never been curious about a person before. She had never wondered what Hans was thinking, never desired to plumb his depths. What she saw on the surface she accepted as the whole person. It had never occurred to her that secrets and passions could run beneath. But now she could not stop wondering about this enigmatic stranger who seemed, day by day, to be not of this world but to dwell instead in the interior landscape of his soul.

Her thoughts startled her. It struck her that they were the wise and lofty thoughts of an adult. She considered the hundreds of miles she had traveled, and all the towns and people she had seen, and now she was on a vast ocean, and it made her feel suddenly mature. She had celebrated her eighteenth birthday on the Amber Route and now she felt no longer like a girl but a woman. She liked the feeling and she believed that she now understood everything about life. She had been through so much in such a short time, losing her mother and learning the truth about her birth and identity, and now halfway into the Adriatic Katharina was convinced she had seen most of the world. And when she thought of Jerusalem and the dramatic reunion with her father and family there, she imagined herself going back to Badendorf, being received as a special person because she had traveled so far and now she was a wise woman. She already knew how she would describe Jerusalem to everyone, with its magnificent churches standing in rows, the people all pious and religious, everyone speaking Latin and conferring benedictions as a matter of course. And because she would be the most worldly person in Badendorf, people would come to her for advice, even Father Benedict whose sole claim to fame rested on a single trip to Rome. But he had never been to Jerusalem, where Jesus himself had walked.

As the days passed and the horizon stretched before them, Katharina became terribly seasick but Dr. Mahmoud eased her discomfort with a remedy made of ginger. She also felt uncomfortable beneath the stares of the crew, who kept looking at her with unreadable expressions. And when the ship had gone for a long time without a sighting of land, she felt a special panic in her heart. For solace she frequently drew the miniature painting from the leather pouch Friar Pastorius had given her, and which she wore beneath her Egyptian robe. Sitting on the deck, knees drawn up, cradling the miniature in her hands, she would rivet her eyes to the blue crystal and wonder what was there about it that had made her father leave his baby daughter to go in search of it. Had he found it, and was the power of the crystal such that it had wiped his mind clean of all memory, making him forget his obligation back in Germany?

She wished she could also hold the stein Hans had given her because in these unfamiliar and frightening surroundings she would draw comfort from such a familiar object, and from the feel of the clay of Badendorf beneath her fingers. But the stein had been packed with her bundle of clothes, protected deep in the folds of skirts and bodices, shawls and scarves, to ensure that it didn't break. She wouldn't see the stein till she reached her lodgings in Jerusalem. Her father's house? They would share a drink from the stein, and her father, being a German nobleman and so long away from home, would weep at the sight of so exquisite a beer stein.

A week out from Venice, the storm hit.

Half the sailors wanted to hoist the mainsail, the others said this was not the time as the wind was increasing. A dispute broke out; they decided to hoist the sail but then it was too late, the canvas tore in two. All fires were doused: the cook's stove and the lanterns. The seas rose. Dr. Mahmoud and Katharina held on to each other. Thunder was suddenly upon them, lightning, and heavy rain pouring down. The wind increased until the main mast gave way with a mighty cracking sound and crashed to the deck. The sailors fell to their knees and began praying loudly. Gigantic waves rose up and swept over the sides, sending the decks awash. Barrels and bales, breaking loose, were swept this way and that and finally overboard. The ship was actually swallowed and went under the water, but in the next instant rose up again as if on a spout. Up and down it went, through the tempest, with her frail human crew and cargo screaming and praying and holding on for dear life.

*K*atharina woke to find herself on a sandy shore, her clothes soaked, her long hair tangled with seaweed. The sky was gray but no rain fell, and the ocean roiled like angry fluid metal with foamy points. Wooden planks and scraps of sail floated on the waves. She looked up and down the deserted shore and saw the remnants of ship and cargo strewn among the dunes. But she saw no people.

She struggled to her feet and looked around in bewilderment. Where was the ship? Where was the crew? "Dr. Mahmoud!" she called. Her only response was the mocking howl of the wind. Staggering along the beach, her galabeya tattered and trailing in the wet sand, she presently came upon a body. It was the captain, and crabs were already making a feast of him. Farther along she found remnants of a wooden chest, but few of its contents remained. Sticking out of the sand she saw a shard of white ceramic. She pulled it out and brushed it off. It was part of the beer stein Hans had given her. She searched for the rest of it but found no other pieces. Still numb with shock, Katharina cradled the small oval in her hand—the miniature painting of Badendorf nestled in the mountains.

Then she saw a figure ahead, stumbling along the sand, his cloak billowing and swirling about him. Don Adriano! Katharina broke into a run, waving her arms and calling out, tripping on the hem of her torn galabeya.

"Praise God!" he cried when they reached one another. She fell into his arms, sobbing. He enveloped her in his damp cloak, and they cried and shivered together until he finally drew her down to her knees and they offered prayers of thanks for their survival.

"Where are we?" she said, her lips cracked and crusted with salt.

He squinted out at the dismal ocean and invisible horizon. "I have no idea, señorita."

"Have you seen Dr. Mahmoud?"

His eyes were filled with sadness as he said, "I saw him go under. I reached into the water but he had gone down. I am sorry."

She cried anew, sitting in the sand and drawing her knees to her chest. Don Adriano draped his knight's cloak about her and went in search of dry wood for a fire.

It was some time before she remembered her small painting of St. Amelia. She cried out with joy when she found it still around her neck in its waterproof pouch, and when she brought it out into the light of the flames from Don Adriano's struggling fire, she drew hope from the comforting image of Amelia and the blue crystal.

Adriano explored their environment and learned they were on an island that was little more than a rocky outcropping in the sea with no greenery or wildlife. But he found casks of water washed ashore from the ship and enough dry driftwood to keep the fire going. Together he and Katharina dug for crabs and other shellfish, which they steamed between hot rocks and wet seaweed.

The sky darkened so they knew the sun had gone down, but clouds blocked the stars, and a mist crept in from the ocean. Don Adriano banked the fire and got it blazing. Katharina stared into the flames like one in a trance. She kept picturing Dr. Mahmoud as she had last seen him: being swept over the side of the ship, his turban flying off, a look of terror on his face. She thought of their weeks traveling together, his gentle patience, and the things he had taught her. She had hoped, back then, that she could persuade him to stay in Jerusalem with her instead of going on to Cairo, for the Arab doctor had been the closest to a blood relative she had ever known. She was also overwhelmed with grief for the death of her mother, and it surprised her for she had thought she was over it. But new death, it seemed, renewed old grief, so that Katharina, weeping into her hands, was mourning not only for Dr. Mahmoud, but for her mother, her birth-mother, the crew, and the captain of the Portuguese ship.

*O*ver the next few days, more bodies of the crew washed ashore, and as the stranded pair gave them Christian burials, Adriano with-drew into deeper silence, and Katharina's grief and despair grew. Fi-nally, one morning she came across the pale corpse of one of the boys who had played pipes and drum on the ship, and she knew she could not go on. Believing that her survival had been an accident, that she belonged in the watery deep with Dr. Mahmoud, she waded out into the surf, intent upon drowning herself in the waves.

But Adriano ran after her and, following a brief struggle in the water, managed to bring her back and deposit her on the sand. There he took her by the shoulders and said with passion, "We do not know God's purpose. We cannot begin to guess at His design. We must only do His bidding. He spared us, señorita, for what reason I do not know. But to give in to despair is to defy God's will. For His sake, you must stay alive." They were the most words he had spoken in days, and the mere speaking of them seemed to revive his strength.

Katharina cried for a long time afterward, and although she still felt she should have died with Dr. Mahmoud, she made no more attempts to drown herself. She ate little and drank a little, and wan-dered the small shore with her eyes set to the far horizon, deciding that she and Adriano were probably as good as dead anyway.

*T*hey slept together for warmth and finally the morning came when Katharina awoke to feel the knight's arms around her, his solid body against hers, the firm beat of his heart beneath her head as it lay upon his chest. Lifting herself up, she studied his face in the pale dawn, noticing how sand and salt crystals clung to his thick brown eyelashes and brows and closely cropped beard. What troubled dreams, she won-dered, made his eyes roll beneath their lids? What passions drove him to stay alive, and drove him to keep *her* alive as well, because she knew that without Adriano she would surely have killed herself. Then she remembered waking during the night screaming, and Adriano there to hold her and comfort her. What had made her scream? Dreams of drowning.

For the first time in days, dawn brought sunlight, for the clouds were dispersing and the ocean even sparkled in places. While Adriano managed to spear some fish in nearby shallows, Katharina scavenged the shore and found yet another cask of ship's water. She wondered how long they could survive on an island where not even a single tree grew. They had seafood but nothing else. No birds came here to roost. No vegetation struggled among the rocky fissures. And then it crossed her mind to wonder if it was proper for a man and woman to live together and not be married. Did the church take shipwrecked people into consideration when it catalogued sins?

When another sunset seemed to mock them in their stranded state, for it was apparent the storm had knocked their ship far off course and out of the sight of other passing vessels, Adriano found voice and words. "Why do you go to Jerusalem?" he asked as he stoked the fire.

As Katharina braided her long hair that, to her surprise, was still brown as the dye had not been washed out by the sea water, she told him her story, ending with: "So I go to search for my father."

"A man who abandoned you?"

"I am sure he did not intend to. He meant to come back for me."

"But this young man you mentioned, Hans Roth. You could have married him, lived very comfortably. You would risk losing all that?"

She looked at him with steady eyes. "My father might be hurt, or in the hands of cruel men. It is my duty to find him."

This gave him something to think about. If truth be told, Don Adriano felt bitterly toward women. He had only ever loved one woman in his life and when she had betrayed him with another man, he had sworn he would never love another as he had loved her, nor would he ever again trust a woman. Once he had entered the Brotherhood of Mary and taken a vow of celibacy, he had put women from his mind.

Katharina pointed to the blue cross embroidered on the breast of his white doublet and said, "Are you a priest?"

He gave her a startled look, and then his face softened into a smile. "No, señorita, I am not. Just a servant of the Lord." He fell silent and stared morosely into the flames. Presently he said, "I killed a man who was not my enemy, and I ruined a woman's life. For a day and a night

I lay prone before an altar, asking the Blessed Mother for a sign. She came to me in a vision and spoke of a brotherhood dedicated to restoring her throne in the Holy Land. I sought them out and joined their membership. That was twenty years ago, and I serve both the brotherhood and the Blessed Mother still."

He brought his soulful gaze back to Katharina. "Who is the old man you call Mahmoud?"

"When I was orphaned he became my guardian."

"A heathen?"

"He believes in God, and he prays. Even more frequently than we do. Dr. Mahmoud is a good man." Tears sprang to her eyes. "Was," she corrected softly.

Don Adriano had his own opinions of good men and godless men, but he kept them to himself. What an innocent this child was, to be out in the world on her own with no protection other than a frail old heathen. Don Adriano felt a rare emotion stir his heart, one he had not felt in a long time, not since a woman named Maria had destroyed his life and made him vow never to love again.

And then he quickly remembered himself, and turned away. Thoughts of women had no place in the mind of a man on a religious crusade.

As Katharina watched sparks rise up to the indifferent stars, memories drifted up in her mind: her mother telling her the stories of Rapunzel and Little Red Cap. The two of them going for walks in the snow. The night Isabella had hurried home from delivering embroidery to a patron, bearing strudel still warm from the oven, and the delicious feast they had shared that night. Sleeping together on cold nights, Katharina watching the snow fall beyond the window, and feeling safe and loved. She poked the embers and said quietly, "My mother could have taken the gold coins and left me at the inn and maybe found a rich husband with those gold coins. But she didn't. She kept me and raised me and loved me. She went hungry while we had gold coins hidden in our room. She sacrificed and went without and kept them safe for me, but now I have lost them, in that ocean. I have let her down."

Adriano nodded gravely. "Mother is the first to love us, and the first whom we love. Father always comes later." His set his eyes to the horizon. "I serve God, but it is the Blessed Mother whom I love, and to whom I have dedicated my life and my soul." He brought his eyes back to Katharina. "I feel as you do, that I have let my mother down. But we shall leave this island, señorita. We shall not be left here to die."

Katharina looked at the barren rocks behind them, craggy and dark and forbidding, and she thought, *Nothing grows here, nothing survives here, how can we?* Then she looked at Adriano and marveled at this man who had the faith of apostles.

Adriano kept watch while the girl slept, his eyes fixed to the black sea, watching for the dangers that he knew lurked out there. He did not tell her that although they had survived the shipwreck, there was more for them to fear, for the threat of being found by Barbary corsairs or an Ottoman naval vessel were all too real. And the likely fates for either of them—a helpless girl and a Christian knight—were grim. Nonetheless he prayed and drew hope from thoughts of God that a Venetian ship would be the first to come along.

Their rescuers turned out to be neither pirates nor Turks but scavengers aboard a Greek caravel, one of the many independent opportunistic mercenary ships that scoured the Mediterranean for anything that could be traded for a profit. In this case the captain was a man who sold slaves to the sultan's court. He saw value in keeping the girl a virgin and so threatened to kill any of his crew who touched her, and likewise in keeping the knight in sound condition, for he knew that the Turks reserved a special torture-death for Christian knights.

And so instead of continuing eastward toward Jerusalem and the blue crystal of St. Amelia, Katharina found her course suddenly changed as the caravel pointed north and sailed for Constantinople, center of the Ottoman Empire.

*W*here are you taking us? Please, I have to go to Jerusalem. If it is money you want, my father—"

Katharina's pleas fell on deaf ears. Shackled and ignored, she sat huddled in dark bewilderment and misery, praying that Adriano was safe, and that this nightmare would soon end.

The Greek caravel had stopped at the nameless island in hopes of finding freshwater. Now, chained in the hold and facing an unknown fate, Katharina didn't know whether to thank God for their good fortune or curse their bad luck. After all, they were no longer stranded, but now they were on a slave ship. If the Greek caravel had never happened by, she and Adriano might never have been found and would have lived on that barren outcropping until they died.

By the time the caravel docked at Constantinople, its hold was filled with human goods ranging from children to elderly people, of all nationalities and tongues, for it had stopped along the way to raid, kidnap, steal, and buy slaves for the sultan. During the voyage, Katharina had been kept below like the others, crammed into a lightless, foul-smelling space with little water and food, no communication with the outside world, violently seasick, and certain she was about to die. She did not see Adriano until they were dragged out into the sunlight of the busy harbor. With the light stabbing her eyes, she saw him shackled to a row of wretched looking men, Adriano standing out because of his height and bearing. He was half-naked and looked abused, but still he held his head high, and she saw him bend to help a fellow captive who had stumbled. Katharina tried to signal to him, but whips drove them in separate directions until Katharina saw him disappear into a noisy, colorful throng.

The sunlight and fresh air did little to revive her. Her dyed hair matted and crawling with vermin, her galabeya stained with vomit, she stumbled barefoot over searing cobblestones along with her weeping and wailing companions. The trek was not far to the imperial gate, an imposing white marble arch open to all and standing three hundred feet from the hippodrome and the basilica of Hagia Sophia, which had been converted into a mosque. Strung across the front of the gate were the rotting heads of criminals as a warning to the population. Through this massive entrance streamed people of all kinds, from high-ranking dignitaries to the lowest of classes—Muslims and Christians, citizens and foreigners—all watched over by fierce guards armed with scimitars, spears, and arrows.

Driven by overseers with whips, the weeping girls and women were crowded into a smaller courtyard guarded by large black men with pikestaffs, and there the captives were stripped and left to shiver naked beneath the sky. Katharina wanted to cry out in protest. They had taken Friar Pastorius's leather pouch that contained the miniature of St. Amelia and the oval ceramic of Badendorf. It had been her little piece of Germany, a bit of pottery made from German soil, fashioned by German hands, and painted with German love. Wherever her body might be, that was where her heart was. But now it had been taken from her, along with the painting that would identify her to her father. How was she to get them back?

A formidable looking woman appeared, tottering on very high platform shoes and wearing a conical headdress that made her look even taller. She stopped before each captive female and said, "Believer or nonbeliever?" To the muttered replies she then performed a cursory visual examination and sorted the poor woman or girl out with a single word: "kitchens," "laundry," "barracks," or "slave market." By the time the woman reached her, Katharina had deduced that those who claimed to be believers were given jobs in the palace whereas nonbelievers were sent to the slave market or, possibly worse, to the nearby guards barracks to serve as pleasure-girls.

Before the woman could even pose her question, Katharina blurted, "La illaha illa Allah!", which meant, "There is no God but God," the essential Muslim prayer she had learned from Dr. Mahmoud.

The woman's eyebrows rose. "You are Muslim?"

Katharina bit her lip. Dr. Mahmoud had taught her enough of Islam and the Koran that she knew she could pass for one of this woman's faith. But then she thought of Adriano and his devotion to the Virgin and his vow to assist Christian travelers, and knowing that he would be tortured for his faith, that *he* would never pretend to be other than a follower of Christ, she bent her head and murmured, "No, Lady, I am a Christian. But I can read and write," she added quickly, hoping this would spare her from the fates of the other women, for she suspected that life in the palace kitchens and laundry was hard and short.

The woman took a moment longer with Katharina than she had with the others, inspecting her hands and teeth, and inquiring about her bloodline, to which Katharina replied that she was of noble lineage. Finally the woman signaled to an assistant who led Katharina away through a doorway that, to Katharina's surprise, opened onto steaming baths where women and girls were socializing in various forms of undress. Here she was scrubbed and checked for lice, the attendant grumbling that it was well known that Christians did not wash with great frequency. And then to her further shock was forced to suffer complete removal of all her body hair, which she later learned was required of all Muslim men and women, according to Koranic injunction.

She was given fresh clothes—a curious costume of long robes, trousers, and a veil to cover her face—and after brief questioning and a demonstration of her skill with a needle, Katharina was assigned to the entourage of the Mistress of the Costume. She soon discovered that this position, lowly and menial though it was, allowed her to travel all over the women's side of the palace with a group of seamstresses, each of whom had a specialized job. Katharina was told that if she did well, she might someday be elevated to the position of Keeper of the Thread, whose sole job was to organize and keep track of embroidery thread, with herself having assistants. Although this piece of information was clearly meant to be good news and to help cheer her up, to Katharina it was a prison sentence, for it meant she was going to spend the rest of her life in this place.

Thus did she begin her new life in the great sultan's palace in Constantinople. No one cared that she was a German citizen searching for her father, that she was a freeborn woman with rights, that she might even be of noble blood. In fact, no one cared anything about her at all, not even her name, for the sultan's palace was populated with thousands of slaves and servants who had all come as captives at one time or another. They lived out their lives within these high walls with an air of resignation, and many even turned the situation to their advantage, rising high in their own ranks, gaining wealth and political status.

A complex of pavilions set in green surroundings and encircled by high walls, the seraglio stood on a hill overlooking the forum of Theodosius and the sultan's fabulous stables that housed four thousand horses. Within this isolated, exotic world Katharina tasted rice for the first time and learned to drink coffee morning, noon, and night. She also learned to fall to her knees five times a day for the call to prayer, and each time her heart wept with the memory of Dr. Mahmoud who had prayed this same way in their garden in Badendorf, during their journey along the Amber Route, and on the deck of the ill-fated Portuguese ship. In her prayers she also remembered Adriano, whom she desperately hoped was still alive and somewhere nearby, and her father, renewing her determination to go to Jerusalem and find him.

The women who lived in the imperial harem were divided into two classes: the concubines and those who served them. The concubines were women who, having met strict criteria of beauty, poise, and charm, had been set aside as sexual partners for the sultan. The servants, who ranged from hard laborers to those with skill and education, saw to the myriad needs of the concubines. Katharina was put to work adding flourishes and embellishments to fabrics and textiles that were already rich and sumptuous beyond imagining. But at least she was not put to work in the kitchens, or under the baths where they kept the water hot (in other societies, this work would be done by men, but no men were allowed within the walls of the seraglio).

Katharina knew that another world—the *real* world of commerce, science, and men—existed in another part of the palace. There was a secret room at the top of the Imperial Gate for the sultan's ladies to watch parades unseen, and from there Katharina saw the endless processions of foreign dignitaries, visitors, ambassadors, heads of state, scientists, and artists. This was an age of exploration and discovery, and as the sultan considered himself to be an enlightened ruler, he welcomed the world to his doorstep. Beneath the marble arch strode conquering Spaniards with their Indians from the New World, making gifts of Aztecs and Incas to the sultan. Emissaries from the court of Henry VIII brought books on astronomy and musical works composed by the king himself. And from Italy came artists with new ideas for painting and sculpture. When she saw these Europeans on their horses below, Katharina wanted to shout to them, "Here I am! Please take me away!" But though that real world lay beyond only a few high walls, it might as well exist among the stars for as accessible as it was to the women in the Imperial Harem.

Although at times Katharina thought she would go insane in this gilded cage, and although she often wept into her pillow late at night, she kept her silence and blended into the routine of this world of unreality, following the seamstresses, doing her fine sewing, watching and listening as she counted the days and waited for an opportunity to escape. She discreetly enquired about a man who had been taken prisoner with her and brought to Constantinople by the same slave traders. A Christian Spaniard knight, she said. She asked, too, about possessions that were taken from captives, for there was something special that had belonged to her that she desperately needed to get back. But her questions were met by indifference and blank stares.

So she would have to find them on her own: Adriano, and the miniature of St. Amelia.

*A*lthough she lived in a kind of prison, it was a prison with its own form of freedom, for as long as she stayed within the walls of the seraglio Katharina was free to go where she wished. The endless corridors with their magnificent stone pillars and fountains, the marble benches and exotic gazebos, the gardens where musicians played endlessly, the sudden, unexpected plazas where jugglers and dancers entertained, the mazes of apartments and baths were all like a self-contained city of imponderable luxury, leaving its pampered inmates wanting for nothing. The whole precinct was filled with a delightful citrus scent as all marble columns and walls were washed down daily in lemon juice to make them shine. But there was one place Katharina was forbidden to go: a beautiful arched colonnade called the Pearl Gate. This led, she was cautioned, to the private apartments of the Sultana Safiya, the sultan's favorite concubine, and only those under invitation may enter.

There was always something exciting going on in the palace, whether it was a religious holiday with music and feasting, or a party honoring someone's birthday, or a festival venerating the sultan, with parades and trumpets and visiting entertainers. Within the Imperial Harem, the most exciting moments were when a girl was selected for the sultan's bed. Although the women of the palace, from lowest slave to the sultana, were all the sultan's personal possessions to do with as he wished, few women ever actually saw him. That was why there were so few children in the harem: just little girls who had been fathered by the sultan. Three boy babies had died in infancy, leaving only one living son to the sultan, by a concubine whom Katharina had never seen. Such women as did get pregnant (usually by a guard or a visitor who had managed to sneak in) were put to death. Girls entered these walls as virgins and lived out their lives without knowing a man's touch. Therefore when the sultan chose a girl to come to his bed (and no one quite knew how the selection was made since he never visited the harem), the days of preparation were among the liveliest of celebrations, with much excitement and gossip and speculation surrounding the event as the lucky candidate was bathed and massaged and clothed in the finest garments and jewels, treated like a queen and given whispered hints on how to please the sultan. The next morning, excitement continued to run high as everyone anticipated the gifts the girl would receive, speculating on the generosity of the sultan, everyone genuinely happy for her, celebrating her good fortune and eager to hear how the night went. Although the girl would never be called to the sultan's bedroom again, she was nonetheless a special person now for she had been chosen, and her elevated status in the harem was secured.

Another favorite entertainment among the women was riding in little boats on an enormous indoor pool, knocking turbans off the eunuchs' heads and seeing which team could knock the turbans farthest out onto the water. There were endless diversions with pet monkeys, parrots, and trained pigeons that wore little pearl anklets and performed tricks; eternal hours spent over backgammon games and chess; never-ending afternoons trying on dresses and veils, slippers and jewelry; brushing each other's hair, or experimenting with cosmetics, mixing perfumes, trying this cream or that, and tweezing imagined hairs from anywhere on the body.

Gossip, too, was a mainstay of the harem, as the concubines and their servants gobbled up rumors the way they did candied fruits: who was sleeping with whom (Jamila and Sarah), who had broken whose heart (that witch Farida and poor little Yasmin), who was jockeying for favors with Sultana Safiya, who was getting fat, who was getting old. The main topic for weeks had been the scandalous love affair between Mariam and one of the African eunuchs—when they were caught both had been beheaded, their corpses strung up on the Imperial Gate as a warning to the others.

The main pastime, however, it seemed to Katharina, was simply to while away the hours doing nothing. A great deal of this nonactivity was spent in the baths—washing, being massaged, having body hair removed. The women lounged in the saunas for hours, snacking on fruit and drinks while they gossiped. There were no tubs in these baths, for the Turks suspected that evil jinn lurked in standing water, so the women sat on marble benches and were soaped and scrubbed by slaves. Katharina was astonished at their lack of modesty, for these women wore not a stitch but lay about naked or paraded back and forth to show off firm breasts and buttocks. Since these sensuous women were so seldom in the arms of a virile male—the eunuchs being generally of no interest—they sought sexual pleasure with one another and frequently formed passionate romantic attachments that lead to violent jealousies and hatreds.

So much tedium and languishing and lack of purpose filled Katharina with a vague uneasiness. These women had all been brought here against their will yet now they seemed satisfied, happy even, as if their hearts and memories had been numbed. They were leading lives that were a kind of pleasant death and Katharina feared that if she spent long enough in this enchanted place, she too would succumb to its magic. And this must never happen. She had made a deathbed promise to find her father. And she owed her life to Adriano.

Haunted by visions of what might be happening to him at that moment, Katharina was consumed with guilt over the luxurious life she was leading. Every morning, with the first of the day's five prayers, she reminded herself that on the island, Adriano had not given up on her. So now she was not going to give up on him. One way or another, she would repay the debt.

*H*e was there again, the disfigured eunuch, watching her. Katharina was certain now that it was no accident. After weeks of encountering him in odd places, she was convinced he was following her. And it frightened her.

After eight months in the Imperial Harem, Katharina had managed by wit and cunning to keep herself from getting drawn into the myriad tangled relationships, crushes and jealousies, politics and conspiracies, plots and counterplots that constantly seethed between the cliques and rival groups. Pecking order was crucial, and it changed and shifted like sand dunes, with concubines rising or descending within the harem hierarchy, gaining favor with the majority, or losing it upon a whim. Only the Sultana Safiya, the sultan's favorite, remained above it all, and Katharina had yet to even glimpse this lofty personage. While others had tried to draw Katharina into their various factions, she managed to stay neutral, and after a while they respected her for this, for they knew they could trust her and depend upon her honesty. She had also managed to stay in favor with her temperamental mistresses—of the Silk, of the Thread, of the Slippers—and while she had not exactly made any friends in the harem, neither had she made enemies.

But the eunuchs were another matter, and even after eight months of trying to adapt to this impossible world that was unlike the world outside, she still could not fathom the strange creatures who guarded the women.

The harem was overseen exclusively by black eunuchs who were purposely ugly or deformed in order to discourage any romantic interest on the part of the women. Captured in Africa as youths, they were castrated along the way, usually in a desert where the hot sand was the only remedy against the high incidence of fatal hemorrhage, the operation being so extensive: for a eunuch to qualify for the Imperial Harem he had to have undergone complete removal of the penis and testicles (resulting in the need to urinate through a pipe that the eunuch kept concealed in his turban). Eunuchs could rise to great power and themselves have a staff of servants and slaves; they could be formidable enemies if one fell out of favor with them. Which was why Katharina was worried about this one that was clearly following her around and spying on her. To whom was he reporting, and why?

Her suspicions were answered late one night when she was awakened in her bed in the dormitory by a hand suddenly clamped over her mouth. It was not unusual for girls to mysteriously disappear and never be heard from again—the gossip was always about infractions, disfavor, jealousy. Where these luckless girls vanished to no one ever knew, and no one dared try to find out. Katharina was carried from the dormitory while girls watched under the pretense of sleep, fearful that even being witnesses could bring this same fate upon themselves.

But once outside in the moonlight, the eunuch put her down and gestured for her to be silent, indicating that she follow him.

He took her to an apartment in a special wing of the harem, where only the most highly favored ladies lived, and Katharina was astounded at the sumptuousness of it. This inner sanctum was grander than anything she had seen so far, with its rich carpets and tapestries, pillow-strewn divans and gold furnishings. Whoever lived here had wealth and power.

And then Katharina saw her—a young woman not much older than herself, slender and lovely, dressed in shimmering silks of crimson and vermilion, all edged in gold. "God's peace," the young woman said with a smile. "Please remove your veil."

Katharina did so, exposing her long hair that was bound up in intricate braids around her head.

"And your hat," came the second order, although it was more of a request, and Katharina removed the little boxlike silk hat that covered the crown of her head. The concubine studied her for a moment, then she broke into a pleasant laugh. "You look as if you are wearing a yellow skull cap!"

Katharina blushed. All the girls teased her about it. They loved hearing her tale of disguising herself as a boy, and dyeing her hair to make herself look Egyptian. But what was even more hilarious was that now that her hair had partially grown out, the first few inches were her natural golden color while the longer tresses were still muddy brown.

"My eunuch told me you were blond," the young woman said. She held out her hand. "Please sit. Be comfortable." Then she gestured to servants to pour coffee into tiny cups and that Katharina still found undrinkable.

"I have been watching you," her mysterious hostess said. "Or rather, my eunuch has been watching you and he has been reporting to me." She daintily sipped her drink. "You have not joined any clique. There is not a concubine who can, as the saying goes, claim to have you in her pocket. This says something of your character, for some of them can be most persuasive when recruiting minions. You are your own person, which is rare in the harem."

She spoke Arabic, which Katharina had grown proficient in over the months; she was able to understand her hostess and make herself understood. "What does the sultana wish of me?" she said. Katharina knew that the Ottoman sultans had ceased bothering with marriage and that there hadn't been a wife in this dynasty for centuries. Favorite concubines, however, could rise to special status, and for lack of a better title, the current favorite was given the honorific of sultana.

The young woman corrected her: "I am not the sultana. But I *am* the sultan's second favorite woman. My name is Asmahan and I have brought you here to ask a favor of you."

Katharina was immediately on her guard. "A favor, Lady?"

Asmahan spoke in a soft, mellifluous voice. "I was kidnapped eight years ago from my home in Samarkand and sold to the sultan's house. Like you, I became a prisoner in the harem, to spend the rest of my days here. But I was lucky—I was chosen to spend a night with the sultan. As you know, such women are elevated in status, even though they never see him again. But in my case, God be praised, I became pregnant. For nine months I was pampered and cosseted and watched as everyone waited to see if I was going to produce a boy or a girl. If it was a girl, she would be raised in the harem and groomed for a future political marriage. But if it was a boy . . ."

Katharina had already heard the sultan had a son by a favorite concubine. Asmahan was the envy of the whole harem. "The sultan must be very happy," Katharina said, for lack of anything else to say, and wondering what favor this powerful woman could possibly ask of her.

"Yes. He dotes upon our son. Bulbul is often collected and taken to the sultan's apartment for days at a time." Another thoughtful sip of the strong brew.

Katharina waited.

Asmahan leaned forward and her voice grew tense. "The sultana is also pregnant. Surely you knew this."

Katharina wanted to say that a robin didn't lay an egg in the palace without every single one of its thousand inhabitants knowing it. "I had heard," she said. Sultana Safiya, the most powerful woman in the Ottoman Empire because she alone was called back repeatedly to the sultan's bed.

"It isn't her first pregnancy," Asmahan went on in a voice barely above a whisper. Katharina imagined a thousand unseen eyes watching them, a hundred ears listening behind the drapes. "The other pregnancies ended in miscarriages, or she gave birth to daughters. But the astrologers say that this time it is a son. Do you know what has happened to other women who got pregnant by the sultan?"

Katharina had heard stories. One poor creature, only weeks ago, was in her fifth month of pregnancy when she was summoned to Sultana Safiya's apartment never to be seen again. The rumors were that Safiya had kicked the girl in the stomach, causing a massive miscarriage that had ended the lives of both mother and child.

"By various methods the sultana has managed to keep the way clear for her own child. I was lucky—and smart. When my time neared, I asked the sultan to have his personal physicians at hand. Safiya could not touch me or my baby. I know she hates my son. But even she has not had the brazenness to try to remove him. But once she gives birth to a son, then she can *legally* remove mine."

"She will kill him?" Katharina said.

"Wish that were so! But a worse fate awaits my little Bulbul if the sultana gives birth to a son." Asmahan glanced around, even though they were alone in the luxurious chamber. "There is within this palace a room called the Cage. It is a very small room at the end of a long corridor. The doors and windows are sealed off so there is no access to the outer world. There live Turkish princes who are not allowed to inherit the throne. They are raised in complete isolation by deaf mutes, and after many years they usually go mad."

"But what cruelty! Why is this?"

"There is a law under Turkish rule that the son who inherits the throne must eliminate his brothers. But the removal must take place without bloodshed. Life imprisonment in the Cage is their sentence. This will happen to my Bulbul should Safiya give the sultan a son."

"I do not understand, Lady. Your son is older."

"But I am of lower birth than Safiya. She comes from a very noble and ancient Turkish family, whereas my family are nomads—we are rich and powerful in our own country, but that does not count here. Safiya reminds the sultan of this at every opportunity, and already I see his mind changing."

"But how can I help you?"

"God willing, you will take Bulbul back to my family in Samarkand."

Katharina drew in a sharp breath. "Samarkand! But, Lady! Why me? Of the hundreds of women within these walls—"

"Because you are the only one who wishes to escape. I have seen in you a passion to leave this place. Something awaits you beyond these walls. Mostly, the women are happy here, as you surely have noticed. Many were kidnapped from dreary villages where they faced a life of hardship with domineering husbands. Here, they live in luxury and, within these walls at least, enjoy freedom. And those who are not happy, nonetheless are resigned to their fate. I also chose you," she added as she lifted her arms to draw back the elaborate scarlet veil from her head and revealed golden hair, "because you are fair-skinned and blond like me. Bulbul could be your child."

Katharina marveled to see hair a color so like her own. Blondes were not unusual in the Imperial Harem, but since blond hair was considered a sign of weakness and lack of passion in the blood, fair-haired women went to great pains to dye their hair red.

"I would do this for you, Lady, for you are right, I do wish to leave. But I cannot do as you ask."

Exquisitely painted eyebrows rose. "Why not? You do wish to leave this place, do you not?"

"Oh yes, Lady," Katharina said with passion. "I am searching for my family. Like you, I was separated from them long ago—I have never known my father and brothers and find in myself a deep longing to know them."

Asmahan nodded gravely. "To be separated from one's blood relations is an unhappy thing. Which is why Bulbul must be with his kin. But why will you not do this for me?"

"There is a man, a Christian knight, who was abducted with me and brought to Constantinople. I cannot leave without him."

Asmahan frowned. "A Christian knight would not last long in a Turkish city, so deeply does the hatred run. He will have been tortured and killed long since, God's mercy upon him."

"But I do not know that for certain. I cannot leave until I know Adriano's fate. And if he is alive, he must go with me."

Asmahan considered this. "I shall make inquiries," she said.

Katharina said, "May I ask one other favor, Lady? When I was brought to the palace, I had a small possession with me, a leather bag containing sentimental mementoes. This bag was taken from me. Might you be able to find it for me?"

Asmahan frowned. "As a rule, the possessions of captives are considered too inconsequential for the sultan and his household to be concerned with and so they are given either in payment to the men who brought the captives to us, or to the poor of the city, as part of the sultan's charity program. I shall see what I can do. It is up to God."

Her tone grew cautionary: "Now listen to me. This is dangerous business. There are spies everywhere. The sultana is watching me. Now that you are my friend, you are no longer safe and must watch your back at all times. Come again tomorrow night. Bring your embroidery kit."

*U*pon her next visit to Asmahan's apartment, Katharina found Friar Pastorius's leather pouch lying miraculously on the divan. She fell upon it and opened it at once. The miniature painting of St. Amelia was still there. And the ceramic cameo of Badendorf.

Pressing them to her bosom, Katharina cried and said, "Bless you, Lady. You have restored my life to me."

Asmahan held her tongue, thinking it would be too cruel to let

the girl know that so insignificant were these items that no one
wanted them, not even the scavengers who came to the charity hos-
pital for free clothing and a cup of medicinal wine. But she sympa-
thized, for she herself would give all her gold and jewels to feel
beneath her fingers but one sheepskin from her father's vast herd. It
proved the old adage that a pearl to one was a pebble to another.

And so Katharina went nightly to Asmahan's apartment after that,
taking her embroidery kit on the pretense of stitching something for
the concubine but in truth to get acquainted with Bulbul, a chubby,
fair-haired, and sweet-tempered little boy who, when the terrible moment came, was going to have to go quietly and willingly with his
new mother.

*I*t was a cool, cloud-cast morning, with a light drizzle falling over
the city of Constantinople. The Mistress of the Costume came hurrying into the Pavilion of Doves, where her assistants were sewing an
ensemble for a lucky girl who had been selected to visit the sultan's
bed, and she slapped the needle and threads from Katharina's hands.
"It is the sultana! She has sent for you!"

Katharina's heart jumped. The sultana! Had she found out Asmahan's secret plan?

A eunuch was waiting to escort her, a formidable looking man she
had never seen before. Clad in elegant robes, his turban richly plumed
and made of gold fabric. His nose had been sliced off long ago and
replaced by a golden beak, making him look like a mythical creature.
He uttered not a word to Katharina as he turned and led the way.
She followed, curious, but when they approached the forbidden Pearl
Gate, she began to shiver with fear. How many had passed under this
archway never to return? If the sultana had found out about her secret
collaboration with Asmahan, she had no hope of leaving these rooms
alive.

Katharina had not thought it possible that living quarters could be
more sumptuous than Asmahan's, but the sultana's private suite took
her breath away. She had heard that the sultana had a passion for
pearls, but the sight that met her eyes surpassed all imagining. The
wall hangings, draperies, footstools, divan cushions, and even the floor
mats were woven with pink, white, and black pearls. And sitting on
a thronelike chair (also imbedded with hundreds of pearls) was a

woman so covered in pearl-studded garments that she looked as if she had stood in a snowstorm. Katharina had never seen so many pearls on one person. How could the woman walk with so much weighing her down?

Safiya's eyes were as hard and fixed as her precious pearls, and they studied the assistant seamstress with inscrutable candor. Katharina tried not to fidget beneath the cold gaze, and she tried not to stare. Heavy kohl outlined the woman's upper and lower eyelids, nearly obscuring her eyes, and she had so much rouge on her lips it looked as if she had eaten jam and forgotten to wipe it off. Despite the heavy cosmetics, it was apparent the sultan's favorite concubine was old—surprisingly so. Katharina had heard that Safiya was almost forty. How strange that the sultan should summon this woman back to his bed when he had his choice of a hundred nubile girls.

Safiya's pregnancy was well advanced.

Her voice was like a scimitar, sharp and deadly. "You have been visiting Asmahan. Why?"

Katharina tried to keep from trembling. "She likes my embroidery, Lady."

"I find your work mediocre. Asmahan has no taste." The black-rimmed eyes bored through her. Katharina felt her heart rise in her throat. "Why are you shaking, girl?"

"I have never"—Katharina licked her dry lips—"been in such magnificent company, Lady. It is like looking upon a goddess."

Katharina had no idea where the words had come from, yet they had an effect. The sultana seemed to soften a little; even a woman so exalted was not immune to flattery. "You are to do something for me," she said, not a woman to waste time. "Do it well, and I shall grant you any wish."

Katharina could barely disguise her shock. "What is it you desire, Lady?"

"You are to spy on Asmahan. Watch what she does, whom she sees, and listen to what is said. Then you are to report to me. Do you understand me?"

"Yes, Lady. Is there anything in partic—"

"Everything," she snapped. "Tell me everything that goes on. It will be up to me to decide what is important." She eyed Katharina thoughtfully for a moment, then said, "Perhaps you owe some loyalty or allegiance to Asmahan. That is your own concern. Do not let it get in the way of this task I have assigned you to. But in case your heart should weaken, remember my promise to grant you *anything you wish*, if your report pleases me."

The sultana sighed and placed heavily jeweled hands on her swollen abdomen. "I carry the sultan's heir," she said, an unnecessary announcement and one leaving no room for misinterpretation: that Asmahan's son did not stand a chance.

As Katharina started to leave, the sultana's hard-edged voice cautioned: "Take care, girl, for as you will be watching Asmahan, so shall *you* be watched. Your every step will be reported to me."

*K*atharina continued to go to Asmahan's every night under the pretense of embroidering for her, but she was burdened now with a new and terrible secret. While she played with Bulbul and told him stories and sang to him, with Asmahan looking on with great sadness for these were her final days with her son, Katharina wondered what to report to Safiya, wondered if she should confide this new development in Asmahan, and wondered if Adriano would ever be found. During the day, wherever Katharina went she imagined hundreds of unseen eyes watching her. The palace was honeycombed with secret doors, hidden passageways, and screens with peepholes. Spies spying on the spy. Each night, when she went to Asmahan's apartment, she asked, "What news of Don Adriano?" And each night the response was, "I have no news," until Katharina began seriously to think that the sultana had more power than Asmahan. *If I report this plot to her, will she rescue Adriano for me and set us both free?* "I will grant you any wish," the powerful Safiya had said.

And then one evening Asmahan said, "The danger to my son grows. Safiya has vowed that he will not be the sultan's heir."

"But what if the sultana's child is a girl?"

"Then she will murder my son out of jealousy. Each day his life is in increasing danger. I grow fearful. My eunuch has found a bodyguard whom we can trust. The man will stay with Bulbul every minute until the day of departure."

"How can you be sure you can trust him?" *You cannot even trust me!* Katharina cursed the fate that had put her in such a situation—to help Asmahan or turn spy and ask the sultana's help in finding Adriano.

"Are you a good judge of character, Katharina? Perhaps you can tell me yourself whether we can trust this man." Asmahan pointed toward her private garden, where Bulbul liked to sail little boats on the fish pond.

Katharina went out under the night sky and saw, standing beneath a weeping willow, a tall human figure draped in a robe—a man, thin and gaunt, with a ragged beard and hair past his shoulders. And when he turned, she saw eyes recessed in dark hollows, and deep lines etched on either side of a mouth that had not smiled in a long time.

He stared at her for a moment, and then recognition dawned on his face. "Praise God in His mercy," he whispered, and he took a faltering step toward her.

Katharina reached him first, and emaciated arms went around her in the most tender of embraces. She felt skin and bone beneath the robe, and wept on a shoulder that had wasted away.

Adriano wept with her, for he had thought he would never see her again.

"How—?" she began, drawing back and drinking in his image with her eyes.

He wiped the tears from his face and said, "While I sat in the stinking hold of a slave ship, I thought of a girl I had met, a very brave girl, who left the safety of her town, left a life of comfort and security to go out into the world to find her father. No dangers or perils would dissuade her from this path, not even being shipwrecked on an island with a stranger. When I heard the determination in her voice, and saw the strength of her spirit, I thought, *Surely I can be as this mere girl.* I offered a prayer to the Blessed Virgin, renewing my vow to restore Her sovereignty in Jerusalem, and to be reunited with my brother knights on Crete, and while I slept the Blessed Mother came to me in a dream and told me that I was no good to her dead for martyrs did not build churches, and that she needed her soldiers alive. So I discarded my knight's cloak while on the slave ship, and divested myself of any evidence of my true status, so that when we were brought out of the hold of that ship at the docks, no one knew my identity. I feigned muteness, but when they saw my size, the overseers sent me to work in the brickyards for the work on this palace is never-ending. Ever since, I have been building the very walls that have been keeping us in."

He took Katharina's soft smooth hands into his hard calloused ones.

"What kept me alive was the vow I made to the Virgin, for I must return to Jerusalem. But also, thoughts of you, Katharina, kept me alive, for I knew that you would have the strength and fortitude to overcome this misadventure." The ghost of a smile played at his lips. "And I thought that surely I, a knight of the Brotherhood of Mary, can do what a mere girl can."

Asmahan came into the garden then, paused to observe the unlikely pair in the moonlight—the plump girl in silks, the skeletal man in rags—and said, "I decided, Katharina, that you should not travel alone, for it might draw attention to you. You should be in the company of a man whom you can say is your husband. He would be protection for you and my son. I have enough money and friends to find a place for the two of you, and Bulbul, on a caravan. I will give you letters to take to my family. My father is Sheik Ali Sayid, a rich and powerful man. He will reward you well for what you have done."

Katharina looked at Asmahan through eyes swimming with tears. All thoughts of Sultana Safiya and spying and intrigue fled her mind. She was aware of only one thing: the rough and calloused hand holding hers.

Asmahan said, "My spies have told me of a caravan that leaves for Samarkand at the first full moon. I will ask the sultan permission to visit the mosque that day. I will tell him it is my father's birthday, and I wish to honor him and offer prayers for him. The sultan will not refuse. I will take my child with me, and of course a retainer of ladies and eunuchs for protection. You and your Spaniard will be among them. We women pray behind a screen in the mosque so that the men cannot see us. You will be able to slip out unseen, with my son, and my eunuch will take you and Adriano to the place where caravans depart. Afterward, I shall return to the palace."

Katharina finally found her voice, though it was difficult on this magical of nights. "But surely the sultan will notice the boy is missing."

"The sultan is currently preoccupied with ridding the empire of the Knights of Rhodes," Asmahan's eyes flickered to Adriano, "and so his visits with our son are infrequent. By the time he learns that the boy is missing, you and Bulbul will be well on your way and no one will know where you have gone."

Katharina did not wish to ask it, but she had to for it was a reasonable question: "Why can't *you* go?"

"If I were to disappear, it would be noticed at once and a search would be launched. The sultan's men would find me within days. But it will be many weeks before it is noticed that Bulbul is gone and by that time, it will be too late to pick up your trail." She handed Katharina a packet. "You will travel first to Baghdad, which is at the edge of the Ottoman Empire. For this first part of the journey you will travel under the sultan's protection. I have had papers drawn up that will grant you safe passage. From Baghdad you will join a caravan bound for Samarkand, and for that part of the journey you will be under my father's protection. I have been in secret negotiations with the ambassador from Samarkand. He has drawn up the necessary documents. My father is a powerful man, his name is feared. You will be safe. Once in Samarkand, he will reward you handsomely for what you have done. And once you have handed Bulbul into my family's care, you will be free to go anywhere you wish."

Baghdad, Samarkand . . . So far from Jerusalem, so many miles in the wrong direction! But Katharina thought of little Bulbul and then of a baby that had been given up nearly nineteen years before by a widowed father who had gone off in search of a blue stone. This little one's plight was much like her own. And here, his life was in danger.

"Lady," she said. "I have no words to express my gratitude. For finding Adriano and for—"

Asmahan held up a jeweled hand. "I do it for my son, and no other reason. Keep him safe, and speak to him often of me."

𝒦atharina did not see Adriano again after that, for as a man he was not allowed in the company of the women and therefore was only with the boy when Bulbul was summoned to the sultan's private apartments. But Katharina continued to visit Asmahan each evening, taking silks and embroidery, and every morning reported to the sultana that Asmahan had gossiped about the other concubines and harem politics, wondering if the sharp-eyed woman could see through her subterfuge. Each night, in her alcove in the dormitory, Katharina gazed at the painting of St. Amelia's Stone and felt her heart race with hope: very soon now, she and Adriano would once again be free and she would be once more on the road to the blue crystal and, God willing, her family.

Two days before they were to execute their plan of escape, word spread through the palace like fire: Safiya was in labor. All activities were suspended as everyone waited anxiously for news. Asmahan kept Bulbul close, while Katharina waited in the dormitory for word.

And then it came: the sultana had given birth to a son.

They had run out of time. The instant the newborn was placed at her breast, Safiya claimed her legal right to have Asmahan's son locked in the Cage. Almost at once the younger concubine's eunuchs and guards deserted her. There was no longer any question of going to the mosque to offer prayers for her father. It was only a matter of hours before the sultana's eunuchs arrived to take Bulbul away.

Although Adriano still believed all Turks to be godless heathens and his sworn enemies, nonetheless this concubine had saved his life and reunited him with Katharina, and so he was her avowed protector. At least, protector of her son, for ultimately nothing could be done to save Asmahan. With the aid of her faithful eunuch, Adriano scaled the garden wall and, with Bulbul strapped to his back—asleep, as he had been given milk laced with poppy juice—went back over the wall, helping Katharina up behind him. Under the cover of night, they followed the eunuch through the maze of outer walls and alleys that surrounded the palace, and eventually into the labyrinthine warren of streets and hovels of the city. Before they left, Asmahan had given Katharina a small wooden chest filled with gold dinars, the coin of the Ottoman Empire. They had embraced and Asmahan kissed her son for the last time. Now, as Katharina and Adriano followed the eunuch to the vast caravan encampment, she knew the fate that awaited Asmahan once her deceit was discovered, it was the same punishment for all harem women who transgressed the sultan's rules: she would be sealed in a sack with a cat and a snake and thrown into the waters of the Bosporus.

The caravan departed at dawn, a thousand-camel train that carried perfume and cosmetics from Egypt and along the way would pick up colored glass in Syria and fur from the Eurasian steppes—all bound for China where the people had a passion for such things—to be exchanged for silk and jade, which would then be brought back to the western nations where people had a passion for such things. Along the way they met entertainers bound for China—jugglers, acrobats, singers, magicians—and coming from the East, monks, scholars, and explorers bound for Europe. Although they would find wildlife along the way, Katharina and Adriano took along provisions of bread, dried fruit, salted meat, and hard cheese, as well as plenty of water. And they delighted in being a carefree threesome: Adriano the protector, Katharina the nurturer, and Bulbul their "son." As Constantinople and its terrors fell behind them, as they rode beneath the sun and in the fresh air, and ate wholesome food and found myriad things to laugh at, the life and strength returned to Adriano. His body fleshed out and his spirits began to shine again through his eyes. Katharina told him only once that he was free to go to Jerusalem now, that he was not obligated to make the long journey to Samarkand with her, but he silenced her with a vow not to leave her side until her promise to Asmahan had been fulfilled. After that, he said, they would return to Jerusalem together.

As the caravan snaked its way eastward, Katharina—who had once thought, just a few miles onto the Adriatic, that she had seen most of the world—encountered the desert for the first time, and the terrible wonder of sandstorms that rose up with such suddenness that death claimed the traveler who was not alert. She and Adriano soon learned to watch their camels; if the beasts suddenly started snarling and burying their faces in the sand, it meant a sandstorm was coming, even though the day was clear. Riders immediately wrapped their noses and mouths with cloth, and all of a sudden the storm was there, fierce and swift, and over in an instant.

Along the way they mostly camped in the open, under the stars, at oases and crossroads, but sometimes they stopped at garrisons and caravansaries, where they found inns and proper beds, and musicians and lively entertainment. As they passed between golden sands and deep blue sky, beneath scudding white clouds and the shade of emerald-green palm trees, the journey took on an unreal aspect for Katharina, who held Bulbul in her arms as their camel swayed and rocked them into semislumber. Ahead she watched Adriano, with his broad shoulders and straight back, a man of deep convictions and devotion to God, a man of mystery, too.

The moment of falling in love, she could not pinpoint. Perhaps it had even been as far back as her first sight of him on the docks in Venice. Or watching him at prayer on the deck of the Portuguese ship. Or as they slept in each other's arms on a deserted island, feeling like the last two people on earth. Whenever and wherever her love for him began, she kept it a secret, for Adriano had his own road to travel, as she had hers. She would never speak her heart, but keep her love close to her, protecting it in the special chamber where she held her mother, and her father, and now even the tragic concubine Asmahan who had saved their lives.

But these strange new emotions startled her, for she had not experienced such passion for Hans Roth. It seemed incomprehensible to her now, as she caught on fire with Adriano's every glance and sound of his voice, that she had once thought romantic love a myth. Her desire for Adriano was greater than any hunger or thirst she had ever known; it was a yearning of the spirit that occupied her mind night and day. Therefore did Katharina's love need an outlet, and she found it in the making of a new cloak for him. Having secretly bartered in the marketplace of Ankara for a new white mantle and some silk thread and needles, she worked on her labor of love at each day's rest, when Adriano went out with the men to hunt or gather wood for the fires. She knew he bore a pain deep within him, deeper than the scars on his poor tortured body, a pain she had first glimpsed in the deep lines that etched his face, and had heard in his voice when, on that deserted island, he had spoken of a woman he had once loved. While Katharina knew she could never hope to be balm to that deep pain, it was her prayer that the new cloak would help restore some measure of his dignity.

Adriano also occupied her thoughts because of something that puzzled her, a puzzle that deepened with each passing day. He had told her that he had taken vows of celibacy and austerity when he had joined the brotherhood, and that these vows had been taken as penance for having killed a man. But now that they were spending nights and days in close company, sharing food and shelter, pretending to be father and mother to the delightful little Bulbul, Katharina was becoming aware of the true breadth and depth of those vows. Days and nights on a Portuguese ship, and a few days stranded on an island had not been enough for her to truly observe the man. But out here on the boundless desert beneath a sky that stretched into eternity, Katharina watched Adriano with a clarity that was as clear as glass. And it seemed to her that his vow of abstinence and austerity went beyond reasonable bounds, for he not only denied himself meat and wine, but food in adequate supply. He seemed almost to starve himself and to need to punish his body, pushing himself beyond daily endurance, continuing to work and hunt and chop wood long after the other men had retired to their campfires. The crime he had committed (and she was not certain it was a crime, for was not fighting for a woman he loved fighting for his rights?) had taken place over twenty years ago. Had he not paid penance enough? Or—and this suspicion grew with each mile that fell behind them as the caravan pushed eastward—was there more to his story than he had revealed?

She realized that her obsession with him was overshadowing the central purpose of her life: to find her father. And so she had to rely more and more upon the portrait of St. Amelia to remind her of that purpose. Like a suppliant in church with a genuine desire to offer prayers but whose wayward mind was straying beyond the stained-glass windows to the fields of daisies beyond, Katharina needed more and more to draw upon will power to keep her heart to its course. Night after night, in what had become a ritual, she brought the little painting to light and gazed at the blue crystal as she silently recited the litany, *This is where my destiny lies.*

As soon as Bulbul was restored to his mother's people, Katharina was going to turn around and head back to Jerusalem, to search for the blue crystal, to find her father.

And Adriano must follow wherever his stars led.

*T*he caravan was a dynamic and ever-changing creature, with people leaving and joining, whole clans or lone riders, causing the train to shrink and expand snakelike as it slithered through desert, grassland, hill country. Feeling safe now in their false personas, and being so far east from Constantinople and the danger of being found out, Katharina and Adriano made friends with newcomers, sharing their fire and their food, and then bade farewell to them along the way and welcomed the company of new acquaintances.

The matter of language started to become a problem as they moved eastward, for they encountered new dialects and mutations of tongues they had thought they were familiar with. Arabic became increasingly difficult for Katharina, and Adriano's Greek became less and less helpful. Although Latin had been carried east for over a thousand years, Katharina and Adriano found it harder and harder to understand as the ancient language had mutated and adapted to local regions. But they understood each other; their private communication began less to rely upon words as upon gestures, facial expressions, and silences filled with meaningful looks. It was, they were beginning to realize as they spent day and night in each other's company, all they needed.

*I*n northern Persia, the caravan stopped in a small valley between two rugged ranges, and here they found a most remarkable stream: no vegetation grew along its banks, all around was rocky and barren, but the water ran warm, and to everyone's amazement, it ran bright green. This was a result of mineral deposits at its source, the caravan leader explained. These gave the water its remarkable emerald tint. But it was drinkable and even, some claimed, healthful. And so they camped beside the emerald spring, a thousand tents and a hundred campfires in the moonlight.

Katherina welcomed the opportunity to give her hair a good washing at last. Although she had, over the weeks, occasionally washed it, the water had been in short supply. To keep her hair clean she had used a trick learned from local Bedouins whose women rubbed a mixture of ash and soda into their hair and then spent hours combing it through. In this way had the dark dye, applied back in Venice to make her look like an Arab youth, begun to fade to a dun brown, with her newly grown roots giving her a blond "cap." But now she used proper soap and lathered and scrubbed and massaged and rinsed, and did it all over again. And when she was done, and drying her hair in the breeze so that it billowed like a golden mane, the effect was such that nearly everyone in the encampment was brought to a halt to stare.

Adriano most of all.

That night, beneath an effulgent moon, Katharina gave Adriano the new cloak she had embroidered and he was moved beyond words. He had his emblem back, the dark blue, eight-pointed cross of his brotherhood that gave meaning to his life. Once again he would wear his dignity as if it were a garment, and proclaim to the world his dedication to the Blessed Virgin.

And finally here, beneath the stars, Adriano told Katharina his whole story.

She already knew that over twenty years ago, back in Aragon, he had been passionately in love with a girl named Maria, that he had assumed they would marry, and that she had then confessed she was in love with another. Adriano had flown into a rage and challenged the other man. They fought. Adriano slew him and Maria withdrew in grief into a cloistered convent where he supposed she still lived to this day. That was what Katharina knew of his story. But this night, with the moon large and fat and majestic in the night sky, and the emerald stream gurgling softly in its stony bed, Adriano confessed the pain that filled him every day of his life.

"I knew," he said softly, gathering his knight's cloak about him, "I knew in my heart of hearts that Maria did not love me. It was pride and arrogance that blinded me to this fact. I believed I could make her love me in time. But the other man . . . if it had been any other man, I might have let it go. I might have turned a blind eye and waited for Maria to come to me. But the other man was my brother, and this I could not bear."

He turned anguished eyes to Katharina. "Yes, the man I killed was my brother. I slew him out of blind jealousy. He was innocent of any crime or wrongdoing against me. I have no right to happiness, Katharina. I have no right to love you or to be loved by you."

He broke down in bitter sobbing and she put her arms around him. He buried his face in her clean, golden hair and felt her warm young body against his, her lips on his cheeks and neck, her tears mingling with his, until finally his mouth found hers, and they both lay beneath the knight's cloak with its blue cross, and found solace in love at last.

Later, when they woke, Adriano rose and took Katharina by the hand to the bank of the emerald stream. Here he thrust his sword into the ground, the handsome gold-hilted weapon Asmahan had given to him for the protection of her son. There he and Katharina knelt, as if kneeling before a cross, and taking her hand in his, said, "Though we are far from priests and churches, we are visible to God, the Blessed Mother, and all the saints. It is before these exhaled witnesses, my beloved Katharina, that I declare you to be my wife, and I your husband, and I pledge my soul and body to you, my love and my devotion, for the rest of my life, and after we are dead and united in Heaven."

Katharina pledged the same oath, and knew that no matter what lay in their future, she and Adriano would be bound together always.

◆   ◆   ◆

They spent a week of love, as husband and wife, both wondering what they had done to deserve such happiness, each promising to God to do good works and favors in payment for this joy, until one dawn, they crept from their tent to go to the river to bathe. Adriano wrapped his knight's cloak about himself, Katharina joined the other women and children at another part of the river, playing with Bulbul in the water and telling him, as she did everyday, that he was soon going to be with his grandfather and all his cousins. When he asked, as he always did, if his mama was going to be there, Katharina answered, "I do not know, perhaps," which at least was somewhat truthful, adding, "But she wants you to be with your grandfather, who will teach you to ride a horse." For the first time, however, she regretted having to give the boy to his family, for in the weeks since leaving Constantinople she had grown to love him.

She was wrapping him in a towel when she heard the first scream. Turning, she saw men on horseback, wielding massive swords, galloping through the encampment.

Katharina picked up the child and ran. She reached the part of the river where the men of the caravan had been bathing and she saw that they had already been taken by surprise. In the confusion she saw Adriano, distinguished by his cloak of knighthood, blazing white in the morning sun, and she called to him just as a sword was thrust into his back, directly in the center of the blue eight-pointed cross. She looked in horror as he flung his arms wide and then dropped to his knees, and then fell onto his face, a ribbon of blood flowing from his back. She saw the sword raised high and come down on his neck. She turned and shielded Bulbul's eyes as she heard the sickening sound of a head being severed from its body.

Katharina turned and ran, but she was caught by raiders. The boy was snatched from her arms. She watched in horror as little Bulbul flew up into the air as if he were a weightless bird, and then land headfirst on a boulder, his child's skull splitting open like a melon.

And then a sharp pain filled her own head, and blackness enfolded her like a sudden night.

◆ ◆ ◆

*W*hen Katharina regained consciousness, she found herself in a compound with other females, some of them weeping, some angry, a few dejected and desolate. She didn't remember anything. Her head hurt and she was nauseated.

Where was she? She rubbed her eyes and looked around. From what she could see, she and the others were in a makeshift pen with walls made of goat hides. There was no shelter beneath the punishing sun, except for a leafless tree that spread dry, brittle branches. Beyond the goatskin walls there appeared to be crude tents, and the smoke of campfires. She could hear shouts and arguments and the galloping of horses.

When her head began to clear and the nausea subsided, but all of her memory not yet returned, she saw men come into the compound and begin roughly to inspect the girls, stripping them and examining them. As they appeared to have no interest in using the women sexually, it occurred to Katharina that they must be slavers.

The Greek caravel! The sultan's palace! *Not again.*

Katharina backed away until she stumbled and fell against the trunk of the old dead tree. Putting her hand to her chest, she felt something beneath her dress. She pulled it out and was surprised to find a small leather pouch on a thong. It was vaguely familiar and she suspected it must be important, so she hastily removed it from her neck and tucked the pouch into a knothole in the tree trunk, making sure she had not been seen.

By then the men had reached her, and began remarking excitedly about her hair. Although she could not understand their language, some gestures were universal, and she knew she had some value to them. They stripped her and looked her over, and finally, when they were done with all the captive women, gathered up all garments and possessions and distributed rough robes of cheap wool. When the captives were left alone, and the sun began to set, and the other women sat in groups to wail or weep, Katharina crept back to the tree and secretly removed the hidden pouch, restoring it to its safe place around her neck.

◆   ◆   ◆

*I*t was during the night that it all came back to her, for she dreamed of Adriano and Bulbul, and she woke screaming, and when full realization of what had happened, and her new situation, hit her with brutal force, she began to weep so bitterly and inconsolably that the others left her alone.

*K*atharina lived in a daze after that, ignoring the advances of the other women, unresponsive to questions, drinking water only when it was put to her lips, but refusing food as she sat and stared at the distant horizon.

Adriano, lying dead with a sword between his shoulder blades.

Bulbul, his brains splattered on a boulder.

Yet she was alive, and once again a slave.

*W*hen one of the tribal women came to wash Katharina's hair, she neither questioned it nor protested. The woman's job was vigorous and thorough, and when it was dry she combed the golden tresses through and brought others into the pen to look upon and remark at the beautiful sun-colored curls.

The next day the woman returned with soap and a sharp knife, and this time she carefully shaved Katharina's head, collecting the hair in a basket. Once again Katharina did not protest, but stared out at the desert that stretched away into infinity.

But a week later Katharina saw a woman, who, judging by the many coins she wore, was the chief's head wife, proudly modeling a crudely made blond wig. In her numb state, Katharina vaguely wondered why these women would bother with wigs when they kept their heads covered. And then that night she heard moans of sexual ecstasy coming from the chief's tent, and she remembered with a pain how Adriano had loved to run his hands through her hair.

The next morning a man strode into the pen, furious. He grabbed Katharina's head and examined it as if it were a melon. Then he began shouting at the woman who had shaved her. Not understanding their language, Katharina could not guess what the argument was about, but the word "Zhandu" kept coming up, and the man gestured angrily over and over toward the east.

She learned from her fellow captives that these people were the Kosh, famous slave traders of the region, a proud, arrogant people who believed they were the first to be created by the gods and that all other races were afterthoughts and therefore created to serve the Kosh. A warrior-nomad society that didn't mingle with other races because they were believed to be inferior, the Kosh had round flat faces and slanting eyes, and the reddest hair Katharina had ever seen. They rode fierce horses that had woolly hides and shaggy manes.

When the camp broke up and they began an eastward trek, Katharina once again did not protest nor question her fate. But as they covered many miles, stopping briefly at settlements to sell their human goods, with herself always being kept apart, she began to realize the Kosh were keeping her while her hair grew out, and that they were taking her to a place called Zhandu.

As she walked alongside their horses and double-humped camels, Katharina was oblivious to the burning sands beneath her bare feet, to the weariness in her bones, the hunger in her stomach. She thought only of Adriano: where was his soul? Had it flown back to Spain and was now in his beloved Aragon? Or had it gone to Jerusalem and was now one of the shadows in a small church dedicated to the Blessed Mother? Or did it hover over the heads of his comrades in the brotherhood on Crete, silently urging them on in their fight against the infidels? At times, late at night when the wind blew mournfully and Katharina looked up at the stars, she almost felt Adriano at her side, a consoling phantom longing to take her into corporeal arms.

And then one night a man came to look her over and he haggled in a most animated fashion with the woman who had become her caretaker. Katharina had heard enough Kosh to grasp some rudimentary words, and realized that the woman was asking an exorbitantly high price for her. When the man demanded to know why, the woman poked Katharina's rounded belly and said, "There is a child there."

And Katharina was instantly brought out of her numb state.

She looked down in wonder and realized that what the woman had said was true, for in her trance she had not realized that her monthly trouble had not visited her, nor had she noticed that though she ate little, her stomach grew.

Adriano's child.

At last she was able to bring Friar Pastorius's leather pouch from beneath her grimy robe and look at its contents, and when she saw the little cameo of Badendorf and the miniature of St. Amelia with the blue crystal, she wept anew. But mixed in with her grief was the spark of new hope—a part of Adriano still lived.

𝓔astward moved the massive caravan of the Kosh, pausing only long enough to sell slaves and pick up supplies, continuing deeper into unknown regions and farther from the world Katharina knew. Although her captors fed her, it was only barely enough to keep her alive, and now Katharina wanted very much to live. So she took to fighting for extra scraps of food, and stealing from others, in order to feed the new life that was growing within her. Katharina thought the Kosh a godless, savage race, brutal beyond comprehension. When a criminal was decapitated, the tribe played polo with his head. Weddings were primitive: the prospective bride jumped on a horse and galloped away with suitors in pursuit. The man who caught her and wrestled her to the ground became her husband. The Kosh worked their slaves to death and left the bodies behind, unburied. Yet they laughed and danced and sang a lot, drinking a brew so potent that just being near the fumes made Katharina dizzy.

And during the whole time, while she watched and listened, she learned their foreign tongue, as she had once learned Latin and Arabic, for it could mean her survival and the survival of her unborn child.

𝓕inally, while the Kosh were wintering on a plateau among ancient crumbling walls built by a forgotten race, Katharina's child was born, a pale-haired daughter that with one mewling cry chipped a fracture in the stone wall around Katharina's heart. She named the girl Adriana, for her father, and as the days and weeks passed, as she fed the child at her breast and held it and crooned to it, Katharina experienced a melting of her sorrow and the beginning of an unexpected new joy. Adriano's child, with hair like fleece. But the baby had been born underweight and was struggling to thrive. Katharina's milk dried up too soon and she had to fight once again for food.

When the chief and head woman came to inspect, they saw the infant's golden hair and nodded in satisfaction, and once again Katharina heard them say the word, "Zhandu," and she knew she and her child were being kept for something special.

*W*hile traversing the Greater Headache Mountains, the Kosh camped in a high pass surrounded by tall snowbound peaks and one night heard a sound like thunder that alarmed Katharina but only excited her captors. At dawn they swarmed ahead on foot, clambering farther up the pass until they came to the place of the recent avalanche. They dug frantically into the snow, a massive undertaking calling upon the work of everyone, captives as well, until their efforts were rewarded. As the slavers gave out yelps of joy, they uncovered the bodies and cargo of the hapless caravan that had gotten caught under the avalanche. Katharina had at first thought they were looking for survivors, but when a victim still living was uncovered, he was clubbed to death, for the Kosh were interested only in booty. As she watched the obscene plunder and heard the muffled cries for help, her captors stripped the dead and the dying of their clothing and jewelry, and carried off much wealth that day, for it had been a caravan from China, bearing gold and silk. When the Kosh caravan resumed its journey it was to take an alternate route for the pass would not be clear until spring, when the snow melted and the bodies of men and beasts were washed away.

Katharina saw wonderful and terrible sights during her sojourn with the Kosh, and she observed them all as two people: the Katharina who marveled at the world's diversity, and the Katharina who clasped Adriano's baby to her bosom and silently wept.

She tried to escape only once. At a crossroads, they had passed a vast encampment where hundreds of horses, camels, and pack ponies were being watered, and the smoke from a thousand fires rose warmly to the sky. When the red-haired slavers camped farther up the river, perhaps ten miles from the crossroads, Katharina waited until the encampment was silent and sleeping before she stole from the captives' tent, untethered a horse and, with Adriana strapped securely to her chest, rode off.

She was caught a few yards beyond the perimeter, dragged back and soundly beaten in front of the gathered company. After that, whenever the caravan came within any distance of other travelers or settlements, someone took Adriana from Katharina and kept the baby until they were on their way again. This ensured that she would try no more escapes.

They crossed the red-gold shifting dunes of the cursed Takli Makan, where mirages and eerie sounds lured unwary travelers to their deaths. Here the sands drifted so swiftly and unpredictably that the trail was quickly lost, therefore when men passed this way they erected towers made of animal bones to mark the way for others. When the Kosh built these desert towers, they were made of human bones. The caravan wound through misty river gorges and across breezy high pasture lands. In the heat of summer they traveled only at night; in winter they fought snows and glaciers.

It took another two years for the Kosh to reach their destination high in the mountains in a remote spot far from the Silk Road where sentinels stood watch in strange stone towers. And when they came at last to the terminus of their route, at the base of a mysterious cloud-covered plateau where they said no stranger could go, Katharina had been with the slavers for nearly four years. Her hair had grown long down her back again and she was twenty-three years old. Adriana, her daughter, was three.

The way to Zhandu was a steep and narrow mountain pass that grew ever steeper and narrower. The climb was single file along this precipice on either side of which rose enormous walls of mountain rock the color of iron. At the end of the perilous trail rose a towering wooden gate, many arm's-lengths thick, topped with spikes and men with spears. There was no other way onto the plateau than through this gate, and only those with permission from the Heavenly Ruler may pass. In this fashion had Zhandu remained for centuries out of touch with the rest of the world.

After being admitted through the wooden gates, the Kosh caravan continued on until it crossed the Celestial Bridge, a marble and granite feat of engineering set upon massive pylons through which a river raged, emerald-green and white with foam, swollen by the melting snow in the mountains. Here spread a plateau that gave one the feeling of being on top of the world—a vista filled with green trees and fertile fields. Katharina's eyes widened in wonder at the acres of fruit and flowers and grasses, for she had seen nothing that came so close to looking like Eden. And in the center of this fabulous plateau rose a city of domes and spires and white walls that seemed to actually undulate in the blaze of the sun.

The Kosh camped on the plateau in the shadow of Zhandu with its dazzling turquoise domes and crystal towers behind unassailable walls. Not just anyone was allowed entry; thousands camped on the plain and could only look in wonder at a city that was sometimes engulfed in low clouds so that it appeared to be floating.

When a representative rode out from the city to meet with the Kosh chief, Katharina asked one of the women what the Kosh, and all the other traders camped on the plain, wanted from Zhandu? What made it worth their while to make such a long and dangerous trek to this place at the end of the world? The curt reply was that the Zhandu had more wealth than they knew what to do with. They paid whatever price was asked and never haggled. And then when Katharina saw yaks burdened with piles of wondrous white furs and was told that they were payment for her, she recalled how precious these furs, called ermines, were back in Constantinople and even in Europe, and was astounded that they should be handed over like common loaves of bread. What her captors had said was true. Clearly the Zhandu paid any price asked, no matter how exorbitant, and did not care if it was a fair price or not.

Katharina was hoisted onto a mule, Adriana in her lap, and tethered to the double-humped camel of the representative, who rode in a curtained litter so that no one could see him. Accompanying them were a hundred guards in perfectly matched uniforms of blue pantaloons and scarlet vests and turbans of canary yellow. As the peculiar procession passed through the massive city gates, Katharina glanced back and saw that already the Kosh were pulling up stakes and preparing to leave, no doubt anxious to get back to civilization and turn a hundredfold profit on their furs.

She and Adriana were not taken far into the city but almost immediately spirited off the mule by a team of servants dressed in blue and red and wearing peculiar slippers with toes that curled up. They were whisked into a door in a wall where they were turned over to a magnificently robed chamberlain who wordlessly hurried them down a long corridor, up three winding staircases, down more corridors, under arches and through doorways many times taller than a man, until they were unceremoniously and without a word deposited in a garden containing the most remarkable looking birds Katharina had ever seen: enormous bright pink creatures that stood on one leg.

From out of nowhere a remarkable looking woman came floating in on a sea of silk. She had the round flat face and slanting almond eyes of the Kosh, and her smile was missing a tooth. Her hairdo astonished: the long red tresses were arranged as two enormous wheels, one on either side of her head, threaded with colored ribbons and ornaments of silver, gold, and pearl. The embroidery on her silk gown was impressive beyond belief, even for Katharina who had seen exquisite needlework in the sultan's palace. The turquoise and gold peacock on the woman's gown looked as if it were going to suddenly spread its tail feathers and strut right off the fabric.

She came in with a happy, hopeful expression, Katharina noted, but her smile fell as soon as she saw the captive. The woman frowned over Katharina's long blond hair, then looked into her eyes. "Bah!" she said, and turned to walk out.

"Please, Lady," Katharina said quickly in the tongue of the Kosh.

The woman turned, a look of surprise on her face. "You speak our language?" she said.

"I have been with your people for four years," Katharina said, surmising by the woman's distinctive looks that she was Kosh. "Please, may my daughter and I go?"

The woman looked at Katharina as if she were a simpleton, made another impatient gesture, and glided out on her cloud of silk.

Turning to the chamberlain, a man wearing a long scarlet silk robe and small black silk hat, Katharina said, "I must leave. You cannot keep me here."

He gave her the same look the woman had, and said with indifference, "You can go. The Supreme Sister does not want you." He also spoke Kosh, but a mutated version that took a moment for Katharina to understand.

She blinked. "I can leave this place? I can leave Zhandu? My daughter and I? We are not prisoners?"

"You *must* leave. We do not keep prisoners and we do not like guests." He wrinkled his nose as if detecting an odor. "The guards will take you back to the gate."

"Now? But we have no money, no food."

"That is not our concern."

"Then why were we brought here?"

He waved dismissively. "There was a mistake," he said vaguely. "You will go now."

Katharina watched him leave, and tried to protest when men in colorful silk pantaloons and vests nudged her out of the garden. They were not menacing, as the guards and eunuchs of the sultan's palace had been, but displayed the impatience of men anxious to get to their lunch. She tried to reason with them: "The people who brought me here, the Kosh, they were leaving. I shall never catch up with them. Where are my child and I supposed to go?"

But they crowded her until she gathered Adriana into her arms and fled down a long corridor that seemed to lead only to more corridors. When she looked back, the guards had vanished.

She looked around in perplexity. What were they supposed to do now? They couldn't leave and they couldn't stay!

When Adriana said, "Mama," and rested her head on Katharina's shoulder, Katharina realized that the ordeal had fatigued her. Poor little Adriana, born underweight and now small for her age, the result of their harsh and deprived life among the Kosh. And as the Kosh hadn't bothered to feed them that morning, most likely thinking it a waste of food since the pair were going to be sold to the Zhandu, Adriana was weaker still. Katharina decided that she must find a place to hide for the night and figure out what to do in the morning.

After wandering more endless corridors, she discovered that the palace of Zhandu was like a beehive, with elegantly dressed courtiers coming and going, women as well, a stark contrast to the segregated court of Constantinople. They all had the Asian features and red hair of the Kosh, so that Katharina wondered if the two races had sprung from the same distant ancestors. The men wore outrageous hats the size of cart wheels, the brims edged with fur, the crowns tall and pointy. The women dressed their long hair in impossibly intricate styles, each more outlandish than the next, and everyone seemed to have a purpose as they bustled past with papers and books, musical

instruments, and platters of food, none paying the slightest attention
to the woman in rags holding a listless child.

Trying to avoid guards or anyone who would drive them out of the
city, Katharina hurried up and down corridors of polished marble until
she came to what appeared to be a deserted wing. Here she found a
doorway with cobwebs on its lintel and, thinking this an abandoned
room and therefore a safe place to hide, she pushed against the door
and slipped inside.

Light poured through tall narrow windows, illuminating a round
stone tower that was filled floor to ceiling with all manner of weap-
onry: swords and spears, axes and javelins, bows and arrows, and many
styles of chain mail and armor. She had clearly stumbled into a weapons arsenal, but there was something strange—everything was thick
with dust and festooned with cobwebs, as if they hadn't been used in
decades.

Katharina stepped up to the window and looked out. From the base
of the stone wall, a precipitous drop fell thousands of feet to a vast
plain below, stretching away to the horizon. On either side, ragged
mountains pierced the sky with perennially snowcapped peaks. Remembering what she had been told about the narrow pass being the
only way to get to Zhandu, Katharina realized that no enemy could
assail this mountaintop kingdom, and probably had not even tried in
generations. So the citizens of this fabulous city hadn't known invaders or warfare possibly in centuries.

She found woolen cloaks stored in a chest, and antique leather
helmets that, wrapped in the wool, could be used as pillows. Leaving
Adriana safely in the room, admonishing her not to touch anything,
Katharina stole back out and made her way to a corridor where she
remembered seeing what appeared to be a shrine to a goddess. The
statue in the niche was a willowy, doe-eyed woman with a compassionate smile; food and burning candles had been left at her feet.
Noting a resemblance to the Blessed Virgin, Katharina whispered a
prayer and took some of the food and one of the candles, knowing
that the goddess would understand.

She and Adriana feasted on figs and cakes and a small flagon of
what tasted like tepid fruit juice, and after they had eaten, Katharina
performed the nightly ritual she had begun almost the moment Adriana was born: she brought out the painting of St. Amelia, and the
ceramic cameo of Badendorf, and told her daughter the story of her

life. She talked about Hans Roth and Isabella Bauer and the other people of her town, and then she told Adriana about the family that waited for them wherever the blue crystal was to be found—a grandfather for Adriana, and possibly many cousins, because Isabella had mentioned the nobleman's sons, who would have since married and had children of their own. "What is your name?" Katharina asked her daughter every night. And every night the child responded, "I am Adriana von Grünewald."

When she saw how her baby yawned, Katharina knew it was time for a story, to help the child sleep peacefully through the night because Adriana often woke from nightmares about the Kosh. "Once upon a time . . ." she began. Katharina had taught Adriana the language of their captors for it might one day mean survival, and so tonight, in Kosh, she told the story of Amelia and the blue crystal. But since Katharina had never heard of St. Amelia before the day her mother died, and did not know the saint's true story, she made one up. "There was a good and kind lady named Amelia, who lived in the woods near Badendorf. Amelia was very poor, except for one precious treasure she owned: a perfect blue crystal that had been given to her by Jesus when he was walking in the woods one day and was hungry and she gave him bread and sausages to eat. Now, in the castle high up the mountain, there lived an evil king who wanted the blue crystal . . ."

Unknown to the fugitives hiding in the abandoned weapons store, an old man in white slippers and long white robe was haunting the palace corridors and, when he heard a voice, drew near out of curiosity. Stopping to listen, he pressed his ear to the door. When, a few minutes later, he heard the words, "And so Amelia and the handsome prince lived happily ever after," he pushed the door open and clapped his hands.

Katharina looked up with a start.

"Tell another story," he said in the variation of Kosh peculiar to Zhandu, and then crossed his legs to sit on the floor.

Katharina stared at the intruder. He was very old and his head was perfectly round, like an orange, and bald except for a fringe of white hair. His eyes were slanted like those of the Kosh, with a squinty quality that made him look like he was smiling, even though he was not. Everything about him seemed round: rounded tummy beneath the white robe, rounded little end on his nose, matching rounded cheeks that lifted when he did smile, which seemed for no reason at all. *Is he a simpleton?* she wondered.

"Another story," he said again, this time a little crossly.

Katharina looked at Adriana, who was staring at their peculiar guest. During her short life among the Kosh, she had learned to keep quiet around strangers and not draw attention to herself.

Seeing that the peculiar little man would not leave until he had heard a story, Katharina decided on "Little Red Cap," which was short, and hoped he would then go.

But when she was done and the hunstman had killed the wolf, the old man clapped his hands and laughed with toothless gums, urging her to tell another. Katharina protested that her child was sleepy. He became cranky. When she said he was welcome to come back to-morrow, he began to shout and suddenly guards with spears materialized from out of nowhere.

Katharina shot to her feet, Adriana in her arms, and backed away from the gold-tipped spears. While the old man carried on so incoherently that Katharina could not grasp what he was saying, another person suddenly appeared as if from thin air, making Katharina wonder if they had been searching for the old man.

It was the woman from the garden, whom the chamberlain had called Supreme Sister, now draped in a silk robe embroidered with such dazzling flowers that Katharina thought they could attract bees. "Why are you still here and why are you distressing my brother?" the woman demanded.

"We had no where to go—"

She snapped orders to the guards, who took a step forward.

"Please, Lady," Katharina said. "Let us stay for just a little while. My child is not well."

"That is not my concern," the woman barked.

"But it is! I was brought here by the Kosh. They sold me to you."

"Yes, but we can't use you. So you have to go."

"I cannot go! My child is not well!"

The almond eyes flickered toward Adriana. "What is wrong with her?"

"We were not fed properly by the Kosh. They gave us scraps their dogs would not eat. She did not have enough food when she was a baby. I need to make her well again."

"The Kosh are pigs," the woman spat in Kosh. "Still, you must go."

"But I can work to earn our keep," Katharina said quickly, desperate. "I can embroider. I do very good needlework."

"Bah! Got plenty of women doing embroidery. I do it myself, and better than you I would say." As the Supreme Sister started to leave, she was stayed by the old man, who tugged at her sleeve and whispered something in her ear. She turned and narrowed her eyes at Katharina. "My brother says you tell stories. What stories?"

Katharina was instantly defensive. Were stories a criminal offense in this place? "I was only telling children's stories, fairy tales, I meant no harm."

"Tell me one."

What manner of people were these, that they were afraid of stories? "But they are only fairy tales. They are harmless, Lady."

"I want to hear," and to Katharina's surprise, the woman crossed her legs and sat on the floor the way the old man had done.

She tried to think of the most harmless tale she knew, in case her stories caused some unintended offense that would have her and Adriana thrown into a dungeon. She settled upon "Rapunzel" and instantly she had a rapt audience comprised of her own daughter, the old man, his sister, and the guards who all leaned close to listen. And when she came to the end and told how Rapunzel had foiled the witch, everyone laughed and clapped with glee, from Adriana to the fiercest of the guards.

The woman's attitude immediately changed. "That was a good story," she said, her round face radiating a smile. "Tell another."

"But, Lady, my child is tired and weak, and we are exhausted."

"Another story, then you go to sleep."

By the time Katharina got halfway through "The Tortoise and the Hare," Adriana was slumbering in her arms. But her peculiar audience was as alert and rapt as ever, barely breathing or blinking as they hung upon every word she uttered. And when she reached the end, they all laughed and cheered for the tortoise.

Katharina marveled at the reaction of these people to simple tales that she had thought were universal. At home, one could only tell these stories to the youngest children, who had never heard them, for otherwise the audience grew bored and demanded something new. Had Zhandu's self-imposed isolation from the rest of the world re-

sulted in a dearth of new stories, she wondered, and as they had grown
bored with their own, they hungered for new myths and legends as
other races might crave gold and wine?

Supreme Sister rose to her feet. "You can stay. You will tell us
stories."

Katharina's mind raced with hope. "May we have a room of our
own?"

"For as long as you have stories to tell us."

"And food for my child?"

The woman squinted, then wrinkled her nose, then said, "She is
puny. Needs fattening. Tell us fine stories and you will have a fine
apartment and fine clothes and fine food." She laughed at her own
play on words. "My brother is very happy," she said, patting the old
man on the arm. "He will see that you are happy in return."

But when Supreme Sister added, "You will live with us forever,"
Katharina's relief turned to panic. "But I must get to Jerusalem."

"Eh? Where is that?"

Katharina was momentarily speechless. Everyone in the world had
heard of Jerusalem. "It is a city," she began, but was cut off by an
impatient gesture.

"After all the stories are done, you can leave."

"I will need money for the journey."

The woman shrugged. "We have plenty of money. Tell stories, go
away rich."

In this way did Katharina learn that she had been telling stories to
Heavenly Ruler, king of Zhandu, and Summer Rose, his sister.

*T*he first night of storytelling, when she and Adriana were escorted
to the royal apartments, Katharina received a shock. Instead of just
the king and his sister, she found herself facing an audience of several
hundred.

She was not daunted. To tell a tale to one child or to three hundred
adults was the same thing: catch their interest, give them a hero, keep
them in breathless anticipation, and then reward them with a satisfying ending. While she spun her tales, scribes sat at ornately carved
desks with scrolls and pens and inks, and recorded Katharina's stories
in the intricate calligraphy of Zhandu. These would be copied, she

was told, and distributed throughout the kingdom for other storytellers to read to the most farflung citizens.

She told Heavenly Ruler and his court tales from the forests of her homeland—"The Frog Prince," "Snow White," and "The Twelve Dancing Princesses." When the German folk tales ran out, she recounted the lives of Jesus and the saints, and then stories of Muhammad she had heard in Constantinople. The favorites were yarns filled with wondrous beings such as talking frogs, dancing donkeys, horses that flew, and ogres that crouched beneath bridges to catch passersby unaware. And miracles and curses aplenty. Each night she delighted the growing audience, and each day she was rewarded with the promised gold coin, abundant food, and the freedom of the city. In this way did Katharina learn that people were the same all over, be they peasants on a farm in Germany, or wizards in an ancient mountain kingdom, for the people of Zhandu laughed when mice outwitted cats, cried when beautiful heroines died, and cheered when handsome heroes were victorious. They gasped in horror when the wicked queen believed she was eating the heart of Snow White; they cried, "Look out!" when Little Red Cap met the wolf in the woods; they shivered when Katharina described the great dark forests where evil frogs and ogres lived; they jeered at the poor-sport fox who said the grapes must be sour; and they clapped when the heroic Siegfried won the magic treasure away from the Nieblungs. But their favorite story of all was the one of the girl whose dying mother told her to go in search of her father, and the girl encountered many adventures and mishaps along the way, and when Katharina did not end the story, and they all asked, "Did the girl find her father?" and she told them that it was *her* story, they clapped and said it was the best of all.

For the first time since the encampment by the emerald stream, Katharina knew happiness. Zhandu was a fabulous spectacle of snowy mountain peaks and mossy valleys, golden domes and ivory spires. Everything had a delightful sounding name: the Jade Gate, the Palace of Celestial Happiness, the Hall of Joyful Contemplations. The few visitors who did come from the outside world were taken to stand before the Mirror of Hidden Truths, and a sorcerer—he was the *Wu*, which in their ancestral tongue meant "wizard"—examined the reflection to judge the person's honesty. Every night an army of chefs created miracles out of food: towers of spun sugar, marzipan molded into flowers and animals, multicolored cakes that melted on the tongue. Rare and costly fish eggs, brought by strenuous stages from the far north, were arranged on delicate breads and biscuits. Wine was chilled in snow brought down from the mountains.

When Katharina had first arrived with the Kosh, she had marveled at the wealth of ermines the Kosh had received for her, and she had wondered if the people of Zhandu were so wealthy that they didn't care about money. But now she learned that there was nothing the outside world could offer: the people of Zhandu enjoyed trees that bore fruit and nuts year round; acres of grain and vegetables; wild game in plenty; a whole forest of honey-giving beehives; and fresh, healthful water bubbling from perennial springs. Few outsiders were allowed in, even fewer were invited to trade. Emissaries rode out, inspected offerings, and more often than not came back empty-handed. Zhandu had all the silks, jewels, rich foods, wine, and creature comforts that it could want.

Except for stories. For the first time in generations, an outsider had brought something new.

Katharina and her daughter were given fabulous rooms with huge beds with silken coverlets, new clothes and jewels, all the food they could eat, and the freedom of the city—as long as they were back at the palace each night for Heavenly Ruler's story. They adopted the ways and customs of Zhandu. And Katharina discovered the secret of the women's unbelievable hairdos: headdresses fashioned from very thin jade were first secured to the scalp, and then the long hair was combed over the frame, with curls and braids added so that no jade showed, making it look as if the hair stood by itself this way, all fixed in place with long ivory sticks that resembled knitting needles. The foreign mother and daughter wore long silk robes and slippers with curved-up toes, and every night, after the storytelling, Katharina counted their slowly growing pile of money against the day they would leave and resume their journey.

As they adjusted to life in this remarkable kingdom, Adriana's nightmares began to recede: memories of seeing a man set on fire for the sport of it, having to fight with dogs for food, of being snatched away from her mother as a form of punishment. She also began to grow strong and healthy. The court physician looked at the child and said she had a weakness of the blood due to undernourishment while in the womb, and so he had prescribed a special Zhandu tea that, along with the water, which Summer Rose said was magical, and the air, which was pure being at so high an altitude, had wonderful healing powers.

But the physician cautioned that it would be dangerous for the girl to leave, for her health was supported by Zhandu and it would fail once she was away from the healthful influences of this place. Katharina took this advice to heart, especially as, after a life fraught with danger, when many times Katharina had not thought her daughter would survive, she saw that here in Zhandu her child was safe and secure at last. Adriana knew stability and a home for the first time, such as Katharina had once known years ago, with Isabella Bauer in Badendorf. Did Katharina have the right to take this away from her?

And so every night, after Adriana was asleep and the palace was quiet, Katharina sat by a lamp and stared at the painting of St. Amelia and the blue crystal. Jerusalem seemed so far away as to be almost nonexistent, and it had now been almost twenty-five years since her father had left his baby in the care of a penniless seamstress. Was he still alive?

*W*hen they had been there a year and Katharina was counting her gold coins and wondering if they had enough to leave Zhandu, Summer Rose came to her and said, "Come with me."

Katharina automatically reached for Adriana's hand, but Summer Rose said, "Leave the child. It will frighten her."

But Katharina never went anywhere without her daughter, and so Adriana was taken along an unfamiliar corridor into a part of the palace Katharina had never visited before. Here, at a locked and guarded door, Summer Rose paused and said gravely, "He will alarm you at first, but he will not hurt you."

"Who am I to meet, Lady?"

"He is my son, the crown prince of Zhandu."

Katharina was shocked. She had never heard mention of a prince, or any heirs to the throne. She was further surprised to find herself ushered through two more locked and guarded doors, and then into the most remarkable chamber she had ever seen.

Not a single window pierced the walls; not a single shaft of sunlight penetrated. Instead, a hundred lamps hung from the high ceilings, and flames blazed in sconces along the walls. The enormous room was capped by a high dome that had been painted blue with white clouds; the floor was dominated by a pond that rippled with goldfish, and even a magnificent white heron waded among the reeds. Trees grew in huge pots, and shrubs and all varieties of flowers flourished around the pond, giving the impression of being outdoors although there was no real sky overhead. Patches of grass grew here and there, and flagstone paths had been laid. Following Summer Rose, they came upon a delightful pavilion just like those in the gardens outside, and it was brightly lit with lamps. Katharina could not believe her eyes: gazelles grazed among the shrubs, and a bird flew overhead, startling her. It was as if, for some unfathomable reason, the outdoors had been brought inside.

"Be calm," Summer Rose said. "He frightens people at first. But I assure you he is harmless."

Katharina wondered if this was a kind of prison where the crown prince was kept, away from sunlight and the eyes of his subjects, and she wondered what his crime had been. She tightened her grip on Adriana's hand and belatedly questioned her decision to bring her.

His name was Lo-Tan, which meant "Fierce Dragon," and it was explained to Katharina that every night when she told her stories to the court of Zhandu, he sat hidden behind a screen, listening. But now he wished to meet the storyteller in person.

Summer Rose went on to say that her son was the reason Katharina had been brought to Zhandu in the first place, because Heavenly Ruler had sent out a proclamation for a woman fitting a certain description, with the intention of marrying her to his heir. When Lo-Tan appeared, Katharina saw at once why she had been rejected as soon as Summer Rose had set eyes on her: for, pale and blond as she was, Katharina was not as white as this young man, who was in fact so white and colorless he was what Katharina had heard called albino.

Had his name been given to him in the hope that he would grow into a fierce dragon? For he struck Katharina as being like a dove, a pure white, unblemished dove, soft and gentle and the color of snow. Katharina was captivated by his eyes—red pupils in pink irises. They held her with a steady, confident gaze, and his smile was friendly and disarming.

Before Katharina could return his softly spoken salutation, Adriana broke free of her mother's grasp and, instead of running away as Summer Rose had feared, she ran to the prince and, tugging on his yellow silk pantaloons, said, "Are you a rabbit?"

"Adriana!" Katharina said.

But the prince only laughed. Dropping down to one knee, he said to the five-year-old, "Do I look like a rabbit?"

Adriana frowned. "Well, you don't have the ears."

He grinned. "That is because I do not wear them all the time."

Her face lit up. "Really? Where do you keep them?"

Lo-Tan returned to his feet and said to Katharina in a voice that was as soft as clouds, "Would the young lady do me the honor of telling me a story?"

As Katharina blushed, and replied, "The honor would be all mine," Summer Rose smiled with tears of relief and gratitude in her eyes.

Katharina and Adriana spent afternoons in the enchanting indoor garden, discovering pools and waterfalls, more birds flying freely, tame deer. Because the royal physicians had warned that any exposure to sunlight could sicken or perhaps even kill him, Lo-Tan never went beyond these walls. But Katharina did not mind, for she found peace and tranquility in his presence, and Adriana, to whom he gave the nickname Happy Flea, loved to play in his make-believe wonderland.

Fierce Dragon shyly confessed to Katharina that he thought her name unbecoming and difficult to pronounce, so he gave her a new one: Wei-Ming, which meant Golden Lotus. Therefore when Summer Rose came to Katharina one afternoon in the Garden of Peaceful Reflections, she addressed her as Golden Lotus, and said solemnly, "You are thinking of leaving us."

Katharina saw the sadness on the older woman's round face, and she realized how fond she had grown of Summer Rose and how she was going to miss her. "Yes. I have enough money to buy passage on a caravan to Jerusalem."

"And you will take your daughter?"

Katharina didn't immediately respond, for she was still undecided. Adriana was now five years old, a happy healthy child with many friends, Fierce Dragon being her favorite. She was such a cheerful little fixture in the court, with her miniature silk robes and golden hair twisted into spires, prattling on in rapid Kosh as if she had been born here, that she was everyone's favorite. But Katharina had said all along that their stay was only temporary, that someday they must leave.

"Let me offer you a proposition," Summer Rose said, in a kindly tone, understanding the young woman's dilemma, for what mother can leave her child behind and go on a long, unknowable journey? "This Jerusalem you speak of is very far away. Many things can happen in the time it takes you to get there. You have already been kidnapped and sold twice, it could happen again. And Happy Flea would be orphaned, if you left her here. Or if you took her with you she could be killed, or sold into slavery, or at the least, grow weak again once away from the healthful influences of Zhandu."

Katharina nodded. Summer Rose was not saying anything she herself had not already considered. It seemed there was no solution: she had to leave, yet she could neither take nor abandon her child.

And then Summer Rose spoke words that, for once in her life, left Katharina speechless: "Marry my son and we shall find your father for you."

When the younger woman did not respond, Summer Rose spoke quickly, "Our dynasty needs healthy heirs. You see that my brother has no offspring that have survived, and Lo-Tan is my only son. Fifteen years ago, when Lo-Tan was twelve, we sent out a proclamation looking for a female like himself. We thought this was the way it should be done. But we think now that we shall never find a woman like him."

Katharina recovered herself. "But . . . I do not love him."

Summer Rose stared at her blankly. "What has love to do with marriage? I did not love Lo-Tan's father."

"And I am already married," Katharina said softly.

Summer Rose patted her hand. "Dear child, the man of your heart is dead. You must live your life. He would have wished it, I am sure. Tell me, are you at least fond of my son?"

"Oh yes," Katharina said, meaning it. She had developed a deep affection for the gentle Lo-Tan. A kinder and more modest man did not live, and he was so good with Adriana.

"If you marry him," Summer Rose continued, "you can remain in Zhandu and we will send out proclamations as we once did for an albino woman. You have seen how far and wide our proclamations travel. We plucked you from deep in Persia, did we not? We can reach

Jerusalem, too. All caravans stop here, and all caravan leaders know of the riches that await them if they bring us what we seek. In this way, Golden Lotus, you need not be separated from your daughter, nor need you hazard the risks of so long and dangerous a journey, and you will still find your father!"

Katharina said, "I must think about it," and that night prayed to St. Amelia for guidance, holding the little painting that had a mate somewhere in the world, another little painting of St. Amelia and her sacred blue crystal, most likely in the possession of a European nobleman with a beard like a golden sunburst, waiting for his daughter to find him. She prayed also to the spirit of Don Adriano, whom she would love for the rest of her life, and finally she prayed over the sleeping form of her daughter, little Happy Flea, glowing in health and free from nightmares at last.

As sunlight streamed through the silken hangings of their bedchamber the next morning, and Katharina heard the whispering of courtiers, and the tinkle of fountains, and glorious birdsong, she wondered that she had even hesitated. For what Summer Rose had said was wise: the proclamations of Zhandu did indeed reach the ends of the earth and if anyone could find her father, it would be the emissaries of this mountain kingdom.

And, after all, Katharina *was* fond of Lo-Tan.

And so she said yes, and on a glorious summer day when all the citizens of Zhandu turned out for the great celebration, Katharina Bauer-von Grünewald of Badendorf, Germany, mother of the child of a knight of the Brotherhood of Mary, Don Adriano of Aragon, Spain, married the albino nephew of Heavenly Ruler and son of Summer Rose, Prince Lo-Tan, and in so doing became Princess Wei-Ming of Zhandu.

*A*s promised, Heavenly Ruler sent men out in search of the blue stone and her father: runners and emissaries bearing proclamations promising rich rewards to whoever came back with information about the blue stone, or the blue stone itself, or a yellow-bearded foreigner.

Word spread. It was carried on camels and yaks, in the mouths of men dreaming of Zhandu riches, in conversations at garrisons, in dialogues at caravansaries and crossroads. Wherever two travelers met over a campfire, the blue crystal of Zhandu and the yellow-bearded stranger were discussed. Like wind whispering across sand dunes the proclamations flew so that within a year the first fruits began to appear: blue stones of all kinds were brought to the plateau at the foot of Zhandu, some as big as melons, some as small as peas; peacock blue and heaven blue, some nearer to green, others nearer to black. Everyday, guards went out to gather up the stones and bring them back for Katharina to inspect, and everyday the reward went unpaid.

Then Heavenly Ruler had his royal artists copy the diptych of St. Amelia on durable paper and they were very good likenesses except they didn't capture the living blue of the crystal, and the saint had an Asian look to her. These paintings went out of Zhandu in the form of scrolls, with a promise of reward written on them in Kosh, Latin, Arabic, and German.

Years passed. While Katharina's love for Lo-Tan never neared the passion and hunger she had felt for Adriano, her fondness for her gentle husband ran deep. She shared his sunless world with him, and Adriana grew and flourished and became elder sister to a brother, a sister, and a third brother. When Adriana was old enough, she attended school with other children of the court, learning to work basic sums on an apparatus called an abacus, and to paint rudimentary letters and words in calligraphy. Though she learned nothing in the way of geography, for the people of Zhandu believed the world was flat and that Zhandu was at its center, there were lessons in astronomy and mathematics, poetry and painting.

Blue stones continued to be brought to Zhandu—big and little, transparent and opaque, from powder blue to royal blue—and along with them came stories of yellow-bearded men. Katharina listened to each with the same attention she gave to examining the stones, but none matched a German nobleman who had gone to Jerusalem looking for a magic blue crystal.

$\mathcal{F}$inally, in the summer of the tenth year after the first proclamation had gone out, and Katharina, while happy with Lo-Tan and her Zhandu children, was beginning to wonder if she should have taken the journey herself after all, a runner came to say that traders had found the man searching for the blue stone.

Katharina, always hopeful, always doubtful, said, "You have found my father?"

"And we are bringing him to you!"

The foreigner was brought to the Garden of Eternal Bliss, where the royal family was gathered in breathless anticipation. Katharina's heart fluttered anxiously as her mind raced with questions: *What will we say to one another? How shall I address him? Are my brothers with him?*

And then he stepped through the archway and entered splendid sunshine. Katharina gave a cry. She saw the cloak first, and although travel-worn and patched, and not as white as it had been at the emerald stream, it still looked handsome and dignified. Adriano's skin was sun-darkened and contrasted against his shoulder length white hair. Although his hair was no longer dark, his eyes still were, and he did not have the face of an old man, merely a well-journeyed one.

Katharina ran into his arms, and while everyone looked on in amazement and awe, Adriano told her he was in Tashkent when he had met a man showing this little painting around. He knew then that he had found her.

Katharina feasted her eyes on him, touched his arms, felt his solidness, and silently thanked God for this miracle. "But you were killed by the emerald stream! I saw!"

Adriano could not get his fill of the sight of her, still his Katharina, and yet foreign in her silk robes and golden hair arranged on her head like an exotic birdcage. "There was a man in our caravan who coveted my cloak, and while I bathed he stole it. It was his poor fortune that at that moment the Kosh attacked. I was wounded and nearly drowned in the stream. But I was found by nomads who took me into their tents and nursed me back to health."

Realizing that a story was about to be told, Heavenly Ruler and Summer Rose, Lo-Tan, and the children gathered close to listen. "After I recovered," Adriano said, "and bade good-bye to my rescuers, I went looking for you, Katharina. But there was no trail, I had no way of knowing which direction you had gone, if you were still alive even. So I went to Jerusalem, for I thought if I would find you anywhere, it would be there. I looked for the blue stone, but it was no longer there. I met a man who told me of a Saxony nobleman, Baron von Grünewald, who had also been in Jerusalem looking for the blue stone. We missed him by fifteen years, Katharina. The man said the German went next to Baghdad, and so I followed his trail there. All these years, I have been following your father's trail, hoping it would lead me to you."

"But you never found him?"

"No, but I found you," he said with a smile.

"But what of your work on Crete? What of your brotherhood? Should you not have gone to them?"

"While I was in Jerusalem I heard news of the Turks invading Crete where my brotherhood were wiped out to a man." He paused and looked at his audience with the air of a man bearing a wonderful secret. "And now the news . . . Katharina, although I did not find your father, I do know where he is."

A collective gasp filled the garden, for everyone was familiar with Katharina's lifelong quest. "Tell me quickly," she said.

"When I was in Tashkent, I met a man who told me of a father and three sons, Germans, carrying a small painting like yours. They were searching for a blue stone. I was told that they learned it had been sold to monks traveling east to Cathay, where they were headed for the court of the emperor. That is where your father went, Katharina, to China, and he is most likely there still."

Food was brought, and wine, and the incredible people in dazzling silks flitted and fussed around him like exotic birds. Though white-haired and care-worn, Adriano still towered over the Zhandu, and he laughed at all the attention for, truth be told, he had had no idea what to expect while he was being escorted to this isolated kingdom in the sky.

But when a young girl was brought before him, and she bowed respectfully and called him father, his laughter died. The garden fell silent, even the birds and tinkling fountain seemed to hush themselves in awe of this man's reaction to news of something he never knew: that he had a child.

It was some minutes before he could speak, and then it was in a voice tight with emotion. "In our home in Aragon there hung a portrait of my mother when she was your age. You could be her, Adriana, the resemblance is so strong."

Father and daughter embraced, and everyone cried, none so loudly as Heavenly Ruler who sobbed like a child and wiped his face on his immaculate white sleeves.

That night, as Katharina lay in Lo-Tan's arms, he whispered to her, "If you wish to return to Adriano as his wife, I understand and release you, for he is your first husband. And if you decide to go to Cathay and search for your father, I give you my blessing. But I pray to Kwan

Yin, my beloved Golden Lotus, that you keep me always in your heart."

But she said, "Adriano and I were never truly married. Not according to our laws. You are my husband, Lo-Tan, and always shall be." As for the other, her heart was heavy as she said, "A blue stone meant more to my father than his own daughter did. He did not just leave me in a stranger's care, he *abandoned* me. And if I go after him now, I would be abandoning my own children. But unlike my father, my children mean more to me than an elusive blue stone. I will not go after him. My place is here, with you, with my family."

The next morning she went to Adriano, who was marveling at all the riches and glory of Zhandu. She took his rough hands in hers and said, "I will not go to Cathay and search for my father. I believe the blue crystal became his obsession, just as he became mine. And I believe that somewhere along the way I lost sight of my true purpose, just as he lost sight of his. My father chose his path, Adriano, and I have chosen mine. I will stay here. But it would bring me great joy if you ended your long journey and stayed in this place. Can you stay here . . . as my dear friend?" she added, for the fact of her marriage to Lo-Tan stood between them, and both knew they could never rekindle the intimacy they had once shared.

Adriano's tone was deep and heartfelt as he replied, "When you first met me, Katharina, I was an intolerant man. I carried hatred in my heart for all men of another creed. I used religion as my gauge to measure a man. If he did not embrace Christ, then he could not be a worthy man. And in my arrogance I believed it was my destiny to bring all men to the true God, whether by word or by sword. But when I regained consciousness after the raid by the emerald stream, and found myself in the company of fire-worshippers, I was on the brink of death and they took care of me, they nursed me back to health and treated me with kindness. In another age, I would have called them demon-worshippers, but during my convalescence I saw that they were just people, like people everywhere, striving to survive, living in fear and hope, and worshipping the powers they believed in. I should be happy to stay here and teach the people of Zhandu about Jesus, Katharina, and if they come to accept Him, then so be it. But I am no longer of the belief that one must knock skulls in order to bring people to the true faith, for I am no longer convinced that there *is* just one true faith."

Adriano went on to say that he had had no right marrying her years ago. He broke his vows and believed that what happened at the emerald spring was his punishment. He had spent the past ten years doing penance for his sin, by seeking the blue crystal and Katharina's father, and by staying celibate.

Katharina accepted this, but when she saw how the ladies of the court eyed the robust stranger, and giggled and whispered behind their fluttering fans, she wondered how long Adriano's renewed vow of celibacy would last.

She marveled at the mysteries of fate. What if her mother, Isabella Bauer, had died before Katharina had reached her? What if she had died keeping the secret of Katharina's birth? Katharina would have married Hans Roth and moved into the house behind the beer stein factory, and she would have lived out her days believing that Badendorf was the world.

She said to Adriano, "I have been disguised as a boy and have lived in a Turkish harem; I have been shipwrecked, kidnapped, sold into slavery; I have been a Christian, a Muslim, and a goddess-worshipper; I have loved a man and lost him and found him again; I have known ecstasy and pain, fulfillment and loss. I have spoken German, Arabic, Latin, and the tongue of the Zhandu; I have traveled to the ends of the earth and seen wonders indescribable. But through it all, Badendorf remained my home. And in a way it still is, with its colorful *marktplatz* and familiar *rathaus*, the river and the forest and the castle. But Zhandu is also my home. And while I doubt I shall ever find my true father, I have a father nonetheless, in Heavenly Ruler. I have a brother in you, Adriano, and a sister and third mother in Summer Rose. Cousins and aunts and uncles do I have now in plenty, here in Zhandu, and a family more extensive than even that of the Roths of Badendorf. And I have Adriana, and Lo-Tan and my children by him. For all these years I searched for my family, and only now do I realize that they have been with me all along. I searched for the blue crystal, but it too was with me all along, in this little painting of St. Amelia. And so here I shall stay, in Zhandu, where I belong."

Interim

$\mathcal{K}$atharina lived the rest of her life in the isolated mountain kingdom, watching her children grow, taking the throne at Lo-Tan's side when he succeeded his uncle as Heavenly Ruler. When Summer Rose died and was laid to rest, Katharina grieved anew for the mothers she had loved. And when Adriano died, at the age of ninety-three, the entire populace mourned, for they had so loved his stories.

Two more generations came and went, telling and retelling the stories of Katharina von Grünewald, until finally Zhandu was toppled, not by an invading army but by nature itself—an earthquake so powerful that it brought down the walls and domes and spires of the fabled city, killing all its inhabitants. And then storms came, both rain and snow, delivering mud and boulders and massive sandrifts to the ruins of Zhandu. As decades and then centuries passed, the climate changed and desert sands came to bury the last tip of the last spire so that five hundred years in the future, archaeologists would pick through rubble and try to imagine the city that had once stood here.

Baron Johann von Grünewald did indeed go to China with his sons, after learning from a merchant in Tashkent that the blue crystal had accompanied a consortium of Christian monks intent upon evangelizing the emperor's court. He never forgot that he had left a daughter back in Germany in the care of a seamstress, and he believed in his heart that he would one day return for her. But the baron was a man born to roam, all he needed was a quest. Like the Grail of Christ that lured other noble-minded men to foreign lands, so was St. Amelia's Stone his lure. But when he finally found it, in the possession of a royal courtesan skilled in the art of love, and he curled his fingers around the object he had been searching for nearly all his life, its purpose died, and so did his. Still vowing to return home and be reunited with his daughter, Johann von Grünewald died in distant China without ever setting foot in his beloved Europe again.

From China the blue crystal was carried on a spice ship to the Dutch Indies, where the gem, having lost all connection to Christian saints, was named the Star of Cathay by a romantic-minded sea captain who believed it possessed love magic that he hoped would convince a certain young lady in Amsterdam to marry him.

Off the coast of India, the spice ship met with misadventure, the captain was sold into slavery, and the Star of Cathay was taken to a temple in Bombay where it was fitted into the statue of a god, so that it was known for a while as the Eye of Krishna. But when the temple was attacked and ransacked during a religious war, the blue crystal was again liberated and carried north to Amsterdam by a Dutch sea captain who sold the stone to a gem merchant named Hendrick Kloppman. From letters written years earlier by the spice ship captain to the jewelers guild, requesting an estimation of the worth of the stone, Kloppman identified it as the Star of Cathay, and deduced from the letters that the lovesick captain had intended it to go to a certain young lady on Keisersgracht Street. Acting honorably and as a man of conscience, Kloppman sought the young woman out and offered her the gem. No longer young and past all desire for marriage, she accepted the crystal with indifference, saying she had only the vaguest recollection of the unfortunate spice ship captain, and sold it right back to Kloppman for enough money to open her own fabric shop and be independent of men forever. Kloppman traveled to Paris where, hoping to make ten times profit on the stone, he played up the romantic angle of the Star of Cathay, inventing a story about a wizard in the imperial court of China and how he had created the crystal out of northern glaciers and dragon bones, the blood of a phoenix and the heart of a virgin.

There were those in Paris who believed him.

Book Seven

MARTINIQUE
1720 C.E.

_____

$\mathcal{B}$rigitte Bellefontaine had a secret.

It involved forbidden love with a dark-eyed rogue, and as she sat at her vanity table, brushing out her hair and removing her cosmetics, she tried not to think of it, for with each passing day, the guilty burden of the secret grew.

A rude sound brought her out of her thoughts. She looked at her husband reflected in the glass behind her. Henri. Sprawled on the bed and snoring. Drunk again.

Brigitte sighed. There was nothing worse than a Frenchman who could not hold his wine.

And he had *promised*. Tonight, after their guests left, he said, he was going to treat her to a special evening under the stars. "Just like the old days, *ma cherie*, when we were young lovers." And then the guests had arrived, and the party had gotten underway, and the wine had poured and poured. And now Henri was flat on his back on the bed, wig askew, his waistcoat stained with samples from the evening's menu: fried codfish fritters and crepes dripping with melted chocolate.

Brigitte set her hairbrush down and gazed wistfully at the piece of jewelry she had worn for the party: a stunning brooch of white gold with a blue crystal at its center surrounded by diamonds and sapphires. The Star of Cathay, that had been so full of romantic promise back in her naive youth.

The Star of Cathay was supposed to bring love and romance into the life of the wearer. Hadn't the gypsy foretold as much? And it *had* delivered . . . for a while. On Brigitte's wedding night—Henri (the man who now snored on the bed) had been a magnificent lover, and seventeen-year-old Brigitte had thought she had died and gone to heaven. But now, twenty years and seven children later, she had all but given up on ever knowing true passion again. Henri was a good man, but he no longer had fire in him. And Brigitte yearned for fire.

Too restless to sleep, she rose and went to the doors that opened onto a balcony off the bedroom. Stepping out into the tropical night redolent with the perfumes of frangipani and mimosa, she closed her eyes and pictured *him*—not Henri but the dark-eyed stranger, tall and noble, of aristocratic features and bearing, impeccably dressed, expert swordsman and roguish lover. He would appear suddenly, unexpectedly, when she was in her garden, or watching the exotic fish in the lagoon, materializing out of the sultry day like the storm clouds that came upon the island swiftly and darkly, drench Martinique with a torrid shower, then dissipate, move on and be only a memory. *He* was like that. And his lovemaking was like a tropical storm—fierce, steamy, irresistible. The mere thought of him sent tremors through her body.

Unfortunately, he didn't exist.

Brigitte thought she would go insane if she never experienced romance and passion again. But how was it ever to happen? It was unthinkable that she should enter into an affair with one of the local colonists. She had her reputation, and her husband's, to think of. And as there was no one else, she had resorted to a fantasy lover, a devilish gentleman of her imagination whose name changed according to her mood and the story. Usually he was French, perhaps called Pierre or Jacques, and he came to the island just for one day, meeting her in the grotto where they made passionate love all afternoon, and as he sailed away he promised someday to return, a promise that fed her soul and kept her alive.

Her fantasies served not only to bring love into her life, but to recapture her youth as well, for in them Brigitte was young and slender and beautiful again, turning men's heads as she had done long ago. Unfortunately, although these fantasies gave her pleasure, they also riddled her with guilt. Brigitte was a good Catholic and believed, as the priests preached, that a sinful deed committed in the heart was as good as being committed in the flesh. Having lustful thoughts outside the bounds of marriage was a sin. If she imagined making love to one of the colonists, then it would be adultery. But was it adultery if the lover did not exist?

She set her eyes to the distant horizon, identifiable only by its absence of stars. Brilliant night sky above, black forbidding ocean below. And beyond . . . Paris. Four thousand miles away, where her friends, family, and children lived in a world so different from the West Indies that they might as well live on the moon.

Brigitte wished she could have gone with her children. She didn't miss the cold or the crowding of Paris, but she longed for the cultural and social life. Born into nobility, she had known the company of kings and queens and the finest of French society. She missed the plays of Molière and Racine, and the spectacles of La Comédie Francaise, those glorious days when the Sun King lavished money on the arts. But what plays were being staged now? Who was the latest wit? What were the ladies wearing at court? The colonists on Martinique relied on mail from home for all their news, and sometimes it came late or not at all, due to the vagaries of the seas, weather, and pirates. Three years ago they had learned that their great king, Louis XIV, was dead—and had been dead for two years! Now his great-grandson, Louis XV, a boy of ten, was on the French throne.

A night breeze came up, stirring palm fronds and the giant leaves of banana plants, ruffling the muslin folds of Brigitte's peignoir. As the breeze brushed her bare skin like a lover's sigh, she felt her ache deepen. And it frightened her. She felt weak and vulnerable. Sending the children away was something all the colonists did, to make sure they grew up as ladies and gentlemen. So Brigitte had sent her lively brood to her sister in Paris for proper schooling in deportment and etiquette. But now that she had done it, she missed them greatly. She had too much time, sunlight, tropical perfumes, and balmy tradewinds on her hands. Henri had the sugarcane fields, the refinery, and the rum distillery to distract him. But with the children gone, and servants to take care of everything else, what else was there for a lady of these islands to do? Brigitte was an avid reader but even that pastime, of late, was reflecting her growing discontent, for her taste ran to pairs of tragic lovers: two French like herself, Heloise and Abelard; two Italians, young but no less tragic, Romeo and Juliet; two English, of long ago, Tristram and Isolde; and a Roman soldier and a Greek queen, Antony and Cleopatra. She devoured these sad, romantic tales as her friends devoured luscious fruits and rum. There was no better sadness, she thought, than sweet sadness. In her private fantasy, she and her lover must live apart, and the delicious ache it conveyed to her heart kept her sighing through sultry afternoons.

She tried to convince herself that dreams were so much more satisfying than reality. Besides, dreams were safe whereas reality could be fraught with peril. Despite Martinique being a tropical Eden, it had its dangers—from sudden, destructive storms, from Mt. Pelée threatening to erupt, from fevers and exotic diseases, and from that worst of dangers: pirates. Only this evening at dinner, when the talk wasn't about the cost of rum and slaves, the conversation had turned to pirates and, lately, one in particular—an English dog named Christopher Kent. One of her guests, a pineapple grower, had suffered a loss to Kent just days earlier when Kent's schooner, *Bold Ranger*, attacked the man's merchant vessel, boarded her, threw the crew overboard and made off with a fortune in gold coin. No one knew what Kent looked like, although the few survivors of his attacks had said he was very tall and looked like the devil.

The night suddenly exploded with shouts from the slave quarters— men wagering on mongoose-and-snake fights. Like the whispering tradewinds and rustling palms, it was the sound of the island calling to her. It made Brigitte think of the native people who had lived here long ago, the Indians with their drums and nakedness, living as God had created them, like Adam and Eve. Their spirits were still here—in the trees and streams and mist-shrouded mountain peaks. New primitives were here now, too, from Africa; more naked people with drums, who filled the nights with their primeval beat and rhythms, chanting and dancing in the firelight.

The air felt heavy, reminding Brigitte that this was the start of hurricane season. She went back inside, closed the double doors, and then went to her vanity table to restore the Star of Cathay to its locked box. The blue crystal had, over the years, become symbolic of the blue seas that surrounded her, the blue sky that covered her. And when she looked into its diamond-dust heart she saw fire and passion. *Her* passion. Trapped, struggling to get free.

She went to the bed and pulled off her husband's boots. Henri was smiling in his sleep. She sighed again. He wasn't a bad man, just an unconscious one. As she slipped between the sheets next to him, she closed her eyes and, although her secret fantasies riddled her with guilt, she once again conjured up the image of *him*, her fantasy lover. When she drifted off to sleep she began to dream, and in the dream he reached for her.

*H*enri Bellefontaine was not unaware of his wife's recent discontent. After all, she no longer had the children to occupy her time. Henri, on the other hand, had the plantation to run. Bellefontaine grew sugar and exported rum, with side interests in the growing and exporting of cinnamon, cloves, and nutmeg, which were in great demand in Europe for use in cooking, perfumes, and medicines. Therefore Henri Bellefontaine was very rich, but he was also very busy. But what did Brigitte have? Fancying himself a loving and attentive husband, but mistaking entirely the cause of her frequent sighs and restlessness (homesickness, he thought, and missing their children), he had come up with what he thought was the perfect remedy.

He bought her a telescope.

It stood on a special rooftop platform, a handsome brass spyglass imported from Holland, fixed to a tripod with a complete 360-degree view of the island and beyond. Henri congratulated himself on his brilliance. Brigitte would no longer feel so remote and isolated for the lens brought the world to her fingertips: the horizon, with France— and their children—just over its edge; islands closer in (patches of emerald green floating on hyacinth blue); Martinique's busy harbors and waterfront settlements with ships coming and going; and finally the seawalls and battlements, narrow lanes and alleyways, and rooftops rising in layers into the hills.

The gesture had touched Brigitte, for Henri *was* a dear man and his heart was in the right place. And it wasn't as though he had brought her to the most godforsaken place on earth. After all, Martinique was the cultural center of the French Antilles, a rich, aristocratic island famous for its gracious living as well as for its lush, tropical vegetation, deep gorges, and towering cliffs. Their own home was a magnificent plantation perched on a spur on the slopes of Mt. Pelée, a volcano that periodically shot up steam and made the ground rumble, as if to remind the humans below of their mortality. The house was designed in typical Creole style with the main rooms on the bottom floor and the bedrooms upstairs. Surrounding it were green lawns like fabulous carpets, bordered by palm trees whose fronds rustled in the tradewinds. Brigitte loved her tropical home, and she loved Martinique. Nobody knew for certain why the island was named so. Some said it was derived from an Indian name that meant "flowers," some said it was named for St. Martin. But Brigitte Bellefontaine, with her romantic heart, believed that when Columbus discovered it and found the island so fantastically beautiful, he named it for a woman he secretly loved.

It had become Brigitte's habit to climb daily to her special rooftop aerie at sunset, her favorite time of the day when work ceased and the evening entertainments began; a time also when changes came over the Caribbean, the luminous sky giving way to a black, star-splashed firmament. Brigitte would give instructions to her kitchen slaves for the evening meal, then she would take a long, languorous bath, put on her underclothes and petticoats, slip into her gauzy peignoir and climb to the roof to watch the sun make its spectacular exit from the world.

As she sipped a small glass of rum, Brigitte kept her eye to the spyglass, sweeping the sea and the bay, the mountains and the clouds, the small fishing villages, and she thought of the coming evening. There would be no guests tonight as it was Sunday. It would be just her and Henri. Would he stay with her, or would the island and its seductions call to him, in the form of gambling in Saint-Pierre? When Henri woke that morning to realize he had fallen asleep before fulfilling his promise, he had been repentant. "*Ma chere! Ma puce!* I am not worthy of thee." Then he had given her a peck on the cheek and, dressed in his riding clothes, had headed out to inspect the sugarcane fields.

Brigitte saw lights going on in the harbor town, doorways being flung open to the sunset, little boats bringing hungry visitors from anchored ships. She could almost hear the music and laughter, smell the cooking aromas, see the smiles of the people. Circling the glass away from the settlement, she scanned the rich green mountain peaks and ridges rising and falling like ocean waves, tropical jungles ranging in every hue of green known to the human eye. And now to the east, away from the crimson sky, to the quiet, windward side of the island with its pristine beaches and lime-green lagoons and hidden coves—

She stopped. Masts? Furled sails?

She focused the lens, bringing the ship into clarity, and peered hard. It had to be an American schooner, judging by the two masts and narrow hull, and the fact that it had to have a shallow draft to be able to navigate through shoal waters and into such a tiny cove.

Brigitte frowned. Why was it anchored there?

She moved the glass slightly, up the main mast, along spars and rigging until she saw the flag.

A pirate ship! There was no mistaking the ensign, what the French wryly called the *joli rouge*—"pretty red"—and the English, the Jolly Roger. Usually they featured skulls and crossbones; this one was designed with a cutlass dripping blood.

"Mon Dieu!" Brigitte whispered. She knew what ship it was—*Bold Ranger*—belonging to the bloodthirsty Christopher Kent. She could see no crew on board.

She began to tremble. Where were they? She had heard of Kent's method—to strike swiftly and brutally. To attack and ravish and be gone before the victims could defend themselves.

Frantically she peered through the glass, scanning the hills between the cove and the plantation, a distance of two miles. Henri and his men were somewhere in all that green, inspecting the sugarcane crop, but she could not find them.

Christopher Kent was every colonist's nightmare. He was one of those buccaneers who did not restrict himself to attacking ships, but made bold attacks on land as well. All plantation owners kept their fortunes hidden somewhere on their estates. It was the only way of guaranteeing its security. Kent knew this. He would come in the night, catch the hapless victims unaware and force them to divulge the location of their gold. Usually by torture.

"Please God," she whispered with a mouth gone suddenly dry. "Let them not be coming this way."

And then she saw them—pirates, making their way up the hillside, prodding overseers and slaves through the sugarcane fields. Henri, knocked from his horse—

"Colette, fetch my musket!" She knew she couldn't hit anything at this range, but perhaps she could fire warning shots. She wondered if the soldiers at the fortress were aware of the pirates. She doubted it. The church bells would be clanging out a warning, and cannons would be firing. Kent had crept up along the windward side of the island and sneaked into the small cove. Two ridges hid the plateau where Bellefontaine sprawled on many acres. The pirates could strike, do their lethal work silently and swiftly, and depart like ghosts, leaving only corpses and a smoldering ruin. It would be at least a day before the soldiers knew what had happened, and by then Kent's ship would be far out to sea.

"What is it, madame?" the young black woman said breathlessly as she came up the narrow stairway, clumsily handling the long firearm. Colette was a third-generation African slave. She had been born on Martinique, as had her mother, but her grandmother had been brought from Africa along with thousands of others to work the sugar and tobacco fields for the French colonists.

"Send Hercule to the fortress," Brigitte began, trying to site the pirates without the aid of the glass. But the sun had finally dipped below the horizon and the light was dying. "Tell him to run, Colette! Tell him there are pirates—"

And then, through the glass, she saw him, Christopher Kent, a tall, forbidding figure dressed all in black. He wore tight breeches and a long coat, the shining gold buttons of his waistcoat flashing in the final rays of the sun. His face was shaded by the broad brim of his tricorn hat, a generous white plume ruffling in the breeze. When he turned and his face came partially into the light, she realized with a shock that he made her think of the phantom lover of her fantasies.

Brigitte's mind worked rapidly. The fortress was ten miles away, over mountainous terrain, and night would fall, plunging jungle and trails into utter blackness long before a runner could even get a good start. The pirates had lit torches, which now burned brightly in the descending dusk, and the flames were making steady snakelike progress up the hill.

Taking a last look at Kent through the glass—he was barely visible now in the swiftly dying day, a phantom figure striding through lush vegetation, like a conqueror—Brigitte said, "Never mind," and set the musket aside.

"But madame," Colette wailed. "Pirates! We must warn everyone!"

"Hush," Brigitte said as she made her way back down the stairs and into her bedroom. "Tell no one, Colette!" The situation suddenly called for another strategy. But it also required a cool head.

She possessed one beautiful gown that she had never worn. It had come with her from France twenty years ago, a very special dress that she had planned to wear when they celebrated the king's birthday. But she had gotten pregnant during the voyage to Martinique and after the birth of that first child, she hadn't been able to fit into the gown. She had gotten pregnant again and the cycle continued until she had given up ever wearing the gown. And anyway, there was a new king now, one whom she didn't even know.

The silk overdress was a dazzling summer pink, the stomacher embroidered in rich scarlet and cardinal hues, with the underskirt a contrasting sun-yellow, as was the fashion back then, when gowns were meant to blind and colors were to be as shocking and contrasting as possible. It looked very much like a tropical sunset: the gold sun blazing against a blushing sky. She had had the waist let out after the birth of her seventh child so that it finally fit (with help from a tight corset) but by then the gown was hopelessly out of date. Such an elaborate, ponderous style had gone out of fashion upon the death of Louis XIV. How could she possibly wear it? And so the gown had become a symbol, of faded youth and missed opportunities, and just the sight of it reminded her of young passions and stolen kisses in summer gardens.

Her heart pounded as she lifted the gown from its storage chest and gave orders to a very flustered Colette. It was difficult to hurry with such a complicated outfit—the corsets and skirts and panniers, and all the lacings and hooks, and with Colette so terrified she was ready to bolt. Brigitte herself was gripped with fear, but she kept Kent's image in the forefront of her mind—a dark, menacing figure. As she held her breath while Colette tightened the last of the laces, Brigitte did a rapid mental calculation: the pirates would be at the edge of the distillery now. The road from there to the main house was half a mile.

Finally she looked at herself in the glass. But she frowned at her reflection. Although the dress was dazzling, she herself still looked old and plump. Kent would hardly give her a second look. And then she remembered the Star of Cathay. With trembling fingers she fastened the brooch to the lowest point of her décolletage, so that the diamonds and sapphires gave the appearance of the blue crystal having fluttered like a butterfly and landed quivering on her exposed bosom.

The transformation was instantaneous. A new woman stood before her in the looking glass. The crystal did indeed possess magic! Brigitte Bellefontaine was young, slender, and beautiful again.

Before she went downstairs, she took Colette's hands in a firm grip and said, "Now listen to me. We are about to have unexpected visitors. Do not be afraid. Do not try to run away."

"But, madame—"

"Colette! Listen carefully, for you must do exactly as I say . . ."

Before she left the bedroom, she took a final look at herself in the mirror and smiled with grim approval. Glancing at the musket leaning against the wall she thought, *Sometimes a gown is better than a gun.*

Although over a hundred slaves worked on Bellefontaine—in the fields, in the sugar refinery and rum distillery—it only took a handful of men with pistols and muskets to keep them all frightened and compliant. As Brigitte made her way through the main living room of her house, she heard the stamping of feet outside, the growled commands, the occasional sound of a whip. The female slaves, whose work was concentrated on the master's family, house, vegetable gardens and hen yards, came running at the sight of their men stumbling at pistol and sword point into the main yard. They immediately sent up wails of lament. House servants rushed to the windows and cowered there, looking out with big frightened eyes.

Brigitte paused to compose herself. She could barely breathe. Outside she heard screams and shouts and gunfire. But she waited behind the closed front door, calming herself, an actress awaiting her grand entrance. Holding herself in check, for her impulse was to run, she held back for another long minute and then reached for the door, drew it slowly open.

The pirates were a frightening sight with their arsenal of weapons: muskets, blunderbusses, cutlasses, daggers, and pistols. Some even brandished boarding axes meant for hacking at nets and rigging. They numbered fifty, Brigitte guessed, and were dressed in an array of rags and tatters, with long filthy hair and mismatched boots. Against the backdrop of blazing torches they resembled, or so Brigitte thought, Satan's army of imps and demons.

Henri was tied up in ropes, and had been pushed to his knees. Brigitte had to steel herself against running to him.

The veranda was arrayed in masses of climbing flowers, all colors of the rainbow, and the pillars were thick with green vines. The combined perfume was rich and heady while the last of a few industrious bees buzzed about the blossoms. Framed thus, as if on a theater stage, Brigitte did not say a word, but stood there until, one by one, the men fell silent and stared.

Captain Kent had just reached the bottom step when he realized everyone had fallen silent. He turned and looked up. Now, in the dusky gloom and by lantern light, Brigitte saw his features more clearly: they were sharp and hard. Kent was wearing a long black coat, generously cut, nearly reaching his ankles. It was richly embroidered with silk and gold thread, and the buttons were shining gold. His breeches were black, and he wore spotless white stockings and well-shined shoes with gold buckles. White ruffles frothed at his throat and wrists. Beneath his wide-brimmed tricorn hat he wore no wig but had his own long hair tied back in a ponytail with side curls over his ears, in the very latest fashion. Every inch the fine gentleman, Brigitte thought, as if he had arrived to attend an opera instead of ransack a house.

When his eyes met hers, a startling thought came suddenly to her mind: *Back in the fortune-teller's tent on the grounds of Versailles, a big celebration for the king's birthday with actors and jugglers and a carnival. The old Gypsy saying to sixteen-year-old Brigitte, "This blue stone possesses tremendous fire. You see? It is trapped inside. One day this fire will be released and it will consume you. In love. In passion. In a man's arms. A man who will make such love to you that you will nearly die of ecstasy."*

Clasping her hands tightly before her, Brigitte glided forward to the edge of the veranda, as gracefully and without fear as she could, and said softly, "Welcome to my home, m'sieu."

He stared. Then he smiled. And the way he looked her up and down—she knew that just an hour ago he would not have looked at her in that way. But she was beautiful now, because of the magic in the blue crystal. It had cast a spell and transformed her.

"Milady," he said, removing his hat with a flourish and extending one leg forward as he bowed.

Her voice was barely above a whisper, yet so still and silent were the gathered men that everyone heard. "We offer you the hospitality of our home."

Brigitte silently thanked God that she and her sisters had had an

English tutor when they were girls, for her father had believed in his children having a well-rounded education in order that they may move in all the best and most cultured circles. Her sister had then married an English baron and had moved to Britain, so that for the past twenty years Brigitte had written letters to her nieces and nephews in English—thank God for that, too. While she was not expert at the language, she could make herself understood.

Kent's eyebrows arched. "Hospitality! We won't be staying, mistress. We've come for the gold and then we'll be on our way."

Several yards away, her husband, having been knocked to his knees, shouted, "Save yourself, Brigitte!"

She moistened her lips. "To refuse hospitality is rude, m'sieu. And I had heard you were a gentleman."

He smiled. "So you know who I am then," he said.

"You are Captain Christopher Kent."

"And you aren't afraid of me?"

"I am," she said in as matter-of-fact tone as she could, but her heart beat in fear. "But regardless of who you are, sir, or your intention here, it is the custom among my class to offer hospitality to the visitor."

His laugh was short and dry. "You think a few victuals will save your gold?"

She lifted her chin. "You mistake my intention, sir. You may have our gold since there is obviously no way I can stop you. But I had thought that as a gentleman you would understand the rules of civilized behavior."

His dark eyes flickered and she knew she had touched a sensitive spot. Pirate or not, Christopher Kent believed in his heart that he was a gentleman. Why else would he dress so when the rest of his men dressed like animals? "I have six sucking piglets, ready to be cooked," she added.

He put his hands on his hips and said with a laugh, "Well this is a new trick!"

While some of the men laughed with him, one of them, older than Kent, with long gray hair twisted into a nest of braids and a cancer growing on the side of his nose, stepped up and said, "Beggin' yer pardon, ma'am, how might ye be preparin' them piggies?"

Brigitte refused to acknowledge the man. She continued to address Kent: "I cook them with cloves and garlic, capers and oregano, accompanied by hot bread soaked in garlic gravy, herbed goat cheese and a cold ginger soup. Mango tarts covered in chocolate sauce for dessert."

"And what's to drink?" the brute said sharply.

"French wine and brandy," she said to Kent.

The man rubbed the good side of his nose and said to his captain, "It might not be a bad idea, Chris. We ain't had a good meal since God knows when."

"And let the soldiers catch us with our guard down? Don't you see it's a trick, Mr. Phipps?"

"I don't think the soldiers know we're here, Chris. But I can check." He added more quietly, "And I don't think it's a trick. The lady's bargaining is what. Thinks we'll show mercy."

Kent gave this some thought. And while he did, Brigitte drew in a deep breath, causing the blue-crystal brooch on her bosom to flash its blue fire.

As she had intended, it caught Kent's eye. He took one look at the white breast and gave a signal to Phipps, who in turn sent two men clambering up trees as lookouts. Then Kent gave another signal and a mob of his men rushed forward, thundered up the veranda steps, past Brigitte and into the house.

She used all her self-control to ignore the sounds of ransacking and vandalism within. Her home meant nothing in this moment; all her precious furniture and pottery, draperies and jewelry. The pirates could have it all.

Mr. Phipps came back to report: "The lookouts report that everything's quiet, no hue and cry has been raised, it's business as usual down at the harbor. What about that feast, Chris?"

Kent went up the steps and drew close to Brigitte. She could barely breathe as she looked up at him, for he towered over her. "How do I know you will not poison us?" he said. "I have been deceived by a beautiful woman before."

She caught her breath. He had called her beautiful! "An understandable caution, m'sieu. Then let your own men do the slaughtering and the spitting, and let them oversee the making of the sauces and bastings, and have my slaves taste everything that is prepared."

She saw the dark currents in his eyes as he assessed what was surely an unexpected situation. "I hope you do not take me for a fool," he said softly.

Their eyes met and held.

The moment stretched; Brigitte caught her breath. This was the crucial moment. And then Kent relaxed, his lips curled in a smile and he said, "Very well, we eat!"

His men cheered and Kent, inclining himself toward Brigitte, said, "Now to the matter of business. Where is the gold, mistress, or shall we wring it from your husband?"

Recalling tales she had heard of Kent, how his men had strung up plantation owners by the wrists in the hot midday sun until they told where their fortune was hidden, she said, "Please do not hurt my husband. If you promise not to harm him, I shall take you to the treasure."

$\mathcal{M}$aking certain first that the roasting pits were being prepared and that her kitchen slaves understood their assignments, reassuring them that as long as everyone cooperated they would be safe, Brigitte led Kent and a handful of his men from the main yard down a flagstone path, one of many walkways scattered in this tropical paradise, leading to gardens and cottages, as well as to the sugar refinery and rum distillery, and, beyond that, the slaves' quarters. Brigitte walked ahead of her "guests" with a graceful glide learned long ago in girlhood, her voluminous pink and yellow skirts skimming along the path as if no human legs propelled them beneath. It was a walk she had perfected on the grounds of Versailles to catch the flirtatious attention of young men; she used it now to guide thieves to a treasure.

They reached a clearing in the lush growth and saw before them a vision that made even these rough men goggle with wonder. It was a gazebo, seemingly spun of starlight, white and shimmering in the night. Brigitte graciously stepped to one side, as if about to serve tea. "There," she said, pointing to the floor of the structure. "Beneath those boards."

Standing their blazing torches into the ground, the men rushed forward, axes going at the boards with a great splintering and tearing. They ripped up the floor and hauled out the chests hidden beneath. Brigitte stood wordlessly as the men dragged their booty back to the compound where a bonfire had been lit, fueled, she noticed, by furniture from the house. By the light of the flames, the plunderers pried open the chests and gave a great shout when they saw the gold coins, for coins were what pirates preferred most.

That was clearly the signal for the celebration to get underway, for from out of nowhere a fiddle was produced and someone began a lively jig. Others had broken into the distillery and were rolling giant oak barrels of rum up the path. Female slaves began going nervously through the mob of men with wine bottles and cups, while on the other side of the fire the roasting pits were already singeing the pigs on spits. Brigitte saw her husband and the other captives being prodded into the pig pen, where they were pushed into the muck while their tormentors howled with laughter.

Somewhere during the rough march from the sugarcane fields, Henri had lost his magnificent wig. Large and richly black it had been, with carefully tiered curls rising high on his head and cascading down his back and over his shoulders. Newcomers to the island remarked that such wigs were now out of date, but Henri didn't care. He held to old traditions, which dictated that a gentleman must look his best at all times, and so he wore his wigs no matter what the weather or what task he was about. But it had been knocked from his head and now he was bareheaded, his graying hair standing up in tufts as the pirates poked and kicked him and made fun of him.

Brigitte dug her fingernails into her palms and kept her composure. She wanted to grab one of the burning torches and run into the crowd of pirates, bludgeoning them as she went.

But in the next instant Kent was looking at her, and she remembered her resolve, and that this night was going to be her only chance.

"Hm," he said, studying her in the flickering torchlight. "What makes you so unafraid, I wonder?"

His comment startled her. Could he not see the pulse galloping at her throat, the fear in her eyes, the tremor in her hands? "I am not unafraid," she said, and it was the truth. But *what* she was afraid of was another question.

"When you came out of your house you did not seem surprised to see us. You appeared almost to have been expecting us."

She pointed to the roof of the house. "On that platform there is a spyglass. I watched your progress from the beach."

He stared at it with great interest. "I would like to see this glass."

She nodded and led the way. They passed through the yard where the piglets turned on spits cut from branches, and Kent's men were happily at work draining the rum casks. Atop two very tall palm trees, lookouts with spyglasses kept watch on the fortress and the town of

Saint-Pierre. At the slightest sign of military movement, they could give the signal and Kent and his men would vanish. Brigitte prayed that no such signal would be given.

The house had been thoroughly pillaged, with pottery smashed on the polished wooden floors, furniture overturned, silver- and goldware heaped in a pile by the door, ready to be carted off. Brigitte wordlessly led Kent through to the rear garden, where purple orchids and orange bougainvillea mingled with scarlet hibiscus and pale pink oleander. She preceded him up the narrow staircase, her back straight, her head held high, as if she were giving royalty a tour of her home. But she was aware of the sharp cutlass that hung from his waist, the pistol and dagger tucked into his belt. The space between her shoulder blades crept with fear. She felt as if she were being followed by a wild animal, like the black jaguar the governor kept in a cage in his home.

When they reached the rooftop and its curious platform with a low guardrail, they saw that the full moon was starting to rise. They also had a good view of the compound below, where Brigitte's terrified slaves were cooking under the watchful eyes of Kent's men, being made to taste everything as they went along. Even the basting used on the piglets was tasted first.

At the sound of so much music, Brigitte gave Kent a curious look. He smiled. "We're a lucky crew, for we've musicians among us. It's every pirate ship that hopes for at least a piper and a fiddler." He nodded as he leaned on the rail and watched the festivities below. "I've a good crew." Phipps, the man with the many pigtails, was the quartermaster—the strong man of the ship, the ship's magistrate and punisher of minor offenses. He was also responsible for the selection and division of the plunder. There was Jeremy, the sailing master in charge of navigation, and Mulligan the boatswain, Jack the gunner, Obadiah the sailmaker, Luke the carpenter. They even had a ship's surgeon, although he was fairly useless in tropical waters where the main causes of death were the incurable yellow fever, malaria and dysentery. His main job was amputations.

Brigitte showed Kent the glass and noticed that he had to bend low to peer through it, he was so tall. She also sensed a body of great physical strength beneath the long coat and breeches. The French colonists, with slaves to do all the work and such abundance of food and drink, were a soft lot; men who had forgotten the sport of dueling and riding. But she suspected that Christopher Kent was held together with strong muscle and sinew.

Kent looked through the glass and then, satisfied that no soldiers had been dispatched from the distant fort, he straightened and turned his attention to his perplexing hostess. His eyes went to the brooch on her breast and he said, "Now there's a fair piece."

"It is a famous stone, m'sieu, called the Star of Cathay. It was created in faraway China by a wizard who, the legend goes, created it to win a lady's heart. It is supposed to bring love and romance to whoever possesses it."

He smiled and reached for it.

She put her hand over it protectively. He mustn't have it yet! She needed to be beautiful, for just a while longer. If he took it now, her beauty would go with it and her plan would fail. "I shall give it to you as a gift when you leave."

He laughed and his gaze lingered on her hand, which protected not only the brooch but her breast as well. "And to what are you referring when you say you shall give it to me as a gift? The brooch or the treasure beneath?"

She tried not to look away, but instead met his bold gaze challenge for challenge. "Is this the way you treat the women on the island where you live?"

He shifted his eyes to the distant horizon and seemed to consider answering her. Finally he said, "I don't live on an island. I have a plantation in the American colony of Virginia."

Her shock was apparent. "You live among civilized people?"

"It is in fact those so-called civilized people," he said with a wry smile, "who support my privateering. After all, plunder is only plunder until it can be sold. Without buyers there would be no reason for piracy."

"I do not understand."

"It's the Americans who buy my goods. In England, pirates are treated mercilessly, but in America we are given protection in their ports, even hospitality. It is the Americans who provision my ship and find buyers for my treasures, for a commission, of course. So the Americans get rich along with me."

She frowned. "It is unthinkable."

"It's politics. By supporting buccaneers like myself, Americans are striking a blow against British rule, a struggle that is growing stronger and more bitter with time. The English made this rule called the Navigation Act, which stipulates that no goods can be imported into England's colonies except in English ships manned by English crews. The Americans don't think this is fair, so they circumvent British law whenever they can."

"And so my lovely candlesticks and my mother's china . . ."

"Will most likely end up on a mantel in Boston."

As he began to unscrew the telescope, Brigitte said, "But that was a gift from my husband!"

He laughed as he hefted the brass instrument in his hand. "Sentimental man, your husband."

"You would not understand, m'sieu," she said with indignation.

"I understand that women prefer gifts of beauty or romantic meaning, but a *telescope?*"

"It is more than a mere spyglass, m'sieu. It is an instrument of power."

"How so?"

"I saw *you*, didn't I? And you were unaware of me."

"Yes," he said slowly. "That is true. You saw us coming and we were unaware. But you did not raise the alarm. Most curious."

He walked to the stairway and indicated she should precede him. So Brigitte descended to the landing below and led the way into the main living room where, to her surprise, Kent swept his hat from his head and demanded something to drink. His hair was deepest black without a shadow of gray or silver, yet she placed his age nearer forty than thirty, for his face, when seen close up, was lined with the creases of life and weather.

Refusing a bottle of wine that was already open and insisting she fetch one that was still sealed, Kent went out onto the veranda where he conferred briefly with Mr. Phipps. Coming back inside, he said to Brigitte, "Still nothing unusual going on at the fort or in the town. We continue to go undetected."

Through the transparent panes of the front window, she could see the moon continuing to rise and shed light on the compound where Kent's men were getting loud and some of her slave women were being encouraged to be friendly. They hadn't started eating yet, but smoke and cooking aromas filled the air.

Kent looked at the portrait over the fireplace—a pastoral scene depicting Henri and Brigitte Bellefontaine seated beneath a spreading oak tree, with their children gathered around them. When Kent commented on the young Bellefontaines, and their fortuitous resemblance to their mother instead of their father, Brigitte said, "They mean the world to me. My children are my life."

"Yet you sent them away."

"A decision I regret." She brought a tray with two glasses filled with brandy. Kent had her taste both before he selected one.

"You insult me," she whispered.

"Milady, there are a thousand ways to kill a man, but poisoning is a woman's art. And there are a thousand ways to poison. Shall we have a fire? The night grows chill." Brigitte called for one of her slaves to build a fire in the fireplace and presently the flames were casting Christopher Kent's tall shadow on the walls.

He tasted his brandy, watching her over the rim of his glass. "So your husband drags you to a godforsaken place where you can't raise children."

"My husband did not 'drag' me. We came here to build something. The Bellefontaines are an old and noble family, but the previous generation mishandled the fortune so there were no lands for my husband to inherit. He accepted an offer from the king to come here and help build the colony. In return, the land would be ours. Here is our real home, m'sieu, which we built for our children, for they will come back to Martinique. Their stay in Paris is only temporary, for their education. And that is why," she added a little breathlessly, "I beg of you not to kill my husband. His children need their father."

Kent looked out the window and saw Mr. Phipps watching as one of the women tasted a chunk of freshly baked bread before he himself had a bite. Everything was under control, nothing untoward. "Men like your husband," Kent said presently in a dark, deadly tone, "men with wealth and power, need to be taught lessons." He fell into a morose silence, his expression growing stormy and unreadable as he watched his men dance around the bonfire. Then he turned, as if suddenly remembering where he was, and said in a lighter tone, "Anyway, your husband's fate is not up to me but to my men."

"But surely you could order them—"

"You clearly do not understand the law of the high seas, milady. I might be captain of my crew, but we are a democratic ship, as are all pirate ships. What my men decide is theirs to do. I give no orders, nor do they take them. What happens is not my responsibility."

He walked to the doors that stood open to the rear garden and, inhaling the night air, said, "What is that perfume?" It was a heady mixture of white jasmine, lily-of-the-valley, purple and pink freesia, lilac and honeysuckle.

"What pirate *does* take responsibility for his actions?" she said behind him.

He turned. "Madam, you know nothing of me, nor of the world I would wager. Think what you will. Why should I care?"

"So you blame the world for your ills?"

"What has the world ever done for me?"

"You kill for revenge, is that it? Even the innocent?"

"It is the law of survival. As the hawk kills the snake, as the snake kills the rat. Only the strong survive, I've learned that much."

"But why do you pick on the French?"

"I pick on everyone. Mankind is my enemy. I make no distinction between English and French, Spanish or Arab. I am a free prince, madam, and have as much right to make war on the whole world as he who commands a navy upon the sea and an army upon the land."

She turned away speechlessly. She saw the flowers in her garden standing as brightly in the moonlight as if it were day. She heard the enchanting calls of a nightbird. The island continued to sleep beneath the effulgent moon. There was no cannon-fire from the fort. No sign of ships, no torches being carried up the mountainside. And the lookouts in the palm trees had shouted no alarms. Below, tangy smoke and aromatic cooking filled the air, and drunken song and loud fiddle playing broken by high feminine laughter.

Kent fell silent and seemed to withdraw into himself.

"Strange," he murmured after a length. "I have visited all of these islands these past years, I have trod their earth and drunk from their streams, I have anchored in their waters and tasted their fruits. Yet I have never actually *seen* these islands."

She waited, and the night seemed to wait with her. She imagined all the exotic birds with their colorful plumage, all the tropical flowers with their succulent leaves and petals, the sparkling stars and fat, ivory moon, even the white breakers on the beach in the distance, she imagined that the entire universe had stopped for an instant to wait with her.

Kent said, "Yet I seem to be seeing them now. Martinique, at least.

What magic is at work in this place?" His glance fell to the blue crystal at her breast. " 'Tis a mysterious stone. The likes of which I have never seen before. Neither diamond nor sapphire. Like a blue topaz, but deeper and cloudier. And what lies at its heart? A cluster of stars, it appears."

When he brought his eyes up to hers, he said quietly, "There *is* magic at work here, but is it the island? Or is it you, madam? What kind of enchantment do you cast upon me?" His brow furrowed and his look turned troubled. "My men and I should leave," he said decisively. "It makes me nervous to stay too long in one place. We have been seduced, I suspect."

Her heart jumped. He must not leave! "Your men haven't eaten yet."

"They can take the food with them."

"The piglets are not quite done. And some of your men . . ." Her voice trailed off a the looked into the dense trees surrounding the house. Kent took her meaning: he, too, had seen some of his men sneaking off into the foliage with slave women.

Kent gave Brigitte another long, curious look. "Why are you not afraid of us?"

"But I am."

"You said that, yet I cannot believe it. I have never seen a woman acting as you do. I am used to screaming, running, fainting. Or hiding behind their men. You are made of different stuff." His eyes trailed from her face to her shoulders, bare and white in the moonlight. "But you shiver, madam. The night has grown cold."

"At this altitude," she said, breathlessly, as if the altitude were making it difficult to breathe, "the temperature drops at night even though we enjoy very warm days."

Amusement danced in his eyes as he said, "And how do you keep warm at night?"

"Martinique has its warm places."

He saw challenge in her eyes. And when she moved slightly, he caught the flash of blue fire at her bosom. Also a challenge? "Show me these warm places," he said quietly.

*A*s they passed through the smoky compound again, some of Kent's men called merrily to him, making bawdy comments about the company he was keeping. By now they were cutting off chunks of bread for themselves, and hacking away at pineapples and coconuts. Brigitte noticed that they were using their own daggers instead of the kitchen knives provided by her slaves. She also noticed that Mr. Phipps had found the crate of brand new pewter goblets recently arrived from France, still in their packing straw, for it was from these the pirates drank, again to avoid the chance of being poisoned. In fact, they took no chances at all, but made sure that every onion, every pinch of pepper that went into the dishes was first tested on a human, and once the piglets were cooked, the men would hack at the meat with their own safe daggers.

But at least they were eating and drinking, which was what Brigitte had counted on, to keep them from bolting as soon as they had the gold. Once they were gone, she would never have a chance with Kent again.

Brigitte kept her head high and tried not to look in her husband's direction as she led the pirate captain through the partying crowd, past the edge of the immaculate green lawn, and into cool, dense jungle foliage.

As soon as the thick leaves and fronds closed behind them, sound was muffled and a strange silence enfolded them. Behind her, Brigitte heard the sound of Kent's cutlass being drawn from its scabbard. But she pressed forward on the trail barely visible in the moonlight. Overhead, a leafy canopy allowed only glimpses of the full moon; unseen creatures rustled underfoot, and golden eyes blinked in the darkness. Finally they came to the edge of the thick green growth and could hear up ahead a curious rushing sound.

Brigitte went first, and when Kent joined her, coming to an abrupt halt at her side, she heard his whispered oath. For they were both gazing at a sight beyond belief.

The lagoon was perhaps a hundred feet across, bordered by large smooth boulders, reedy shallows, grassy dunes, and a short stretch of sandy beach. It stood open to the sky so that the fat moon rode like a gold coin on the water's surface, which rippled out in concentric circles from a most astonishing waterfall. It came from a geyser that bubbled up through rocks high overhead and cascaded in a froth of white foam and hot steam.

Sheathing his cutlass, for he realized no trap lay here, Kent stepped forward and swore again. "Never in my life have I seen such a place! 'Tis like a bathhouse in here! How is this water so hot?"

"It is heated by volcanic springs far below the ground," Brigitte said, noticing that a fine perspiration had sprouted on his forehead. Here, in this sultry clime, wild orchids grew in profusion, and jade vines, flamingo flowers, many varieties of hibiscus, and fleshy succulents with tumescent stems.

Walking to the water's edge, Kent put his hands on his hips and surveyed the astonishing scene. Already the torrid atmosphere was making the ends of his hair curl and beads of sweat to appear around his mouth. He removed his hat and then his long black coat, folding it carefully onto the ground. Brigitte saw how his white linen shirt had begun to cling to him in damp places, outlining muscles.

Kent rubbed his forehead in confusion. The hot mist and floral perfume were confounding his reason. This lush, verdant paradise had robbed him of logic and sanity. In all his life he had never been so seduced, nor ever thought he could be. He stared at his bewitching companion and again the glint of blue fire at her breast caught his eye. Was it the crystal that was casting the spell, or was it the woman? Or both?

He reached her in four strides and, taking her by the arms, said in a husky voice, "From the moment we arrived I had the feeling you wanted to keep us here. I suspected a trap. I thought you had sent runners to the fort. But there has been time now for soldiers to arrive, and my lookouts would have spotted them. You sent no message, did you?"

She shook her head.

"You wanted me to stay?"

She slowly nodded.

"Swear it. On everything you hold dear. Swear it is the truth that you wanted me to stay."

"I swear it," she whispered. "On the life of my children, I swear I wanted you to stay." And it *was* the truth.

He pulled her to him and kissed her. They broke apart for only a moment, to catch a hasty breath, then he drew her to him again while the waterfall plunged and steamed, and the moon looked down with a dispassionate eye. Brigitte, surrendering to his kisses, thought of the gypsy fortune-teller of long ago and realized that the legend was true, the Star of Cathay *did* possess the powers of love and passion. Without it, she knew, this night would never have happened.

◆ ◆ ◆

*T*hey lay upon the damp grass, exhausted. They had swum in the warm lagoon and embraced beneath the tumbling waterfall. Now Kent was murmuring, "You are magical and rare, like this blue gemstone, and just as beautiful. Come away with me, Brigitte. Live with me on my plantation in Virginia. I would make you very happy."

He spoke for a while then of his home in America, and then he drifted off to sleep while Brigitte lay in his arms, looking up at the tropical moon as it made its relentless progress to the western horizon.

*K*ent awoke to the sound of birdcall. The sky was still black but the moon had set and dawn was not far off. He saw Brigitte standing at the water's edge, as dressed as she could be without the help of a lady's maid to do the laces.

Kent dressed silently, wrapped up in the wonder and magic of what had taken place. And as they took the trail back to the plantation and to reality, Kent knew two things: that he wanted to keep this woman, and that he was ravenously hungry.

Most of his men were sprawled around the dying bonfire, snoring, mouths agape. A few staggered about, moaning and retching. The women had vanished. Colette materialized suddenly, as if she had been awaiting her mistress's return, bearing a platter of hot food and a mug of rum.

"She saved you some," Brigitte said to Kent, taking the plate and handing it to him. "Otherwise, the bones have all been licked clean."

Kent grinned as he lowered himself to the grass and crammed the succulent meat into his mouth. It had been cooked and seasoned to perfection. His men, when they sobered up, were going to swear they would never in their lives eat as well again.

He turned his face to the east, where paleness was starting to wash the horizon, and said, "We must set off soon. My ship is hidden, but still there is risk of discovery."

Brigitte looked over at the animal pens where the men had been locked up. Most of them slept, having drunk their fill of rum which the women had brought to them. But they had had no food, under Colette's strict orders, who had received her instructions from Brigitte.

She saw Henri, still chained to the hen house, looking abject and miserable.

"Collect whatever you want to take with you as quickly as possible," Kent was saying as he devoured the juicy piglet meat and washed it down with rum. "You won't be needing much, darling, for I shall buy you all the gowns and jewels you want."

Brigitte saw Colette by the veranda, watching, solemn eyes set in a black face. The young woman stood with her arms folded, as if the night's events had not touched her.

The sky continued to pale and the surrounding rainforest broke out with monkey chatter and noisy birdsong. The last of the pirates collapsed to the ground, but Kent did not notice as he ran a bread crust around his plate to catch the last of the piglet juices. He spoke with his mouth full: "Are you not hungry, my love?"

She knelt beside him at last, her skirts billowing around her, and the colors of her gown resembled a sunrise—gold against pink. She said, "Martinique is known for its flowers, m'sieu. But even so, many of us brought favorite plants from home. Do you know the oleander?" She pointed to tall, leafy shrubs bearing pink blossoms. White stumps could be seen where branches had earlier been hacked off.

Kent sucked on the last piglet bone and then crunched the remaining piece of crackling skin. "Wait till you see the flowers in America, my dear."

She pointed to the discarded spits beside the fire pits. "We cooked the piglets on those branches. I told Colette to make sure the bark was well stripped off before they were skewered into the meat."

He took a long swig of rum and gave her a perplexed look. "What is all this to me?"

"The oleander is poisonous. Every bit of it."

His look was blank.

"Your men are not sleeping, m'sieu, they are dead." She gestured to Colette who, knowing what was expected of her, broke into a sprint. She went from man to man, to all the bodies sprawled in the yard, felt each on the neck briefly, and then moved on. When she was finished, she flashed her mistress a triumphant grin.

Kent blinked. "Dead? What are you talking about?" And then comprehension dawned on him just as dawn broke over the mountain peaks and shot spears of light across the plantation. Now he saw what he had not seen in the smoky light of predawn: that his men lay in unnatural positions, and that they were far too silent to be sleeping.

He shot to his feet, throwing down his plate and cup. "I don't believe you. Every step of the cooking was supervised, every ingredient was tasted."

"You think only of poison that comes from the outside and goes in. You never thought of poison from the *inside* going out. As the cooking proceeded, the sap from the oleander branches was released and spread through the flesh of the pig."

"I do not believe you."

"Look at your men."

He slowly turned, blinking at the sight of bodies strewn in the pale light of dawn.

Her voice came to him through the lingering smoke of the bonfire: "You said there are a thousand ways to poison a man. You were wrong, m'sieu. There are a thousand and *one*. You did not know about the oleander."

He gave her an incredulous look. "When did you decide to do it?"

"From the moment I saw you through the spyglass. Before you and your men even reached the plantation. You were right all along, m'sieu. It *was* a trap. When I saw you coming up the hillside and I knew there was no time to send a warning to the fortress, I realized that our only hope lay in poisoning all of you. But that required you staying here. And the only way I could keep you here was by seducing you."

"By God, woman, you did not seduce me! It was the other way round!"

She pointed to the discarded spits. "Those were already prepared before you even reached the plantation. Have you not wondered why I did not send a runner to the fort when I first saw you? True, the soldiers could not have come in time, but still did it not seem strange to you that I didn't even try?"

He didn't respond, but ran his hands over his perspiring face. He had gone shockingly white.

"I decided not to send a runner to the fort because the soldiers would have started out, and you would have spotted them, and you and your men would have made your escape. For my plan to work I needed you to stay here until the piglets were eaten. So I took a gamble."

His look turned furious. "Then what we shared in the grotto meant nothing to you?"

"It meant *something* to me, m'sieu. It meant saving my husband's life. It also meant saving my children's legacy." She pointed to the chests of gold coins his men had dug up from under the gazebo. "That gold belongs to my children. My husband built up that fortune to pass along to our sons and daughters. Did you think I would let you take it?"

He suddenly grabbed his head. "I don't feel well."

"It should hit you quickly. Unlike your men, you ate little else, just the meat. And you have had little to drink."

"You aren't seriously going to stand there and watch me die!"

"It is of your own doing," she said without a trace of pity in her voice.

"You can say this . . . after what we had together? You *enjoyed* it!"

"Pretense, m'sieu. Your touch was vile."

"Then you are nothing more than a whore."

"No, m'sieu, I am simply a woman who will do anything to keep her family. Even sleep with a serpent."

Sweat dripped from his forehead. "It was my mistake to take you for a lady."

"It was your mistake to underestimate how far a woman will go to protect her family."

He clutched his stomach and cried, "For the love of God!"

She watched him in cool detachment, as she might watch a pot come to boil. When she saw his color go from white to ash, and then a queer purple blush rose up from his neck, she said, "My slaves are already on their way to the fortress to alert the soldiers. It will not be long before they are here. But you will be dead by then."

He reached for her. She stepped back and, as he fell, his fingers curled around the brooch, tearing her bodice. When he hit the ground, the blue crystal was clenched in his fist, its hues of magic and enchantment glinting between his fingers in the rising sun.

M a chou, you are the talk of the Antilles. You are a positive heroine!" They were getting ready for bed. Although they had just entertained guests for the evening, Henri had made a point of staying sober. And now he was looking at his wife with new love, and desire, in his eyes.

"Do you see the irony, Henri? If I had told you the true source of my discontent, you would never have bought me the telescope, and without the telescope that night would have gone quite differently."

"Thank God, then, for my obtuseness."

She climbed beneath the covers and blew out the candle. "Henri, I want to bring the children back from Paris. I know it isn't done. Colonists don't raise their children on the islands. But we shall be the first. We will import tutors, riding instructors, ladies of good quality to teach etiquette and deportment. Perhaps I shall establish a school. Yes, that is what we will do."

He said, "Yes, *ma chou*," deciding he was going to say yes to everything she asked for from now on, she was so enchanting.

He reached for her but she drew back. "What is it, *ma chou?*"

"You fell in love with me because I was beautiful. And then you saw how beautiful I was the night with Kent. But it was the Star of Cathay. It made me beautiful, and so I was able to distract Captain Kent long enough." Henri had tactfully not enquired about what went on at the lagoon and, despite the disarray of her clothes the next morning (Brigitte had clearly fought off the scoundrel and successfully defended her honor), had convinced himself that his wife, being a clever conversationalist, had merely *talked* with the Englishman all night. Brigitte, of course, did not disabuse him of this notion.

"But you *are* beautiful," he said. "No gemstone can make you so." He thought for a moment, then said, "Very well." He left the bed and came back a moment later. In the darkness she felt his fingers on the bodice of her nightdress. "What are you doing?"

"Making you beautiful. There. There is your blue crystal."

And she felt its magic begin to work at once, the Star of Cathay, transforming her. She went happily into Henri's embrace, feeling beautiful again, for what can work on a pirate can work just as well on a husband. And when their passion was spent, and Brigitte was deciding that life in Martinique was going to be paradise after all, Henri turned on the light to illuminate the ivory cameo he had pinned to her breast. The blue crystal was still in its box.

She laughed softly and reached for him again.

Interim

*A*fter the defeat of Christopher Kent, Martinique suffered no more pirate invasions, and the so-called golden age of piracy came to an end soon after when the navies of the world joined together to take back the seas. Henri and Brigitte lived to the ripe old ages of sixty and sixty-three respectively, leaving a legacy of wealth and honor to their children. Bellefontaine Plantation survived earthquakes, hurricanes, and a massive eruption of Mt. Pelée to become, in the present day, a popular tourist attraction where visitors are told by cheerful young tour guides the exciting tale of how Mr. and Mrs. Bellefontaine, armed only with a spyglass and a musket, managed to defeat a hundred bloodthirsty pirates in the course of a single night.

In 1760, Brigitte's son, by then a dissolute old man suffering from gout and venereal disease, was in a poker game with a man named James Hamilton. All Bellefontaine had left was a blue crystal that had belonged to his mother. He had no idea of its worth, only that it had been known as the Star of Cathay. He lost the hand and possession of the crystal passed to James Hamilton, who gave it to his lady-love, Rachel, who bore him two sons out of wedlock on the island of Nevis, in the West Indies. Shortly after the family moved to the island of St. Croix, James Hamilton abandoned Rachel and the two boys, Alexander and James. Using the blue crystal as collateral, Rachel obtained a loan and opened a small shop in the main town, where James was apprenticed to a carpenter, and Alexander, eleven years old, took work as a clerk at the trading post. They prospered and Rachel was able to buy back the blue crystal, for sentimental reasons.

When the youngest son reached the age of seventeen, a local clergyman raised funds to send him away to school in New York. While studying at Kings College, Alexander Hamilton met and fell in love with Molly Prentice, the daughter of a Methodist minister. To Molly he pledged his eternal devotion, sealing his pledge with the gift of a blue crystal that his mother had given to him as a parting gift when he left the West Indies. Molly's father, however, did not approve of his daughter's relationship with an impoverished young man of dubious lineage, and packed her off to live with relatives in Boston, where she later fell in love with and married Cyrus Harding, giving him eight children. She never saw Hamilton again, but kept the crystal as a reminder of her first love, and when she heard of his death in a duel with a man named Aaron Burr, she could no longer bear to look at the crystal and so gave it as a wedding gift to her daughter, Hannah, a girl with mystical leanings who claimed to be able to communicate with the dead. The crystal, Hannah declared, was a great help in this regard.

Book Eight

THE AMERICAN WEST
1848 C.E.

---

*E*ast, South, North and West,
   Tell me, O Spirit, which way is best.
   After he finished his silent chant, Matthew Lively kept his eyes
closed a moment longer, then opened them to see where the spinning
crystal had come to rest. It was how Matthew made all his important
decisions—consulting the Blessing Stone.

He opened his eyes. It was pointing west.

He felt a small thrill of excitement. He had already wanted to go
west, to see the new country on the other side of the Rocky Mountains, maybe even to carve a whole new life for himself there. But if
the Blessing Stone had told him to go east, then to Europe he would
have sailed; south would have taken him to Florida, and north would
have had him packing off to the wilds of Canada.

But the stone was pointing to the word "west," which he had
printed on a large square of white paper along with the words "south,"
"east," and "north," lining up the four cardinal points with the help
of a compass. Then he had placed the smooth crystal, which his

mother had christened the Blessing Stone, in the center and spun it. It had come to a rest with its narrower end pointing west.

He could hardly contain his joy. Crumpling up the paper and returning the crystal to its special velvet-lined box, he hurried downstairs to inform his mother of his plans. But he stopped at the foot of the stairs. The curtains were drawn across the doorway to the parlor, which meant a séance was in progress and so his mother could not be disturbed.

Matthew didn't mind. He was young and hungry and would celebrate with cake and milk in the kitchen until his mother's ghost-seeking clients had left.

As he cut himself a generous wedge of chocolate cake, he hoped his mother's contact with the spirits was a good one this afternoon; he was not in a mood to cross words with her, or to have her refuse to let him go. Matthew needed to go; he would die here in Boston if he didn't.

It was because of Honoria. She had nearly killed him with her rejection of his marriage proposal. His heart was in mortal pain; there were no salves or ointments for this kind of wound. It wasn't just that she had said no, it was the *way* she had said it. With a horrified tone: "I could not live with a man who dealt daily with diseased bodies." Matthew didn't blame her. Honoria herself was frail, spending half her time on her retiring couch where she received visitors. Moreover, he himself was not made of heroic proportions. Matthew Lively knew very well what people saw when they looked at him: a pale, nervous young man who frequently stuttered, and, despite his college education, was altogether too unsure of himself.

Still, her rejection had wounded him, and so Matthew Lively, twenty-five years old and finishing his glass of milk, decided he was done with women forever.

Hannah Lively, daughter of Molly Prentice who had once been the love interest of Alexander Hamilton, came into the kitchen, a plain woman in black bombazine, a small lace cap on her head.

"Was it a good reading, Mother?" Matthew asked. He was proud of the fact that his mother was one of the most sought after spiritualists on the East Coast.

"The spirits came through very clear today. Even without the aid of the Blessing Stone." Then she gave him an expectant look.

"Mother, the stone pointed west!"

She nodded sagely. "The guiding spirit in the crystal knows where your destiny lies."

Sixty years old and considered a true prophetess by their many friends and neighbors, Hannah Lively believed absolutely in the power of the crystal, therefore Matthew didn't tell her that he had had to spin it eleven times before it finally pointed west. He reckoned the stone just needed warming up.

"I have to leave for Independence at once," he said excitedly. "They say you shouldn't leave later than the first of May. Wagons that come after the first ones don't get as good grazing grass along the trail, and it's crucial to get to the California mountains before the first snowfall—" He stopped when he realized what he had revealed: that he had planned to go west all along.

His mother didn't mind. As long as the crystal sanctioned it, her son was free to go where his heart led.

They heard the front door open and close, feet stamping on the mat in the hall. There was Matthew's father, knocking the rain from his top hat—a tall silver-haired gentleman with distinguished bearing, as befitted his profession. He said solemnly, "The Simson boy died. It was the pneumonia, he couldn't be saved," and went into the library. Jacob Lively sat at a desk and, as was his habit, took care of business before anything else. A meticulous record keeper, the elder Lively took out a blank death certificate, dipped his pen into the ink and carefully filled out the details, taking out his pocket watch to reckon the time of death: it was exactly a six minute walk from the Simson house.

Only after he had completed his business did he then turn to his family and, reverting to husband and father, rose with a smile. "Am I to guess from the look on my son's face that a decision has been made?"

"I am going west, Father!"

Jacob embraced Matthew and said with unaccustomed emotion, "I will miss you, son, and that's God's truth. But you were born to put roots down in a foreign land. We've always known that, your mother and me." The Livelys had seen the growing restlessness in their youngest son, and understood his yearning to go to a place where he was needed. They reckoned that out west was where his skills would be needed most of all. "Now that the hour is upon us, son, I wish you godspeed."

His parents presented him with a gift: a black bag with his initials stamped in gold. Inside were scalpels, scissors, needles for sewing flesh and skin, sutures of silk and catgut, dressings and bandages, syringes, and catheters—all brand new. His eyes widened as he brought a prized instrument from the bag. "A stethoscope!"

"Genuine French," his father said with chest-puffed pride. Very few were in use yet on this side of the Atlantic.

The long wooden tube, with one widened end to be placed on a patient's chest, had only been invented a few years earlier. The original creations had been much shorter, and then doctors had realized that a longer listening tube allowed enough distance to keep the patient's fleas from jumping on them.

Before he departed, his mother wanted to do one last reading, for it was her plan to send the Blessing Stone with him, reasoning that in the three thousand miles between Boston and Oregon, Matthew was going to need the crystal more than she.

While his mother consulted privately with the Blessing Stone, Matthew paced in the parlor. His upcoming adventure both excited and frightened him. It was the first time in his life he had taken the initiative to do something on his own. Ever since he was a toddler, he had been a follower. He had even followed his older brothers into their father's profession (and if Matthew had ever entertained thoughts of pursuing another career, he had buried them because such bold initiative was not in his nature).

After Hannah had communed with the spirit in the Blessing Stone, she took her son's hand and pressed the crystal into it, curling his fingers over the stone. "Listen to me now, son," she said gravely. "A great trial is facing you. You must meet it with strength, courage and wisdom."

"I know, Mother," he said gently. "It's a long and uncertain journey to Oregon."

"No, son, I'm not speaking of the journey. Yes, that will be arduous, but what path isn't? I speak of something else—a turning point in that journey. Something"—her face grew troubled—"terrible and dark."

This alarmed him. "Can I avoid it?"

She shook her head. "It has been placed before you, it is your fate. But it is there as a test. Let the crystal guide you, son, it will lead you to light and to life."

And then it was time to leave as he had a long way to travel—by foot, horse, coach, canal boat, and train—from Boston to Independence, where the road to his destiny was to begin.

I've already told ya," the wagon master fairly shouted, "I ain't takin' no unattached females and that's that!"

Emmeline Fitzsimmons glowered at Amos Tice in exasperation. She had spent the past two weeks in Independence, the jumping-off point for the Oregon Trail, going through the massive encampment on the Missouri where families were waiting to start the trek west, and she still had not found a wagon master who would take her along. It wasn't fair. Plenty of single men were finding places in the wagon trains. But one lone female . . .

She wanted to scream.

Capt. Amos Tice was originally a mountain man and his attire showed it: a long, fringed buckskin jacket over striped pants, boots, flannel shirt, and a beaded Indian belt from which was slung a long hunting knife. His sweat-stained, broad-rimmed hat shadowed a face red from the sun and a beard gray with age and hardship. No one knew exactly what he was a "captain" of, but he had a reputation for being fair and for seeing that his emigrants got where they needed to go. Tice looked the audacious young woman up and down: while Emmeline Fitzsimmons wasn't exactly beautiful, and he wasn't partial to ginger fly-away hair and freckles, still she was pretty, he thought, and he liked her plump, robust figure. But she was an invitation to trouble in any man's book. "I'm sorry, miss," he said again, "but them's the rules. We don't allow unmarried women traveling alone."

Emmeline was beyond frustration. This was the seventh wagon master to refuse her and the prospects were diminishing. Already the first wagon trains had left; in a couple of weeks there would be no more leaving because of snows in the Sierras. "But I can be of help. I am a midwife." She waved her arm over the crowd of women and children. "By the looks of some of these women, they will be needing my services."

Tice frowned disapprovingly. No proper lady would make mention of so delicate a subject as a woman's expecting state. He doubted she was a midwife. Too young, too genteel. And unattached. The sort that caused the worst trouble. The journey to Oregon was two thousand miles and with God's help should take four months. That was too many miles and too many nights to have a woman such as this along. He started to turn away, presenting his broad back as his final word.

"If I find someone," she said quickly. "If I find a family that will take me, will you allow me to join your wagon company?"

He scratched his beard and spat tobacco juice to the muddy ground. "Awright, but I gotta approve of the family first."

Independence was a bustling frontier town where all manner and varieties of people mingled: Canadian trappers decked out in furs; Mexican muleteers in bright blue jackets and white pantaloons; shabbily dressed Kanza Indians on ponies; Yankee opportunists selling everything imaginable under the sun; and the thousands of emigrants with their wagons and bright hopes. The spring air rang with the clanging of blacksmith's hammers, the shouts of gamblers in the muddy streets, and the sounds of honky-tonk pianos pouring from the saloons. People in a hurry milled in and out of shops crammed with goods, while Indians gathered in the streets to sell their crafts.

As Emmeline stood in front of the busy dry goods shop wondering which way to go next, she overheard one man say to another, "Yessir, heard it direct from my brother. Says that out in Oregon pigs run about freely and with no owner, fat and round and already cooked, with forks and knives stickin' out a them so all you have to do is cut a slice off now and then when you're hungry."

That was when she spied the young doctor, going into the apothecary shop across the way.

Having a sudden idea, she hurried across and went inside. Pausing to let her eyes adjust to the dimness of the store, she saw advertisements for Windham's Bilious Pills, Dr. Solomon's Balm of Gilead, and Holloway's Ointment. The shelves behind the counter were stocked with tonics and powders meant to cure everything from gout to cancer, all claiming guaranteed results. Emmeline picked up a bottle of Soothing Syrup for Babies. The label said it contained morphine and alcohol. The recommended dosage was "until baby is calmed."

Then she saw the young doctor, talking to the chemist.

She had deduced he was a medical man by the black bag he carried—it was identical to the ones her father and uncles always took on house calls, the ubiquitous black bag of the physician. The young man himself was thin and pale, his suit ill-fitting. And Emmeline thought he seemed nervous. As she made her way through the customers and drew up next to him at the counter, the young man opened his black bag and produced a bottle for the chemist to fill. Emmeline saw the gauze and bandages, sutures and scissors.

"Pardon me, Doctor, I was wondering if you could help me."

He rounded on her, startled. "Are you addressing me?" he said, a flush rising up from his starched white collar.

Emmeline had been brought up well enough to know never to approach a strange man without first being introduced. But these were peculiar times, and this *was* the frontier. So she said boldly, "My name is Emmeline Fitzsimmons and I'm looking to go west. As I am a lady on her own, however, the wagon masters are reluctant to sign me on. Let me travel with you, Doctor. I can be your assistant. I am a trained midwife." She held up her own leather satchel that contained the instruments and medicines of her craft. "But I am much more than that," she hastened to add as he continued to stare open-mouthed at her. "My father was a doctor and I helped him in his practice. I wanted to be a doctor, too, but I wasn't allowed in the medical college." She added bitterly, "Only men can become doctors." Then she smiled brightly. "But I would be a great help to you."

Matthew did not know what to make of the brazen young woman. Unlike his beloved Honoria who had been slender and frail, Miss Fitzsimmons was plump with a generous bosom. She had full red lips and her eyes were fringed with long lashes. She gave off a feminine perfume that nearly made him dizzy. He gulped. Her blatant femaleness made him uneasy, and he was horrified that she would suggest something so unthinkable as two strangers, a man and a woman, traveling together.

"I . . . I'm sorry—" he stammered.

"Look," and she opened her bag and brought out blank birth certificates. "I saw death certificates in your bag. How more suited can two people be? I call this a sign!"

But Matthew just mumbled his apologies, took his filled bottle from the chemist and hurried out.

Refusing to be defeated, Emmeline returned to the vast emigrant encampment on the river and surveyed the scene once again. Many of the wagon trains had already left, few remained. She really wanted to join Tice's company, which was due to depart in the morning. Unlike most wagon masters, Tice had been to Oregon and back, knew the way and knew the Indians. That was why his price was higher than what other men charged; but no matter how much Emmeline had offered to pay, it wasn't enough.

She paused to watch a dapper young man in a checkered vest and cocky bowler hat set up a camera on a tripod while a small crowd watched. The sign on his wagon said, "Silas Winslow, Daguerreotypist. All pictures guaranteed flattering." The new invention was all the rage. Emmeline herself had sat for a portrait before leaving home in Illinois, a keepsake for her sisters. Unfortunately, they hadn't been able to afford to have one taken of themselves in return, so Emmeline would have to carry memories of their faces in her heart.

She continued among the wagons where men were checking provisions and greasing wagon wheels and women were supervising the loading of furniture, trunks, and bedding. When Emmeline came upon a newly arrived family, the wife in an advanced state of pregnancy trying to deal with children, chickens, and a wagon, she approached the harried woman and introduced herself in as cheerful a manner as her mood could conjure. "I am a trained midwife and will be most helpful when your time comes, which most assuredly will be on the trail."

The woman said her name was Ida Threadgood and that she'd be thankful of the help. "You'd be God's blessing if you traveled with us, Miss Fitzsimmons. A blessing indeed. Just as that man," Ida said bitterly as she turned a stormy expression toward her husband who was yoking the oxen, "is a curse."

On the clear spring morning of May 12, 1848, everyone was dressed in their Sunday best, the ladies tightly corseted and wearing flowery hats with parasols, gloves, and fans, the men clean-shaven with hair slicked down, suspenders and belt buckles all new and shiny. The bathhouses of Independence had been hopping the night before, as all emigrants had their one final good wash before hitting the trail. A band played "Yankee Doodle" and "The Star Spangled Banner" while fireworks went off and Mr. Silas Winslow took group pictures of those who had the money to pay for them. Family and friends waved and wiped tears off their cheeks as they said good-bye to loved ones heading off into a great unknown.

And then, placing one foot in front of the other, the emigrants began their walk. It was to be a journey across two thousand miles at a speed of two miles per hour. They set off with sleek, canvas-topped, ox-drawn wagons nicknamed prairie schooners, because when they moved through the tall grasses they resembled ships under full sail gliding across a green sea. The company consisted of seventy-two wagons, one hundred thirty-six men, sixty-five women, one hundred twenty-five children and seven hundred head of cattle and horses. Each wagon was loaded with personal possessions and furniture, plus provisions purchased at Independence: two hundred pounds of flour, one hundred pounds of bacon, ten pounds of coffee, twenty of sugar, ten of salt. Additional supplies included rice, tea, beans, dried fruit, vinegar, pickles, and mustard. The emigrants also carried goods for trading: bolts of cotton for Indians they would meet along the way; lace and silk for Spaniards; books and tools for Yankees already settled in the west. Women brought tablecloths, china, and the family Bible. Men brought guns, plows, and shovels. They were accompanied by an assortment of dogs, chickens, and geese.

The trail went west from Independence, through Shawnee country, following the Kansas River, where they got help from local Indians ferrying the wagons across (the Indians charged seventy-five cents per wagon, which the emigrants called highway robbery). While men rode horseback, most of the women walked alongside the wagons, as did the teamsters driving the oxen, with only old folks and children riding. At the end of the first day, the mass of wagons, oxen, horses, mules, and cattle came to a noisy halt to camp for the night, make dinner, sleep, graze the animals, and then pick up stakes the next morning to resume the trek. This was to continue for the next four months, like a great moving village. They met folks along the way who were headed for California, now that it had been annexed to the United States and was no longer at war with Mexico. But the Oregon-bound emigrants saw no point in going to California, which had been described as a "worthless wilderness with nothing but Mexicans and Indians." One fellow, in a hurry on a single horse, said something about gold having been found, but everyone laughed and chalked him up for a gullible fool.

The prairie stretched before them, flat and grassy and boggy in places where it had rained. The emigrants kept their eyes on the horizon as they walked alongside their wagons and oxen, each family doggedly following the one in front, and leading the one behind: Tim and Rebecca O'Ross and their combined children from previous marriages; Charlie Benbow and his wife Florine, the chicken farmers; Sean Flaherty, the singing Irishman, and his friendly black coon dog, Daisy; the four Schumann brothers from Germany whose wagon was filled with cast-iron plows and other farming equipment (the Schumanns spoke very little English and for a long time thought the word for "mule" was "goddamnit").

The emigrants began as strangers to one another but soon made acquaintances. Because Capt. Amos Tice never inquired into a man's personal business, caring only that he paid the price of traveling with the company and agreed to pitch in and help with chores, hunting, and defense against Indians, it was up to the travelers themselves to get to know one another. In this way did they learn who was from Ohio or Illinois or New York; who was of what profession; who had been widowed and remarried and how many times. One afternoon a Kentucky teamster named Jeb approached Matthew Lively and said, "Mrs. Threadgood said Miss Fitzsimmons told her you're a doc. Can you pull a tooth?" Jeb was rubbing a swollen jaw and looking a little green. But Matthew said he did not practice dentistry but had heard that Osgood Aahrens in the last wagon was a barber.

Ida and Barnabas Threadgood, like most of the married couples in the wagon train, were on their third and fourth marriages, both widowed twice and three times, and had a passel of kids between them. Ida was thankful for the assistance of Miss Emmeline who helped with the cooking and washing and minding the children in return for a bed in the wagon and the protection of a family (for it was quickly noticed among the men that a single lady was in the company and they began to buzz around her like bees). This fact did not escape the notice of Albertina Hopkins who declared, "That girl will stir restlessness among the unmarried men. You mark my word, Miss Emmeline Fitzsimmons will be the cause of fights." The other women agreed, for they were suspicious of a young woman traveling on her own, especially a young woman who seemed to make no apologies for her single state. Miss Fitzsimmons wasn't a bit shy or ladylike and bantered with the men a little too freely for the ladies' comfort. As Albertina turned the bacon in her frying pan, she said loud enough for anyone, even Emmeline, to hear: "No decent woman would go about with her head bare like that, letting her hair fly free. We all know what happened to Jezebel in the Bible."

Albertina was opinionated on other topics as well. When they came upon a Negro family on the trail, trying to make it west on their own with but three wagons, a vote was taken in response to their request to join the Tice Party. Although Emmeline, Silas Winslow, Matthew Lively, Ida and her husband voted to allow the blacks to join them, everyone else rejected the idea. So Amos Tice had to explain to the former slaves from Alabama that they would be better off going to California where black people were welcome. "Oregon isn't admitting Negroes," he said, which was true.

As they left the three shabby wagons, six oxen, two horses, one cow, and a family of five adults and seven children behind on the open prairie, Albertina Hopkins declared, "If the colored want to go west, that's fine with me. I have nothing against those people. I just think they would want to travel with their own kind. And why anybody would go where they're not wanted is beyond me."

Albertina was a hefty woman with a bulldog face and a voice as loud as she was large. She was as equally vocal about her Christianity as she was about the dubious morals of Miss Emmeline Fitzsimmons, and had even named her children for the two Aramaic phrases in the Bible—the girl, Talitha Cumi, which meant, "Arise, little girl," and the boy, Maranatha, which meant "The Lord is coming." Albertina, always talking about her good works—perhaps because no one else did—believed she was being called west to bring the Lord and civilization to the heathens (although just who the heathens were in Oregon she was never clear on).

Mr. Hopkins, on the other hand, was a quiet man, pleasant and agreeable. As both were widowed, he had brought another set of children to the marriage, by his first wife, and Albertina likewise had brought three children, plus they had two young ones of their own. The whole mob were brats in the eyes of the rest of the company, running free, grabbing food, tormenting the animals. But Albertina turned a blind eye to her children and loudly declared what angels they were. Every man in the company felt sorry for the quiet Mr. Hopkins and wondered at the source of his suffering patience until one night a few days out of Ft. Laramie the Schumann brothers found him sitting behind a cottonwood tree, secretly sipping jug whiskey.

During the fourth night at camp, Albertina said over her hot biscuits, "That Emmeline Fitzsimmons told me she was twenty-five years old. Can you imagine that?" Albertina went on to use phrases like "passed over" and "left on the shelf." "I consider it most improper that an unmarried girl should attend childbirth. I don't care what schooling she has had in midwifery. A girl who is still a maiden has no understanding of these matters." She added with a sigh, "Poor Ida Threadgood," and the others agreed.

Matthew Lively couldn't help overhearing, Albertina's voice carrying the way it did. He had a strong feeling that Mrs. Hopkins was wrong about Miss Fitzsimmons being passed over. In these first few days on the trail he'd had plenty of opportunity to observe the young woman with the wild ginger hair, the Threadgood wagon being just three up the line from his own, and he had a suspicion that Miss Fitzsimmons didn't let men choose her but did the choosing herself. And if she was a spinster, it wasn't because she hadn't been asked.

He didn't know why Miss Fitzsimmons should catch his attention so. He didn't particularly like her. She seemed too unladylike, and when he watched her eat with such manlike gusto, it repelled him. His beloved Honoria had barely let food pass her lips. She was so thin her cheekbones and collarbones were painfully prominent. And she was so weak she could barely lift a fan to cool herself. It was no wonder half the young men in Boston were desperately in love with her. But there was something compelling about Miss Fitzsimmons all the same, and he suspected it was because her motives for going west were the same as his—to find a place where her skills were needed.

*A*s the wagon train moved relentlessly forward across the flat Kansas plain, Ida Threadgood pressed her hands to her swollen abdomen and said to Emmeline, "Thank God you're along. This wasn't my idea. That brainless fool husband of mine up and sold the farm without so much as telling me. There I was, uprooted with five young 'uns and one on the way."

Emmeline tried to hide her shock. She had never heard a woman speak so disrespectfully of her husband before, but she was learning very quickly that Ida wasn't the only one with such sentiments. Many of the women in the wagon train were there against their will, following a husband or father out west because they had no other choice. They quietly grumbled their grievances over cook fires and laundry tubs, out of the hearing of men. It was all an adventure for the menfolk, to go journeying like this. But women needed roots, a permanent place, especially once the babies started coming. Since there was nothing else they could do, they comforted themselves with the belief that the better life of tomorrow would be earned by the hard work of today.

A hundred and sixteen miles out of Independence, when the company had traveled twelve days, Mrs. Biggs went into labor. When Emmeline went to assist, Albertina Hopkins shoved past her, nearly knocking Emmeline off her feet and blocking the way into the wagon. Emmeline, wanting to go at the self-righteous Albertina tooth and nail, held herself in check out of consideration for the poor laboring Mrs. Biggs.

The next day a massive storm appeared on the horizon and as it rapidly approached, the company drew the wagons into an enormous circle, fencing in cattle and horses, then sat shivering beneath flapping canvas as thunder broke over them and lightning forked down. Having gotten caught in a sudden downpour as she was helping to unyoke the Threadgoods' oxen, Emmeline dashed for cover under the nearest wagon, which happened to belong to Matthew Lively. They huddled close together in awed silence as nature menaced the livestock and threatened to overturn wagons, causing women to shriek and children to cry. And then just as quickly as it had come, the storm rolled on across the plain, leaving behind the most spectacular rainbow anyone had ever seen. Albertina Hopkins, descending from her wagon and shooing her unruly brood to play in the mud, faced the break in the clouds and said, "Ah, the sun's out," exuding a kind of pride as if she had engineered the phenomenon herself.

As she crept out from under the protection of his wagon, Emmeline found her curiosity growing about the young Dr. Lively. His long face made him look like he had attended too many funerals. *Did he lose a lot of patients?* she wondered. Emmeline did not know that at the same time Matthew was thinking: *Why is Miss Fitzsimmons always smiling? Where does she get that energy? Didn't anyone ever tell her it is unladylike for a girl to talk so much?*

On May twenty-ninth, after two and a half weeks of traveling, they reached the banks of the Big Blue River that flowed into the Kansas from the north, and the emigrants were dismayed to discover that heavy rains had so swollen the river that it was impossible to cross. Since the wagon train was forced to stay put, the emigrants took the opportunity to do their first laundry and take their first baths since leaving Independence. Tallow soap was vigorously applied to bodies and clothing alike, children being scrubbed along with grimy shirts, dresses, blankets, coats, and "unmentionables." That evening a crescent moon came out and the emigrants entertained themselves with music and stories, and innocent flirtations across the many campfires. Silas Winslow, eligible bachelor with a lucrative profession, found himself the focus of the attention of mothers of unmarried daughters, as was Matthew Lively, now that word had gotten around he was a doctor.

But whereas Winslow was thoroughly enjoying being treated like a prince, and gobbled the pies and allowed the ladies to do his mending and washing, Matthew Lively was nonplussed by it all. Shy by nature and awkward in social settings, Matthew had never before found himself the center of ladies' attention. On top of that, frail Honoria still tugged at his heart and he continued to suffer from the pain of her rejection of his marriage proposal. So the eager young daughters of the farmers and settlers, actively on the prowl for husbands, made him skittish. The only exception was the remarkable Miss Emmeline Fitzsimmons who had been overheard to say she did not believe in marriage. Matthew had heard her telling this to Mrs. Ida Threadgood, explaining that marriage was an artificial institution, invented by men as a way of subjugating women. And so while she did not discomfit him in the same way the emigrants' daughters did, by bringing him pies and flirtatious smiles, she discomfited him all the same.

Finally the river was passable, but ferries were needed to haul the wagons across. And so big cottonwood trees were cut down to make an enormous raft of logs and timbers, big enough to carry a prairie schooner. The work was hard as the current was deep and swift; and forcing the horses and cattle to swim across was a nearly impossible task. The emigrants worked for two days, in a fresh downpour, to get the whole lot across; during that time tempers flared and two teamsters nearly killed each other with knives.

On the other side, muddy and wet and exhausted, the disheartened company tried to get oxen yoked, horses and cattle rounded up, and some sort of fire going to cook food, when Barnabas Threadgood suddenly gave out a cry and slumped to the ground.

Everyone gathered around the unconscious man as Emmeline went running to fetch Matthew Lively. Ida stood over her husband, hands on hips, and said, "He ain't never done *that* before."

Matthew pushed his way through and, dropping to one knee, felt Barnabas's neck. The onlookers stood in silence as Matthew opened his black bag and drew out the stethoscope. No one had ever seen one before. Their eyes widened as he placed the end of the tube to the stricken man's chest and listened. After a moment, he looked up and said sorrowfully, "Your husband is dead, ma'am."

"Is that a fact?" Ida said.

She spent one minute looking at her husband's face, then, shifting her gaze westward, pondered that direction for another minute, then she shifted her gaze backward toward the east, looked a little longer, and finally said, "After we bury him, I'm headin' back to Missouri."

To Emmeline's shock, four other wives joined Ida, along with their children and six teamsters. If the husbands protested, they did not do so out loud. But now Emmeline was without a ride again, out in the middle of nowhere, 160 miles from Independence. When Amos Tice told her she would have to return with Ida, Emmeline dug her heels into the mud and insisted she was going to Oregon.

What happened next surprised even the seasoned Tice: four teamsters, two widowed farmers, Silas Winslow the photographer, and a gangly teenager all rushed forward offering to escort Miss Fitzsimmons to Oregon. Seeing that a fistfight was about to break out over who got to take over the protection of the young lady, Matthew went back to his wagon and secretly brought out the Blessing Stone.

As he held it in his palm, he pondered his unexpected actions. The decision of what was to be done with Miss Fitzsimmons was up to Amos Tice, or up to the headstrong young lady herself, it certainly wasn't Matthew's business. But something inside him, unfamiliar and disturbing, nagged at him to step in and take initiative. His conscience was calling upon him to make a decision, and Matthew was not used to that.

Still, it wouldn't be completely his own doing. He would do whatever the Blessing Stone told him to do.

He had made a ritual of looking into the crystal every night before he went to sleep and every morning when he woke up because he couldn't get his mother's chilling prophecy out of his mind, that a great trial lay before him, "terrible and dark." He was hoping to find a way to avoid whatever it was, but the Guiding Spirit wasn't telling him anything. But he had another question for blue stone now, and he took out a child's school slate he used specially for asking the crystal questions, and a piece of chalk. On one edge of the slate he wrote "yes," on the other, "no." Then he placed the crystal between them, asked "Should I offer to take Miss Fitzsimmons to Oregon?" and spun the crystal. It pointed to "yes." He spun it again. And again. When it kept coming up "yes" he decided it wasn't good to question the Guiding Spirit as he might be inviting bad luck on himself. So he went back to the fracas that Miss Fitzsimmons had unwittingly ignited, with Tice trying to push two brawling men apart, and, with heart racing and palms sweating at this boldness that was not at all in his character, offered to take Emmeline along with him in his wagon.

She accepted at once.

They buried Barnabas Threadgood at the side of the trail, said a hasty prayer and got the wagons moving again. Behind them, heading back along the way they had come, Ida Threadgood and her brood, along with another three wagons with women and children, and teamsters who'd changed their minds about going west, started the trek back for civilization.

As the Oregon-bound wagons got underway, Albertina Hopkins let everybody know that she did not approve of two unmarried people traveling together.

"It's none of her business," Emmeline fretted as she climbed onto the wagon seat to ride at Matthew's side.

Matthew said nothing. Secretly, he agreed with Mrs. Hopkins.

*A*lbertina continued to furiously oppose the arrangement and let Captain Tice know at every opportunity. A few of the other women joined her, but some didn't mind and told Tice to leave the two medical people alone. "We might have need of them both," Florine Benbow said, not knowing she spoke prophetic words.

As they crossed the sweeping, tall grass prairies of eastern Kansas and Nebraska that seemed to stretch into infinity, Emmeline and Matthew came up with an arrangement in which they made sure they did everything proper and above board, with Emmeline sleeping in Matthew's wagon while Matthew slept in a bedroll on the ground, maintaining decency and propriety at all times. But they ate together, made camp and struck camp together, worked the oxen, fixed the wagon,

and collected water together. They fell in with the daily routine of
the wagon train: at dawn a bugle blew to waken the camp. The men
who had been on night herding duty brought the cattle and horses
in from their grazing while the women started their cook fires and
prepared breakfasts of bread, bacon, and coffee. After everyone had
eaten—generally a congenial time—the tents were taken down and
everything stowed in the wagons, oxen rounded up and yoked in their
harnesses. The company was underway by seven A.M. to take advantage of the coolness and to cover miles before noon, when they
stopped for an hour's rest before getting underway for another five-
hour trek. When Captain Tice finally signaled the stop of the night,
it was met with groans of relief and a few weary cheers. Now the
wagons were drawn into a circle and chained together for protection
against possible Indian attacks, although the Indians preferred to attack wagon trains that were on the move and in a straight line. Animals were set out to grazing and women cooked dinner. The hours
after the meal was the best time of the day, the visiting time, maybe
with music and dancing, certainly gossip and a few good stories told
around the campfire.

It seemed a dream to people used to the confinement of farms and
houses: the days were hard but the nights were peaceful and the en-
campments were like picnics, with people making friends, children
running free, food generously shared. Jealousies had not yet broken
out, envy had not begun to seethe, complaints had not yet started to
make their way to Amos Tice's tent. In time to come, a very short
time, tempers were going to begin to flare, nerves were going to start
to wear raw, and Tice was going to be accused, as all wagon masters
eventually were, of being unfair and having favorites.

His was a thankless job. It was Tice who determined every aspect
of wagon company life, the order of the wagons in line, the assigning
of duties of wood and water gathering, watch duty, herding. In days
to come, those down the line in the train would begin to complain
of having to breathe the dust of the wagons up ahead, and even
though Tice rotated the order of the wagons so that everyone got a
turn at the head of the line, no one was satisfied.

He also had to dispense justice. When Sean Flaherty's dog got into
the Benbow's chickens and killed six before the dog could be captured,
the Benbows demanded that the dog be shot. But Sean held Daisy to
him and pleaded with tears on his cheeks that she was all he had in

the world. So the company voted and Daisy was spared with Mr. Flaherty paying Mr. Benbow a fair price for the slaughtered fowl.

They had their sorrows as well. Jeb the teamster from Kentucky finally succumbed to the abscess that had festered in his jaw after Osgood Aahrens the barber had pulled the bad tooth. They buried him at the side of the trail and moved on. More graves were added as children died of measles, men were crushed beneath wagons, and babies did not survive birth, sometimes being buried with their mothers. The company encountered more graves along the way, dug by emigrants who went before them. In the decades to come, the Oregon Trail was to be dotted with thousands of crosses and headstones.

As Matthew's wagon rolled along behind his team of horses, Emmeline sat at his side, her face to the sun, and pictured the promised land ahead where men and women were going to live as equals. Matthew, handling the reins and keeping enough distance behind the wagon up front so as not to breathe their dust, reveled in the broad sunshine of the plains, showing him an existence so different from the dark séance parlors of Boston's spiritualist community. There, life focused on the dead, here it focused on the living—on the grazing cattle, the soaring hawks, children running and laughing, Daisy the coon dog barking at rabbits and turkeys too stupid to fly.

They spoke little, the doctor's daughter from Illinois and the young man from Boston, as they rode side by side in the wagon, keeping their eyes on the horizon ahead, never imagining an earth so vast, a sky so limitless. They felt their souls expand with each passing mile, as if they had lived their youths compressed in an attic trunk and now they were being aired on a sunny clothesline. And as the horizon continued to stay distant and elusive, and the wagon rocked, it seemed to Emmeline a good time for conversation. She was curious about the blue stone she had seen Dr. Lively take out and look at once in a while, and so she inquired.

"It's called the Blessing Stone," he said, squinting into the sunshine as he handled the reins. "It was given to my mother on her wedding day. She says it is very old, as old as the world itself maybe, and that it possesses the powers of all the people who owned it, down through the ages. My mother always consulted the stone for guidance, and so do I." He didn't go on to say that his mother had also used it to contact the dead. Nor did he tell Emmeline about his mother's dire prophecy of a great trial that lay before him, dark and terrible. Perhaps it had already come and gone: maybe the test of his soul was deciding to take Emmeline along, because it certainly hadn't made him popular with the others—men and women alike.

Her interest was sparked. "And the crystal really guides you?"

"Without it I would be lost. I sometimes fear," he added self-consciously, "that I was born a coward. I can't seem to make decisions on my own."

"You are simply cautious, Dr. Lively," she said. "My problem is I'm too brave. Nothing frightens me. And sometimes it can get me into trouble."

She removed her bonnet and shook her long hair free in the breeze. "You don't know how lucky you are, being a man. You can pursue any career you wish, without prejudice. I wanted to be a doctor but wasn't allowed because I'm a woman. It isn't fair. That's why I'm going west. The atmosphere will be more tolerant out there, and democratic. A truly free land. There is a new spirit in the nation, women are waking up. I attended a wonderful convention at Seneca Falls where a Declaration of Sentiments was drawn up listing sixteen forms of discrimination against women, including the vote, equal wages for equal work, control of our persons and our children. We women are starting to mobilize, Dr. Lively."

Matthew shifted uneasily on the wagon seat. He was already familiar with Miss Fitzsimmons's radical views. Though they were but a short time out of Independence, Emmeline had already begun receiving proposals of marriage—from each of the Schumann brothers (with Mr. Hopkins acting as interpreter), from Sean Flaherty who declared he was going to have the biggest potato farm in all of Oregon, from young Dickie O'Ross, whose voice broke as he proposed. But Emmeline had turned them all down, saying that it was not because of faults in them but because she planned never to marry. She explained to anyone who would listen that she had no intention of being encumbered by an artificial institution that was invented by churches and society to keep women in line. If she had children, she would do so on her own without having to answer to a husband.

The wives in the wagon train, simple farm folk or village women who had never heard such radical ideas before or read a book titled *A Vindication on the Rights of Women* by Mary Shelley, thought Emmeline was either too young to know her own mind, or perhaps touched in the head (although some secretly envied her spirited independence and wished her luck). But Matthew had encountered women like Miss Fitzsimmons in Boston, who called themselves feminists and who had made him uneasy. How he longed for his quiet, pale, frail Honoria who barely spoke and who certainly didn't have a political thought in her head! Every night, when the camp was asleep and he was alone and tried to consult the Blessing Stone to see the Guiding Spirit his mother had seen (but somehow failing), he also took out the daguerreotype of Honoria, so thin and hollow-eyed that she was almost ghostly. She hardly ever ate so that gowns hung on her. Her wrists were as delicate as bird bones, her cheeks so sunken they gave her an ethereal look: the beautiful, emaciated Ligeia of Edgar Allen Poe.

"What do you think of anesthesia?" Emmeline said now, changing the subject so abruptly that she caught him off guard. "Chloroform, ether!" she said before he could respond. "It is going to revolutionize surgery. My father attended the removal of a breast tumor. The woman was asleep the whole time! And the next revolution will be allowing women to become doctors. There is too much prejudice in the east. Things will be different in the west."

She paused and said, "Dr. Lively, you need to smile more."

He silently thought, *And you need to talk less*.

*W*hen they entered Pawnee Indian country, the men kept rifles and sidearms ready, flintlocks, and percussion-cap guns loaded and half-cocked. But the Indians merely came by out of curiosity and hoping for handouts.

As the heat and dust increased, and patience began to wear thin, it became increasingly difficult to maintain civilized and genteel ways, but the women were determined. Many continued to wear corsets, although some quietly packed the restricting garments away. Flowered hats were stored in trunks in favor of the more practical calico bonnets. And although table cloths were now dispensed with and the good china (such as had made it across the many perilous river crossings) was safely stowed away, still the children and men were made to wash before meals and to say grace before they wolfed down their food. And when a man was found hanging from a cottonwood tree—

dead three days or so, which meant he had been a member of the wagon train ahead—with a sign about his neck that read, "Cheeted at cards," they paused to build a coffin and give him a decent burial.

As they stopped to make camp on the Little Blue River, Victoria Correll went into labor with her first child. Albertina Hopkins, self-appointed midwife, dominated the event despite the efforts of two other wives who offered to help. Her voice could be heard through the wagon canvas as she admonished the screaming Mrs. Correll to stop acting like a child. "Hush now. What a silly thing you are being! Doesn't the Bible tell us that God made women to bring forth children in sorrow and pain? All this carrying on is an offense to the Almighty's ears."

When Albertina left the wagon to visit the latrine that had been constructed for the women in a poplar grove, Emmeline slipped into the wagon and, uncapping a bottle she had brought with her, said to the poor laboring Victoria, "God might have given us pain, but he also gave us the resources to alleviate it. This is an herbal elixir my father always gave to birthing mothers. It will ease your labor and help make the passage of your baby into this world an easier one."

Albertina was outraged, but after that women came to Emmeline with female problems, for Emmeline carried a supply of medicines to ease pains, nerves, and general malaise.

When they reached the eastern edge of Cheyenne territory, the company came upon a swollen river with a dangerous undertow. They would have normally camped until the river went down, but the men were nervous about being so close to unfriendly Indians, so they voted to attempt a crossing. Albertina Hopkins's protests that it was Sunday and they had no business engaging in such work on the Sabbath fell on deaf ears, so that when, midway into the afternoon, the Corrells' wagon overturned, throwing Mrs. Correll and her newborn baby to watery deaths, Albertina's triumphant look said, *I told you so.*

Emmeline and Florine Benbow took care of the corpses, dressing them, arranging Mrs. Correll's hair and swaddling the baby in the prettiest blanket that could be found, and Silas Winslow took their picture, free of charge, a keepsake for Mr. Correll, who sorrowfully accepted a horse from the Schumann brothers and headed back to Missouri, never to be seen again.

The wagon train moved on.

Silas Winslow, in his wagon that rattled with copper plates and

bottles of chemicals, continued to ply a lucrative trade in daguerreotype keepsakes of the dead as more mishaps overtook the company:
pneumonia, dysentery, children falling from wagons and getting killed
beneath the wheels. No one faulted Dr. Matthew Lively for not being
able to save any of them. Everyone knew that there wasn't much a
doctor could do against devastating illness and extreme injury. But
he helped build the coffins and filled out death certificates for the
families to carry with them on to Oregon—another keepsake.

On June ninth they reached the Platte, a broad and shallow river
three hundred miles by trail from Independence, which meant the
emigrants had completed the first stage of the journey. From now on
they would be traveling through a new kind of country, a land of
short grass, sagebrush, cactus, and of ever increasing aridity. Here the
company encountered a strange form of communication for the first
time: bleached buffalo skulls on the side of the trail with messages
written on them by members of wagon trains up ahead. One such
skull alerted those who followed that there was trouble with the Pawnee up ahead, and much mud on the trail.

The traveling grew difficult. The heat of the summer was oppressive
and brought sickness. Wagon breakdowns increased due to shrinkage
of the wheels and splintering of the wood. Trees and vegetation were
sparse and so they had to gather buffalo dung for their campfires.
When dung wasn't available, they trudged in clouds of dust behind
the wagons to collect weeds for burning. The women gathered wild
berries and managed to roll dough on wagon seats and bake pies on
hot rocks to lend variety to meals that consisted mainly of beans and
coffee. Occasionally the men went hunting and brought back elk, but
often they came back with nothing and so wound up having to trade
shirts with the Indians for salmon and dried buffalo meat. The emigrants encountered more fresh graves along the way but remained
undaunted, and when Blind Billy, the night scout (who could hardly
see in the daytime but who had better night vision than any man
alive and so it was his job to watch the herds while everyone else
slept), was found dead one morning with an arrow in his back and
his horse missing, the emigrants didn't panic but merely left a message
on a buffalo skull for the trains following behind.

Between wagons breaking down and oxen bolting, food poisoning

and dog bites, snakes and measles, dysentery and fever, death in childbirth and death by angry knife, gradually Matthew's supply of bandages and sutures diminished. Emmeline likewise found herself busy at
her profession, for many of the women had grown to dislike Albertina
Hopkins and requested Miss Fitzsimmons's help when their labor pains
began. As Florine Benbow had predicted, the "medical couple" were
proving to be indispensable.

And, despite themselves, Emmeline and Matthew were starting to
become a couple in other ways as well.

Most folks retired early at night, but some stayed up, mainly the
younger ones. Matthew liked to use the quiet time in the camp to
read by lantern, poetry mostly, sometimes the Bible. Emmeline liked
to stare at the stars. "How do we know we're going the right direction?" she asked one night.

He laid his book down and pointed to the night sky. "Do you know
the Big Dipper? Those stars there, that form a giant saucepan? See
the two stars at the end of the handle? They point to the North Star,
and the North Star is always within one degree of true north."

Emmeline settled admiring eyes upon him and said, "I declare, Dr.
Lively, you are an educated man."

Two nights later, Matthew was trying to sew a button on his shirt
using a curved suture needle and silk surgical thread. He was hopeless
at it. When he looked up to see Emmeline watching him, he thought
she was going to laugh. But she didn't. Instead, to his surprise, she
came over with a small sewing box, took the shirt and, sitting next
to him, said tactfully, "I myself am all thumbs when it comes to mending, but perhaps I've had a little more experience." She did a perfect
job.

Over the miles, through days plagued with heat and dust and flies,
and nights filled with the howls of wolves and mournful winds, Matthew altered his assessment of Miss Fitzsimmons, who never once
complained about having to do a man's work. When creeks were
swollen and wagons got stuck, Emmeline plunged into the water without thought for herself, her skirts billowing out about her as she
pushed with all her might to free the wheels from the mud. She "hee-
hawed" the oxen along with the men, she labored over laundry and
broken axels, skinned buffalo and stitched canvas like any experienced hand. As the days went by, Matthew began to feel a budding
admiration for her. Less and less did he look at the daguerreotype of

the frail Honoria, and when he did he wondered how long she would have lasted on this trail. Certainly she would have been a burden instead of a help.

Matthew was undergoing changes in other ways as well. He found muscles growing beneath his shirtsleeves, saw his face grow increasingly tanned in the mirror. The paleness of dark parlors had been vanquished by a vigorous climate of sun, heat, dust, and storms. Calluses grew on his hands as he worked side by side with Emmeline Fitzsimmons.

And then came the night when Sean Flaherty's coon dog, Daisy, stole one of Rebecca O'Ross's meat pies. The sight of the dog racing around the camp with a big pie in his mouth and diminutive Mrs. O'Ross chasing him with a rolling pin, put everyone in hysterics. As Matthew joined in the laughter, he looked over at Emmeline and saw that she was laughing so hard tears ran down her cheeks. And it struck him that passion ran deep in every aspect of her character, not only in the way she ate, or voiced her opinion on women's rights. Emmeline Fitzsimmons welcomed and embraced and experienced life with all the exuberance God had given her. And in the next instant an unbidden notion flashed in his mind: that she must also be passionate in love.

He felt his cheeks burn, and the breath caught momentarily in his chest. When she suddenly looked his way and their eyes met, he felt his heart skip a beat.

On June twenty-sixth the wagon train camped near Ft. Laramie beneath warm, clear skies. Bands of Sioux Indians, preparing for war with the neighboring Crow, visited the encampment where they shared the emigrants' breakfast of bread and meat in exchange for beads and feathers. Everyone parted in a friendly spirit and a little of the Americans' fear of the natives diminished. But when a French trapper named Jean Baptiste joined the train for a day and told them of possible early snows in the mountains, new fears sprang up (everyone had heard tales of earlier emigrants getting trapped in winterbound mountains and dying of starvation) so Amos Tice informed the company that it would be wise if they picked up their pace.

◆ ◆ ◆

*O*n July fourth the emigrants celebrated the nation's seventy-second birthday with ale and fireworks, patriotic speeches and prayers. Two thousand Sioux warriors, resplendent in buffalo skins decorated with beads and feathers and riding like an army to meet their enemies the Crow in battle, paused to watch the curious celebrations of the white strangers. Matthew Lively, accepting a glass of Mr. Hopkins's brandy, which the quiet man had been saving for just this occasion, turned with the rest of the company to gaze eastward and remember friends and loved ones left behind. Matthew thought of his mother and her séances, while Emmeline Fitzsimmons, standing at his side and holding a cup of Charlie Benbow's wine (from a cask that had survived a river crossing), thought of her parents in their twin graves on the farm she had inherited and sold. Sean Flaherty raised his glass to Ireland; Tim O'Ross was thinking of a redhead in New York; the Schumanns recalled family in Bavaria. Together they all saluted the home they had left, then they turned to face the west and drank to the new home to come.

*J*uly seventeenth found them camped on the summit of South Pass, the broad passage through the Rocky Mountains, backbone of the continent. This was a time to do fixing and mending, to repair and shore up, and to ponder the momentousness of this point of no return, for South Pass was the halfway point: on the eastward side of the great divide, rivers ran to the Mississippi, on the other they ran westward to the Pacific. Checkerboards and decks of cards were produced, a harmonica and a fiddle played a spirited tune. Mr. Hopkins quietly drank whiskey while his imperious wife held her usual court and let their children run wild through the camp.

Emmeline was mending her skirt by the light of a lantern when the Hopkins's eldest daughter came shyly up. She was the child of Mr. Hopkins's first wife; Albertina was her stepmother, and the girl was terrified of her. Therefore she brought her secret fears to Emmeline, the midwife. After hearing the first halting words of the shamed confession, Emmeline quickly grasped the situation—the girl had been spending time alone with one of the teamsters and the inevitable was bound to happen. "I'm afraid it might be true," she said quietly, patting the frightened girl's hand. "That's the first sign that a baby is coming, when your monthly show does not happen." As the girl began to weep, mostly out of fear from her stepmother's wrath, Emmeline grew practical. "I heard tell of a preacher in the wagon train just up ahead. I shall ask Dr. Lively to ride up there and bring him back. You'll be married and no one will be the wiser."

The preacher, who had been presiding over more graves than he ever thought possible, was only too happy to retrace the miles to conduct matrimonial services in the Tice Party, and in fact a few families came with him, for the diversion and the need for celebration. After the Hopkins daughter and the teamster spoke their vows, presided over by a queenly Albertina who was none the wiser of her stepdaughter's secret, a merry party broke out, with fiddle music and dancing under a starry sky, and Silas Winslow took the happy couple's picture.

During the festivities, as they ate unfrosted cake and drank warm cider, Emmeline looked at Matthew in the light of the campfire and thought, *He has gained confidence. Not the nervous young man of three months ago. And the sunburn suits him.*

She went on to analyze exactly what it was about Dr. Lively that made him seem special to her out of a company of so many men, most of them stronger and more rugged than Matthew. And she thought, *It is his kindness.* Because no matter what the circumstances, how dire or stressful a situation, Matthew could be counted on to help out without having been asked; he willingly shared his food and his wagon, frequently giving rides to exhausted women when their own husbands were oblivious to their needs; and inquiring after everyone's health and comfort when others were too weary to give a damn.

In that same moment, as Emmeline was thinking of Dr. Lively and starting to allow that he wasn't so bad looking after all, and maybe even handsome, Matthew was also thinking about Emmeline Fitzsimmons. But his thoughts weren't so broad or encompassing as hers. His mental focus was very singular: now that he thought about it, Miss Fitzsimmons's curvaceous figure was rather fetching after all.

◆ ◆ ◆

$\mathscr{F}$t. Bridger, so named by its founder, Jim Bridger, had served as a trading post for the past five years—a settlement of crude log buildings, Indians in buckskins, trappers, woodsmen, and emigrants heading west. As they neared the fort, the Tice Party encountered a wagon train heading *east*, the dispirited emigrants having given up and decided to return home. For the most part, it was severe loss of life that had broken their dream, and the party of twenty wagons consisted mostly of women and children and a few old men. The Tice Party itself was lighter by twelve wagons and thirty-two souls, and after nearly three months on the trail, they were a more ragged bunch than when they had left Independence, despite efforts to maintain certain standards of civilized behavior. The children were barefoot and in shameful disarray, men sported long unkempt beards, clothes were soiled and torn. Even Silas Winslow, dandy and photographer, sported stains on his fancy checkered waistcoat and smears of axle grease on his once expensive clothes that no amount of soda and ash could remove. Nor were they in the merry spirits that had once regarded this trek as a lark, for jealousies and hatreds, arguments and feuds, resentments and bitter rivalries had erupted along the trail so that many once-friends were now enemies. But they were happy to have arrived at what they saw as the jumping-off place for the final leg of the journey: from here they would turn north toward Oregon.

And here, too, some would make a decision that would turn out to be their death warrants.

Passing through the fort was a mountain man who had made it all the way west and was now headed back east, a man who was warning anyone who would listen that they might hear tell of a new shortcut and they should avoid it at all costs. "Take the regular wagon track and never leave it," he advised Amos Tice and other wagon masters. "Taking the shortcut could be fatal."

But Tice countered: "If there is a shorter route, then taking the roundabout one is foolish." He spoke as if he were thinking of the well-being of his emigrants, but something had happened to Amos Tice in the last miles before reaching Ft. Bridger—he had undergone a complete change of heart, although none of his fellow travelers knew it. Jean Baptiste, the French trapper who had visited the wagon train for a day, had been traveling with more than furs from the Sierras, he had also been carrying a poster that he had brought with him from a place in California called Sutter's Sawmill. To keep the Frenchman from showing the poster to any of the other members of his wagon train, or the members of trains that were coming behind, Amos Tice paid Baptiste handsomely for it. This was because at heart Amos Tice was an intensely greedy man. His sole reason for leading folks to Oregon had been to claim as much free land for himself as possible, and to make a profit on emigrants' hopes and dreams. But all that changed when he saw the poster the French trapper carried, for it announced the discovery of gold in California.

Tice bought the poster, the Frenchman rode on, and Amos kept the news to himself. He had been mulling the problem over the last few miles to Ft. Bridger, wondering how to get to California. To abandon the wagon train would mean he would have to travel alone, a highly dangerous proposition. There was safety in numbers, it was why wagon companies had been formed in the first place. Getting his people to go with him to California was therefore Tice's secret objective. Once there, he would abandon them and set about the business of getting extremely rich on gold. But how to convince his party to agree to change the route? The blessed solution had come ironically from the mountain man who was warning everyone *against* listening to rumors of a shortcut to Oregon.

Tice fanned the flames of the rumor, saying that he had heard the alternate trail was not only shorter, it was a more pleasant route and that Oregon-bound emigrants needn't suffer the hazards and hardships of their predecessors. Next, Tice invented a map. It looked authentic— he labored over it a day and a night in secret, making sure it looked used, well worn, and reliable. He also made sure that the trail they took steered well clear of Mormons who had settled just the year before near an area they would be crossing. Amos Tice had been among the militiamen who had arrested and jailed (and then murdered, although Tice himself was not the executioner) Joseph Smith just three years prior, and so no love was lost between Tice and the Latter-day Saints. Then he presented his new plan and the "genuine" map to the gathered company in their camp outside Ft. Bridger. The enthusiasm and excitement in his voice wasn't fake, for his mind was filled with visions of streams running thick with gold nuggets.

"It's as plain as day," he said, spreading the map out for all to see. "The Oregon Trail goes up this way across perilous mountains and then there's a long and hazardous river journey on rafts where many folks have already perished. I propose this here route. Look, it's straight across nice open flatland, then a hike through a mountain pass. In California we turn north and follow the flattest, most pleasant route cooled by sea breezes, where there's fruit trees as far as the eye can see."

"But isn't it longer?" asked Charlie Benbow.

"In miles, yes, but the other route is longer in time and misery and danger. Remember South Pass through the Rockies? How easy and pleasant it was? Well, the Sierras ain't even nothing like the Rockies. Crossin' them will be like a stroll in the park!"

They believed him.

However, they wanted to think it over. After all, this was the last outpost, and beyond was untracked wilderness. So while Tice's people mulled over his proposition to take the shortcut, they used the few days of rest to make further repairs to wagons and harnesses, to rest and feed horses and cattle, and to make up food for the trail ahead. Their mood was optimistic. Paradise lay just over the next ridge of mountains, the California Sierras. Tice's group could almost feel the soft breezes of the Pacific against their faces.

But several had their doubts. Matthew Lively did not jump at Tice's new plan, preferring to consult the Guiding Spirit in the Blessing Stone (although his gut feeling was that the shortcut was not a good idea). He allowed Emmeline to join him, for he was now used to showing her the stone and explaining how it worked. They sat on the tailgate of his wagon, encircled in the warm glow of a lantern, while the rest of the camp went on about its noisy business beneath the stars. Matthew used his slate again, with the words "yes" and "no" written on it. As he quietly enquired, "Should we take the new cut-off?" Emmeline sat solemnly watching the crystal twirl before coming to a rest before the word "yes."

Matthew frowned. He hated to doubt the wisdom of the crystal, but something deep within him said they should continue on the old northward trail. Emmeline agreed. While believing herself to be adventurous in nature and willing to try anything new, it seemed folly to abandon a sure trail for one untried, no matter how promising it sounded. "Spin it again," she said.

The answer came up "yes."

Matthew rubbed his chin. "The Blessing Stone says we should follow Amos Tice."

"And what do *you* think we should do?"

Matthew had no idea. He had never really made a decision of his own in his life. Even when he was a boy and his mother made the decisions for him, she consulted the crystal first. "My mother always said the spirits guide us, and that we should heed them."

"Even if your own intuition tells you otherwise?"

"My own intuition, I am ashamed to say, has always been weak. When I was a boy, I let my brothers lead me around. When I was older, I imitated my peers. I'm afraid I am a follower, Miss Fitzsimmons, and I shall go wherever leaders such as Amos Tice, or the Guiding Spirit in the crystal, tell me to."

He regarded her in the golden lamplight and noticed the beautiful amber color of her eyes. "What will *you* do, Miss Fitzsimmons?" He asked it with a lump in his throat, for he was afraid of her answer. It was only this moment of tremendous decision that Matthew realized his feelings for Miss Fitzsimmons ran deep.

"I find you a comfortable traveling companion, Dr. Lively," she said quietly, "and I believe we work well together. If I leave your company now, I should be hard pressed to find someone else so amiable to invite me along. Therefore I will go wherever you go, Dr. Lively."

Matthew felt his heart race. He swallowed and licked his lips. "Miss Fitzsimmons," he said quickly, "there is something you should know—"

"Hoy there," came a voice through the darkness. They saw Silas Winslow saunter up with his trademark swagger, bowler hat tilted forward on his brow. "I am not going with Tice, Miss Fitzsimmons," he said, ignoring Matthew, his rival for Emmeline's affections. "I'm heading north with a new company that is forming under Stephen Collingsworth. If you find yourself without a ride, I shall be happy to escort you to Oregon." He laid a hand dramatically on his chest. "And I assure you, my dear Miss Fitzsimmons, of the utmost gentlemanly propriety while I am your protector."

Emmeline blinked at him, and opened her mouth to speak, when they were suddenly interrupted by shouts.

"Dr. Lively!" came a voice through the camp. "Dr. Lively! Joe Strickland's been hurt bad!"

The teamster lay moaning in his wagon, unconscious from pain. It was explained to Matthew that his foot had gotten stomped by an ornery ox that didn't want to go back into its yoke. One look at the foot told even the most inexperienced eye that Joe was in serious trouble. Bone jutted through skin, and while the blood was beginning to stanch, a horrible purplish color was spreading from the toes up. With Emmeline's assistance, Matthew bathed the wound, applied salve and then covered it in clean bandages. When he tried to press the jutting bone back into place, Joe cried out and sank into even deeper unconsciousness. His face turned an alarming gray and he sweated profusely. As Joe was traveling alone, Emmeline volunteered to take care of him.

That night decisions were made. Various wagon companies were divided up, with some of the original Tice Party deciding to go with Collingsworth on the northern trail, and newcomers from recently arrived wagon trains opting to join Tice on his shortcut. Silas Winslow, smitten with Miss Fitzsimmons, decided to join the Tice Party after all.

They said farewell to people they had traveled with since Missouri, promising to meet up with them in Oregon. Although new members had joined, with wagons and cattle, wives and children, the Tice Party was smaller now, consisting of thirty-five wagons, sixty-nine men, thirty-two women, seventy-one children, and three hundred head of cattle and horses.

Hopes were high as the wagons made their way past streams jumping with trout, fields carpeted with wild flowers, groves lush with aspen and willow. The company felt stronger now that there was new "blood," for the recently added members were strong and healthy. But Matthew Lively was filled with misgivings; something was wrong and he couldn't put his finger on it. He wondered if his mother's dark and terrible prophecy were the cause of it. But he kept his doubts to himself. Everyone else seemed to think Tice had a good idea and spirits were high.

The idyll did not last long.

After the first few pleasant days of travel, the wagon train came to the Wasatch Mountains, a range of high, snowcapped peaks and deep canyons. The sides of the canyons were clogged with willow, dense berry bushes, thick cottonwoods, box elder, and alder trees, and the riverbeds were narrow and full of boulders. It called for every able-bodied male in the company to help clear the route.

Armed with hatchets and axes, chains and spades, they fought and hacked their way through willow, cottonwoods, aspen, and box elder. Each night the men fell exhausted on their blankets while their women nursed their husbands', brothers', and sons' blisters and scrapes with ointments and words of encouragement. At least they had water, Tice pointed out, and grass for cattle. But they also had swarms of mosquitoes and biting flies.

Progressing only five miles a day, they were finally forced to double-team the oxen in order to haul the wagons over the Wasatch summit, and when they descended to the other side, the emigrants stared at the formidable obstacle that lay before them: the Great Salt Lake Desert.

Night camps were less cheerful now and wrapped in sober silence. Travel during the day was slow going, for temperatures soared and roasted the desert. Injuries incurred in the Wasatch mountains held up travel as there were fewer able men to hitch and unhitch the oxen, and frequent rest stops were needed. While the women worried over their menfolk—Joe Strickland's foot started to fester although Emmeline did her best to take care of it—Amos Tice harbored a secret worry of his own: that they were falling behind schedule. Up ahead lay the Sierras and the threat of snow.

Across the barren lake bed they trudged as a merciless sun pounded down. As the heat grew searing and ovenlike, the emigrants believed they had entered a new hell. They bathed the animals' tongues with wet towels for so waterless and devoid of the slightest moisture was this arid land they feared the oxen and cattle would go mad from thirst. It was a desolate alkali wasteland where not a living thing could be seen. The wagons up ahead looked gigantic through the magnifying heat waves. The mountains in the distance seemed to float on air. The midday sun was like a hammer. Vulcan's forge, the more educated among the party thought. At sunset shadows stretched for miles. The night air was like cold tongs pinching through blankets. Children cried, cattle moaned. The surface of the plain was so compact that the animals' hooves left but little impression in the hard salt and alkaline crust, but when the wagons reached the center of the desert, they found a shallow lake that turned the alkali into mush. Now it was like walking through oatmeal. Each footfall requiring effort to pull the next foot out of the mire. The gluey muck covered their feet like cement casts, it clumped around wagon wheels and made oxen stumble.

Still the emigrants tramped on through the furnace, parched, sweating with heat. Joe Strickland's foot got worse. As infection and fever ravaged the poor man's body, Emmeline rode in the Hammersmiths' wagon with Joe's head cradled in her lap. Other members were now likewise ailing, but they knew they had to keep going, that it meant death to stop.

A group of men, elected by the others, announced to Tice their intention to go to the Mormons for help (although no one had any idea exactly where Brigham Young's people had settled), but Tice, knowing he had a bad reputation among the Latter-day Saints, declared authoritatively that they were too far out of the way and it would be suicide to try even to search for them.

Onward they went, through the scalding heat of the day and the bone-crunching cold of night, lips cracked and bleeding, tongues swollen, water doled out in spoonfuls. The Schumann brothers' oxen finally gave out, dropping to their knees and bellowing with thirst. So the four Germans buried their plows and farm implements right there in the sand with the intention of coming back for them after they found land in Oregon.

The Biggs's new baby, delivered three months prior by Albertina Hopkins, succumbed to the heat and was buried in the sand. The Benbows' chickens began to drop with heat and thirst, and even Daisy, the otherwise excitable coon dog, drooped alongside Sean Flaherty's wagon.

They thought the Great Salt Lake Desert would never end.

But it finally did, and as the weary wagon train drew up to the first watering hole in the foothills, as the hot day gave way to cool evening, as cattle stampeded to the water and people tried not to get trampled in the rush, and as Matthew Lively was thinking that this was the dark and terrible trial prophesied by his mother, Emmeline came to him and said, "Joe Strickland has gangrene. His foot is going to have to be amputated."

Matthew suddenly felt as if he carried the weight of the world and all its populations on his shoulders. Sinking to the ground, where he had been trying to start a campfire, he shook his head and said, "I cannot do it."

Emmeline sat next to him and laid a hand on his arm. Like herself, like all the others, Matthew's face was red and blistered, his eyes bleary, his clothes stiff with sweat and grime. "I'll help you," she said. "I once assisted my father in the amputation of a leg. I am not squeamish, Dr. Lively."

He looked at her and felt like crying. "Miss Fitzsimmons, I am not a doctor."

She stared at him. "What do you mean?"

"I mean that I am not a medical man. You made that assumption back in Independence, and I did not correct you."

She frowned. "Then what are you?"

His voice was small and weary as he said, "I am an undertaker."

She blinked. Her frown deepened. "An undertaker? Like a mortician?"

"Exactly like a mortician."

"But . . . your medical bag—"

"The tools of a man who heals bodies are the same as those of a man who lays bodies to eternal rest. Especially when the demise was caused by injury. We have to do the same sewing and bandaging as any doctor. And the stethoscope—that is how we can know for sure the man is dead before he goes into the ground."

"But I saw you buying medicine in the apothecary shop!"

"It was for myself. I have a chest weakness in the winter."

Emmeline was so flabbergasted she could barely speak. "Why did you not correct me? Why did you let everyone believe you are a doctor?"

He gave her a woebegone look. "If you had a group of people depending on you for their lives, would *you* tell them you were a mortician? Miss Fitzsimmons, you have been complaining of prejudice and stigma because of your gender. Well I face the same prejudice and stigma—because of my profession."

Emmeline's expression grew thoughtful. "Yes," she said. "I suppose I see your point."

"I make people uncomfortable," he said miserably. "I remind them of something they'd rather not be reminded of. But it's our family business! My father is a mortician, and so are my two brothers. I had no choice but to follow them."

"My dear Matthew," she said gently, addressing him for the first time by his Christian name. "Do not be ashamed and embarrassed of the profession your father taught you for there is nothing shameful about what you do. It is an honorable profession, a necessary job, and people need men like you who are respectful of the dead, and of the grieving, because I have seen how you are when someone dies. My father and uncles told me of morticians robbing corpses and cheating the families, undertakers selling families caskets they can't afford, preying upon their grief and guilt. You can make a difference, Matthew, and fulfill a very important need because you are called upon during one of the most dire and vulnerable moments in a human life."

He could only stare at her, and recall Honoria's words when she rejected his marriage proposal: "I could never live with a man who dealt with diseased bodies."

"So . . . my profession doesn't bother you?"

"I would be the worst of hypocrites if it did. I made my decision to go west when I saw how steeped in prejudice and outmoded tradition the east is. People are squeezed into molds and expected to stay in them. I wanted to be a doctor but all anyone could say to me was that women were meant to be wives and mothers. So I decided to go where thinking is free and unhampered by blind bias. Now what sort of feminist would I be if I demanded open-mindedness of others and did not hold that same open mind myself?"

"And you don't think"—he cleared his throat and his cheeks reddened—"That there is a problem with my name? I would prefer not to change it."

She stared at him for a moment, and then, understanding, said, "Oh!" and her hand flew to her mouth.

"So you see not only will I be a pariah, I'll be a laughingstock, too."

She smiled. "The name doesn't bother your father, does it? So it should not bother you."

"It's different," he said unhappily. "In Boston, the Livelys have been morticians for generations. Ever since the original colonists. No one gives the name a second thought. But out here. Can an undertaker named Lively expect to gain respect?"

Emmeline granted it could be a problem, but now was not the time to worry about Matthew Lively's name. Joe Strickland was going to die if something wasn't done to save his leg.

They went back to the Hammersmiths' wagon and although Joe Strickland had been unconscious for two days, he opened his eyes and, in one of those moments of clarity that sometimes come to a man on the threshold of death, said, "I appreciate what you done for me, Doc, and while I know you just want to help me, I can't let you take my leg. I've been driving livestock since I left my mother's knee. Don't know nothing else. And there ain't nothing more useless than a one-legged muleskinner. So I'll say my good-byes now, if you don't mind."

Joe died that night but no one blamed Matthew—they said he had done his best. Emmeline discovered a new admiration for Matthew Lively that night, because though it pained his conscience to keep his profession a secret, he put other people's feelings before his own. She kept his secret and continued to call him Dr. Lively.

As for Matthew himself, in the weeks to come he would look back on this night and realize that this was the instant he had fallen in love.

They plodded onward. More oxen collapsed on the salt flats and cattle wandered off in search of water. Four more wagons were abandoned as family members buried goods they could no longer carry, intending to come back for them someday. Into the barren ground went trunks of clothes and keepsakes, family heirlooms and quilts, butter churns and frying pans. The emigrants had devised different ways, during the journey from Independence, for keeping their money safe. Some simply packed it away in trunks with other possessions, but some drilled holes in the wagon planks and secreted coins in there. Silas Winslow had a special tin box labeled, "Caustic chemical! Will cause instant burning of the eyes and skin if opened." Here was where he had hidden all his coins. Having to abandon his wagon now, and all his cumbersome photographic equipment, he strapped the heavy gold-filled tin to his back.

There was a sense of urgency in the party. They had lost days in the fruitless search for the lost cattle, summer was waning, snow now crowned nearby peaks, provisions were getting low, and they were still facing hundreds of miles of Nevada desert.

Once out of the Utah wasteland they encountered mountainous country. From a high pass they could see another desert valley, and beyond that another mountain range, with another valley beyond it. This was the topography of Nevada: a rhythm of valley and range, valley and range, stretching from salt desert to the Sierras, each valley a desert, each range a wall. And there was nothing for the emigrants to do but put one foot in front of the other and hope that the last of the oxen held out.

They entered Paiute Indian country where raiding was a way of life. Cattle were stolen during the night, horses snared in broad daylight. And as the number of oxen diminished, more wagons had to be abandoned. The majority of the members were now walking, having left most of their possessions behind. Youngsters doubled up riding on horses while remaining provisions were piled into the last of the wagons.

More of Charlie Benbow's chickens perished but he still had some good breeding stock left and he guarded them day and night. The Hopkins daughter who got married at South Pass came privately to Emmeline with a complaint of pains. As the girl was four months pregnant, Emmeline was alarmed. But she hid her fear and gave the girl a soothing tonic. Sean Flaherty still had his dog Daisy but fewer potatoes with which to start his Oregon farm. And Osgood Aahrens lost all his barber tools in a bog. When the party finally began the trek up along the winding Truckee River, the remaining cattle were gaunt and stumbling over rocks, the people weak and malnourished with supplies dangerously low, and when they finally saw the Sierra Nevada, the range was cloaked in dark, ominous clouds.

In the third week of October the exhausted party straggled into a broad mountain valley where they found snow swirling among the pines. Here they regrouped and rested, making camp as best they could. But they awoke the next dawn to a light snowfall and realized they must hasten their ascent of the Sierra summit, on the other side of which lay California.

Five days later they reached a mountain lake, beyond which lay the pass through the Sierras. They tried to cross but snow thwarted their efforts, forcing them to retreat to the shore of the lake, where there was level ground, timber, and the prospect of game. Here they built makeshift shelters constructed from tents, quilts, buffalo robes, and brush. One hundred fifty nine people huddled in the crude dwellings, hoping that the early snow would melt and they would be able to cross the pass. While they waited and prayed, they made an accounting of all that they had, and found they still had a few wagons with cattle and horses, and some provisions: beans, flour, coffee, and sugar. It was decided that everything would be pooled, including the Benbows' chickens and Sean Flaherty's potatoes, and distributed equally among the families.

That night, when Albertina Hopkins protested that the unmarried girls, her eyes going pointedly to Emmeline Fitzsimmons, should all sleep in a separate shelter, her husband quietly said, "Shut up, woman," and she did.

$\mathcal{M}$atthew was unable to sleep. A chill wind cut through the cracks and crevices of the tent, making it impossible to get comfortable. But something else kept him wakeful as well: the nagging presentiment that had followed him in the ten weeks since leaving Ft. Bridger, that something was terribly wrong.

Stepping over sleeping bodies, he shook Amos Tice awake and demanded in a harsh whisper to see him outside where, by good fortune, a clear sky and bright moon illuminated the snowy landscape. In unaccustomed assertiveness Matthew insisted he be allowed a look at Tice's map, saying that this was not the easy trail Tice had promised.

The wagon master grumbled but produced the map, which he secretly hoped Matthew could not read well in the moonlight. But as the paper snapped in his hands, and his own icy breath clouded his vision, Matthew could see well enough. And what he saw was something he had not noticed back at Ft. Bridger: that this was an amateurishly drawn map and not to scale.

"Where did you get this, Amos?" he asked suspiciously.

Tice didn't meet his eyes. "Got it at Ft. Bridger."

"You mean where that old mountain man was telling everybody to ignore rumors about a shortcut? You saw this map and you *believed* it? Why, it's fake, Amos! Anyone can see that!"

Something flared in Tice's eyes, a glint of power in a weary face. He laughed in a way that alarmed Matthew, and said, "Guess it don't matter now." He reached inside his fringed buckskin jacket and brought out a thick, tattered paper that, unfolded, turned out to be a poster announcing the discovery of gold at Sutter's Sawmill.

Matthew stared in shock. "You should have asked the rest of us if we're interested in gold!"

But Tice only laughed again and returned to the shelter. The next morning, the wagon master and five other men were gone.

The emigrants had been abandoned.

They broke camp, loaded the remaining wagons, and slogged on, determined to crest the mountains. But they encountered more snow and suffered more unsuccessful attempts to cross the Sierras. The weather was getting colder with heavy clouds hanging low over the ponderosa pines. The emigrants' clothes were cold and damp as they shivered in their bones, panic and despair were barely held in check, and everyone prayed that the weather would hold.

When a surprise downpour drenched the party, some said the rain was a good sign, but Matthew was reminded of something he heard Jim Bridger say back at the fort: "Rain in a Sierra valley means snow at the pass."

For the first time in his life, Matthew felt genuine fear. He had dealt with the dead many times in his young life, both in his father's mortuary and at his mother's séances, but he had never had to face his own mortality before. And it terrified him. He recalled how brave he had felt, sitting atop his wagon as they had left Independence, Missouri, an exodus of courageous people off to conquer the wilderness. But he saw now, through freshly bleak eyes, that there had been no real bravery among them for they had all regarded the trek as a lark, a merry adventure with picnics along the way.

No one had anticipated this.

As they made a new camp with makeshift shelters, their spirits low, the emigrants prayed that the rain would beat down the drifts, but they awakened the next morning to see the snow even deeper.

The mountain ahead was daunting but they knew they must press on. The oxen were weak from a diet of pine branches, and yet more wagons had to be abandoned. They piled what they could onto the remaining oxen and carried the rest themselves, with even the children shouldering small burdens.

The snow was now three feet deep.

◆ ◆ ◆

*T*hey tried to press on but the last mountain peak rose before them like a white wall. Dispirited and exhausted, the weary band could go no farther. So they retreated to a small lake where, during another snowstorm, they again constructed shelters out of wood from the wagons, canvas tops, even adding quilts and buffalo hides to keep out the cold. They lit fires within and were quickly overcome by smoke and fumes, requiring them to scramble outside, coughing and gasping, to cut ventilation holes in the hides, which also let the cold in. Hunting was poor here. Matthew managed to snare a coyote, and the stringy animal was devoured along with an owl boiled down to a broth that was given only to the young and the ill. Hunting for deer proved futile as the deer had gone to lower elevations. Beans and flour were stretched out and apportioned in meager mouthfuls. The last of the Benbows' chickens were eaten, and Sean Flaherty's potatoes were all gone. Despite this, they still elected to say grace before each meager meal.

At seven thousand feet above sea level, they struggled to kindle fires and keep them going. The weaker members were having difficulty breathing at this altitude. And the poor newly wedded Hopkins girl, five months pregnant, suffered a miscarriage that nearly cost her her life. The fetus was given a Christian burial and Albertina Hopkins, lighter now by many pounds since Independence, and more quietly spoken, grimly nursed her stepdaughter.

After seven straight days of snowfall, the sun came out and the heartened emigrants voted to send a party on to the pass in the hopes they would make it across and down to Sutter's Mill, from where rescue relief could be sent. The eight strongest men were chosen, but when Matthew Lively volunteered to go, everyone agreed that the "doc" should stay with the women and the sick. The party was dressed in the warmest clothing and given packs of dried beef. Everyone tried to give them a cheerful send-off.

They were back at sundown. There was no advancing, they said. The snowstorms had blocked all paths.

◆ ◆ ◆

*S*omeone reckoned it was around the fifth of December when the emigrants began to slaughter their remaining cattle, but many animals had wandered off in the storms to get buried in the snow. And the men had such little success hunting that a new, chilling thought began to infiltrate the emigrants' minds: if they were stranded here for the winter, there would not be enough food to go around.

Charlie Benbow's wife Florine was found frozen in her sleep. As the ground was too hard to dig a grave, she was wrapped in a shroud and laid between two planks and then covered with stones.

Another escape attempt was made, this time with women in the party, but they were again driven back by a snowstorm. They sat huddled in their flimsy shelters, frozen and bitten, trying to draw warmth from fires that were growing smaller as dried wood became harder to find. Bibles that had been used for spiritual comfort were now put on the fire for physical comfort, as was anything that couldn't be worn or eaten. They watched in bleak despair as Psalms, the Song of Solomon, the Gospels and the letters of Paul went up in smoke. The children were given the thickest blankets and slept with the few remaining dogs for warmth. Fresh snowfall during the night buried their cache of meat and it took a day of searching with long poles to find the beef. The next morning, the cached meat was gone altogether, wolf tracks leading away.

In an unaccustomed fit of heroic inspiration, brought on mostly by hunger, Silas Winslow decided to strike off for the summit on his own, determined to bring rescuers to the camp. He was found two days later, still alive but snowblind. When they carried him back, they wrapped his eyes in calico to prevent further damage to them. His spirits were high enough for him to quip that he hoped the loss of sight was temporary because of what use was a blind photographer?

Emmeline did her best to try and keep the company cheered. She led them in songs and stories, and asked each to talk about their plans for Oregon. The first evenings were successful, but as the cold deepened and everyone shivered with teeth chattering despite the fire and blankets, they grew less inclined to talk.

Matthew's fears heightened, along with everyone else's, for there was an unspoken horror hanging in the air. The landscape—including boulders, pine trees and the little lake—was now completely white. There was not a bird, a fish, a pine nut to be found. When the supplies ran out, other things were going to have to be eaten.

And when even those—the remaining dogs, the Schumanns' apple seeds, boiled leather—had been consumed, something else was going to have to be found.

Matthew clutched the blue crystal in his mittened hand night and day as he stared into the hollow eyes of his companions. Starvation was drawing closer. They were all suffering from frostbite. When Daisy, the last dog still alive, was slaughtered for food, Sean Flaherty dashed out of the shelter in a paroxysm of grief and tried to hang himself from a tree. But the frozen branch broke and the men were able to bring him back inside.

The Blessing Stone held no answers, no matter how hard Matthew gazed into it. He felt none of the spirit power it was supposed to possess, he heard no answers whispered on ghostly breath.

More people began to suffer from fever and pneumonia. Two young men, Freddy Hastings and Abe Waterford, with mothers back home anxiously awaiting letters from Oregon, plunged to watery deaths when they tried to cut a hole in the lake ice for fishing. The others were too weak to haul them out and so they were left there for the spring thaw. When the Schumann brothers managed to catch mice, which they scorched on hot coals, there was an obscene fight for the food—bones, tails, and all. Nonetheless, Osgood Aahrens managed to lead the gathering in grace before they forced down the repulsive meal.

Finally there was no food left. They boiled leather and ate the residual glue that formed at the bottom of the pot. They baked leather shoelaces among the embers and ate the crisp strings. For the first time, they did not say grace.

They grew weaker. They dreamed of food. One man, mad with hunger, ran out of the sodden tent and was found hours later, dead in the snow. They left him there, to be covered by drifts. Charlie Benbow began to hold conversations with his dead wife, Florine.

Matthew and Emmeline slept entwined in each other's arms. They entertained no thoughts of romance or physical intimacy, but simply drew warmth and touch and love from each other.

◆ ◆ ◆

The dawn of Christmas Day brought a new blizzard. The wind cut through the tents like swords and howled like pain-racked phantoms. The glassy-eyed occupants of the frail shelters had difficulty getting and keeping fires lit. They ransacked their possessions, searching for anything edible. They tossed away gold and money, for these no longer held value or meaning. They had now gone for two weeks without any food whatsoever, subsisting only on melted ice that they drank in sips.

Rebecca O'Ross, not a strong woman to begin with, was the first adult to die of starvation. Her husband Tim was so beside himself with grief that he had to be dragged off her grave by four men, for fear he would freeze to death there. His son, Dickie, curled up in a corner of the shelter and wept until he was silent, glassy-eyed, and staring.

When, a week later, one of the Schumann brothers died of pneumonia, there was, for the first time, hesitancy among the survivors over his burial. The words weren't spoke, and people could not meet each other's eyes, but the terrible, unspoken thought hung over them all the same, as loud as the howling wind that never let up its ceaseless torment.

Here, in the person of Helmut Schumann, lay fresh meat.

"My God, no!" cried Matthew when the full meaning of their silence struck him. "We are not animals."

"But we are," Mr. Hopkins said softly, sadly. "Humans, perhaps, and God's children. But animals all the same, and we need to eat." His wife, Albertina, was sobbing with her face in her hands. One would not recognize the skeletal creature in the loose-fitting dress as the same domineering woman who had departed Independence eight months prior. But her two children were dead, her spirit broken.

"And what will *I* eat?" cried Manfred Schumann. "I cannot eat my own brother!"

Another silence filled with meaning answered him: Helmut was only the first, more were sure to follow.

Matthew ran outside, stumbling in the snow, tears freezing on his cheeks. He fell to his knees and wept with great heaving sobs. When Emmeline joined him, he drew her into his arms. Despite the layers of clothing, her coat made from a blanket, he felt the skin and bones beneath. She was no longer a robust young woman. But there was still life in her eyes as they searched his face with anguish and compassion, and life in her lips as they sought his and kissed his mouth.

"We cannot do it," he sobbed into her neck. "We cannot reduce ourselves to that!"

"Have we a choice? Should we let ourselves die? Matthew, we are trapped here. And we shall be here until the spring. There is no food. There is no—" Then she too broke down weeping, and they held each other in the snow, rocking back and forth, their wails of despair rising up to the frigid, indifferent sky.

Finally, taking control of herself, Emmeline drew Matthew to his feet and said, "They need a leader. They need someone to hold them together in body and spirit. They respect you."

"I am not a leader. You're the brave one, Emmeline. You have been from the start, back in Independence when you were determined to make this journey on your own."

She looked at him with hunted eyes. "I am not brave, Matthew. Not any longer. I am frightened out of my wits. All that courage—it was all talk because it was so easy. But now that I am faced with the necessity for real bravery, I find that I have none." She said, "You are lucky, you have the Blessing Stone to guide you. I have only myself and I am a very weak guide indeed."

He took the crystal out of his pocket and tried to see the Guiding Spirit his mother had always seen in it. Suddenly, all hope and pretense of belief in the stone gave way to hunger and despair. "It's a fake! A humbug!" he cried, and he flung the stone with a mighty throw.

"No!" said Emmeline, for though she herself did not believe in the crystal's magic, she knew that Mathew still did. She stumbled through the snow after it, frantically searching for the crystal.

"Wait," Matthew said, going after her.

When they found it, and Emmeline was bending to pick it up, Matthew saw something in the snow. He frowned. He squinted and bent low. He rubbed his eyes and blinked. There was no mistake: they were bear tracks.

"What is it?" Emmeline said when she saw the look on his face.

Matthew drew up straight and looked around. The landscape was blinding white and nearly featureless. He watched for movement.

Then he wrinkled his nose. "Do you smell that?"

She sniffed the air. "What an awful stink!"

"I think I know what it is." He took off through the deep snow and Emmeline followed.

They came to a small pile of bear scat. It was still steaming, which meant it was fresh—the bear was nearby.

"We have to tell the others!" Emmeline said. "We can kill it! We'll have food—"

"No! A group of people will scare the beast off and then we might never find it. If I can sneak up on it with a gun . . ."

"Matthew, you're no huntsman."

But he knew that this was something *he* had to do, alone, and quickly. His heart pounding with fear, he dashed into one of the shelters and quietly grabbed Charlie Benbow's gun. He wouldn't tell the others, who were too listless and lethargic anyway to notice or care that he was taking the rifle. It would be too cruel a thing to get their hopes up. He told Emmeline to wait for him inside, in the warmth. And to pray.

Matthew knew it was folly for a man to face a bear alone with only a muzzle-loading gun, but reason was not part of his thinking right now. He cocked his rifle and tucked the only other rifle ball into his mitten for quick reloading. Then he followed the bear tracks with great difficulty, for the snow was blinding and his sight grew blurred. Each intake of breath stabbed his lungs, and he no longer had sensation in his feet. He stopped every so often to listen; but the snow-white forest was silent.

He grew desperate. He had to find the animal! He had to stop the others from going through with the unthinkable act they were contemplating. Matthew had been raised to respect the dead. Desecration was an abomination. The dead couldn't defend themselves; it was up to the living to protect them.

But the people back at the camp were barely living now; they were walking corpses themselves.

Suddenly he froze. There it was, about a hundred yards ahead, an enormous grizzly bear digging in the snow. Matthew moved slowly forward, then he crouched behind a tree, cocked his rifle, took careful aim and fired.

The bear gave out a roar and reared up on its hind legs. Seeing Matthew, it charged. Matthew hurriedly poured powder into the gun and rammed the second lead ball home. He leveled the rifle and fired again. The bear bellowed and staggered. Then it fell to all fours and ran away. "Wait," Matthew said weakly, not believing that he had been so close and was now going to lose it. "Please!" He began to weep. All that food. He could have saved everyone. But his aim had been poor. He had failed.

Then he saw the bloody trail in the snow.

He ran back to the camp as fast as he could, stumbling and falling in the snow. He found several men gathered around the corpse of Helmut Schumann, Mr. Benbow holding a butcher knife. The women were crouched around the fire, sobbing. "Stop!" Matthew cried.

When he hurriedly told them about the bear, saying that they should follow it, not everyone agreed. "A wounded bear is too dangerous," said Aahrens the barber. Charlie Benbow added, "I seen what a hurt bear can do to a man. It's suicide, doc."

Bret Hammersmith said, "Why don't *you* go after it? Take a look see. Then come back for us."

Matthew looked into the hollow eyes and gaunt faces etched with the madness of hunger. He knew they would not wait for him to return with news of the bear, that they only wanted to get rid of him. "I am weak," he said, and it was the truth. "I can make but one more walk through the snow and then I will be done for. I ask all of you to make that trek with me. I shot that bear good. He won't live long. And where we find him, we'll find food. And we will survive. Here," he looked around at the hell they had descended into, "even if our bodies survive, our spirits will die."

But Emmeline was also terrified to leave the camp. He took her by her frozen hands and said, "You have to have courage now, Emmeline. For the others. If you go, they will follow."

"But I'm afraid."

"I'll see to it that we're all right. Don't worry, my darling."

In the end, they followed him, starved people holding onto one another, carrying loved ones on their shoulders, staggering through snowdrifts, half dead from hunger. They carried only a few possessions— blankets and quilts, cooking pots, and carefully protected hot embers from their fires. Several times they wanted to give up, for it seemed they were lost in a blinding white limbo. But Matthew found the drops of blood, scarlet in the snow, and he urged his ragtag group onward, promising them a feast of roast meat at the end. He described fat sizzling in a pan until they all smelled it, and their saliva ran. Emmeline joined in, taking each person by the arm, lifting them up from their knees, telling them how she had seen the wounded bear—a lie—and that she was sure by now it was dead. It was just up ahead . . . a few more feet . . . a few more steps . . . just one more step . . . no, no, don't stop, don't fall, here take my arm. . . .

Ruth Hammersmith sank into a snowdrift and lay there like a dead-weight. Her husband dropped by her side and told the others to go on. He stared up at them with sunken eyes circled with dark shadows.

The half-dead people pressed on, not even really thinking now, barely hearing Matthew's words of encouragement, plodding mind-lessly through snowdrifts, hands and feet frozen numb, faces white with extreme cold.

More fell, holding their children in their arms. Emmeline tried to raise them up, but was too weak herself, having only just enough strength to follow Matthew.

And when it seemed even to Emmeline and Matthew that their trek was a hopeless one, they found the cave, the bloody trail going inside.

While the others waited at a safe distance, Matthew and Manfred Schumann went cautiously inside, listening, sniffing the air, rifle cocked and ready. They found the bear inside, and it was dead.

Manfred and Osgood Aahrens found the strength to plunge knives into the animal's belly and slice it open. At the sight of tender raw innards spilling to the cave floor, the others came straggling in, falling upon the steaming, bloody morsels in a mindless feeding frenzy. They glutted themselves on warm, raw bear meat and blood, and then, feeling strengthened, went back along the trail to retrieve the people who had fallen behind. The Hammersmiths were both dead, but everyone else was brought back, packing the cave with their human warmth, filling their bellies with grizzly bear.

That night they slept exhausted against the carcass, children crawl-ing inside to get warm. And when they awoke, they built a fire from the embers, offered a prayer of thanks to God, and began to butcher the bear.

They ate directly from it, throwing chunks of meat onto the fire, but then also began cutting long thin strips and hanging them over the smoke until it dried, in this way preserving the bear meat for the cold weeks to come. They buried the bones and skull, to discourage wolves, and then used the stiff hide, which nearly covered the cave floor, as a rug for warmth.

Six more people perished, despite the food and warmth, but when it appeared the rest would survive, Matthew took a count of the company: there were now fifty-five men, twenty-four women, and fifty-three children. Forty souls fewer than had left Ft. Bridger.

And one day when the sun felt warm for the first time, and they encountered the first snowmelt beside a stream, Matthew turned to Emmeline and, taking her face between his hands, said with passion, "I love the sound of your voice, Emmeline. Don't ever stop talking. Don't ever be silent. When we started this journey, I was gloomy and much too serious. And I thought you smiled too much. But your buoyancy kept me from sinking. I grew up among the dead and the dark, but you brought light and cheer into my life."

"And you keep me from flying off the earth, dear Matthew, for I was frivolous and overconfident. You are my rock and my stability."

$\mathcal{T}$he rescue party from Sutter's arrived in the middle of March, led by one of the men who had run off with Amos Tice. Once they had reached civilization, the man had been stricken with a guilty conscience and told the authorities of a stranded party of emigrants up by the last pass. Volunteers had immediately signed up, loaded with arms and provisions, and had made the trek in record time.

Of the 172 men, women, and children who had left Ft. Bridger in August, fewer than 120 had survived.

Everyone told the rescuers that it was Doc Lively who had saved them, through his courage and wisdom to make the right decision in the face of extreme adversity.

Not one of them mentioned the incident over Helmut Schumann's corpse.

$\mathcal{W}$hen they came at last into Sutter's Mill and they saw it was a place of growth and new starts, with gold fever everywhere, Matthew took the Blessing Stone out of his pocket one last time. "I don't see it," he said decisively.

"What don't you see?"

"The Guiding Spirit. Do you see this clouding at the crystal's core?

Like diamond dust. It changes shape when you turn the stone in the light. My mother said it was a spirit, but I see only mineral deposits." He handed it to Emmeline. "What do you see?"

She peered into the heart of the crystal and said, "A valley. The lush green valley where we are going to settle and start new lives." She handed it back to him.

"I wonder," he mused, trying to see Emmeline's valley in the Blessing Stone. "All this time I thought it was the crystal telling me what to do. But perhaps it was me all along, *I* was the one making the decisions, not the stone. I wanted to go west, so I spun the stone eleven times until it pointed west. And when Ida Threadgood left you at the river and you needed someone to ride with"—he turned a smile to her—"I had already made my decision to ask you to join me. If I hadn't wanted to, I never would have consulted the Blessing Stone in the first place. But I did not have enough confidence in myself to make my own decisions. The stone was my crutch. I don't need it anymore."

"Don't be too hasty in your judgment," she said, having given a great deal of thought to the miracle that took place at the mountain lake. "It was the Blessing Stone that led us to the bear tracks. Without it, we would all surely be dead now."

He nodded, deep in thought for a moment, then he said, "I have been thinking, Emmeline, that Lively might be a strange name for an undertaker, but it's a perfect name for a midwife." Then in all seriousness: "I know you vowed never to wed, but—"

She placed a fingertip on his lips and said with a smile, "Of course I shall marry you, my darling Matthew, for we do make a perfect pair, midwife and undertaker. I help folks into the world and you escort them out of it."

She took the Blessing Stone from him once again and held it to the sunlight. "I wonder about all the people who have held this crystal, who looked to it for guidance or protection or luck. And I wonder if they were like you, Matthew, blind to their own strengths, giving credit to an inanimate piece of mineral. But you discovered your own power in the end, the spirit that is in all of us, the spirit to overcome adversity. People are strong, Matthew, I know that now. We can meet whatever trials are put in our path, and we can be triumphant."

"You're right, we won't be needing it any more," she said, slipping the stone into his pocket. "But perhaps someone in the future can use the Blessing Stone and let it help them to find their own inner strength, wisdom and power."

Matthew kissed Emmeline, then he snapped the reins and got the wagon moving, toward their future in the green valley, toward new hope.

Interim

The Livelys bought land, invested in gold mines and railroads, and grew rich. Matthew became a leader in his community, and in his later years ran for state congress, and was a powerful and commanding figure. When asked what advice he would give to future emigrants taking the Oregon and California trails, Matthew said, "Don't take shortcuts." Both he and Emmeline lived to old age and were buried in Livelyville, California.

The Blessing Stone was inherited by their eldest son, Peter, who passed it to his daughter, Mildred, upon her graduation from medical school. Dr. Lively carried the good-luck crystal with her to Africa where she spent thirty years in medical missionary work before returning to the United States to undergo treatment for a rare disease she had contracted while on safari in Uganda. As Mildred Lively had no children, she bequeathed the crystal to the woman who was her dedicated nurse in her final months, a Japanese-American woman named Toki Yoshinaga.

Toki and her family were removed from their San Francisco home after the bombing of Pearl Harbor and sent to live at a place called Manzanar. After the war, the family was forced to sell whatever valuables they had left in order to get back on their feet. The blue crystal fetched a hundred dollars, considered quite a sum in 1948.

The buyer was an accountant named Homer whose hobby was gemology, and when he examined his new purchase at the workbench in his garage, he realized with a thrill that he might have found a new mineral. Subjecting the crystal to its first scientific scrutiny since a Dutchman named Kloppman analyzed it in Amsterdam in the year 1698, Homer found it to be a hard stone, 8.2 on the Mohs' scale, with a sharp luster and very low cleavage. The blue reminded him of varieties of topaz and tourmaline, but it had a "star" at its center as sapphires sometimes did. Feeling excitement for the first time in many years, he packed the stone along with others and took it to a gemology convention in Albuquerque, New Mexico, where he hoped to confirm his new find, with the possibility of naming the new gem after himself—"Homerite" had a nice ring to it. One day into the convention, Homer met a young lady who was *very* interested in precious stones, and he was persuaded to take her back to his hotel room to look at his collection. Unfortunately, the unworldly accountant mistook the intentions of the buxom young lady and, in anticipation of sexual intimacy, suffered a massive coronary.

Homer's collection lay neglected in the garage by his widow until, deciding to move to a retirement village in Florida, she sold the "whole worthless lot" to a free spirit named Sunbeam, who made beaded jewelry and antiestablishment paraphernalia for the head shops on Hollywood Boulevard, which was how, in 1969, the Blessing Stone ended up in a place called Woodstock, wired into the handle of a marijuana roach clip owned by a hippy named Argyle. After Argyle's death in an undeclared war in Southeast Asia, his sister went through his possessions and, finding the clip, cut the thin wires to set the blue crystal free. Thinking the stone nothing more than a piece of glass, she gave it to her eight-year-old daughter who, using aluminum foil and glue, made a crown of it for one of her dolls.

When the little girl came of college age and moved out of the house, she donated all her old toys to the Salvation Army, where the blue crystal was rescued by a woman who regularly scoured thrift shops and rummage sales for items of worth that were overlooked by less keen eyes—in her opinion, anyway. She saw possibilities in the crystal, for she was a New Age believer, and felt definite vibes when she clasped it.

And thus the blue stone that had sailed through galaxies and nebulae to land on a primordial Earth—a cosmic crystal that had given a protohuman named Tall One the wisdom to know when to lead her people from danger, that had comforted Laliari, and enlightened Avram, and bestowed Lady Amelia with faith, and had given Mother Winifred the courage to stand up to an abbot's order, and Katharina the hope to search for her father, and channeled Brigitte Bellefontaine's buried passion into practical use, and finally made Matthew Lively the master of his own destiny—thus did this blessing stone come to reside in a small shop in a California beach community. It sits today in the window in an unpretentious display of healing crystals, Tarot cards, and incense. If you do not walk by too fast, or are not too distracted by your Palm Pilot or newspaper or cell phone, you will see it.

And if you feel you need to find your inner strength, or courage, or wisdom, go inside the shop, look at the stone, hold it in your hand, and see what it tells you. The proprietor is willing to sell it at a reasonable price . . . to the right person.

READING GROUP GUIDE

THE BLESSING STONE

1. What do you think of the time periods the author chose to write about in *The Blessing Stone*? Were there any you liked more than others? Were there any you would have liked to see? Which came the most alive for you?

2. In Tall One's story, there is no actual dialogue. Did you notice this? Were the characters' motivations and intentions still clearly delineated?

3. What aspects of the ancient Middle Eastern section do you think still have resonance today?

4. Have your ideas about fate and destiny changed after reading this book? If so, how? If not, why?

5. What do you think the author is trying to say about superstitions and the power we give objects?

6. Did any historical fact or idea in *The Blessing Stone* surprise you? If so, how?

7. Which character in *The Blessing Stone* did you find the most heroic? The most villainous?

8. The author compresses time in the "interludes." How did the use of compressed time work for you in the story?

9. How did the book make you think about the history of seemingly ordinary objects?

A Bracelet
Ronai ~~Gcul~~ Garrison
P.O. Box 514
Hague, NY 12836